JOSHUA
FRAGMENTED

BY BRUCE LEWIS

RABBIT HOUSE PRESS

Versailles, KY 40383

www.Rabbithousepress.com

Cover Art: "Personae" by Rick Bennett

Formatting and Interior Design: Corbyn Keys

Edited by Erin Chandler

For inquiries about author appearances and/or volume orders contact: Rabbithousepress@gmail.com

ISBN: 978-1-7351727-1-2

I have long respected Bruce Lewis as a virtuoso Jazz guitarist. A close cousin to Blues, Jazz is dissonant, unstable and like the music he has mastered, the author's prose follows suit. In the tradition of Thomas Wolfe, Lewis's words are a cry to the very soil that birthed each character. In lyrical outbursts, Joshua Celeste remembers and is remembered. We are introduced to the characters that make up Joshua's life from the fields of his boyhood home at Water Maple Farm in Kentucky, with a cattle rancher father and misplaced, glamorous mother to the streets of Budapest, Hungary as a traveling guitarist, a melancholic ex-pat.

Bruce Lewis moved to Budapest on May 4th 1993 and stayed until May 22nd 2012. He played with some of the best European musicians in the world, traveling with his guitar to twelve different countries. His insight into the culture and people of the ancient city make Joshua Fragmented part travelogue and history lesson along with a beautiful, philosophical lesson on the sacrifices of art and the pull of home.

This book resembles the dissonance of Jazz as a cast of brilliantly articulated characters sing angular harmonies in the reader's ear. We hear the passionate railings of his academia-minded brother, Doc and his loyal, sex-obsessed and jealous bandmate, Crip Kovacs right alongside his grandmother Bertha, mother Agnes and the steady stream of women in which Joshua searches for meaning. It is a testament to the lost, nomadic quality of an ever changing modern world. I am most proud to have a small part in bringing this powerful and original work of fiction to light.

Erin Chandler

"... as if things were instantly changed by memory.

… he looked back to retain as much as possible.

Which means he knew what was needed for some
ultimate moment.

When he would compose from fragments a world
perfect at last."

—Czeslaw Milosz

"These fragments I have shored against my ruins"

—T.S. Eliot

"Hate on and love in unrepining hours"

—Yeats

"Ephemera"

DEDICATION

For Katherine and my sons

PART

ONE

ONE

1

JOSHUA CELESTE

The yellow light burns off the fog. The gravel road the color of fog winds through the farm. There is no sound for a long time and then the deep bellowing of a young steer comes from down by the creek, mouth wet and green from grazing, thick tufts of grass cling to its legs, wet with thick dew. A red-tailed hawk leaps from the great oak tree, talons dangling in the air. A groundhog, small arms held as if in prayer darts into the sanctuary of its hole. The sound of water rushing under the stone bridge as the truck passes over it with a tympanic thud. The yellow light rises, becoming thicker while the dew recedes. The truck moves up the hill, past Bertha's house cupped in a hollow. Three silver silos rise in different heights behind a great red barn.

A young boy walks across the blue field. His canvas tennis shoes are soaked from the wetness of morning. Grass blades and seeds stick to them. He likes the feeling of the water squishing between his toes and knows that soon the hot July sun will dry them and he'll look down and all the seeds and Spanish needles will be gone, dried and flaked off. His shoes will be as clean and white and warm as when his mother, Agnes, gave them to him this morning out of the dryer. He stops for a moment and looks out over the fields. He can almost see the whole farm. There's Ricky Boy's house in the far corner. His father, Marshall, takes him there sometimes in the evening. Marshall gives Rickey Boy money or they just talk. Sometimes Marshall gets mad and Rickey Boy laughs and this makes his dad even madder and he says, "I'll get Money Joe and Shine!" Sometimes Rickey Boy gets mad and they drive away but the next morning they are friends again and talk about work and money. Rickey says he bought a real good car off his cousin that runs good for almost nothing.

The young boy sees Marshall's old gray Mercedes come down the gravel road from the other direction. Doc, the boy's brother, is riding with him. The young boy turns to look up toward the blacktop road and sees a line of cattle trucks crossing the cattle gate, coming down the old farm road that his great grandfather built when people still rode in buckboards. Down the hill, Bertha comes out on her porch to wave. He sees the rising sunlight glinting on the creek where the spring running under her house trickles down. A herd of cattle move across the creek. Marshall's Mercedes comes up behind them. Doc gets out and flails his arms at the cattle, herding them up the hill toward the barn. His father honks his horn at them and shouts instructions to his brother.

When he reaches the gate the young boy that Marshall and Agnes named Joshua sees that the whole barn lot is filled with trucks and truckers standing around laughing, spitting and waiting.

A caravan of cattle trucks rattle the cattle gate as they cross the old limestone bridge. Bertha, an old woman in a torn gingham dress, comes walking slowly up the hill to flag down the passing fleet but to no avail. "Heeeey! Whoooooa!" she screams. The terrified eyes of the cattle show through the slats swaying on the truck beds as July dust swirls in the heat.

Crew-cutted, stocky and overweight truck drivers lean out the mud-smeared windows shouting curses intermingled with instructions. "Get the fuck out the way then if you don't know where you're going you candy ass sonnuva bitch."

"Open the goddam gate and get yer ass the hell away!" said the one Marshall pointed out had been a preacher once.

Marshall said it didn't matter to him, a preacher cussin'. He didn't think too highly of it but figured a man had the right to change his mind about bein' a preacher and talk like he wanted to... except of course around women.

The cattle are unloaded down a stone chute and herded into pens where they are packed into a strange writhing bovine jigsaw puzzle, heads fusing into necks twisted at impossible angles, nostrils into flanks, flanks into heads. A steer is not an aggressive animal but because of its massive size, it can be dangerous when frightened. Cattle are playful in fact and very tranquil. When not frisking around they seem to almost be daydreaming. It's very rare that a cow or steer will attack a man, but when afraid the animal will do anything in its power, which is considerable, to free itself of any danger and would not hesitate to charge. Any creature in this volatile state should be regarded as potentially lethal. Dogs seem to bring out the playful part of a steer's disposition.

It was the moment Joshua saw the cattle trucks that he ran downstairs and out the backdoor screen with its familiar thwack against the aluminum siding. He had to run a quarter of a mile, just like my horse, he thought. Quarterhorse: faster than a thoroughbred for a quarter of a mile. Hot summer wind whistled in his ears. Big grasshoppers dove in every direction. He grabbed one on the run fascinated by the sheer abundance of them, inadvertently squashing it under his sneakers he stopped morbidly curious of its spilled guts, and mangled body parts resembling an astronaut's suit.

When he and Marshall checked the herds in the evening, hundreds would be sprawled writhing over the hood jumping from the full ripe seed heads of the tall bluegrass. Sometimes they would be intermingled with beautiful cicadas and locusts whose wings had strange lines on them Bertha said could tell the future.

He ran until he reached the front door of the feed barn where he saw more men standing around. They took no notice of him when he came up out of breath. One of the younger drivers smiled his way but quickly turned his face back to what one of the truckers was saying to Marshall's hired men, TLC and Rickey Boy while waving his electric cattle prod.

"Just take the stick like this and push it in. Can ye feel it? Naw, that ain't it, TLC, y'dumb sumbitch. Hold it like this!" The trucker adjusted his grip. "Now watch close now," he squeezed the two ends of the prod together. "I'm taking all she's got right now!" He grimaced, neck muscles bulging out, sweat beading on his forehead in a kind of watery glow.

"Aw, shit! Duane, you ain't gettin' no shock!" said TLC.

"The hell I ain't! I'm taking all of her right this minute! Here, grab my hand."

As soon as TLC grabs the proffered hand, he gives a little yelp and jumps away. The truckers all laugh.

"You didn't think I was actually gonna shock myself did ya, T- boy?" They all laugh again.

"Naw, really, you tell him, Rickey. I'm one of the few people in this world thats can take a shock. Ain't many people like me in this world that 'lectricity can't hurt."

With that, he grabbed the prod again at both ends like a strong man doing isometrics. He grunted at each jolt. "I'm takin' all she's got right now!" The preachin' driver, a short, stocky man, suddenly runs up. "Rickey, Marshall's yellin' for you over at the cattle pens. He don't seem real happy. Just got his boy over there right now."

"Tell him I'm comin', Revren', I jes wanna see if this geek can do 'at shit with TWO cattle prods! I'll lay money he can't!"

"Aw, shit, Rickey, ain't time for that."

"YOU shit, yer ass is a lot closer to the ground than mine is!" All the cattlemen laugh.

"Here! Get up here and help! Don't stand around thinking 'bout beatin' yr meat, boy. Get up here!" Marshall shouted from the barn loft. Some of the other work hands turned around to see what all the commotion was about. Josh felt embarrassed. Had someone seen him masturbating that other morning out behind the tobacco barn? Why this public abuse? That was weeks ago when Doc had stolen that STAG magazine outta Tilton's Grocery. But it was all in his mind. How could Marshall have known? He breathed easier. That was just the way his father talked when he was mad.

"Here now! Don't chuall look up here!" Marshall shouted at the cattle-men." Watch the goddamn cattle! See, you let one get back in the wagon. Close the goddamn gate on that truck and move away from the chute. See, you just cost me ten dollars. That's how much weight that steer lost tryin' to find his way back outta that truck and back into my pens. See? We got a dollar waiting on a dime. I'll tell y'all this: when she's gone she's gone, there ain't no more! And you! You get your fanny up here and help Ricky Boy rick this hay!" Josh crawled up the barn loft ladder and pulled himself up the rest of the way by a stout oak beam that supported one corner of the loft floor.

2

CRIP KOVACS

The way Josh told it, or the way he heard Crazy Reddy tell it, was that the Equation could never be explained. Or if it could it would have to be explained twice, once for you and once for me. Once for each side of the equation. See?

It's part of the equation I guess that I ended up the one who wrote it down. My name's Crip Kovacs, or Crib, since I spent so much time in my own "crib" see? And Crip for cripple. See? I look pretty good in the face, like Don Henley of the Eagles some chick told me once. I play pretty fuckin good bass guitar, get my share of pussy, whatever, but I'll never be completely all there. See? I'm a cripple. I walk with a pretty noticeable limp even when I try hard not to. If I come down wrong on my bad leg it hurts like a mother fucker. This happens when I'm loading my amp or going downstairs, especially the ones that ain't got handrails. You probably don't notice shit like that but I do. Like what subway stops got handrails and which don't. It's about half and half. I never understood the logic… the equation you might say.

Josh said people are judged by how well they mastered it or avoided it. He was an avoider he would say. But I don't know, it's hard to say. Josh loved people. Later on, he got to where he didn't trust them. That's what changed him. He seemed to get further and further away. Some people who knew him 'fore I did said he was always that way. Always quiet. He could be real quiet sometimes. It could be scary. He loved to sit in the dark. I'd ask him what he was doin' and he'd just say that he was thinking. I never did ask him what about. He sure did like to read that weird poetry shit. Only now do I get an idea of what that stuff was

15

about. Bein' a crip, although sometimes chicks would have pity on you and give you a sympathy screw, was not that much fun. So there was alotta times I just stayed in my crib and read and wrote shit like this because there was nothing else to do. Like maybe that's how Michel Petrucciani (you all dumb mother fuckin' jazz illiterates probably don't even know who that is) got so great on the piano. Fuckin' crippled dwarf. Wasn't much else hapnin' for him was there? He sure ain't gonna be dancin' like Michael Jackson.

So, I figure that's how it come to me to write this, for my own salvation. Who can say who planted the seed? I'm just a hack musician. It's been almost twenty years since I got it in my head to do this, my memories, my memoirs. Still, Josh, my friend, my blood brother, why did I wrong you? Josh, how can I say it? What were you to me? There are no words… yet. Some kind of hate and some kind of love won't go away. So I keep on keepin on doin this weird thing. Writin this weird half bullshit thing. Who can say who planted the seed?

This won't be a family chronicle. This wasn't my family but I almost felt like it was. All the stories Josh told when we were on the road. It wasn't ever boring like some people get when they talk about when they're growing up. Compared to just a straight road life. I learned everything from Josh and then somewhere we got shy of each other and I didn't see him for forever. Then we ended up on the road with you name it… bluegrass bands, reggae bands, rock bands, blues brothers-type R&B show bands, everything.

> *We called ourselves the Latin Lovers*
> *Hawaiian shirts and top forty covers.*
> *Didn't think I could sink so low*
> *drugs and booze ate all my dough…*

> – STING

In the beginning, sometimes we'd go out on the road, just the three of us, guitar, bass and Hector playing fiddle and mandolin, even a little banjo. We'd make better money this way. We'd have a big time in some rented bus going across the country. But we weren't that good back then. Things got heavier later. We got into all kinda shit, musical and otherwise. We talked about pussy constantly. Always made up dirty songs by taking some old tune we all knew and then add the word "pussy" in just the right place. Like instead of "Preachin', Prayin', Singin' Everywhere," the old gospel song we'd done a real good arrange-ment of, we'd sing, "Preachin', Prayin', Pussy Everywhere," you know, just to pass the time. We didn't mean any harm by it. "On the Comode Again," instead of "On the Road Again." Later, we used to work with Sylvester Moore's band. He would call "Honeysuckle Rose," "Honey, Suck My Toes," "When Sunny Gets

Blue," "When Sunny Sniffs Glue," and "Misty," "Musty."

It was a world I never knew completely. I was too young. All I know is the city. They all look the same to me after two million, Europe or America. Medina, Kentucky used to be a small town in the forties. I remember Josh's grandma, Bertha, bringing the two boys from Edgeton into Medina, comin' to see my Aunt Pearl. I was a little too young to remember it all but I remember some. "Gone with the Wind," Josh'd say, on the bus, imitating a swelling orchestral movie theme. And he'd laugh about it, but it was gone, lost forever.

Joshua Celeste was my friend. A strange cat, in a way. A strange case. The world rejects what don't balance out in the Equation. Kills it. Doc says he thinks the equation rests on the Mystery. Death rules the equation and they say God rules the Mystery. But Josh wasn't a misfit. That's not the right word. Maybe he just lived for other people. Natural to him as breathing or playing his guitar. Music was his inner life and it was deep and full of sun… and shadow… but outwardly he just wanted to offer it to someone. Sometimes with success. Sometimes not.

3

MARSHALL

Marshall Celeste toiled in the fields. Sometimes sun-up to sun-down and into the night he harvested, "strippin'" they called it, the heavy seed head from the thin stalks of bluegrass, fed his cattle or, working late into the night with a hook light, repaired some farm implement pushed beyond its capacity. These were daily chores.

Marshall looked taller and heavier than he was. He had a kind of stockiness that, when he put on his cowboy boots, made him seem big and tall. In the evenings, he would sometimes drive his old beat-up Mercedes along the gravel road beside the ripening hay fields, checking on his cattle and the condition of his fence rows, fields of the grasses of great prairies, fescue, bluegrass, alfalfa, red clover, fields full of nectar-seeking creatures like bumblebees and hummingbirds. Josh always remembered the sound the grass made bending beneath the old car's chassis as if it were being harvested only to spring back to life as the car passed over, leaving moist tire tracks of bruised grass in its wake from which a sweet smell arose.

Great swarms of grasshoppers sprung onto the hood of the car, writhing, spitting a brown juice some said was from the tobacco and looking to young Josh as if they were wearing green tuxedos, peering out of Hapsburg fin de siecle spectacles with magnified eye. This was like the Disney character, Jiminy Cricket. Whenever Josh put his face up to the rounded chrome of a car side-view mirror or saw his reflection in the faucet of the school water fountain he thought he had the egg-shaped face of Jiminy Cricket.

"Awright, let's be real easy now and see if we can find ol' mama cow," Marshall said.

Marshall had been in an unusual mood that night. He had asked all the children to get into the Mercedes and go riding with him across the vast meadow behind the old house on Edgeton road. He even asked Agnes who seemed surprised enough to say yes. He knew his wife rarely cared for such outings or for much of anything connected to the real running of the farm but tonight for reasons he would have been unable to fathom, he wanted his family with him.

They started down the dirt back road that wound through the farm but soon Marshall steered the Mercedes off the half-washed-out mud and out into the field. Instantly the sound of the grass underneath began to beat out its rhythm. They pitched and swayed like a boat. Marshall peered over the steering wheel mindful of groundhog holes. In summer these holes were easy to spot because the freshly dug, bright soil was laid out in a glorious complex of entrances and exits the groundhog had assiduously tunneled out. Doc and Josh called these groundhog hotels. They were huge and deadly to horse and axle, often lurking unseen because the varmit died or moved on to other pastures. Intervening years partly covered the holes with weeds and dirt piled in front which gradually washed it back down, mother nature's healing of the small scar the groundhog made in the earth.

They rode on into the twilight, the taste of supper still in their mouths when Marshall, whispering to himself finally spotted the pregnant cow lying on the ground. They stopped for a moment.

"There it is, Dad". Doc cried out.

"Just be easy, now. I see it". said Marshall.

"Poor thing," said Agnes. "Is she in pain?"

"No, I wouldn't think so. Their nervous system is not as sensitive as ours."

Marshall knew a little about the physiology of cattle, but he followed instead a kind of intuition about them, their feelings, even their thoughts, and he trusted only in this. Suddenly, the belabored cow stood up, fearful of the approaching car.

"She's gonna have that calf," Marshall whispered, cutting off the engine. Sure enough, just as he said it the birth sack filled with the young calf and all its protective liquid came pouring out onto the ground. Josh and Angelika sat wide-eyed in the backseat.

"Will it be hurt?" asked Agnes.

"No, that's just exactly the way it should be," Marshall said.

He got out of the car and walked toward the calf and Mother solemnly, a priest approaching an altar. By now the calf was already standing shakily as its mother licked it to a pure white, whiter than Bertha's freshly bleached bed sheets.

"Everything's fine," he said, walking back to the car. "It's a little heifer. Mama Nature's the boss now. Let's go home".

He started up the engine and they rode in silence until reaching the gate to the yard. Doc jumped out to open it.

"Well, what ch'all gonna name her?" Marshall asked.

"It's white like a dish," said little Angelika. "Let's call her 'Dish'!" Everyone laughed.

"Ok, sweetheart," said Marshall, "we'll call her 'Dish.'"

The sun went down. Marshall fell asleep in front of the TV. Josh stared at the ceiling above his bed wondering if the calf would be cold.

4

AGNES

When the car wouldn't start Agnes called Marshall. He was sitting at Bertha's kitchen table drinking his black coffee looking out at the Rose of Sharon bushes thick with bumblebees covered with yellow dusty pollen doing their morning work.

The phone rang, Marshall sensed it was her and let it go for three rings, jealous of his reverie. On the second ring, he was still thinking about Rickey Boy's cousin, TLC, the simple boy, being left alone to mow the hillside above the lower creek. Poor feller hasn't got sense enough to do it, he thought. But there wasn't time to do it himself. He had to meet Ol' Man Gene at Billy's Grill. Billy's was a hamburger breakfast joint frequented by cattlemen, stockyard flunkies, and tobacco yaps, and it smelled of cow manure and fried onions. Twenty years later it would become Billy Fudpucker's Go-Go dance hall where chubby, down on their luck country girls with faint cesarean scars would don washed out bikinis and do dances that looked like they were trying to bust outta a buncha chains by jerking their elbows into the smoky air. Then it turned into an insurance agency, but the onion smell never quite disappeared. That's what Josh said when he had to go in there and get his driver's license. The onions couldn't be painted out of the walls.

The yellow light sifted down onto Water Maple Farm, a fine pepper of dust and sun. Grasshoppers rattled from the purplish grass stalk heads. Shade covered the cow tracks still filled with a rain three days past. The cattle stared blankly in the shade, chewing, swishing hungry flies with their manure and mud-encrusted tails. Some laid down in the muddy water to keep cool. Doors and side panels of the long blood-red tobacco barns were flung open, aired out and swept of pigeon droppings before being filled to bulging with pungent green tobacco leaves. It was summer. The sulfur butterflies rimmed the mud holes in a unified circular flight. A barn swallow shot arrow-like from the loft, a piece of hay in its beak. Money Joe's rake was the only sound in the yard. Over the hill, TLC's mower rumbled and hummed quiet in the distance with the bees.

On the third ring, he answered it. It was her.

"Honey, the car's broken again. Rickey Boy was just no use at all. It worked for fifteen minutes after he left then pfff! Gone. It's doing the very same thing it did yesterday. RRRRR-unk! RRRR-UNK! Then it just stopped."

"You probably flooded it," Marshall said.

"No, hon," answered Agness. "I did just what you said, put the pedal to the floor, pump twice."

"Aw, goddammit, Ag. I've got work to do! I've got men waiting on me!"

"Well, I've got children that need to be taken to school."

"School's not important!" he lied, trying to shock her. "Work's all that matters. They'd learn more in one day in the fields than ten years in that friggin' school!"

"Well, how is it, dear, that all your sacred time in the fields has culminated in so little knowledge?" She said snidely.

"I ain't talkin' 'bout that kind of knowledge." Marshall gruffed.

"Oh, Marshall, I can't believe you're saying this. I refuse to listen to such childish nonsense. Does your pursuit of the almighty dollar ....,"

"Who else is gonna pursue the goddamn thing? Not you! You never had to pursue. But by God you're a goddamn GENIUS at spending!"

"Oh, Marshall, please. Spend what? Your money? HA!"

The fight was on but Marshall paused, collecting every fiber of his patience. He wanted to cry out, wanted to scream. I need Money! Oh God please remove the weight of this debt from the middle of my chest! I hate my mother! my wife! All Women!

"I'll be right there," he said calmly into the phone.

5

SYLVESTER

Sylvester Moore opened the door to the tack room, brushed a cobweb from his face, and laid the saddle across a sawhorse. He put the wet saddle blanket over that and hung up the bridle on a nine-inch nail that was driven halfway into the plank wall. He blew on his hands and wiped away the dust, locked the feed barn door behind him and started down the hill. Snow lay on the bitter cold ground. He watched the sun set for a moment across the crystalized field. The cattle huddled by the salt house in the frozen dirt they had trampled into mud and made into a wallow by the heat of their bodies. The "curing slats" were closed on the full tobacco barn but he still smelled the aroma of leaves even in the cold. A few crows walked on the snow crust, picking through dead stalks that were yet unburied.

He saw a thin line of smoke coming out of Bertha's chimney before getting in his car. It was a dilapidated Malibu Classic with a chrome side strip and a side-view mirror missing. Still a good car, still able to cruise 85. Agnes had sold it to him for four hundred. He turned the key and sat back a moment, rolling a joint and waiting to turn on the heater. He popped in a cassette, Bird and Diz, the one Josh made for him for Christmas. That Miles tune, "Half Nelson" was playing. He started tapping his finger against the dashboard like it was a ride cymbal and made a snare pop with his other hand using his ring finger against the steering wheel. He could get a pretty good floor tom sound with the whoosh of the brake pedal. Thinking nobody was around he started whistling Bird's solo and grooving to himself when there came a tap on his window. It was Josh. He rolled down the window but not too far so he wouldn't lose much heat.

"You gonna run that battery down or asphyxiate one," Josh giggled. What you smokin' there bebop man?"

"C'mon in here, man," when Sylvester said it, it sounded like 'mein.' "And I'll show you."

Sylvester laughed and leaned over to open the passenger door and Josh got in. The sun was disappearing. Suddenly Josh was in another world. Not only a black man's car but one filled with hard bop and marijuana smoke. "Man, I sho' do dig this tape. Hadn't heard dis shit in ages. This was definitely the shit. Still is the shit. These cats was playin' they black asses off. Who the drummer? Max Roach? Course you wudn't know nothing 'bout that you bein' lilly white and all!" Sylvester grinned and the last of the sunlight sparkled off his gold tooth.

"Aw, c'mon, Sylves, let up on me. I didn't ask to be white." He said. "Yes, it was Max Roach. The only drummer."

Sylvester paused and looked at Josh. "Naw, I guess you didn't. But don't keep thinking this bein' black thing is so got-damned hip. Still 'bout half a pain in the black ass if you ask me. But nobody ask me." There was a sudden seriousness in his voice that made Josh look away and down at the floor.

"Hey man," Sylvester said, "I ain't about nothin'. Don't pay no 'tention to me, you know I'm' bout half fulla shit most of the time. They ain't but damn few folks black, green, white or blue even listen this shit anymore. Hey. Look up here. You allright, dough. Man, yo' daddy right! You IS damn sensitive, ain't you? Like a Collie dog, ain't that what he said?" Josh smiled. "C'mon, let's you and me take a little ride and finish this roach… this Max Roach… and listen some of this shit." He shifted into gear and steered down the long driveway across both cattle gates and out onto the country road. The snowplow had been through so it was clear. Twilight was over them. Venus was bright.

"When I was little none of this wudda been cleared. Didn't have no snowplows. Not out here. We just hook up the mules and go to school or out to town or any damn where. At night wudn't nothin' but the movie house no way.'

"You musta been bored, man."

"You about a smart little motherfucker, ain't you? Hell yeah, we was bored. But see back then we didn't think so much about it. Didn't have time to. Too busy getting stuff ready for this here." He pointed out to the snowy fields. "This here winter for one thing. Just put a couple of hot bakin' taters in our pockets 'den lit out walkin'. We worked as a family. Did things together. Didn't have no time for that thumpa thumpa shit dese brothers up there in town listenin' to now. In my humble , the groove done got too heavy. Too Strong! Too strong fo' OOBAH! We Stripped tobaccah, pulled plants, topped it, hung it, cured it, smoked it. But they ain't no money in it, now. Yo Daddy'll tell you that. Dat's why we gots de herb! Here hit that, but be careful 'cause it's the fire."

Josh carefully took the roach from Sylves' thumb and forefinger and took a hit. He breathed the smoke deep into his lungs and held it in for a moment. He exhaled. Bam. Snare pop. Rim shot. The music never stopped but played on into the darkness as they moved down the winding country road and into the cold Kentucky night. They descended down toward the Kentucky River and Frankfort, passing over a small rusted bridge at Millville and back toward the Capitol Dome. The moon shimmered like a Zildjian cymbal lightly touched with a brush.

"You playin' tonight?" Sylvester asked.

"Naw, the gig was canceled at the last minute."

"You gonna get your money?"

"I doubt it."

"What you mean you doubt it. You ought to try and get at least half."

"Yeah, but the guy who hired us is a friend so…"

"Yeah, I know all about that friendship shit. Ah, ol' Josh. You a goodin', man. But always let people know you're for real. Learn the fundamentals, then tell your story… that's all you can do."

"Well, I try to keep a air about myself!" Josh laughed.

"Hah, aw, I bet you do, man. I bet you do, haw. Where'd you hear that? Haha!" Hearing a kid like Josh put that tinge of jive in his voice cracked Sylves up. "How many in y' band now?"

"Just guitar, bass and piano. You know, standards."

"Ain't nothing wrong with that. That's the best way to learn it. Dat's how I learnt piano."

"You think I need to learn some piano?"

"Well, it ain't my main ax either but you gotta know the chords. Piano's a percussion instrument, too. Ain't no short cuts. Well, you oughta know that… bein' a GETar man. I like 'at 'ol Wes Montgom'ry." Josh agreed.

They drove in silence under the awesome virtuosity of the moon, brightening white and cold as snowy linen, it made its arc across the sky. The harmony of saxophone, trumpet, the conga-like thump of the double bass, the cascading, starry shimmer of the cymbal, all this wove itself into their thoughts.

Then it occurred to Josh, "You ought to come out and jam. We ain't been using drums on account of the noise, you know how all 'em rock guys play, and hell we can't afford to pay another piece. But I could talk to Crazy Reddy and he might be able to come up off another fifty or so."

"Aw, me and Reddy goes way back. He still talking 'bout that 'three hundred seat room' he gonna build?"

"Yeah."

"Is he? No shit? Well, I will say one thing. He does love the music, bless his crazy soul, but he's one them dudes that just gotta try and take your money or he don't feel right."

"Like that night Yuseff Lateff was playing at Reddy's old place out on Limestone and he made so much at the door he started giving it away to all his relatives and shit, payin' debts and smilin' and shit. End of the night come and he don't got enough to pay Yuseff. He tell Yuseff, I pay with a check, OK? But ol' Yuseff just shake his head say all elegant, 'Sir, (called ol' Reddy sir!) 'Sir, I do not accept payment by check. I play organic music. I want organic money!' Then later on these two big mutha fuckin' black Muslim motherfuckers shows up sayin' 'The master needs his money!' Motherfuckers callin' him 'the Master' and shit… sayin' 'He will not accept a check. That is the institution of the white devil' (or some shit) and said, 'No one leaves this room until the debt is paid in cash.' Shine and Money Joe was there. Ask them about it. I don't know what all happened but Shine said Reddy was callin' e'body he knew in Medina to come down with the cash. All nervous and shit."

"How much you think Yuseff Lateff got for that gig?"

"Probably not as much as you would think. Them cats never did make no kinda big money. Well, now I ask Dinah Washington once how Yuseff made his money and she just look at me and said, 'God takes care of Yuseff.' So there it is. Cats put in some miles out there, man. Yeah, God did, man. He did take care of him. Made sure he got enough organics!"

"Tell the story about the time Eddie Harris played his club," Josh asked.

"Aw, Eddie Harris? (Sylvester lisped the S' of Harris) He'd say, 'People up here think I'm thinking 'bout music and shit. But I'm thinkin' 'bout fartin', jackin' off, that kind of shit'. 'Course people just fell out over that."

"Didn't Reddy ask Major Harris to tell the crowd who was playin' there the next night?"

"Yeah Reddy all bent down behind the bar lookin for some damn thing. Eddie say, 'A band. That's who's playin' there tomorrow night!' and then he say, 'I can't be bothered wif no tellin' who gonna be here tomorrow night. I don't give a fuck if this motherfuckin' place burns down tomorrow night long as I got MY check!'"

Their laughter echoed up the hill toward the barn and into the moonrise and the green sky.

"I 'preciate the invite, man. Maybe I will come up. I don't know if I could do it regular 'cause I gotta stay up late foalin' them mares this spring and my artheritis is comin' back on me and shit. But you know I would love to play."

"Just if you want. And Sylvester?"

"Yeah, man."

"Would you, like… teach me? Not only drums but…like.. harmonies… Jazz? You know?"

"Man, I ain't playin' down your gig, man. I'm liable to show up, no shit."

"Oh, I know but…"

"Agnes still got that piano?"

"Sure does."

Sylvester Moore took a long toke off the dying joint. The smoked curled up past his nostrils and under the brim of his button-down cap.

"I'll see you tomorrow night 'fore supper, how that be?"

"Aw Right!"

6

BERENICE

The band finished a lethargic musaky sounding version of 'Satin Doll' and took a break. Josh strayed away from the bandstand and walked toward the cool stones embedded in the hill above the creek. He stood before this fountain where water trickled down from a spring somewhere over the wall of limestone shelving, turning stones the dark golden brown color of wet sand. The air was cool and a thousand locusts began to whir and chirp across a luxurious old antebellum lawn.

The mansion that the club now occupied had once been owned by the Durais family. Josh's mom, Agnes played there with the Durais children when she was a little girl, she always told the children whenever they drove by the old place. Kate Durais, who later married John Prudent, had been her friend since childhood. They spent many languid summer afternoons in later years sipping lemonades on the upper veranda, looking down and watching their children.

"Oh Aggie, little Albert and Josh are so cute. When I knelt down to ask Josh for a kiss, after he cried so, oh my, he kisses like a real man!"

"Oh, I know, and your Aloysius is so precious, Josh, Albert and Angelika all love him so!"

Josh also remembered the Laramies, a family of eight children whose father, Mr. Xavier Laramie, came down from the North with IBM. He devised elaborate, ingenious Easter egg hunts complete with maps given to each child along with hints and riddles. Ones like: "If you stand beneath the old catalpa, you might find a genuine Indian scalpa!" or "In the hollow tree above the nub, there secretly hangs an old golf club."

Josh found that one. He took it down from the tree and walked back toward the house afraid when he saw the other kids had found more hidden toys than he had. He remembered looking into the tree and at first seeing nothing but the black boughs of tulip poplar splitting off from the main trunk wrapped in a wreath of new spring flowers. The trunk was like a torso and the old bent golf club hanging slightly askew in the tree seemed like the arm of a dark woman forever petrified among the limbs, head drooping, melancholic.

He walked up and Mr. Laramie, smiling said, "I thought nobody would ever find that one, it was my favorite hiding job of the morning. Way to go, Josh!"

Josh smiled shyly at the praise. He never knew a man so relaxed and happy with his lot in life. Mr. Laramie was creative and thrilled to spend Easter morning hiding strange objects he'd found in the old mansion's attic just for the delight of the children.

Years later when Josh was a teenager, he and Hector and Carlo and Bobby Paganini (whose father bought the place when he came down from the North to be director of the new mental hospital in Medina) snuck up those same attic stairs and found old Civil War uniforms, sabers and portraits of the Durais' who had long ago departed. One of the uniforms they found was an old-style British Army uniform from before the Revolutionary War. This might have belonged to Isaac Shelby Durais, a decorated veteran who fought with George Rodgers Clark in the French and Indian War and whose great-great-great-grandson was still alive at the Edgeton old folks home. The oldest daughter, Louise, Kate's half-sister, married Abercrombie the Texas oilman but they rarely visited Kentucky or the old man anymore. Now the old Durais place was converted into a country club for the faculty at the university. Doc, then a professor at Medina, got him the job.

Josh walked alongside the creek thinking of the Indian arrowheads that rested in its bed. Birds fluttered in the twilight, a small flock of thoroughbreds grazed on the green hillside. Then he saw it, Lilian's ring. Was this where they walked? The little diamond setting shone under the water. He bent down to pick it up and thought of his old roommate at Kentucky Academy, Steinbach, who'd thrown a penny into the creek that ran through the woods below the school grounds, saying, *think of it Josh, that penny will be there long after we're dead and gone. Even after civilization and all humankind has vanished!* Maybe it wasn't hers. Had she lost it there that night? It was so long ago. It was as if, one night, he pulled the ancient Book from the shelf, scrawling something in the flyleaf and some desperate poem flung like the I Ching onto the available white space, then like an adolescent, he was ashamed of it in the morning.

Josh walked, hands shoved deep into his father's navy peacoat, back to the bandstand where he could hear Carlo tuning his bass and Sylvester fluttering his brushes over the snare. The bride and groom, bouquet and garter thrown, were waving farewell to everyone in a shower of rice as they sped by in a Mercedes limousine. Time to go back, play a few more tunes for the last drunks hanging on each other like weary autumn trees, then call it a night.

In those days, Josh was looking for a job again. The bookstore gig he had taken at Berenice's insistence was starting to fade just like their love affair. The owner had gotten rich on the little downtown shop but when he tried to open a mega shop out in the 'burbs he became another casualty of Reagan era over-extension. Josh was never the aggressive managerial type so when it came time to lay people off he was the first to go.

By then Berenice brought up the subject of marriage less frequently. She became distant and spent most of her time with her girlfriends hanging 'round with Jean and Joan and who knows who. They were living in Medina around this time, had a nice little place over near the park. One night he walked into the Joyland Club looking for Carlo and she was there talking with some dude he didn't know. He felt something clench in the pit of his stomach but still didn't have much instinct about break-ups and Berenice came over smiling and acting like there was nothing unusual about it so he pushed it outta his mind.

But it wouldn't go away. He'd sit up at their apartment trying to practice guitar when suddenly a sense of panic came over him especially if he'd had a few hits of dope and he'd wonder where she was.

Josh was so heavy into the jazz thing at this point he'd almost quit listening to his Doc Watson and Norman Blake records. He quit going to hear J. Byrd and his Bluegrass Boys over at the Ramada. He even got real bored with funk stuff. His craving for harmonic complexity got so bad, he realized how right Hector was about the greatness of Django. And Sylvester and Carlo got him listening to 'Trane and Miles. He would lean on his spiritual link with 'Trane, Bill Evans and Monk on the darker nights of his soul.

Carlo told him about a workshop on Long Island where people like Jim Hall, Larry Coryell and Donald Brown were teaching. He thought it might make Berenice love him again if he showed some initiative for his music career so he decided to go. This is where Josh learned the music. He practiced hard. Coryell said memorable things, *"There's nothing easy about this music...don't think when you improvise...try to fly."* Josh liked that. It felt like church when he was an altar boy in Edgeton handing the chalice of consecrated wine to Father Hozni opening the box of communion wafers with the yellow light of Sunday pouring through the stained glass window. Jesus knocking on the door of the soul, *"take, eat, this is my body..."*

He remembered Berenice's project for her adult ed. class in stained glass, beautiful birds and flowers. They hung them in the bedroom of the apartment they shared. When he'd call her from New York she seemed distant. He asked over and over if she still loved him. She answered yes but still his stomach clenched.

When he got back after eight weeks of intense study, he came home wondering if she was proud of what he had done, or if he even still lived there as her boyfriend. He felt relieved when she answered the door and they had a nice chat about all he had done at the school. Like an electric shock, the phone rang and she took it into the kitchen.

Somewhere far away and deep inside Josh heard the old hay conveyor rattling, cattle screaming, wild-eyed as they were driven into the chute, and Marshall yelling orders at them. A crow sprang from a dead elm limb down by the creek below Bertha's house.

"Who was that, honey? "

"A man."

"Really? Who?"

"A man I'm in love with."

Josh was too numb to move. As the fist turned in his gut and, as if he'd flown down into the dead cow gulley of Water Maple, an aimless dove, he heard himself ask "Do you... kiss this guy?"

"Honey, let's not talk about it. You're obviously upset."

They slept together in their old bed alone and apart. He heard her faint breath as he watched the windows lighten with dawn and wondered what he had done to lose her love. He watched her sleeping for a few moments. She had aged it seemed. Perhaps he had not really seen her. Ever.

He did not know this person sleeping there. Never knew her dreams, her anguish. She started awake.

"Don't go," she said in the morning. "Can't I make you coffee?"

"Yeah, okay. Thanks." He couldn't leave the years they'd spent together.

"Berenice? What did I do?"

"It's not what you did. It's what you didn't do."

After thinking over those mystical, silly-ass words that have passed over lovers' lips for thousands of years, tears poured forth like a sick man coughing, the final loss that evened the equation hovering between them like an empty expression of a lunatic.

"Please don't. Don't."

"But, Berenice. Oh, God. What do I do now?"

She held his head against her breast.

A few days later still clinging to hopes of getting back together, Josh went to buy her flowers. He couldn't afford a dozen roses so he settled for a bouquet of daisies and black-eyed Susans the shop keeper made up herself. Can florists tell when a man's heart is broken?

He went up their old sidewalk as he had so many times before in happier days and knocked, with the flowers hidden behind his back like in the movies. A man answered the door. He remembered now, the instructor at the stained-glass workshop she'd gone to before he left. He handed him the flowers. Stomach clenched, he stammered a few courtesies, shook his hand, the hand of his own death, turned and never went back.

7

Josh fooled himself into believing that the ordered world, the world of Water Maple Farm, the days of his high school romance with Lilian, the life he'd known with Berenice, was not over. Like anyone he'd ever known, he'd lived a domestic life imitative of his parents, a normal childhood, education, job. But the imitation became impossible when he began earning his living playing guitar. He became a musician and this would separate him forever.

He saw this in the aftermath of his failed relationships. It was difficult to play artist in the white American middle-class world he had always known. Sylvester always said, "You can't play music to the cows." Now that world and his ability to function in it was disappearing. It had clearly rejected him and he hardly knew what to do with this newfound freedom. The responsibility for another person that a relationship entails, the responsibility for himself, was gone.

Sitting alone in the little house where they had once been happy, he felt Berenice's power over him, her spiritual presence, begin to fade. Quirks of inconvenience, her rules and demands he once endured with a smile and later detested were suddenly gone. So, too, the necessity of keeping up a pretext of sexual attraction for her which he had lost. Especially upon realizing he had become another Jerry, her ex she dumped to be with him. O, what karmic repetitions are all our loves and O, how under the shadow of our unchangeable self! He would have been willing to fake it indefinitely. Mercifully, after a year of living in the same house, in the same bed, rarely touching or even speaking, they managed the courage to split up.

The giddiness of freedom was tempered by all-consuming loneliness that came upon him in the dark, staring at the ceiling. He replayed the scenes of life with Berenice. Five years! Five years! Again and again on that ceiling as if it was a movie screen with a projectionist gone mad. He would wonder perversely where she was, who she was with. "I vander who's kizzing her now…" Aunt Pearl sang when they were little. In the end, he fantasized about Berenice making love with other men. At the brink of orgasm, he would imagine her fucking a whole bed full of old rivals or even close friends, Hector among them, even Lacy Corman, and being overcome with a pleasure, like his own, he could no longer provide.

When Josh woke up alone in his bed the next morning, he knew a new life had begun. Sleepy, he walked into the bright living room. Berenice's paintings still hung from the walls. Clay masks she had sculpted no longer laughed or cried, they were simply objects staring emptily into space. Her furniture, the sofa with the cat-clawed upholstery that reminded him of the color of her hair, a kind of light peach, like the frescoes on the walls of Venetian villas he would see years later, was just as she left it. The cane rocker, the antique radio, all in place. But she was gone. He realized, perhaps for the first time, the love they had known was irrevocably lost. He imagined her driving down a western interstate with a truckload of essentials to the new life she built with all her secret phone calls.

"It would never have worked," he said to the four walls, half weeping. "Well, it did for a while. No. I've cried enough. Enough crying."

He threw on his clothes and bounded out the front door. It was late August. The air was thick with the detritus of summer but somehow light and clear like Karo syrup. Soon, September would deepen to a dark yellow, then October to light brown and pumpkin orange. November was burgundy. December, black and white. In January the sun would start to reappear with a touch of pine green. February was brown and white and patches of laced snow on rolling hills and the red of returning cardinals. March was light green and yellow. April, pink. May, lavender. June, dark purple. July, dark green and blue with the reds of roses. This was the rhythm of the year he had come to know and clung to. The colors Berenice taught him to see. The beautiful, ominous colors Sylvester painted. Just as, in a moment of clear despair of lost love, he heard 'Trane's saxophone voice in a dream chant, "Spirit-chul shit, man! Spirit-chul shit!"

He heard that same voice after their night of arguing when he woke on the couch with his clothes on and whispered mantra-like to himself, Spiritual shit, Spiritual shit, Spiritual shit.

8

The wan light of Budapest comes through his bedroom window at dawn as he lays on his back staring at the ceiling. The lost, other world of his past life comes to him, appears before him as if engulfing the shadow, creeping across the room like a curtain being drawn slowly across a stage. Each character motionless in some remembered pose.

Only the man who has left his past utterly behind is able to see that same life as a complete whole. For hours, months, years Josh could stare into that past peeling layer after layer away until a certain truth appeared, at least for himself, a truth almost too much to bear. He is Lazarus. He has seen the end of something. The end of it all. He becomes a seer. He sees what others cannot, the end, the end of a time, a life. He alone can tell the story.

Perhaps the cowardice that made him lose that first life, in the beginning, is the same cowardice that now distorts that vision. He can only go on remembering, peeling away yet another layer but coming no closer to what... justification?

I gotta think, after all those years, Josh was just too good for this world. See, e' body comes outta the Dipper. But Josh, he was like put BACK IN the Dipper and poured back over the earth. Over the years a kind of tranquil resignation settled over him and the more the world and all the love he couldn't find leaned in on him, he got swept away in the flood. Josh was a saint with no God. The Saints of old had a power Josh never had, an active God. Still, the God Josh found at St. Jude's when he was a boy in Edgeton stayed with him all of his life.

When he knelt on the right side of the altar and Father Hozni raised the chalice of communion wine that altar boy Josh had helped him consecrate, when he raised it in prayer to the big brass cross under the stained-glass Jesus knocking on the Door of the Soul, he knelt in the light of grace of a silent God, not the one St. Francis had access to. Seems like to me it's easier to believe in something you KNOW is there than something you're always having to look for a sign of. The old Saints found their God. Josh never did find his. But it wasn't 'cause he didn't look. He was a lonely seeker. Maybe I'm wrong. I never did know much about theology. I guess those Saints had their moments of doubt, too, it's what let themselves be killed.

Seems like to me it was those same moments got Josh in trouble. He lost the thread of such a silent God and began to look for other kinds of love, love of women. But ol' Sylves was a real artist, painting, music, poetry, everything. He said women can't save you. Doc, Josh's brother, the professor, said women were only one of many wounds to our youth. Maybe Josh found peace when he realized they wudn't meant to save nobody nohow. I guess you got to save somebody, might as well be yrsef. Carlo said, "It's too bad women gots to be people. Pussy is some POWERFUL shit!"

One wound after another, Lilian and then his long love affair with Berenice ending. He never would forget that sound of the door closing for the last time and her getting in that big U- haul truck with all her furniture, getting ready to drive to New York. What Josh didn't know was that Hector was hiding in the back of that truck. He was gonna drive—not Berenice. So, she was lying when she tried to ease his mind about her driving such a big unwieldy vehicle. She was afraid he'd get his feelings hurt or get mad and yell at Hector like the night he lost his temper when he found them together by accident. Josh had come home early from a gig in Cincinnati with Larry Young on Hammond organ when the last set got canceled 'cause this audience of old folks thought they sucked which they did 'cause Othello was playing drums and he forgot his sticks. Larry wasn't even playing the B—3 but had this little Yamaha guitar-lookin' keyboard. They weren't doing nothin' but sitting kinda close on the sofa. When Hector left, Josh kicked over a table and the corner of it put a dent in the floor.

Berenice was wrong to think Josh wudda got mad. She didn't understand the way of his rage. She'd never grown up in a house with alotta yellin' like Josh had. Maybe it came from that feeling of not having anyone to fall back on or that awful feeling of being unable to escape from the pain he knew other people was gonna give him even if they didn't mean to. It's like sometimes you're happy that you're alive and it feels good but the other side is you know yr alive and that the pain is inescapable. Josh's rage was like a kid finally screamin' to get his mama's attention. Maybe Josh was trying to get God's attention. That's what Doc said— always taking a deeper look.

Berenice didn't see this 'cause no matter what a smart girl she was and a sculptor who made beautiful things with her hands, when something was too awful to see, she had a way of not seeing it or calling somebody "negative" if they did. Like almost any woman Josh ever hung out with, she didn't believe in God or any afterlife. I never knew a pretty girl who believed in God. God was invented by men, Doc said.

When Berenice left, the world of Water Maple Farm, Josh's parents and his adolescent dreams of fame and glory left with her. Visions sent him into a wistful, sad feeling. He'd fall asleep on the couch with all his clothes on, then, wake up from a dream where Berenice had come back and was saying something he couldn't understand. Anxious and depressed he'd stumble to the toilet and urinate in the dark, then fall into the bed and sleep fitfully.

The pain eventually faded in the bright yellow light of mornings and he'd feel a surge of joy in his newfound freedom. So began his life as a bachelor playboy. He had an almost continual desire for contact with women but this new freedom to flirt with any women he saw with no recriminations frightened him. Josh didn't understand how much the end of his life with Berenice would change him. Freedom's other side in the equation of love was gut gnawing loneliness.

For the first time, Josh was without the motherly kind of love that had comforted him all his life. First Agnes and Bertha, Aunt Pearl and Millicent, then Lilian and Berenice, they had all been his mother. Like a young woman who decides to get pregnant and decides whose gonna be the daddy and where they're gonna live, they got the apartments, the jobs, the cars, the groceries. Josh was still a kid. They bought him clothes and told him how to wear them, cut his hair, washed his clothes, made his bed.

When he was with Berenice he started to get better gigs so he had the power to play breadwinner. She was the first woman in his life that, though fiercely independent, was financially dependent on him. Joshua made the down payment on the house and put it in his name. Agnes was happier that way since she thought all his girlfriends were trying to steal from him. Years later, he saw buying the old house in Medina, which his parents tried to discourage, as the most decisive act of his life. Hadn't he bought the place to make Berenice love him more?

Sitting alone in that house on the bronze-colored sofa, frayed with aged cat clawings, he stared into the TV, daydreaming, changing channels with the remote Berenice left. It was her TV. A black youth with no shirt and a backward hat undulated to a heavy backbeat, gold chain dangling between glistening well-formed pectorals. With the sound off, Josh could only read his lips. It occurred to him that the world had changed. The warmth of Marvin Gaye, James Brown and Stevie Wonder had changed into something ominous, cynical. Or maybe it was just fear... anger. He realized with half a laugh he could no longer imitate the current dances. Only a gymnast could.

Kids were getting bigger and stronger, tougher, louder. The new world was raw, chaffing over some old wound. He was getting old. The bullet that killed John Lennon, that killed Marvin Gaye, struck down his youth. Something changed. *Hello Walls*, Josh said as they closed in on him. Entranced by the twilight, he sat for several hours in the dark.

Suddenly Joshua felt the urge to embrace his youth with both arms, to stop the horror of time and hold the past tight to his breast. He struggled into an old pair of jeans. They fit over his still youthful-looking legs but he could hardly button them over his stomach and faint love handles. He kept his shirttail out so he could breathe easier and hide the roll around his waist. He donned a dangling earring and his old Jimi Hendrix-style "Indian Joe" hat, and played air guitar into the mirror. He didn't look bad. If someone had frozen that moment on film, Josh would have seen himself, because of strong Welsh features, as a kind of aging Pete Townsend with a much smaller nose. It wasn't what he wanted. It was not Jimi Hendrix. Josh had little of the classic rock star's body, wiry build with spindly long legs and mounds of hair. His oval face gave away his Celeste features and a drop of Cherokee blood, and his bulging midriff belied his Demeter ancestry. He had changed. He had aged. He was alone.

9

Josh awakened as if out of a trance speeding down I-75 North heading toward Cincinnati. A thin film of October rain covered the highway. Tractor-trailer trucks moved in beside him like train cars and he sped by the poor little farmhouses of Northern Kentucky. Long red tobacco barns were filled with curing tobacco, glowing with the light of the coke stoves underneath low hanging leaves. As he descended toward the river at Covington, the misty skyline of Cincinnati rose before him and he crossed the high arching steel bridge into Ohio.

His instincts guided him to the Blue Wisp Jazz Club. Perhaps he would know someone there. He went in, ordered a beer and sat down. Jimmy McGary the local legend tenor sax player was on the bandstand and Josh heard the last few bars of Coltrane's Lazybird disappear into the air. McGary was a mentor to many great players who went on to stardom like Fred Hirsch and Wilbur Longmeyer and Larry Young and, yes, Sylvester Moore, years before he'd come to work on Water Maple, had been his drummer for a few gigs. When Josh had asked Sylvester about it, curious of stories from the endless secret layers of other people's lives, he acted like he didn't remember.

Josh introduced himself on a break but McGary seemed bored and distracted and less than enthusiastic about Josh's sudden, almost desperate, attempt to sit in. He didn't have his guitar so asked if he might sing something. Right away Josh knew it was a mistake. Singers are the most suspicious of jazz animals. Most musicians are wary of them and rarely grant them the title of 'musician' at all.

"Well, look," said McGary, "we're doin' alotta arranged stuff tonight, not just standards. Maybe later, okay?" Josh nodded and smiled nervously, half expecting the rejection.

He wanted to talk to someone. Anyone. This was the first night of his total loneliness. He thought of Kiki LaSalle. She had become in his mind the dark side of his Mom, this classic chick singer who worshiped Billie Holiday, talked jivey like a black dude and was really just one of the guys. And she could sing. It was as if the soul of every boy who'd jilted her in high school came oozing outta each note. She had a thing for slow torturous ballads but like so many unschooled singers she couldn't handle scatting be-bop at up-tempos. It was as if she was saying, "See? See? I've suffered more than you!" She'd had a thing for Josh, too, years before when she'd come along with her drummer boyfriend to a gig Josh played at the Queen City Club. She knew Josh from Edgeton High and also the Medina music scene. She remembered how pretty he'd sung James Taylor's "Don't Let Me Be Lonely" at one of Wanda's parties. She gave him her business card but Josh never called her for gigs since Berenice would've been too jealous of him hanging out with Cincinnati jazz chicks, but he remembered her card with the rose and a teardrop falling from it.

The card was still in his wallet and he asked if he could use the phone but the fat lady with too much make-up behind the bar pointed to the street. The rain was really coming down, that classic soaking autumn rain that falls in the Ohio Valley. The phone had a hard plastic awning over it. He hadn't seen Kiki for years but asked her to meet him at the Blue Wisp. There was a pause on the other end. The noise from the traffic on the street made Josh think he hadn't heard her reply so he almost yelled into the receiver, his jacket getting soaked from the rain. "Kiki? You there?"

"I heard you, Josh. I just kinda wonder what the scene is. You know I'm seeing Eddie right now, right?"

"Eddie who?"

"Eddie Firstman. You know, the trumpet player."

Josh suddenly remembered. They were to be married. The new guy who had produced her record. All the old memories of the Queen City Club, Gemma's Interstate Lounge, the whole thing came rushing back. "Oh, yeah, Eddie. What happened to Othello Shy that drummer you used to date?"

"Oh, him? He's on the road with the Basie Band. That was awhile back."

"Was it? Well, how's Eddie?"

"He's right here. You wanna talk to him? I thought you got married or something?"

"No, listen, Kiki. I'm sorry. I'm a little drunk and out of it right now, dig? Just forget I called. Tell Eddie it was just somebody calling about a gig you can't do or something, okay? See ya 'round, okay?"

"Yeah, Josh no problem, man, anytime. Take care of yourself."

When Josh first started getting big at the Joyland Club, Berenice already knew who he was by the way she came in and looked at him. It was the beginning of summer so she'd had time in the Kentucky springtime to working on a deep, velvety tan. She came in wearing a sherbet green mini-skirt and white top that barely covered her tits. There were yellow flowers on the skirt and she had on yellow sandals which enhanced her lovely brown feet. Her hair had that same peachy blondness to it along with the peach sheen of her wet lipstick. Man, she was a dish of peaches.

I don't think Josh knew, seeing how green he was at the time, that she was laying out the prospect. The band was digging on her from the stage and the place was packed with lawyers and yups with their ties still on and secretaries stayin' late on a Friday after work getting a buzz, knowing they didn't have to get up the next morning. Then later came a wave of college kids with check shirts and Neil Young sneakers, a kind of upscale punk grad student crowd, the jeunesse doree as Doc called them, who knew jazz from old movies and tolerated it. All these people were there to get drunk on overpriced downtown drinks and dig the scene of which Josh's band was the musical background.

That had been the perfect gig, a built-in, money-spending crowd not there to hear you play, some of those folks didn't have the faintest idea what he was playing, but they were willing to go along. The dude who owned the club just knew having "live jazz" was hip. He didn't know what they were doin', sayin' things like, "Can y'all play somethin' that doesn't sound like you're practicing?" Ain't it strange how Americans, even most black Americans, don't know jazz. Like that story Cecil Mcbee told him in New York years later about the club owner who wanted "danceable funk" but the band just kept on playin' bop, convincing the dude that bebop was funk! Eventually, tolerance began to wear thin and Josh would see the club owner eyeing the "low numbers," like that dude who owned The Cantina, the club on the other side of town, said one night, "Boys, the numbers just aren't there." So Josh started cranking up the ol' Motown, which we all loved, and the Blues and R&B stuff which was such a groove, in order to save the gig.

It worked. He stretched that one to some two or three years. But the days of pure pouring forth of soul and intellect that was bebop were over. Now it was all entertainment and the scene got weird and loud and finally, the "alternative rock" crowd got so big they started bringing in their own bands. Those dudes would even play for free long as the beer was free! That was the end of it. That was the first crack in the whole thing. Jazz no longer spoke to the people. It turned inward into a more dangerous territory and spoke only to the individual soul. Nobody believed in its prophecies, maybe too many dreams, especially after 'Nam, didn't come true. Nobody listened to anything anyone had to say about nothin' anymore.

Another one of those lost nights, soon after Berenice left, Josh drove to Louisville and called Sheila, the chick who'd worked at the art museum. He'd seen Hector out with her a few times but figured there wasn't much to that since Hector was on the road playing bass with the Holmes Brothers most of the time. Josh hadn't seen her for years and heard she had moved to Louisville.

When he finally got her on the phone she immediately sounded distant like she already knew he was recently divorced and single. What an uncanny sense women have for these things. They chatted about nothing. How was her new job? Did she like Louisville? Did she miss Medina? Then he let it drop, "hows 'bout meeting me for a drink somewhere?"

"Nah, sorry. I got other plans, Josh. My boyfriend…" the word sent a mild shock through him, "is coming soon to pick me up."

He muttered through a few apologies of the "well, I was just in the area" type and hung up. His head bowed in the phone booth. Right hand brushing over his high forehead, he let his fingers hang for a moment in his hair like a comb. Tears sprang to his eyes and he felt a sudden need to talk to Berenice. She was so far away. Further than LA. Out to sea, lost forever in a mist.

He knew that Sheila was only part of that imaginary world he had woven over the past few years to console himself for his lost passion for Berenice. It was filled with women he thought wanted him and people who considered him a great musician. He had never grounded any of these fantasies in reality… a few random glances, girls watching him on stage. *You're the kinda guy that will always make a beautiful dollar in this business, you know what I mean? You're what I call a perennial, you get better looking as you get older.* Just like in "Broadway Danny Rose," "It's true when I'm out there singing, I can feel the women mentally undressing me, it's true." The Stage. That slightly raised height which allowed him a kind of B-movie, God's-eye-view of all that went on in the nightlife. The Scene, a sea of faces, some vacant, some desperate, playing itself out before him.

He drove through the dim streets of Louisville, hardly knowing his way around.

He was free. Free to flirt with any chick who came his way without recriminations, without guilt or fear of jeopardizing a relationship where happiness faded like a long Indian summer. It was over.

He drove aimlessly, popping in at the Bardstown Tavern for a moment walking through the Friday night crowd. Someone he vaguely recognized yelled, "Hey Josh, how come you ain't playin' tonight?" But he only dived deeper into the horde and pretended not to hear. It was a rare weekend off Crazy Reddy at the Joyland Club had given him. They were remodeling, putting in a new patio bar. Now he was on the ground looking up at the stage from the crammed dance floor. It was impossible to order a drink. Big buzz headed jocks and tall thin guys in leather jackets, jostled him as he tried to make his way through. Chicks with three nose rings in each nostril and a chain runnin' to their ear, hair braided Stevie-style, like an African princess and painted peach and lady's feather blue, or shaved slick as Isaac Hayes, gave him bemused or outright disdainful looks that brought a tightening to the pit of his stomach. He was not one of them.

He reached the other side of the dance floor almost gasping for breath. He felt a sense of panic as if the energy of the dance was literally pushing him out the door. Just like the feeling he'd had at Aloysius Prudent's house when he was eight years old and dared to get in a pick-up football game with his older brother's high school friends. After getting battered around by these cold-hearted, bloodthirsty boys, he proudly hoped for recognition, and their respect for injuries he'd suffered and endured. What an honor to be accepted as their equal! The young upstart with the fleet moves… small but fast. Instead, they played keep-away, forming a circle around him, laughing convulsively as they lobbed the football over his head while he gave little boy leaps to try and reach it. Once he stumbled and one of the boys threw a bullet pass that soundly smacked him upside the head coming in at him like the flight of a bat. He lay still for a moment as the laughter faded into a smattering of guffaws. Then he heard, Kate, Aloysius's mom yelling, calling everyone in, "Hec! Jared! Skeeter! Stop bullying the younger boys this minute! Someone's going to get hurt! It's getting too dark to see the ball anyway!"

Josh looked out over the strobe-lit sea of faces. The flash of human gesture. He thought he might try to find the booking manager, usually some thick-necked yup or some chick with stiff spray, moussed hair and a vicious slash of rouge that looked like it'd been laid on with a putty knife. Thought he'd try to hit 'em up for a gig but changed his mind. He reached the door feeling the sting of cigarette smoke in his throat. Outside, in the parking lot, he threw his head back toward the night sky and saw the Big Dipper leaning toward him as if each star could pierce through him. Behind the wheel, he took a few deep breaths, fastened his seat belt and drove home.

10

Maybe this was the first time Josh felt true freedom coupled with panic. No job. No band. His old friend, Carlo Everett, was working with a blues band that worked all the time around Medina. Somehow Carlo always managed to find a gig. Especially 5 night a week hotel gigs. The Fairy Gig Mother came through and often for him. Everybody needed someone who could play different stuff and Carlo played bass, keys, horns and played them well. The perfect musician with enough chops to do the job, read well. He was also dependable, loved to get high but could hold his dope, never got metaphysical on your ass or tried to lay a trip on you. Not like those virtuoso cats who blew into town on some college tour and flamed out all over everything before they blew out. Head-cutters. Dudes who liked to come into town and set the local hero up on the bandstand didn't matter if it was guitar, piano or saxophone, then blow his ass away. Carlo had the chops to do that but never used them. He wasn't that kind of dude.

The cool thing was, he had a way of never letting you see him look bad. Like, he wudda never got his head cut 'cause he'd never let hisself be set up. He was protective of his image but didn't show it. You couldn't tell he was conscious of not wanting to be made to look bad, dig? Most of the time he was real open, like, enjoyed hisself at a jam session or a party. Loved to smoke reef.

If things got too anarchistic for Carlo you know, silly, like Josh and Hector and Jared Smallwood used to get sometimes making prank calls and driving weird or imitating that scene in 'Chinatown' when Faye Dunaway gets a bullet in the eye and falls dead onto her car horn that keeps blowing, Carlo would just slip away.

Stable. Didn't think much of things people did just for kicks. Once in awhile he'd get into kicks if he was into it. He realized earlier than the others, there wasn't much in it for somebody to be standing around checking out other people's kicks. Their trip. He figured nobody cared about his trip much either.

Josh did. In those days, he did care. As if he dug other people's lives more than his own. That's where they were different. Joshua never had that self-confidence. He wanted to do what everybody wanted him to do and everybody wanted him to do something different. That's why everybody loved him I guess. He was into everyone else's trip as much as his own 'cause in those days it seemed like everybody and everything was connected. You could take a hitta acid and feel it… the Connection. Beyond the Equation.

Josh never lost that feeling like the rest of 'em did. He kept up with everybody, even all the jazz players, country players, songwriters and rock stars. Anything he couldn't do he wanted to learn. When he saw something creative, he wanted to be part of it. He led people even though he thought they were smarter and better than him. People loved him but no amount of love was enough to make him love himself.

When I think of all the bitches I had in my old crib, I see now there was something feminine in it too. Perhaps the graceful part. I waited for them like a spider. We called the place the Web of Love. As to a woman they came to me, a cock-bearing mother. Wasn't I watching myself being fucked as well? Like I was the chick I myself was fucking. A spider engulfing it all. Mind. The girl I'm subtly humiliating as I watch her suck the cock I've just unsheathed from her asshole is Me! C'est Moi! That's what Doc said. Said he got it outta some book. Women chased Dionysius, he didn't have to chase women. He blow that flute and womens would follow!

Crazy Reddy said, "Yeah, you know I never could go out with women. I'd get 'em to come over here, especially after me and my girlfriend split up. We was together fifteen years, man! So, for a long time, I never went outside my crib. Just for food or cigarettes or something. I was like a damsel in a tower and these bitches was knights in shining armor trying to get me to come down. I was in my emotional fortress, so to speak. Only they didn't know it. I'd fix a delicious fish dinner with white wine, turn the lights down, put on Marvin Gaye 'Sexual Healing' and that was it." I knew what he meant.

All them faceless chicks were like parts of my own self. When I made love to them it was like traveling backwards and forwards in time. I got caught in the present. The future stopped luring me on and the past got too painful to look at anymore. As if my mind couldn't think itself forward anymore, I sank.

Wanda was the bottom. Even when I ran my hands across her ass and up along her ribcage and under her tits I felt like I was stirring up the sediment of seashells and sand. Strange fish swam before my eyes like the time Jared and Josh told me about snorkeling in the Bahamas. Now she's abandoned me to the depths.

I've now been "clinically," that's the word on the Questionnaire, diagnosed as a sex addict by this chick shrink who says I need to get on Xanax. I took four of 'em and felt so good I canceled my appointment with her. She said don't kid yourself, it's the drug. You're gonna be depressed again when you come off 'em. Damned if she wudn't right. They knocked something loose maybe shouldn't a been. I had this dream about Kiki LaSalle with all her long curly white-blond hair coming towards me in the old junior high gymnasium like a statue of an angel, only her see-thru nightgown blowing back like a bad horror flick. Like a chintzy old romance drawing of a prophetess pointing the way to damnation. I would wake up right as it felt like we were being pushed off the back end of the highest bleachers in the same gym where I fell and broke my leg. Then I dreamed I had leaves on my back and Carlo (just a little twelve-year-old like me) saying, You alright, man? You alright? Then I woke up. Xanax triggered it.

11

Dear Wanda,

I can't sleep. My head is full of ideas. It occurred to me that twenty years have passed (your whole life!) but I've always been the same person. The same person you stopped loving is still me. What happened to me with every love I ever had SEEMS LIKE YESTERDAY! Still keeping it all in the same file cabinet. Sift thru data of passed life w/ flick of finger. Always my mind drifts back to you and Medina. The night Lacey Corman was sooo witty and drunk? "Josh, the most dog-eared book on this shelf is "Alcohol and the Writer." He'd read me as an alkie but I never was.

As I look back, I see how I always read traits into people. Not out of a desire for control but out of loneliness.....what I wanted in a father I read into Lacy. What I wanted in a friend I read into Crib or Hector or Carlo. Yet, it was like the great wall of their own lives, their jobs, their hidden souls in everyone I've ever known that was so impenetrable.

I also read into myself. Delusion is a cunning enemy, taking you into a labyrinth that leads away from your true self, showing you a host of imposters. But I am SOMETHING! This is what delusion tries to smash into fragments. Lost in a hall of mirrors, you go from one project to the next, one self- image to the next, infatuated and full of hatred and rage and love all at once. But the idea it wants most to deny you is that you exist. You. Individual. A something in the universe that cannot be broken down! (MUSIC SWELLS HERE). I HAVE THE RIGHT TO EXIST! I, JOSHUA CELESTE disappear from that universe? Preposterous! I need not gather here, steal there, patch here, pluck there to piece together a self… this one made in the image of others not in god's… as it should be. NO! I steal only for aesthetic purposes to clothe the majesty of what already stands naming itself into eternity!! ME! ME!

Yours,

Joshua

My God, she was so young! Lovely as a child is lovely and she was childish and bright but vague like a child. Crossing Jonquil street, laughing with her friends on the corner. Her hair dyed sunlight yellow, buzzed on the sides, the rest Prince Charming neck length and pushed back behind her ears. A spray of bangs the color of a freshly cut hayfield covered her forehead. Jeans hugging long, slim muscular legs. She was smoking a cig. Not intentionally sexy. A lost post-hippy punk kinda girl. It was her. Somebody called her name. Wanda. She looked at Josh again, then looked away shyly as if he saw her from the stage.

She'd been to high school in Pennsylvania and had that northern girl wariness in her eyes. She wore a black Italian style leather jacket and tight blue jeans, and those clunky fork-lift driver type work shoes. Josh recalled a gold ring on the middle finger of her left hand and a silver one on the pinky of her right. Her lips fuller than most blond girls and gorgeous green eyes with the slightly faded glow of a smoldering emerald. And she was tall, maybe a half-inch taller than Josh, who was over six feet. This gave her body a boyish look.

Josh looked down at the Marlboro burning between his fingers, raised it to his lips, took a deep drag, then made himself pull up alongside her and say hello. It had been a year since his first clumsy pass. They talked. Her classes sucked, she said. She hated Business English. Anthropology was kinda interesting.

"You wanna come up and have a cigarette?" she asked. Only northern girls say "have a cigarette." It reminded him of Lilian's roommates at Smith. He let her go first up the stairs and couldn't take his eyes off that shapely muscularity of her buttocks as he followed a few steps below. He smelled the soapy fragrance of her skin as she stepped back to let him in. There was another guy there, a little red-haired college kid name Mickey The shock of the appearance of the stranger. The other. You thought you invented her. Behold! The flesh of her own life!

Her apartment was one of those student hovels that racketeer landlords make a killing on. They cram three or four kids in there, then charge them a thousand bucks and never show up except to collect the rent. Her friends were lousy housekeepers, always dirty dishes in the sink covered with hardened tomato sauce, the kind you buy in a jar and pour over pasta. Waiting for everyone to do "their share" so nothing ever got done around the place. Finally, one of the girls would clean up so it was livable for a few days. The guys would sit in front of the TV, ashing cigarettes on the floor or in a big Maxwell House coffee can in the middle of the room. It's weird seeing a Maxwell can full of butts. Finally, someone would dump it.

After a clumsy intro and a brief look of dismay in Mickey's eyes, they sat down to beers and a fresh pack of camel filters. No one had any dope. It was too expensive. And the local marijuana harvest was still another month away. A cheap black and white TV sitting in a straight-backed chair had an afternoon soap opera on it. Tony on Days of Our Lives had just knocked up his girlfriend, Ursula, who was, if he remembered correctly, the wife of some old business scion, the kind with one of those distinguished grey perfect box haircuts. The girl has a miscarriage. Theme song comes up, credits roll.

"Yeah, I loved that gun the guy pulls out," the guy said. "Guns always look so stupid on daytime TV."

"It feels weird, sometimes, watchin' this stuff," Josh said.

"I guess people don't have that much to fill their lives up with," Wanda said,

"Yeah, I know," said Josh, "Bertha and Judge Daddy have both been watching this for twenty years!"

"Really?" Wanda asked, her huge eyes opening wide, "That's longer than I've even been alive! Whoa, that's cool."

Wanda got up to go to the bathroom, but when she came back she moved her chair toward Josh a few inches before she sat down, and when she sat down crossed her legs and let her toe point toward him a little. She leaned forward to light his cigarette. They smiled at each other. Mickey, by subtle male instinct, began to see his opportunity disappearing, so he stood up abruptly and blurted out two or three things he had to go and do, reciting a list of people who were awaiting him. Wanda gave him a sisterly hug and a peck on the cheek and mentioned some inside joke about her archaeology class.

Mickey made a last-ditch effort to salvage some of his hard-fought territorial gains, mentioning an incident involving some people they both knew, crisis averted at the last moment that might have cost someone their college career, or at least their driver's license. Then blew it by referring to someone she didn't know as if she knew them, and his, "I'm Somebody You Really Know Well" schtick was exposed as something of a stretch. This put him out there stuttering a few "Guess I'll see you in class" styled remarks, and after a lightning quick look of despair toward Josh, he was out the door. Josh could no longer see him as Wanda leaned, almost swinging, on the door saying something he couldn't hear. There was a laugh and then the smallest moment of silence.

Wanda came back in, apologizing for the intrusion. He's a nice guy, she said. Josh agreed. She moved over to the sofa and fiddled with the TV.

"I can't seem to get 'Cheers' to come in clearly."

"You watch Cheers?" Josh asked, thinking of all those years he and Berenice had watched it. Yeah, the Woody Harrelson character, what's his name? Sam says, 'So what's your mother's dream?" and Woody says, "To play lead guitar in a power trio!"

"Yeah, sometimes, either that or Jeopardy. But I get a little burned out on answering questions, or excuse me, asking them." They both giggled.

He sat down beside her to have a look at the TV antennae and miraculously got it to come in pretty well. She looked pleased. They looked at each other. He inclined his head ever so slightly toward her and she leaned closer and gave him a quizzical look, cocking her head ever so slightly as if making sure it was ok. He kissed her. He pushed her lips apart further with his tongue and let it dart over her teeth. He felt her tongue and sucked on it gently. When they took a breath at the same time their tongues were still dancing greedily and their lips met again and he let his mouth roam with little kisses over her face and down her neck. She closed her eyes and smiled, letting her head fall back slightly so he could more easily kiss her throat and her temples. He had a raging hard-on by now and his own throat filled with joyous internal squeals of, She's mine, I can't believe it!

12

Slouched and tired in front of the old Russian television in his small Budapest apartment, Josh switched channels at three a.m.. He found the old movie channel and Treasure of the Sierra Madre or some other western, dubbed into Hungarian. He liked to watch the late-night talk shows, Letterman, and now that new kid Conan O'Brien. Still dreaming in his peaceful post-gig reverie of being one of the featured guests, telling how he had "made it" in show biz. In moments when all life, on stage and off, seemed so embraceable, Josh would laugh at these relaxed conversations. He knew that these guys making it look easy was the mark of a true professional. And they were so quick! So smooth! How frivolous and beautiful American TV would then seem. So far from his real life. Humor was his salvation. Like the night Karl Lewis, the great Olympian, was on Conan O'Brien. How full of life he seemed, so buoyant at the end of such a fulfilling career. And all at thirty-five. A comedian named Mark Chilson came on and Josh even after all these years would still try and imitate routines and imagine doing them for friends he had bumped into on the street, in a bar or at a party. "Well, if you ask me… and you DID ask me, right?" (light chuckles) "all this fuss about drug testing in the Olympics is silly. What they oughta have is drug TAKING! Hey, look at Karl's last long jump! You gotta remember, now, he's had four beers, a hit of weed and a Jaeger!"

Josh would fall into the familiar dream of floating down the streets of Edgeton feeling like Jimi Hendrix, when he and Carlo and Hector and Jared Smallwood had their little band that played every Friday night at the church coffee house,

(*My God, I've had a gig every Friday night since I was twelve*, he once told me on the band bus), of listening to JR Byrd, the great bluegrass fiddler at the Ramada Inn in Frankfort, Kentucky. His first real up-close look at stage performers, his first real experience of being in a bar, a place he had once feared. Half-buttered people who seemed loud and desperate frightened him, especially a drunk redneck on a Saturday night.

But he learned, after years of playing in them, it was the upscale, slick, fern-covered bars that catered to tie-wearin' bidness men, that were the most dangerous. Sylvester said, "A rich white man can be a deadly mother-fucker."

To his sister, Angelika, he was funny. He had been making her laugh since they were kids, especially with silly things like goofy faces or writhing on the floor in hysterics, fake-vomiting, or just saying something like, "waka-waka" over and over at the right time. Making her laugh gave him a sense of well-being. It meant that everything at that moment was good. It released them, all of them, Josh, Doc and Angelika from the tension that Marshall and Agnes' arguing created in the house. Making Angelika laugh, withdrawing into his room with his guitar and singing into the side yard twilight, the light of the evening star coming off his guitar—these were his sanctuaries. And so they remained.

Josh thought about the day Agnes was shopping on Faulkner Street in Medina and saw a guitar propped up in a shop window. Young Agnes knew she wanted her sons to get interested in something. The window dressing was a popular one of the day, it was the "guitar craze." There were pictures of guitar celebrities like Chet Adkins and Gene Autry and even more obscure faces on the covers of sheet music like Eddie Lang and Lonnie Johnson with titles like "Hittin' On all Six" and "Tickling the Tuners." Agnes feared Bertha's influence over them. It was a critical point in their lives. Children's toys made of plastic would not keep them occupied anymore.

Doc and Josh were slowly coming out of the "playing army" stage even though they still crawled around the yard on their elbows imitating the machine gun noises they heard on shows like "Combat" and "Twelve O'Clock High." Josh so perfected his machine gun sounds during this period that he would later wow schoolmates at parties, those basement make-out parties where everyone slow danced and once he touched Hillary Fox's bra strap. He was good at imitating machine gun fire that sounded far off like distant thunder. He would wait just long enough, then hit 'em with the sound of one distant gunshot from a lonely rifleman. It was a nice touch. Anything macabre or that mocked death appealed to Josh and Doc. As if somewhere, far away, an execution had taken place. They loved explosions and imitating being blown up. "The field was quiet. The Germans thought the time was right to move out of their foxholes when suddenly,

ChuhCHOOO!!!! A single shot rang out." They narrated the story in voices like John Cameron Swayze or Walter Cronkite, "The strategy proved to be wrong on that fateful day in…" or more britishy, like Alexander Scourby. Once, at Christmas, Agnes brought them home a record of poems read by him, "Lord Rrrandall, Lord Rrrandall were have you beeeen? I fearrr you've been poisoned, my son. I fearrrr you've been poisoned."

Perhaps that's why Agnes walked into that shop that Saturday in May, with the yellow light all around, and bought a guitar for Josh. Tim Bogle was their teacher and they took lessons right there in the shop. He found that the first hurdle was getting a callous on the end of their fingers. You see, all stringed-instrument players must go through this maiming ritual. Mr. Bogle said he cussed and fumed over an F chord for weeks. That's the one where you press down two strings at a time with one finger. But Josh quickly learned it and D minor. He promised his mom he would practice fifteen minutes every day.

Coming out of his daydream for a moment, in a small room in Budapest, Joshua felt the sudden welling up of anger. Maybe it's true, he thought, no one cares. The old bitterness returned. The fact was nothing ever really happened that was that miraculous. He felt lost and afraid for a split second, then, would sigh heavily and resign himself to forget it, roll with it. Hadn't he done that with Lilian? Berenice? Hadn't that been the source of sudden shock that struck him down to the bottom of his heart when the routines of life had lulled him to sleep?

On the way back from a gig, he had one of those late-night Interstate "epiphanies." Turning on his car radio, looking for jazz and hearing a fatherly-sounding German accent saying, "All life is loss, culminating with the ultimate loss of our own life. At some point in our lives, there is no longer the earthly, parental 'warm hand' that once reached into our crib to comfort us in our helpless infancy." This reminded him of when Lilian made him go with her to see Robert Lowell read at Wellesley. He had quoted Yeats, "We wither into Truth," then added, "I think we wither into Untruth as well."

13

Josh stared into the TV and thought of the bright sky, a cloud casting a shadow across the bluegrass field, moving like a huge bird. Air wet and cool. Bertha's car horn trumpeting across the tobacco field heavy with blooms. Bertha's old house that sat up under the hill. The spring ran under the limestone masonry running the length of the back wall covered with ivy. Three doors were built into it. One led down a damp corridor to nowhere. Marshall said his folks'd kept ice down there and things that needed cooling. Another door, to a large limestone reservoir for her drinking water. There was always a salamander frozen still on the moist wall or a black snake or cow sucker laying peacefully in the rafters. This door was always fastened with an old wooden-handled screwdriver in the latch, probably just to keep possums out. The last one led to a stone-floored shower room whose squeaky on/off faucets were connected right on the pipe and where Bertha had her old-fashioned wringer. Doc and Josh spent hours sticking things into it until Josh caught his finger once and couldn't play his guitar for a week.

In the fall, dry leaves clung to their wet feet in crumbs. They would run naked to the backdoor only a few feet away, giggling as they dried their feet on the thick

burgundy carpet. Bertha was a small, round woman with a slight stoop. She would give them cokes and candy bars on a tray and not even bother sweeping out the leaves.

"It won't bother nothing," she said.

The car horn was Bertha's revenge on those who questioned her ability to carry out important farm business. In fact, her white-finned Dodge was, Doc recalled, a perpetually beleaguered unpredictable ship that kept the oncoming drivers of the county roads wary of her. Ricky-Boy called her "Wiggles" 'cause she drove to town like… he'd make his hand go like a snake in the water. Cattle began to prance, jumping and snorting away, banging into the fence row. Bertha wore an onyx ring with a gold band and three diamonds in it. She kept three more in a box of a drawer in the old house.

She got them out and showed them to Josh and Doc, "When I die I'm gonna give this one to you and this one to you. Don't tell Marshall or Agnes."

"What you gonna do with the other?" Doc asked.

"That one belonged to my mother," Bertha said.

"Let's you and me gope the mall." She would slur those two words together like that. "Go" and "up" became one.

"Now, Bertha, you know Dad told me to chop out this fence row," said Josh.

"Do it tomarrie! Let's you and me gope town… Marshall said for us to."

Josh knew that was a lie. But he also knew that his father wouldn't be angry for skipping weed-chopping as long it was for Bertha's sake.

"You drive," Bertha said.

Josh got behind the wheel. He was only sixteen and had just gotten his driver's permit. The yellow summer light was all around them. Edgeton on a Saturday morning. Josh felt the joy catch in his throat as he giggled and gripped the steering wheel. No time for daydreams now. He looked at Bertha in the passenger seat. A smile of girlish joy gently curled her upper lip. Doc once said that "the plenitude of the Mall was compensation for the austerity of her Appalachian childhood."

So, spoil the boys. Marshall could not break her.

On the way through Rylton, Josh waved to Shine and Money Joe, sitting on the porch of their old broke-down mansion that looked like it was once a rich white man's house even though it was down in a swag with paint peeled off and the front porch with big rotten columns was busted down, wild weeds and vines growing everywhere.

At last, the three grass strippers were hooked together in the shape of a trapezoidal flying V. Ricky Boy pulled the throttle out in the old Farm-All tractor and with a jolt and clinking of chains slipped it into gear and, front wheels rearing up a little from the back weight, moved on toward the field.

The front of a bluegrass stripper consisted of a broadsheet of thick tin set at an angle back up to a set of gears that ran up on both sides, the teeth of which pulled chains just like a bicycle chain only thicker and longer. Narrow wooden slats lay across the tin sheets at ten-inch intervals and moved up the sheet, powered by gears which themselves were connected to the main large gear turned by the wheel of the machine itself, which was turned by the motion of the tractor wheels. The slats carried the seed up the slanted sheet and dumped it into two large square holes fitted with burlap sacks.

At various intervals, the stripper riders would holler at the driver to stop when their sacks were full, remove them from the hooks around the square holes (chutes), tie them up and lay them aside in the field to be picked up later and ricked on a wagon or Marshall's big International truck with the removable black side slats.

The main part of the stripper was the set of teeth that spun down along the ground and looked like a big metal hair curler full of teeth. The teeth turned in a rapid motion, like the spinning of an old-time lawn. The ripe seed-filled heads of the grass were combed off their stalks in the V of the sharp, knife-like teeth, much like if you ran your hand palm down along the tall grass and caught the seed heads between splayed fingers. But the seed was then caught in the tin trough, curving like a harlequin's shoe at the bottom of the slanting tin sheet to be scooped up by wooden slats and carried up into dangling burlap sacks.

The rider's job was to shake down the sacks and clean the chaff of stalks, weeds and lost seed from the gears as he rode, looking down into the sacks, pushing the seed and stalk down into them, pulling up the bottom like stuffing a pillowcase with a pillow. While doing this the rider could lean against the metal sack rack behind him using it as a stool while keeping his feet firmly planted on the small wooden floor of the stripper.

To fall off would almost certainly mean getting run over by the stripper and cut to pieces in the spinning comb of metal teeth. Once Josh, hypnotized by the drone of the machines, inadvertently stepped off the small, wooden floor of the platform but darted into the narrow corridor between the oncoming stripper and narrowly escaped. Marshall looked back from the lead stripper and shouted at Ricky Boy to stop the tractor.

"Goddamn it, I told you to watch what you're doing! I don't wanna be stuffin' parts of you into these goddamn seed bags! Besides yourself, who you tryin' to kill?" Marshall's face went white with fear. The workmen were amazed by the power of his rage. Sylves, TLC, Ricky Boy, and the migrant workers who had come down from the eastern mountains all pitied the boy his humiliation.

Josh began to cry and his older brother came to him and Marshall reprimanded them, "When you boys gonna start payin' attention to what you're doing? I thought you could do a man's job, work on a man's machine but you all acting like boys out there carryin' on with all that silliness." Josh still sobbed softly. "What are you crying about, Joshua? You gonna let all these men here see you act thatta way?"

The men had left their respective machines and were lying, smoking in the shades of them. "Well, I always said you had fine feelings... yessir, fine feelings like a collie dog. How old you boys now?"

Doc muttered, "Fourteen."

"I'm nine, daddy," said Josh.

"Now, you see," continued their father, "In India you'd both be considered a man, able to work like a man. Just like some of them places I was at in the south Pacific during the war. The children would go out and follow their mamas and daddies right on out to the field and work all day right beside of 'em."

Marshall paused a moment and looked out over the field. It was nearly harvested. He looked into the row of tall, black cherry trees and the apron of shade they provided, undulating faintly in the early summer breeze. He seemed to Doc, who looked up at him for a moment, to be recalling some of the awful scenes of those battleship fights he'd been in in the Navy. Bodies floating in burning, swelling seas. Marshall was only seventeen then, fatherless for seven years. Fresh out of the military school Bertha had thought it was best to send him to.

Dexter was dead. Dead. To know the discipline of men. To stand watch on a battleship deck. There. A torpedo approaching. Torpedo! Torpedo! Marshall couldn't scream. Couldn't scream it into his mask. Sweat. Heart pound. No, it was a fish. A fish. Not a torpedo. War. The end of it. Sailing into Tokyo Bay. Where's Tokyo Rose? She vowed to sleep with every sailor boy who made it into the harbor. Where's Rose? Over now. The Rose of Sharon of home. Edgeton. The big shiny new "Indian Head" '46 Pontiac. Go out drinkin' and ridin' around in it with Sylvester. Getting wild. He looks over at Sylvester in the shade, smoking, laughing with the mountain boys. 25 years since we come home. Boy, we had us a time. They said his daddy and my daddy made the best whiskey in Water Maple County. Then him going out to LA playin' that damn piano and them damn drums. That's what fucked him up. Had him a good job on a horse farm, then got out there with that ol' Redd Foxx and all them crazy mother-fuckers. That and that crazy shit he smokes he brought back from Korea. Ain't nobody else gonna say shit bad about him, though. I'll do the shit givin' that needs givin' 'specially if it's give out here on this farm.

"Yessir boys you all'd be considered men where I was overseas. Expected to work a full day like everybody else…" he paused a moment, "of course those slant-eyed bastards can live a month on one damn bowl of rice!" Marshall laughed. "Reckon we could get along on Bertha fixin' us a bowl of rice for dinner?" The boys smiled at the thought. "There you go," said Marshall. "Life ain't so bad, is it? No, boys, you gotta work for a livin' in this world, ain't no gettin' around it. Now, let's get this field finished."

Doc looked at him and thought about how he'd asked, "Which one of us you wanna kill?" You, Doc thought to himself, You.

The sun rose hot into the morning in an arc across the sky. The men and boys on the machines went around and around the field in circles. The patch of unharvested seed began to grow smaller and smaller with each pass. The bare stalks left in their wake shone gold, slanted and glinting in the sun. The shadows from the trees, oaks, wild cherry, elm and poplar began to shorten as the sun rose and the cool dewy air was burned away and became lava-like. The tops of the boy's heads began to sting with the sun and Sylves tied a colorful handkerchief around his which gave him the appearance of a Caribbean pirate on a sea of bluegrass. The last pass was made. The field finished.

Sylves jumped off his stripper and threw each one back out of gear and the caravan of men, boys and machines slowly began their return to the tractor barn. The bladed combs no longer turned and now, no longer hungrily churning and whirring through the field, seemed almost like broken toys, almost like gentle crones gone in the teeth.

The men stood in the shade brushing the dirt and dust and seed out of their hair and clothes, washing their hands and necks with cold water from the hand pump on the hill above Bertha's house where she had prepared the noontime dinner. These elaborate country repasts were not that frequent. Most of the time the workmen piled into Marshall's pick-up truck and went to Bogles' grocery for boloney sandwiches, RC's and hostess cupcakes. But Bertha's noontime dinners were forever burned into Josh's memory.

Fried chicken was of course the centerpiece. The men walked down the hill on a pathway of stones that over the years had sunk down smooth into the earth. The right side of the yard was lined with rose of Sharon bushes full of bumblebees and hummingbirds. Through the rest of the spacious yard, which took the boys sometimes two workdays to mow, stood oaks and locusts and elms and chestnut trees among which scampered squirrels below every variety of songbird. The mockingbird, Robin and Kentucky Cardinal sang out, the cackle of the Starling and scream of the Bluejay.

Further down on the right just before reaching a small stone staircase leading to the porch and Bertha's side door stood a rock garden filled with chunks of bright limestone, sandstone, feldspar and quartz that sparkled in the sun. No one, except the occasional stranger, actually used her front entrance bordered by trellises of Chinese ivy and morning glory, there was no real pathway to it. Among those rocks lay fossils of sea sponge and shell creatures, a testimony of antediluvial Kentucky uncovered by the plow and tobacco setter. Bertha followed behind in the black earth finding Indian arrowheads, pieces of adze and millstones, remnants of vanished people.

The east side of Bertha's house was lined with picture windows that looked out onto more Rose of Sharon bushes and up the hill toward the large red feed barn. The yellow morning light shone through her house onto a light pine floor scrubbed clean with scalding water and pine-sol and ammonia so the whole house smelled like a hospital standing in the middle of a forest. On a pine breakfast table under the row of windows sat a wooden tray with her silverware. Josh was always fascinated by a spoon from the 1938 Chicago World's Fair and a knife with John F. Kennedy's face on it. He stared at it for hours over the years waiting with Doc and Marshall for Bertha to bring food.

Joshua, his brother Albert 'Doc,' his father Marshall, son of Bertha and now deceased Dexter Celeste, and all the work hands, after removing their heavy muddy shoes, enter the house below the hill. Marshall goes past the pine breakfast table and down another little staircase to the room he calls his office. The men and his two boys go on into the little dining room to sit down to dinner.

Marshall sits at the long cherry desk perhaps writing checks if this is a Friday or shuffling through bank statements or feed, fertilizer and equipment repair bills. This was once his parent's bedroom and he gazes in solitude. He stares at the antique four-poster bed that one almost needs a ladder to climb into. Sometimes he slept here warm between his parents. Marshall Celeste sits alone with his financial burdens. He hears TLC ask for another piece of fried chicken, what Marshall said was the only thing Bertha ever took much time to cook, and their laughter over some remark he couldn't hear. The sound of ice dropping from a pitcher of iced tea into a glass, silver against china.

"There's nothing to be done," he thinks. "Let the will of God prevail. Let the boys stay in after lunch. Let them stay with Bertha. Watch TV. Sleep. No homework to do in summer. School never did me much good. Hard work never hurt nobody. Still, they's just boys." He looked up at their baby pictures Bertha had arranged to nearly cover the entire wall before his desk. Little Angelika, his only daughter. The boys in paper cone party hats and Josh's cheeks puffed out blowing out candles on the cake, surrounded by beaming child's faces. Josh, Jared, Carlo, Harriss and Hector on stage at a school talent show. Agnes holding the little Angelika. The little boys in 1958 standing with Agnes' father and the gray-faced black and white photo faces of Judge Daddy and other white-haired dignitaries in dark suits surrounding them, guiding their little hands holding scissors to cut the ribbon opening the new road between Edgeton and Medina. Bertha with the two boys. She considered them hers while Angelika conceded to Agnes. The boys playing in the sandbox with Aunt Pearl, Millicent, Bertha and Marshall sitting around in the lawn chairs. Was that old Schwartz in the background? He'd never noticed before. Doc as a newborn, eyes wide open. Hundreds more adorned the wall.

Marshall got up from the desk and walked toward the dining room to join the others. He stopped in the hall and looked up the hill where the old mansion once stood, where he'd lived with his parents and their parents, his beloved Grandaddy Ryly and Grandmama Fanny. The night it burned to the ground. Christmas night. He sees the little boy standing barefoot in the snow watching it burn. "Why don't the snow put it out, mama? A match don't light in the snow. Then daddy drinkin' too much. Oh lord the stories how Mother and I would pour out his whiskey, him on a three-day drunk. And bustin' the bottles so they wouldn't make more. There's a good story in that. The boys need to hear all of 'em. And Angelika.

That feller uptown, Doc's teacher, wants me to put all this on a tape machine. Doc says he's a folk singer. Or no, a folklorist! That's what he is! That's what I meant to say. I loved my daddy so so so much. The old big house is gone now. Then Daddy died. Then my grandmama lord how my grandaddy Ryley loved that woman. Didn't survive her thirty days. Ol' Logger Ryly logged all of Heater Mountain, Kentucky. Everybody in the mountains knew him and loved him. Came down the mountain on buckboard with twelve thousand dollars in a ceegar box and bought him this big ass bluegrass farm. Then Mother and I had to live in town and we brought fresh eggs and milk in that little red wagon, the same one the kids play in now, back from the farm. It was so cold, every bit of it would freeze on some mornings. Nobody hardly but Garvis Stepp, the barber, bought from us. I'll tell you to this day I won't let nobody else but him cut my hair. That's the way people did for each other back in the depression. People don't do that way no more."

"Then we had to fix up the old slave house down the hill up over the spring running out the bottom of it, where I'm sittin' right now, to live back on the farm. Nobody helping us since they said it wasn't nothin' but an old black person's house but Sylves'daddy, who Bertha didn't mind and ol' Schwartz who said he was an "Old World NEGRO." Where was little Sylves? probably out there in LA playin' his drums in that Redd Foxx's club. He wudn't much older'n me, sixteen, seventeen. We'd both be gone to the war in a few years. But they helped us. There's black people I can take or leave but I wouldn't say nothing against them. But I ain't Jesus Christ and I ain't no goddam bank. If a man don't like the way I do, well, go work someplace else. Look at these floors, these walls."

Marshall stood in the doorway of the dining room. The platter of fried chicken had diminished down to half a dozen or so pieces. The bowls of green beans cooked in bacon grease, fresh butter beans and sweet corn were nearly empty. Years later, Josh and me hungry as hell on the band bus, he told me that Agnes made the best corn pudding you ever put in your mouth. Platters of Early Girl tomatoes, cucumbers and green and red onions with a salad dressing made of oil and vinegar and ketchup that Mandy, Kate Prudent's cook, concocted; plates of fresh cornbread for sopping the green bean sop or dipping in the bowls of sawmill gravy (aka bulldog gravy) or crumbling up in a glass of fresh cold milk Bertha kept in a turquoise-colored pitcher in the icebox. There were boiled sugar beets and deviled eggs the mountain boys swallowed one after another like candy drops, baked cinnamon apples with candied ten-cent store red cinnamon drops (aka whiskey killers), candied yams, collard greens, stewed tomatoes in wonder bread and sugar and a bowl of mashed potatoes, butter standing in pools on top.

"You better get in here and eat, boss man," TLC said, "these mountain boys eats like they misses they mama's!" Laughter poured from the dining room.

"Now, Mr. Celeste I 'spect us boys'll go on out and smoke while you get your dinner," said one of the older mountain men.

"Y'all go on and finish your coffee and get a piece of that mincemeat pie."

"Well, sir, we sure do 'preciate the fixin's, but we're plumb full as ticks. We sure thank Miss Bertha for the hospitality."

"Oh, he'll work it off of ye out in the field, don't y'all worry none 'bout that!" said Bertha. The men laughed and shuffled apologetically out of the room.

"Well, you shore got two mighty fine boys," the old man said.

"Well, we try to do with 'em as good as we can," Bertha said.

Marshall Celeste gazed down the empty table, sunlight glinting on the silver and pooling up saffron on the floor. He sees the men moving up the hill toward where the old house stood. "Oh Lord the times we had there. If walls could talk. If this old farm could talk." A little boy again, Marshall sees the poor mountain relatives shuffle into the big dining room of the old big house up on the hill before it burned to the ground. 'How come it to burn down, mama?' "Logger Ryly was known to them. Need a job? Go down and see Ryly Celeste in Edgeton, KY. He's a mountain man. He knows us. Granddaddy Logger Ryly and my Daddy Dexter, in their Sunday suits. Little barefoot mountain girls helping young Bertha and her sisters with meals and washing the clothes. My daddy gets up to carve the roast pig and he takes out the heart of the ham, the tenderest part of the whole hog and sets it smack dab in the middle of my plate. I can still see those ol' mountain folks fallen faces when they see they ain't gonna get nothin' but the hind parts. That's just the way my daddy was. He took care of his own first. Marshall watches the men climb the hill. Doc and Josh have fallen asleep in front of the TV downstairs. He smiles from the steps. They're good boys. Little wild. Let them stay with Bertha."

POCKETKNIFE : A STORY JOSH TOLD ME ON THE BAND BUS.

Dexter Celeste, my father's father, was an alcoholic. A bad one. My father always said that we children had no concept of just how terrible his father's alcoholism was. "He might lay in the grass back over behind the house for 3 days and just lay in his own shit and piss, too drunk to move!"

I always pictured a gray Edgeton day, late fall, early evening tho the light was fading. Then at nightfall when the windows of the little hick town's poolroom windows went black with the dark night outside, little 6-year-old Marshall, my father as a child, had had enough. He had stood on the stool beside the big pool table and Money Joe and Shine had let him practice shooting pool balls, shiny as faces of the old men beside the roaring fireplace, into the pockets; they had given him quarters to put into the jukebox—all that had been done and he was ready to go home. Dexter sat at the old greasy bar, which was spattered with years of hamburger grease and enveloped in years of nicotine clouds. He sat among his friends and swapped big wild tales of drunkenness. Fragments would come to Marshall's ears as he periodically walked to the bar and begged his father that he was ready to go home. "Yeah, Dex," one of the men said, "he walked outta here, and when he rounded the corner I heard him squeal. Damned if she didn't stab his black ass with a ...." The sound drifted away in the hubbub.

Knives. Dexter had given one to little Marshall as a gift. Little Marshall had it in his pocket. His boredom with the poolroom intensified,

"Please, Daddy, can't we go home"?

"Just a minute, son. Just a minute". Marshall pulled at Dexter's old coat. This went on and on through the night. The night grew cold and sad and colorless and damp in late December, a glaze of rain on the cracked sidewalk outside and in the empty.

Marshall took out his pocketknife and approached his father saying, "You puss-gutted old sumbitch, you take me home right now or I'll kill you". And with that he poked Dexter in the belly with his little pocket knife, startling him and making him jerk away. Dexter rubbed the sting left on his belly through his heavy overcoat. "Alright, son. Alright. Let's go."

Bertha had been waiting at young Pearl Rabinowitz's house. They had sat and talked of many things. Dexter's whiskey still, his drinking. She had been sitting with Bertha's palm in her hand, telling her fortune. The phone rang. Dexter said come get me. She drove the car around to Crazy Reddy's Poolroom and Marshall and Dexter got in. It was a model T Ford.

They went down the country road and Marshall could hear them talking softly. Finally, they came to a stopping place by the roadside and Dexter got out and walked out into the field. He came to a fence row where hedge limbs hung down and he found one, reached up for it and broke it off. He walked back to the car holding the stick. "Mother how come Daddy's got that stick?" Dexter motioned for Marshall to get out of the car. "Mother, why's he got the stick. Mother, no! "Don't worry, boy, he's not going to hurt you." "Uh, uh, Mother, I ain't opening that door!" But Dexter came in from the other side suddenly and grabbed the boy out of the car. With one hand he pulled down the boys pants, exposing his pale thin legs, and with the other he raised the hedge limb glazed with rain shining in the faint moonlight over his head. The thorns on the limb glistened in the starlight. Marshall screamed as the limb came down, came down and slapped against his legs like the sound it made at night when he would listen as the wind scraped the locust branches against the house. Bertha's expressionless face is pale in the moonlight, through the car window, staring straight ahead into the black field.

"Get down on the floor! Don't you bleed them legs on my car! Don't you never pull a knife on me like that again, boy! You hear me? Don't you never do that again! And you quit that sniveling or I'll whip you some more." Bertha gave Marshall a hot bath and dabbed methylate on the wounds and wrapped him in a white towel. The little boy wept in the little bed in the moonlight, listening to their voices, and fell asleep.

14

Wanda and Josh went to see Sylves at some prefab new apartment complex in the black end of Medina where Sylves was living with a sister while he was recovering from surgery. The southern end of Medina experienced a rapid population increase in the early 80s. It's now predominantly black. In fact, the field that was cleared and bulldozed to make room for the complex, backed up to the extreme northern corner of what was once part of Water Maple Farm at the edge of Edgeton County. The same field where Shine and Money Joe and Mr. Dex made their whiskey, where even Sylves had grown some of his marijuana, was now covered over in a maze of parking lots, drives and open-staircased buildings like a motel with numbers down a hallway of doors.

"Come in here! Come in this house this minute!" Sylves said, in a mock-scolding grandmotherly tone. "How y'all doin? I ain't seen you in a looong time!" Josh recognized what he thought sounded like the old Coltrane record "Coltrane Jazz."

"That Trane?" he asked.

"Who else, man? Who else?" Sylves replied, eyes widening as he grinned. "And how you doin' girl? You must be Miss Wanda."

"Yeah, nice tuh meet ya," Wanda said, a little nervously.

"Kept wonderin when he was gonna bring you by here sometime. Josh told me alot about you."

"He did?" Wanda replied, her eyes flashing that slightly scared little girl look they often got.

"Oh, now, it was all good. Don't worry 'bout that," Sylves said reassuringly, "I told him hey you my man I ain't gonna 'low him to go 'round with somebody wadn't good to him."

"Well, I try to be." She smiled, child-like.

"You know when he had that other girl I tol him, look, ain't but two things you gotta do in this world, believe that Jesus Christ is the Son of God and leave 'at bitch you with!! What was her name?"

"Lilian."

"Yeah, that's the one. Never did like her. Angelika called her "icy eyes." Went to that big fine school way up north somewhere. I knew she was playin around on you up there. Havin' Sunday guests, that's how we say it. Her daddy owned all them horses out on Darcy Farm. I woiked for him out dere. Not very long. Man, he was a son of a bitch. Liked good music, tho. Had plenty of money. Finally struck it rich. He had my man 'ol George Benson play down there at her debutante party. Biiiig wingding. I bet George come outta there that night with twenty g's in his pocket, cold cash. Grinnin' like a possum."

"Yeah, you played drums. That's where I met her sort of. Well, a few weeks before at Bunny's graduation party."

"I remember. George talked to me about goin on the road with him. But I said forget it. I'll just stay down here with my mares. I lost my taste for that life. So many things… then there was that other'n, Berenice. Don't EVEN get me started on her!"

They all laughed. Wanda smiled at Josh, at the past and its mystery, its anger, and held his hand.

"Life goes on, Sylves. I guess I grew up," said Josh, a little embarrassed by all those stories. He glanced out the window over the parking lots and into the fields.

"But YOU 'bout half fucked that one up didn't you?" said Sylves, winking at Wanda.   "Messin with that piano teacher over at the University."

"Ha-ha, I hadn't heard about that," Wanda giggled.

Josh smiled, "Well, we started seeing other people."

Sylves laughed, "Now, ain't that a white person thing, 'seein' other people!' Lawd, don't that beat all!"

Josh smiled and shook his head, resigned to the army-like, yet good-intentioned ribbing from this man he loved and who was like a father to him.

They all sat down and drank coca-cola. Sylves apologized for having to get up every few minutes and go out to the bathroom. The medicine they gave him, he said, made him sick.

When he went out, Josh and Wanda glanced around the room for a moment, taking in his humble abode. His sister, he said, had gone away for the weekend to see a cousin in Dayton. On the wall just above the TV and a little to the left, hung an old framed photograph, wrinkled with a bit of moisture under the glass, of Sylves with Frank Sinatra and Red Foxx, their arms flung around each other. Sylves came back in and eased his gaunt frame into an easy chair, looking a little embarrassed.

"Smoke some, Sylves?" asked Wanda, pulling a bag of pot out of her purse and smiling at Josh. Josh smiled back and shook his head at her.

"Aw, shit. Doctor said I wudnt 'sposed to do' at shit. But hell, they say C patients can get it for depression now so... Lemme smell it. Uh-hummmm. That's the shit. That's the fire there. Don't gimme none of that. Naw, man. Nyooooh buddy. Das some shit you can keep right there. Dashit would fuck me up more than twelve motherfuckers. If Miss Wanda don't mind me sayin so."

"Oh, you can say anything in front of her. She don't get offended," said Josh.

Wanda smiled and nodded her head in agreement.

Sylves leaned forward. "Fuck that white doctor motherfucker... lemme just have one hit. Jush one!"

They laughed about so many things in the beautiful life passed. The young time. Soon it was time to go. Sylves insisted he walk them to the car. "I wanna see this new French ride Cotton told me he saw you drivin around in."

"By the way, how's he doin'?" asked Josh.

"Aw, he's fine. You heard about him gettin mad at TLC, didn't you, when they come up on him with some white girl in the Avenue one night? They doin all that shootin' and scarin' people. One of them bullets ricocheted, I heard Ricky tell it. Cotton come back by the cornfield wantin' to give TLC a good ass-whuppin'. Me and Marshall had to come out there through the cornfield and break it up. You 'member that night, right? You was a pretty young fella back then, but I guess you do. Cop cars flyin through the farm at all hours. Something changed in him after that. I guess time just kinda beat all that anger out of him. He don't act like he used to. That mad at the world coz he half white way he had. You know all that pretty blond hair he had? They shaved it all off in the Army. He said he likes it that way now."

After a moment, as Wanda walked ahead down the hallway to the parking lot, Josh turned and asked him, "Sylves, why do you think you're getting sick?"

"I can't hardly think about nobody no more." His modern black accent kicked in and the jive talk posturing faded some. "It doesn't feel right somehow anymore. The old jokes just aren't as funny now that so many have gone on. My brain is getting too tired to work and it seems it hasn't been taking good enough care of my body."

His eyes seemed filmed over with a vague sepia color.

"I can't hardly think about anybody anymore. It doesn't do any good. Nothing does any good anymore." The last note of "Some Other Blues" drifted through the open window.

"That's what it is, nothing does any good anymore." There was a long pause. He looked at Josh and for a brief second saw the young boy with his music books and records under his arm, the little cardboard guitar case, yellow school bus pulling slowly away, walking down the long avenue, past the spring and Bertha's house at the bottom of the hill, the waves of dark grass that smelled of wild onion, the jonquil- lined avenue, the enormous Elms and Oaks and Catalpas shading his young form.

Somewhere a horn blew and awakened him back to the present and now he saw Josh the man, approaching middle age, with Agnes' eyes, but hair thinning, and he wanted to say, to cry out, Stop, Time! It's enough! Take me and let this boy go!

"Yep, that's what it is. Don't nothin do no good no mo'.... 'cept this reefer we just smoked! Makes everything seem cool."

They all laughed loud and long.

A few years later, on a snowy Sunday night in Budapest, Josh would remember the call from Carlo in Philadelphia. "Hey man," he said, "I'm sorry if I'm callin too late. I didn't know the exact time dif between Europe and the US but... hey, man, Sylves died this afternoon. Peacefully in his sleep. The cancer had spread all through his lymph system. He just faded out. No pain. He'd been stayin at a friend's house here in town, even playin a few gigs with my band at the Rose Mill. Yeah, it's ok, man. He went out on a groove. Had a picture of your Mom and Dad said he wanted me to give you. Gave it to me a week or so ago. I think he knew his time wasn't long. I talked to Lacy on the phone and he's gonna get

DownBeat to do an obit.

FINAL BAR

Drummer Sylvester Moore has died at age 62. A longtime drummer at the Redd Foxx Club in Los Angeles in the late fifties, Moore became an important figure in the early west coast avant-garde scene and was particularly known in jazz circles for his cymbal work on up-tempo pieces. During this period and into the early seventies, he worked with every major name in jazz, mostly in touring ensembles. An accomplished pianist, as well as painter, Moore's first break came when he and regionally known singer, Agnes Demeter (Celeste) daughter of Sen. John Xavier "Judge Daddy" Demeter, received scholarships from the High School of Music and Art Jazz Program in Los Angeles, which included a recording contract with Capitol records. Mrs. Celeste later appeared in several feature films and Moore played a prominent role in their musical scores. Their success was marred by what many saw as veiled racist reactions to their personal relationship, especially from elements politically opposed to Sen. Demeter. Moore's flamboyant lifestyle came under police scrutiny, but he was later acquitted of drug charges. Celeste and Moore both eventually rejected the show business world. Moore spent the remainder of his life working with thoroughbred horses on a farm in Kentucky, though he never gave up music entirely. At the time of his death, he was working part time as a drummer with the Carlo Everett Quartet in Philadelphia.

15

"Crip what the fuck happened to your leg?" Remember the guy who worked at Crazy Red's poolroom before Red bought the Joyland? The ol' one-armed Mac. We never would say anything to that guy for fear of not only hurtin' his feelings but 'cause he might get mad and come across the bar after us. But we were curious how he'd lost his arm. Then one night that drunk guy comes in talking real loud and being generally weird, Mac walks over to take his order and the drunk guy says, "Hey Mac were the hell'd your arm go?" Mac didn't seem to mind, just turned away with a growl. We couldn't help but laugh. "Crip, I didn't want to hurt your feelings by greeting you in such a fashion... you fuckin' CRIPPLE!"

I remember when Carlo, Jared and Hector would come down summers to the farm and work for Marshall and Rickey. None of them could understand a word he said. Doc called it "authentic frontier gibberish." We figured, it didn't matter if you understood him or not, just smile and nod yes to everything he said. Bobby Paganini, the kid from way up North, Milwaukee, whose dad was director of the nuthouse came down to make a little summer wage putting up hay mentioned he'd worked all morning with Rickey and hadn't understood a word. We recommended the smile and nod method. After lunch, we went back to work and there's Bobby smiling and nodding unloading hay bales off the wagon with Rickey Boy, agreeing with everything he said. Rickey Boy just laughed and got a big kick outta Bobby showing him the easiest way to slide bales onto the conveyor.

All of sudden there come the awfullest commotion you ever heard in your life.

We all ran to the barn loft window to look out and see what it was and there was Rickey a-straddle of poor Bobby, yelling, "I'll kill you you Yankee sumbitch! I'll kill you!" Looks like Bobby agreed with something he shouldn't oughta. Like he nodded when he should've shook. Rickey Boy was a little sensitive on the subject of his wife who had a rep for staying in town a little later than she should. I 'spect she did what she had to do. If she was looking for a rich guy, she wasn't going to find many in Edgeton. Her choice of Rickey Boy as a husband was ill advised to say the least. Most folks in town knew the story. Rickey joked about it but you could tell it hurt him. Lord knows he wasn't a saint in matters of fidelity. He related to me stories concerning his relationship with a fourteen-year-old girl. "She just work her little laigs!"

My response to which after repeatedly but unsuccessfully trying to change the subject was also simply, what else? A nod and a smile. I can only imagine what she looked like if she engaged willingly in such sport with a toothless and hygienically-challenged Rickey Boy.

The way Doc pieced it together was that Rickey asked Bobby in a joking, quasi-self-deprecating but half-serious way, "I 'spose you wanna go uptown and get a piece of it like e'body else?" Referring to his wife not his concubine, to which, Bobby, thinking he had been referring to his penchant for the homemade apple pie at Crazy Red's, nodded vigorously in the affirmative. Thus, the failure of smile/nod method. By the time we managed to get down from the loft to pull Rickey off him he got away with only a bloody nose and lump on the back of his head. Bobby got lucky.

Doc wrote that Rickey Boy fell into the archetypal category of the "Seemingly placid Hick who unexpectedly turns on you." - Albert Celeste, Stories of Farm Life: Confessions of A Gooberologist and other Imaginary Writings. Water Maple Publications, 1984.

There came a time after the guitar lessons with Tim Bogle Agnes paid for after hours strumming and singing to the evening stars shining through the bedroom window, Josh thought about getting in a band. One day Tim invited him to stay after the lesson and watch a rehearsal with his band. There was an older boy there, maybe sixteen, who played a robin's egg blue strat through a fender twin reverb amp. This was around 1969 and yet this kid knew Hendrix's solo on "Hey Joe," the lick on "Fire" and many other wonders Josh had never heard before. What kind of music is this? The boy's tone was round and full. "I gave her the gun! I SHOT her!"

Josh was mystified by every move he made. Tim, with his pimply face and hair down over his Buddy Holly glasses, smiled to see his pupil so inspired and was quick to make a mental note of the credit he was due for steering him toward such beneficent influences.

As suddenly as these rehearsals ended a disagreement as to whether the band should play rock and roll or (Tim grabbin' his nose between two fingers) acid rock. Adolescence of electric guitar. Neighbors complained. Josh's first glimpse of fragile band relationships. The world's intrusion. These failures would preoccupy him for the rest of his life. Tim slowly faded from his life and the mysterious guitarist disappeared.

But the bug bit. Josh couldn't put down the guitar. He hugged it against his chest. It so happened at this time that Bobby Paganini's dad, being a wealthy shrink from up North, gave his son a charge account at Madison's Drugstore, the only place in Edgeton where you could buy Lp's. Josh and Bobby stood in front of the painted chipboard record bins flipping through albums, Herman's Hermits, Freddie and the Dreamers, that rare gospel recording of Elvis, the one where he's sitting solemn in his choir robes at the Hammond B-3 organ. Herb Alpert in a bull ring, another Herb Alpert record with a sexy girl on the cover covered with whipped cream, Cream's "Goodbye Cream." Then he flipped another record jacket. There they were. The Jimi Hendrix Experience. "Are you Experienced?" Wearing coats of fish eyes staring in a convex lens. The wavy Afro tousled eccentrically. It scared Josh a little. A mixture of predetermined knowledge and fear. Sweat sprang to his palms. A clairvoyance. Yes, the Orphic one had arrived. But a lost feeling. The lyrical, romantic gathering for its final discord. The chord that sounds when the instrument explodes. A lost airplane humming over India. This was Hendrix's guitar. Josh worshiped him.

The consummation of his godliness was coming. Bobby charged a copy of "Goodbye Cream" to the account his parents had given him. When he noticed Josh looking at the Hendrix album, he said, "Oh that guy's cool. Come on over to my house, I got one of his records I'll give you."

With the yellow light of afternoon streaming through the windows, on a day with nothing much to do, Josh placed the vinyl disc on the little stereo and into the room rushed the eternal benevolent spirit, the same one from Coltrane's horn he would cling to desperately years later chanting in lonely tearful shower, "SPIRICHULL SHIT! SPIRICHULL SHIT!" Berenice gone and the house so empty. "Have you uuu, have you ever beeneeeyeyyn to electric ladylaaannd... Look up in the sky turned hellfire red y'all... somebody's house is burnin'... down down down down."

Like one who now held the secret of All Things, he stayed in his room until night fell. The room was pitch black except for a tiny light coming from the turntable. He stared at the light as it began to move, pulse, waver, "a merman I should turn to be... not to die but to be reborn away from the world so tattered and torn… orororor... to the OTHER SIDE..." Orpheus riding out to sea. Born like Venus on the surf. Stereo light like the green evening star. Darkness all around. What was LSD like? he thought. He saw shapes in the air. The sound went in a circle from speaker to speaker creating a vast world. Circle. Parabola. Arc of Sound. A silver spoon melting down a stone wall. Inward. Look inward. Left-handed Orpheus weeping in a well. Image wavering in water. The tiny light. The moon. The boy lay in bed frightened and exhilarated listening to the thump of needle against label. The tone arm lifted. Report of distant explosion. It cut itself off. Pitch black.

Jimi walked with Josh everywhere, bringing in wood for the evening fire in the huge old limestone fireplace Marshall built from stones taken from the farm. To Madison's Drugstore after school where he and Doc ate hamburgers and drank milkshakes. The same place he would see Kiki La Salle, through the glass door so dark in her white dress, walking down main street to the library, long silky chestnut hair hanging down her back. Jimi was with him as he drove the wagons from barn to field and back again. And as he walked the streets of Edgeton.

Then one day, walking through the living room of the house on Edgeton Road, he saw his face, a strange pencil drawing of it. And below it the dates of birth and death. Jimi Hendrix, the something something something, said David Brinkly, was dead.

Josh went to do some homework. Ate dinner with Agnes. The ceiling above the bed. Dome of heaven. We'll meet up yonder some sweet day. I will see him again. Gone. I done changed addresses on ya. What loss is this? Fragment of prayer… then Josh cried a little and went to sleep. Jimi waved to him in the astral plane.

16

"Reach and grab!" Marshall yelled, "Find out what you want in this world and take it!" Josh was beginning to think he never did figure that out.

One day Marshall was ridin' in the old International truck, routinely checkin' for a broken-down fence, stray cattle and groundhog holes. He spent a lot of time alone but sometimes he'd take a notion he wanted company and ask Josh to go along with him. He'd put his shotgun between the two seats, barrel pointing down at the floorboard just to the right of the gas pedal. He got to carryin' it that way all the time. They rode through the twilit fields, lush green and unmowed.

"I just might let this field grow out for hay this year", Marshall said, almost to himself. "Yep, I just miiiight do it."

His mountain accent lengthening the sound of the "I," he looked off into the distance catatonically, tired from the day's work. He slowed the car down to a crawl then stopped it very gently. He reached for the shotgun. Very quickly he pointed the barrel out the window and cradled the stock into his cheek, resting it gently on his neck.

"Groundhog," he whispered. Way up the rolling hillside, far beyond a thick grove of trees, a small shadow of a creature stood up on its hind legs, its little paws held up as in prayer, sniffing the air.

A sharp pop seemed to crack open the whole valley and it fell to each side like a walnut being hit with a hammer. Pow! another shot. The poor running creature flipped in the air like a tossed coin but fell on its feet and kept runnin. Pow! another shot raised a little mist of dirt beside it a few feet away. "Well, goddamn, if I can't hit him after three goddamn tries, little sumbitch deserves to live!"

They drove on in silence. "If I don't get rid of 'em, they'll destroy a field. A man can die if a tractor wheel rolls down in one of their holes. Holes bigger'n one on one of them whores up in Medina that Money Joe and Rickey Boy screws around with all the time. Bigger'n one of them bomb craters I used to see on the beaches in the South Pacific after they'd wasted them Jap sumbitches to hell and gone. Used to climb down in 'em. Nice and cool."

They stopped beside the field up by Sylves's barn, chest-high in corn. The wind rustled the top leaves and tassels ever so gently. Josh and his dad got out and walked to the fence. Crows, a small band of them a hundred paces away, dispersed as they drew closer. Josh leaned on the rusted barbed wire sagging, loose and strung over top of the old fence built by his great grandfather, Ryly Celeste.

"Your mother and them like it up there at that church and that's fine with me." Marshall told him. "You go on up there and help with the service and keep playin your music if that's what you want. Do it for yourself though. Don't nobody really give a shit about nobody else. Guess you figured that out by now." He looked at him and smiled, his eyes wise. Josh knew he didn't mean what he'd just said, not completely.

"Hell, it's worth it just to go up there to that church and hear Sylves play the organ.'"

"He just plays sometimes," Josh said.

"Well, I figured. Maybe if he played every week I'd go!" He smiled again, took a camel out of his pocket and lit it.

"I used to go on some of his 'tours' with him," he said, chuckling. "God, we had us a time. We shoooore did."

He let go a laugh then stared out at the field for a few minutes in silence.

"But this is my God," Marshall said, sweeping his hand out in front of him. "This is my God."

Josh set his guitar aside, the old martin d-28 Brazilian rosewood. He noticed how lovely it was there against the wall like one of those William Harnett still lifes he and Berenice saw at the Art Institute in Chicago. Beneath the glare of the lamp in the little Budapest apartment room he slept in, every nick, scrap and bump the old guitar ever absorbed seemed visible. As he looked at his reflection in the dark rosewood back of the guitar, he saw his past life swirling Oz-like around his face. In every nick and gouge of the finish, came a drunken party at Lilian's, or the night it dawned on him that he and Berenice were finished and he jumped into his pick up and drove straight to the farm and played his guitar cross-legged half lotus position in the gravel driveway, gravel scratching the wood as he tilted his head back to see the milky way and Venus. The hairline crack put there years later by Dragan, Helen's old boyfriend. The bigger crack was made by the affable guy from Pennsylvania. After he and Lilian split up, and he rode a bus as far as Pittsburg, then hitched the rest of the way home, the guy who picked him up dropped the case as he was trying to get it into the trunk. Sleepy and stoned, Josh thought maybe the guy would kill him and stuff HIM in there too but he turned out to be cool and generous, especially with his Camel cigarettes. When he and Berenice drifted apart, he played hard, frustrated against the strings, attacking the guitar, putting scratches just below the pickguard. All the years of Django rhythms backing up flashy dudes in Budapest bars and playin' Bluegrass into a cheap mic in a noisy bar in Edgeton, being too rough with it. He remembered carrying it out of the case which was doubling as a speaker stand that night at Crazy Reddie's and up the stairs where he nicked it on the wall several times so stoned and drunk he couldn't judge the steps.

The whole story seemed like it was there in hieroglyph, scratched on the top of that Martin guitar. He hugged it, put his ear down to it, against it, like a shell, carried it a million miles it seemed. Now, what more could he do? It was as if, kneeling, he caressed his little son standing before him, held the instrument firmly in both hands as you would someone by the shoulders. He closed his eyes and listened to the watery sound.

17

Josh,

The artificial reality I built, the foundation for "The Perceptions of Doc Celeste" is gettin a whippin from Reality little brother, one which gets bigger as my brain power shrinks. I pit My World against The World with the ill-founded hope of becoming the victor. But I denied, never overcame, its influence over me. With age and the certainty of my death, resignation comes and the artificial world I was king of, disappears.

"I'm takin all she's got!" that's what that old trucker used to say when he shocked himself with an electric cattle prod. I'm facing the music now but I'm a man without a conspiracy to hatch, without a dream. Loneliness and heartbreak make you fear death less. You're actually stronger, Josh, if you think about it. When I'm happy, fat and sassy, sometimes my anxieties about mortality increase. Pain and joy must balance out in the equation of psychic logic, or cancel each other out. The idea of death mars the complacent tranquility of the happy man, but it brings joyous hope of release to the lonesome. The weakness that ushered "lonesome" metamorphoses into the strength that fearlessness of death can bring, just as the strength and health that led to joy and happiness, becomes the weakness of the fear of its loss.

And at bottom, like a wild-eyed phosphorescent sea fish, lies the awful self you don't want to face, knowing that now, at rock bottom, it's all you've got. Remember how Dad used to say, "Have a place to land"? Hope to see you at your show if I can get out of the office... or should I say recital since you mentioned a few classical pieces with Lacy.

And Josh, don't be like Crip. He seems to think the world fucked up his leg so it owes him something. He's an okay guy but can't you see the path of vengeance he sometimes takes? He's casting about for something to blame his failure on. Play some gigs but I wouldn't hitch my wagon, etc. Blah blah and so on... You get the point. All true all true.

As ever,

Doc.

P.S. Sylves told me: "lower you sink, lower you WILL sink. Don't be lookin for no help from nobody. They don't feel sorry for you when you get old."

As I sit here in the middle of that old European capitol, Budapest, it seems like many lifetimes ago that Josh, when he was just a boy, wandered the lush bluegrass fields of Kentucky. The songs he sang to the trees, to the cattle, to the fading sun were, I can see now almost like prayers. Even at nine he knew where God and Jesus lived... just above the Black Walnut tree, behind the garage and below the evening star. Josh wrote me, "I remember Christmas in the big house on Tranquility St. The tree was in the hallway one year and then over in the living room the next. I must have been really small."

Years later after Mom had gotten out of show bizness, she came back to Edgeton and bought the old mansion that's separated from my old childhood house by a large green expanse of yard. When I visit her there now I find myself staring through the second story window at that huge mansion of childhood across the large wooded garden and the little brook that runs through it where I used to fish for imaginary fish, safety pin for fish hook. It seems to almost float above the ground, not tethered to any reality or Time, a kingdom of heaven already realized and unchangeable, its mass so dense with memory, so solid with green yard, limestone rock foundation, white boards, green roofs and gables. It seems, for a moment, greater than Earth's.

In the back of the house was a second story glassed-in porch where eastern sunlight poured in like safflower oil. There was a child's breakfast table and a TV. Dad's tobacco-colored leather upholstered easy chair was in one corner. My big pastime was sliding around in my footie pajamas, yellow ones with grey foot pads. It was there that cartoons blared in the morning and we were forced to eat spinach "Just like Popeye!" in the evening. Mom always said, "Eat a bite of everything!" Hey, I love spinach now, Greek salads, the Hungies eat it pureed over noodles, or with big pieces of egg-dipped toast. But at that time there were few foods that could make a kid toss his cookies quicker.

We stood next to Mom in church and learned how to sing harmony because she always sang the alto part while the rest of the congregation was singing, or trying to sing, the melody. So we heard both going on. All those great Episcopal hymns! I think Josh's first exposure to music was in the cartoons. There was one Bugs Bunny one where, whenever the Myna bird appeared, this weird Moussoursky-like theme would play. Josh couldn't have been much more than two but he would run to the TV screen and put his nose up in it and squeal with delight! It was the kind of song that raised the hairs on the back of your neck. A warm feeling came over me. And we marched around the room screaming. I wrote about it:

SOFTLY... A WOMAN IS SINGING

A memoir by Dr. Albert "Doc" Celeste

"Softly, in the dusk, a woman is singing to me: taking me back down the vista of years... in the flood of remembrance, I weep like a child for the past."

– FROM "PIANO" BY D. H. LAWRENCE

My first memory is of a Christmas tree. Two Christmas trees. One year, it must have been 1958 or '59, my parents put it up in a corner under the staircase of our house on Water Maple St. but the next year they moved it into the living room. These are the only Christmases I remember in that huge old Victorian house in our little town. The next year we moved out to the Farm, only a few miles away, where my father had grown up and where his mother, my grandmother Bertha, still lived in the old house down the hill beside the spring that fed the little creek.

My father had decided to remodel an old farmhouse that stood on the other side of the farm, a half-mile or so away from my grandmother's. It was here that I lived a significant part of my life, almost fifteen years, and where the foundation you might say was laid for the adult I would become.

Yet, somehow it was in the old Water Maple St. house, the house of the two Christmas trees that another foundation, a foundation of a self, the poetical self, first formed. Even the house itself, which had originally stood on Tranquility Ave, was literally picked up off its foundation and carried the fifty yards or so across to Water Maple St. where it now stands. Recently, I came across a few snapshots my mother had kept of this curious feat of engineering involving ropes and palettes, pulleys and wheels. There is the house, a huge boat, floating, like an Emerald City toward its new destination.

It was here that I spent so many afternoons, still too young for school, pretending to be the legendary Zorro, galloping thru the kitchen and up the stairs in one of my father's black hats, a safety-pinned towel for a cape, a pair of my mother's sunglasses for a mask and a pencil for my sword. I cut quite a heroic figure.

It occurs to me it was then that I had also first become Don Quixote, tilting at an adult reality I could only then vaguely perceive, and which I have never since fully assented to, my pencil metamorphosing into a sword and then back into a pencil, a pen, a writer's pen.

My mother's father, the great Kentucky politician, Judge Daddy Demeter, must have been the driving force behind this idea of picking up a house and moving it. No one with the least bit of heart would have wanted to tear the lovely old thing down, and my grandfather was no exception but he wanted to build a new house on the spot where the old one stood so, of course, something had to be done. This project, this big house switcharoo, like so many things Judge Daddy did in his long, charmed career, was successful. Both homes, the tall, three-story wooden one on Tranquility St. that was to provide a kind of theatrical backdrop for my early childhood, and the rambling, one-story brick one of a Williamsburg colonial type, I never liked the look of it much, though it did have an austere beauty, are both still standing and in excellent repair today.

The public life of my maternal grandfather, Judge Daddy Demeter, is well documented and need not be touched on here, tempting though it is to relive those past glories as I sit here writing so many years later, far from that magical corner of Tranquility Ave and Water Maple where the heavy yellow light of so many forgotten sunny days and so many memories remain.

I was old enough to remember the glories, the fairy tale years at his mansion where my brother and I rode our tricycles over, what seemed to us then, endless acres of flat smooth asphalt. Where huge birthday parties were given for us with huge cakes and ice creams and where projectors and screens were set up in sumptuous drawing rooms of antebellum mansions so we could watch Donald Duck and Mickey Mouse cartoons. Returning there years later, as is often the case with people revisiting childhood places, I was shocked to see how really small it all was, especially compared to some of the Italian and Austro-Hungarian villas I would see in later years when I visited my brother in Europe. My brother Josh and I were like two princes in a folktale. A black servant would make us our favorite lunch, tuna fish sandwiches and Hawaiian Punch. I remember the servants as being kind, playful, yet sometimes stoic and pensive. Many were convicts serving prison terms. Judge Daddy was a grand, expansive man who loved everyone, until, of course, you crossed him. He was particularly fond of his servants and was pleased to be able to give them a second chance to better their lives. He was Judge, "Senatah," the master of the house, yet he was still of them. He himself had risen from poverty. He'd worked with black people all his life, played with them as a child, was impressed with their strength and tried to impress them. The rhythm of his speech, his stories, his country wisdom, his jocular style—all this he shared with his servants, all this was close to the black way of things. This closeness to black culture that I inherited from many of my relatives remained with me as my interest in the old stories began to grow years later.

Yet there remained an undercurrent of shame in black/white relations which is still with us in America. Judge Daddy wasn't a social innovator. He had no power, no magic wand, to change the status of the African American in society. He was generally not one to severely question the status quo, though when his instincts, which were keen as all country people's are, called him to act, he invariably did the right thing, and remained loyal to principle, even if it went against the grain, or cost him his job, as witnessed by his controversial authorization to allow Johnnie Simpson, Medina University's first black athlete, to play basketball in the Southern Conference). For the most part, he tended to side with prevailing Authority. He'd, after all, spent much of his youth trying to win its approval. Perhaps he felt that ultimately it was right.

He was not a rebel. He simply met the world on the field of endeavor with an energy equal to that which confronted him. His handshake was legendary. And, for him, if you worked hard and played by the rules, the shake the World gave in return should be fair. He had no idea of the possibility that, at the core of that morality, inherited from his English and Scottish ancestry, something might be rotten: that the black man, especially in the South of the Fifties, was damned if he did, damned if he didn't. "A black man got to fly to the place where a white man walks," Sylves use to say. "But I did it," Judge Daddy must have thought, "I raised myself up. They can do the same." In the Great Game of Life, which he'd learned to play beautifully, he simply couldn't imagine that the field might be uneven. He'd known bad men. During his three terms as Senator, he'd had the nerve to send men to the electric chair. He was tough enough, certainly not a naive man, but the subtle, sinister roots of racism, of slavery, was simply beyond his comprehension. His segregationist tendencies, "separate but equal," the empty slogan often bandied about the dinner table, his conservatism, was nigh on unshakable and he scoffed years later at mine and Josh's liberal views. His position, indeed, the whole region's, the whole country's, became more irrational as it became more untenable.

As I write this, the entire world groans in its chains and it becomes apparent that more than political solutions are required. A great love, Love itself, might be needed to emerge from the World and save it in the end. If my Grandfather, "Daddy," as us kids liked to call him, Judge Demeter, that grand old man of Kentucky, that Great American Character, could return from the spirit world and bring back wisdom from Beyond, he might agree with me or else now prophesy a fateful End Time.

Perhaps the most wondrous thing about Daddy and Milli's house on Water Maple St. was the basement. It wasn't a cellar with must and mold and dust but a splendid series of spacious rooms with a shiny tile floor, cool in summer, warm in winter. I'll never forget turning the latch that unbolted the door, turning the bright brass knob a little to the right and descending the well-built wooden staircase made of butternut wood, as was indeed the whole interior paneling of the entire house, the rarity of which I often heard Judge Daddy brag to visitors about. It did have a rich unique color, a kind of light-colored walnut, yet richer than poplar or pine. At the bottom of the staircase was a Spenser coat of arms hung in a cheap black frame. Judge Daddy cared little for such things. Although he loved his father dearly, little was known to his immediate family about their Demeter ancestry, his mother had abandoned him at age four. Judge Daddy viewed himself as the first of a new line, and in some ways he was, caring little for ancient relatives he considered inferior to himself. His wife Millicent, though, whom he affectionately called Mama, a pet name that belied the fact that he'd known little about his own mother, descended from the Raleigh and Spenser families of Virginia, who traced their ancestry back to Renaissance England, and the powerful nobles of those names, and even before. Milli's mother, whom we all called Mama Raleigh, was an amateur genealogist and author who wrote a book about the Apostle John and claimed kinship to Nicholas the Dispenser, an old Crusading knight from whom her maiden name, Spenser, is supposedly derived.

Judge Daddy viewed such rigamarole coming from his wife's family with not a small amount of incredulity, though perhaps a Demeter coat of arms also hung beside it. I don't remember. Years later, as I visited Southern families from time to time with their own visions of grandeur, I noticed that almost everyone had some sort of rigged up coat of arms proudly displayed on their wall.

On the right side, at the bottom of the stair, as you turned to go into the first room, there was a framed picture of Daddy and Milli and their California friends, the John Geislingens— who were Jewish—with Pope Pius. I found myself staring at this picture for hours as a little boy, somehow connecting my grandparents to holy things, to God and His Church and His Saints, to the magical light of photographs from the 1950s. Now, in my imagination, it almost seems as if this picture had been a kind of publicity still taken with God.

Continuing across the room, a narrow window on your right letting in a faint ray of yellow light from the front yard on the Tranquility St. side, there were many other large framed photographs, Daddy with Winston Churchill, Daddy with FDR, Daddy with Babe Ruth. He had been baseball coach at Medina U. for a time, even played in the Red River league with Earle Combs, the famed center fielder of the 1927 Yankees. Sports were his true love and the great metaphor of his life. There were photographs of Daddy with Jimmy Durante, Daddy with Hoagy Carmichael, with Redd Foxx (Sylvester in the background behind his drums!), with every famous person who had ever lived, it seemed.

Entranced by these fading icons of the adult world hanging upon the wall, it became almost de rigueur that my own life should somehow also be connected to the power of celebrity. As I first began to make my way in the world, whenever the quest for fame would go on around me it felt like something I had already experienced, almost old hat, something an indolent teenager would find too boringly familiar. It was only many years later in life that I realized my Grandfather's fame, and the many famous people with whom he was connected, couldn't guarantee my own. In fact, their celebrity was only loosely connected to the reality of my life. I had to live my own but for a long time I didn't know this, so secure I was within the world my Grandfather had created.

Turning away from that wall of Fame, looking behind me, there were many other even more wondrous things. My grandfather, long before I came into existence, had traveled the world. And everywhere he went he was given souvenir gifts. A long mahogany case with sliding glass doors stood against the opposite wall. Inside were all manner of geegaws: a 1930s Hohner harmonica from Berlin, silver spoons from the Brussels world's fair, a bible from David Ben Gurion, you name it. Upstairs in the library there stood an amazing four-foot wooden sculpture of the head of a North American Indian Chieftain in full wood-carved regalia, which I often ran my fingers across, feeling the rough wooden grooves of his face, downstairs in the basement there was something even more amazing: a full Indian headdress of long cascading feathers and a thickly beaded headband. The pane of the long glass case serving as a mirror, I would put it on, it fit perfectly, and strike various poses, staring at myself narcissistically for hours. But there was more. After the war, in the early fifties, Daddy had made a very memorable trip to Japan, escorting an American baseball team on a tour of exhibition games. The Japanese loved my grandfather and he loved them. And they were baseball crazy. He was given a souvenir there that enchanted me: a mask, something straight out of the Kurosawa films that would fascinate me years later. It was one of those warrior masks that covers the top half of the face, a shiny, patent leather-like, obsidian black, with holes for the eyes, the face of some oriental demon of war, probably meant as much to scare one's opponent as for protection, though the solid helmet with its protruding goat-like horns would have afforded plenty. It gave me a bit of an adrenalin rush looking at it, the horror of war fought by a race of men from the other side of the world—the strangeness of another culture. A culture where soldiers, instead of protecting the innocent, which I had somewhat naively believed was the only motive of the armies of my own country, would create a face, a mask of horror to strike fear into their enemy. There was something so alien to it. To don the face of a devil to defeat your opponent was something almost blasphemous to my frail fledgling inherited Christian sensibility. The images of Japanese soldiers killing GI's with machetes came to mind, the war movies we would watch. TV was full of war movies in those days: the struggle against the Germans, against the Japanese in the South Pacific, where my father had been in the Navy, explosions and machine-gun fire we would try to imitate in our games. I put on the mask and saw myself suddenly in the glass pane of the mahogany display case. I, a demon. Scary. Take it off.

Looking around for other curiosities, a wooden bucket full of signed baseballs grabbed my attention. A stack of paperbacks, Faulkner, Erskine Caldwell, John O'Hara, with racy thirties- style book covers, sat mildewing in the faint dampness. Shelves of old files, Life Magazines, a rack of old dresses—Milli hated to throw anything away. I'm glad she didn't. Walk back around now to the next room and see a real pinball machine, some shelves with a few odds and ends, some old school notebooks, a ping pong table where endless games and arguments would play themselves out well into my twenties. But the greatest thing was a regulation size basketball goal taken from a US Navy aircraft carrier. There wasn't room to actually hang it up at the official ten-foot height, so it just sat there a few feet off the ground. But it was still fun to shoot baskets on, hours and hours and hours. Time passed. The long glorious daydream of childhood drifted away as I stood there looking, hours and hours, at time's objects fished from its endless river and put on a shelf to look down upon my little life from their eternity. The afternoon sun plunged on down into the sky. I sat in a darkening room trying to see how long I could last before having to turn on the light. Suddenly someone would call to me from upstairs. Come up they would say. Come back to the Upper World. Supper's ready.

Whenever I ascended that staircase, I was returning from that basement world, the nether world of the past and its photographs and odd souvenirs stored away there, to the world of the desires and maneuverings of men and women. But I found out that those desires, those hopes, dreams... they are rarely fulfilled. Yet, as I write this now, so far away from that world, in time and space, as a delicate

Spring dawn creeps into my windows on little cat feet, I cannot say that, in my life, Fortune has been cruel or unfair. There have been shocks and scrapes, but the hand I was dealt was playable. And somehow the way things turned out seemed to carry its own logic that sprang from a depth no mortal could fathom. No victory could ever be savored too long and no defeat was ever permanent. As my Grandfather himself said toward the end of his life, " I have no regrets. I meant to do everything I did".

At the top of the basement stair, you turned left to the kitchen, a huge classic American one, with the stove right in the middle of the room and Formica counter running nearly its entire length, filled with the smell of bacon grease and frying chicken and steaming hot-buttered yeast rolls and bowls of mashed potatoes and green beans swimming in fresh butter and dollops of lard. Here ruled Cassandra the cook who, in her apron and pearl-rimmed glasses and wooden spoon, seemed like a fairy godmother of food, a conjuress calling up spirits, steam rising around her. Vida, a big Bessie Smith-looking woman, who had once killed a man with a razor, could usually be found helping her.

Next to the kitchen was a large yet cozy-feeling dining room with a rich Persian carpet, a large portrait of my grandmother over the fireplace and a chandelier over a long dark cherry wood dining table that we gathered around for Sunday dinners and holidays. To the right, you could walk through the double doors into a hallway. You could then continue on across the hall, through another set of double doors, into a sumptuous living room wherein lay many wonders, a portrait of my grandfather as a young man which he referred to as the "boy Senator," a piano, which Millicent sometimes played as we sang carols on Christmas eve, or as Judge Daddy sang his legendary version of *My Old Kentucky Home*, with Millicent adding a harmony. This shared talent for singing and their cute, cutting repartee with each other charmed audiences on the old campaign trails of the Thirties. *Gold Mine in the Sky* was another tune in their repertoire.

If you stopped in the hallway and looked down the length of it to the right, you would look out the windows by the front door and see the magnificent oaks of the front yard. Looking left your gaze might pass by a spacious uncarpeted room with a cool tile floor where Milli kept a flourishing array of house plants as well as a liquor cabinet. From there you could look further out into the back yard toward the swimming pool, built in the Forties, trimmed in lapis blue tile, and the lovely brown paneled two-storied guest house they called "the Cabin." It was here in May of 1963 that my life would suddenly change forever.

One of my strongest memories is of the softness of the grass. Although, as in so many yards on Tranquility St., the towering pin oak trees and pines gave off such thick shade that it was difficult for the grass around them to grow: fragments of twigs and bark and acorns and pine cones, all the detritus of their growth and living process, were strewn beneath them, letting only patches of tousled wild onion grow in the crumbling earth. In other parts of the yard, where the full sun had shone down on sunny southern summer days, thick green patches of bluegrass flourished. There I would lie for hours, hands behind my head, daydreaming figures, and perhaps my future, into the endless caravan of cumulus clouds moving eternally by. The little drama that played itself out in this yard on the third Tuesday of May 1963, always primary election day down South, has played itself out again and again in my memory. And the curiosity as to how my life and the life of my family might have been different has never much left me. What might Josh have become?

It was one of those lovely May Kentucky evenings, the air feeling almost like lotion and soft as the grass of my daydreams. All the friends, neighbors, their children, dogs, cats, prominent local lawyers, preachers, judges, sports figures, even a few Hollywood celebrities (Tony Curtis? Peter Falk? Natalie Wood? Surely Angelika remembers) were there. Everyone I had ever known in my eight years on the planet were all there in that lovely back yard. The atmosphere was festive. A doting old man leaned down to shake my hand, while I stared at the gnarled roadmap of arteriosclerosis on his cheek, brought into sharp relief by the tightness of his collar and tie, the sweet smell of bourbon and branch water on his breath. "Son," he said," I remember when you was thiiiis big." He held his thumb and forefinger apart slightly, indicating my previous size, "but lawd look at you now. Why, yer all growed up!" Matronly southern women, black and white, picked me up and kissed me, leaving little smears of lipstick on my cheeks, nearly burning me with their lipstick-smeared Lucky Strike non-filters they held between their fingers. "Yeay-uh, peed in his paints one time, went upstairs didn't wanna tell nobody. 'That's how he learned to change his clothes!" Then came their loud laughter. Finally, I managed to get back to my mates where badminton or touch football was the center of the universe, a few pine twigs stuck in the ground for goalposts.

I could hear my uncle Dennis' almost maniacal Indian whoop of a laugh, his face flushed with beer and whiskey, his cronies, former stars of the University football team, convulsed with laughter over Dennis' immaculate imitation of their old coach. A heated billiard game was stirring up among some of the young campaign workers. People began to grow restless for the final news of the victory my grandfather was heavily favored to get. But as the polls closed at six and the tabulations began to filter in, the mood became more somber. Something had gone wrong. I could sense it in my child's way. The burnished saffron light of evening began to fade from the sky and from my once innocent world. I went inside and found a crowd of grownups gathered around the television. Lovely, freshly tanned women in Chanel perfume and summer dresses, bejeweled in pearls and gold, standing beside handsome young husbands in blazers and seersucker suits, bent down to give me conciliatory hugs.

What was wrong? I couldn't quite tell. I left the room, that lovely old TV room paneled in the rich butternut wood Judge Daddy was so proud of, and walked down the hall, at the end of which was his large master bedroom. Before I reached the room, one hallway intersecting the other I mentioned, right at this crossing point, at this crossroads of life, you might say, I found my mother. I'd been looking for her among the crowd of strangers. I remember tugging at her skirt and asking, "Mama, is Judge Daddy losing?"

"Yes, sugar," she glanced tenderly down at me and then at a friend standing by. "Judge Daddy's losing."

My grandfather suddenly came in from the yard walking briskly, surrounded by aides though somehow looking completely alone in his thoughts, down the arm of the crossing hallways that led to his bedroom. Right at the crossing point, just before he turned left toward his room and the end of his career as holder of political office, my mother called out to him, "Daddy, you'll live ten years longer." He gave a brief smile, his eyes toward the ground, and disappeared.

Just as vividly, the house of my father's mother, my grandmother Bertha's house, still stands out in my memory, though it stood half-hidden under a hill. Those very words together, the sound of them out loud, "Bertha's house," even at this moment, echo deep reverberations of memory. As a child, I heard them spoken together so much. Her house and the huge rolling yard that surrounded it were truly the center of my childhood, "Go down and wait at Bertha's' house," "I'll be at Bertha's' house," "Where are they?" "Down at Bertha's' house." Everything, all activity, especially in the sphere of my Father's life, seemed to emanate from that point.

She, more than any woman I've ever known, was a woman of the country. A real country girl, Appalachian version. My father often said that none of us had ever known the real Bertha he had known. It would be difficult to disagree. What mother/son relationship can be fathomed by anyone else in the end? He painted a picture in our minds of a wild youthful Bertha who cared little about her appearance. She had wild curly black hair and in summer often just wore a flimsy country dress that, according to him, barely covered her ample breasts. She almost always went barefoot. And only when she needed to take that inevitable "trip to town" for business or groceries or a funeral or a wedding did she dress up with typical (albeit, slightly eccentric) female decorum. It's possible that at least some of the clothes she wore she had made herself, making alterations as she increased in age and weight. I say this only because her clothes had the same straight-forward, practical look as the many handsome rugs and blankets and crazy quilts she sewed. They all partook of a similar, no-frills, handmade style. I remember one pinkish, peachy colored suit of matching skirt and waist-length jacket and a similar one in green, red (she loved red) black and brown. She often knitted little matching caps to go with them. One of my girlfriends, when I was in my twenties, in the days of Bertha's very old age, thought that these little knitted beanies she wore were particularly cute, though a little silly looking. This same girl also reminded me not so long ago, in one of our e-mail exchanges, about Bertha's' penchant for "Swiss Miss" hamburgers at Frisch's, a popular restaurant chain in the South, which she mispronounced, as she did so many words, "Fischer's." She was probably dressed in one of these eccentric outfits when, in her eighties, she drove her car into the front wall of an insurance building on Main St in Edgeton. Amazingly, she survived that crash with only a broken arm and a badly blacked eye.

She became a sort of laughing stock of our little town after that, the brunt of jokes, most of which were good-natured. But much of the gossip about her possessed that subtle element of cruelty that only small town people possess. But even long before that unfortunate incident, her driving had become notorious, although she never drank a drop. Tranquility Pike, the road which led from our farm gate, if one turned east towards town, was as undulant as the rolling Bluegrass fields surrounding it. Quite a roller coaster in places, the roads were built over the fields as they were found in nature. Only years later were the rolling hills flattened for the coming of the Superhighways. If you turned West and went down to the Kentucky River toward Crowville, you reached, by way of some of the most picturesque countryside I would ever see in all my worldly travels, the state capitol at Frankfort, the dome of which reminded me of the Hapsburg royal palace in Budapest, where years later I would visit my expatriate brother.

Bertha had a habit of drifting into the center of the road just as an approaching hill obscured her vision of cars in the oncoming lane. Riding with her as a boy I had no idea this wasn't the correct and safe way to drive. I thought everyone drifted into the oncoming lane as they drove. Frequently, as we drove home from school, I would look up from my textbook, or from simply daydreaming out the car window, to see the look of alarm, indeed, terror, on the farmer's face in an oncoming pickup truck as he swerved dangerously to avoid being hit head-on by my grandmother's drifting, beat-up old dodge! The skilled driving of the local farmers—they were a stern, hardworking lot, only rarely given to excessive drinking—and the fact that in those days there weren't as many cars on the road, were probably the only things that saved us from a gruesome death in the twisted wreckage of a large American car.

One of the tobacco foremen of the farm, a stout man of few words who had that hillbillie habit of sipping Pepsi early in the morning, always made me chuckle in later years when he called her "Wiggles." This was in reference to the patterns she often wove in the road on trips to town. Eventually, when as a teenager and got my own driver's license, I tried to drive her where she needed to go as time permitted. It became one of my most important duties, taking her around town to do her errands, even driving her to the mall in Medina, to a big Super Market like Winn-Dixie or Kroger or to a store called Cloth World where she could get sewing supplies. She, of course, pronounced it in her Appalachian accent, "World Cloth." There were a few other endearing mispronunciations she always made, Diet-Rite cola became "Diet-ette." On another occasion she told Josh and me that sometime soon she intended, Japanese cars having just appeared on the scene, to buy us both a brand new Toyodia!

I think Bertha's dependence on me, a suddenly more smart-alecky, back-talking twenty-something with long hair and moustache, to get her from place to place, irritated her. I was too slow-witted and daydreamy for her, as I was for many women in my life. Sometimes when, self-importantly, I was unwilling to give up some part of my own schedule, probably a date with my girlfriend, she would become very angry and sometimes let out a blood-curdling scream. If this was done in the confines of the car, resulting from my refusal to drive toward the main highway and, instead, resolutely driving her back home as my father insisted, this scream was deafening and nerve-shattering. Josh, once thinking he was alone in her house, found that he had to climb up on one of her old Shaker style antique beds in order to fix a curtain that had fallen. As he was straightening it up and feeling satisfied with his repair job, he got one of her screams from behind, piercing as a whistle, "Don't you staaaaand on that beeeed!" His heart nearly leaped out his mouth, he was so startled. Often she would outwit me by coquettishly getting me to take her on a very small errand and then, once she had me behind the wheel and out on the highway, suddenly remember a much more convoluted and time-consuming errand she pretended to have forgotten. More often than not, I would like to think, I gave in. If I refused, she screamed, like the warrior squaws of her Cherokee ancestry, at the top of her lungs.

On another occasion, when I refused to take Bertha somewhere, she simply looked over at me from the passenger seat and said, "Why don't you shave off that goddamned moustache? It looks like a girl's pussy!" But these outbursts were exceptions, usually, she coddled and spoiled us terribly. Even after my brother and I were grown men she would often say, in a gentle tone of voice, perhaps in contrition for one of her tantrums, "You'll always be little boys to me."

One of my most outstanding memories is of her sitting in that bone-colored poplar rocker next to her door, it was actually her back door, no one ever used the front, which faced up a steep hill and was intentionally allowed to be overgrown with wild hedge, sitting there quilting or crocheting for hours on end. The east wall to her right was all windows, so in the mornings it was flooded with a watery pale yellow light that "en- sapphired" the dew on the meadow as it rose slowly to the top of the hill towards the sprawling red feed barn. In the evening, the window of the backdoor to her left, and another smaller one in the adjacent room, which contained a large faded black, nap-friendly chaise longe and a floor covered with a black crocheted rug with flecks of yellow and light blue in it, allowed the rich western light that sifted through oaks and maples down the hill to the house, to shine in. My grandmother was not a particularly spiritual person, but here she sat, rocking and sewing for hours in her meditations. Sometimes, as a young man, I would sit across from her at the table, which we used for breakfast and lunch, and just stare for hours out the window and gaze up the hill toward the barn, musing on a horse grazing near the back fence or cattle in the fields beyond, lost in my own meditations, occasionally glancing at her sewing or remarking on this or that. But more often than not we were just as comfortable not saying a word for hours.

She would make a quilt by first snipping up her departed husband's, my grandfather Dexter's, old ties then sew them together using old newspapers for backing. Surely a Freudian would squeal with delight if allowed to rummage through a case history like this. After sewing the pieces into the paper with what she called a feather stitch, which resembled a small network of bird's feet, she could then carefully remove the paper and then sew the quilted pieces onto a stronger cloth backing. She covered big spongy pillows the same way which, along with her quilts, adorned all our beds. Even now, after so many years and miles away from that life, from that world, I am looking at one of her quilts, folded on my bed. I stare at it and into the years.

It occurs to me now, as I write in this one room apartment in a faraway city, my dear brother Josh sleeping on the sofa, that perhaps it was her separation from the town, her many hours of solitude in her house under the hill, her many years of widowhood, or the resignation, or even rage, toward what life had not given her, all this created the eccentricity of her old age. She lost her trust in the male-dominated world. She believed everyone, including her son, was out to steal her farm. And it turned out that, presciently enough, the frail little world of her finances that she had for so many years fretted over and tried to protect after her husband's death, did indeed collapse. In the end, not a penny was left. Mercifully, she died before the complete financial ruin and foreclosure, the real estate agents, the trucks and shovels.

But it was the long, winding farm road that led to my grandmother's little house under the hill that I recall so vividly. It traces a kind of trail of dreams and memories. As it turned from the public road, which itself was just a country road, it gently descended a hill for some hundred yards, lined with all manner of oaks, maples and catalpas, toward a creek called Moore's Creek, a large stream that started from a spring in the little town of Edgeton that everyone, even the Indians of old, had used as a water source for hundreds of years as it flowed down, down for another five miles or so, to the Kentucky River. At the foot of the hill, the little farm road crossed a twenty-foot high bridge, whose worn, wooden trestles were dry and gray with decay, and then gently ascended again toward the main barns and the general day to day activity of the farm.

I remember that in March, as traces of Spring were first felt, starting from this point, as the road made its way up the hill above my grandmother's house, it was entirely lined on both sides with glorious waves of jonquils, thousands of butter-colored blooms on deep green stems. Sometimes, as a boy, after tiring of throwing rocks off the old bridge, I would wander up the little road (everyone on the Farm called it "the avenue") and wade in among these silken yellow cups, staring down into them, listening to the loud buzz of black and yellow striped bumblebees at their work, the sudden gurgling throttle of a distant tractor or, as afternoon shadows lengthened, the soft moans of the mourning dove.

Sometimes I picked a few of these lovely flowers and took them to her house but just as often as not I whacked off their heads with a stick or crushed them under my sneakers, fascinated by the yellow powder they bled. I was a boy after all. I hope I have become worthy of their forgiveness, these things which now live only in the imagination.

In every garden, there is a Serpent. Water Maple Farm was Eden. But the debt that my father had assumed when he re-purchased the "other side" of the Farm, as we called it, the part his own father had squandered on drink and general neglect... this was the serpent. And very slowly, all through my childhood and well into my adult years, that serpent spawned another more venomous serpent, my father's rage.

Marshall, paradoxically, was a boisterous man in public, often given to ribbing his cronies and business associates in the local establishments in an almost too loud and forceful way. He had lived in Edgeton all his life, he knew everyone and everyone knew him. Yet, he was a very quiet, private man, a loner, with only a few close friends. His displays of gregariousness, which often seemed forced and artificial, were most likely a cover for his basic shyness and lack of self-confidence, no doubt rooted in having grown up without a father. Grandfather Dex died when he was only ten.

As a farmer in the modern, mechanized world, my father had to venture out into the market place and make his mark as a businessman, to sell his tobacco, his cattle, his corn, and keep abreast of new methods to stay competitive. The old quasi-feudal days of the Family Farm as an almost self-sufficient world unto itself were rapidly fading, when bartering was a common practice and large sums of cash were unheard of, when poor tenant farmers worked the landowner's land for very low wages in exchange for free, though primitive, housing, when farm families all "put in" a huge garden, miniature Edens full of beets, purple as black eyes, big fat red Early Girl and German tomatoes, sweet corn, cabbages, leaf lettuce, carrots, half-runners and bulging green pods of lima beans. I sometimes think I've never researched it statistically so this may be a bit of romanticised narcissism, that I witnessed, as a child, the final twilight of the old Southern Rural America. I distinctly remember how, around 1970, farmers and even their children, rich or poor, in larger numbers it seemed, began looking for work in the factories that had come down from the North like Kulman and Rand McNally, International Paper and Trane. Old farm trucks were replaced by bigger shinier Ford and Chevy pickups. The old, round, small-bodied Farm-All tractors metamorphosed, overnight it seemed, into huge, square-bodied Fords and Cases and Massey Fergusons, with twice the tire size, ten times the capabilities. It was progress, alright, but there was something funny about it, like a weed or some mushrooms that sprang up overnight. Something that came from the outside. Like the way Sylves began to complain about "all these outside brothers" coming around town. It all seemed to my teenage eyes vaguely connected to the oil wealth America was importing. Big cars and high riding, jacked-up trucks were suddenly everywhere. Energy-thirsty America was growing, growing! And ruining the air, the soil and water.

During this perceptible change in the rhythm of country life, I was a little boy waking up every morning and dealing with things as I found them. The farm was divided into two different worlds: The Tranquility Pike side and the Edgeton Roadside. After leaving the Water Maple St. house at the age of six, that house that made the aforementioned journey from the corner at Tranquility Av., the one that still floats, like Dorothy's did through Kansan skies, over the "dream of ocean" between Europe and America, through my memory, we settled into Route Three Edgeton Rd. That was the place I would call home off and on until my twentieth year. It was a simple little structure surrounded by gorgeous bluegrass pastureland, the aesthetic equal of which I have never seen in all my worldly travels (perhaps a few places in southern and eastern Germany, a valley in Ecuador might've come close). The first time I ever saw it, I might have been as young as five, it was just an old run-down, dilapidated farmhouse. I remember the family who lived there. The old tenant farmer patriarch was a heavyset man with long white hair and a long white walrus moustache, stained faintly brown on the handlebar ends by his chewing tobacco. He looked a bit like Mr. Darling on the Andy Griffith Show or a heavier Leon Russell in his Mad Dogs and Englishman phase. People called him simply "Rue." I was fascinated by the sound of it. "Go see old Rue," someone would say. "Better go up and see Rue." Surrounding him was the typical hollow-eyed, solemn-faced wife and a brood of dirty-faced little children in patched, ill-fitting clothes. The John Prine line from Sam Stone always brought back images to me of those children, *"while his kids went around wearin other people's clothes."*

Rue appeared at the door, barefoot and overall-clad. I remember how strange his big toe looked, crooked, yellowed, the nail badly in need of trimming. The yard was filled with an anarchy of old tires, a child's rope swing slung over a stout arm-like limb of the thick-trunked water maple, the hollowed out portion of which would become a nest for endless kittens, a rusting car body, a stack of wood, a scythe. He and his wife scolding their children with little mild threats as they ran around giggling, almost swatting at them like flies. Was my father asking them to leave? Or was it they would move to another old house on the Tranquility side of the farm? They were a migrant family. Had they been here only to help harvest the tobacco? I couldn't tell. They were moving on.

Soon my father, would completely remodel the old house, landscape the half-acre of yard that surrounded it, restore the orchard on the hill beyond the back yard fence that slanted gently down to the creek and put in a spring house that would pump running water up the hill to us. The old hand pump Rue and his family had had to use was carted off. Years later, Dad even added a two-car garage with a regulation basketball goal tacked up on it. Almost no trace of Rue's old house was left.

This was our new home, soon to be freshly painted snow white, with pine green shutters and a bright red front door. Somewhere in the depths of memory, a rich saffron light shines. There is a blue Kentucky sky and a rolling green pasture. On summer mornings, I woke up and ate my cereal. We ate Gerber's Baby oatmeal till I was fifteen! I put on my fresh washed sneakers, still warm from the dryer and bounded out of that house and head down the dirt road, through half a mile of fields toward Bertha's house. Along the way, which to me, at age eight or nine, seemed like some epic fairy tale journey, I would see all manner of natural wonders. Sulphur yellow butterflies flitted along the edges of small pools of water, still standing in the bright heat after a hard summer rain the night before. Squatting down at the edge of the mud baking in the morning sun, looking at my reflection, I could see a universe of water bugs darting across little miniature ponds. I would take a stick and stir up the mud at the bottom or throw good throwing-sized rocks of ancient limestone fragments into them just to watch the splash. On rare occasions, I might see a red-speckled salamander dart into a hole. A bumblebee whirred by; huge winged grasshoppers leaped awkwardly from purple Canadian thistle to ironweed bloom. My father always said that the amount of ironweed in a field was a sign of the richness of its soil. Our fields were full of it.

The cows were my dear friends. Mostly Herefords and Black Angus huddled together beneath the shade of a fence row full of tall wild cherry trees or a majestic elm or oak. I could often recognize the ones whose faces had become familiar to me on past walks. I gave them names. I called out to them, but they only swished their tails at flies swarming around the traces of dung on their haunches and stared catatonically in front of them. I stared back, fascinated by their stoicism and peace of mind. But like any boy, I sometimes teased them. I tossed small limestone rocks at their thick-skinned shanks, I never wanted to hit their head or eyes. It barely phased them. As I walked closer, to scare them more effectively into engaging me, a startled look would gradually register in their faces and they would lumber up on their feet and trot away. Sometimes I would chase after them. They never turned around to attack me. Cattle in a field are completely docile and harmless. I remember now how comical it was when friends of mine from the town would come to visit. They were always deathly afraid to get out of the car and walk in a field of cattle, even if there were but a handful standing around a hundred feet away. They would draw back in terror and amazement as I waded through a herd, touching one here or there on the head or rump, even grabbing a tail or two. "Fear not," I would say, mocking them, "I will guide you through this den of monstrous beasts!" They would be embarrassed by their ignorance of the behavior of such common domestic beasts.

There are exceptions to every rule. Once I was almost the victim of my own smug self-assurance. When I was around twenty I spent a summer working at a stockyard. It was an awful place, full of the smell of shit and piss and screams of frightened animals being whipped, kicked, beaten and prodded with electric cattle prods as they were loaded onto trucks or moved from one pen to another. One morning, as we were sorting out a rowdy truckload of young Hereford steers into their proper pens, one frightened steer saw an open gate and headed for it full speed. Only I could rush into the gap, wave my arms wildly, yell and shoo it back to the herd. Yet, even as I did, the steer was still headed right for me. In all my childhood experiences with cattle up until that moment, if you stood in front of a moving cow to herd it in a different direction, waved your arms and yelled "Heeey!" it always veered off. Not always in the direction you wanted, but it never went right for you! This was different. We weren't out in an open sunlit bluegrass pasture. No, this was a maze of chutes and pens, men and trucks, and a concrete floor covered with hay and mixed with urine and excrement of all kinds. Here, a cow's sense of place, its natural state of serenity was completely shattered. A desperate sense of self-preservation reigned in its stead, much like the difference between a man in the country and a city dweller beset by the million stresses of manic urban life. Our eyes locked for a split second and, though I desperately clung to my belief in a steer's cowardly nature, suddenly I knew he wasn't going to veer off. Miraculously, I managed to jump out of the way and onto a fence that ran along beside me. The steer blew by, inches from me. It would've been like getting hit by three Hershel Walkers at once. One of the other boys later remarked as we were having a smoke, "Boy, I thought he HAD you!".

But my love of these doe-eyed beasts of the field, the companions of my childhood memory, hasn't faded. Not long ago, when I took Josh's children to the Budapest petting zoo, seeing cattle standing there in rope halters, being petted, it transported me, once again, back to that lost time. Standing there, amidst the joy of giggling children, tears sprang to my eyes. I think it was at that moment, standing at the far side of Europe, looking at cattle put into a kind of museum for the well-intentioned enjoyment of kids, at that moment I knew that time moves and the past is lost forever. Only in stories can we recreate it in fragments.

"The way I see it," Sylvester Moore said, "the dinosaurs had their shot, then we had ours, then the insects gonna get theirs." The grasshopper was a stranger companion, yet just as integral a part of childhood. I remember they were so abundant and completely covered the hood of my father's car, shaking and popping and jumping like popcorn kernels in a frying pan, as we drove through the fields of tall grass, checking for a broken fence or stray cattle. Perhaps I only want to assuage my guilt, but every little boy is a kind of sadist, isn't he? I'm afraid I treated my grasshopper friends rather cruelly at times. I was fascinated with the masked mechanical-looking armor of their faces. Suddenly one would fly into my face and drop down clinging to my shirt by its strange barbed feet. I grabbed it and stared into its strange eyes and tentacles, observed its robot-looking jaw. What was it trying to say to me through a billion years of evolution? It seemed aware of me. I held tight, holding down its dinosaur wings and powerful, struggling frog-like legs. Its pincers tried nibbling into my fingers but were impotent against the thickness of my skin. It slobbered a brown juice, which as children we called "tobacco juice," into my hand but that had no effect on me either. I gloated in my power over it. This thing that might have scared me if I were five, but now I was eight! With my little thumb and forefinger, I popped off its head. It bled a green liquid, head still connected to a kind of insect spine. I watched with a mixture of sudden guilt and fascination as the headless torso continued to wriggle its legs. How can that be? I wondered. I looked around thinking his million companions might now attack me en masse but they seemed unaware of the murder that had just taken place, that or the biblical creatures still lacked the unity as a species to unify against me. I looked proudly across the fields I now ruled. But I decided to run the rest of the way to my grandmother's house. Lunch was ready and I was late. I was a gentle king, a gentle tyrant. I didn't want to make anyone angry. The shadow of a great red-tailed hawk passed over me. I watched it land high in a great oak a half mile away.

The loveliness of the grounds around the Prudent's home, as well as the house itself, is a childhood memory I go back to so many times that, as John Prine sings, *My Memory is Worn*. They called the place Soldier's Rest. Countless hours I spent there in the bright humid days of Kentucky summer, playing tennis with Aloyisius. We got quite good. His mother, Kate, a beautiful woman who tanned as brown as a Cherokee, could have been a drop in her blood, was an avid player and had the court put in. Its upkeep must have been difficult even for a grand old aristocratic family of the Water Maple County, landed gentry as they were. Aloyisius' ancestral blood, certainly on his father's side, was much bluer than mine, Nicholas the Dispenser notwithstanding. His great-great-great-grandfather had been given the land by George Washington himself for services rendered as a Revolutionary War soldier!

We played and practiced our tennis technique every day. Kate entered us in tournaments, which either he or I frequently won. There would be a little ceremony and we would be given a shiny fake gold trophy of a tennis player playing a passionate point, his feet set in a veneer pedestal, with the words, Twelve and Under Singles Champion written under it. I think I beat some girl who kept double-faulting a lot. It would turn out to be my greatest sports moment. I spent hours fiddling with the little fake gold racquet that you could remove from the metal molded hand, poised to make an overhead smash. Eventually, the cute little miniature racquet got lost. A racquetless figurine attached to a wooden base sat on one of my bedroom shelves at the Edgeton Rd. house for years, long after my interest in tennis faded.

Back to wasp's revenge, which I'm sure, dear reader, if you are one of those current day animal/insect activists, practically unknown in my youth, you are waiting happily to applaud. It was a typically hot, humid Kentucky summer's day, but the grand towering Oaks and Elms of Soldier's Rest provided enough shade for us to stay cool. We sipped on lemonade or iced tea in big sweating glass pitchers all day. At lunchtime we took refuge in the tall cool hallways and high ceilings of the early 19th-century house, a house whose door sills and latches and ornamentation resembled, as a contemporaneous counterpart, Helen's Hapsburg Era apartments I would visit many years later in Budapest. We sat down to a lunch of fried chicken or roast beef and all the assorted southern-style vegetables and breads, green beans and fatback with cornbread, mashed potatoes and gravy, fresh sliced tomatoes and sweet Vidalia onions, sweet corn. Well, there wasn't always such a varied selection but damn near! Mandy, the cook, whose swept-back, salt and pepper, broomstraw hair, and kind crinkly eyes made her resemble a Miss Mousey character, or Little Bear's mother from the old stories, had a delicious but simple recipe for salad dressing. She would make a good oil and vinegar dressing and then add ketchup. Everyone loved it. Josh used to laugh that it was "too American" for continental European tastes!

Sufficiently fattened on southern food. I threw myself to the wasps. There's nothing unusual about boys being stung by wasps but this was interesting if for nothing else than the ingenious way these industrious little creatures managed to conceal their nest in the shell-like husk of an old sycamore leaf that had gotten itself stuck in the mesh of the tennis court backstop. Aloyisius discovered it while retrieving a ball stuck in the web of mesh, proof of the speed with which we were, at eleven or so, hitting the ball, and called me over to take a look. It was fascinating to see how they had attached the nest, by just a thin daub, to the inside of the curled dead leaf. He sent a quiver through the wire as he dislodged the ball, exciting the buggers and they flew all around. One whizzed by our heads and that was enough for us to declare war on our underestimated enemy. We soon realized that, because of their tight mesh, our rackets were excellent wasp swatters. We mowed them down as fast as they came at us like Jap fighter pilots. Once they hit the ground, a good stomp would finish them off. As I say, they kept coming right at us, diving in flashes of speed. Funny, it never occurred to me that they might attack our "flank." Just about that time small explosions of pain hit the backs of my legs, timed one after another like a terrorist bomb attack. The pain was so sharp and sudden that I instantly started crying like a baby and fell to the ground, my leg swelling badly, lucky not to have fallen on a few stomp survivors with stings left in them. Aloyisius' Mom heard my yelps and came running. If I remember correctly, she put baking soda on my war wounds. The coolness of the moisture relieved the intense heat of the stings. They eventually scabbed over but itched for weeks. All the insect spirits we had so cruelly dispatched no doubt now stood avenged, laughing from the halls of insect heaven.

Southern culture never died. As someone said, Nature transforms but never extinguishes. Even a hundred years after the end of the "War Between the States," as my father liked to call it, eschewing the term "Civil War" and downright fuming at the term "Great Rebellion," a drab kind of poverty still gripped the deep south. Many of the issues that sparked the war, remained unresolved. The cotton industry sank as more textiles were produced in the Orient. But in the Old Upper South, Kentucky and Virginia, the tobacco industry had steadily grown, the cancer scare of the 70s was still nearly a decade away, and remained strong. As I've said, I believe that I witnessed the final glory days of the Family Farm era, right before the advent, mostly from the North, of the new industrial era that brought in so many factories into Water Maple County. In kindergarten and grade school I played with the children of the landed gentry, the ones that allowed their children to attend a public school, and those of the old established bourgeoise of central Kentucky. But by high school, in the seventies, I was rubbing elbows with the sons and daughters of engineers, lawyers, educators and industrialists from the North.

The Family Farm of even mid-century, mid-continental America was a fascinating thing. The Grand Patriarch would live, with his wife, the Grand Matriarch, in the Grand original house on the Farm, sometimes on a picturesque hill gently rising behind a serpentine line of stone fences. On another corner of the farm, connected by a lovely shady road, stood the, usually oldest, son's house. Down the road on a newly purchased expanse of land, stood the house of a younger sibling, his head filled with capitalist dreams and modern farming techniques. This could be a kind of basic outline of the feudal system in place around that time. For example, my father resembled to some extent this brief description of the "younger brother." Though he was in reality, an only child and also the "older brother" who lived in the bigger house near that of the patriarch. In some curious way, he was all three, the youngest, the oldest and the middle. I could imagine, if permitted to continue my fictitious construct, a daughter, perhaps educated at a Northern school, like Radcliffe or Wellesley, like Josh's old girlfriend, Lilian, building an experimental house, baiting the "provincialism" of her neighbors. It might be of an oriental type, on some far off corner of the farm where she lived with her husband, an affable bohemian sort, who would begrudgingly let in, by her brothers, on the day to day dealings of the farm. Truth be told he was a pathetic failure trying to perpetuate the image of the detached "artist" and doing a good job of it. This is only a sketch, of course, but not one completely devoid of accuracy. Somewhere in the New South and elsewhere these characters in some form or another strutted and fretted their hour upon life's stage.

In "real" reality, the women of this time, to be sure women like my mother and Aloyisius' mother, liked to throw parties. And the grandeur of them was something right out of Proust. On a Saturday evening, our car would turn up the long driveway and Soldier's Rest would appear there on its hill, bright as a candle on a cherry wood supper table. Already, the field beyond the black wrought iron gate, just outside the grounds around the house, was lined with huge American cars, black, blue, cream and red. On one of the dark magnolia trees that stood on each side of the old Palladian portico, the "Greek Revival" style that dominated the antebellum period, a giant white flower had bloomed, spread out as portent as a lotus. Roses and lilacs hung from trellises. Gnats and mosquitos hovered in the fading light, fireflies flashed in little droplets of light over the pungent dew-soaked fields. Locusts began whirring a long saxophone cry.

There was the food, spread out upon the long wooden country tables. Potato salad, only in the South does it seem to taste right, this single concoction remains the most memorable dish, even though it was just a simple provincial thing, full of cheap grocery store ingredients like bright yellow American style squirt bottle mustard and Hellman's mayonnaise. There were many variations, some of which no doubt approximated more closely their original continental models, particularly the less sweetened "German" version, which I sometimes found, even years later when I began to travel extensively in Germany, with bratwurst, or just about anything, for that matter, you could always get Kartoffle, too runny and vinegary. I preferred the tacky American version. My Mother's was the finest. She always made it in the same big yellow bowl and always managed to give it a marvelous creamy texture, but with plenty of tasty potato chunks inside at the same time. There was always the perfect delicate hint of celery, something which less accomplished potato salad makers eschewed. In Mom's potato salad, you could taste the potato, unlike some other inferior versions where the potato taste was masked out of existence.

On one occasion, I must have been around twelve, some members of a tennis team from a provincial part of the state, Somerset, in the southeastern region, came to Medina and Edgeton, the central portion of the state, to play a tournament against us. I use the word " provincial" again though that word does little to convey the uniqueness, arising out of hundreds of years of isolation, of Appalachia and its people. Their accent is just one notable thing that sets them apart. Linguists and ethnologists and other academic types once combed the hills of East Kentucky and Tennessee, searching for connections between the mountain dialects and their British ancestors. They weren't dumb hillbillies, the liberal and well-intentioned professors from Harvard argued, but the direct linguistic descendants of Shakespeare! Of course, that did little to stem the tide of the exploitation of Appalachia by mostly Northern industrialists, a tragedy of Shakespearean proportions. In my time, it was more the music of the South that was exploited, misused and misunderstood.

The sound of the long "i" in their pronunciation is particularly striking. Night, fight, sight, light. You have to hear it to fully experience it, but in order to get a working idea, it's necessary to lengthen the "i" sound to an absurd length, open the mouth very wide and squint by raising the muscles of the cheekbones up toward the eyes as closely as possible.

There are many other fascinating idiosyncracies in the Appalachian accent too numerous to discuss here in-depth. Suffice it to say that the human voice can twist vowels and consonants into unimaginably bizarre shapes if it is so disposed.

Back to the tennis tournament. Aloyisius' mother was part of the organizing committee to see that every young Somerset boy and girl tennis player was assigned a family to stay with during tournament time. My mother welcomed the idea and volunteered to take in one of the children. I recall being excited about it in that typical way children have when meeting a child of their own age from a different place. The boy arrived like a new puppy to great anticipation. Tyrone Funderburke was his name. He was a beautiful boy, I recall, a bit tall for his age, with lots of curly blond hair, very full pink lips, a slightly tanned pink skin tone and bright blue eyes. He remains in memory now, untouched by time, as a kind of god of summer, a summer that never ends and the sad autumn followed by a dull school year never begins.

Of course, the first thing that's necessary for such occasions is a cookout. Grilled hamburgers and hot dogs, sweet baked beans, fresh sliced tomatoes, plates of hot buttered corn on the cob, my mother's tasty coleslaw, unsweetened with no carrots and lots of celery seed and black pepper, very unusual, but so good. Most of all, there, in its big yellow bowl, the one thing that stands out in my memory most vividly, her potato salad.

We were on our way to one of those indescribably gorgeous evening picnics on the grounds of the 18th century presbyterian church they called "Hebron." It was an idyllic place. The small stone chapel stood behind a low stone fence near the winding country road, Hebron Pike. Behind it, some sixty yards or so, lay an old country graveyard, shaded by Kentucky's plethora of Hardwood trees, Pinoak, Watermaple, Wildcherry, Sweetgum, Hackberry and ornamented by Dogwoods and Rosebuds, Forsythias and hedges of all manner.

The graveyard descended down the hill behind the Church, towards the curve of the road, while up the hill, away from the road, on the front side of the church, a flat expanse of lawn extended, shaded by the same sumptuous trees, bordered by two lovely and well- kept tennis courts. This is where the famed Water Maple County Tennis Tournament was held every year. Here, Aloyisius and I, if we weren't smacking balls and torturing insects on his home court, spent many a summer's day honing our forehands, backhands and serves. It was also here that every Sunday summer evening, people of the county, members of St Jude of Our Childhood Church, farmers, tennis players, preachers and sinners alike, gathered together over some of the best goddamned food I would ever taste, even in all my subsequent worldly travels.

I was what my mother referred to as a "good eater" because I, unlike many children, liked most of what was put on my plate. At that age a child could simply say, when being asked to try a particularly healthy food like broccoli, for instance, "But I don't like it," at which point he would either be forced to eat it or let off the hook, depending on how much energy the parent had at the time.

It was on one of those evenings that my mother's potato salad sat waiting on the dining room table that young Tyrone, freshly showered and rested from a hard day of hitting tennis balls, quietly and shyly strolled into the room, as young boys will when they're away from home, perhaps for the first time, and upon seeing the glorious bowl of salad sitting in the exact center of the table like a bouquet of flowers the like of which Van Gogh himself could never have accurately painted, exclaimed, in all the ancient glory of his Elizabethan ancestors, "Gaaawleee! Potato salad! Too bad I don't liiiike it!"

Other pronunciations I recall: "Tractor" becomes " Cractor" and another friend swore that hillbillies pronounce every s as a sh."I'm the luckiesht girl, in the whole U-SH-A." It seems they do.

As I said, Water Maple Farm was divided into two very different worlds, the "Tranquility Pike side" of the farm and the "Edgeton Roadside." The farm sat, in its almost trapezoidal shape, between these two country roads, the one forming its eastern border and the other its western. Its North and South borders were formed by neighboring farms. The sun always went down behind the fish pond below the Edgeton Rd house just below the field where I batted rocks for hours on end with a baseball bat, pretending I was Vada Pinson or Frank Robinson of the Cincinnati Reds. The rocks gouged chips and dents into my pine Louisville Slugger.

The sun always rose in front of me as I ran through fields, past my cattle companions towards Tranquility and Bertha's house. I say the Farm was trapezoidal-shaped because it had been rendered into map form. A map my father drew himself with his own surveyings. A small version of the map, in a simple black frame, hung on the wall of the little half staircase leading downstairs in Bertha's house, to the room, carpeted in dark, rich burgundy, that my father used as an office. The wall in front of his massive desk was covered with framed photographs of ancestors, parents, children and grandchildren, scenes of bygone days. Bertha always went to the Olon Mills Studio to have portraits done of my brother and sister and me. I still recall, as if it were branded on my mind's eye, the Olon Mills insignia at the bottom right corner of almost every family picture. Strange name, "Olon." I've never known anyone else by that name.

My favorite was a photograph from the turn of the century, of maybe fifty or a hundred mountain men on horseback, gathered round a huge tree trunk, tethered in rope to a mule, purported to be the largest poplar log ever to come out of the Cumberland Mountains. In the center, in a black hat and jacket reminiscent of the old Circuit Riders, astride a gleaming black quarterhorse, sat my Father's grandfather, Logger Jack Ryley Celeste, with a little boy, Dexter, in his lap. A great handlebar moustache under his classic broad Indian nose. He more than anyone, perhaps because of my father's, probably exaggerated, stories of him, stands out as the hero of my childhood, though I never knew him. Logger, moonshiner, lady's man, devoted husband and, according to my father, the first sheriff of Ryly Co., Kentucky. Not an undemanding job considering that people in Manchester, KY carried guns openly even as late as the Second World War. Logger Jack rises larger than life above the Family Mythology.

The Tranquility Pike side of the Farm was older. You could tell, although as a child I didn't think of such things. The trees were more gnarled, shadowy, the barns so old they seemed to have always been there. Dad put in new white plank fence in places around the big feed barn, which formed a network of pens necessary for sorting the cattle and loading them onto trucks for the trip to Medina Stockyard where they were auctioned, but the old wire and post fences were more prevalent out into the outer reaches of the farm. Many of the old posts were rotten and moss-covered, the original white paint chipped almost completely away, exposing the grey weather-beaten, insect-eaten wood underneath, and the fencing rusted. Yet, they maintained their resiliency and usually only had to be patched here and there.

Occasionally, a rambunctious steer would bust out onto the pike. They always seemed so out of place, grazing by the roadside. They could easily outrun even the fastest man, but we usually had our car and Dad would head them off. I often fantasized about one of them eventually making his way into town, booking a room at the old Colonial Hotel, ordering a beer at Crazy Reddy's Poolroom. I made up my own Disney-like script, "the Cow Goes to Town" complete with a Rex Barker narration, the whole thing gone to vapor in my daydreaming mind within a few minutes. Occasionally one of Mr. Moreland's wild sons would get drunk and drive through the front fence on Tranquility, the police would come, the boys would spend the night in jail, the fathers of a couple of cute chesty blonds would strut and fume and threaten lawsuits. Finally, they would think better of it and whisk the cursing girls away in their cars. The next morning there would be poor old Mr. Moreland, a rounder himself in days of old, according to Dad, dutifully repairing the damage with a pair of wire clips and a post hole digger. He'd give a big wave hello as we passed him Sunday morning on our way to church. The wild Moreland brothers, especially the one everyone called "Free" became heroes to me and to Josh too. They would be the first people I'd ever actually see play good rock guitar live.

On other rare days, the Tower blessed us poor mortal townspeople with its seemingly inexhaustible bounty of pure clean Kentucky Springwater. Taken from the spring that ran out of the ground below the hill, it was the same spring that Indians of old drank from. When the Tower would go dry, a train car would pull up alongside it and water would be pumped in. Often times, in those days of crude instruments, it was difficult to gauge the exact amount of water needed to fill it. Too much water would be put into the Tower and it would overflow, much to our delight as children. Rain-like droplets of water rained down upon us passersby. Angelika and I would giggle with delight as our Mother would have to switch on the windshield wipers of the old Plymouth, even on a perfectly sunny summer day, as we drove by. The finned, two-tone car making an unforgettable "ka-bunk" sound as it crossed over the train tracks. For a moment, in our child world, it felt to us as if a great beneficent Spirit had turned some cosmic hose upon us.

The marvelous silver paint of the tower lasted a good many years. I got through junior high school it seemed, and then came that watershed first year of high school that we always remember. We always remember, years later, the most beautiful girl, the wildest boy, the geeks, the heroes, the cliques, the little internal popularity wars, and the harmless epithets scratched hurriedly in revenge on a toilet door: "Ever wonder why you can't find the books you need in the library? I've got them!" or a simple, terse, "Fuck You." Was it a crowd of concerned adults we saw as Mom drove us to that first high school day, scratching their heads and appearing distraught as they craned their necks and looked upwards at the Tower? There! A hundred feet up, something in canned red spray paint had been scrawled across the beautiful black letters and gleaming silver paint job the city council was so proud of. The new letters, for the whole town to see, and ponder, read simply, "Jared Smallwood Sucks!"

Ah, such is Youth's respect for the adult monuments bequeathed it. For years that bold red indictment, which now only elevated to local celebrity status the delinquent boy it was meant to deride, remained a hundred feet above the town for all townspeople and strangers passing through to read, gawk and guffaw at. I don't know why it took so long for someone to finally paint over it. Perhaps the city council lacked the funds to pay the Spray Crew to come back and repaint it all. Perhaps their spirit was simply broken. And it would fall to a new administration to repair the damage.

I'll never forget the first night we spent in the Edgeton Roadhouse. It was finally finished and ready for us. The yard was a kid's paradise, for the moment, huge piles of dirt, great for playing Army, where plumbers dug ditches for new pipe. Much of the furniture had been brought in, sofas, tables and cupboards but it was all helter-skelter in the large central room of rich walnut paneling that we would call the living room. It was here for the next few years that Josh and I sat and watched the Andy Griffith Show, Outer Limits, the Danny Thomas Show, The Dick Van Dyke Show, Twilight Zone, Saturday Night at the Movies and all the countless other shows, Truth or Consequences, the Price is Right, that the amazing new medium would provide.

There was a smaller TV in my parent's bedroom. They liked to watch Carson in bed without waking up us kids. It was on this TV that I remember watching President Kennedy's funeral and three-year-old John-John's famous salute to the coffin while my mother cried. It was on the bigger living room TV that I sat on the floor and watched Jack Ruby suddenly appear among a police escort walking down some Dallas corridor and shoot and kill Lee Harvey Oswald. I remember how Oswald, dressed in that drab mock turtle neck sweater, doubled over and bellowed in pain. As three shots rang out and he fell to the floor, the announcer, all completely live, began shouting, mantra-like, "Oswald has been shot! Oswald has been shot!" I sensed even at eight years old that something terrible had happened. Yet, it seemed like just another scene from a cop show, so uniformly does television shape everything that happens on it.

On that first night when evening fell, the wind whipped up and the lush green leaves on the trees shimmered as the treetops swayed to and fro. Josh and I were in our new beds, not yet arranged as they would be in the coming years, headboards against the eastern wall, my bed closest to the window that looked out toward the pond, past a field and a hundred meters down the hill, the locust tree branches tangled in a horses head shape that for years I could always find if I stared at it for a few moments. For now, the beds were just put askew in a haphazard fashion. As my brother and I whispered into the night, we could hear the low murmur of our parents talking in the living room. Ganglia of lightening would crawl across the sky like electrified silver veins, lightening up the whole world as bright as day for a split second and then just as quickly the room would be plunged back into pitch-black night. The supply of electricity to the house was suddenly knocked out. None of the lights worked. We were ecstatic, ducking our heads under the covers with each reverberating peel of thunder. When a bolt would strike and light up the whole room with light we would shout out, "Day!" Then, when a brief moment of false light went out, we would just as quickly, but in a lowered voice, say somehow disappointed I suppose that the light couldn't remain, "night." For hours it was Day! night. Day! night. Day! night.

As the storm subsided we ventured out of our beds, it was impossible to sleep in all the excitement, and found our parents having a bowl of cereal in the living room on a little coffee table, the one with white tiles and blue butterflies painted on them, surrounded by an anarchy of sofas and chairs and tables and cupboards. We thought they'd make us get back in bed but instead, we got to sit down with them and eat cereal even though it must have been past midnight. It was a wondrous night. The first night of my new life as a full-fledged farmboy.

Once, on a lovely summer evening when we were still a happy family, my mother, father, brother, sister and I walked up the hill together. We took such walks on occasion, but this particular evening stands out in my mind. My father had freshly showered and shaved and had on a clean white oxford cloth shirt and khakis. What was Mom wearing? We had had a pleasant supper, everyone seemed in a good mood. Perhaps some argument had been resolved, some wrong forgiven. My parents kissed and made up and stopped fighting, deeply in love again. Bertha's meddling in her son's life had ceased for the moment. My father's ridicule of my mother's family, mother's disdain for my father's mother and her odd country ways, all this for the moment had subsided. Somehow, on this evening, Venus rising above the sunset, there was a soft air of family perfection. My father stopped for a moment and grabbed a sprig of crabgrass. We walked along the dirt road when he suddenly squatted down on one knee and motioned for all of us to come over to him. He placed the sprig of grass down about halfway into a small hole in the packed dirt of the road and worked it around a bit. Then, after a brief moment, let the sprig stand there on its own and told us to keep watching it. Just as we were growing impatient watching a spear of grass in a small hole, it began to move. Just a slight wiggle at first but then it started turning around and around. My sister giggled with delight. My brother and I were amazed. My mother grimaced squeamishly. Dad, smiling now that he had gotten the effect he'd wanted from everyone, reached down and pulled up the sprig. Dangling on the end of it was a huge whitish maggot-looking grub worm with black eyes and great brown pincers the color of tobacco juice. "Fishing for doodlebugs!" Dad said, laughing. Man walks the Earth but above and below there lives a tumult of creatures barely seen.

There was a lovely old church that radiated the old Anglican heritage of Water Maple County. The bricks had darkened to the color of dried blood. And a thin film of blackened moss covered many of them. The main church house was quite spacious on the inside, somehow gave off, to a young boy at least, a Cathedral-like austerity. The colors were darker than in the interiors of other brighter more freshly painted Protestant churches I had been to on occasion with my classmates, whose parents were of other denominations, Baptist, Presbyterian, Church of God. Yet, inside St Jude, the colors seemed warmer. The flooring was a rich hardwood, brown with age. The carpet was deep burgundy. The bright Kentucky sun of the 11 o'clock service was dimmed slightly by the dark stained windows, adorned with the beatific ceramic faces of angels and saints with hopeful yet melancholy expressions as if what they ached for had not yet come. The moats of dust shone in the curtain of late morning sun, like particles of gold on the robes of God Himself.

From the outside, St Jude seemed much smaller. There was the little rusting sign nearby, in traditional blue and red colors, that had St Jude's name printed on it. The main door, shaped like a child's drawing of a house, was of a blackened wood and after the service, Father Hozni, the vicar, stood beside it smiling, shaking hands and nodding thank yous to the ladies' compliments on an excellent sermon. He wore a many-faceted purple hat that had something of the mysteries of the east in its roundness. After all, this was the High Church of England. As I sidled away from the cheerful priest I often stood listening to what seemed to me, as a boy, inane adult conversations, wondering how the things they spoke about could be of interest to anyone.

I sidled away and walked in the direction of the courthouse and Edgeton Drugstore. There was a little courtyard just to my left covered with ivy, an ivy-covered rock garden, adorned with statues and little stone fountains dedicated to Saint Someone and a prominent citizen or two. Someday Judge Daddy and Millecent's names would be carved into the stone.

There was a narrow brick walk that ran through the middle of beds of ivy, little statuettes here and there, a Madonna and child, a shepherd holding a lamb. Up the small half staircase that led to the door of another wing of the church, I entered and looked up and down a small hallway lined with portraits of former rectors, some even going back as far as the faded black and white, wan light of civil war era daguerreotype in their priestly attire. Milli and Judge Daddy had known many of them. In the country, there would be picnics and saint's day festivals, and Milli spoke of how Bishop Montague once, in a revival of English custom, had blessed the hounds before a hunt. He had even written a history of the Episcopal Church in Water Maple County. I met him once as a child, perhaps he touched Josh and me on the forehead at our Confirmation service, softly making the sign of the cross between our eyes. Kindly Father Hozni following close by with the wine-filled communion chalice. I sometimes stared at these framed pictures, the wan faces and bright eyes, on my way between Sunday school lessons and the main church service, wondering what these men born in the nineteenth century must have been like as they walked the leaf-strewn streets of Edgeton, or looked into the summer sun, or rubbed their hands before a fire at Christmas. Surely they must have lusted after women.

As you came through the door there was a sumptuous meeting room lined with books, church histories, theologies, Aquinas, the Works of John Wesley Vol. I-V, Calvin, Plato, Aristotle. On a higher shelf almost hidden from view, Wordsworth,

Byron, Shelly, Emerson and Whitman. Father Hozni had been a lit major at Vandy. I could keep going left and I would be in the large breakfast hall, filled with good old fashioned long tables and solid chairs. At the far end was a small stage for amateur theatricals. Josh played Christmas songs on his guitar there once. Another time the church board got together and asked Josh to play the song he wrote for that famous Lacy Corman album, with a small band, Sylvester Moore, Carlo Everett and Hector.

Beside a rack of church pamphlets announcing various bible study classes and upcoming summer camp programs and the like, was a set of swinging doors. I still hear the slight creaking sound they made. You entered a dim hallway where, in my mind, all Spiritual Events took place. It was a medieval-looking little hallway of cool limestone and arched doorways, the place, in my imagination, where Aquinas pondered Aristotelian questions, St John of the Cross, in his prayers and sufferings, composed many of his poems, Bach composed many a cantata, where Athanasius sought refuge from the Romans, where lusty Charlemagne was crowned Emperor, where Richard the III, Hamlet, Lady Macbeth and Lear all acted out their moments of crisis, where Jesus himself preached the Word, all things of God in my imagination, all the gentle things of my brother and his voice, his guitar, his poems, all marriages, all christenings, all funerals, all things seen or unseen, as they passed through my mind's eye, they came through this place, the tiny chapel of St. Jude in Edgeton.

Eternity lies just on the other side as if I could reach out my hand and pull back this veil. Beyond the golden mist and the sapphire and diamond waters, the "marshy grass," there are the departed, Judge Daddy and Milli, Bertha, Marshall, Agnes, Sylvester—Joshua, all waiting to embrace me, among the virtuosic song of the mockingbird, the trill of the meadowlark, the sweeping shadow of the Great Blue Heron's wing.

18

"Look, man," Jared Smallwood was saying, "I need a piece of ass, you need a piece of ass. Let's get on this windjammer cruise and GET A PIECE OF ASS! When you go on these freakin' things, you get a piece of ass. It's in the brochure, airfare, seven nights room and board, bar privileges… PIECE OF ASS. It's in the contract. It's guaranteed!" Josh smiled at his friend's sales pitch.

The summer of 1982 was the end of something. Berenice was gone. The pain had faded like the first hurtful light of dawn turning into one of those hot summer Kentucky mornings. The journey held out her arms. They snorkeled in the big aqua blue with the secret barracudas in the pink corals.

It was like the cold bus ride from West Mass. Ten years before when Josh and Lilian said goodbye at the little stop in Amherst. How many times would he come back to that bus stop in his memory? He'd had to call Bertha to wire money for a bus ticket back to Edgeton. Marshall or Agnes wudda got too mad. He didn't have it in him to hitch back. Now that love was dead and there was no one to be romantic for. There was no reason to be the "lonesome picker" for anyone anymore.

Poor Josh never was any good at letting go. This occurs to him sitting in front of the Television in Budapest years later. Strange, he thinks, how lovers get rid of each other. *Fifty ways to leave your lover*. Some little radio of the guy 'cross the bus aisle barreling down I- 80 on a Greyhound outta Pittsburg. The cold refusal of the guy he tried to bum a cigarette off of. Windows icing up from the inside black with Eastern winter. Why did he look that way at me? My hair's not that long. The driver woke him up for a pit stop near Cincinnati. He put on the jacket he was using as a blanket and walked out for the first time in his life to the cold cruel womanless weird world. "Life is weird" became his mantra.

See, for Josh, Lilian's love was love sent from God. What had he done, he wondered, to upset the universe? Suddenly, every song on the radio was about him. For the first time it seemed, he heard them, little angels coming out of radios everywhere. Someone else had always lost love, *"the daybreaks, your mind aches..." "ain't it time we said goodbye"*—that was one Lilian cried over all of a sudden one night when we were all driving around. And, *"Can't liiiive if livin' is without youuuuuuuuuu..."*

The sorrow of love never lessens with age. He stared from the dilapidated Budapest easy chair into the late movie fire. The poison settles down into the blood.

He moved to Boston with Carlo so he could be near Lilian. Carlo and him in a U-Haul. When Josh asked for his father's blessing, Marshall said to his young prodigal son, "You ever driven a car with a trailer on the back of it?"

"No, Dad, don't reckon I have."

"It's different, Josh. It's different."

"It's different, Josh." Stanfield doing his imitation of Marshall's mountain voice as they barreled down the interstate. "It's different."

They laughed a lot on the way there. Laughed at the State Trooper after he caught Carlo speeding on I 80. "File 'at under, 'Shove it up your ass with a fork, Smokey!'" While the trooper stood in back of the car to check the license number, Carlo's face got red having to hold back a laugh when Josh said, "Go on, Stanny, back over 'at sumbitch!'"

They laughed at the world. Visions of becoming great musicians danced in their heads. They took a place on Revere Street. *Remember the Robert Lowell short story in freshman English?"*

One night, comin' home from his day job a dude approached him on a street going up Beacon Hill coming out of the shadows, "Look here, man. You into turquoise? Cause if you is, I gots a piece right here that's worth five hundred bucks in a shop but I'm gonna give it to you for fifty, dig?" Josh kept walking as the dude pulled out a piece of blue rock that looked like a chicklet.

"No, thanks, man."

"Hey, man I…"

Just then a car, one of them big Fairlanes cops used to drive, drove by and the dude disappeared. Josh was lucky then that way. What had the dude wanted? For Josh to reach in his pocket for the bread then PAYA upside his head?

There was a time three dudes in long black coats and umpire hats stopped him in the Public Garden at 6 am on his way to his security guard job at Bonwit Tellers.

"What are you," one of 'em asked, momentarily startled by the stripe down his uniform pants, "some kinda cop or somethin'?"

Josh, heart-pounding, answered simply, "I'm a security guard."

"Well, Mr. Security Guard, how much money you got in your pocket?"

"Not much."

"How you know? You ain't looked yet."

"Maybe a buck and a half, see, I don't eat lunch at the… "

"Yeah yeah yeah, right. Well, let's have it."

As he reached for it one of them said, "We don't need a dollar and a half that bad, mein. Let's just fuck it and go on." Miracle of pity?

"We need it pretty bad, man," the other said.

Musta been something in Josh's eyes. Like that sleepy, innocent look they got when they was all stung with cigarette smoke in the dives they played. Some kind of compassion and pity for everyone's misery. That's what they must of seen and let him go.

Josh and Carlo washed out in Boston. They were too green to cop a real music gig. One day they just up and left in Carlo's Camaro. Carlo from his 7-11 cashier's job, and Josh, from his security guard gig. They drove back across the Alleghenies in silence. Something changed forever.

Carlo went back to his music studies at the University of Medina but Josh missed Lilian and one day hitched back to Western Mass. From Medina, all the way up I-75 to 71 at Columbus, Ohio, then back on across Pennsylvania. It seemed far across as Texas. on I- 80, where he could then head up I-84 to upstate New York then through Hartford with its strange, uneasy visions in the swirling snow of the night-lit Capital, and up to Springfield, Mass. on I- 90. James Taylor on the radio, *"O the Berkshires seemed dreamlike on account of that frostin'…"*

Then Bam! Soon as he got out of a short ride into the middle of the Poconos outside Brooksville, the air changed all of a sudden, the temperature dropped and Boom… a late winter Pennsylvania mountain blizzard dumped on his head like oats outta a slashed feedbag. The folks who'd let him out had been tellin' him how much they admired guys like him for having long hair. In those days Josh's grazed the sheep's wool collar of his roughout leather jacket that Doc, a master hitcher before him, had let him borrow for the Road. Travelin' with a guitar and protesting war and livin' free to a different drummer and all that shit, they had this weird look of pity on their faces Josh couldn't figure out until he got out and tried to walk across the vast meadow of Interstate median and found himself ass-high in wet snow, only his torso visible. He'd been daydreamin out the window thinkin' 'bout how good Lilian was gonna feel in his arms and hadn't even noticed the coming deluge. Trucks were roaring and skiddin' and jacknifin' into their cabs like giant lizards tryin to eat their own tails. Cars were pulling over in shock.

Finally, he made it to the truck plaza walking up the ramp the wrong way and climbing the wire fence that had been made climbable by the driftin' snow that surrounded in a pitiful way the asphalt lake where the ice-encrusted dragons were buoyed. *"Driftin'.. on a sea of forgotten teardrops… on a lifeboat… sailin' for… your love…"*

Road-weary, he walked through the restaurant lobby, past the postcard rack and cassette tapes, not even noticing the Truckers Only sign on the counter, he pulled off his coat and sweater and sat down. A kindly- looking waitress with a face like a roadmap came up to take his order.

"Funny, but you don't look like no trucker."

"I ain't," Josh said, surprised. "I'm tryin' to find a ride to Massachusetts."

"Well, you'd better sit over here at the waitress table. Some of the fellas might get a little riled. They're kinda proud of their personal space. What's in Massachusetts? A girl?"

"Naw… how'd you know?"

"Guess you learn to spot these kinda things over the years. What'll ya have?"

"Just coffee. I gotta get back on the road."

"In this storm? You'd better have something to eat and cool it, kid. She can wait another day, can't she?" Josh laughed.

He'd never known a woman like this, someone who'd seen (or seen through) all the tricks life could pull. "In the meantime, while yer waitin' out the blizzard, ask some of these truckers if they'll give you a ride."

After he worked up the nerve, Josh approached them one after another. They'd stop, listen to his story, give him the up and down then shake their heads. One guy with a funny Yankee accent he'd never heard before offered to take him as far as the George Washington Bridge.

"Where's that?" Josh asked.

"New York City. It's a little out of yer way but yous otta be able to get a ride straight up I- 95 from thir."

"Okay, I'll think about it and if I can't find something else I'll meet you back here in an hour."

"Suit yourself."

Who were these people? Josh thought wandering around this new snowy purgatory. These people didn't understand his weariness, how much he needed Lilian. He wondered what Marshall was doing right now. Probably asleep. Not wondering or knowing where he was out on the lonesome road. Thinking his son was somewhere safe and sound. And Bertha. She'd know what to do. He could call her and she'd have Ricky Boy come and get him or even take him to Massachusetts! Nah. It was impossible. Besides, Ricky'd never find him now. He laughed as he thought of Bertha's face in the crystal ball like in the Wizard of Oz, *Dorothy, Dorothy, come home dear, where are you?... Auntie Em! Auntie Em!*

He called Lilian, "Hey, sugar pie, I'm stuck in a truck stop in PA. *Stuck inside Mobile with the Memphis blues again.*" He did the Dylan impression she used to laugh at.

There was a long pause. She still laughs with me, Josh thought, but she waits a second too long. And the sky is black and still now... came the John Prine lyric in his head.

"Josh, you sound so listless."

"Well, I been on the road for 24 hours, Honey, and I still got a ways to go."

He heard static on the other end, "You wanna come all this way, Josh?"

"Huh? I didn't hear you. I'm so tired I think I'm starting to have those weird auditory hallucinations you have when you trip."

"I don't trip," Lilian said.

"I know. I meant like me and Hector and Carlo and Jared."

Nothing. Followed by, "When do you think you'll get here?"

"Hard to say. Probably tomorrow morning."

"Okay. Well… take care. I got a big paper to do tonight so love y~~~" More static.

"Just think of me as your lonesome troubadour. I…"~~~ beep beep beep... "Lilian? I Love you, too," he said to no one as he let his head rest against the glass of the phone booth.

He searched for the George Washington Bridge guy but never found him.

How lucky I was not to have gotten that ride. Josh muttered to himself in the warm glow of the TV. *Maybe it would have been better if I'd never made it to Massachusetts.* But he did make it. He conquered his fear of hitchin' and the road. *But how many miles were still left to go on the roads of the world!*

Sweet Lilian had been a wallflower Josh never noticed. He always wanted Jennifer Gardiner or Kiki La Salle, buxom lasses whose shapely asses made their cheerleader uniform skirts jut out. But chicks like them always went with the jocks. Then on the last day of high school, senior year, now or never, she followed him around like a puppy. She wasn't beautiful but had gorgeous long brown hair that fell almost to the hems of her short summer dresses. She was brainy. She wrote poems in the school paper. That's how Josh learned about Yeats and Eliot. It was because of Lilian that he tried to read "The Wasteland" in the Margaret King Library years later when he first met Berenice. She had this Upstate New York accent she got from her Dad in Yonkers. Her mom was a pharmacist who worked nights to support the family. She had been a beauty in her day, as Josh saw in old photographs on dingy walls of their suburban cracker box house. Lilian's Dad had been a rich doctor in Miami but a malpractice suit drove him out so he brought them all to Kentucky to pursue his dream of owning a horse farm and winning the Kentucky Derby. It came to nothing. Marshall always said horse racing was the sport of kings, meaning you already had to be a king before you could afford that shit.

Lilian was a little princess who had ridden show horses in Miami and continued on in Kentucky but she was, at seventeen, getting a little wise to the whole set up, starting to see her dad as a lazy loser, which he wasn't, just unlucky. She was tired of being poor. It was hard for a young girl like her to go from the Miami "horse set" to a Sears and Roebuck house on a street of many, a street of broken dreams. She went on to a smaller but just as exclusive horse set in Medina and nearby Lexington that gathered around the Idle Hour Country Club and the old venerable Keeneland Race Course.

He hadn't thought she was that good looking at first. In September she was thin-lipped, pale and bookish. By June she had blossomed. Her hair had thickened. She was tan from days at the pool with Kiki La Salle and Jennifer Gardiner, girls Josh had craved. Every evening all that Spring, with the orange light fading over the fields he would lay on the dark yellow bedspread and fantasize about Jennifer. He saw her practicing with the cheerleading squad. *He met her by surprise in the gym, coaxed her behind the bleachers.* Like a scene in Penthouse he'd seen the first issue a few years before in the lobby of the Hyatt Regency when Marshall took him to Atlanta on a business trip, *he lifted her perfectly pleated cheerleader skirt and felt her ass against his thighs.* The sound of his grandmother Bertha's key in the door broke the spell and he pulled the cover over him and pretended to be asleep.

Once he actually talked with Beatrix Loveless and Hillary Fox gave him a ride home in her yellow Thunderbird convertible. Another time, near the spring break when afternoons got hot in KY, he saw them laughing hysterically at Kiki as she gave her ice cream cone exaggerated licks. Josh never knew these girls might have enjoyed making love to him. He thought of these girls as something sacred.

He and Lilian loved each other more than they thought possible.

On senior night, they went to Big Bunny's party. When they arrived in Josh's mom's powder blue Pontiac Catalina everyone was drinking and talking loudly and red in the face. Someone said Big Bunny's dad, a Santa Claus looking man with tobacco juice stain on his white mustache, a ruddy face and a nose the color of a Bloody Mary, had pinched Beatrix Loveless on the fanny and she'd gotten mad and cried and went home. Some of her friends were mad since they'd wanted her to stay and they felt some of the guys shudda come forward and helped her or cussed the old man out. One thing men never do and I think rightly so, is cuss a man in front of his son and Big Bunny was mostly the affable all-star left tackle and everyone loved him.

"Women seldom understand the depth of male friendship," Doc said. The guys mostly laughed and teased the girls about bein' mad 'cause their asses didn't get pinched. They didn't think it was funny but later they got drunk and all danced with Gene Headley, the drama teacher who had once met Marlon Brando and lots of famous people. "You know what Brando once said to me backstage?" "No, what?", we asked. "Who are you?" They laughed and then he told them it was he himself who had written the lyrics to Mr. Tambourine Man. Bob Dylan had stolen them from him. Later, Beatrix came back and laughed about it all. Big Bunny's dad nodded in the corner, head bowed, mouth sprung open, a vision of the twilight of Norse Mythology, Gene Hadley said.

Beatrix and Kiki and Jennifer Gardiner all got drunk and winked and elbowed

Lilian, giving Josh the once over sayin' mmmm mighty fine, hey hey hey. Always the brainy ones gets the fellas, ain't that right, girls? That's when he knew he loved her and they would make love. It made him thirsty and his tongue ached.

Maybe he was drunk when he skidded off onto the gravel, stopped and scooted over in the large smooth front seat to kiss her. They kissed.

"There's a better place," she said.

"Yeah, I guess we shouldn't just stop on the side of the road," Josh whispered.

19

Josh walked across the newly plowed field under an April sky. As he approached the long narrow tobacco barn, standing blood-red up the little hill, he could see where Sylves had set up a small living space in the tobacco stripping room. It was still redolent of last year's tobacco leaves, dry and strewn about the dirt floor. As he walked past he saw that the ancient red door to the room was warped and couldn't close all the way unless you fastened it through the latch with a big flathead screwdriver. Sylves had a TV, a record player and a standing easel next to his cot where he slept between his vigil of the mares in foal.

Sometimes they did their lessons there in Sylvester's new studio. He had room for all his canvases plus a small upright piano. Sometimes they'd meet at Josh's mother's house where she had a nice Yamaha baby grand she'd been given by the great songwriter Vernon Duke, an old friend from her Los Angeles days. Sylves remembered playing on it once at a private party at the Duke's home in Beverly Hills even before Agnes had arrived in LA, and before the drumming gig with Redd Foxx. Agnes always arranged to be somewhere else during their lessons and Josh never really thought much about it, though he sometimes wondered why. Sylves never mentioned it. The first lessons dealt with the rudiments of scales and arpeggios, but it wasn't long before they got to jamming on standards from a few fakebooks Sylves had accumulated over the years. All this became part of Josh's Sunday afternoon jazz reveries, his favorite day to practice for the rest of his life.

When the lessons were over, they'd spent the evening listening to Art Tatum on Sylves' old stereo. Sylves playin his licks slowed down and discoursing how best to improvise over an altered dominant chord. Josh would bug him into getting down the old scrapbook. THE scrapbook, the one with all the snapshots, loose clippings, fragments of charts and chord changes, everything. Sylves posing with Sammy Davis Jr, Red Foxx, Paul Robeson, Ethel Waters and Dinah Washington "Now'at bitch could sho nuff sing her ass off! Voice never crack or nuthin'!"

"Don't care about that fame shit too much, man. Them folks ain't about nothin,' They just like you and me or anybody else."

"Yeah, but look at the joy and songs, stuff they gave the world," Josh said.

Sylves smiled and looked at him for a moment. He saw Agnes so clearly. Tears welled up sharply in his eyes forcing him to turn his face away, toward the solace of the keyboard, "Yo Mama and Papa always said you was a goodin.'"

"I know," said Marshall. "I know everything. And little Josh, he reminds me..."

Josh remembered his mom singing. She sang along with the car radio. She knew all the great old standards. In the confines of the huge old Plymouth, with the fins, on the way home from school or church, she did her duets with Vic Damone and Jack Jones, Dinah Shore, Tony Bennett, Edy Gorme and Steve Lawrence, *"I wanna be around to see how she does it—when she breaks your heart to bits—I wanna see if that puzzle fits... so fiiine."* She went to NYC once and sang on Arthur Godfrey's show. An agency booked her gigs all over the country for a year or so. Sylves was the drummer in her band for a while. She began to hate it.

They had that huge old mahogany stereo in the living room. Josh came upon Agnes sometimes looking out the big picture window, Marshall out in the field, mowing, or over at Bertha's across the farm. "The very thought of you makes my heart sing, like an April breeze in the..." She always sang a little behind the lyric phrase. Frank or Tony, her favorite, would sing, "I've been around the world in a plane..." and somewhere about the word "world", she'd come in with, "I've been around the world..." again, overlapping what had just been sung. It sounded strange but cool to me in the front seat. She had this cool, whispery, alto, 40's style standards voice. "Never get too far ahead of the accompanist!" she would say. She learned tricks like that from some of the great songwriters she worked with like Jimmy McHugh and Matt Dennis. She sat down at the piano with them and they taught her all the alto parts to the one great role she played in the Broadway musical, *Fly Little Angel*, about a girl who falls in love with a fighter pilot.

"Look," Sylves went on, "them songs and shit wudda got wrote by somebody, somehow if it was meant to be. Wudnt nuthin in heaven or earth could stop it. They was just lucky. Right place. Right time. It don't mean shit. What needs to get played is gonna get played somehow. But like a dude get up on the bandstand

and don't know the tune, if he can hang, fine, but if he can't hang man, he's going against GRAVITY! The force of the tune is gonna crush his, pardon me, Lilly white (usually) ass! It don't mean shit."

"It's gotta mean somethin, right?" Josh asked.

"What makes you think that? People just do what they gotta do. But… it's all a mystery. Music's mystery makin sense for a minute, that's all, if you ask me. YOU gotta make it mean something. It don't mean shit in itself. Usually don't nobody ask me so I don't give a big hairy rat's ass, like your grandaddy Dex usetah say. So I don't gotta tell it to nobody."

"You told it to me."

"You different. You just keep practicing that whole tone scale and them melodic minors over them flat five chords. That's the onliest mystery you need to be worryin 'bout now, Mr Art."

They looked at Sylves' paintings. Wild red streaks through purples and greens. Explosions of color. They looked at other pictures on the wall, Sylves with Ray Charles at a recording session in Nashville. Sylves with Merle Haggard and Jethro Burns, Stanley Turrentine muggin in the background.

"Onliest reason I got that gig was cause of playin' at Crazy Reddy's. I was in the house band at Reddy's. Yo' Mama used to come up and sing there, too, sometimes. When Ray Charles come through, he just said, come on and go on with me to Nashville. That's how I got on that record. That's how Redd Foxx heard about me. Then he heard your Mom sing. Pure Luck. See, Ray was 'fraid of white drummers. Scared he might get a bad one. But you know all that ol story."

"But I like to hear it."

"All pure luck."

"But you were good."

"Bein good ain't no guarantee of a gig though. It don't matter what kind of music it is. It's what you say in whatever style. You could be the baddest beboppinest jazz cat in the universe, but if it ain't a good song it ain't gonna say shit. And if the feelin ain't inside….

Sylves and Josh say together in prayer-like unison, "IT AIN'T GONNA COME OUT YO HORN"

"A-men," Sylves nodded. "Now you go on home. Put that guitar down and play some piano every now and then. It won't kill you. And work on your readin. Say hello to your Daddy for me. Seems like I never see him or your mother no more since she moved to town."

20

Sometimes, on the road, traveling with the band, Josh would stare out the bus window into the twilight vision of his past. One Saturday morning, sun shining, he got up and fixed himself a huge cup of strong tea, Josh only drank coffee in the afternoon and even that was never that habitual until he moved to Europe. He had a pleasant breakfast with Berenice and decided to walk the two miles to work. It was his first day of being in charge of opening the bookstore. He was a little nervous but the watery yellow morning light over-powered him and he sat at the bay window of their little apartment sipping his tea and stroking Berenice's long auburn hair.

I have to go. One last long kiss. She tasted like toast and strawberry jam. Wanna hit of dope? Nahh. Maybe this evenin' when I get back. Let's go see, "The Ruling Class" with Peter O'Toole. Get stoned before.

He thought about the dark green sticky tropical lushness of the Kentucky ailanthus- leaved jungles of yard and roadside, how the grass was glowing now pond-green in April. The pink and white dogwoods thickened as he turned down Sweet Gum St. The fallen saffron petals of the March-bloomed forsythia had started to form a dark, leafy, yellow sponginess on the ground as he turned off the sidewalk pavement up into a thin-trailed short-cut along the periphery of Old Governor Marcellus' (the legendary abolitionist) vast yard full of towering tulip poplars and purple beeches with elephant skin bark and exposed roots like the toes of dinosaurs.

Among the dogwoods hung full bee-filled white balls of viburnum, heads drooping under the weight of their dew, undried by the sun because of the thick morning shade against them. By noon they'd be dry and bursting fragrance everywhere. Josh whiffed a faint honey smell of the locusts and pungent wet grass. Fierce robins scampered about and the shimmering dominant starling. A lone blood droplet-red cardinal darted almost humming bird-like down the row of fragile green lilacs. Old Marcellus' carriage path was now nothing but a fading depression in the spongy forsythia and pine needle ground.

The grasshoppers trill… they buzz by your ear in trills of Latin percussion sounds, like snips of Santana songs and the drone and Doppler effect of the bumblebee drenched in pollen. A little striped chipmunk the color of layered caramel ice cream scurries down a hole.

The first Spring and the last and all of them! And I am alive in the alive world! The cardinal alights on the cord of cut wood. Chain saw in the shade. And there stands the aboriginal tree that he sat under so many years before, breaking up with Lilian. "These are the dimensions of the great tree," he'd written in his notebook. Now off to work! A new Life! A new job! A new love! A new broom! Health to the new people…"

A hot Medina day in April was approaching. Joshua Celeste in full harmony striding down Medina Road, the same one old Marcellus, on his way to Washington to speak before the senate, must've been driven down one hundred and thirty years before.

There was the tree. There was the carriage path. "Koch" engraved in brass on the hard enamel red and black paint of the carriage door. "Coach" is derived from the Hungarian, "Kocs." The trees. He thought about secret walks with Berenice, her husband Jerry still at work. But the caretaker seeing them, but only wanting to talk in his loneliness about the trees.

That pecan tree there was probably planted by Marcellus' father, Agnes' maternal great, great grandfather, thought Josh. "It's over three hunnert year old," the old caretaker said. The Versailles-like hedged in garden Old Marcellus' wife had done in European copy. "I know just as much about landscaping as that old billy goat Thomas Jefferson does!"

Josh entered the garden and looked into the glass tabletop sitting on the wrought-iron table. Walking toward the street again towards the bookstore he saw himself in the crystal glass, movie of the future, sitting at this same table with Crazy Reddie, Wanda and the old caretaker's banjo-pickin' son, Buddy, having just eatin' some LSD, watching the sunset on a tranquil summer evening, bluegrass music sifting up into the trees.

But now he's alive again. Winter. Greyhound bus of New England night. Wounds almost healed. The Resurrection of Joshua Celeste. J. C. It fit. Jesus Christ.

"I never made the connection," Marshall said when Josh asked him about it. "What's wrong? It bother you? Hell, you can change it if you want to. Wudn't bother me a damn bit. You always gonna be my little boy, that's all I care about."

The soil pungent with insects. The towering poplars with small hands. *"And no one, not even the rain...."* Lilian had read ee cummings to him in bed. Jonquils still in bloom.

The same trees grew on Water Maple Farm. The same flow to the fields as at Marcellus' estate, a National Historic Site. This garden, this huge front yard was once a great meadow that reached "all the way to Main St." All of Medina was once Old Marcellus' farm, or else he hunted deer through all of it. Some Shawnee a hundred years before, led by Simon Benje, had killed a white hunting party somewhere not far from here, near the grave of Marcellus' father. A farm like Water Maple but, here, Medina had grown and encroached, the highway snaking in slow and encircling old Marcellus' fields one by one, till they got about twenty acres from the house and the city said no more, they placed a limestone monument in front of it with a plaque that said:

"In this place, in 1819, the first Hereford steers were raised in the New World by Governor John Marcellus, farmer, statesman, writer. Commemorative speech given July 1936. 'May Almighty God bless this, the New Garden.'" - National Historic Register.

When Josh unlocked the bookstore door, he went straight to the "Kentucky" section, got down a biography of John Marcellus and thumbed through it. It was his day to vacuum the floor but he still had a few minutes before customers would be coming in. He wanted to write the poem of every spring, of all time, the dimensions of the yellow sunlit tree with the leaved halo of green like a hand against the morning sky, this first morning of his life.

Now, Josh, home off the road after so many years, after all the loves of his life. Marshall's old house. He stares at the undulating, bluegrass meadow that was once a sea. No man changed this field. They plowed it, cleared it of a few trees. But here, where a sinkhole curves into the limestone mound, a half cup of out-cropping, stones bursting through the ground, too dangerous to plow, too steep, fox and mink caves, like dark eyes, this has remained, all this as far as he could see. Up there to Rickey Boy and TLC's house, it's always been this way. A piece of farm that was and is the seabed covered with loam now and everything dried down to the trickle of Moore's Creek, flowing to the palisades of the Kentucky.

21

When he opened the door he knew she was gone. She tried to tell him in the bar that it would be better if she got her own place. She'd never had her own place and now she had her own money and then they argued but when they got home he'd taken a couple of codeines and a glass of dark red wine, smoked a joint and fell asleep on the sofa, "Beware, the couch of Pain," Sylves said once. He shut his eyes.

The crying seagulls swooped around his head. *"Josh, he's just a friend!"*

He walked to the closet where she once hung her clothes. Empty. The few dresses, the jeans tossed on the floor, her leather sandals. He cried one night months before when she hadn't come home. Working Upstairs. He smelled the strong sweet smell of her feet and the grass and the street, the few old high heels, one broken- heeled. He'd never had money to buy her clothes. All gone. Gone. He knew. But then it hit. A tiny ball at the top of the gut. Back of the jaw burning. This is it, man. Gone. No trace.

He shivered and shook on the floor. Nowhere else to go man down, down! Hurry! There's nowhere else, man! Only hell of mind inside. Pierce of cascading fender strat and tenor sax. Spirt-uall shit! spirt-chuall shit! Don't lose touch with Jesus! Don't lose him now. Her bein gone grabbed him like a fever and held him. Thoughts backing up. Too much. Mind gotta go somewhere. Look out! Just get down... down! He panicked for a moment. Can't breathe. Old Hag world face smell enveloped him and then it was gone. Everything. His soul felt like suddenly it flew onto the roof into a bitter cold wind and looked out on the ice of the city. It swirled once around the little flat place above the porch they made love on one night then whirled back into him. That's it, man! You can kiss that pussy goodbye motherfucker! Those young girls don't like all that bein cooped up! They gotta flyyy, man FLLLYYY! Hay!!! Hayayh! You pissed in a well you shall not drink from again!

Some red-faced sweating stubble of beard in wet lips blubbered towards him. Walking in the supermarket. They know! Everybody knows! She ain't coming back to you! You pitiful, man... pitiful. *They call me Mr. Pitiful* Walkin by the drug counter in the Rite-Aid he sees a box of condoms on the shelf, a couple making love on the cover, faces toward heaven with enraptured expressions. But not you! Not you! Somebody else is gonna fuck her. But NOT YOUUU! Never ever again! Can you dig that? Just walk on past. Don't look at those people in ecstasy. You will never know it with her ever again. Just walk on by, motherfucker! Just walk on by.

My sweet little baby's gone forever! Something horrible has happened. "Maybe people get weird about sex because it's so good." Buys some codeine. Walkin' (Miles' tune: dut du-duu dut dut du-duuu dut dut du-duuuuuuu... can't save you. Go with the fountain of tenor and Jimi driftin o but God No! not my little Little Wing where is she man o god o goddammmmm. Twisting on the big empty bed. He vomited every moment back out into nothing and rolled over wiping his mouth salty with tears. He's crying for real, man. Heavin' Grievin' Dark Emptiness of lost house. "O O O those sleepless nights... will break..."

He switches on the light and crawls to the couch. Sleep. Sleep. It's ended. Sleep. Goodbye Wanda. At dawn, he lay in bed... remembering. He's gonna call her. She's not gonna be there. She's just gonna say... she's gonna come by sometime when he feels better and say good-bye.

Suddenly, Medina seemed dry and dead. Life there, all of a sudden made no sense to Josh. Yesterday he was a young man in love with a beautiful young girl who swore her eternal love and then... ain't it strange how things can turn themselves around? He drove aimlessly around town, feeling sorry for himself, headed back to some purgatorial square one of human relationships.

Her flesh became a drug. Secretly hooking Josh. He always thought, I've got her, and looked to other realms to conquer, secure in her devotion to him.

"I just want you, Josh. I know I was wild before but now it's all out of my system." Woman selects. Man collects. That's what Doc had said. His desires go on multiplying, impossible to satisfy: riding, riding across desert after desert finding for a brief moment that oasis of ecstasy. It's hard to remember, like women recalling labor, how he survived. There's that moment you see that yo' real good thang done gone! Out the door. Back to Mama.

He opened the closet door. Old ghosts fluttered out. Memories. The bright day standing by, helpless. Empty. Cleaned out. Faint smell of her. Something balled up in the pit of his stomach. Involuntary, like wretching. He cried out. Like he'd touched a flame. Or a wound. He wanted to vomit something substance-less, metaphysical. A sudden deep encompassing nausea. He wandered like a man gut-shot into the living room, sank to his knees and wept.

Josh tried to make sense of it. They had an argument. He was jealous of her spending time with her friends, her clique before he'd lured her into the pleasure dome of his bachelor pad. He was becoming the classic imperialistic boyfriend. Yet his eye had begun to roguishly wander. Why not another nubile wench? Three? Four? A hundred?

The drug had so strung him out. Who was he? He wondered when he saw himself in the mirror. He could see why people blew their brains out. It was the opium of her sweet flesh. He feared going out of the house. Surely the dogs were layin for him out there.

Then came denial. She'll be back, he thought, chain-smoking in bed. He tried calling her but she had wisely and maturely cut him off. Cold turkey. She was hiding out at a girlfriend's apartment. Josh imagined them fucking this guy, that guy, having fun, free from him now! And they were.

Josh stalked her job. Waitress at an Applebees type place but a notch down. College boy co-workers snickered when they saw him peering through the window from the back alley where the trash bins were lined up, trying to catch a glimpse of her. Once, one of them had asked, "Hey Josh! Or should I call you Mr. Celeste? do you remember polio!" She came out looking more beautiful than he had ever seen her. Soft skin seemed sugary as cocaine. Brown lips and sweet pink gums above her candy cane teeth, even in her dopey waitress uniform. Knowing he would never have her again, ever. She was a scared little girl... or boy, her hair was now cut so short. Her huge emerald eyes broke his heart and he wept again like a child. "How could one not have loved her great still eyes"

"You've got to be strong about this," Wanda said.

"But I just can't accept it," Josh sniveled.

"God, it amazes me that I've got this kind of power over someone. It's scary."

22

His best tour was with the Lacy Corman Band who had a hit on the radio at the time. Unusual for a band with such a decidedly jazzy sound. Lacy was a great player, great singer/songwriter, full of emotion, sometimes beyond orthodox technique and delivery. He was sloppy but he could still "get you right here," Josh would say as he touched his breast with the fingers of his slightly upturned palm. Josh loved listening to Lacy's guitar solos night after night, though his role was merely that of rhythm player.

The tour was a flop even though the critics liked it. It was canceled halfway through, but not before Josh played places like Avery Fischer Hall and Sweet Basils in New York, The Birchmere in DC and a buncha other cool rooms. He dug hanging out with Lacy, were they the only guys in the band who smoked reefer? Might have been, since the Reagan Era sent a real straight vibe through the whole scene. It kept Lacy off the sauce. But sometimes there was no time. Lacy's agency (was it William Morris?) who booked people like Miles and Carlos Santana, kept him busy.

Josh learned a lot from him. Once in a hotel room in Cincinnati, Josh remarked to him that he dug his version of Ravel's "Pavanne Pour une Enfant Defunct" and wondered where he could get the score. Lacy took out his trusty composer's pen and sketched the entire guitar adaptation out for him there on the spot using hotel stationery when he ran out of staff paper. He still had it. And he was a decent guy. The music biz circus made him a bit aloof and distant. Almost arrogant. Josh said his greatest thrill was just being accepted by him and hoped a few other gigs of similar glory would come out of that one, "But – alas," he would laugh to himself in that mock English accent he and his friends picked up watching Monty Python, "it was not to be." Show business has no benevolent patron saint, except the Fat Lady at the End, the big Fairy Gig Mother. He made a few calls. No agency was acquiring new acts. Nothing happened. Eventually, he and Lacy, who had become a kind of guru to him, fell out of touch. No Warm Hand.

He went back to Edgeton for a while and stayed with Marshall who was living alone in the old house on Water Maple and needed company. Or he slept over at Agnes' new apartment. He started playing in Medina again. It was as if his brush with the big time had never even happened.

Gigs afterwards weren't like the ones of the Lacy tour days. Much of the time, as I remember, out of boredom he would stare out the window of some rented mini-van barrelling down the interstate to some smokey roadhouse or some midwestern college coffeehouse, playing covers in some rock/blues/country band. To pass the time, he would go back in his imagination to childhood places. Tell me stories.

Someone opened a door. Agnes picked him up to carry him in. A staircase rose up the right-hand wall of the gracious twenties-built front hall. The ceiling was old-house high. They came in from the porch where Doc, who at that time they called little Allie, short for Albert, had cried in the early morning when Agnes had to go to work as an announcer at the local radio station. Allie sobbed into the little blanket he had named By-Ya. Years later in a moment of psychoanalytic revelation Doc would figure out that the blanket's name came from his infantile recollection of his mother saying over and over through his screams, "Bye Allie! Bye-bye Allie!" as she tore herself away from him, handing him to the colored baby sitter. One year the Christmas tree was in the front hall. Another year, the living room. Josh was three. Then four. He remembered Agnes on rainy days working a jigsaw puzzle on the oval-shaped dark cherry wood table.

Little Allie, Doc, was with Bertha. Agnes resented her spoiling the boys. Luring them away to her house down the hill with soda pop and milky way bars, ice-cold in Bertha's old icebox. Marshall let his mother have her way. But Agnes wanted him to stand up to her. A man's first duty is to his wife she wanted to say, but kept silent, shying away from any competition for her son's affection.

Josh, restless with the rainy day, walked slowly toward his mother and waited. She felt his small child's presence in the room and after a few moments spoke gently to him without looking up from her puzzle, "Why don't you look at the book Millicent gave you? Or go upstairs and play Zorro?" This was his favorite game, to imagine himself as the Spanish Robin Hood, running through the upstairs bedrooms, up and down the halls on his horse's back, protecting the family, tilting at villains with his pencil sword, a towel for a cape Agnes pinned to his back with a safety pin.

Tiring of this he opened what seemed like a forbidden door that led up to the attic. A different color from anything else in the old house. As he walked up the narrow wooden stairs with the yellow afternoon light streaming through the transom, he slowly forgot his Zorro game, his bad guys. He took off his hat and cape and put his pencil in his back pocket as if they were childish things that needed discarding. He felt a nervousness and yet a thrill, it made him suddenly want to pee. But he held it. The urge passed as he fell into a daydream. What wonders there were here: racks of old clothes, discarded toys from Christmases passed, stacks of magazines that, Agnes, like her mother Millicent, could never throw away for fear of losing an important recipe, a pattern for a dress or an article about an old friend from her showbiz days. He picked up a copy with Betty Hutton on the cover. A brown spider ran out and down a crack in the floor. He tried to fish it out with his pencil but the spider was too fast. He remembered Kiki LaSalle at the kindergarten playground, how she wasn't afraid of spiders, she liked them because they tickled when she put them on her arms. He wanted to know if it was true. It made him feel sad that a spider should run away.

He tried on his mother's hats, her high-heeled shoes, Marshall's heavy winter coat, his old cracked boots, his worn-out slippers. He looked into the warped dusty mirror. How strange he looked to himself. He placed the veil from his mother's velvet hat over his face. He liked the dark, shadowy look it gave him. Like his father's blue jaw, yet he was a woman like his mother. He sat down in an old easy chair, the stuffing coming out the sides, and sighed. He looked at the grown-up coat sleeves that covered his hands, the grown-up shoes that swallowed his feet, the womanly hat that covered his face and smelled of his mother's perfume. Was he a grown-up now? He found a box of jewelry and ran his hands through it like a pirate he'd seen in a pirate movie on TV. Was this bad? Pirates are all dead now, he thought, and if there were any, the good guys would shoot them all. He saw a ring with a circle of diamonds around it and tried to put it on his finger. It was too big. He tried his thumb. It stuck. He pulled. It still stuck. He panicked for a moment until he remembered seeing Marshall use a little spit to take off his ring one night in the bathroom when he came home shouting, laughing and stumbling and didn't know Josh was there. Josh tried a little spit. It came off. He giggled. Mama will never know! His heart leaped.

He looked up and saw the sun glare red against the windows. The huge limbs of poplar, elm and pine swayed in gentle evening breezes that smelled of the coming rains. The sky darkened. What secret did it hold, refusing to tell? What secret lay in the silence of the attic? It made him want to pee again. But he dared not. He knew his mother would fuss and make him change his clothes.

The center room, built into the east-facing wall, that looked out over the yard, was the smallest. This was his favorite. Here was the big toy box made of wood and cardboard and covered in red plastic with animals and circus characters drawn on the sides. Three lions standing before the lion tamer with his whip. The lady acrobat with full curved breast diving into space, her crinoline sequins costume like a bird's wings. A monkey swinging from its tail. He looked out the little window, just his height and watched the sky darken over the luxurious, rolling expanse of yard. He noticed a little bird's nest in the eaves. A robin, its breast the color of sunset, flittered in with a piece of straw in its mouth. It looked at him fearfully. Why? He lunged at it playfully and it flew away. For a moment he felt sad. Why did it fly away? We could play. He craned his neck to see what was inside. The need to pee rose in him again. He looked. He was startled to see the three little blue eggs. He wanted to possess them. He saw the mother robin come curving back in flight through a grove just across the yard. What if he could reach them? Hatch them? Become a bird himself? Then he saw his father's truck pulling slowly into the asphalt driveway.

"Josh!" he heard his mother call." Come down! Your father's home and supper'll be ready soon. Come down, darlin'."

How did she know he was up there? he wondered.

"Josh! Oh, Jah-yash!"

He didn't know why but he always waited for her to call once more before he answered.

23

Bertha was old from as early as Josh could remember. Yet there was something of a little girl about his grandmother, deep in the shine of her onyx eyes. She made the boys mind her, but her principal means of coercion was to get them hooked on Milky Way bars and the endless supply of RC colas. Josh figured he and Doc drank fifteen pops and twelve Milky Ways, not to mention a Baby Ruth and maybe a couple of packs of M&M's, in one afternoon! Her old porcelain fridge was a kid's paradise of Three Musketeers, Heath bars and tinfoil-wrapped Hershey's kisses, sugar sprinkled jellied Chuckles, and an ice-cold disc of semi-sweet chocolate mint called Cool Mint that made everything you ate or drank for a week taste like peppermint. She even bought beautiful, hat box-sized tins of Leo's brand peppermint sticks the boys and Marshall would suck on after a big midday farm lunch they called it "dinner." The boys even dipped them in the colas or iced teas while Marshall would sit back in his chair and listen to the farm weather report on the radio or gab with business partners on the telephone. Amongst all the Pepsis and Cokes and Diet-Rite colas, Bertha, in her confusion over all the influx of new products in early sixties America, in her mountain way, pronounced it, "diet-ette." She also interspersed a few Nehi Grapes, Orange Crushes, Ginger Ales, Seven-Ups and, not so long after, that soon-to-be greatest of hillbilly thirst quenchers, Mountain Dew. In the TV ad, the cork pops out of the moonshine jug and is propelled through the barefoot hillbilly's hat brim as he prepares to take a swig.

On sweltering summer days, the boys would walk down a little staircase from the front room of her small house built into the cup of the hill, and into the cool of a living room where an old rusty air-conditioner dripped droplets of water very slowly onto the dark burgundy rug that covered only part of the butterscotch poplar floor. The floor often smelled of the Pine-sol cleaner that, on cleaning days, which were frequent, stood foamy in buckets and chalk-white as the seawater Josh would see in his later travels. The rest of the house smelled of mothballs she put inside over-stuffed closets and trunks of clothes too dressy to ever wear, satin bedspreads and throw rugs she made herself.

In their games, Josh and Doc would sometimes stumble into those back rooms of her house where nobody went anymore, not since her married days with Dexter. Except on those rare occasions, she fixed a fried chicken dinner, what Marshall said was the only thing she cooked worth a damn, for some relative from the east mountains, or some local politician or the farmhands when everyone would eat together in the main dining room. There was a dark cherry chest-of-drawers with gold-plated handles, on top of which she carefully arranged her baroque-copy porcelain figurines. They were pale green-faced fauns with wreaths around their necks and laurel leaves in their hair, leaning against a fragment of tree trunk, or Mozartian figures of the Old Empire, grey wigs braided down the back, or in three-cornered hats, or Hungarian hussars promenading in their soutache, ladies on their arms, all smiling from a dead era. On two walls behind Marshall's dark antique cherry office desk, hung mural-sized tapestries, depicting the pale, cherubic, lamb-like faces of courtiers and courtesans walking arm in arm through gardens or singing around a harpsichord, some strumming lutes or mandolins.

The two boys wandered as if in a museum of their own lives. Was Bertha like these people? This was the lost world of her dead husband's parents that all mountain girls revere, that all widows preserve. For these frontier people, these were proper furnishings so she kept them intact, having saved them and many other things from the fire that had destroyed the old family mansion on the hill above. She kept this world in separate rooms from the day-to-day goings on of the rest of the house. No one slept in these bedrooms with their high satin-sheeted beds and lace pillowcases though they were kept immaculate as if waiting for the lost people to return, resting after a long journey. Only on those rare occasions when Bertha had, as she would say, comp'ny comin', or when covetous ladies from town would come to oogle her antiques (Bertha enjoyed deceiving such ladies with promises of leaving them certain prized pieces in her will) only then would anyone who was not a Celeste by blood, marriage didn't count, be allowed to enter. In this world, time stopped after the first world war.

As you walked downhill to her little cottage, past the rock garden on the right, down the cool, damp stones of her small stone stairway, you could find her shelling half runner beans and enjoying the breeze, but when the hot July weather began, she walked up the hill to the elm shade tree and sat in a metal rocker, waving to Rickey boy or TLC or any field hand or tobacco yap who might be passing by with a load of hay, tobacco, silage or cattle, yelling for them to stop if she felt like giving orders... impractical things that sometimes went against her son's wishes. More likely as not, they pretended not to notice her. Marshall told them to ignore the old woman unless it was an emergency. From this vantage point, she was most likely to catch Marshall on his way home to the Edgeton Road side of the farm where Agnes had his supper waiting. On days she tried to avoid him, she hid down on the porch behind the heavy hanging cascade of Rose of Sharon with the bumblebees, yellow and black and drenched in pollen, and a garden of rocks around her. But he knew she was there. She might of had some kind of plan going that day or the next and seeing him might ruin it for reasons only she knew. They argued quite a bit over how Water Maple Farm should be run, but some days they just didn't have the heart to, so he drove on.

I remember seeing them once on an early autumn evening, Bertha and the two boys, walking down Main St., I was staying with my Aunt in Edgeton at the time. Aunt Pearl had a little apartment above Madison's Drugstore on Main Street. I would see them walking in the full light when the sandy granite walls of the corner bank looked shell pink and a Maker's Mark whiskey red seal bottle beamed from a wall advertisement in the background. I'd see 'em comin. The boys friskin around her in rocking horse leaps and cat-like crouches like she was a maypole and it could have been May it was so warm. I looked out Aunt Pearl's window that looked across the street at the courthouse and watched Bertha walking with Albert (Doc) and Josh, coming to let my Aunt Pearl read their palms. They'd hold out their little hands, restlessly turning their sun-tanned knees in toward each other.

They sat down and Aunt Pearl would bring a cold glass of milk for Bertha and soda pop for the boys. The drone of the fan drew in the few remaining sounds of the streets, making them louder than usual for that time of day, honking horns and hollers from sun-burned yahoos tryin' out rusted, resurrected trucks they'd traded some hapless cousin out of and got runnin' again. Pearl would bring out a book at Bertha's urging and listen to little Albert read out loud from the encyclopedia. He'd been reading since he was three. The whole town knew about that since sometimes Marshall would set him up on a table at Crazy Red's poolroom and little Allie would read the menu on the wall. Well, that about flipped everybody, and Crazy Red and even his son, little Red, started taking bets on what words he could spell. They'd say, especially to someone who didn't know anything about the kid's uncanny talent, "Wilbur, ten dollars says that boy can spell collard greens and vie-eener sausage."

So, they'd bring Albert over and he'd turn his back to the menu, they'd give him the word and he'd spell it right every time. Pretty soon they'd just think up the hardest words they knew, not sayin much in small town America, and Allie did the same thing. Spelled 'em right every time. Some nights, when Marshall was in town havin a beer, ol crazy Reddie might come over and say, "Marsh, how 'bout you and me we go up this year to the State Fair in Louisville and see if we can get Allie in one of them sideshows. I bet they'd pay good money to see a little boy like that read and spell all them words. I got the perfect name, Wizard Boy, five minutes to see, a lifetime to forget... or Brain Boy, have you ever seen two heads on the same booooody. Alive alive Alive!' Wudda you think? I'll take him up there myself if you ain't got time. Give you ten percent."

And Marshall'd say, "Red, you been drinkin your profits again? My son ain't no friggin Geek! You oughta be ashamed schemin' over a boy ain't even four year old yet."

"Well, it's just a thought," Red would say.

Marshall'd look down in his beer and mutter, "ten percent... shiiit." They'd have this same conversation for years, 'til Allie got to be almost thirteen. Then it didn't make sense anymore to take him up to the Louisville Fair.

One day when Allie was still just a boy, Red asked him what he wanted to be when he grew up and Allie said, "A doctor!" so everybody, even Marshall, laughed and Red always called him "Doc" after that. Pretty soon everybody picked it up. But how they, Agnes and Marshall, first figured out how he could spell words was funny. They used to spell words to keep him from knowing what they were talking about. Like, she'd say, I'm going to the s-t-o-r-e to get the c-a-k-e. but then one day Allie said, If you go to the s-t-o- r-e please get m-e some c-h-o-c-o-l-a-t-e.

Doc knew all Aunt Pearl's encyclopedias backwards and forwards. They would eat cookies and she'd fix cold chocolate milk from a Hershey's syrup can and Pearl would hold Bertha's plump wrinkled hand in her hand.

"Well, you've got a good long lifeline, Miss Bertha," she told everybody, "And these little lines are your children. Only one stands out strongly."

"That's Marshall"

"That's right, Miss Bertha."

"Read the boys."

Doc held out his hand but Josh stood behind him like he was a sapling a rabbit might crouch behind. "Well, let's see, Doc, you've got a good strong lifeline and this is your love line, and it is strong, too."

"He's the smartest boy at the school." Bertha then asked, "Does it say anything else? Is he gonna be rich and have lots of children?"

"Well, let's see," said Pearl. "These strong lines here indicate prosperity. Josh! Jah-yash! Your turn, come in here".

Josh wandered over to Aunt Pearl's bookcase to stare at all the bulging shelves of books he barely understood. There stood her battered cherished collection of first edition novels, books of poetry, philosophy and cultural history: Spengler's Decline of the West; Heidegger's Language, Poetry and Thought, Simone Weil, Marianne Moore, Virginia Woolfe, a memoir by her "Uncle" Schwartz, stuff like that all over the house.

She loaned Bertha a book about William Henry Becknall, the frontiersman she claimed they were kin to. It was a book full of daguerreotype pictures Little Josh said looked just like the ones of Bertha's father-in-law, Ryley Jackson Celeste, Marshall's grandfather, Josh and Doc's great grandfather, pictures of a time-worn silver look, except the eyes shone out strong, almost like the phosphorescent paint you find in dimestores.

"I'm readin a book now called "Look Homeward Angel" by Thomas Wolfe!" Doc piped up suddenly.

"You are!" said Aunt Pearl, "That's an awful big book for a little boy. What's it about?"

Aunt Pearl had read it herself because Mrs. Knopf and other ladies in their Tuesday night book club talked about what a shame it was Wolfe died so young. But Aunt Pearl, always so good with children, even if she never had any of her own, wanted to let Doc talk.

"It's about a man who tries all his life to make a beautiful angel out of stone," Doc said. "And did you like it?" asked Aunt Pearl.

"It's ok. I ain't hardly finished it yet but I think only God can make an angel and they are invisible".

"No," she said, "you and Josh are two little angels and you're real and I can see you!"

There was a faint light of the Edgeton dusk as they went down the old wooden staircase of the same drugstore years later Josh and Jared marveled at the cover

133

of the dusty old Elvis gospel album, faded with so many afternoons, and Jimi Hendrix's "Are You Experienced" beside it. Pearl watched from the window as they got into Bertha's Olds Cutlass and drove away.

One thing I forgot to mention about all of Pearl's books was that many were in Hungarian. That's where she grew up, Hungary. That was the language she spoke when she was a little girl. I only heard her speak it a few times. Only, it seemed when she was mad about something, like when Mr. Madison never would put salt on the icy sidewalk in front of our apartment in the wintertime, or Mrs. LaSalle would leave her car running under our window when she was parked in front of the drugstore, waiting to pick up her kids at the soda fountain, and the exhaust would drift up into the house. Only times like that I would hear her muttering Hungarian under her breath. It was a strange but pretty sounding. Like nothing you'd ever heard. She tended to avoid bringing up the subject of teaching it to me. It was the language of my mother, her sister. Sometimes, late at night around holiday times, I'd hear her speaking it on the phone to someone. It was our secret subject. But, like I said, I was never much of a student anyway so I never learned a whole lot. I spent most of my time daydreaming, fooling around on my guitar or mandolin. I even played a little fiddle, and of course, tried to learn electric bass so I could be in a band. I thought about girls a lot.

Aunt Pearl played piano quite well, even showed me a Hungarian tune or two. Josh later used a few of those old songs in his shows with Lacy Corman, a big thrill for me, gave their show a taste of the new "world music" trend. People ate it up. She took me back to Hungary a few times when I was a teenager. She had inside connections within the Party then so we could travel pretty freely. I'd meet fiddlers and guitarists, all sorts of musicians. Many were gypsies, a few who played a big piano-like instrument called a "cimbalom." I'd learn tunes and some Hungarian words from them. I'd even teach them the Appalachian fiddle tunes I learned from local guys when Aunt Pearl had been a librarian for a while at West Virginia State University. It was when I went wandering around the Hungarian countryside with my fiddle that I got drunk for the first time in my life on Hungarian "pálinka," a kind of plum brandy.

Now, only the sounds of Budapest waft through the open window, a gunned motorcycle, a siren, a dog barking, a firecracker going off.

Pearl had to leave Hungary when she was barely a teenager. "Uncle" Schwartz brought her to Yugoslavia, the part near Italy, where he made a deal with some men from Bosnia to get them on a boat bound for New York. Mr. Swartz didn't like New York much and after a few years, he saved enough money for him and Pearl to move to Kentucky. Schwartz was a milliner by trade so he opened what soon became a thriving hat shop on Limestone Street in Medina, KY. She learned the business and got heavy into reading novels and poetry, what she called her "literature," things Schwartz gave her to read.

Schwartz was a poet and he wrote in another language, Yiddish. In Hungary, he'd written many books and was well-known and respected until the war. Then everything changed. Even though his poems had little if any political content to them, they were mostly what Pearl called "lyrics," the government considered them a threat and had all existing copies of his books destroyed and new printings banned. He managed to smuggle a copy of his most famous one out, "Dal" (song), sewn page by page into the lining of their clothes. I remember Aunt Pearl keeping it in a hand-sewn, leather-tooled cover where company could see it and marvel but not touch the pages. They were sacred, all that was left of her girlhood.

She never saw or heard from my mother or any of my relatives again so it was assumed they perished in the camps. She never talked about it unless I asked her what my mother had been like. She was very beautiful she said. But turned out she had never really known my mother who was much older. She hadn't known her well at all, since she went to University at Szeged and then to study in New York where I was born. I was put up for adoption and my mother returned to Hungary, a fallen woman. My father never resurfaced. There are no photographs from this time. Nothing. Aunt Pearl and Swartz by some miracle had been able to obtain custody of me when they reached New York. Mr. Dallberg, a mysterious figure in their lives, must have arranged it. Swartz and Pearl often spoke of the money they owed him. Some said he had been involved in illegal gun trafficking during the war. Or maybe it was the recognizable development of my leg deformity that made my original adoptive parents change their minds.

Life in Kentucky was like a paradise. The little hat shop thrived and I grew up healthy and happy. After a time, I no longer needed my leg brace, though I still had to drag my leg along after me a bit. Kind of like Marty Feldman in "Young Frankenstein." It was as if my aunt and Mr. Schwartz had been given a place in the Garden of Eden of the New World as recompense for all they'd suffered in the Old. But our luck didn't last.

Schwartz made an innocent enough blunder when he wrote a mildly sarcastic book about his Kentucky experiences. It was all in fun, Aunt Pearl told me years later. Something out of the Beverly Hillbillies. Some prominent townsfolk in Medina didn't take it that way. They recognized, or thought they did, themselves, and were offended. What right did an "outsider", a "Jew" even, have to comment upon their decent God-fearing lives. *Why don't he stay where he belongs—in the bible!*

Schwartz was threatened with several lawsuits until he finally agreed to have the remaining copies he'd had printed, at his own expense, pulled from circulation. I remember coming across a few boxes of them once, playing in a closet at the Main St. apartment in Edgeton. The newspapers got wind of it and that only fueled the flames of what Pearl called "xenophobia." Business at the shop suffered. Eventually, Schwartz went bankrupt and we were forced to move to Edgeton for the cheaper rents but Schwartz couldn't find decent work. He grew despondent, sickened, and one night, a copy of "Dal" spread over his chest, he died.

Pearl did various jobs, laundry, babysitting, even working in the tobacco and bluegrass seed fields of Water Maple Farm, which is how she met Bertha. Her favorite past time, which eventually got her to where she could make money, was writing. She wrote stories and essays and poems and sent them to magazines like Life, Saturday Evening Post, Look and New Republic. She entered writing contests, contests off cereal boxes and matchbooks. And she'd win money, all under her pen name.

24

The yellow light sifts green through the black walnut leaves. If you look up, the sky is blue as a maid's uniform. Angelika's bonnet is white with a pink glow. Black asphalt streets. Black asphalt driveway. Grey sidewalks. The brick is dark as communion wine, sparkling with a thin film of moss, trimmed with white ornamental sills and shutters. The recently painted door is golf course green. I think of an old stately Victorian place, like pictures of the "old brokedown palace," where Sylvester grew up when it was new. Shine and Money Joe still sit on the rotted porch in the evening.

Many of the others are antebellum mansions white as horse farm fences, arrayed with green trim, a maze of hedge and garden in the side yard. Irises and Lillies and lilac shoot up like roman candles, the color of a rich socialite's eyelids. White clover, violets and yellow dandelions. The old slave house of matching brick is now used for storage. Agnes' brother Dennis once stored a hundred and sixty-two cases of aspirin in there that never got sold. Some failed business venture. "You gotta HAVE money to MAKE money!" I know coz one night we got Shine to buy us a fifth of Ripple wine and we counted all of them. That's probably when Uncle Dennis got out of the drug salesman biz and back into fooling around with sound equipment. We'd hide in that old house, where slaves once slept a hundred years before, and smoke camels. Playing games with the pictures on the pack that Marshall said he'd learned in the Navy. The lion on the camel's back, the sexy woman on the camel's front leg, the camel driver out of the picture because he'd gone around to take a piss at the oasis on the flip side.

Luckies were awful tasty, too. L.S.M.F.T. "It's Toasted!" Jared kept saying the night we cheated and won all those packs of cigarettes off the guy at the county fair. Jared drank a pint of Heaven Hill that night, or was it Ancient Age? He blew lunch, tossed cookies, earled, upchucked, kept saying, being the nice guy he was, you'd better get back! You'd BETTER get back! Then BOOM! all over the place. Really arched it. Me and Josh both giggling, covered with puke.

There was Agnes' Derby Party, Labor Day Picnic and Miss Millicent's birthday that sometimes fell in conjunction with Thanksgiving. All-day preachin' and dinner on the ground, all the black folks in her circle, if they wanted to make a buncha money of an afternoon, ladies would put on the white uniform, men, the white jacket and black trousers, black bow tie, shiny black corfam shoes, and serve guests. They probably got at least a hundred and a quarter and that was pretty good, seeing how Sen. Demeter was a tight ass about these kinds of goings on. Sylves said, "Rich white folks didn't get they money by givin' it away!"

We'd play jazz standards at those dinner parties. This was before Carlo moved to Philly and he would loan me his acoustic bass. Must have been around the time he started playin' electric with a blues band over around the college at Medina for extra cash. Of course, I couldn't play it as good as him. It seemed to have sacred significance for Josh. Sacred stories of its acquisition. I'll tell them someday. Ryly and Gordon should know them. I suppose I defiled it. But that day it looked so beautiful sitting next to the piano in that big colonial-style drawing room. As Doc put it, "like a still life by Harnett." Agnes' folks liked anything British or anything from Williamsburg, Virginia, where Millecent's people were from, those mahoganies and cherries and walnuts.

Carlo taught me how to walk a bass line through the chord changes to, "Sunny Side of the Street." Agnes would sing and Josh lay down those Joe Pass style chords on guitar he'd learned off the piano from Sylvester. Nobody cared if it was Easter Sunday. They weren't fundamentalist. You could sing loud and swing real hard on some old tune out of a fakebook and no one would mind. Agnes' brother would record it all on his old Teac recorder and vintage German microphones.

Hi Crip,

There are also some boxes of tape (reel to reel?) that belonged to Uncle Dennis that I found in Mom's attic. Doc says they can be transferred to CD?

Best, Angelika

Agnes was brilliant. Billie Holiday or Anita O'Day. Night. Day. God. She could sing. The ol' Senator's eyes would redden on "Skylark" and he would think back to his campaigning days when he sang with Millicent on all those front porches of the sunny South of the 1930s. When youth and love were still alive!

"You know, Doll Baby," the old man would say, "your mother and I met Hoagy Carmichael one night at the Regency in Atlanta." Those southern "l's" rolling lazily off his tongue. "We had us a big time. He knew who I was! Everybody knows yo' 'Tah- Tah!'" That was Agnes' baby-talk name for him. "He was playing at Harry Truman's birthday party. Aw, he was such a fine boy. Loved me to death. Smart little sumbitch he was. But I couldn't hardly keep Milli's hands off of him. You' member how yo' mama got when she got a few drinks inner. But he said he'd always wanted to write a song about ME!!! My god what a talent. Can you imag…"

"Yeah, Daddy, we know. Everyone loved you," Agnes interrupted. Then cupping her long white-gloved hand against her cheek she would whisper to everyone, though the old man was almost stone deaf by then, "we've only heard THAT story a million times."

At those old Sunday get-togethers we weren't just listening to all the gone years but also about the lined, washed-up showbiz faces at Hollywood dinner parties teen-aged Agnes had been where Georgie Jessel sang "Mammy" and Sammy Fain whispered, "Love is a Many Splendored Thing" at the piano, and Harold Adamson coughed through, "It's A Most Unusual Day." Agnes thought all men in Hollywood gay.

Dear Senator Demeter,

Thanks again for gracing us with your delightful presence, Sir, at the premiere of "Ol' Kaintuck." Rob Taylor really enjoyed having an authentic southerner on the set. The word I'm getting is, "Come on back out here! And bring that knock-out daughter of yours!" That is if your busy Washington schedule will allow. Agnes is a pure natural on screen and we have much to talk about. Just between you and me, (and I know I can speak frankly with you, sir), I thought the picture was complete bullshit but we have a project with Hope and Lamour on the table that Agnes would be perfect for. Hope to see you soon.

Best, Felix Onstein.

"Hey baby don't do that to all those pretty records. They all broken?" Agnes remembered her father, Senator Celeste, 'Judge Daddy' say, "Your Daddy's here, baby... Milli too. We thought that's what you wanted, Sugar. Onstein said Hope and Lamour, big names Sugar, a screen test Sugar! Isn't it wonderful? We oughta try. Come on baby, come down from up there, supper's cold. Come on down... I said COME ON DOWN OR I'LL WHIP YOU TIL THE BLOOD RUNS DOWN YOUR LEGS!!! Yo Daddy's had it with all this foolishness. Now, the train's leavin!"

Josh and Agnes took a trip back out to LA and had a reunion with those Hollywood dudes. Old Onstein, now sixty and fat, "So what's goin on on the farm in Edgeton? Is that it? Great! So that's how you make a front yard, harvest all that Bluegrass seed with a "Stripper?" and tobacco hangs like that? Way up inna barn? Look, Aggie, you had it all, Universal contract, the woiks and ya went and married the hick. That's okay it was your life. You say your son can sing and play? fine. I believe I can take him over to Capitol just like I did for you and that black boyfr... friend of yours and maybe he can make a record I know just like the Beatles or Feliciano. If little Josh was only blind! We'd make millions! If he was only blind!!" Scotch-breathed laughter. Teardrops of rain, hatred, ingratitude carving lines in the window, looking out onto the green eyeshadow of pain and death.

"Doll Baby, don't you remember?" Judge Daddy said. "You sat right down beside him on the piano and sang.... what was it?"

"Yeah, Daddy, I remember." Agnes conceded.

We didn't know what it was all about then but we would. One by one the poison drops of life came. Josh looked out the van window and asked Hector if we can smoke and crack the window, headlights melted Dali-like over his face on the dark road like a movie screen. We already knew even then what was going to happen. Women, then songs, then stupor then... so we tried to twist it outta the instruments.

Sylves and Josh would do four-handed piano stuff on something like "Invitation" That cool melody at the beginning really knocks me out. Tough changes. Then Sylves might sing "Laura" really, really slow like Billy Eckstein or Arthur Prysock. Big ornamental crescendo at the end, sputtering these half fucked notes.

Agnes would walk up beside the piano. That Billie Holiday turban on. She nodded pensively. So simple it was. The tone. Just sang it straight but with that perfect grace note. If she scatted a few bars it had a Paul Desmond cool about it, volume but not overbearing. Not too strong. Don't get too strong Sylves used to say. It can't be described by these silly words! Doesn't even matter anymore. All gone 'cept for some plastic tape.

I can still hear her. The Voice. Josh had the same except, like looking through the other end of a telescope. It was as if it said, come closer. Come closer to me. Love me. I love you. I love everyone I ever laid eyes on. I'm mute if I can't give.

Then Josh hit that little intro on "Darn That Dream" and here she'd come, flowin' in on that tricky chord change on the second bar. From GMAJ7 to Bbmin7 for all you dumbasses who know squat about chordal relationships. Sang the baby out the mama's arms Sylves would say. Marshall'd come in from the fields poking his head in, clothes still sweaty and dusty before he'd had a shower and put on that pinstriped suit and the burgundy tie and shiny alligator cowboy boots comin in to listen a spell, shake his head and say "if only it put tobacco in the barn!" Laughter and then somebody handing him a bourbon and branch water and beaten biscuit crumbs still on his strong chin shouting out, "Hey, honey ('hahnee'), sing 'Hey Lawdy Mama'!"

When Josh put in a harmony or two, just like at St Jude's, I can still feel it. The Touch. Human Touch and... fuck it... it didn't make it to tape. Fuck it. It's gone forever. What difference does it make?

I could go back there, to that empty house. Some stranger would greet me at the door with a puzzled look, yes I remember them very talented people. Would he recognize me with the limp and gray hair falling out? Dennis lived there alone at the end, got fat on inheritance, filet mignon and Maker's Mark. Divorced. Kentucky basketball game on in the background, Caywood Ledford's voice from the radio because Kentucky fans only listened to him. The big-time TV announcers were always biased against Kentucky, so they turned the TV sound off. Everyone knew they hated us and thought we were all Ku Kluxers and wore no shoes and our eyes don't match. "Real tough loss for the Bruins, Jim. Yeah, that's right Ralph, they managed to stay with the Cats only losing by 20 this time." Caywood god/voice rolling over the rolling hills.

Autumn rain on the windshield. Poor little church on an Edgeton Easter morning, Josh and Doc as acolytes helping the priest prepare communion wine and bread. "That we might keep a perpetual memory of his death and sacrifice... until he's coming again." Josh knelt down and rang the sanctus bell. Ding. Jackhammers pounding outside my window.

Josh looked up past Father Hozni's robes rustling close to his shoulders as he stood by the altar or knelt together in prayer. The service of the Holy Communion had a fancy ritual attached to it where Josh, just as Doc had done when he was the same age, had to hand Father Hozni the golden chalice of wine. It was consecrated by the priest by first raising it to the large golden cross in the center of the altar. Then, kneeling, always uttering prayerful words in a low voice, then Josh handed him the silver box. "Never grab it by the little silver cross on top! It might come off! Just unscrew it gently counterclockwise!" Years later Josh tasted the legendary wine of the Tokaj region of Hungary, he'd swear it was the same as the communion wine at St. Jude's.

White pringle chip-like wafers with IHS printed in the center of them were then broken and fed to the parishioners. Josh looked up and saw the homely face of Christ. Looked like guys who are good-looking but have something missing, some lack of cuteness or charisma Josh imagined girls might find empty of sex appeal. Nice guy, though.

In the stained-glass rendering, Christ's hand softly knocked at the heavy, medieval-looking door of Eternity that seemed like something out of Grimm's Fairy Tales. He said Agnes use to read 'em stories from that book, but thought his Dad brought it from Bertha's house who got it from a lady in Edgeton. Christ's long brown hair hung down to the shoulders draped in a blue robe that reminded young Josh a little of Muhammed Ali's boxing outfit. The colored glass, illuminated from the back by a lamp and the light yellow eastern sun, reminded him of the hard candy sitting around in bowls at Bertha's house. The new young priest, Fr. Hozni's assistant, walked young Josh through the altar boy routine, got upset and said, in his Yankee accent, "Josh, ya look suh lost, I don't know what we're gonna do with ya!"

Josh knew that after church he must go, freshly blessed, to the field that stretched out beside the road to Medina and play football. He loved the game, the autumn feeling, proving his strength, his speed, his heart. But he dreaded the yelling, the frustration that brought some boys to tears. He cried, knocked down, the ball fumbling away, as he lay helpless on the ground. Torchy Kiraly, the star of the other team, scooping it up and running 60 yards for the Touch Down. The pressure. The Desire to win. Those men, those coaches, scared him with their obsession with discipline, the green pulsing veins in their necks. They seemed angry and temperamental like his Dad could be but these men were further from the soil. They weren't farmers. Sometimes they even spoke with strange accents and were from places like Michigan and Indiana. The very field they strutted upon was a contrivance with silly white lines and iron posts, not to mention the candy-colored uniforms and plastic helmets. Sunday crowds brought children, gathered to watch their other children, run around bored under bleachers, kissing and smoking Marlboros. Angelika and her friends hid there and put on make-up, stuffed their bras with toilet paper and mock walked like Mrs. LaSalle, who Agnes said was not a good mother.

Josh thought of Christ's face in the St. Jude stained-glass window above the altar, looking hurt but still a little happy, tired, knocking on the door of Eternity like he'd been waiting for someone, maybe like a girl at the picture show, that kind of face. He had the face of someone who was usually nice even if he occasionally got mad, someone who would always be around if you got in trouble. Josh found himself walking with him everywhere, the fields of Water Maple, the halls at school. He talked (to himself?) as he stared at the dark ceiling that, as he was falling asleep, headlights from the road would creep slowly across and illuminate, for just a moment, the spindly locust tree out the window beside his bed, whose ornate, thick curlicues of branches formed into the faces of animals and monsters.

It occurred to him Jesus would love and save him from the field where boys butted heads. He would play where friends moved together in spiritual union and there was no need to keep score. Too bad most people didn't act like Jesus. *Mama, is everything alright? Why are you crying?* Maybe he always looked for people who tried to… or maybe they just were.

25

BUDAPEST 1989

When I think about it now, throwback the sash and the light of October morning pours through the window of this one-room apartment, I see things. I see that Josh's inner life, that inner voice that kept him talking to God even while he was talking to us, is what kept him going. He kept searching for that perfect love. Some folks just give up and live out their lives, stop looking for anything. Josh couldn't keep from searching. When he first hit town, still stinging from that thing with Wanda, I told him where to find whores. He had to walk down to Rakoczi Square and go left. Other times we hit the music clubs and looked for women and gigs. He hit on lots of girls but never seemed to get very far. He was too honest to be a good playboy. But sometimes I'd see a bike fastened to some light pole outside the door of some apartment I'd managed to find for him, making me think he had a few visitors from time to time. I would lose touch with him for a few months. Then there'd be that late-night phone call. I managed to find him a few gigs, mostly solo things, just his guitar but I found a few band gigs for him, sometimes I even played bass. We worked up some nice tunes, played some nice clubs. He was always on the look out for babes, there were many in Budapest, but in that child's way, he had. Like he was looking for a mama.

First, there was Paloma from Crete. I'll never forget how open we all felt walking through the streets of Pest with the crumbling facades no government raised a hand to repair since the end of the War. After living so long in the pristine safety and newness of suburban America, it felt dangerous to walk beside the old buildings let alone actually enter one, the feeling they might collapse was ever present. Many of the soot-blackened decaying walls propped up with boards were riddled with scars from blasts of flack and bursts of machine-gun fire in the bombing runs and street battles of '45 and '56. The pavement of blackened, hand-sized, hand-fitted chunks of stone, quarried from the mountains to the north, glistened in the misty fall evenings like the scaley back of some mythical dragon, part benevolent, part ominous. Often a portion had been gouged out by time or vandal, giving you the feeling that the dark streets of midnight Budapest were flashing a quick, sly, gap-toothed smile. They knew something you didn't. The street was a jigsaw puzzle with an important piece missing.

One night, after listening to Josh sing at this little club, a gig I got him at the Mona Lisa, we came back to my apartment in the Kelenföld district with Paloma in tow. She was this cool half Armenian chick, a little fat, but beautiful with classic dark eyes and black hair, always joking in a smartalecky kinda way. She was brilliant at school and was finishing her degree in medicine at Budapest University. I dug her and we hung out often but she really took a shine to Josh. I went to the kitchen for some beers and came back to see she had thrown her leg over Josh as they were sitting, backs to the wall on the bed. It was the only piece of sit-uponable furniture in the room. I was a little crestfallen and realized there was no point in me hanging around so I yelled down the hall that I was going out for more beer.

I took a stroll in the cold autumn air. My curiosity got the better of me later and I snuck back in, turning the key very slowly and quietly. I heard Paloma's moans as I stood motionless in the kitchen. I bent down to the bedroom keyhole and there she was brown-skinned and lovely in the dim light. Her breasts sagged down more than it seemed when she'd had her shirt on and white stretch lines were faintly visible. Still, she was beautiful. They kissed and hugged for a long time, hours it seemed. Then I heard Josh say as he entered her from behind, Fuck me! C'mon! Fuck me! And then she said joking, No, You fuck me! Then I heard giggling.

"I love your black hair," I heard him say.

"But every Armenian girl dreams of being blond," she said.

After a few more minutes, Josh came bounding out. He saw me but didn't seem to mind if he even knew I'd been peeping at them. He laughed, "Look what an idiot I am! I kept fucking her without taking her panties off, I was so fucking horny I just pulled the crotch of em off to the side and look now the elastic band has rubbed a blister on the side of my dick the size of a baseball. I'm too sore to fuck anymore! Sorry rover" he said, "maybe you can take over."

And let Jimi take over, I thought to myself, thinking of the Hendrix song we played. I crept in like a shameful dog and started to undress. Can she see me in this light? Then I heard her. She was softly snoring.

They went around together for a few weeks and Josh told me he was really starting to fall for her. "That's not to say you can't fuck her, too, man, if you want." Good 'ol Josh! "I mean if she doesn't mind…"

Paloma had no intention of staying in Budapest. She kept talking about what an asshole her father was. It turned out that he called the shots and when he demanded she return to Yerevan and study medicine, she obeyed. She left a number that turned out to be an old boyfriend's. Josh called and the guy was nice enough to give him her parent's phone number. He spoke with them but they acted like they didn't know where she was.

That was only the beginning. We met up with lots of bands, even did several "interesting" tours of neighboring Austria, which at that time felt almost like getting back to the States, much more "western" than Hungary felt. I remember one incident in particular. I'll tell it all someday.

Mostly we stayed in Budapest, wandering its dark cobble-stoned streets, going from bar to bar. On some deserted side street in the wee hours, you might see our little entourage of expats walking past, someone telling a story, doing an impression from American TV, girls and guys endlessly flirting, making moves on each other. I was usually the ringleader standing at the front, stopping now and then to tell some tidbit of Hungarian history or to take a vote on which bar we would visit next. I spoke better Hungarian than anyone and knew my way around from all my visits with Aunt Pearl when I was in high school. Doc used to say I was a Virgil in Josh's Dantean Inferno.

As I say, I found him a little gig at a pizzeria/bar called the Mona Lisa. It was one of the first commercial live music venues to open in Budapest after the fall of the communist regime. It was run by a bunch of affable Serbs, all running away from conscription into the Yugoslavian civil war.

I remember they paid him two thousand Hungarian forints (10 bucks) and dinner. And that was one of the best paying gigs in town then! The pizza was decent and so was the pasta, though they had to use Trappista cheese instead of mozzarella or parmesan. There wasn't any in Budapest in those days. It gave the pizza a more bitter taste and I remember how they used to grate big slivers of it over the spaghetti Bolognese. Still, it was delicious. Even if they were pretty stingy with the tomato sauce.

My favorite thing was the lepény. Very middle eastern. A kind of hot pita sandwich with fresh garlic and cheese in the middle. You ate it with a fork instead of picking it up like a gyro. And the pita bread seemed crunchier and thicker somehow. You can still find a good one here and there.

The Mona Lisa became a kind of meeting place for all the Americans and Brits and Dutch and Germans and French and Italians and just about anyone looking for a bit of a party in this strange city with the strange language on the edge of nowhere. Josh played his songs in the background while the old Europe faded further away and a new one awakened. The Wall had fallen and here came the "civilized" hordes of those who wanted to see what was going on behind where it used to be. If you listened to the talk at the tables around you, you could hear a dozen languages, people burning to know the future, businessmen, journalists, soldiers, exiles, those who wanted to risk it all and those that just wanted to watch it go by.

26

I think it was Josh's wife who was the center point, the point from which his whole life in Europe would ripple out. The first time he saw her, it wasn't a momentous event. Though looking back he said he felt something, some attraction and some repulsion. We walked around the city and I pointed out interesting things, getting him oriented to the way the streets are laid out like spokes in a wheel within two ringed boulevards. I think it was near the corner of Hajo and Dessweffy st. where there's a nice sculpture in the doorway of #13, I think this is where he first laid eyes on her. She was with her big red-headed Serb boyfriend who had grown up in Boston. He had a reputation for mistreating her and being very jealous. There were many stories of him getting into fights with fellow expats he suspected of flirting with her or even Hungarian taxi drivers who he thought might have glanced at her lustfully in the rearview mirror, or took her hand helping her out of the cab and glance too furtively at her full breasts and shapely legs.

She was beautiful alright. No argument there. A cross between Penelope Cruz and Natalie Wood. She wasn't tall. She wasn't small. She was shapely. Her dark brown hair was cut page boy short and curled under just below her ear. Her complexion was dark but not too dark. She didn't look ethnically exotic to a white middle-class boy. She didn't look Mediterranean. She had a very broad classic European nose and dark round eyes and full pink purplish lips. She wasn't Jewish. Some gypsy blood? Maybe. But gypsy girls have such underdeveloped calves. Hers weren't. You could see that as you saw her now standing in a gauzy spring skirt that stopped well above her tanned knees. Her veins stood out on her forearms. Her shoulders were wiry and boyishly muscular. What then? Some mystery. She was Hungarian.

She was a small girl. But all of her smallness was filled with a quick kind of energy that made her seem almost tall. The way she cast her slightly pointed chin downward a little into her collarbone while her eyes widened and her eyebrows arched, this was her half pretended shyness, her seductive look, a look that could not be denied.

Years later, he would see that look, unaffected by it. But tonight it was the first time. He met her by chance through friends. He'd noticed how pretty she was, the dark-complexioned, dark-haired, brown-eyedness I mentioned, but wrote her off as out of his league. Besides, she had a boyfriend. A powerful business man who owned an ad agency. He dabbled with handling performers and when Josh arrived in Budapest, he was told to speak with him about trying to book gigs. That was when he first saw her. Helena.

"You can call me Helen."

"What's wrong with "Helena"?

"Well, I just thought you'd wanna say it the American way since you're American."

"Well, it's just where I grew up. Is there really an America? It's not like Europe, all those different nations bunched up with national pride. Besides, it's also the capital of Arkansas, I think."

"What is 'Arkansas'?"

"Not important."

He talked to her boyfriend after she introduced them in his office. He was a very tall man, broad shoulders and big hands he held in front of him explaining the difficulties of working as a musician in Budapest.

That's why it surprised Josh when she came up to him after a charity Christmas show. Just a freebie I had managed to book him for the exposure. It was a large hall but in the early days of the collapse of the communist regime, mics and amplifiers were hard to come by. He got up there and belted out Chuck Berry's "Merry Christmas, Baby." Then he did that quiet guitar piece that Tim Boggle showed him called "E'er a Rose is Blooming." Everything got real quiet. He drew out the last few notes, the audience went wild. At the end everyone came out and sang "Silent Night" in German and then Hungarian. Then Josh sang a verse in English.

"You were great!" Helena said. "Don't go away. My friend and I are going for pizza. Would you like to come with us?"

They went to a place that was popular during the early years of the regime change, big plain, pine, beer-hall type tables and benches. It was decorated with old commie propaganda posters and red stars. People had sketched in obscene remarks in fake thought bubbles above cartooned heads of Lenin and Marx, Stalin, Janos Kadár and the evil Rakosi. All silenced now, sealed over with the quick-drying new cement of regime change, political upheaval and death. There would be others of course. It was naive to think otherwise. But for now, Budapest awoke to a new era. So much was changing.

On a late December night, Josh and Helena walked under the lamplight. He couldn't resist glancing over at her. She was beautiful. A strong, prominent, gorgeously large nose, reddish-gold hues of hot coffee seemed to froth up in her dark hair. Her lips were full and brownish red with perfect wrinkles. Her breasts protruded up largely and gently beneath the soft Kashmir cloth of her sweater, and a brown creamy curve shone briefly at the V of the neck of it. He imagined suddenly the brown-red wrinkle of her nipple, but then thought, Where was Dragan, her boyfriend? Gone home to Boston for a few weeks, she said.

It was cold and they walked closer together. Her father was very ill, she said. Cancer. She wanted to be alone, so Dragan had gone home. "I sent him home you might say," she said. But then when she had heard the music at the Christmas concert...

Her body heat, he could feel it warming him. They laughed about something. Then stopped. Somehow their faces got closer. They looked at each other. Her eyes were so deep and brown. He held her shoulders and turned her towards him slightly and then kissed her long and deep, feeling her teeth and her lips and her tongue inside his mouth. Her lips seemed to fit his, to fit the night, the bridges, the water, everything. Everything in him and the world.

"You don't realize what you have done," she said.

"I kissed you," Josh said. " I liked it."

"I liked it, too... but..."

They kissed again. And again. Everything seemed submerged. Water everywhere. A fine mist settled over the walkway. Chilly but her lips were hot. Her coat was warm as he thrust his hands inside it and put his arms around her and held her tight and kissed her. They walked to her apartment, stopping to kiss from time to time in front of a shop window or in the shadow of a stone stairway. The river flowed, slow and quiet.

She'd had a tempestuous relationship with Dragan. We'd see them in the clubs, him snatching her up by the wrist and staring fiercely into her eyes, and her staring back at him, hurt, eyes welling up with tears. He worked hard and established one of the most successful ad agencies in Budapest. Working with musicians, developing the Euro-pop music scene was his passion, a new direction for his company. Helena was drawn to his power yet seemed to know how to manipulate him with her own. She feared his rage yet somehow craved it, began to live for their shouting matches. They started to hate each other. One night she nearly wrecked her car, driving drunk, distraught that the affair was at an end, this just as her father lay dying in a dingy Budapest hospital room. Her world seemed to be crumbling before her eyes. At twenty-eight all seemed lost.

It was the simple, soft way of Josh's voice that she fell in love with. She imagined what it would be like up close. The warmth of its breath. Breath of Spring. The sun. Sun coming up in my heart. Such a cold city. And this cold man she could no longer make love to. When the sun came out bright and suddenly on a dark European winter's day, Josh seemed the answer to everything.

They were inseparable. They tried to keep their love a secret and not display too many overt signs of affection in public but it was difficult. They walked everywhere together, staring into each other's eyes in the cafes, kissing in the little recesses between buildings. It was all they could do to keep their hands off each other. Yet there was always a sense of foreboding, knowing Dragan was due to return in a few weeks.

In the meantime, Josh went on playing at the Mona Lisa, feeling all the time like he'd never stolen away someone's girl before (ah, poor innocent Josh!). He was completely intoxicated with the perfume of love, forbidden love. They made love in his apartment. They made love at her parents' house. It was often the case in those days in Budapest that children continued to live with their parents, no one could afford another apartment. They spread their love all over the town, giggling like mischievous children.

Then, one night, holding hands in the Mona while Josh took a between-sets break, there he was. He walked toward their table, took one look and knew everything that transpired during his absence. He stood for a moment looking down at them. What did his face say? Anger… and something else. We know that feeling of the shock of the Earth. The earth jutting up into our insides. The great leveling power of Death that Woman carries in her eyes, in her hands, in her arms. Josh looked away. Some light went out. Something fell. Down. Down. Dragan turned and walked out.

They stayed. Holding hands. Talking. She telling him not to worry. Stroking his cheek. The sadness of guilt hovered around him. I'll talk to him, she said. It was due. He'll get over it. But we must take care, she said with her faint Hungarian accent.

But he was waiting for them outside in the street.

There was the look of, "I can't fucking beLIEVE you!" Then he grabbed her by the shoulders and flung her into a garbage heap of cardboard boxes the city left uncollected for weeks. Josh knew he was next. Dragan approached. Josh thought maybe he should at least protect his hands. So he put them into his pockets and crouched down. But Dragan merely shoved him over with a push that seemed to hold back something, as if he were trying to say, get down and STAY down and you won't get hurt. He turned on Helen again, said something Josh couldn't hear, then turned and walked back out into the night.

"Are you okay?" Josh asked, taking her by her warm hand.

"Yes, of course. Perce," she said in Hungarian. "He's done this before."

"What will he do, now?" Josh asked.

"I don't know. Probably go somewhere and get very, very drunk."

A few nights later, in the wee hours, after getting back from a gig, Josh's phone rang. He picked up the receiver: "Hello?" he said, always his voice like a little bird. "Josh. Take the next plane. Leave Budapest immediately." he heard a strange voice say on the other end. Click. He was gone.

Dragan had a rep for violence. He liked to flaunt Helen in front of men, and then when they looked at her lustfully, he would challenge them to a fistfight. The element of surprise was his. Most cab drivers or bartenders weren't used to having customers shove beautiful women under their noses, then, take a swing at them. Dragan got the upper hand very quickly. There were times he forgot the extent of his drunkenness and took a sound beating. They would stumble home together and make love desperately, then she would dab the wounds on his cheeks and eyebrows with cotton balls and Q - tips, kissing him, speaking softly and holding him like a child.

No one knew for sure if Dragan was serious. He had beaten alotta guys up, that was well known among all the expats, but he never killed anyone. Still, the girl he loved had left him. Who could know what further action he would take and if he'd take it out on Josh?

The city was still so new for Josh. He'd never ridden much public transportation before. Even when he was a schoolboy, Agnes would always pick him up because if he rode the bus, as the rolling green Water Maple countryside went by the yellow school bus window, he would often get lost in a daydream and forget to get off. At the end of the bus line, when every other child had gotten off, Josh sat alone in the emptiness, waiting. The driver would slowly, curiously, walk to the back and ask the little boy where he wanted to go. "Home," said Josh.

Looking around over his shoulder, Josh hopped on at Templom St. in front of the Synagogue. The hissing sound of the bus doors. The blast of exhaust as it roared its way back into the sea of flowing metal and rubber and asphalt. All this was a shock for Josh and he began to wonder if Dragan was watching him. The tumult of the city seemed to wash together with the idea of a sudden gunshot or stab of a knife, a shove from behind to start a fight, the unstoppable beating of the enraged, jilted lover.

Colors seemed more vivid. The winter light was the bluish-grey of dreams, of the sky in faery tales or Cezanne paintings. The rain-washed city streets were like the sea. The traffic splashed by like surf. Then the sun would come dimly back. Neutral yet all-seeing. The snow came down in a fine soapy powder. Josh began to think that the confrontation with Dragan was inevitable and that somehow he would be physically changed forever after it. Probably killed. Big physical change. He laughed to himself. He didn't know what to think. He only knew that loving her was so sweet it was worth death. He thought of her smooth coffee skin, her muscular legs, loving arms and her thick rose- dark lips. Most of all, the bell-like tone of her voice. He had fallen in love with her. For the first time in his life, he felt so truly alive he was ready to die.

Yet day after day nothing happened. Helen once worried that Dragan might kill himself. That thought saddened Josh but he couldn't give her back. He wanted her too much. Wanda seemed like a distant memory, so much deeper did this new love seem.

One day he saw Dragan walking far across a large square. Josh shivered at the sight of him. He told Helen about it when he'd gotten back to their apartment. She seemed nonchalant about it. He will do nothing, she said. Then one night, many months later, he slipped out of the apartment and headed down to the Mona Lisa. There was no one there he knew. He stood alone at the bar, leaning a little on his elbows, lost in a daydream of the droning stereo, the cigarette smoke and half a glass of red wine. Someone beside him brushed against him and he looked up. There stood Dragan. Josh's heart started beating quickly. Dragan looked over, seeming almost surprised to see him. "Hey, Josh! How's things?" He ordered a large "Corso" mug of beer before Josh could stutter out a reply and then added, "And another glass of red for my friend, here. Cheers, mate. Say hello to what's-her-name for me." He disappeared into the crowd.

Years later, even after Helen had split, Josh saw Dragan again at one of his concerts. He had a hard-nosed, not unbeautiful wife with him and three lovely young daughters. He seemed happy. I saw them chatting during a break and still felt a twinge of anxiety over what the old maverick Dragan might do. When we came back for another set, Josh played a long slow blues solo. As the notes came out pulsing, preaching, whispering, I found myself daydreaming back to the old days. Dragan smiled, content, but then left early since he'd brought his family. We never saw him again.

27

Josh came to Europe to find me. He found death instead. After Wanda, after Berenice, after Helen, he seemed only to want to move. Searching. Now all I have is fragments. Notebooks, demo CDs, letters, emails, poems, pictures, it seems like either he's looking away or else his back is turned. Maddening, part of a novel, "the yellow light burns off the fog…" I can't tell what he wrote and what I filled in, trying to make sense of it. The story. He didn't need to produce art, he was Art!

I found some notebooks. His sister sent me others. I read them on a hundred afternoons in all that October light, yellow and orange, leaves the color of Hereford cowhide, the hides of steers we had herded on ol' Water Maple Farm.

"Your partner gets killed, you just feel like you gotta do something!" You know even if Josh had got a big record deal or something it mighta been worse, coz Josh wanted to do whatever you wanted to do. Not what he wanted to. He would empty his ego into whomever fellow human being's ego he chose to satisfy. It wasn't that Josh didn't have direction. He had All Directions. He was going everywhere all at once! So maybe if hotshot producers had known what he was doing, which they didn't, they wudda made him go in even more different directions and we wouldn't have seen all the patterns of Infinity behind it all.

Dear Mr. Kovacs (Should I call you Crip?) I guess I know that's your name through Josh. Enclosed please find the items I mentioned.

It's funny because I never thought of him as having a Will but it specifically says you should get these things…. Please stay in touch,

   Angi (Angelika)

FRAGMENTS FROM JOSHUA CELESTE'S NOTEBOOK ONE:

Don't judge me. Too harshly. Its late. Every day seems a little further from the old sense of well being. The net below was always Mom and the Celeste/Demeter estate. Mom and Dad are dead. So there is no net. I'm free falling now. It's a feeling I have. I just want to get this all out, all down ("All down now! All bets down now!" said the Rat man at the county fair) but there's no way to get it all down. I feel like a bad Proust. Didn't he almost make it? What else can I do? Every day I wonder: is there some horrible reality I'm refusing to acknowledge the existence of? If so, let me see it full force. I'm ready. Who but myself can take me there to see this horror? The horror of my own mind. Therefore… cast them out ye that would make me see horrible things. Be gone! I think often now, I must prepare for the boys' future.

Leaving the boys is my greatest dread. I will stay here a few more years. Then I can go prepare a way for them into America. But if I found love here again I might not want to go back. Wanda is in Medina. Carlo lives in Philly. Sylves is dead. Is he here with me every morning? Every morning I see the light across the easel. Painting my life every day. Just like I used to watch over his shoulder in his studio. Big circus rides of hay fields and portraits of people—even my mother —my mother in Paris, singing, in New York, but hay fields and tobacco fields swimming in her hair. And Marshall. No, it can't be true. I'm just old. Memories. Crip is here in BP. I could always play with him if things got bad. He's a decent player. And a nice dude. That's the most important thing.

But there's no net. Maybe there never was. Of course, there wasn't. It just seemed that way coz I grew up in farmland's last metamorphosis into suburbia but I just listened a lot and then I had to just sit down with the guitar and remember everything. It was all I could do.

– Joshua

NOTEBOOK TWO:

   How utterly lonely I so often feel. Am I all alone in this world? My children need me. But can I give them enough? No mortal thing has given what I crave, peace to all mankind and boundless love of all things.

Yet Jesus is not apparent in the world. He can only be felt for brief moments. The liquid sun drips orange and dips behind the hill. When I wake up in this odd little country I feel apprehension. I have to face the coming day. I rise from my sofa bed, greeted by my wife's tight lipped silence or curt "good morning" and my little sons are slurping their breakfast cereal.

It's winter in Budapest and my 6 year old son and I bundle up for the walk to the subway station and a short one-stop ride to his school. His bright little pale face, like a little ET emissary, astronaut-like in his down hood, seems too fragile to be jostled by the grey over-coated throng shuffling to work, so I hold tight to his hand and mostly give him little hugs and we make small talk about who his friends are and what they do in school. He kisses me good-bye at the bottom of the washed-out staircase leading up to his classroom. I've grown used to leaving him now… to his inevitable indoctrination into a European culture I'll never really feel part of. Alone, the subway itself is fascinating. I never knew anything like it back in Edgeton, of course. I'd been on the one in NYC with Lacy a few times. But these were the faces of another people with pensive, tired, disgruntled expressions on their way to the day's drudgery.

Every face, not just the pretty office girls, holds some fascination for me. When I first came here, the Hungarian Face seemed distinctly different than the American one I knew back home. The effect produces the same feeling one has when looking at oriental faces, it's difficult to tell them apart. They all, men's and women's, seemed to fall into a broad category of dark-eyed handsomeness or almost teddy bear-like cuteness. They seemed to huddle together in a uniform flow across the platforms and public squares and shops and cafes, up and down the machine tedium of the escalators, those awesome conveyors that plumb the depths of the underground urban world.

These escalators were great facilitators of my "face fascination," and I was able to study those coming up in the crowd that exited the train as I was going down or vice versa. I especially sought out the frequent pretty girl's face. Most men seem to agree that the prettiest girls in Europe are in Hungary. Our separate sets of moving stairs pass each other, making any conversation impossible, and eye-contact fleeting. I made a little game of it, which I called "Count the Babes." "And now!" (with Bob Barker-like game show host voice) "it's time to play COUNT THE BABES!" The object was to see how many attractive faces I could count before reaching the top of the stair. Sometimes it was as many as fifteen! Hardly ever less than ten. Usually, I employed that trusted silly male rating system based on one to ten, ten being drop dead beautiful and anything below six being unattractive. Pretty crass I know, but I will say this, Hungary's got an awful high concentration of eight's and nine's.

Listening to Sting's "Mercury Fallin" record the other day, it occurred to me how I used to dream of sounding like that on stage. Here I am with headphones on, singing along, thinking, "I could do that!" I'm beating out Vinnie Caluita's rhythm on my thigh, but it doesn't sound the same. Suddenly, I get this vast vision across my past, across Time, of all the times I put a band together and we tried to cover our favorite tunes. But come gig night and we mounted the stage, our heads full of new, challenging material, it just didn't sound the same. All the keyboard textures and guitar effects, all the thousand intricacies of the modern recording of a great song, somehow we left that all out because… well… we didn't know how to do it. I can still hear, will always hear, that dry, snare pop ringing in my ears, mixed too loud by the tin-eared soundman. the rumbling bass drum, the missed chorus, the wrong bass note, botched lyric, uncertainty and wonderful stuttered rhythm of not knowing when to come back in after the bridge or after anything, really. The untogether ending. Yet, there we were, human beings, each of us crying his Death into a half-listening audience that milled around, crying theirs into us.

NOTEBOOK THREE:

Sometime around the middle of December (as always, it seems, since childhood) the spirit of Christmas descends on me, seeps into me. Is it the light that triggers it? A sudden weakening silver, yellow light, the dim sun, the feeble breeze rattling the husks of leaves? It seems to shift to the darker green smell of pine, the white clean smell of snow. Then the memories of Edgeton start. Water Maple. My sons' little pink expectant faces whenever I come to their mother Helen's house for a visit. People shopping. Thinking of friends. Talk of parties. Getting together for a drink and a laugh amidst all the goings on. Ideas for presents that of course I can never afford. Pretty girls in shops. Thinking of calling some girl whose phone number I happen to have. Starting some holiday romance. It never happens.

Then the music. The carols come rushing down that snowy hillside of memory like a hot spring. I grab my guitar and run through them all again, O Christmas Tree, Away in a Manger, O Little Town of Bethlehem, God Rest Ye Merry Gentlemen, While Shepherds Watched, Hark the Herald, Angels We Have Heard On High, Come All Ye Faithful, E'er a Rose is Blooming…

For a year they all lie dormant and it seems I've forgotten them, then they all spring open and alive and I'm standing in St. Jude of Our Childhood singing my heart out with Doc and Angelika and Mom and Milli and everyone. It Came Upon a Midnight Clear. Then the jazzy ones, w/ the lush changes, Have Yourself

A Merry... (with that cute lead in), The Christmas Song (how Sylves used to goof, "Jack Frost roasting on an open fire…"). I'll be Home for Christmas, Santa Claus is Comin' To Town, and the Rock and Roll ones, Rockin Around the Christmas Tree (How many years I tried to get Brenda Lee's "hillbilly hurt" in my voice!!!) Jingle Bell Rock (what happened to Bobby Helms?) I never really dug White Christmas that much tho I love a lot of Irving Berlin stuff. That jazzy Vince Guaraldi version of O Christmas Tree on the Charlie Brown's Xmas record. Then the slow Charlie Brown's Xmas Theme. Wow. Such Beauty. Perennially returning. Suddenly, I buy a tree. The kids come over to help me decorate it. Every night I come home it's a treat to turn the Xmas tree lights on. That misty light. Lamps on the Eternal Road.

Music and chocolate and wine and light and candle wax and incense… it all blends. And builds and builds. I'm doing some concerts and my head is full of music and dreams and silver light. Then, just as suddenly, it's over. I awaken as if from a long winter's sleep and find the bleak winter world, its dull light, its boredom, its restlessness all around me. One drop of sun on a droplet of icicle point is all you've got to steady your faith in Spring. I can't help but cry a little when I take the dry tree out to the curb. Goodbye Christmas, it's only a year away.

Today I decided to take the whole day to myself. Only later did I realize that my wanting to do some errands in fifth district Budapest had been only a subterfuge for my true hidden desire, to revisit the old neighborhood where I once lived with my (now estranged) wife and children. It had only been a few months since I helped them move into a new, even lovelier, apartment on the Buda side near the foot of the Castle Hill. This was my first trip back to the old place, knowing I now no longer had any connection with it. No one I loved lived there anymore. In that lovely Hapsburg era apartment owned by Helen's family, on its little street. We called it home for twelve years. Now it was empty.

What is it that drew me back to that old neighborhood, sitting there on the #2 tram watching it go by? The bittersweet passage of time. The radiant yellow dust of a new spring day so full of memories. It occurred to me as I looked out the slow moving tram's window, that my first years there were the loveliest days of my life, as lovely as my days on the old farm and the years I lived with Berenice on Ankor Ave. Perhaps, the high point of my life.

Something in the light of Spring is taking me back gently, leading me by the hand. It was here that I first awakened in the bright spring light. A man with a beautiful woman who loved him. It was here I would wake up, dusty yellow light pouring through the tall Hapsburg windows. I would open my eyes, look around and say, "Another day of Love." The alabaster Angel adorning the beautiful baroque facade opposite our apartment smiled down upon me. Every morning I would open my eyes and look into his face through the window. It was the stone face of a Grecian mask, like the man in the moon expressing joy and despair at the same time. I had never been happier in my life.

So there I was sitting on the 2 tram, stations going by, Vigado Square, Eötvös Square, Roosevelt Square, Kossuth Square, Jatszai Square, astonished by the scenes of joy and heartbreak that lovely neighborhood had provided the background for.

When something is irrevocably gone one asks Whence? Whither? What did it mean? But no answer comes, only stinging tears seem as if they might spring to one's eyes. But tears don't come. Not now. Not yet. Later in the evening, alone, they might come, but not now, here with the crowds and the pouring yellow light. Can there be a lovelier city than Budapest in the Spring? Could I have been luckier than to have been loved by her once, even though love fades, disappears all together like the sun going down over the hills of Buda to the West? Could I have been luckier than to have such lovely sons?

NOTEBOOK FOUR:

Music has been my life. Everything I remember comes from it. It is the great source I swim back to like a salmon to spawn. I'll never make it back, of course, but I feel compelled, I don't know why, to try. "Everything comes of thee, O Lord, and of thine own have we given thee." Oh music, not that I studied her diligently, not as a child, not as obedient schoolboy, though she was everywhere and I loved her like a mother, not as a teenager, though I was an avid record collector like anyone. Far from it. I never really studied anything. I just sat in front of a stereo dropping the needle on sudden bursts of bluegrass or bebop, trying to decipher some code vibrating in the wood of my guitar.

But in every step I took and even before when my mother sang as she rocked me in her arms, burning with fever, music was there. Music was sun and rain, warm coat against the chill, cool drink of water in the desert. Music was sobriety, music was drunkenness. Lover, Hater, Father, Mother, God and all I could conceive.

Could it be I feel the time she rocked me during fever, singing Daddy's Little Baby or Mary dontcha weep, dontcha moan. It's not a real memory. Perhaps it didn't happen. I see white clothes. Sputtering cough. My red pinched face. But then Agnes told me about all this. I'm filling in the blanks now. It's only feeling. In Millicent's big library.

LETTER FROM JOSH:

Dear Berenice,

I suppose I could talk about all the normal stuff ... weather, family, gigs, books, movies, tv ... or I could go deeper... after all, we did live together for five years. I guess the dominant feeling (somehow I can't help but remember yr Kandinsky prints when I see that word before me—dominant—violet dominant—but what is the color I feel now? I'm not sure. I'm not sure if I can be that visual. Even though it's one of your paintings I picture not the Kandinsky one. I saw yours more. Right over the sofa.) The dominant feeling is... I sometimes feel overwhelmed by the speed dreams are dying in. Doors are closing. It's as if time not only passed but narrowed. Even tightened its noose, maybe (sound too Poe-ish.?) And the body seems frailer. But the mind! How it soars to nowhere ... since it hasn't the body's legs to carry it! It's all memory memory memory because nothing more can really happen. Except more danger. And fear. You get claustrophobic when you realize the room is shrinking. The blue skies that beckoned in our childhood now just indicate another day of the miracle of ... survival. Nothing or nothing else but the sky if we let ourselves have that momentary childlike pleasure of savoring the beginning of a day, if there's time, will deliver us. We know that now. Before, I was almost certain someone would appear like a biblical character and whisk me away to success and stardom. But that wasn't so selfish. I wanted to get laid but I wanted to unite with god, too. Make everything right. Make the world a better place. Become the virtuosic mystic that used his power only for good... and then, of course make love to all the women. Not ALL the women. That would have been too pure, too "saintly", too democratic. No, only the ones I seemed to have always gravitated towards even though "looks were not important—only spiritual values! I lied. (I thought I was so good—but I hardly even noticed unbeautiful women! When I found myself single, I thought of myself as some great liberator of the souls of women and when I was "married" I pretended to have risen above all that. My libertine notions faded away into some comfortable living room with a tv, a cat, and a guitar. Then, inevitably, the curtain fell or, better, a character appeared for whom I had written no lines. I had no control over what speeches he might deliver, movements he might make, an interloper from a world that suddenly, meteorically, swerved into mine with no warning. Or did I want it to happen? I ignored pain so long that it silently plotted its revenge against me. Remember when we went to see "Fanny and Alexander"? I keep remembering the old mother's phrase "... it shattered reality..." and then, "The beautiful life is going away and the horrible life is beginning". That's what it felt like. We all want to go, when our minds are healthy, to the next moment. We come to expect that feeling of floating forward. Our mothers carried us this way; in fact, the future is like a drug....a dependency on something that doesn't even exist ! That's how addicted we are to it! Like a beam of light shining into a fog that isn't really a fog, just the present getting misty. We sense that the ground under our feet continues but we only see it when we have come through what once only appeared as mist, and a new cloud stands before us just as mysteriously as the one we just passed through. But then the moments stop coming. That's what happens. That's what I seemed to experience when I felt heartbroken and abandoned. (And there was no recourse or comfort in the flippant way the world —those around you who weren't feeling what you were feeling—treated that whole subject.) There's nothing to look forward to except the next cigarette. The next cigarette makes the future, which has shrunk down to nearly nothing, hang on to its existence. Like sending up a flare for itself (or my ridiculous light beam image above) it lets us know its approximate whereabouts. Thanks for being there..

Take care,

Josh.

ANOTHER LETTER FROM JOSH:

Dear Doctor,

If all life is a dream, which you said it might be, then my life in Budapest, Hungary is a dream within a dream. I came here one year ago running, I suppose, from the pain of trying to continue living in Medina. My life there as a musician, and a person, had run itself out. My last few months seemed like something dry and dead. Those faithful, precious feelings from the "yellow light" I could never describe in words to you, stopped nourishing. They broke my heart. Everything I saw did. I had to go before this crippled stranger inside became the new me.

I arrived in Budapest on Angelika's birthday (a good omen) with a guitar, one suitcase (mostly full of demo tapes and some clothes) and very shaky self-confidence. My old friend from Medina, who I call Crip or Crib (he got the one name because of his handicap, the other because he stayed home a lot) met me at the airport and we went by taxi thru the run down outskirts to his apartment in South Buda. I passed the first few days smoking too much staring out the window. That's been a favorite occupation of mine all my life, now I stare into the tv, and writing letters to the woman who was, I guess, my main reason for leaving town. I didn't have the balls to go through seeing her with someone else. It was like asking a heroin addict trying to go cold turkey to watch people shoot up and get off real good.

One good side effect, though, was that I felt compelled to write. At first, just my own thoughts about losing her love as you suggested I do for therapeutic reasons but then I started inventing fictitious characters to represent different emotions. I didn't have the balls to attach my name to things I wanted to express. Like so many other things in my life, I let someone else say it for me. I found out I liked it better that way.

My letters were long wistful apologies to her for any neglect I'd shown in our relationship and I'd hope we could see each other again someday. Looking back it seems strange that I could have been so shattered by the break-up. After all, I was much older than her. I reached an impasse, as you said, an existential wall, in coming to terms with it. I simply couldn't accept the end.

As I told you, I'd been through other relationships but this one, perhaps because I was older and weaker and more desperate to finally find the answer to love, had a finality to it I'd never experienced. Something in me disappeared. Or my soul was sculpted around her or her around it. When it crumbled some vulnerable wound of myself was exposed. A chasm opened. I couldn't stop the swallowing motion of my descent toward self destruction. Something involuntary starts, as when the pumping feeling of an orgasm starts and one is no longer in control of the body's stopping and starting, like choking. The Involuntary. Some defense mechanism I'd always relied on failed me. I told Crip about it but all he said was, You're twenty-seven and you just now hit bottom?

Maybe she felt sorry for me. I remember she asked me once, looking desperate and lost, to give her a ride to her landlord's office before it closed. By the time we got there, she convinced me to loan her the money, so I paid her rent, late fee and all. They were all so broke. There were no decent jobs. It was hard to make any tips working in these little college town beer joints. Only the bartenders downtown got rich. Kiki LaSalle had one of those gigs for awhile. That's how she got started in Cincinnati. Otherwise, these kids had to scrape together enough loose change to get wasted on pitchers of lousy American beer then go to class. Somehow they managed to get drunk on that stuff with the help of a few joints which cushioned the blow of the boredom of their classes and their lives. I kept playing guitar in these places just to keep from having to dig into my tour money.

I didn't see her for awhile and then I found out she'd got a gig waitressing in Crazy Reddy's place downtown. He'd opened the upstairs and made it into a Mexican cantina. He hired a couple of Mexicans who worked with Sylvester on the Abercrombie horse farm to manage it. Sometimes I'd drop in to hang out with Wanda, catch a rap as they say, and I'd see the Mexican manager's sons chatting her up and buying her shots of tequila.

Jared said, "American girls, no woman is ever easy to pick up unless she wants to be. But sometimes you get lucky. It happens. Men are like dogs, they'll keep coming back if you feed them anything at all. And when you stop feeding them they still come back for a long time… hoping. Men are full of useless hopes. Women don't waste time. Men are dogs. Dogs are male, loyal and stupid especially when on the scent of that same thang. Women are cats, man. Totally independent.

I would come in and sit by Wanda acting casual as I could. After a noticeable pause, Wanda introduced me. The Mexicans looked a little uncomfortable and the one sitting closest to her asked, "You liife togetter?"

I started to answer but then Wanda blurted out, "Nah, he's just a friend. A good friend," she added quickly, giving herself away, then a little clumsily trying to cover herself, looking around the table, the desperate, lost look again. "A good friend, okay?t We all fake-laughed nervously. I think it was at that moment that the whole crazy thing started between us. She was young enough to give it a go. But we didn't go. Not just yet. I still had to climb that arduous hill of love.

Thanks for your call. Best wishes,

Josh.

JOSH ARRIVES

I went to pick him up at the Budapest airport. His plane was late. Turns out the Queen of England was on the plane in front of him. She was here to dedicate the new Jewish Memorial on Temple St. But there was a bomb scare at the airport. It turned out to be some meaningless prank. Probably some right winger guy just being weird on the telephone. He had to sit on the runway for hours while they cleared the situation. I wondered if he'd still recognize me. I came walking up with my familiar hop-along gait, which I hoped didn't seem to have gotten worse since our old gigging days in Medina all those years before years that seemed like a dream now.

We rode through the streets of West Pest. He said later he had thought things would look older and more uniform. What had he expected? The Middle Ages? I think so. It did have a run-down 70's vibe: rows and rows of gray sooty or brownish stucco facades, cracked streets and old beat-up cars which I told him were E. German, Serb or Romanian. I felt tense. We spoke little on the subway ride. We got to my flat.

"I already got us a gig, heh heh, one of the early afternoon acts at the new memorial dedication tomorrow. 50 bucks each. So let's get settled and rehearse later".

"You mean, for the Queen? Wow, just off the plane and I'm already a star".

"Don't have delusions of significance. All the shops are having different activities going on. We are just one of many. Kinda like a street fair, you know. I'll play bass and we can do some standards or whatever the fuck we want".

My flat was pleasant enough inside but dingy and sooty in the stairways. The walls were covered with graffiti. He asked me to translate and I said it was mostly nasty remarks toward the Russian occupiers. But they'd all left the city 5 years before.

"Get ready. Just drop your bag in here for the time being. The lady next door has a small kid so we gotta be kinda quiet. She's Romanian, hiding out from customs agents. You know me, the Patron Saint of Strays".

On the rollicking trolly ride he brought up some old stories from back in our Medina days, and I faked an interest. At one point I said, "I'm pretty much finished with all that sentimental stuff."

The market was like nothing he'd ever seen: lots of people milling about, a few classic ladies in scarves and old men in berets, but mostly young people, many of them gypsy, I told him, many quite handsome and beautiful. As we shopped he talked about the girls and said he already fantasized about me introducing him to them: "You see, here is the American boy you always wanted!" The memory of his fucked up shit with American chicks back in the states was starting to fade. Suddenly, I elbowed him in the ribs: "Hey! Watch where you're going? Didn't you see that bus coming? Gotta be careful. People here are zombies. They're so into their automatic routines. They hardly see you." The stalls were just huts built over a concrete floor. Slabs of raw pork were piled onto palettes tilted toward the customer; fruits and vegetables in crates, sausage of many types hanging from strings attached to the hut roof. I gave the butcher orders in a not impolite but firm Hungarian staccato: "No, not that one. That one. Up there. Jo lesz. That will be good". I explained later that I had asked for a specific piece of tripe. "I told him I wanted the one, hehe, where the poo is made!" As he laughed I could tell we were relaxing and getting used to being around each other again. At first, his presence triggered memories of Medina I wanted to forget. I remembered again my phrase: "We committed suicide in America and were karmically reborn in Budapest!"

Next, we went through the fruit and vegetable stands. Smallish red tomatoes that turned out to be sweet as cantaloupe, endless stacks of spring onions and big balls of red and yellow onions and fresh garlic still on its long green stems, potatoes, carrots still mud-caked, huge beetroots, huge barrels where beets, cabbage and cucumber sat in pickle brine that smelled as strong as urine.

The ground shook as the yellow tram cars rolled by. A fiddler stood beside a stall, his case open with a few coins and small bills scattered through it. It's kinda like Blues in a way: desperate, plaintive, high and lonesome. A large hammered dulcimer they call a cimbalom was played by an old man beside the fiddler. The metallic sound of the zither, ecstatic yet slightly sinister, like the soundtrack of a black and white movie, set in Europe, full of shadows. Like "The Third Man". A fat gypsy woman with dimpled elbows ran her hands through mounds of pickled cabbage, putting it into plastic bags for their customers, another hosed chicken and pork blood off a table.

"Hey, I've gotta go run a few more errands", I told him. You should sleep. Can you find your way back to the apartment"?

"I always manage to get back home somehow," he said.

Which is worse? losing the love of someone who loves you or the love of someone you love?

But one morning he awoke with a high fever. I don't know how it happened. It was probably due to all the anxieties he felt leaving Medina, staying with Agnes in Edgeton, arranging with Angelika for his house to be sold, carrying stuff down to his Mom's basement, and his fear of flying, the blue rocks and dead volcanoes of Greenland under the metal underside of a metal bird rocketing through ocean mists. Then the strangeness of European light, the thinner watery yellow of it— not the thick amber of southern light—the strange smells and polluted air. His fever shot up and he shivered beneath the blanket and sweated out onto the sofa bed. My neighbor began to fear for her baby.

"We cannot let him to stay for here any longer," she said. I hoped Josh couldn't hear us. "He may be bringing strange strain of flu from the Amerika the baby cannot ward off".

And so it was decided that he must be moved to a hotel. I was reluctant to make him move out. I wanted to appear master of his house but the anger and resolve of a young mother is hard to stare down. I felt sorry for her. He didn't mind moving, really, but was sick and aching. His teeth chattered and his eyes looked swollen as we climbed into the taxi with his small bag of belongings. He left his guitar behind.

The white paint and scrubbed limestone of American houses is not to be found here. There are no manicured green yards. The walls are a sooty gray, cut from a darker stone. The streets, too, were made of this dark stone, quarried from the northern mountains, cut into small hand-sized cubes and fitted together, one by one, side by side to form a rough and uneven pavement that rumbled beneath the taxi tires. Whenever possible the taxi driver would veer onto the smoother asphalt between the tram tracks and drive down the very middle of the street. The rumble of stones would then cease for a moment, like a radio going dead when you passed under a bridge. In this way, the driver saved the wear and tear on his tires.

The illness and disorder of his mind seemed reflected in the streets. They turned at strange angles. Grass and weeds sprouted, unkempt, up through the cracks. People's clothes seemed washed out, colorless, their facial features so different than the pink/ white British faces of provincial America. Here it was Oriental, dark faces, the high Slavic cheekbones of the fairer-skinned girls and young men, stunning eyes and large noses, strong chins and everyone so tall. The lobby appeared dreamlike in a nicotine cloud and a gray man wrote down his name and looked at his passport. I took my leave and gave him an apologetic look, and said I'd return early the next day.

Josh's notebook

"I got into bed and shivered. My fever became a kind of white blanket over me and there was a ringing in my ears. The gray sky was visible through the riverlets of rain running down the transom window. The light bulb in the bathroom shone down in a dull yellow curtain of light on the floor. I listened to the ringing in my ears. I felt like I had reached the end of something, or that if this was the end, a yellow light in a cold room with metal furniture halfway round the world wasn't so bad. My fever created a rhythm of tension and I would moan rhythmically, trying to work against it and then there was a release when I felt for a brief moment that it might be subsiding. But then a wave of heat and ache would roll over me. My eyes burned when I closed them as if they were full of saltwater. I kept picturing a black dog. A wolf? Far off he whimpered in answer, at long intervals, to my rhythmic moaning. I thought, So I've come all this way only to die in a Hungarian hotel? I slept."

I awakened him the next morning on the phone.

"How ya feeling?"

As he tried to answer some phlegm caught in his throat and he coughed.

"I think I just got my answer," I said. "I'll be over in a sec with some aspirins I rustled up". When I came into the room I sat at the foot of the bed.

He looked like he was totally vulnerable to all the Earth, the air, the light, the pigeons. I shuffled him into a cab.

"Had to get you out of this place. Expensive. All kinds of flu bugs here you ain't used to. This girl, I know, Helen, said you could stay at her place for a few days. And listen, try a little of this smoke." I handed him a joint. "After awhile you'll say, 'I'm not sick. I'm hungry!'"

28

Fucking Wanda was like going back in time, moon or dawn pouring over her in a milk-white stream. The glow of the past I relived. I didn't just fuck her, I fucked them all. Not just my lovers. All women. All people. As if I could shed my being and give it back to someone. Who? Thank you, here's your Being back. I fucked them all. Their faces rising up in planetary phases, waxing, waning. I always wondered why I chose one face over another when I finally came. Why the one final image that could bring me over the top. It was revenge, haha I fucked you again! If you could only see me now with this obviously sexier chick than you, you stupid bitch. I'll teach you to hurt my buddy! I'd look down to see one whole hand up her cunt and the other one halfway down her throat, then she would roll over and sit down squarely on my tongue running her asshole and cunt over it faster and faster as if she was trying to paint my face. I would delight in my humiliation as well. Is that what it was? It occurs to me now that I was also fucking myself. A female vision (version) of myself. I was wading deep into a pool of narcissism. Only the sudden smell of sex, of her vaginal juice, would startle me back into the awareness of what I was doing. The awareness of an Other.

Equation: mother is the first and last part; lover brings death, delayed by Venus, the giving wife, mother is old.

To be aware of it. What? Josh said he'd like to be with Carlo, Angelika, Doc, Helen, Harris, or me if he started dyin.' He panicked, he said, only if he thought too much about being with no one he loved and trusted. "Once I Loved," he crooned on one of those wedding reception gigs we used to do. He did Jobim stuff great. "Once upon a time I loved and trusted over and over, always thinking the 'one to be trusted' was out there, somewhere, waiting for me if only I'd go on searching. I never changed," he said, looking out the bus window, me half dozing in the next seat. The cute little talented boy grows up.

One by one: Lilian, Berenice, Wanda, Helen, Gudrun, Samidha. Maybe he "niced" himself into a corner until, geez, they just couldn't resist finishing him off. Life is for the living. Truth and Love for the dead. Did Sylvester say that to me once? Why do I need to remember all this? Oh, God have mercy on my miserable soul.

Women psychically paralyzed Josh. Assertion of self is a gamble for the shy. He must have thought, just lay low and Helen's agitation, her disappointment in seeing his vast unrealizable talent and potential wasted, would blow over. The lone, forlorn wolf appears at the damsel's doorstep. She pities it, falls in love with it, pets it for three or four years. Oh those motherly caresses! I remember them, too! Then, boredom, distractions, separation, six, seven, eight, ten years go by. Then, they rarely speak. He said he slept in the same bed with Berenice for a year before they broke up, and they never touched. "Sometimes, I still daydream out this god awful bus window, before it all changed, about the way she looked on cold mornings when she'd lean over out of bed to get a sweater from her dresser then snuggle back in with me under the comforter."

It was so wonderful, and all so long ago, when they sprawled in each other's arms filled with love, naughtiness and hatred.

Looking out the window Josh said, "Where did it go? Where are they all? Where is the better place, the necessary place that life took them to, away from my arms? She smelled like the freshly washed sheets. The cookie smell of her hair. But that morning we hadn't touched in the bed for a year. She was leaning over and I could see the little round nut of her pussy. Her reddish-blond hair. Like the soft hairs of an acorn. I felt a stab of longing in my groin. Another two years went by and finally, I just went out and got laid. I can tell all dis shit to you now, it's been so long ago." Darkness fell and we both nodded off to the vibrations of the road as the bus plunged further into a flat oblivion.

I found an unsent letter on the back of a Denny's Placemat:

Dear Josh,

Then somehow I knew I'd reached the lower rung of myself. I cheated on Helen... and who with? Why, your x-girlfriend. Destroy my most cherished friendships all at once. Poof! But I never confessed, of course. Then the guilt... well, it dissipates. But I could feel something eroding in me. I never was the same.

I lost faith in myself. Do I still have a self? It might just be a collection of impulses like Doc said some people become.

29

"I don't know why but when your Daddy died I just kept thinking about that song we sang one time when we got our heads all boined up," Sylvester told Josh at the North End Projects. "Got him to even smoke one with me that night. I 'member he said, 'Sylvester, is this how you get talkin' to them horses and winnin' all that money at the track?'"

"And man we was fucked up. This was some of Money Joe's besshit he was growing down there behind Bertha's house. And I 'spect we'd finished off the better part of a bottle of Maker's as well. He was going thru the divorce and all. This been maybe thirty years ago. Anyway, we was singin' that ol' song we sung when we was kids. I remember my Daddy playin it for us all on that rusted out banjo we found up in yr all's attic. Just bewshittin' really, the one about ol' black Ned that went, 'O there was an ol' man who's name was Ned and he lived long ago, long ago. And he had no wool on the top of his head in the places were the wool ought to grow.'"

"But I was singin' it drunk at one of those art opening receptions like we play sometimes, singin' it just for a joke, you know just to see how people react. I always was kindly mischeevus like that. Here come some white dude come up to me and said he wondered if I minded singin' that n-word in the song and for some dumb drunk reason I got so mad I hit the motherfucker right dead in the mouth. Weird. Right in the face. Bled like a stuck pig. They called the cops and shit. Didn't nobody up there in Cincinnati know who the fuck I was outside bein' 'the drummer' so maybe they thought oh shit this black mother-fucker done gone crazy he gonna kill somebody. I had to spend the night in jail on that one."

"But here he come next morning bailin' me out and shit, apologizing like white motherfuckers do sometimes for even uttering the n-word and not being more sensitive to my feelings and this and that bullshit. I thanked him for getting me out. But then it hit me later, he was a nice dude. I don't know why he infuriated my ass like he did but it dawned on me that motherfuckers like him would be getting me INTO "jail" for the rest of my life but I couldn't say why. I told Marshall about what happened, one morning on my way to the barn, and he just smiled and went back fixing one of the bluegrass strippers. The next morning he called me up and when I picked up the phone he just said, 'Hi there, blackie.' He could crack my ass up sometimes, no shit. Don't exactly know why but he was the onliest dude who could say shit like that in front of me and not make me mad. It goes back to Money Joe before I was even born and back to your granddaddy Dexter. I know your daddy told you about how they used to make whiskey back in that backfield and one night the still blew up and Money Joe come runnin' down the limestone stairs through Bertha's garden yellin', 'Miss B! It's Mr. Dex! Mr.Dex!'"

30

The scent of a woman awakened him. Flame of lust, singeing him. Lonesome reality of another person. The scent of the impenetrable soul. The first morning after. She's awake and putting clothes in her closet. Josh is watching her. Watching her naked ass that looks different than he thought it would when he first saw her walking through the Medina campus. Not quite as Penthouse Magazine-like.

Still, the long reddish, Francois Comerre hair falling over the shoulders of that fox-colored, leather jacket she'd worn. The full, round, lower lip, the thinner upper one. He held it with his teeth and tongue. They looked into each other's eyes and made love in a tent they pitched on the campground. They always made love the same way, coiled around each other, then he would go down on her until she came, then she would suck him for awhile, then, when he couldn't hold back any longer, he'd drape over her and fuck 'til he came in her, her breath in his ear. She always came first. He seemed to think this was the most polite way for her. He was always a good, fair-minded boy.

Then he played his guitar and she rolled joints, blowing smoke into each other's mouths and endlessly kissing. Her incense sticks and massage oil, the sound of drums far away.

31

Josh lay in bed freezing in an Austrian hotel room after the *Forgotten Eclectic Guitarists of the American Midwest* gig, even though it's July— fuckin' Europe, man— watching some Chuck Norris rerun. He gets up to go to the bathroom. Looks in the mirror for a moment and suddenly it hits him,

"Me and Crip, Carlo, Berenice, Jared, all of us have been victims of our desires. At first, I thought I'd just thought of these four people at random but come to think of it these are probably four of the most decent people I've ever known and they gave selflessly to me."

"But it was our wanting something that drove us away from each other and our home. O how we might have found a smaller happiness had we not wanted and shot for The Big One. The one outta da movies, images gluttonously consumed from the time we were kids. It's a shame we couldn't have all lived two lives, one for ourselves and one for others. Some of us tried to live both. It made both impossible. Doc drunk at parties saying, 'We poets in our youth begin in gladness whereof in the end, comes despondency and madness.'

I couldn't stand to hurt people, Lord, look at my face. Yet, I and those I should have had the courage to hurt were hurt anyway from the turning away. What you leave undone, time will eventually do for you. I didn't want to act in a world. I didn't want to see that I was really here. I touch nothing. Nothing touches me. The guitar and the voice lull the cobra audience. I feed on the poison. But it was impossible.

I went to Sylvester's studio to say goodbye when I was moving to Europe. He gave me a big hug and said, 'We are not here to realize our dreams. Only to live as decently as we can, so, fuck it, man'."

"Crip, you remember how you once sayeth unto me: We committed suicide and were reborn here in Budapest! How many rebirths? No. Old age is the room to accommodate ugliness and the staging ground for the spiritual crucible that precedes eternal life. Okay, so, let men have affairs. Let married women have affairs. With immunity! That's what I saw in her eyes now that I think back on it. It was, like, Rita Moreno said, Okay, give me the five hundred bucks expenses and I'll go home to my apt on West 60 something and look thru the West Side Story scrapbook and nod off. Desirable. We want to be desired by youth goddamnit! What else is there? But constant prayer, Oh Lord God have mercy on my miserable soul. 'Chastity was not Charlemagne's most conspicuous virtue. After his death a monk had a vision of him crowned in glory in Purgatory, a vulture gnawing at his genitals' (Gibbon's, The Decline and Fall of the Roman Empire).

So What? Now I think, yes, we can rise, we must rise against the animal. It's no good following an animal's instincts. Ain't that what Sylvester said Jesus said? There's a Higher Love. Don't waste your motherfuckin' time. The flesh ain't the whole story! But then What Is?"

You. All day long.

"Hey, Sylvester, What's Hapnin'?"

"YOU," Sylves said. "ALL DAY LONG."

32

Tuesday was Josh's night at Crazy Red's. I was playing bass for him then. So, I could no longer be cattin' around looking for his women. Our crowds seemed to be dwindling. He told me one night he walked past the club window and peered in. He wasn't much of a socializer. He walked by the club thinking, "How come on the nights I play, the night seems different, more important, like the whole town is thinking about coming to hear me? Just a lowly weeknight but the whole universe seems to be bending down to listen. Does God bless me?" But then he looks in the window walkin past on his night off and sees a different rockin' crowd checkin' out another band. They don't just come to hear me! Josh is thinking to himself. Even more people than he gets were in there—a lot more. A cookin' band of dudes he don't even know and playin' great. Students from the university with much greater technique than his—and playing for nuthin'! He'd thought the dwindling crowds meant the club was going under and he was not gonna bother asking Red for a raise. Then BAM! He walks by and the place is packed. He felt a stab of lostness in his gut as he walked away from the window. *Lest they turn and rend you.* A roar went up from the crowd. It suddenly hit him, when he wasn't playing, the world still went on. He turned away and walked into the silent parking lot filled with empty cars, into the empty night toward home. *The world that is before you are and will continue when you are not.*

33

Josh:

We'd finished cuttin' tobaccah one evening and the other hands, Rickey Boy, TLC, and another new guy down from the mountains was there too, givin' us extra help. Dad always hired abuncha dudes from the mountains to get the tobaccah in. It was hell to get the stuff in the barn so we needed more help than just Rickey Boy and TLC. Men would come down and work two weeks or so and stay at Bertha's sometimes sleepin' down below the house near the spring that ran under the big ivy-covered stone foundation and out beside the limestone walkway that ran from Bertha's door back to her cellars where we used to take showers in the summer.

It was on this patio that the men could pile hay or bring some palettes from the barn on the hill above Bertha's and make their beds and build a fire and hang the big soup cauldron over it and make brown beans and fatback and Bertha or one of the other women would whip up big pans of cornbread. They'd sit around the fire and shoot the shit, tell stories usually about hunting or runnin' from the Law.

This was one of the first times I ever heard real mountain music, what I guess most people now call Bluegrass but it had that older, primitive sound like it had just grown there wild and hadn't been really cultivated in any way, just remembered and preserved for what it was. But some of the younger ones knew rock and roll and all that. And they new blues licks, too. One guy said there was a dude in Medina who could sound just like Jimi Hendrix and did I know him. I'm pretty sure he was talking about, Free, the dude that played at Tim Boggle's house that time. I'd go get my ax and they'd show me a few licks but mostly I just tried to play a solid rhythm behind the fiddle and banjo.

I was only fourteen or fifteen years old. I didn't know much about lead guitar yet. Maybe this was what really kicked it in for me. I don't remember. I just remember it was the most wonderful music I'd ever heard. It woulda been a few more years before I'd have started studying jazz with Sylvester. I don't remember if he was living on the farm then or not. I was up roaming the streets all the time with Jared or Carlo, gettin' in trouble for this or that so maybe I was outta the sphere then. Typical teenager stuff. We smoked Millecent's Salems, drank cheap sweet wine talked about girls and dreamed about being rock stars and we'd come back at dawn and spend the night in their backyards in a tent.

We'd sometimes meet up with other outlaw kids and go do stupid meaningless stuff like toilet paper Jared's grandmother's viburnum bush. We'd heard about settin' fire to a burlap bag of shit on someone's porch then ringin' the doorbell and watchin' em stomp it out but we never tried it. The funniest thing was to call some old lady tell her a man was working on her phone line and would she please not pick up her phone for the next five minutes or so because the lineman might be vulnerable to electric shock. We'd wait maybe ten minutes then call back and when the lady would pick up the phone to answer (thinking the "danger time" had passed) one of us would let out a blood curdling scream into the receiver, what we hoped would sound like the scream of an electrocuted lineman plummeting to his death. We'd then call back and pretend to be the appropriate authorities making their case to press manslaughter charges.

People would actually believe this shit but every now and then you'd get a dude who'd seen through all the crap and recognized kid's voices and he would say something like, 'I know who the fuck you are and if I catch you I'm going to cut all your fucking balls off and feed them to my fuckin' German Police dog!' Of course we'd call him right back at Jared's urging but somehow it always put a damper on things hearing a grown-up say shit like that and we'd go do something else ever watchful for any ball-eatin' German dogs.

From the hard road, Tranquility Pike, which was up the hill from Bertha's house, all the way through Water Maple to the other side of the farm where it ran to Edgeton Rd, a paved farm road, lined on both sides with Catalpa, what we called Indian Ceegar trees, and Oaks and Maples and Elms and Hackberrys, snaked its way, connecting the two. We just called this farm road the Avenue. Everybody, Bertha, Marshall, Agnes, for as long as I can remember, called it this. When you turned off Tranquility onto the Avenue, you crossed over the cattle gate that rattled with the weight of the pickup truck and it went down toward the creek, crossing over the limestone bridge from where I spent hours tossing handfuls of gravel into the gently flowing water below, watching the tiny rocks make ripples on the surface like a spring rain shower.

A few summers before, Marshall and Rickey Boy, with TLC helping out, built us a play house sitting up on stilts to keep it dry, drug it by tractor and chain out past the tobaccah barns to the middle of one of the bluegrass fields and put it under the shade of a clump of wild cherry trees. We played in that wondrous place for years and as we got older, Carlo, Jared and Hector started using it as a base of operations for our big camp outs. Marshall figured it was better for us out there than in town since I suppose the temptations of vandalism were less. There was nothing out that far off on the farm for us to fuck up. Marshall said we could smoke and drink wine but no marijuana. If any us of us smoked that shit he'd call the cops. 'I'll be checkin' on you all thru my beenoculars so don't do anything funny or the poe-leese will be on your ass like white on rice.'

'Course I knew he was 'bout half kiddin' but Jared probably didn't. You know how kids take their friend's parents more serious. And he looked at Jared while he said it. He knew he was the trouble maker cause Millicent, who played bridge with his grandmother had tipped him off. I'd gotten up to go to the bathroom when I heard all the commotion and look out and see my own grandboy with that little ruff-neck a-wrappin' toilet paper 'round my viburnum!' One evening after we finished cuttin' tobaccah and were headed down to Bertha's shower to wash off, Rickey Boy asked me did I want to come with them up the avenue this evenin' and have a little fun.

34

One summer evening, Josh and Lilian drove down Edgeton Pike toward the river. The shadows of the elms were long across the asphalt and the green meadows rolled in waves away from the road. Warm green grasses shimmered in the fading light. Hereford and Angus cattle dotted the hills in black and auburn above the catfish pond. Josh waved at Shine and Money Joe as he drove by, glancing at Cotton, muscular in his white sleeveless t-shirt, struggling with his line caught in the over-hanging willows. Shadows of willow leaves danced like the minnows on the water. Bream sprang into the air with one sharp plash, or a catfish after a fly or carp up from the bottom for the sun, gleaming white muscle in the orange light.

He didn't want to make eye contact with him. Money Joe called him "belligerent" so he glanced back at the dough-ball shack to see Shine and Money Joe baiting their hooks. FISH ALL DAY 1$, the sign said. The Chevy droned by. The top was rusted out but it ran good and it was roomy enough for Carlo to stick his big bass fiddle in the back seat when they had a gig playing at the church coffee house on Sunday evenings. Carlo would start in on that bass lick they called "The Ghetto" and then Josh would break into that James Brown strum on an E7 sharp 9 chord, ting-a-ling-a-link, like the Jimi Hendrix Foxey Lady chord and they'd start in funkin it up, Sylves start clappin his hands real fast in funky rhythms saying he learned them from Mexican Indian dudes out in LA.

They found a place to park under a big elm. Josh kissed Lilian and then buried his nose in her fragrant brown hair, which he lifted up in handfuls to kiss the downy hairs on the back of her neck. He moved her on to the back seat and she started unbuckling her pants. The breeze was fragrant with honeysuckle and river mud, the color of the red hawk's tail.

The river kept its ancient ocean smell, shells encrusted in the limestone, the bones of fish layered for ten million years. She scooted her ass up on the seat and put her feet high up on the headrest so he could have room to move into her freely. His cock brushed against her face as she lowered her head to kiss his chest, her tongue reached out for it and her lips searched out the head like a young deer drinking from Moore's Creek. The car smelled faintly of honeysuckle, sweat, fish and shit as he breathed in the smell of their bodies. He held up her ass cupped in both hands for a moment as he licked in long licks from the first cupped line of her ass to the hole, where he lingered for a moment with his tongue and then began licking her cunt with slow strokes along its entire length, stopping every few moments to lick the pale pink dot of her clitoris. Her breath quickened and he knew she was coming. He entered her and moved in a hard slow rhythm in and out. She moaned in oh's like someone encouraging a racehorse and a creaky sound was in the back of her throat as when you've forgotten something you wanted to bring to someone. She smiled and they kissed some more.

35

Up the road Cotton cursed and laughed "Ain't no white motherfucka.... said I didn't give a fuck... oh, I just fucks they women! Das whatta said!.... Yeah, I take 'at white bitch downair at Marshall's gate and.... it don't HAVE no MERCY! And crackers downair shootin guns, whew laaaawd! And Shine and Money Joe loading the car that Marshall gave them. Marshall said to try and keep it picked up round here but these black mother fuckers be throwin beer cans an' shit everwhar. I best bring Sylves' pickup down here munny moinin."

He picked up the sign saying Fish All Day for 1$. "Somebody'll steal 'at shit if I don't..." Money Joe said.

"Them damn crackers downair who done it. I aint lyin'. Wudn't no black mother fucker, I know 'at shit," said Cotton.

"It don't matter," said Money Joe. "Aint heavy at that much layin around".

"Shit man, you gonna be cleanin some serious fish tonight."

"Damn straight," said Shine.

"Sylves sure as hell aint gonna do it. Just eat it. And up there playin his music with all them white kids and paintin them pictures all day long," Cotton made a face like he was observing a crazy man who wasn't there.

"Well, Sylves was born to it," said Joe.

Work is done. Your muscles ache from stooping to cut tobacco stalks but the summer air is still humid as the big orange sun goes down and the clean, after-shower feelings you had from washing in Bertha's spring house soon gives way to the fine layer of sweat that pours back out onto your skin, soothed by the gentle breeze. Along this old, rutted crudely paved farm road, Catalpas, Oaks, Elms and Maples rise majestically and cast huge evening shadows on the rich green meadows that undulate gently in all directions, down to Moore's Creek, up to Tranquility Pike, south down to the border with Tootsie Broward's farm, north up to the Abercrombie's, owned by the rich Texas lady who's never there and whose managers drive the finest trucks and don't associate with the other farmers up and down the pike.

Cattle graze and swish their tails against the flies, they twitch their hide in small bursts. They chew the rich bluegrass to a thin layer of green saliva around their mouths. A blackbird lands on the back of one hops once and flies on. Silence. Then the brief distant trill of birdsong. Cardinal. Starling. Meadow Lark. Scream of Jay. The startling drone of bumblebees whizzing by, drenched in pollen and faint traces of dew. The sharp report of a rifle. Bam! Cattle jump and stare, then chew

"Boy, you got him!" One of the men yells. "You blew 'at sumbitch clean tuh hell and gone!"

The new guy, Burt, had shot a starling that briefly hopped onto a Catalpa limb. Completely disintegrated.

Dusk. Two lovers drive carefully over the cattle gate which rattles like a stack of pool cues falling. It's getting dark enough to need to turn on the headlights, but the man driving pulls in, stops and turns his lights off. Josh, TLC, Ricky Boy and the new guy crouch down behind a big oak. It's getting dark fast. They see the parked driver, fifty yards away, put his arm around the girl.

"Who is that? Tim Boggles the music teacher?" asks TLC. "And damned if that ain't Dotty La Salle's daughter… what's her name?"

"Kiki," says Josh.

"Ain't that her?" asks Ricky Boy.

"Looks like her," says Josh. "Oh God, I hope they don't see me."

"Oh, don't you worry, they ain't gonna see us in these bushes. But they damn sure gonna hear us!"

Slowly Kiki turns her head toward Tim and scoots along the expansive front seat of the Chevy Bel-Air. They neck and Tim runs his hand along her t-shirt covered breasts. They seem to talk awhile and the men obediently watch as if they could hear what they said to each other, probably imagining themselves in Tim's place and wondering what seductive things they would try to say. Josh looks over at TLC and Ricky Boy. Their jaws are slack, their eyes hypnotized by the stillness. Off comes Kiki's shirt. Josh recognized the territory. The skin that tans well. Dark pink aureoles. Summer haircut. So, that's why he was asking about her during lessons. Josh didn't care. He didn't get sore. In a moment, Tim moved his hips up off the seat and began unbuckling his belt and sliding his pants down. Don't slide 'em off, Josh thought to himself, half wishing now he could disappear. But he didn't take them off. They must have been just down around his knees. Kiki smiled and her head disappeared behind the windshield. Tim leaned back smiling with a lustful sneer. Well, thought Josh, it's all in fun. Dusk seemed to almost sigh a big sigh one last time, coming close to all God's creatures. Then came the beginning of the dark.

"Open up, boys!!" Ricky Boy yelled. With that command, everyone began firing their rifles into the air. Blam! Ka bam! Quickly the headlights came back on. Thrown quickly into reverse, the Chevy screeched backward, sending smoke from the ornate tires, although Kiki didn't seem afraid and peered around trying to see out into the dark. Tim was visibly shaken and his naked white buttocks clearly visible, too, as he frantically tried to pull up his pants. Kiki held the wheel. She seemed to be giggling, her head thrown back, looking around curiously as the car sped away over the hill. The men fell out onto the ground around the towering trees, laughing hysterically. Josh watched them, amused, but apart somehow.

"D'you see 'at sumbitch's little white ass and him justa jerkin' up his britches tryin to get the hell outta thar," said Burt, the new guy, whom TLC and Ricky Boy looked up to since he once had a factory job making good money and had finished high school.

"Run for your life," TLC mocked. "Them rednecks is gonna kill us!"

"Betcha he won't be trying to get no pussy in Marshall Celeste's avenue no more." Said Burt.

"Oh, he'll be out here tomorrow night, the way I hear that sumbitch chases pussy. I'd come out here and shoot at myself if I thought I could get hold of some of that shit," said Ricky Boy.

"Think ther'll be anybody else comin tonight?" Burt asked.

"Oh, don't you worry none about that," said Ricky Boy. This farm's the only drive-in in town that don't show a movie."

"Or maybe it does show one," Josh laughs. "And we're the ones in it."

There was a silence. Far down the hill you could hear the creek gurgling and then a screech owl hooted. TLC laughed, "That's kinda funny to say, Josh, but I reckon you right."

36

FLEUR-DE-LYS: AN EVENING IN BUDAPEST

from the Life of Joshua Celeste by Krip Kovacs

I started to hail a taxi but then something came over me as if some lovely specter of autumn had suddenly approached like a gypsy prostitute out of nowhere putting her arm in mine, whispering seductively, picking my pocket. I couldn't resist walking through the leaf-strewn streets of Budapest at two am. Yet you're alone wandering solipsistically, celebrating a Halloween night that Hungarians don't celebrate. Not really. They save the costumes and laughing at Death for Mardi Gras (Farsang). Tomorrow, tight-lipped, they will visit graveyards and weep. Maybe I will, too.

Final curtain call of the leaves. The passing of the sycamore touches me deepest. The leaves are so big, broad, dry, brittle. Human. They disintegrate in the first rains.

I started out the evening in a tiny little expat bar called the Mona Lisa 2. I saw my good friend Tamas Papp and we proceeded to get bombed on pints of beer. Good man. What a wonderful place, really. A small dog sat nearby doing impressions of Groucho Marx "Why, hello Delores. I didn't recognize you standing up!" A lot of the same old faces I'd remembered were still there. Damon, the Scotsman, tall, thin, hair cut shorter than the afro-like hippie frizz I'd remembered. He'd been a founding father of this place, one of the first barkeeps. Good man. It felt like a good night. It had been six or eight months since I'd been in and seen a few of the old buddies. Little had changed except the paint on the walls. It was now a more vibrant yet soft orange, almost peach with various abstract, artsy squiggles running along here and there at random. Still, an improvement over the old nicotine-soaked dull green paint previous.

Eventually, as the evening went on, the short-sighted new management ran out of beer. I was happy to drink wine but my friend Stan arrived and insisted we slake our thirsts elsewhere, even though it was rumored that another keg was on its way.

Back out into the Old Jewish Quarter Night! How delicious, how awe-inspiring the crumbling imperial facades of Old Pest! I couldn't begin to describe them with any accurate architectural vocabulary. As I grow older, I realize such knowledge is out of any realistic sphere for me. I could get a dictionary and throw some terms around but would it be real? No, only the ache of the alley that curves out of sight, the dragon-skin cobblestones, the sapphire star just to the left of the spire… those would be. I'm fascinated by the tidbits of history that have come my way. Gibbon's Baroque prose remains a favorite. There's a section on Attila the Hun. It stands before me as a section of this wall. All of Europe is suddenly enclosed in it. A river lined with seagulls runs out to a camp where a warrior made his speech, then died of having too much.

Recently I stumbled across, in an antikvarium across from the Opera, a copy of Joseph Lengel's, "The Bridge Builders" which I read in the Goethe Institute cafe one afternoon with nothing to do. Interesting insights into the real Istvan Szechenyi: madness, revolution. Dark eyebrows like a Turk. Two hundred yards away from where I am the bridge still stands.

But tonight it's Halloween and the leaves are dead. Tomorrow the Dead are dead. But the streets! Leaves blow across empty boulevards. On nights like this, it seems the whole city is asleep. Perhaps everyone's dead but me, or motionless like a Twilight Zone episode I saw once. Rod Serling's voice: Your mind. Your mind. Your mind. He died, right? Your mind.

Actually, everyone's probably in a smoke-filled bar or a cellar disco. Everyone's asleep. No, a group of Hungarian kids is coming toward me, dressed in black. Is that white face makeup for Halloween or is that their natural pallor? They're beautiful with the European paleness of winter. One girl with astonishing blond hair passes me and I get a whiff of intoxicating perfume and like Pepe Le Pew, I turn for a moment to follow it, participating in their youth. It's no use. I am already drunk so I stumble homeward from square to square.

Before, when I was drinking with my mates, I remember thinking as the alcohol buzz washed over me on the way to the pissoir, or even as I stood before the sweet fragrance of the urinal, deciphering drunken hieroglyphics on the wall, it was sad that such an evening should have to end. My first few beers with Tamas, which somehow seemed long ago, were like the opening bars of a great song, potent, joyous. Then, meeting Stan and a friend of his I didn't know, interesting chap, getting settled in yet another bar, all that heightened the effect, the grandeur of the European night. Soon conversation, after a time, it happens with everything, began to dull a bit. The horror of today's political scene, our jobs, pursuits, women, marriage, tastes in music, books read, movies seen. Then, leave-taking, a twinge of sadness. A tipsy whirling around to walk away. Something drifting apart?

Friendship has limitations and like women or drugs or God, cannot save you from yourself. Perhaps I'll curl up on your sofa tonight, or inside your Mother's womb? One mustn't be demanding of friends unrealistically. Each separate little life. Down a separate street or into a separate cab. My temptation is to lose myself in another person, to live my little life for them and make a deep emotional, even physical bond secure. This is impossible. At least people say it is.

Alone with the street, such delicious thoughts escape the cold autumn wind down a side street. Autumn rain brings winter in. The ornate doorway at 13 Dessweffy is a favorite meditative spot for a cigarette and mindless gaze toward the lights of Bajcsy- Zalinczky Boulevard. When I finally get up to its expanse, I'm nostalgic with the thought of 1993 and fallen walls and of how disoriented my earlier view of this city once was. I once thought that the Vaci Ut viaduct was a bridge over the Danube. For years this illusion persisted in the City's coquettish way of hiding itself from me. Which way is the river? It's whirling around in your brain? Taxis stood at wheel spoke intersections with the boulevards and my dear friends (I didn't know where the fuck I was half the time, reeling with imitation Baroque as I was) put me into them and I'd be whisked away to my apartment in Buda to a street I couldn't pronounce, tipsily looking at the magnificent and directionally correct view of the Erzsebet Bridge through cozy cab window. Just let your head slump into a pre-dream loll. The sky over east Pest lifts me over the water at dawn.

Once, I was on a business trip in the States (my first trip home for four years) and we drove past my aunt's house. But I was only scheduled to meet her a few days later so I couldn't just turn off the highway and go see her even if it had been so long ago.

"Let's go visit my aunt," I pretended to say to my business associate, slumping in a pre-dream loll in the passenger seat. "What?" he would have said.

We were already terribly late for some important appointment. Besides, I would see her in a few days for a brief visit before heading back to Europe. Still, strange to see the little sign and arrow for my hometown and, after all these years, not be able to go there.

"Oh, Dennis…"

"Yeah?"

"Fuck all this promotional material. I'm going home."

"Okay."

Could it happen like that? Three years later my aunt and I hugged goodbye at Ferihegy Airport. For the previous week, we had been dealing with the "aunt stuff" of Budapest hotels, restaurants, taxis. So comical. Like we were the goofball comedians and Budapest was the straight man. Budapest as Dan Rowan: "Say g'night, Dick." Us as Dick Martin: "G'night, Dick." Americans learned comedic timing from watching so many sitcoms. But the native banging his gavel. The foreigner banging his gavel.

There comes a time when you feel the chill of a reality you hadn't suspected and are numbed into old age. Even at twenty-eight. Suddenly the stain of death is on everything. Why not me? The Pattern looms large. Like the fleurs-de-lys shadows from the banister of the baroque staircase. Down in the crowded Metro, every face a symbol of fragile mortality. Budapest is a vast fossil shell network of buildings built for a race of giants that no longer exists! We smaller beings have curled up into the void they left. Cut up into apartments. We built on top of the Ruins. But, like a palimpsest, the ruins still show through. We are at play among them. The deserted street is the meeting place of every human equation… fleur-de-lys.

I always come back in my mind to that ol' farm. Even as we're drivin through the night in the tour bus and the moon is riding with me out the window, I look out across snow-covered fields and think about that ol Farm. I can't help it. That's where I started I guess. That's where my memories begin. It seems impossible that it's all gone. Seems like yesterday I roamed those fields. Watched the men, Rickey Boy, TLC, all of them, put up the tobacco, climbing up in those high barn rafters, covered with dust and sweat and dirt from the leaves, or out in the bluegrass field carrying those sacks of seed, stacking them up on a truck and taking them to that ol hot warehouse and spreading all that grass out on the floor to cure in the sweltering heat. I remember those big ol black dudes, but just teenage boys, Marshall would hire off the street up in Medina, ones Sylves didn't want anything to do with. How I watched them work, yellow seeds, clinging to their black skin, white t-shirts darkened with dirt and sweat, ladies stockings tied around their heads pirate style, the strong smell of onions they'd eat on their lunch sandwiches and then sweat it out into body funk. The smell of them and the mountain men bunched up with me and Doc in Marshall's car as we'd take 'em back to some cheap motel at the end of the day, Kentucky sun sinking orange behind a soft sinking hill.

One would say to Marshall, "What's a fahmah like you doin' drivin' a Mercedes Benz?" Marshall just laughed and me and Doc tried to sound just like him, "what's a fahmah like you" especially when Marshall would tell us to do something we didn't want to. He'd frown and shake his head. It felt cool to think the black boys would let me hang out with them. They'd say, "Hey Josh, go get me a drink of water! Us Soul Brothers gotta stick together!"

We'd tell Sylves all about it and say, let's go up to Ryly-town and find em, and he'd say, "Naw, problee just a buncha jive-ass brothers."

You got to our farm by going out Tranquility Pike about two miles out of Edgeton. Soon the pretty green yards of the town would start to peter out and turn into farm fields. You realized if you thought about it a little bit that, well, the whole thing was just once a forest that became farms that became a little town. A farm, then, a grocery store, a church, a schoolhouse, a tavern, a gas station, a factory. All of a sudden the Forest becomes a Town. At least that's what it seems like sometimes to me now that I think about it.

But I remember one night after we'd worked real hard in the bluegrass fields, this was when Rickey and TLC and some of the mountain boys would get it into their heads to get their rifles and go over by the old road that snaked thru the farm, up by the big entrance cattle gate, and hide behind one of them big Indian Cigar trees (Catalpa) and wait for lovers parking up there in their cars. Once a car would pull in and turn off its lights, Rickey and them would wait awhile all crouched down then when the time was right, jump up firin their rifles in the air and whoopin and hollerin and scarin the shit outta those poor boys and girls makin love in those big rusty chevy cars they'd drive. Girls runnin round screamin tryin to gather up their underwear, dudes hoppin' round tryin to get it back in their pants, whatever. You remember that story.

One evening Rickey and TLC took a chain and hooked up the playhouse they'd built for us to a tractor and dragged it way out in the fields, way off from Bertha's house so we wouldn't be botherin anybody with our guitars and car radios blastin and singin and all that while we were campin out back there with all our friends like Bobby Paganini and Jared Smallwood and Hector and Carlo and everybody. They'd put the playhouse up on runners so it was easy to drag along, just like draggin' a cattle salt house.

The only rule Marshall laid down was no pot smokin. He said, Catch ye pot smokin I'm gonna call the law on ye. He was probably bullshittin us of course but we couldn't be sure. Well, it just so happened that later that night, back over on the other side of the farm, about a mile or so from where we were camping out, here come ol' Jimmy" Free" Moore, one of the meanest, nastiest guitar pickers in Water Maple County by the way, The Jimi Hendrix of Edgeton, Medina, too, for that matter. Here he come all drunk in his VW hippie van and run right into the ditch and his girlfriend breaks an arm or somethin against the smashed-up door. Somebody calls the cops and the ambulance. Well, to get her over to Edgeton Hospital a little quicker the cops decide to put her into a cruiser and zip thru the old dirt and gravel road that snaked through the farm from the Tranquility Pike side, you know, the one called the Avenue, where the Big Entrance Cattle Gate is, all the way to the Edgeton Roadside.

We'd parked our playhouse about midway across, not far off the farm road and we're havin a good time, regular high school boys drinkin and carryin on. Then Bobby says hey screw your ol' man let's roll a joint. I said fine by me. Well, no sooner than he gets that joint rolled, in his mouth, with the lighter lit and him ready to smoke, here comes that cop cruiser flying by doin seventy, gravel flyin, on its way to the Edgeton Hospital carryin Free Morton's girlfriend, who we have no idea about, with her broken arm. We all jump up when we see those blue lights flashin and somebody yells, "Hide the dope!"

Bobby just stands there, takes the joint out his mouth, lookin real bewildered and says, "Guess your ol' man wudn't bullshittin was he?" We're all preparing to do some fast talkin, thinkin the cops are comin to bust us and suddenly the cruiser just roars on, not payin the least bit of attention to us, except maybe when Chief Freeman catches a glimpse of a few of us still standin outside by the clubhouse and gives a smile and a wave and toots his horn.

Bobby's really puzzled now. But he just scratches his head, relights the joint and says, "Wanna hit"?

About that time ol' Hector comes shufflin out the clubhouse, been hidin under some old boards, and him scratchin his head, too, sayin: "Now, don't that just beat all." We just had to laugh.

37

We'd been pretty nervous about Tim Boggle's band playin at the Catholic church basketball gym for the Spring sock hop. I couldn't play guitar as well as Josh but I thought maybe I'd fool around on Sylves' congas when the band took a break or whatever, but we wanted to see "Free" Moore. He was in Doc's class and everybody called him the Jimi Hendrix of Edgeton. He kinda looked like Jimi.

It was one of those soft Kentucky evenings when the air feels like lotion, the sun setting behind Edgeton Road. You could see the line of kids waiting to get in, forming in front of the gym door. We found a place off to the side somewhere and sat down on the wood floor.

Shine and Money Joe and Ricky Boy and TLC all helped set up the sound equipment, speakers and amps and mic stands and Sylves' drums and Stanfield's bass, etc. Dennis Demeter ran the soundboard. Suddenly, the lights went down and you could hear Carlo play the beginning bass lick of Miles' "So What." Then Sylves came out and started jamming on the electric piano. They went into a cool jam and some of the teachers clapped. But a lot of the kids didn't understand what they were playing. Pretty soon, Sylves jumped over to the drum set and Carlo switched over to electric bass and they started in on this cool blues groove when suddenly there he was, Free, the Jimi Hendrix of Edgeton.

Like droplets of Mercury, the notes came out. Clear singing sounds and fast clusters of bursting notes like somebody talking or screaming. Then he sang, "There's a red house over yonder... that's where my baby stays..." Guitar siren sounds billowed to the back of the gym wall, like a loon screaming or somebody drowning. And then weeping.

All the way home we kept trying to imitate that liquid sound as we walked back to Aunt Pearl's house on Main St. We stopped a while and sat on the courthouse steps and smoked a few Marlboros (or "marbs" as we called them) not caring if anyone saw us. Hell, we're sixteen. It's legal. We watched the cars pass by and dreamed of a time we might learn to be as good as Free or Sylves or Carlo. How could we know then that it would be all buses and crazy meaningless trips around this Blue Earth? And all the lost people, masters and slaves, betrayers and betrayed.

Suddenly, a car went past and they slowed down almost to a crawl. The guy on the passenger side yelled, "Hey, ain't you Josh Celeste, ol man Celeste's boy out there on Water Maple?"

Josh looked inquisitive then we both yelled out, "YEAH!"

It was Free himself. With his friend Harris at the wheel. I'd seen them clowning around in the halls together, always chatting up chicks.

"Y'all wanna ride around some with us? We got beer."

I jumped up for pure joy. Ride around with Free? It was like being asked to play guitar with Carlos Santana. Hell yes, we wanna ride around.

"Get in the back," he said.

I started telling them how great the concert was. I did most of the talking. Josh sat shyly back in his seat. Free grinned at him and handed him a beer. He took a swig just as a cop car went zooming by.

"Hey, don't be turnin one up when the fuzz goes by. Keep it down in the seat till everything's clear, then you swig it, see?"

He took a big draw on a can of Pabst Blue Ribbon and then hit a big fat joint of Kentucky Blue homegrown pot.

"My cousin down in Leslie County grows this shit hisself. Yeah, I thought that was you standin out there. You dudes look kinda lost."

The cut stung a little but then Free saw our reaction and quickly added, "Hey I didn't mean no offense. I mean that as kind of a compliment, really. Hell, I'm about half lost misself. Let's get lost. Ever heard that song? But I figured that was you. You came to hear us before didn't you somewhere? And Tim's always talking about you, sayin how good you are on guitar and all that. Maybe we better take em out in the country and kick their asses, huh, Harris ol boy? Don't want em gettin' TOO good…"

For a second a flash of fear went through us. Oh no, they wanna beat us up? Then Free grinned and said, "Hey I'm only kiddin. I aint no violent redneck type. I ain't no Ronnie Rongo. I heard about that, too, from Tim. Hey, I know a dude who'll kick his ass for ya if you want him to. But, hell, might as well forget it. It wouldn't do anybody much good. Unless you just want revenge for the hell of it. But I can look at your face and see you ain't that way. Besides, everybody, even Harris here, fucked Kiki LaSalle. Oops, hope you don't mind me tellin that. You ain't still in love with her or anything like that is ye?" Josh shook his head. He wondered if he might be talking about someone else.

"But, hell, like I say, Tim's all the time talkin' about you. Sayin' I should teach you and all that but I ain't no good at that. I'm sorry. He handed Josh a joint.

"Go on, smoke it. It'll make you play like Jimi Hendrix!" He and Harris laughed out loud at that.

"But everybody says you sound like Hendrix," Josh said shyly.

"No way, man. Nobody can play like him. He's some kinda Shaman or something. Jimi was the greatest. I got to see him in 'natti one time. Boy, that was a helluva night wudn't it, Harr? Guess it don't matter now, him bein dead.

"We took 'at little LaSalle girl up there with us that night didn't we?" Harris said.

"Oh, hell we passed her around like communion. Which one was it? Kiki LaSalle or that one really cute one that used to work in the blow job place?

"I bleve it was Kiki," Harris ventured. "Wudnt this before that damn place was even built?"

"Hell, I don't know. I don't have time to keep up with all 'at shit." He looked back over his shoulder at Josh and me.

"Anyway, as I was sayin' before Harris started interjecting (he pronounced the "ing" at the end of the word in a kind of mock British intellectual way) his theories of identity into all this, Whoever it was, we gave her a ride home one night from that ol' Bunny dude's house that use to give parties a lot."

"We got to her house and started to sneak down the basement so her parents wouldn't see us. Well, I couldn't help but try and kiss her as we got outta the car but she didn't get mad, she just wrapped her legs around me and started hunchin like a dog, so I reached up under there and got a big handful of ass and man! Hot as fire! So I said, "Can you give Harris some too"? Fuck, I was drunker'n twelve motherfuckers. And I thought, "Shit, she's gonna think I think she's a whore or something, which she ain't, really. I mean, hell, a woman can get a bee up her butt same as a man, right? Well, she said that'd be fine, so all night long I'd fuck her a while, then Harris'd come in and he'd fuck her for awhile. Thought about both fuckin her at the same time but then I thought lookin at Harris' ol pimply ass hunchin up and down, I wouldn't be able to keep a hard-on, so I'd step into the tv room and smoke cigarette. Hell, this was in her basement rec room or whatever you call it. Her parents were upstairs doin' whatever they was doin', maybe listening to all the fuckin goin' on. Hell, I don't know, like I say I'd slip into the TV room, maybe catch some news, nod off or somethin' but then here'd come Harris lumberin' in sayin' it was my turn and all and I'd peek back in at that sweet little body and those pretty blond curls (and blond pussy hair, too, I'm here to tell you) well, hell, I'd get a hard-on big as a zit on Harris' ass, then I'd fuck her, then he'd fuck her, then I'd fuck her... went on like that all night.

She told me in school the next Monday morning that she'd slept like a baby, and that she felt sore but it was good sore, she said. I felt the same way. I'd slept like a baby too.

"I didn't," Harris said. "I jacked off the rest of the night, couldn't sleep."

"What's a matter?" Free asked, "You not get enough?"

"Naw, I just kept thinkin of your cute little hairless ass bobbin up and down and you goin ' uh-uh-uh ' like a sick cow when we worked for Marshall Celeste out there on Water Maple Farm. 'Member me shockin you with that cattle prod?"

"Wait a minute, fucker, you mean you watched?"

"She told me to! Said it turned her on. But you didn't see coz your eyes was all squinted up and you was gruntin' suh much. Man, that gruntin was sexy, you bet!"

"Oh, fuck you, man," Free said, smiling.

"You promise?" Harris laughed. "You gonna get that beer or what?

Free slowly opened the passenger side door and, turning down the corners of his mouth and shooting a glance of good-hearted mock-disgust at his old friend. He walked a bit woozily up the pathetic little subdivision sidewalk toward his parent's drab little brick house, that looked like every other little drab brick house on the street, went around to the aluminum side door and snuck into the kitchen to pilfer another six-pack of beer from their icebox.

We watched him a moment from the car. And when he had gone inside, I said, "Man, he's got some stories, dudn't he? And a fuck of a good guitar player, too."

"Yeah," Harriss sleepily replied, "He's a good ol boy. Little wild. If he only had a pussy."

38

LETTER FROM DOC:

There were many women in my life. Not perhaps an abnormal number. I had normal obsessions, I think. Normal fetishes. I fantasized about women quite often. I still think that there is nothing more wonderful in the world than a beautiful woman—and a beautiful woman who is attracted to you—well, that is an ecstasy that cannot be surpassed. Still, my inherent shyness and lack of self confidence (I recently read in Freud that it's all, that and agoraphobia, which I also mildly suffer from, connected to a fear of castration!) kept the many that I desired, for the most part, out of my reach. I was fortunate that many charming women I have known, and a few that I have loved passionately, overlooked all that and still found something to love in me. Indeed, men who are shy and have no confidence in themselves and are generally inept at even getting along in the mainstream of life can still be seen as worthy of love in the eyes of some women. This is particularly true in America where women are the most "empowered" and independent of any on earth. In Europe, particularly in Eastern Europe, where I've had the pleasure, as you know of visiting my brother from time to time, although infidelity is more common, woman is used to being submissive to the male will, and it is still seen as inappropriate that women should be too powerful, though this attitude is changing.

When I started dating again after a relationship collapsed and I was still in Budapest, I remember an occasion when, conversing with a young lady on the phone, asking her out on a date, I asked, "Where would you like to meet?"

thinking, in an American way, that I was being very considerate of her time and of how far she might have to travel in the city, etc.

She shot back a terse reply, "Well, you are the man. You should decide!"

As one who begins to understand what sort of man I am by reading this might expect, she was a very conservative woman, though very independent. She had a very high position in the state lottery, who expected to be "cared for" by a very self-assured man. A classic Eastern European woman, she was, in short, a terrible match for me.

This is the most engaging, yet shocking thing about attraction, a girl who by her looks alone is so irresistible you feel compelled to try and get to know her somehow. Her looks provoke such dreams, such hopes and fantasies in your mind, particularly the hope that you have finally met your soul mate, it's always shocking when you perceive a personality underneath that has almost nothing in common with you. One that, indeed, might cause you great harm. You see clearly then that what a woman's beauty arouses in you and what she is as a real person, are two very different things. Or is it that Desire is a fluid thing and that the perception of beauty and the Reality of another person are always changing? One says: "She's changed. She's not the person I knew." Yet, might she have really been that person for a time, however brief, and falling in love with her a completely legitimate thing, not a mistake at all? It's this idea of a perpetually changing Self that seems to render the concept of marriage as very flawed. Relationships cannot be governed by something so rigid. Modernity is defined rather by such concepts, though they seem to me rather cold and inhumane, as constant change, and the fact that things in the Modern World become obsolete and irrelevant very quickly. In the end, I'm once again reminded of a favorite quote from Simon Weil:

"What we love in another person is the hoped-for fulfillment of our desire. We don't love their desire. If what we loved in another was their Desire, then we should love them as ourselves".

Perhaps in the old agrarian order of the world, a world I caught glimpse of in its last American manifestation because I grew up on a farm and it was clearly visible in the ways of our grandmother, Bertha, Desire had been a less egotistical thing then it is now in urban society.

All this might seem appalling to a believer in the selflessness of marriage, yet, the intensity and variety of the modern urbanite's Desire must be reckoned with realistically. Our Believer must admit that the negotiations and contracts of marriage, and all the supposedly selfless things that are done "for the sake of the family" do not blot out completely such urban compulsions, some of which are mechanisms of Survival. In Christian terms, one must acknowledge that a tremendous amount of biblical "exegesis" has been necessary to make Christ appear as a staunch advocate of the Institution of Marriage. The truth is he seems to have been rather ambivalent about it.

But such discussions can go on interminably, and so… my best to you and your musical pursuits…

Doc

Yo dude—

I been wanting to write to you for awhile.—This doesn't mean anything, perhaps, in the big bad world out there, the back drop to our consenting to be alive and take what comes. That's it isn't it? We get up every morning (or afternoon if you're a musician like us, particularly if you got laid the night before, or maybe have plenty of gigs in the cupboard and you don't have to go "out there" until say 8 pm to pack in your stuff—you know what I mean?) and we go out there and meet life in all its myriad manifestations.

I mean what I'm writing probably won't ever be turned into a script for a Hollywood movie. That's because I want to say everything and nothing whereas a script has to say something – using all the trickery of plot devices—but often ends up saying nothing. Well, sometimes movies say very profound things. I'm not sure I can say anything profound now that I feel like I've found my place in the world. But I keep wanting to "say something straight." Telling a good story is great for kids and for that insatiable kid inside me—but there comes a time when only the Truth will do.

The world is such an amazing place. You have to admit it's pretty impressive. One day, after we were coming out of a movie, little Gordon came up to me and said, just out of the blue, "I love the World." But I read where Sarah Teasdale, that rather sentimental poetess, once said, "Life can only give so much."

Ultimately it's true, isn't it? What I expected from life is far different than what I got. I'm not saying it has by any means been a big disappointment. Oh God, I've been so much luckier than some. I could just have easily, judging from the world's unpredictability, wound up at the bottom of a mass grave in Iraq or some such god-forsaken place. Add to that bit of good fortune my upper middle-class upbringing in one of the state's most illustrious families, and the word lucky is hardly apt to describe my life. "Charmed" might be much more adequate I would think. I've hardly had to do an "honest day's work" in thirty years, I've been blessed with that most sacred of all talents, "Musicianship," I've been given two beautiful children, and I've had the good fortune to have slept with some of the most beautiful women that ever drew the breath of life.

It's about them, and the emotional shocks that seem to generate from them, that I'm often most compelled to write about.

To speak about love of a woman, one must learn Poetry and the old Mythic language. For a long time I didn't understand it and I don't pretend to speak it fluently now; yet, every old man becomes a Master if he lives long enough. And the reason for the pain he has suffered, becomes, in the end, clearer to him. My hope is to contribute in some way to this clarity.

Still, I think I was just getting to the heart of the matter. I am completely infatuated, fixated, fascinated, addicted, obsessed, etc... with women. Well, you know, before I left Edgeton, my obsession was just kicking in an all-consuming way.

Yet that was merely the prelude for what was to come: my last wife was that sexy, intelligent soul mate I'd always fantasized about. Before I left everything behind, the instinct, that "I must go —go somewhere—get out there—find her" that instinct became very strong. And I found her. And I was able to channel a lot of sexual energy into that relationship. All women became reflected only through her. She became a mirror I saw the world and my old sexual impulses through. Yet, after a time Desire, some caged beast in the breast desires to break out, venture forth.

I still think we could've managed those impulses—giving them a controlled release, so to say. But alas she was there with her home culture, the familiar surroundings of her childhood. She had less to lose by walking out. I had everything to lose. And I did lose everything I had in Hungary—especially the time I'd invested in my career, my marriage—everything but my kids. Yet, the "way" that I must see them, this was controlled, for the last five years since our separation, to some extent, by her.

Soon that will change. The boys will be able to come and go between us as they please. They already can in some ways. Time is unraveling the dilemma I never could. Perseverance has provided me with that consolation, and now, though it's not a wholly uncomplicated matter, the freedom to chase skirts all over hell's half acre, the old "Web of Love" days in Medina lasted for a shorter time comparatively. Berenice split in '79, so we had my whole crib from then until around '81, minus the year I was trying to be faithful to old flame Kiki LaSalle (big mistake!). Not that long. But Medina is such a small town, word gets out and the mystique fades: girls would stop coming to the Web since they didn't wanna be seen as whores.

Doc once told me that he once overheard two girls talking at a club one night, "I'd like to go to this party at Josh Celeste's house," one said, "but I'm kinda scared coz I hear things can get kind of wild there!"

On the other hand, girls who DID wanna be seen as whores were still attracted to the place! So, sometimes image can be interpreted in different ways. Things got wild a few times. Certainly Nikoletta, Free's old nympho girlfriend, would add some unpredictability to the mix on occasion. But things never got weird. My cousin Dennis, uncle Dennis' son, was more into "weird." He liked seeing people squirm when taken out of their comfort zone… unwittingly taken out. Suddenly out came the coke, the wads of cash, the drunkenly driven car, and then, just to fuck with one's composure, the guns.

With the exception of being a father, and that's a difficult state of being to explain to a non-parent, sex is for me the most fascinating, most life-inducing thing about being human. Yet, from the first impulses, the first conscious ones, if I may give Freud his due since, of course, he theorizes that sexuality begins much earlier, and I tend to agree with him, that began forming in me at the age of eleven or twelve, sex has always been something incomprehensibly consuming, unpredictable and the source of intense pleasure and anxiety. The dynamo of life itself.

This is funny and cute I guess: Do you remember your first conscious sexual feeling? By that I mean not the first masturbation but the first conscious twinge of attraction to the opposite sex? I do.

It was the last day of school, sixth grade. Carla Jenkins stood in the hall by her open locker door wearing a scotch plaid skirt. It occurs to me now that I've always found the Scotch Tape insignia pleasant to look at. Her legs were tanned from the early summer sun and she wore those cute little ankle socks with the white bobs in back that you sometimes see lady golfers and other women athletes wear, with a pair of brown loafers. It was as if I was seeing her shoes, her socks, her legs, suddenly her cute nose and lips and eyes and hair, her young womanly Being for the very first time.

I breathed out an ethereal kind of sigh of quiet ecstasy. Suddenly the shape of her thighs and calves, the wrinkle of her instep, the protrusion of her ankle bone above the leather line of her loafer, all this welled up in me into a… well, probably a big boner the size of Florida! No, later perhaps, but at that moment It welled up into something like the imperceptible change of a season. A deep internal sigh came over me. I was never the same. None of us are. Soon, well, months later, I worked up enough nerve to put my hand on Lucy Stark's thigh during a movie and then finally, at another movie, first kiss with Mindy Higgs.

That tasted much saltier than I expected. I thought it would be more like candy, that's what all the songs on the radio said it was like. It was the popcorn.

Sexual hunger and shyness became the two sides of the scale. Just recently I've been reading Freud's theories on the connection between shyness/ agoraphobia, fear of going "outside", which I suffer from in a mild way and fear of castration. This fear begins when the child first notices his mother's lack of a penis. And of course, perverse illustrations of this "complex" can be seen in ancient myths, American Indian ones, e.g., where a vagina is depicted as having teeth. The whole sex experience and its related anxieties, heavy breathing, sweating, fear, ecstasies, increased heart rate, etc., all that is connected to Death.

The French refer to orgasm as "la petite morte," you know all this, of course. I'm far from a Freud expert. Still, I find his explanations fascinating. No one seems to have gotten closer to some deep truth but I know he's not the last word. I'm just a fan. Yet, why does Woman represent something so desirable and yet so foreboding?

Kiki La Salle once told me, never underestimate the wisdom of a twenty year old girl. "Maybe the reason sex is so weird is coz it's so good!" The sexual hunger is natural enough, but the shyness, where does it originate? The not wanting to trespass laws of society, yet needing to feed that hunger. Accepted ways of sexual satisfaction seem always slightly inadequate. Doc has said, "There IS no sexual satisfaction."

He's probably right. But there are moments of it… no?

Not that what follows is really one of those moments, but I've always wanted to try and capture this incident to the written page. It was a beautiful Spring afternoon. My last year of junior high school was reaching its final few weeks. School had just let out and I walked the short distance into town. I was standing in Madison's Drugstore at Main and Lexington St. From there through the big glass front door next to the magazine rack I could look northwest up the street, towards Frankfort. I had at least a half an hour to kill before my mom was coming to pick me up. I gazed, daydreaming, up the street towards Uncle Dennis' dime store and the austere granite pillars of the public library, half aware of the 4 o'clock traffic passing through afternoon shadows as the pavement gave off a moist fragrance.

Then. There she was. Kiki LaSalle. Fourteen in a white mini skirt. Her long brown hair, with beautiful blond sun-bleached streaks in it, streaming down her back all the way to her incomprehensibly cute fanny. It was just like subsequent instincts I would feel throughout my life: I knew, as she was turning to walk into the library, with her lovely honey-colored arms, quite hairy for a girl, and one so young, laden with books and, though I had known her from kindergarten, not having ever really spoken to her before, much less touched her, as I say, I knew that I would walk up the street, enter the library, find her in a secluded place among the stacks, put my arms around her, kiss her, then run my hand under her white dress, lifting it slightly (it was just a scanty little jumper) to find her white panties and slip my finger, very gingerly, into her vagina. I knew I would do all this. And I did. And as I lifted my fingers to caress her cheek, I smelled her body, part soap, part perfume, part sweat, part urine, part vaginal juice. The salt smell of the sea.

My first impulse was to take her upstairs, still out of sight, in the spacious old antebellum building, of the watchful librarian and lay her gently on the floor and lose my virginity. As she would most probably be losing hers. Maybe not, if, in hindsight, I base such speculations on what later transpired. I knew nothing of condoms. We moved toward the staircase and the possible scenario of her getting knocked up, resulting in my marriage to her at fifteen, a factory job, more children and then. perhaps... suicide, but then I suddenly remembered, My Mom!

I kissed her quickly and ran out the door, down the street to Madison's, as fast as I could go. There was Mom in her powder blue Pontiac Catalina waiting at the corner. I got in and we drove away towards the farmhouse on Edgeton Rd., which btw, is no longer standing; it was razed about ten years ago.

When we got home my mind was teeming with confused thoughts. Had I done something wrong? It was the first time I'd ever touched a vagina. I felt guilty. And yet somehow, good. I had kissed and "fingered" (albeit clumsily) Kiki LaSalle. A lot of guys would have liked to have been in my shoes. I told my brother about it and he seemed to concur with the latter opinion. Nix the guilt trip.

Yet, Spring passed. Then Summer. I thought of her. I have a faint memory of trying to call her, her father's name was in the phone book. Yet the thought of leaving my name with a parent terrified me. "He's the one who fingered me and then ran away! Father! We must crucify him and let wild animals feed upon his genitals! Trace that caaaaallll!" The seeds of agoraphobia were taking root, if you'll pardon the pun, along with my new sexual awakening. Yet, I couldn't wait for school to start in the Fall.

There were so many girls. Kiki's just one of a hundred faces that intrigued me. But now I was a freshman. A nobody. It was routine for an upperclassman, once he spotted you in the hall, to call over as many of his friends as he could and they would grab your arms, hold them behind your back, and take turns punching you in the chest. And these were guys who had let me hang out with them just this past summer! Gangs of upperclassmen roamed the halls looking for freshmen to humiliate. Law of the jungle.

It turned out that I wasn't the only guy who got to feel up Kiki; in fact, anyone who could sit next to her in the science lab could put their hand on her thigh and then slowly work their way up. But just at the point of reaching her panties and searching for her tender vaginal lips with your fingertips, suddenly, down came her hand, and yours was put back at her knee again to begin the arduous journey back up her thigh all over again. The upper echelon of The Feelers of Kiki's Leg, Jared Smallwood, Carlo Everett, Hector Endicott and we would discuss our frustration with this new situation over cigarettes furtively smoked in the school bathroom. Jared seemed particularly disappointed at not getting any, as he called it, "stinky on his pinky." What was the problem we wondered?

Then the answer came: she had a boyfriend. A boyfriend? Jared chuckled. Yes, a real boyfriend. Someone who holds hands with her, takes her to movies, and probably fucks her in the back of his Chevy, we were loathe to admit. Ah, how far away were the innocent days of fingering and kissing in the library stacks! I would soon find out.

Strange that Benny Will and Jared's brother, Jimmy Smallwood, and Ronnie Rongo would offer me a ride to basketball practice, which, being across town at the old high school, was a long walk but one I usually made. Strange because I didn't hang out with them that much and they weren't on my team. Wasn't Ronnie Kiki's new boyfriend? Even with my instincts beginning to tingle I somehow still thought of Kiki as a beautiful land of Spring days and, being thirteen, where I was allowed to roam free. The thought that she, now at fourteen, "belonged" to someone else, I don't think, odd as it sounds, that it even crossed my mind.

"Josh," Benny said turning his eyes from the road for a quick glance at me in the back seat, a big stack of books on my lap, "I know someone who wants to kick your ass." Perhaps it was the filthiness of my retort that determined at least part of the events about to unfold. It wasn't that out-of-the ordinary, what I said. A thirteen year old is capable of spewing out an astonishing line of invective: he doesn't mean what he says much, he's mimicking the older boys or things he sees on TV for the most part and he often doesn't have the life experiences to inform him that what he says is, indeed, terribly filthy, even for adults.

"Yeah," I replied. "I know someone who wants to lick my ass—french it!"

Looking back after all these years I'm certain that the boldness of this retort could very well have caused my ill wishing classmates to rethink their original plan, which was probably to simply drag me out of the car at some secluded spot near the old school, we practiced in the old gymnasium, allow me to raise my fists to defend myself and then beat me into a bloody pulp. I think that the severity of what I said, its scatological content, full as it was of lurid image and innuendo as to the sexual preference of its recipient, was shocking enough for a high schooler, and possible proof enough of my fiestiness, that my assailants must have scrapped the idea of a fair fight and decided to go with a plan "B" that assured them of victory. Ronnie Rongo cold-cocked me.

I vaguely remember a car door opening. Sliding across the back seat of Benny's beat up Ford, my books in hand. I think I must have also thought that my flippant remark had pacified them. I hardly felt "in danger." Then after… nothing.

When I came to, my head throbbing, I noticed late autumn leaves clinging to my jacket. I had been rolling across the ground. Why? The basketball practice had been underway for quite some time. But I didn't know that yet. Vast lacunae of time had sprung up in my brain. Like a robot I went to the dressing room and began suiting up. But then Jared and a few other friends came in.

"Hey man. What happened, man? No, man, put your shoes back in the bag, man. You ain't practicing today, man. Practice is over, man. We was waitin for you, man. Wonderin where you was at? But now I see you been laying in the grass out front somewhere, man. You been hit, man. Somebody done hit you, man. Who was it?"

Later, a rumor went around that Ronnie had a list and was gonna get us all, all the upper echelon of the Feel Kiki's Leg Club. But he only got me, then I guess he got tired of it. I never tried to get revenge. He was pretty big. He would've killed me in a fair fight. Maybe cold cockin me was merciful. Nobody fooled around with Kiki after that, at least until after high school.

Still, even now at fifty, I haunt bookstores in Budapest. Yes, looking for that book that will give me all the answers I never found, that will change my life, I keep thinking she's still waiting there, somewhere in the stacks, waiting for me to kiss her, to run my hand up her beautiful white dress.

Ahhh, another Spring. How can I describe the tumult in my mind over the last few months? How shall I sort out the prominent thoughts from mere fancy? How can I learn to be utterly candid? What is it I am feeling?

Aging. Thoughts of it, fear of it, is perhaps the dominant theme running through my thoughts and actions these days. Everywhere I look I see lost Youth. My yearning for sex with young women is so intense sometimes I feel sick with it. Normal social outlets for dating are mostly denied to the foreigner. He simply doesn't fit in. He sometimes meets a local female outcast, or libertine, sympathetic to his situation. But this is rare. And sometimes dangerous. Masturbation of course provides some relief but only for a few hours then lusts return! Ha ha!

For a number of years I thought I might simply be able to find a sex partner by just walking around town. It worked several times! But more often it just resulted in some embarrassing rejection. Or worse, a rather protracted wild goose chase.

It's interesting to see yourself, especially as a foreigner, as simply a sort of free electron, unconnected to the host culture. Just walking around. I have no one I would call a true friend, just some guys in the band I'm with now. But their Hungarianess separates them a little from the true inner recesses of my heart. That's a complex judgment I hope I can clarify further at some point.

I tried valiantly to develop close ties with fellow expats here, but without real success, though there have been moments of generosity and affection beyond that of standard decency, moments of what Maugham called, in his autobiography, "loving kindness." I've always needed the practical help of others to find my way in the world but when I tried to return the favor with niceness, affection, attention, even compassion, I found it wasn't always accepted or even needed; thus the phrase in one of Angelika's letters to me, "People don't need nice." At least not as much as I might have thought back in my young manhood when I went around being nice to so many around me, craving their affection and attention in return.

Of course, I was just following the gut feeling of what I thought of as my true nature. I loved, I empathized with, I felt compassion for my fellow creatures. But somehow it was mixed with simple attraction as well. Could I simply have wanted to win the favor of those I was attracted to? I suddenly found myself useless. The strong and beautiful, I found out, didn't need my niceness. It would have better served the truly needy, the poor, the sick. But I was too egotistical then to make such a sacrifice. Eventually, I saw my niceness as a result of my own need for attention. I was particularly interested in the attention of the strong and beautiful. This, I must have hoped, would give me security in both a practical and erotic way. The Strong would see my usefulness and the Beautiful would be moved to grant me certain favors!

I always craved a mentor, to learn some complicated craft as an apprentice. I never really found one. To have had a mentor lover! That must of been my deepest craving. But who can say? The traces of that time are found only in fragments strewn through the memories of Youth: half erased, illegible grafittis of thought and conversation, headless torsos of forgotten meetings, shards of artifacts, of places. To this day, whenever I pick up my guitar and sing, "There are places I remember...", etc., a chill runs down my spine.

Outside my window, the bounty of Spring is beginning to collect. Soon the overabundance of summer is upon us, almost boring us with its plenty. Then suddenly an arrow shot from somewhere pierces thick humid air. A fierce wind whips up one day. And when it disappears my face in the mirror has lost its rosiness. A paleness settles down upon it. Ashen. The hair, the twigs, the leaves, after one last burst of color, they turn vaguely silver, the color of Autumn clouds. Then the destroying rains. The shrouds of snow. Why did God make me, make such plenty, only to take it all away?

Boethius says the "taking away" is illusion. Only because I am a creature in Time do I see the dearth of summer's plenty. In true Eternity there are no longer any seasons. But perhaps something even more beautiful, what the Beauty of the Seasons only hinted at. Why do I have a clouded vision I cannot fully understand? But as I age I begin to see the culprit: Desire. I want love, life, lust, fame, fortune. I have a vague concept of the Eternal Heavenly Reward but it's too abstract for my animal mind.

Only in fragments do I glimpse it. In my children, my sorrow, true sorrow, when one has reached the utmost of his humanity and is full of pity and compassion for himself and others, or when hate destroys the little faith one had nurtured like the little plant in my kitchen that never grows but refuses to die. Then I see a sudden glimpse of the end. My Death.

I find myself hoping this or that person will at least be at my funeral and will at least eulogize me in some way that pushes my infinity forward even if ever so slightly. Then lust withdraws a little and seems momentarily useless. Quickly in my self pity I long for the comfort of a woman's voice, her touch. I am Adam once again alone in the Garden. But it's only the Garden of man's self made myth. The Real Garden is, maybe, yet to come. Perhaps as an old man I will finally believe it. And be willing to go there, to pass through the Dark Wood of my Death and enter into the Eternity of my ancestors.

Evening falls and I feel restless. I've kept myself in all day, not for any reason: I had nowhere to go. The paralysis of being broke creeps into you in subtly sinister ways. Such loneliness, though, sitting in this little apartment day after day, I have never known. So, it's time to get out there and look around. Take a walk.

If you walk up the lengthy little street beside my building, you eventually reach Fehervari Road. When you get there you've arrived at a kind of Frostian crossroads: go right and you will soon enter the city center in all its cosmopolitan-eity, the many bridges over the river to the other side of the city, the boulevards, the bars, the clubs, the churches, the restaurants, people in vast squares standing around waiting for buses, chatting on benches, or disappearing down a subway stair. The shopkeeper standing by her door in the twilight lull, savoring her cigarette and looking out incredulously at the cheap-skate world, shaking her head, or suddenly letting go with a harrowing laugh as some friend passes by with a story that confirms their joint dismissal of mankind in general and their fellow citizens in particular.

The shops along the boulevard are like cells in a prison that has somehow let its inmates rebel and disintegrate into anarchy. Yet by Seven everything closes and the shadowy nightlife begins to stir. The tourist, the hotelier, the musician and the pimp suddenly appear as the set changes and new props are put in place. The city paints her lips and dabs on a thick slash of rouge. She's beautiful even in her tasteless whore's tight clothes.

But instead, one turns left, the other way. Under the train trestle and the other side of the tracks, it's a different world. Or should I say it has nothing to with THE WORLD but everything to do with this world, the one before your eyes. And ears. The freight train screams as it roars by over your head. The neighborhood cafe, automotive repair shops, offices of small struggling companies and government agencies, a video rental shop, a rough bar with zombie wineheads standing at chest-high tables, eyes rheumy with cheap wine, despair and something beyond despair that can't be described. The walls the color of stagnant pond water. Some young boys sauntering down the street as the traffic begins to slow to an evening trickle, one might stand in front of the cafe embracing a big blond that no longer belongs to him, yet might be seduced into one more night of lust in the upstairs flat, her boyfriend off working late somewhere, probably seducing the boss' wife. The school girl strolling dreamily home, a small plastic bag of groceries and cosmetics in her hand, her protective father waiting impatiently for her, her mother chain-smoking in front of the stove.

This is the life denied to me, the outsider. And they quickly cover themselves who suddenly perceive me as one. But there isn't time for them to put on their rougy mask and I see into them at a crucial moment. It's almost too much. To see so deeply into the seductive twilight of their real lives reveals the sorrow of all life—especially life in a European city. The City, the destroyer of Youth.

Wishing you many gigs—

Josh

39

The sunset stacks up orange layers against blue. Clouds are like fragments of a broken-down stone fence with rocks dislodged and bulging. The green of the hollow, rolling meadow is dark as the eastern sky toward Medina and out over the highway where planes come in low to the runway. Thoroughbred racehorse grazing land surrounds on all sides as far as you can see.

These were days before the advent of big pick-up trucks jacked up on huge tires, when people could still walk down a country road without getting blown off, clinging to their lives. Doc would say that something changed after Jimmy Carter, something that had always been the same before. An old world was shoveled under as a new one began to appear. I see Agnes going through old photographs, her eyes tearing up as she sits beside the vase of Jonquils, "The pretty world is dying and an ugly one has taken its place."

Then when Reagan got in it all disappeared for good. People didn't have things like they do now. Didn't know they needed them. Back then Marshall still used a 49 Ford truck with a water tank on the back for irrigating the tobacco. In the cool of the late summer evening, Rickey Boy and TLC would drive down the alley cut between the fields of yellow broad-leafed burley tobacco leaves and TLC would lean out as far as he could to spray into the rows from the truck bed with the hose so water could reach all the plants. There wasn't much room to stand on the truck bed, the water tank was so big. Rickey Boy kept the truck tight to the tobacco row with one hand, rolling a Prince Albert cigarette with the other. You could hand-roll about a hundred more cigarettes from loose tobacco from a can at about half the price of store-bought readymades. People used the can for different things. The deep red, flip-top tins, embossed as they were with an austere portrait of Prince Albert, work hands didn't know who he was but of course, little Allie (Doc) did make great toothbrush holders.

This was before the automatic irrigation sprayer, an ingenious device that turned itself 360 degrees powered by its own spray. Shiny aluminum pipe zig-zagged through Water Maple like the Tinker Toys Doc and Josh played with on the cool burgundy rug on Bertha's floor after taking a bath under the rusty shower nozzle in the cellar of her house under the hill. "There was an old woman lived under a hill. And if she's not gone she's livin' there still"

The orange Highboy tractor was parked in the shade of a huge solitary oak waiting for the moment when it would be called forth to exterminate the insect population bent on devouring the crop. - Edgeton Examiner, October 15, 1990, reported from the proceedings of the Kentucky Environmental Protection Agency; Dr. Albert " Doc" Celeste, Chairman.

"As I look out at the distinguished scientists, politicians, environmentalists and concerned citizens gathered here to determine the fate of our land, something my old Transy professor Jimmy Broadus once told me comes to mind. He said we are in a great war, a fight to the death, with the insect world and, man, they are winnin'!"

The tuxedoed grasshopper with cane and monocle. A carry-over from Old Empire fashion. The Planter's peanut symbol or Jiminy Cricket. These were the things grasshoppers reminded Doc and Josh of. The highboy stood some nine feet high so it could easily clear the tops of the hearty Burley leaves. They brushed against the shiny orange underside of the metal platform where the driver stood and here the paint had been chipped away to a glossy gray sheen by the shuffling of his feet. The highboy carried the insecticide tanks, gray with plastic tubes filled with urine-colored liquid coming out of them. The tubing then ran down to bottom rubber nozzles arranged around the periphery of the driver's platform.

Marshall once had a dry type of insecticide so lethal that merely throwing a handful of it onto a swarm of flies in the feed barn would kill them instantly on contact. "They don't bite! they don't even light!" said the TV. But they were talking about mosquitoes, then outnumbered on the dew-wet summer nights only by the fireflies.

Once there were so many more insects. Waves of moths, white in the headlights would wash over the car in a constant barrage like snow, car grills caked with an oatmeal of moth wings.

- Josh, July 1967

The highboy's black rubber nozzles hung down, brushing the tips of the ripening leaves, hung down like the arms of a robot in a bad sci-fi movie Josh would go see with Jared and Carlo and Harris and Hector. Maybe Free, the Jimi Hendrix of Edgeton would be in the front row.

"Josh, don't you sit in the front. It's bad for your eyes," Agnes said. In the movie theatre, they would make out with girls in the back row. Jared with Anita Thrush and Josh with Kiki La Salle. If the girls couldn't get out of the house the boys went alone and threw popcorn at the screen and filled in dialogue with dirty words. Randolph Scott would say something like, "Well, whadda ya want me to do about it?" And Jared would jump up from his seat and yell something like, "I want you to eat me!" Or this: Lil, the obligatory prostitute dance hall girl in westerns says, "Goodbye, Kid, you know I'll be waitin' when you pass through this way again." Scott: "Yeah, be careful, Lil..."; Jared: from the crowd, "Yeah, don't take any wooden dicks!"

Now, these boys are walking toward the edge of the field that becomes the old high school grounds, silhouettes against the blazing western sky, walking east to where the traveling carnival has set up their tents and tables and rides. KISSELL BROS. CINCINATI, OHIO. Swarthy roustabouts, their thick black hair slicked back like Free Morton.

One night, when Josh was still a kid, he heard Free play "Green Onions" at a jam down on the Kentucky River. He played on an old, beat up sunburst Stratocaster. Josh would never hear anything so beautiful until the night Bobby Paganini played "Electric Ladyland" on the little stereo in his room. Sylves had played drums that night and Duke Madison, Sylves' old band mate in LA, had also sat in on alto sax. Medina seemed full of great rockabilly country pickers in those days who later realized they didn't have to keep banging their arms out of whack on old high-action Martins, playing Bluegrass, but could switch to country-style chicken pickin, move to Nashville, and make a lot more money. There they played electric guitars with lower action, lighter gauge strings, and amps which enabled them to be heard over loud drummers. The great country star, Ricky Skaggs, with whom Josh, years later, would play a few gigs, was of this tradition. And though they made their way over the years through the irrational world of the music industry, they would all, Josh too, come back to their old Bluegrass roots in Kentucky.

Marshall said you could always tell a Kentuckian away from home by the sad homesick look on his face. Judge Daddy said, "In all my travels, I never met a Kentuckian who wasn't on his way back home." But other than being aboard ship in the south Pacific in WW II, Marshall had only been away from Kentucky once himself. It was a business trip to Washington with Senator Demeter. Sylvester

Moore had also gone and driven the big silver Cadillac in that fine Count Basie-looking hat he wore. Marshall got too drunk in the Hungry I night club one night, the teetotaling Senator had retired long before, listening to Phil Harris, and teased Sylves about getting white women. Sylvester was high and drunk and perhaps paranoid but, out of character, got offended and they almost came to blows. Later they walked arm in arm down Pennsylvania Avenue at three am singing improvised scatological lyrics songs of that era, "Honey Suck My Toes," the old prison classic, "I Hate to Leave My Buddies Behind," and "When Sunny Sniffs Glue," sometimes still taking drunken roundhouse swings at each other but missing.

And now four boys approached the Water Maple County fairgrounds. Josh spoke out first. In the distance, a Ferris wheel careened through the air like an animal out of control but that always seemed to right itself at the last moment and avoid crashing into the poor hillbilly souls underneath.

"It was such a coincidence. I saw her going into the library while I was waiting for Mom to pick me up from basketball practice. I only had about twenty-five minutes or so to spare but I saw it all in a flash. I was going to go in there and kiss her."

"Well, what could you do? We're male. We've been programmed to seek out new female realms of flesh," said little Jared. Then quoting the guy in Dr. Strangelove, which they'd just seen at the Edgeton picture show, "'Women sense my power. They seek it. But they shall not get my essence —my…'" and then everyone chimed in, "'MY PRECIOUS BODILY FLUIDS!'"

"O no, she'd never get that of course but no… there she was, standing where the science books are. A place I'd never been. I just can't read that stuff. Not saying it's not important. But what would a scientist have said. She was so beautiful. A white dress that came down about mid-thigh. A jumper? We both knew I was going to kiss her. I said something first after I walked up to her which I've forgotten, it was probably so stupid and irrelevant to anything. I kissed her, put my tongue in her mouth, etc…"

"That's called 'frenching' by those less ingenuous, Josh," Jared said flippantly. "Is this supposed to be interesting? How many times do I have to hear this story?"

"It would be interesting for some of us if you weren't such a quare, Jared," said Carlo, growing impatient and trying to suppress a smile. Jared then calmly walked over to Carlo and began simulating a kind of dog-style sex act which Carlo scooted out from under in a besieged female way giggling and cursing at the revenge bent sex-crazed plaintant.

"Get away from me yew fuckin' Quare!"

"O you thilly boy, you," said Jared, "'I'm in yer chair and I love it there.'" quoting some country parody hit back during the CB craze. "Ten-four back door. Put yr pedal to the metal whatcha waitin' for? I done been grounded my rig impounded." Blah blah blah.

"No, listen, you latent homosexuals," Josh interrupted. "She was so beautiful and the sun coming in the library window. And I just reached up my hand into her panties and I didn't know what to do, it was my first third base and I put my finger around in her pubic hair kissing her all the time 'cause I think any second she's gonna stop me but she didn't. I couldn't believe it. I still feel weird about it. Her breath was salty but she had gum in her mouth, which was cool. And I could smell her thingy a little on my fingers when I touched her cheek. Her face was so soft. Her thingy..."

"Thingy! Can't you just say PUSSY, Josh," said Jared, exasperated. "Wait a minute! Did this really happen?"

"...didn't smell bad but I wouldn't say it smelled pleasant. That wouldn't be the right word. It smelled like... being afraid, like morning, like the pond below the house on a fall afternoon. It all just hit me and I thought now we're going upstairs and fuck but I don't know how to fuck so I'm feeling scared and then maybe she knows we'll never get to the upstairs and someone walks by and frowns, a grownup, and I look at the clock and it's all over. I'm walking in a dream back to Madison's drugstore and my mom is waving at me and yelling for me to hurry up. And Kiki gives me a smile through the window as I float by and points her chin into her collar bone you know that real cute way girls do it."

"HZZGAW HZZGAW," fake snored Jared. "Is this the epic Russian novel version of your first finger fuck?"

"Yeah, boys, I reckon it is," Josh said in that resigned cowboy voice of the Walt Disney narrator.

They reached the gate of the carnival which was no more than a few bales of hay, a card table and a short picket fence strung together with chicken wire. A fat man with red eyes Josh had never seen before was taking tickets. It seemed a lot, a buck and a half to walk into a place.

"No, Josh, I got a better pussy story then that'n. My big brother Hart said one Saturday night in Nashville he'd just got finished eating a big ol' steak (he pronounced it "shteak") and some girl came up to him on the street and said she liked his looks and they went back in an alley right down town and he fucked her standing up against the wall! Now, that's the way to do it!"

"That's the way quares do it, you mean," said Carlo, getting ready to run. "I'll getchee later, boy," Jared's sharp eyes faking anger seemed to say. Carlo saw that he'd burned out the joke.

"Abandon ship! Abandon ship! Routine getting boring! Boredom alert! Boredom alert!" Free runs up.

"Hey, boys, come quick, there's a guy over here whose ball toss game is screwed up and he don't know it yet. E' body's winnin' cartons of Marlboros and Kools and Camels and everything! Come on! You gotta check it out!"

The boys ambled over incredulously but sure enough there was the ball toss man looking perplexed and Kiki LaSalle and Anita Thrush with some guy they'd never seen laughing and stacking up their cigarette carton winnings. Josh was a little nervous since he knew the guy must know he and Kiki used to make out in the library and the picture show. But the guy seemed older and not much concerned with such things. He kept spinning a set of keys around his finger and chewing gum. Those were car keys! Josh realized. This dude is old enough to drive a car, Josh thought.

He looked at Kiki. She seemed changed since they'd stopped seeing each other two months before. He didn't know how. He supposed he'd changed too. One night talking to her on the phone, it just didn't feel right. She talked funny. Then she'd said she was going with her mother to visit her grandmother but he saw her the next day walking with Ronnie Rongo, a guy on the football team. It was weird enough to see her with someone like that but now THIS guy. He felt a clinch down in his stomach, a feeling that he'd never known the real her, that he knew no one. Deep in his heart he was nothing. Who am I? Look up at the sky. Cold distant stars. Sun gone down. No refuge. Look. There's Free. He's not lovesick. Just have fun. Walk home. Tranquility Pike in the Dark. Red cigarette fire. Win a buncha cigarettes. She saw me. Just pretended not to notice. Jared. Carlo. Doesn't matter to them. They don't really know her. Guess I didn't either.

"Well, boys," said the Louisville guy, giving Josh a once over with a good-natured smirk, "I 'spect I've won about all the cigarettes I need for the rest of my life!" and let go a hearty laugh. Kiki hung on his arm and giggled still pretending not to see Josh. They walked away to another booth.

"Guess it's time to go see the 'rat-man,' said the Louisville guy. " Gotta earn a livin' somehow" (another healthy laugh).

"Sounds good to me, boys," said Jared, "let's win some smokes and follow suit." The ball toss concession man looked unconcerned as the boys tossed the ball into the sagging right corner, always hitting black or red and winning dozens of packs of Kools, Marlboros, Chesterfields and Camels, which they crammed into their pockets and rolled up in their shirt sleeves.

The rat man ran the most popular concession at the fair. Under his tent stood a large circular table with holes in the top of it big enough for a rat to crawl into. Each hole was set into larger squares, each of a different color. In the center of this circle of colored holes sat the rat, a small black and white Norwegian looking fellow (not like the cat sized gray urban denizen Josh would one day see in Budapest) under a dome-shaped, perforated metal covering. Around the perimeter of the table, maybe two feet from the rat's set of holes, lay another circular strip of colored squares. Here the townsfolk, bumpkins, hayseeds and yahoos, farmers, preachers and printers, bankers and children barely able to see over it, gathered 'round the table, lay their nickels, dimes quarters and sometimes even dollar bills down on the squares and waited to see what the rat would do. Gambling was illegal in this bible belt town but somehow nobody ever said anything.

The rat man, the old carny who kept the rat had worked with the creature for so many years that, like couples long married, they'd begun to resemble each other. He stood now in a gap between the two circles of colored squares, the inner one for the rat, the outer for the shouting gamblers, and shouted over them, "ALL DOWN, Now! AW DOWN! AW DOWN! then lifted the perforated metal covering. (Doc said he thought the perforations were there so the rat could look out and see which colors had been most bet on and then go to a different one, thus assuring a bigger take for his rat-ish partner.) The exposed rat paused in the center for a moment, sniffed the air, stood up a little on its hind legs, and then, as the rat man rung a cow bell hanging over its head, scurried down one of the holes.

"RED!" the rat man shouted. A groan went up from the crowd. The rat man strode around the circle with a whisk broom sweeping the many loser's nickels and dimes into his apron, stopping here and there to give a small payoff, always it seemed two to one… a winning nickel paid two nickels, a dime, two dimes, a twenty dollar bill… bet by the lawyer with a beer or two under his belt, forty dollars and so forth. Did anyone ever really win anything? Nobody beats the ratman. The rat man went around the circle of colors sweeping nickels and dimes into his apron, but Cotton, the light-skinned boy with the wild blond afro grabbed him by the arm. "Hey, cracker, I had a dollar on red, now, you pay me my two dollah"! The rat man's beady eyes narrowed down on the man. "You put it down after the rat went in its hole, pal. I saw you. Now, go on, blow"!

Cotton looked hard at the old long-nosed carnie. He put his faceup close to him and started to draw back the flat of his hand to strike, when he saw the county deputy in street clothes walk by with his kids. He thought better of it. The rat man had winced and drawn back his head anticipating the blow. Instead, Cotton turned and walked quickly away. Looking back over his shoulder he said, "I'll be back, motherfucker! I'll fit your fuckin' head in that rat hole!"

40

TLC held up the iron tongue of the grass seed stripper and waited for Ricky Boy to back the small Farm-All tractor toward him. It was early June but the shade from the maples, ailanthuses, and walnuts was thick and cool behind the machinery shed. TLC stood bent over with a hand over his brow looking into the morning sun holding the linchpin in his mouth. The popping sound of the tractor came nearer but Ricky Boy's curses could be hard over it.

"Come on you half-wit sumbitch, hold the goddam thing up! This thing ain't no magnet. How you 'spect me to see something you hidin' in the grass?" TLC adjusted the hitching tongue even higher than he had originally thought suitable for his old field mate, waited until the holes in both the tractor hitch and the seed stripper's tongue were lined up and then smoothly, as he had done it a thousand times, dropped the pin through.

Without even the slightest hesitation Ricky Boy was off like a shot. TLC had to almost leap free to avoid being run over as the jolting snap of metal sounded and the two machines meshed: Ricky Boy pulled out towards Marshall and Sylvester and the two boys who were pushing another stripper towards the first one TLC had just hooked up. They pushed it to the right back corner of the first seed stripper, lined up the holes as TLC had done, dropped the linch pin, hooking the two strippers together. They did the same for the left corner of the first stripper and so, looking straight on, the configuration of tractor hooked to three bluegrass seed strippers resembled a kind of flying "V."

The delicate cornmeal yellow light of the morning sun was already burning off the misty dew as the V-shaped processional of seed strippers moved toward the field. It stopped at the edge. Ricky Boy impatiently stopped the tractor and waited while Sylves leaped off the lead machine and threw each of them one by one into gear so that now each machine was powered by the turning of it own wheels as they followed behind the motion of the tractor. The tractor moved on again, Rickey Boy singing, "Whiskey, whiskey ruin of men, that's the reason I drink gin" and then, "Don't monkey 'round with someone else's monkey…" but no one seemed to hear it. Instead their eyes seemed to be watching the now rotating teeth of the stripper combs and random bits of useless chaff they spit into their tin troughs as the machines skirted the edge of the field.

They reached the meat of the field, the thigh-deep, amber stalks of ripe bluegrass stretching out to the horizon in gentle undulations, interspersed with snatches of wild flowers, daisies, queen Anne's lace, purple thistle and iron weed (a flower Marshall always said was a sign of rich ground) and beetle sized bumble bees with tails of dew- drenched yellow fur whirring through the air among the drunken flight of sulphur butterflies. Atop each single stalk of bluegrass sat the prize, the gold the harvester coveted: the ripe, amber seed head, fat as an asparagus tip, still wet and heavy with dew. They pulled up slowly to the edge of the field.

Suddenly, like racehorses from a starting gate, the flying V of harvesters was off with a jolt of metal and rattling chain. Dust and seed and all manner of field chaff began flying every which-away as the men and boys, Doc was fourteen but Josh was only nine, began attending to their separate machines, cleaning out the weeds from the grease-daubed gears, stuffing the lava flow of seed and stalk, scooped from the bottom of tin troughs by the wooden cross slats, deep into the burlap sacks. All that could be heard was the clicking of the sharp-toothed seed combs as they went around and around the field, bringing everything up that caught between the wedges of metal teeth, and the occasional shouting of Marshall's instructions from the lead stripper to Ricky Boy just above him on the tractor. A complex labyrinth of ground hog holes suddenly loomed in front of the tractor and Ricky Boy slowed and swerved to avoid them. Marshall had said that these were man killers if the front wheel should fall into one and turn over. "Old man Gene Morton's boy was killed thataway. The steering wheel went into his chest so hard it knocked him off and he fell under the big side tires. Killed him deader'n four o'clock. They say ol' man Gene never got over it. Just drank all the time. Last I heard he's still up at the feeble - mind institute in Frankfort." Josh and Doc called them Ground hog hotels. The dirt 'round this one was freshly dug, grave-like in the heaping mound. "I'll get back over here with that thirty ought six and see if I can't kill these bastards this evening" A brace of meadowlarks flushed from the tall grass.

Dear Crip,

My life seems to plod along, though a Hamletian/Prufrockian voice, as Doc would say, of "quiet desperation" keeps whispering in my ear. Since the birth of our child, Helen and I have grown more distant from each other. I remember I had come to the hospital to visit her one morning (late morning, since in those days she indulged me in my habit of sleeping late). We were sitting in the waiting room which adjoined the recovery room where she was allowed to sleep with and nurse the child for the next few days. I remember I was telling her some probably inane story I had deluded myself into thinking was important when suddenly she held up her finger and shushed me in mid-sentence to better hear whether the baby was crying. It was a normal enough response for a new mother yet it shocked me in some strange way, especially when she returned and did not inquire as to the end of my story but only reminded me to bring several packages of diapers on my next visit. And when we would go in together to the baby's room she not only seemed annoyed with every footstep I made, no matter how softly I tried to make them, but she also seemed to take no pleasure in my joyful reactions to the baby, his little coos and squeaks, but was evermore irritated and vigilant against my coming too near or touching it the wrong way, etc. A strange sense of... what? humiliation? crept over me as I descended the hospital stair. Quickly, of course, it dissipated as I returned to the lonely apartment and plunged into my work or lost myself in the newspaper or some book, but over the last few years as the boy has grown, and you know what a great kid he is, that sense of rejection has never disappeared. The distance between us has only grown. Our lives are completely centered around the boy, and the life we once knew—our romantic life – has disappeared. We are both over-protective and neither of us trust the idea of a sitter, but even when the child is asleep or being watched for as briefly as half an hour —in that time we rarely say much to each other and when we do the conversation is only mechanical.... I guess this all sounds pretty dull to you. How's music going? I noticed the review of your record on some indie website. Good for you! And thanks for sending that CD. Love to hear from you again sometime.

As ever,

Josh

41

JOSH ON THE BUS

It had been a tough summer for Dad. Lots of steers got shipping fever and the market was down. The least little thing could set him off. Tobacco market was getting stacked against the small farmers and bluegrass was down to almost nothing.

The trucks were coming in ready to load up the vaccinated steers and take them to the big stockyard in Medina. Many had been de-nutted and de-horned. Pretty painful for the steer but at least it's pretty quick. It has to be done if you're gonna raise cattle. A steer with his nuts and horns is wild and unpredictable. Tear up a fence, ride the ass of other steers. The weak ones get sick and beat up. (What would YOU feel like if a 700lb steer tried to climb up on yo' ass all day long every day? A steer who still had his nuts would literally break down a weaker steer's back and kill it). Marshall used to look at a load of steers and say, "I wonder how many riders they got innair?" It sounds cruel and it is but if you eat McDonald's or steaks or whatever, you're in on it. So it ain't just the farmer's fault.

Fried steer nuts with bulldog gravy is as good a eatin' as they is! We calls 'em calf fries. Or yer daddy called em Rocky Mountain oysters". – TLC

It was one of those typical hot humid July Kentucky days. There was so much blood everywhere all over the barn lot, it really squirts when the horn comes off. I remember Marshall takin' swigs of rubbing alcohol and rinsing his mouth out, he got so much steer's blood in it. A pile of testicles and severed horns laying everywhere, bloodied, flies crawlin'on'em. Steers hot, fly bitten, slingin' their heads wild, snot flyin' out their noses.

I remember Marshall taking me to Morehead once to get a load of tobacco sticks once in that old red pickup he had. I was about 16 or 17 I guess. Pretty much grown you might say. I can remember part of the deal was the guys who sold us the sticks threw in a case of moon shine that had been buried in the ground. They said that improved the taste. Lotta yankees ask me what moonshine tastes like and all I can say is that this was like a clear fine scotch. It wasn't sweet like sour mash. The fellas we bought it from, their grandfathers had known ol' Mr. Dex and Money Joe and Shine. If I think about it maybe I can remember one of the stories the old man told.

But on the way back I remember Marshall (he didn't want me sneakin' and drinkin' any of the shine and we hid it all from Agnes, but said he'd give a jar or two to Sylves) I guess maybe he was a little ashamed at having it but I remember as we were driving back to Edgeton he turned to me from behind the wheel, ceegar wet and rollin' in his mouth, and said, 'Farmin's kinda fun ain't it ? Don't make much money but you have allota fun.' He was like a kid like that sometimes. Before we got home tho' we had a flat (all the weight of the sticks) and he fumed and fretted it over so I thought he was gonna blow a gasket.

Always hated to see my Daddy get so angry but it was, like, in those days of mortgage and debt and interest payments, the least little thing. The old world of Water Maple Farm, Bertha's big fried chicken dinners with all the mountain people, the black men in their white jackets carryin' plates of Bar-b-q, sitting out under the big oak beside the old big mansion smoking, shootin' round ball, the old meadows and groves, the days of one Farm-All and the old Ford water truck—all that shit was changin'.

Ricky Boy and TLC still livin' up in the old block tenant houses with their hollow-eyed wives, pumping the waterspout handle on the old cistern, water pouring over their sun reddened necks, fish belly white backs, farmer's tanned brown arms from short- sleeve bottom tricep down, a bowl of steaming brown beans and corn bread waiting on the table, they and MJ and Shine and Cotton— they all got factory jobs now or else workin' for the prison, or Cotton, I heard was going into the army, bees drone in the rose of Sharon: And he knew it, Marshall knew it was gone, we all did and everything washed down to a gulley of anger and the stagnant water gave off a stench when something stirred it up.

Marshall used to, when we were kids, tell us stories about this Indian warrior:

The great Creek warrior, Simon Benge (Wandering Deer Runner) rode his painted pony through the brush, snapping an Osage Orange branch with a loud snap. He stopped to listen and wondered if he'd heard some little boys and girls crying because since they were bad or if they ever were, the Indian mamas and daddies would make them sleep in a hollow log and wear shoes too big for'em. And the warriors would steal little boys and girls and take them far away to where Indians lived and there wudn't any telephones or crayons to write letters with. Maybe it was the singing of the wind. He rode on til he came to a big flat rock and he tied up his horse and pulled out his lunch which was tuna fish sandwiches and Hawaiian Punch and Milky Way bars and...King Leo peppermint sticks and cinnamon whiskey killers. He was sittin' thar eatin' when he heard voices and he looked out and a- way off down in the valley come a wagon train of white settlers with a herd of cattle and cowboys woopin' and hollerin' movin' 'em through so they could graze on the far hillside. Ol' Ryly Jackson "Logger Jack" Celeste stood tall in the saddle at the front of the caravan with his rifle cradled in his arms like a baby. Then Simon Benge looked down and saw the most beautiful woman he'd ever seen sittin' on the buckboard with coal black hair and pure white skin like marble and cherry red lips and eyes like a Hershey chocolate drop.

Simon Benge rode down to meet the settlers with a white cloth for peace and gave the settlers many things : Hawaiian Punch, Hostess cupcakes, baseball cards and Leo peppermint sticks he wanted to give the girl. She looked a lot like Angelika and Bertha too and she smiled as she crunched on a peppermint stick. Simon Benge said you have come to the land of the spirit of my father who came from far over the mountains. Let his spirit guide your steps aright through this land and give you safe passage. I ask only that you let me ride with you to gaze upon the beauty of this face like the endless bright sky.

"Daddy, Yuuuuk! You know I hate boys!!!"

Well, then they all went to Simon's teepee and had lunch which was (then we'd all chime in) Hawaiian Punch, Tuna fish sandwiches and Milky Ways. "And I put my peppermint stick in the Hawaian Punch like a straw," said Angelika. Then they watched cartoons all night long.

"Now, get in the bed," Marshall would say. If he got impatient he'd look down at us (he was a big man, really) and say, "Watch my mouth! Go pee! Brush your teeth and get in the bed!!! Don't make me come back in here again or I'll... I'll..."

"Make us wear shoes too big for us?" asked Doc.

The stench of the rotting silage. The truckers standin' around with their cattle prods, shocking each other, shockin' themselves to see if they could take the pain, tobacco spit, green trails of nervous cow shit smeared on the gravel here and there. Then a great pile covered with flies. Actually, cow shit is not that bad. We always just said it was like bruised grass. Not near as pungent as dog shit for example. Marshall always had a particular contempt for human shit. One day we rode horses down the Bluegrass Parkway before it was finished, before the endless flood of metal over the black ribbon of asphalt. Then it was just smooth dirt and sand down to the Kentucky River all the way to Lawrenceburg. Little Doc, my big brother, said we were like Daniel Boones of the highway!

Then we tied the horses and rowed across the Kentucky. Well, Dad saw some guy takin' a shit behind a big gravel pile (there was a rock quarry down there) and thought he shudda gone on back up in the woods. How's he gonna wipe his ass? No trees close down here. He huffed contemptuously. Yeah, I can see that sum bitch's little pile from here, he said.

*****

KRIP

The cattle trucks rumbled in and out, rattling the cattle gate as they drove into Josh's family's farm, leaving the hard road and climbing the big hill up past Bertha's house cupped into the hill above the spring, toward the huge feed barn that rose in the clear sky above a network of cattle pens.

Because of the high cost of veterinarian labor, like many cattle farmers, Marshall had decided to learn to administer necessary vaccinations to the cattle himself. This meant that all cattle ready to be shipped to market in Medina had to be rounded up from all the far fields of the farm and put into pens which were connected to a maze of chutes. This is how we did that shit. The big steers were run up the narrow chutes in single file and at the end of the chute there stood a V- shaped opening made of two slabs of oak painted white (like all the rails of the chute were) which hung on runners attached to a cross lintel over the "V". A man (usually Rickey Boy or TLC) could stand to the side and, as a steer approached to leap thru the V, pull the rope attached to the pulleys and runners and catch the steer's head by closing it just tight enough so the big steer couldn't get his shoulders thru—only his head—and the V closed behind his ears, like a pair of scissors, making it impossible to back out either. The steer still had the ability to toss its head up and down the slit of the closed wooden V with considerable and dangerous force (you had to watch your ass coz its head was like somebody slinging a concrete block around) but you could restrain him by simply hooking the steer thru the nose, pulling his head to the side and tying it to the closest post. To secure the steer's back legs ("they can kick hard as a mule") an ingenious system of notches was rigged up behind him, carved into both sides of the chute. After catching the steer's head, somebody would slide a length of iron pipe through a notch and across the length of the chute (maybe 4 feet —and the chute narrowed as you got closer to the V point) and into a notch on the other side one notch closer to the steer than on the side you were standing. Once the pipe was secure against the steer's back legs, a man could work it up one notch at a time, thereby pushing the steer snugly up against the V and severely limiting his movement in any direction. The adjustable V held his head, the pipe, secure in its notches, was pushed up into its back legs, and the walls of the chute itself (also standing in a wider V shape) made lateral movement impossible. With the steer immobilized in this way and other steers packed into the chute behind it, waiting their turn, Marshall could administer what medication the animal needed (or shear off its horns and /or testicles—-both bloody jobs) before it was released and run into another holding pen or turned back out into the field.

The reason I know all this shit is cause I worked for Marshall that summer down there. It wasn't 'til years later I tried to learn guitar but Josh was so good, I got intimidated and just gave up. But then I saw Carlo play with him once. That's what got me on a bass kick. Later, I just happened to be playing with Josh the night Lacy Corman came to town and he just took us both on as part of his road band. It was a cool gig cause he'd made records for major labels and shit. But, in the end, it never really went anywhere.

Steers gettin' more and more nervous in the network of pens. Goddamnit Doc! Marshall said, get that damn steer in line 'fore he…. woop! goddam it! There he goes! Getchee cane and beat him back! I said hit him upside the head 'fore he…! There he goes! There he goes! God damn ! I'll be a son of a bitch! Give me the motherfuckin' cane you candy ass! Quit pussy footin' give it here! Every time that goddam steer shits it costs me a dollar. Did you know that? Josh, quit thinkin' bout beatin' your meat and pickin' that goddam guitar and runnin' round sniffin' those goddam girls you bringin' down to the pond and all that shit and help me get this sumbitch turned around. He's caught his head on the side of the chute. If he gets turned around the other way we'll never get his ass back around we'll have to turn the whole goddam load of 'em out! You hear me?

The steer made a valiant leap but Marshall caught it with a direct blow into the side of his head. But it scared the steer even more and he leaped up and got his legs in one of the notches and was trying to actually leap out of the chute—which would have been better than if he got turned around. (It's amazing how cattle can maneuver considering their size in such a small space). But Marshall wouldn't have it and, man, he just kept beatin' that steer…

He hears the transistor radio over by the chute. ("It shudda been me with that real fine chick…" clkkkkkkkkkkssshhhhhss… that same little cymbal sound I heard. That's when she looked at him on stage that night. "I'm so glad I have you," she said back to me, "But, honey, are you alright? We never seem to talk or anything anymore"… shhhhshshshshshgrrrr… That goddam radio! Those fuckin' drums. I can't hate him. He's like a brother. She doesn't know what or who she wants. "Marshall, I love you so much…. but I can't always be IN love with you. I've known you so long. You're like a big brother." (Young Senator Judge Daddy Demeter picking her up from the ground! "O, my little Aggie!")

Marshall remembers her crying, "Why do you look at me like that? What do you want from me?!!! What do you GODDAMN MEN WANT FROM ME! I've given you everything I know how to give — my heart my voice my ass my tits my cunt my womb! And you still want more!"

Beat that friggin steer silly... and that steer still wouldn't move his head around the right way so we could catch his head and doctor him and cut him... and so he started beatin' his own head into the post thrashin' around and I saw how he'd hit his head so hard one of his eyes had popped out of the socket and was just hangin' down on his cheek all bloody and flies bitin' it.

Marshall came runnin over to Doc and me and yelled, See there! See there! That's what fuckin around does! How many times have I told you boys to keep their motherfuckin' heads turned toward the V-opening! Now look! He grabbed our heads and shoved 'em into the steer's face. Look! Look! Look at that eye! You like that! Look! Then he grabbed us by the hair took us around to the steer's ass and shoved our faces up to his shit covered anus and screamed, neck vein poppin' Ricky Boy turnin' his head away, TLC slack-jawed bewildered rageless-looking, sharp stab to the gut, Look! said Marshall (I smelled the rich odor) That's our goddamn money going out his ass hole! Look! look! The whole fuckin' world is goin' out his fuckin' ass! Look!

42

Those days were hard for Bertha and little Marshall. Lawyers in Edgeton, busy with foreclosures were circling for the kill. Dexter had left a sizable debt. But Rickey Boy's father, Buddy, scavenged around for timber and brought in truckloads of limestone rock from the Kentucky riverbank five miles down the road and tobacco hands and folks all around helped build a new place. Meanwhile, Marshall stayed at Money Joe's in Rylytown up the road. I guess they felt guilty about bein' ol' Dex's moonshinin' buddies (and "co- owners" of the still so black folks would buy whiskey, too) but Bertha never brought it up nor paid much attention to them. She worried that townspeople would belittle her for Marshall stayin' at a black person's house but then she decided after a time that she didn't give a damn (or "a hairy rat's ass" as Dex put it) what people thought.

"Dexter, did you know we was part indian?"

"I'd just soon be kin to a black man as kin to an indian."

43

Bertha More Deerrunner Celeste was a loner. A little girl at the turn of the century who walked the fields around Edgeton, Kentucky alone through the wildflowers, bronzed leaves and snow. She could divine events from the way the flocks of red wing blackbirds dived and divided as they flew or what the mockingbird sang within his song. She had known when Dexter would come walking up "the Avenue," she was only fourteen, to tell her that one day he would marry her. And he gave her a ring. She wore something red every day. She felt she had already seen the great fire that would consume everything, the noise, the trucks and the whiskey. She lost the thread of spinning visions among the trees and soft voices in the wind. Something shook her faith in the worth of her fellow creatures. She was the middle twin of five sisters. Her mother was the center of her life. Everything she did she did for her. She watched her do the cooking. She liked to watch her make clothes. She used a feather stitch in everything she made. Her mother said she'd learned it from her mother, a full-blooded Cherokee from North Carolina. So the day that Bertha put the final touches on her first handmade dress was a big event. The joy welled up in her throat and escaped in little giggles as she ran to show her mother.

She ran across the green circle of yard up the hill from Moore's Creek that sat on a circular limestone foundation covered in spring with a thousand jonquils. Her mother was kneeling in the late March sun looking for something she'd lost in the yard, her black hair shining. She put the wooden clothespin in her mouth and tucked a corner of white sheet under her chin. Her eyes lit up when she saw the dress. "My lawd child, what have you made? Why it's just darlin'!" She held it up against her into the light. It was a dark wine color but with red and emerald bangles and beads sewn in around the neck and wrists. "You know," her mother said, "your sister's prom is comin' up pretty soon. Why don't you let her wear it? It would look soooo pretty on her."

Bertha sits in the rocker now by the window that looks up the hill toward the big maple standing like the Healer Man, crow-colored hair, in his moccasin dance step he danced at the Water Maple County carnival, arms out, pleading to the sky. The children laughed. She sees herself walking to the tree at twilight, the last doves and swallows flittering away. The sun is liquid orange over broad green of tobacco leaves. She pants like a dog in the summer shade as the boy Dexter steals another kiss and puts his hand on her breast.

Shaking, now, as with both arms she raises the lovely dress high over her head and it falls a little around her black braided hair around her head and white neck. Her teeth bare a little as she breathes in and with a moan, a moan the frightened, thirsty cattle make tromping to water or collapsing from the heat, the dove making its long ooou woo ou moan, brings the pathetic little cloth thing down as hard as she can, like a man, against the tree. When she sees it's been torn and ruined with only one blow she becomes infuriated even more as if to punish the little dress for being so sweet and frail. To punish. Punish. Punish. Punish. Again and again she whips the dress against the moss-covered bark, a small wind rustling the leaves a hundred feet up. Flap, flap a dying bird. Waterfowl. Great Blue Heron. Splash. Kagoosh! Until the dress is a shred of bark-stained cloth and thread, pointless buttons dangling. She steadies herself against the great tree, pale and sweating, and vomits.

She sits in the rocker looking out at the great tree in the yellow light. She has remembered every pattern in the tangle of limbs. She lays scraps of silk pieces in her lap and looks at her arthritic hands, the knuckles swollen and red. Pieces of Dexter's ties hundreds of them she snips with the scissors and stitches them back together into crazy quilts and pillow coverings.

"Something useful come from that boy after all." She holds a quilt to the light, smiles satisfied at the red silk backing and thinks of her little Josh and Albert warm under it.

The big house standing splendid in the sun. The horrible night far off.

BERTHA 36

My handsome Dexter left me at the house him drunk going to meet that ol'
Shine and Money Joe and me just cryin. And they laughed sayin', We's kin to him
Miss Berf. He'd get on top of me in that big four-poster mama'd give me and I'd
just lay real still, him huffin' and puffin' and after while I'd say get off Dexter you
can't do nothin' any way. Him always drunk you know. I never did nothin' to him
but I bit his ol' tally whacker one night cause of what he said to me and made
me do, not bad just made a little place but he howled and I tasted the little bit of
blood and then him spewin that stuff all over my pilla cases. But that night I made
sure he'd gone off to meet up with them with that little Martin guitar under his
arm like he loved so much more'n me I 'spect. I went down in the cellar where
now my little grandboys they take their showers, and poured out all them whiskey
jars and broke 'em all too, me and little Marshall. Oh, lard how he yelled and
carried on when he got back. Threw a fit's what he did, clawin' up the hill on his
knees callin' AW naw! Aww Naw! She didn't do it to me and runnin' threw that
door ready to hit my little Marshall with the back of his hand and momma at the
door with that ol' pump action twenty-two papa had sayin' Dexter, if you strike
that child it'll be the last thing you do on this earth.

Bertha snips another piece of necktie and sews it into another. Feather stitch.

She sees her mother's stricken face, the ruined dress at her feet. "Child what
have you done? Oh, lard! Bertha what did you do to it honey? Why? Why?
Honey, come back!" The dress all torn and ruined.

But, one time, after Dex hit me and little Marshall, his Papa, that's Ryly Jackson
"Logger Jack" Celeste, took me up to the doctor, and he asked me so many
questions, and he asked me after awhile with the police standing there if I still
had an active sex life—that's what he said—and I just told him, No, I just lay real
still.

One Saturday morning, sun shining, he got up and fixed himself a huge cup of
strong tea, Josh only drank coffee in the afternoon and even that was never that
habitual until he moved to Europe, or after a big evening meal, had a pleasant
breakfast with Berenice and decided to walk the two miles to work. It was his first
day of being in charge of opening the bookstore. He was a little nervous about it
but then the watery yellow morning light simply over-powered him and he sat at
the bay window of their little apartment sipping his tea and stroking Berenice's
long auburn hair.

I have to go. One last long kiss. She tasted like toast and strawberry jam.

Wanna hit of dope? Nahh. Maybe this evenin' when I get back. Let's go see, 'The Ruling Class' with Peter O'Toole. Get stoned before.

He thought about the dark green sticky tropical lushness of the Kentucky ailanthus- leaved jungles of yard and roadside and marijuana and how the grass was glowing now pond- green in April. The pink and white dogwoods thickened as he turned down Sweet Gum St. The fallen saffron petals of the March-bloomed forsythia had started to form a dark, leafy, yellow sponginess on the ground as he turned off the sidewalk pavement and up into a thin-trailed short-cut along the periphery of Old Governor Marcellus' (the legendary abolitionist) vast yard full of towering tulip poplars and purple beeches with elephant skin bark and exposed roots like the toes of dinosaurs.

Among the dogwoods hung full bee-filled white balls of viburnum, heads drooping under the weight of their dew, undried by the sun because of the thick morning shade against them. By noon they'd be dry and bursting fragrance everywhere. Josh whiffed a faint honey smell of the locusts and the pungent wet grass. Fierce robins scampered about and the shimmering dominant starling. A lone blood droplet-red cardinal darted almost humming bird-like down the row of fragile green lilacs. Old Marcellus' carriage path was now nothing but a fading depression in the spongy forsythia and pine needle ground.

The grasshoppers trill… They buzz by your ear in trills of Latin percussion sounds, like snips of Santana songs and the drone and Doppler effect of the bumblebee drenched in pollen. A little striped chipmunk the color of layered caramel ice cream scurries down a hole.

The first Spring and the last and all of them! And I am alive in the alive world! The cardinal alights on the cord of cut wood. Chain saw in the shade. And there stands the aboriginal tree that he had sat under so many years before, breaking up with Lilian. "These are the dimensions of the great tree," he'd written in his notebook. Now off to work! A new Life! A new job! A new love! ("A new broom! "Health to the new people..." He remembered the night Lilian, up from Smith in his old Boston days, had taken him with her to see Robert Lowell read at Wellesley. He'd read, "My Old Flame…" "My old flame... my wife..." Had it meant anything then?

A hot Kentucky day in April was approaching. Joshua Celeste in full harmony striding down Medina Road, the same one old Marcellus, on his way to Washington to speak before the senate, must've been driven down one hundred thirty years before.

There was the tree. There was the carriage path. "Koch" engraved in brass on the hard enamel red and black paint of the carriage door. "Coach" is derived

from the Hungarian, "Kocs." The trees. He thought about secret walks with
Berenice, her husband Jerry still at work. But the caretaker seeing them, but only
wanting to talk in his loneliness about the trees.

"That pecan tree there was probably planted by Marcellus' father,
Agnes'maternal great, great grandfather, thought Josh. It's over three hunnert
year old," the old caretaker said. The Versailles-like hedged in garden Old
Marcellus' wife had done in European copy. "I know just as much about
landscaping as that old billy goat Thomas Jefferson does!" Josh enters the garden
and looks into the glass table top sitting on the wrought- iron table. Walking
toward the street again towards the bookstore he sees himself in the crystal glass,
movie of the future: him sitting at this same table with Crazy Reddie, Wanda
and the old caretaker's banjo-pickin' son, Buddy, having just eatin' some LSD,
watching the sunset on a tranquil summer evening, bluegrass music sifting up into
the trees.

But now he's alive again. Winter. Greyhound bus of New England night.
Lilian's love dead and gone. Wounds almost healed. The Resurrection of Joshua
Celeste. J. C. It fit. Jesus Christ.

"I never made the connection," Marshall said, when Josh asked him about it
once. "But what's wrong?- it bother you? Hell, you can change it if you want to.
Wudn't bother me a damn bit. You always gonna be my little boy, that's all I care
about."

The soil pungent with insects. The towering poplars with small hands. "And no
one, not even the rain..." Lilian had read to him in bed. Jonquils still in bloom.

The same trees grew on Water Maple Farm. The same flow to the fields as
at Marcellus' estate, a National Historic Site. This garden, this huge front yard
was once a great meadow that reached "all the way to Main St." All of Medina
was once Old Marcellus' farm or else he hunted deer through all of it. Some
Shawnee a hundred years before, led by Simon Benje, had killed a white hunting
party somewhere not far from here, near the grave of Marcellus' father. A farm
like Water Maple but, here, Medina had grown and encroached, the highway
snaking in slow and encircling old Marcellus' fields one by one, till they got about
twenty acres from the house and the city said no more, they placed a lime stone
monument in front of it with a plaque that said:

> "In this place, in 1819, the first Hereford steers were raised in the New World by
> Governor John Marcellus, farmer, statesman, writer. Commemorative speech given July
> 1936. 'May Almighty God bless this, the New Garden.'"

NATIONAL HISTORIC REGISTER

When Josh unlocked the bookstore door, he went straight to the "Kentucky" section, got down a biography of John Marcellus and thumbed through it. It was his day to vacuum the floor but he still had a few minutes before the customers would be coming in. He wanted to write the poem of every spring, of all time, the dimensions of the yellow sunlit tree with the leaved halo of green like a hand against the morning sky, this first morning of his life.

Now, Josh, home off the road after so many years, after all the loves of his life, Marshall's old house. Stares at the undulating, bluegrass meadow that was once a sea No man changed this field. They plowed it, cleared it of a few trees. But here, where a sink hole curves into the limestone mound, a half cup of out-cropping, stones bursting through the ground, too dangerous to plow, too steep, fox and mink caves, like dark eyes, this has remained, all this as far as I can see. Up there to Rickey Boy and TLC's house, it's always been this way. A piece of farm that was and is the sea bed covered with loam now and everything dried down to the trickle of Moore's Creek, flowing to the palisades of the Kentucky.

44

SYLVESTER

After I hit the joint and then that Vodika, the place got real empty even though they was a big crowd in front of me. Before that it was horn sections that shone yellow with the cymbals and dudes actin cool goin backstage of this little concrete slot of a dressing room smokin reef. I swear that white dude lead singer cat musta laced that water bottle with XTC or something. Why was he passin it around, that still water, to every one?"

"No, not that," I said. "You had that dizzy spell that time coz you'd been sleepin strange hours and smoking so much crack. You got so dizzy I thought you had a mild heart attack or something. And Josh, God bless him, saved your ass."

"My BLACK ASS!"

"Right. Nobody else wanted to be part of your death, they turned away."

"Most people didn't notice you," Sylvester said. "You never make eye contact with 'em. Just a few chicks you eyed down, and washed up music buddies out there. It's been a long time since you played with them. But Josh, he's a saint, ain't no doubt.

"The sad thing about musicians is they think the rest of the world is like music. They wrong. Music is the oasis, man, not the desert endless yellow of nothing in the light of day.

"Maybe that's what happens to somebody like me. Can't make it in the US. Can't make it in Europe. Game over. Periodicity. Your body is lookin' for a way out coz it knows you can't look out for it. Explore the possibilities. Maybe what happened to me that night was, like, Hendrix musta said: "Hey, I'm Jimi Hendrix... maybe I can even die." And so he went into his Alpha Jerk, you know, the way you jerk right before you go to sleep, and just kept on going right out. Anyway, I wasn't feelin' too good.

"Where is Josh tonight? Playin' somewhere? I kept thinkin' to myself. Then it was just that one thing: he said, "Dig, dig" when he came in the club saw me all laid out, passed out and shit and they told him how I'd fainted behind the drums. And I heard his voice and came out of it.

Sylves,

Yo, O Great Sage,

Permit me the impudence of this crude mode of communication. I feel as if I should've learned telepathy—that would be my mode of choice. Someday people will just download the entire contents of someone's brain, person to person. All conventional analogue forms of communication will become irrelevant.

Not long ago here in Budapest, I came across a drab looking paperback of American poets explaining their methods of composition in a book apparently sponsored by the US government—probably their way of injecting a morsel of provocation into the oppressed Hungarian society of the Cold War era—a book I found in some second hand shop. (English books other than best sellers are still kinda hard to find here). Of course I went straight for the Gregory Corso essay. (Remember when Wanda and I visited his grave in Rome? We saw you right before we left). The rest were interesting but mostly the same old tired aesthetics. His was as bombastic and iconoclastic as one might expect. I have to agree with him that (this was written in the 70s) the world and the artist/ poet's role in it is changing. (At least the phrase "the world's changing" hasn't sounded less like a cliche in a number of years). The artist's great risk... he seems to say, is irrelevance. It's funny how so much of what he implied has in some ways come true. And now as I wonder how I can best express myself to you, I really have to pause and think what info or even inner landscape I can render that can't be "accessed" (when I was young that wasn't a verb—neither was "party") somewhere on the net or through some form of digital entertainment. What can I give you that isn't just something, as so much is nowadays, cosmetic. I mean, how can I really describe this place, for example, and my situation here, because it is exceptional and should probably be documented somehow, and not just in a Millerian way. But can't someone just get anything like that they'd be curious about on the Net? (Why should I, one out of a million Joshua Celestes—

write down my experiences)? It seems that way sometimes. The plethora of information that is accessible (the old version of that word worked just as well— just like "impact" used to be just a noun, right?) has very gradually... well, I mean since the beginning of the digital age... changed the way people talk to each other and just generally relate. Like, playin in a band, playin geetar pretty good, etc.. It just seems irrelevant sometimes. The era of the 'band' is over. People said the machine was comin, man. It's here! People say, Oh, I can get that on the Net but then don't really know what it's about. No one wants to know... that's too risky emotionally... they just want information no matter how disconnected it is. I guess now there's just so much of it, media of every kind, people even respond to it now much less eagerly. Someone needs to come along and turn the whole thing upside down on its head again like Hendrix did.

Just as narrative poetry was usurped by the novel, the novel usurped by cinema and in turn lyric poetry usurped by popular song (well, it got so academic and distant from its origin as something literally meant to be accompanied by music, "lyre," it brought some of its irrelevance down on its own head, not to mention the indirect ushering in of a brief era of vulgar anti- artistic "performance poetry," a sure sign that it was in trouble. I mean pretty soon everything was "punk" something. That was only to be expected in periods when an art form feels it "has nowhere to go." As I say, just as all this seemed to be happening, enter this curious, slightly sinister? Maybe that just belies my bible belt upbringing, technology, this blue screen, this smart phone, this satellite ping pong table, this info about anything at the touch of a button, this "Zardoz" come to pass.

And the world is being asked to go to Second Level (particularly the 3rd World) and many people like "Friend" in the movie are not feeling that comfortable with it. But they will probably just get bulldozed. "So you better start swimmin or you'll sink like a stone..." only Dylan meant that in an opposite way as a kind of warning to those in power. Still, it has a kind of double meaning because now everyone, politicians, artists, rich, poor, everyone is gonna have to start swimmin because of what this technology of the instantaneous has wrought.

There's a guy on a beach in Acheh who makes three bucks a week but has as much or more access to a computer and all its wonders than I do and/ or he's using that knowledge to know more than me and will probably eventually get what I have (not that it's much) by some sort of instantaneous global default. And the fate of the lyric poet (hey, people like Pound and Eliot and Dylan Thomas and Joyce were once read by the general public so, yeah, it has sunk a bit) is the fate of the live human performer/ musician, etc. today. How much more outrageous must he/she be, how much more clothing must he/ she remove, how much more compromise to "survive in the industry" must he/she make, how much more rich and famous does he/she need to get, how much more money does he/she need to raise for the general good ("The plea for the general good is the plea of a scoundrel." Blake) before we all see that ain't nobody sayin that much. For example, to make a tv show about something, say, like the reunion of, say, Duran Duran... hey man, that's not pop culture, that's grounds for insanity.

That is too much info. Do we need to see that? Or better, should we really allow ourselves to be sold that kind of programming? C'mon, 15yr olds! Rebel! I really think that insanity is out there in a much bigger way than we wanna admit. I mean real insanity. Lookin thru a PEOPLE magazine at my Mom's house once years ago there was one cool bit, they asked Allen Ginsberg what his least favorite personality trait was. He said: insanity. I liked that. I play gigs in packed bars now that sometimes suddenly segue into a feelin I'm in an Oliver Stone film like Natural Born Killers and something really weird is gonna happen. (Got a bit of that feeling in Milan, which I'll describe later in more detail). Youth today has "been there done that" and they're looking for fresh meat. The Consumer seems destined to overrun the Producer and then turn on him. Once, there were 2 sets of people in the computer info industry: ones who programmed in the info and those who "provided content" (the so called "creatives") The latter group appears to me to be shrinking. Though the charlatan of that group flourishes! There IS NO CONTENT. CONTENT IS AN ILLUSION. There hasn't been any for years but no one's really noticed apparently. We've reached the saturation point.

Ironically, the computer just gives us the same stuff we already know—over and over and over again. Ok, we got the info but what do we DO with it? It ain't cured cancer yet. But it's supposed to be just a tool—right? Now it just keeps telling us the same shit only faster and faster. Like, that's a big discovery. More space, more space. The only problem is: has it increased the level of loneliness in the world? I think it has. It has dehumanized. It has destroyed as many media figures as it's created. I grew up in a kind of renaissance of warmth—post WWII wealth and brief release from war horror. There seemed to be other foci besides the sensual and guilt about the sensual. But perhaps I'm just lamenting the fact that the affluence of my youth disappeared and, so, glorifying a past which maybe wasn't so great... certainly wasn't great if, say, you were black. Or was it? Is that me ... or the record? Remember that time Ricky Boy kept asking you that when you all gave him a hit of acid while we were listening to records? Or maybe I'm rejoicing in the perspective it gave me. I saw up close some of the destruction caused by money and power although on the outside it was all smiles. Judge Daddy's house was always full of successful business men and politicians and celebs.

Uncle Dennis had pictures of himself taken with all of 'em, got all their autographs. But when I realized (or at least it seemed that way to me) as a teenager that their lives were really kinda empty and that they really didn't do stuff that was that admirable (eg. nobody dug or was as cool as Hendrix to my teenaged mind) I decided to show them with my guitar that money and fame weren't that cool. But now I see that they were simply tryin to get over with the animals they'd been put in the same cage with and with out money and fame and its inherent power you can't do shit... certainly not in the music bidness, or in their political world. So I forgave 'em. They were men of action. They didn't know it was all going down down. Ahhh, big cars and the fifties and America. It shall never again come to pass. And deez kids tuhdaye, day just doan unnerstind it. People just don't need or talk to each other like they used to. Nobody cares. Am I wrong? Not that they ever did maybe but now they really don't care. Maybe it's just survival mode. There's a desperate quality to all my friends here. Maybe it's just, Is there anything fun to do while we wait for death? Anyone got any ideas about how to assuage a deepening inner loneliness? No? Feelings of irrelevance, the coming plague the...

But hey man I didn't even wanna say all that shit: What I wanted to say was thanks for your care package and that I am totally in awe of your Werke, your Oeuvre, and I'm not saying that so you'll write back and stroke my ego about the cheaply recorded... sorry, got no bread no more... collections of songs I send ye from time to time). No, really, you more than anyone I know are unrelated to the dilemmas delineated above. Humanity is in the pointing out of the "weirds" of the world inside your head, and the poignancy of it that comes through in your paintings and your music, man!

THAT is HUMANITY. THAT'S what is missing from the digital world because people are willing to say ANYTHING and do anything especially for money or power or oil... just control. It's always gonna be master/ slave, man! Except, "Hello brother, weird dude. I see you. I see you in me. I have no money no blanket for you: only my fellow humanity... which I'm not afraid to show."

THAT is what nobody seems to say anymore. That is what you say to me: WARMTH THRU WEIRDNESS. That's what, ultimately, I take away from the characters in your pictures, your piano, and shhhhh of your cymbals. The "strange" is thereby neglect as much as by choice. And so compels us to see what leaks out of the everyday world we thought was the only one. And also depicting the bizarre opens up our sense of possibility, of what lives alongside us. Theopolis Riggins, the nutty tenor player who shellacked his horns with dayglo spray paint, TLC and his odd voice, Cotton Moore and his revolution talk... of what people do to survive. My, my how masterly your technique's become. Your colors and your themes seem made for the global society to come, though they take some of their origin from the local, things Appalachian, things Kentuckian, things southern (though you've gone well beyond "local artist,") things AMERICAN CLASSICAL! I've tried to cop that sense in my music, but it's difficult. Like, you don't wanna add congas to bluegrass, but you do gotta try and stay innovative or simply relevant and communicative of a shared humanity. (Like, the weird is what is. It ain't really weird, ain't nothin to be afeared of. The pageant of fleeting life. Somehow your instincts have taken you there. Prehistoric wall paintings. "This is the wildabeast we hunted and killed. Remember? Pretty cool, no?? The Great Mother accepts our sacrifice."

Well, man, it's an overcast April morning. So many things have suddenly been hapnin'. Maybe there's a gig at a hotel for two months in Crete. I'm definitely going to Germany for a little "tour" (The "Unfamous Jazz Heads" tour: 2 gigs in Stuttgart, 2 gigs in Hamburg starting May 16th (sis Angelika's b-day) and then Italy May 27 (an ancient little village near Udine) for just the one gig. And then up to Slovakia for the Eklektika Guitar Festival on June 3rd. But it's all up in the air ('cept the German tour—that's etched in stone) if I take the two months in Crete. Feels weird to be on hold for all this cool stuff. Wish I could do it all. Life's tough.

The German tour is one you'd be perfect for. Your piano would add so much. The only problem is airfare. That's what they won't pay. Otherwise, each man gets around 6 hundred bucks per gig. The Slovak fest (via US gov grant) paid for Carlo and Harriss' plane fare back in 02 but we got a very small concert fee. US gov grant paid for our reunion concert, essentially. Sorry your illness prevented you from coming. That was the fruits of the rare juxtaposition of forces which might never occur again. O well, maybe down the road. At any rate, one cool thing is that I'm working with a new agency called North Country Blues out of the Hamburg area so maybe the Josh/Sylves Tour is not a pipe dream. I'm gonna mention it to them. I'm serious. You'd be required to play the blues and consume large fish dinners. There ain't much money, man, but we'll... pack yer nose!

Well, it's weeks and weeks later: the Crete thing never came through but I ended up doin my share of traveling in May anyway. I played in Austria, Germany, Italy, Slovenia, Slovakia and Hungary. Funny, back in mid-March things got so slow I was contemplating chucking the whole biz and coming to Edgeton for awhile. German tour was cool. Gotta chance to finally see some of northern Germany around Hamburg. The contact folks consisted of old blues hippies and young dudes who worship old blues hippies but who also have degrees in music management. They took care of bidness while the others provided the aesthetics so to speak. Looks like I might be going back in the Fall. Can't wait.

I only played one gig in Italy (Udine) but it paid well enough that my old friend Crip and his lovely girlfriend Wanda, (you remember Wanda, right? My ex.? Yeah, I know, it looks weird, but it's all cool) who had accompanied me to the gig from Budapest, decided to jump in my hot French ride (the Citroen Xsara Picasso) and head with me for Milano. N. Italy has a KY-like feel to the landscape... a similar green... but the huge lush trees of KY, the poplars, oaks and elms, simply dont exist here. It's rainy enough but perhaps they were all simply cut back over time certainly more heavily than in the North American forests. There are few places here... in all of Europe for that matter, like the Red River Gorge or the Smokies. Still, the hazy blue purples enchant as we wizz by in my Citroen. And Crip turned me onto his passion for Friuli wines: "You can taste the grape!" He's right. Deelicious. On the AutoStrada A4 we passed by Verona and Vicenza and dear old Soave where in 96 Helen and I and little son Ryly had stayed in a little apartment loaned to us for a month by a friend (Soave as in the famous white wine Soave Bolla) and from where we had made frequent little sojourns to see the (Andreas) Palladio-designed villas and chapels that dot the area along with frescoes and paintings by Paolo Veronese and Giambattista Tiepolo. Driving by again after so many years, I remembered how our cute little apartment looked out over a huge vineyard (Soave bolla ripening?) and toward rolling foothills of the Italian Alps in the distance.

Ryly was so cute! He loved pulling out this drawer in the living room, taking everything out of it... keys, passports, money, whatever he'd find and then sitting down inside it (he was that small then! Hard to imagine since he's like a beansprout now) and playing with all the stuff he'd just taken out. He'd do it for hours and hours. It was a memorable time. What possessed us to take such a trip with our little child, I dont know. I was trying to break into the Italian scene a bit and Helen was probably just burned out mothering in Budapest and wanted a change of scene. At that time we were driving her Dad's bright red Fiat/ Zastava (made in Serbia) He had died the previous year at 68.

As I look back I realize how overwhelmed I was. Suddenly a father with a beautiful wife in Italy. My head was spinning. But it was all common place for her, a European. And all our exotic adventures of the years before the birth of our first son were coming to an end. (The weird scene back in the old BP days with her old boyfriend, Dragan. It all seems laughable now). In those earlier days, after taking the train from BP we had hitch hiked to Venice after I had played a few nights at a club not far from Trieste, in Piran, Slovenia. (Once the Italian town of Pirano). We were so madly in love with each other and everyone seemed in love with us. We were always given royal treatment. We were always kissing and hugging in the cozy little club I played in Piran, in the streets of Venice, everywhere. I remember one stone staircase overlooking the Adriatic Sea near our room in Piran. From there you can walk down to the village which was once part of the old Venetian empire and which looks for all the world like Venice in miniature—only with the sea and not the canals.... For me Venetian means stucco smeared in palimpsestic colors trying to show thru... and dark brown wooden shutters framing the windows looking down at narrow, twisting streets. At the top of the stairs I took a snap shot of her with the wine dark Adriatic in the background. We were so in love. Maybe this is the Zenith of my youth! A lot of fantasies, jazz fantasies, Europe fantasies, they all came together at that point. She got pregnant on that trip.

Venice itself had been amazing. Pages from the old art history books staring at you, live, right in the face. So, it really did happen, you seem to keep saying to yourself. The city is almost empty in the fine twilight mist of October rain. The tourists have all gone. We have the city to ourselves, Venice is so in love with us. It felt that way. Strange. Things seemed to unravel from that point. We were never quite so close again, in spite of the joy, we seemed to be in separate worlds.

By 2001 or so, things started crumbling very rapidly. I no longer knew who she was. She seemed to be working against me. I started going into a kind of survival mode. I kept a flack jacket on at all times. By the time Carlo and Harris came to visit in Sept. 2002 she and I hardly spoke, except to argue about something. (Felt bad the guys had to stumble into such a tense situation but still it was so great having them there for a few days. Poor Carlo got briefly caught in a coupla crossfires). But by December she asked for a separation. I talked her out of it but then by April some more weird shit started hapnin and I realized it was hopeless so I just said fuck it I'm outta here and moved in with the piano player in the new band for a few weeks before I found my own place. For the next 6 months or so I went into a hell which I myself (with the helpful illusions of others all around me) had carefully constructed. I floated up to my chin in turd infested waters while the devil in my head came along at various intervals in his motorboat. Only the band allowed me to reach the shore and wash off the shit. It took awhile to get it scrubbed off and I was pink and red and raw from the doing of it. I mean, come on: stranded in a foreign country with a buncha Hungarians, two precious little boys who wonder what's goin on, a few misfit expats for friends, and no sense of real home anymore. (Let's just say going to a foreign country, falling in love, having children and then divorcing after 10 years is not something I'd recommend. I've never seen it in the travel brochures).

Ah, but the worst is so far away now. It's been over two years since we split. There are whole other sets of problems. I wanted so often to die. But I lived. I keep thinking of that Williams poem (Danse Russe?) where he's standing in front of the mirror naked waving a shirt around his head. Doesn't he say somewhere,

"I am lonely.... I am best so." Well, well, here's the book here in front of me on the shelf. Let's have a look from the source itself:

It must be the May morning sun pouring into my window that brings back those memories. The good ones, I mean. The bad ones just kinda filter in from time to time: the "poison" you once spoke of that just "goes on down into your system," as you said it would. The postcard versions of your paintings you sent really buoyed me up. And mother always sent emails saying, "Keep your Spirits up!"

But a fascination persists: why do people do what they do? What is the nature of change? of Pain? Whence emotional pain? O Great Sage, is there a light you can throw onto such ignorance? Is there a clarity that drives away some of the frustration? All is loss: love, life, light. And is it that we keep experiencing fragments of this loss until the final loss of everything at the end?

I dunno but this appears to be so: there is a world out there and a world in here and often they dont match up. (If they do, it's love?) But why should that be so painful?

As I say, it's late Spring 2005, Crip, Wanda and I are in my hot French car, barrelling past the old Soave memories (Free and I used to sing, in Bob Hope croon, "Thanks for the mamarries!") It reminds me of how all the Italians, when they saw little Ryly, they all said, "Bello! Bello bambino.! Esplendido!" Poor Helen. Such a beautiful young mother. And so nervous and overwrought. Me, too. But I learned alot from her about what it takes to take care of a little kid. Thought I was making straight A's. But then later she flunked me). But it's now and we're headed 130km/hr for Milano.

I sit here a few days later not knowing what to say, really, but knowing that in some way I've mastered my life here. Divorced, single father. Today, after almost a month of traveling, I knocked around the hood, went to the I-net cafe next to my Arab buddies' grocery/currency exchange (illegal!) office, still can't afford my own computer) to see what was shaking in gigdom. Or the way just now in my kitchen ("You better come inna my kitchen") I whipped up a coffee, knowing just how long I could write before going into the kitchen and turning off the boiling water.

I can now, after years in front of my Wok, chop up an onion a carrot and a Hungarian sweet pepper in the wink of an eye, steam rice and have it steaming on my table in minutes with a little soy sauce and Thai garlic sauce... mmm mmm.... Crip (or Crib – you remember? The kid who subbed on bass for Carlo sometimes?) who in our narrative is headed down autostrada 4 with me at 130kmph for Milano, has got a gig (in real time) downtown tonight at Castro's cafe with his Klezmer band, (The Klezmoes) I thought I might go check it out. Drink a glass of wine with a few friends.

Thinking back to American days you might remember: I met Crip again after many years. He's the one w the slightly bad leg—hence "Crip" –but also stayed home alot, hence "Crib". You remember him, right? Met him again at Boston University in the Fall of 1976. I'd known him in Edgeton because of Bertha and his Aunt Pearl from New Joisey as he pronounced it bein' friends. We used to ride the bus together to Medina when we were kidsa long time ago. I had a gig in Boston once and looked him up.

I guess it all started one day I happened to be talking to a theatrical rake of an acquaintance in a bar near the concert hall in Boston. He happened to mention a decent jazz bass player he knew. I had, like, zero bread to pay the really heavy cats.

When I entered Crip's room I'd swear (but of course I can embellish with twenty years' knowledge now) that the curtains rustled with the winds of Karma, Nirvana, the chants of monks, mutterings of Cabbalists, shamans, the ecstasies of orgasm, the cries of childbirth, and wails of the damned, farts of the empty. Or just a windy day in Bean Town. It made me think back to the days I rode the Edgeton-Medina bus to guitar lessons with Tim Boggle. Little Crip would tag along.

45

Dear Angelika,

I retrieved this from his computer. I thought that you should have it, if anyone should. I didn't read it and have deleted it from my files.

Thanks,

Krip.

THE AMERICAN: *A FRAGMENT*

I've been feeling almost a new kind of loneliness— a second layer beneath the wounded tissue of my original one. I'm still crazy after women, of course. But I've begun to wonder if it might be time to hang up my playboy robe, five little flings in four years… Whoo! and start trying to lead a more respectable life—at least a more serious one. I'm on the verge of being in some serious financial straits. But isn't everyone in this little nothin' burger country, as Dad on the phone from the States put it. But they don't eat burgers here. At least not the kind Americans are used to. It's funny, when I first came here, I had no fear of the street hamburger, but as the years have gone by, now I do. They weren't very good, anyway. Crip always says, "There's only one thing wrong with them—they suck!" Only Americans can cook them right I guess. Just like only the Syrians and Turks and Greeks can fix gyros. But there I go again, thinking in unintentional mild ethnic slurs. Anybody can fix anything. There should be no nations. Now I never eat hamburgers, or gyros either for that matter, it's too expensive. I've had a plate of rice and a croissant in the last three days. Food no longer tastes good… not like it once did. Not like tasting Cassandra's toll house cookies or Wanda's Pesto or Berenice's eggplant. I'll think of more.

I feel alone. I stay at home a lot. I feel like everyone looks at me now as some sort of loser. Even the natives. But the real truth is: nobody looks at me at all. I'm invisible just like the black dude in that novel you gave me once. But I'm not black, I'm just old and broke.

When I finally get out into the City I feel more alone than ever. Conversation seems forced with old expat friends here because so much has changed. I always feel like what we talk about is trivial—but what I really want to talk about—why I feel so empty all the time… do we all?—isn't a fit topic.

And it isn't, is it? Nobody wants to hear that shit, yet it's all we really feel. Where's home? is what I hear everyone asking even when they're talkin' about the latest football scores.

Home is where somebody loves you.

Therefore Jesus ends up being the only person who listens but he doesn't answer back. Or if he does, he's more obscure than those poems you used to read. Was getting mixed up with all these situations a sign? I asked for guidance but I swear I've passed some of the same marked trees in this forest. I've been here before, again and again. I'm going 'round in circles! But there won't be many circles left. I might be too sick to get well. That's what I meant earlier: if a good woman… or even a bad one… can't save you, what can? Poems? Wine? Pot? young chicks? What? That's what I wanna know. That's a lie. That's not what I want to know. I know. I know what to do. Just be quiet. Empty your head of thoughts. Endless cart wheeling cascades of thoughts. That's what they say saves you. So, I'm doing that now writing this.

KRIP: *MOHAMMAD SPEAKS*

Somehow it seems to me now that Josh and I were always meant to ride the bus together. After the time we met at Aunt Pearl's I saw him in Madison's drug store a few times looking through the lps Mr. Duncan kept in the back by the magazine rack. One day I noticed he had a guitar. I asked him about it because I was interested in taking lessons and he said I should come with him now because he was going down to the Edgeton bus stop to catch the bus to Tim Boggles' music store in Medina for a guitar lesson.

I'll always remember the ride to Medina. You went past Judge Demeter's big house and out along Medina Road where the endless rolling green fields of the horse farms stretched out as far as you could see and then past the graveyard and the big statue of John W. Marcellus, who Aunt Pearl had told me was Josh's maternal great, great, great grandfather, the Confederate general. There was scaffolding at the statue top and I asked Josh about it. "Lightening blew the top off his head off last Saturday night I heard," Josh chuckled.

The bus went past Medina University and some small streets in the old part of town. As we walked through the station I always remember how Josh poked me in the ribs and we laughed to each other at the little stooped over black guy looking all around like he was nervous. He wore a snow-white, short-sleeved shirt 'cause it was so hot and muggy, and black pants and a little thin black tie and he had on a little black hat, the kind old time jazz musicians used to wear. He asked us if we wanted a newspaper. I gave him a quarter and he gave me a copy of MOHAMMED SPEAKS. We read it on the way back from Josh's guitar lesson and wondered at all the pictures of African people in long robes, and a guy with glasses speaking in a room of black people at a podium, and we laughed at cartoons showing white people as devils with horns and rat legs coming out of white people's bodies, people who looked like famous white people, politicians and soldiers. And there were pictures of dead African people killed in a war. The bus always dropped us back in Edgeton at 4 o'clock and I said good-bye to Josh and he smiled and said, Let"s play sometime, and I showed Pearl the paper when I got home. She said people have different beliefs and I remember she said, looking at the pictures, "There's so much injustice in the world".

JOSH'S NOTEBOOK (FACSIMILE)

Then a few years later I saw Crip again in Budapest on a trip there in 91on a jazz tour with Lacey, but really to kind of clear my head from the whole Berenice break-up (ah, nothin like puttin a few hunnerd miles between yrseff and paaaiiin, not that I was the model boyfriend) and that planted the seed of my going there a few years after that. But it's so interesting to renew a friendship that had lain dormant for so many years. And he had changed. He had lost all his innocence, his affable tolerance, his faith in humanity, his sense of humor. We drifted apart rather quickly. All of us Americans—we coined the term 89ers after the year the commie regime fell—we needed each other to survive in some ways. So we've maintained a sacred place in our lives for each other even though for the most part—we have little real contact anymore.

But before we drive into the heart of Milan, I just wanna say this: lately I've been interested in just one thing: inner states of mind. I meditate now and I feel like I know what's gone wrong with the world. And I can change it. I know it's crazy. I met these dudes from the UAE (currency exchange dudes) I should tell you about—next letter). I realize now that what happened is simply not as interesting to me as what I was thinking about WHEN it happened. Dig? Somehow that's what I think I'm more suited to write about. I don't want to doctor up my memories, but capture Time just as it happened. I know it's impossible. Anyway that's my current BIG REVELATION. The only thing that's real is what's in your mind while you know you're alive. Otherwise your in a kind of sleep.

Living in a foreign country gives you a remarkable perspective of your native country. You see the wisdom in the idea of cultural relativism. Everyone pursues the art of life in their own way. But it's the same as when you first realize that your parents are just people... not emissaries from God (though they may be that... but you wudnt know it necessarily) not wholly at your disposal, sent to guide you forever through life's vicissitudes. Earth is just a tiny planet in an unremarkable galaxy, in a very plain jane star system. I will die. When all this hits you, you can easily transfer that logic to, yeah, Americans really are kinda America-centric (whatever the word is, I'm losing my English vocabulary and not really replacing it with a Hungarian one! So pretty soon I'll just grunt and snort and guffaw a lot!) You see the way the Hungarians see you. And you become acutely aware that you are a foreigner and will never be anything else to them. (A sudden identification with black dudes in the States. It's hip to play with ethnic identities in the US. Wear a moslem hat. Tell people you're part Indian. Listen to black music. But if it came down to it, you could always run back to your majority caucasian ethnic group and be safe under the long arm of their laws, their economics, their politics, their racial power. But here whatever statement you make, it better be who you really are and what you're willing to back up otherwise keep quiet and just do your job. People have little time for frivolity here. (So you can see why I've hit a few snags!!) They have very little play around with income time. They're used to a drab life with little purchasing power except the usual staples. Free time is usually used to get sloshed on wine (some great red ones) or beer.

But things are changing. The market revs up a little more every year. And the reality of globalized hi-powered capitalism hits you like a shot of brandy (the hungies call it "palinka") on an empty stomach. I've seen such sweeping changes. Perspective again. I saw a region metamorphose into something else before my eyes. Many changes were too fast to catch. But some were very observable and enlightening. Malls sprang up like mushrooms. Traffic jams. Now your free to buy whatever car you want, not just E. European made ones. The new generation is more American than I was. But they appear to be concentrating on the superficial

Americaness. Products. The older generation (mine and those a bit older) talked lovingly to me about "American feeling" in music, in movies, in life. I liked that phrase. Young people today are less aware of what that is (or was, maybe). Many of them hate America now. But every culture sees itself as a kind of center and can never be totally stripped of that illusion. To try and take it from them just makes them cling to it tighter. Breeds nationalism and intolerance. Still, there were many good things about America that I saw for the first time. We really do have greater faith than the Europeans. But we need to be careful about what that faith is in. Americans are more utopian and, in regard to an earthly paradise, more visionary. But could it turn into a dark vision? Americans are doers and givers, but too motivated. They expect you to motivate to THEIR motivations! Europeans aren't that way. Americans give way more to charity, and not just as tax write-offs. Europeans pay much higher taxes. There's a feeling of "let the government take care of the needy." The socialist mantra. But somebody's got to actually do it!

Well, they've certainly put alot of mula into that system! 35, 40, 50 percent of their income! No wonder you can't find an ice cube in Europe or get change! Still, you can see where an attitude of not being your brother's keeper flourishes. The government is a keeper but not a brother. Magnanimity withers into dry, apathetic sophistication. Yet, Americans are too involved. "Be good! Be generous! Be transparent!... or go to jail." They're always trying to sell you something that "improves" you.

I'll say this for Europeans: at least they leave you the fuck alone. They don't care if you drink (not behind a wheel of course). Everybody in Europe is half buttered all the time, but public transport is much broader and more efficient here. It hardly exists in the US outside of New York or Philly or Boston, SF, and you can get as sloshed as you want on it. You can smoke everywhere. It was as if someone really had put up signs in public places saying "Thanks for smoking"! Or 'Screw your neighbor's wife!' or 'Kill yourself!' (Catholic countries are a little more hesitant about legitimizing that. Fucking your neighbor's wife is fine though, just go to church, confess, no big problem. We're only human. In E. Europe. they don't even bother with that part. Hungary has the biggest suicide and divorce rate in the EU. Even beat out the Swedes). Hungarians are a beautiful race. The women are legendary. Akkor, mi a baj? What's the problem?

Hot chicks everywhere. "How do young Hungarian couples handle it?", Crip asks rhetorically on the rollicking subway. Mass infidelity. Monica Lewinski couldn't happen in Europe. Nobody gives 2 percent of nothin' over who you fuck and when. The Brits are child diddlers sometimes. Seems to happen very rarely on the continent. Yet their continental lack of caring has a coldness to it. An emptiness. "God is dead here," a Belgian girl once said to me in one of those post joint "deep" conversations near some Morrocan neighborhood of Brussels. American "niceness", "Have a Nice Day", is unknown or scoffed at. The southern European will smother you with food drink flattery and besotted brotherly love, but he will come begging to you later, in need of more than he gave. The Northern European rarely ventures that far. The stiff Englishman is a fair stereotype. Though, as my brother once said, once they've sorted you out as a decent chap or "mate" ("Cheers mate!," always said among good drinking companions before guzzling beer, Brits know squat about wine, usually). They can be incredibly loyal even to a fault. "MYYYY Mate!"

There's something gritty about yanks and brits: One can see why they once ruled the world. America as a concept will continue to dominate (maybe for a longtime) but the world is changing! The white man's Euro/American art grows more irrelevant to a growing mass that simply can't understand it. Or they have no use for it! It's da funk and gadgetry from the East the youth of the world, craves. Not Shakespeare. Not Whitman. No... nobody wants to hear 'at shit anymore. ("Coz Wong the chinaman don't like 'at shit either." I bet you remember that from the bluegrass fields!)

After the gig, sitting in my car, after having gotten absolutely nowhere with the ladies, I can't help but meditate on the splendor of the European streets opening out beyond my windshield: the twists and turns of one of the old quarters, the Jewish one in this case. The gypsies are on the other side of the boulevard. It occurs to me that it's all of a piece, a shell, a shell that ossified around the human heart. An old shell another animal has appropriated for his own dwelling. The original worm has long since died, moved on, gone clear, changed addresses. Though he was a god of sorts, a Hapsburg prince standing six foot three, with his entire entourage.

These are his buildings. A Jewish merchant in his robes peering over bifocals. He stands by the exquisite Art Nouveau window casings. His building. The doorway to the old courtyard where people park their cars, now, amazing mahogany carved gate right out of Aubrey Beardsley. Only the City exists at night. The countryside, the village disappears at sundown. Crip wrote a nice piece about it when he worked for the expat newspaper: "Evening in Budapest". I'll send it to you.

And the night is your self inflicted reward for daytime stress endured. The City has the night. And you will go anywhere it tells you, to find your Faustian treasure (a brief sip of immortality/ immorality). Or, to reverse Free's method of how to know how many mushrooms to eat, ("Don't worry- they'll tell you") you tell it where to take you. And sometimes you find it. But you'll end up like

Sidney Greenstreet, standing there with a pocketknife shaving off shards of fake Maltese Falcon. Whatever you find is never what you were looking for. Not getting what you want both kills you and keeps you alive. I'm nodding off, but one last thing: how can I overcome irrelevance? By wanting only to write what's in my heart, with complete sincerity, which is impossible too, btw. (but you said, once, "if you don't feel it! IT AIN'"T GONNA COME OUT YOUR HORN!... I remembered!) How can such an attempt at expression become irrelevant? Poetry is feeling. Blues is feeling. Is it time for a little erotica? No, I am getting no pussy to write home about. And this morning light? Doesn't it diminish the petty love pursuits (euphemism) of a middle-aged man? No, not really. What is their connection? This light through the sycamores and lindens in front of this huge apartment building is decidedly blond. I keep dreaming of some blond, some Wanda or Kiki but prettier, smarter, a musician. Brunette is bad ju ju. But one must have a life, or the life one wants—before one can share that life with someone.

I've been a very bad boy... stupid boy. I've developed a weakness for fat girls with pretty faces. But no matter what human being you become involved with, well, you mingle poisons. As you say, mess with the girls and they will mess with you. But women are so beautiful. Yet, apparently they represent the impossible. I'm fifty and I still ain't found it. Probably never will. Or, it's all over the place and actually I'm runnin from it. And she constantly changes her shape. Just when I got her in my arms she turned into a tree. Her image falls with every piece of fruit. I looked back and lost my little Eurydice forever.

But she went into the underground. Or just be friends but she swoons to the guitar. Wondrous shaking asses seen from the stage. Ah, to strum the jangling strings, vibrate lip against cunt and ass. Holding the cups of her insteps. Taking the long journey home. Horse throws her head from side to side. I give her a slap across the ass. Red welts. Across the face. She's gone hysterical. I see the village in the distance. Riding. Riding. Bitch, get yo ass in de air. He's like a bat swooping down on some livestock. Sitting on top of her. The double-backed beast riding thru the forest. Images go backwards in time, flying by. Strip down to basics. Other women's faces splash up from the seawater like dolphins at play or they are drowning in the irrevocable. I recognize them. Then clouds. I'm still on horseback. Absolute possession. Take no quarter! The village must be burned and everyone put to the sword! Put them to the sword! Riding riding... the blond... running. I grab her as she's trying to get away, pull her up onto my horse. She's juicin all over the quilt Bertha gave me and Doc brought to me all the way from Edgeton!! "It's beautiful," Emese, the cute fat girl with the ancient Hungarian name says when she sees it laid over the bed.

Sickish fantasies flash through my mind as I start through the endless movement toward orgasm with a condom on. Destructive images that fuel a constructive act forward. These little soap bubbles create life! Adoration and Defilement! I'm like a soldier. A Hungarian knight riding thru the Turkish-occupied village. Put them ALL TO THE SWORD!! Run away! Run away! someone screams. But I seize the tall blond one with the amazing legs. She's in my saddle lap. She will be my wife. No, I open my eyes and it's Emese. She's holding her legs by her toes in a huge V. If Free could see me now. If only her legs were long and slim. Yeah, but you ain't no George Clooney yr seff. Goddam I'd forgotten just how great fuckin was. I close my eyes again for a long time and now Blond Diana opens completely and I flood her womb, as far as the end of the plastic condom. The village burns. Now, when I open my eyes she's brunette and petite and round, sighs and cool touch of silk quilt around me. Tomorrow we rebuild and start again.

You know why I'm writin this? Nothing inspires me more than a woman's body. Let's sit down at the cafe and I'll tell you my troubles. But you're 4 thousand miles away! What's it all about? Just gigs/ horror life? So strange, 'cause she's just one last hit of bein' hot enuff to go nuts over her looks. But… she's just a little too fat and the fat pulls down just a tiiiiny bit her jaw and get a flash of her at 60 and huge. And I see she's just a fat little lamb. I can't go on. I'm not ready yet to admit my own corruption. So I get cocky and tell her (Cherist she's got a freakin cock/ boyfriend in Milan!!!) that I could never be satisfied with only her. She gets angry but then I manage to get her to hang out and eventually she's got that almost too fat rosy ass of hers in the air again and I'm fuckin the holy shit out of it. I can tell when she comes coz her cunt's grip around my dick is so strong it almost pops out or it's like suddenly her cunt hardens and you're bangin on a closed door.

I gave her a lesson today. After I sucked her off for an hour! What is she? She's hip and speaks perfect English but you can tell she's been somehow just a little sheltered. Hungie gals got no time for perversion. They fuck straight and then gotta go to work. But I'm just her father. He played sax it turns out. Probably a part gypsy guy. Died at 50 something. Drank a lot. She was too young to understand it then but now at age 32 she's gettin hit with it. Only a strong hard working Mom between her and that wild card of being on your own. And nobody gives a shit. Party of youth is over. Youth, youth party of 4 yr tables waiting. Youth? Youth? Same with me. But I don't know which side of the turnpike to jump towards, a possum on Tranquility Pike. We've fucked now for about 3 weeks. I'm gonna have to pull out of this. But maybe I'll wait and see if I can just add to the… We fucked and sucked again and then she said go ahead and shag whoever you want it's ok. Lie, but it sounds good. I'll see what I can do. Hell, I do that anyway (in my mind at least, constantly) but the hot ones just don't show up. But it's the Equation. Dig a little below the gorgeous exterior. Ever wonder how difficult it must be bein a beautiful woman??? She just doesn't even conceive of the world like me. Great! That's variety. Why is that a drawback? I dunno.

But now I need a small ass for sure. It's all I can do to keep fuckin this big ass girl. But her eyes are so pretty. Dark circles like Sophia Loren, Penelope Cruz-like cutsiness but a bit big in the thigh "Thunder Thighs" Free used tuh call 'em. But that's why she's hungry. We're using each other. We're both ugly. But isn't everybody in a way? Chess Game (Eliot's "Waste Land")

She just left and already I'd like to go get something else. Sex is Holy. Sex is a drug. This blond I met later, after insisting that I write down her number now puts me off when I call. She would be heavenly but doesn't have the Soul of Emese. Those are the breaks. Often happens. Homely girl cool, Hot girl, not. Front hole money hole back hole cornhole. (What joke is that the punch line to???) Why is that? But I gotta wait til I find the hot girl at 55. She's got some money. Kids. But then again I got nothin to offer HER. She goes with the gigolo, instead. Kids are off to college. Then who? I mighta gotten in too deep here to get out gracefully. I can see her vagina growing teeth eventually. Gigs got scarce and then it was all pussy and depression about money for a few days, all up in it. It had been a year since I'd fucked anyone. Gimme a break. But this just ain't the one. Just lay back, chill, disappear.

Waves flood the shore. I awake from the dream and look around. She's right on the border of too fat. Her breath smells vaguely of salt, skin, cum, juice, farts, garlic, wine. Odalisque. Ingres. Rubens. Renoir. Nice chats. She's very nice, really. But then some sort of desperation settles over everything. Phone calls. Petty jealousies. Woe to them that fall in love with a casual fuck. Suddenly she has so many expectations of me. I was once her.

Now, I have no expectations. The certainty of my own death, that others can give a shit about only so much. Except the blond musician girl of the future. She's coming. I can feel her. "I can't see ya... but I know y'theh." Only when you think that love doesn't exist, that's when you begin to feel it in it's truest form. I can't cum with the rubber on so I pull it off and come on her face. She rubs it over her tits and dabs some on her lips. A little afraid to just slurp up a big blob. Hey, I drank your juice, baby. Flighty girl playing sophisticate of love. Silly cunt. Yet, I love you in a way. You are all Creation. You're 'bout big enuff tuh be-uh huhhuhuhuh (hillbillie laughter). Nice kissable lips. What is more wondrous than a kiss? Tomorrow you will find a nice Hungarian guy and, O I'm just a self-indulgent old man. I get up to get her a towel.

It's weeks later and I just perceive stuff (all very beautiful) around me. My death follows me around everywhere I go.

Some quotes that wont let go: this, a blurb by W.H. Auden on the back of a book of Theodore Roethke' poems...a collection called "Words for the Wind" "Mr. Roethke is instantly recognizable as a good poet. Many people have the experience of feeling physically soiled and humiliated by life: some quickly put it out of their mind, others goat narcissistically on its unimportant details; but both to remember and to transform the humiliation into something beautiful, as Mr. Roethke does, is rare."

"Everyman should be able to live two lives: one for himself and another for others" Italo Svevo, A Life.

As I said somewhere: when Jack Kerouac was my age he'd been dead three years. Suddenly it all seems so obvious, yet I'd had it all wrong. Dope can do that (and maybe it's not always a good thing): turn everything into the mythical. Your life is the life. Your love is the love. A Quest. A Quest for the answer. Aren't we all Faust trying to get out of it all alive, waiting for Science to transform it all? To conquer Death. But it is the very nature of that which seeks eternal life... to die. Quiet quiet... save your own skin. That's what we're thinking. One cliche: the answer is in the Quest itself.

Why did I want to go to Milan? Crip said hey why not, I gotta friend who can put us up. Movement. Plain and simple. Just movement.

Ivan put us up, Italian father/Russian mother, hence the Slavic name, grew up in Milan. Works as a translator from Russian to Italian and plays bass in a blues band. A shithole of an apartment though kept reasonably clean by bachelor standards. The filth of the neighborhood reminding me of the Lower Eastside or Washington Heights in Manhattan. Tiers and tiers of clothes drying on clotheslines strung across filthy porches.

End of May and temperatures soared to ca. 40* C. A blueish haze of smog, humidity and strangled yellow light permeates everything. It occurred to me that I could croak in this heat. Many older people do. Air-conditioning is wimpy in Europe. But usually it's not this hot. Summers, by Southern standards, are pretty wimpy here. And only in July and August do you sometimes think, yeah, it's hot.

But this is late May. We're caught off guard. But nobody croaks. Evening brings scant relief as we take a subway ride 4 or 5 stops. Ancient city quarters have a certain look like cow paths cut deep into meadows leading down toward creeks. Some big canals run right thru the city center. On the waterfront, just like Canal St. in Manhattan, tall black African dudes are selling watches, sunglasses (Gucci, 25Euros... yeah, right.) jewelry. But this is no art fair. This is their life, man!

Later we will buy 10E worth of dope from some dude down in a condemned warehouse that dudes and hippie chicks are squatting in, turning it into an art gallery/performance space, hang out. Everyone with weird hair and faces and bodies pierced everywhere you can imagine. It's like punk backed up a little and went back to the sixties. Political activism mixed with bad photography. Anti-globalization. Some drop the anti-US schtick a bit since its influence is so all-pervading and one sees Europe's complicity so clearly.

Once again, like the Oliver Stone film vibe in the Budapest club I mentioned earlier, one feels as if it's too much for everyone now. No solution, just letting go. A pruning of dead hopeless limbs. No one knows where to begin to recover the Irrevocable. And once out of control, no one will know how to restore order. Asian toy-sellers with crazed smiling faces entertain passersby, demonstrating their remote cars, and teddy bears drinking blinking green potions. I start to buy one for the kids but then I realize it's all a dream and the toy won't be there when I wake up.

There are no essences. People just do things. What you can do in Milan and Edgeton are vastly different. Yet here we are- 'da Earth. What happens to all the cars? God, there's alotta cars out dere. And not much love. Woman. Never see her. A girlfriend came over for dinner. She'd been to India where she fucked alotta young beautiful Indian men.

But whadda ya do when you get back to BP? I suffer, she said. My offer to relieve her suffering was not accepted, though. I'm trying to convince her that we should just be good friends who fuck. No "relationship." I fear however that it's gonna be all or nothing. Friendship or sex. Never both together it seems. Not for very long. Ah, the riddles of love. Nice girl. I'll take "friend" rather than nothing. I've had two or three silly affairs, that each lasted about three months or so since me and the old lady split over two years ago.

Yet, somehow in the darkest hour I felt Jesus protecting me, protecting this fragile consciousness from any further harm. Some beneficient spirit. But it's impossible to know. One feels something... that's all. "And forgive us our trespasses as we forgive those who trespass against us" etc. I like that. I chant it as I fall asleep. In the morning, it gives me a bit of strength. The Forgive me, I'm all alone 'cept for my kids. No, that's not true. Got a few buddies here. Like, Crip finally got in touch again. Guess he felt guilty. He shouldn't have. But often there's this big emptiness. But I did get myseff inna fix. No way back to Edgeton without having to leave the kids. Daunting to think of re-building a US life without them beside me. Yet, to stay here is to fade too long into exile. And there's that woman I no longer know: my ex-wife.

Yet dealing with it everyday sharpens your perceptions. I accept it, now. Anger flickers away. There are worse things others must live with. The perception that something terrible happened to me, something much more painful than anything I'd ever experienced (coz of the kid factor, if it'd just been the chick, no way... not at my age, now, after so many similar experiences) fades away when I see that the hand I was dealt was so much better than some.

Another lesson of the City, the vision of hopeless poverty (and the surge of energy I felt in Milan just under the surface, like a BOMB, like New York without the verticality, a Merry go round 'bout to fly off its axis, and yet everyone's down with that). To see that that possibility of hopeless poverty exists for some. It widens the world, the worlds of possibilities. I accept the existence of the dark side. I.e. you can get into, or OUT of, eternities of situations. It might take some time. And something beyond mere self-reliance seems required (heard a U2 song the other day, "Sometimes you can't make it on your own" that's what I meant by that hint of beneficient spirit emanating from Pater Noster chant).

One needn't always have to put on a funny hat worn by ethnicities one knows nothing about in order to connect: your own funny hat from your own Myth works just as well. You just have to get it in the right perspective. One's own Myth obviously hurt one's feelings in adolescence and so in a huff one took up with another Myth. Everything about the Myth you were born into, your parent's Myth, was wrong. All other Myths, you say in anger, (though they're just the distortions you see in your rear-view mirror as you're driving madly away in the opposite direction) were right. But age and time begins to settle back over everything (one sees one's old fetish for the exotic as a flight from something?) and you begin to see that they were all the same, all One: dead gods ("But they're all dead, Monster... died of boredom." – Friend, Zardoz) and the One one hopes is There. Mama. Family. Father. Sons. Daughters. Spirit. What is life without this holiness?

Well, man, I've had several days here in town all by myself in my little flat, Kids are at the little cottage in the countryside (Carlo and Harris were there once) with their Mom (Krip drives them down) and I can't seem to come up with a big finish that ties it all together and makes that ever elusive "point." All I really wanted to say was thank you so much for the pictures and for your existence. A man dies if he runs out of the Possible. In my life you've increased it.

Forgive the CD. Remember this was all done in a few takes for a few hundred bucks at a garage studio. But there were a few nice licks. This is what we play mostly at clubs and private parties here locally. I still only eek out an existence though. Still, it's gratifying to think you might pop this in the CD player once or twice while dabbing on a little paint. (It would be nice to spend an afternoon babbling in this same philosophical manner at your crib while watching you paint). Hey man, love ya madly. Come visit me. My instincts tell me Europe might inspire you even further.

Bye for now,

Josh

46

FROM *MY LIFE IN MUSIC* BY KRIP KOVACS

Different men are driven by different impulses. The majority I've met in my life seem reasonably comfortable with meeting the world straight on as it is (or appears) and tend not to trust thinking about it too much. They move ever outward into the outside world and seem happiest when keeping themselves busy no matter how serious or trivial the task—there being, for them, little difference between the two. I've known lawyers and judges who could sentence a man to death in the morning and come home and work contentedly in their gardens the same evening. A doctor might lose a patient on the operating table yet still attend the theatre the same night. Not that their consciences were untouched they simply, because of a kind of professional and, in many ways, admirable discipline, didn't allow themselves the luxury of too much reflection, particularly reflection that might stifle action. They are able to assure themselves quickly that life goes on and one mustn't upset the flow of it. Such men are the foundation of the world we see in front of us the buildings, the bridges, the highways, the crops, the fences. They, with their women and children beside them, have made it all.

I am not one of those men. Nor was I, as I recollect now in middle age and begin to divest myself of so many youthful pretensions, ever one of them. Or rather, I was on track to become one—a typical middle-class white American man—but something, something I am still trying to uncover as I write this, steered me in a new and different direction. My old school chums, my sports teammates —I began to drift apart from them. Suddenly, I became an artist.

I can still feel the wind. It was October wasn't it? I had just very badly broken my leg playing Little League football and my leg was in a cast. Could this be where a sudden sense of my own vulnerability, my own mortality, entered my life? I'm walking up the hill behind our Tranquility St. house —just before the little subdivision of tiny little crappy houses turns into a meadow going far out to Josh's house. I look out across the undulant grass. Grey clouds and the wind roll in with fine mists, hints of rain. The smell of the turning leaves is in the air. Perhaps a sudden ray of October sun shoots through the clouds. The wind soon blows a cloud over to cover it. Evening is coming. A nameless sadness falls over me.

Somewhere deep inside I must have thought, I'm all alone in this world aren't I? But at the same time I felt the joy of being alive. Still, there was something sad in these revelations, these self-revelations, and my eyes welled up with tears. But I didn't cry. Something had passed. My childhood? I must have become a man that day. But I also knew somehow then that, as I turned to go back to my mother —I never knew my real mother —I mean, Aunt Pearl, calling to me from way across the field to come to supper, and my home that now seemed somehow strange to me, I would have to spend my life trying to tell this story. The Story.

Angels seemed to appear after that day to help me. Josh. Carlo. Wanda, Doc, Angelika—and Jimi Hendrix's music. I craved it again after I first heard it at Bobby Paganini's house. Love is the KEY, Jimi seemed to keep telling me, in some language I can't quite get. At fifteen, I wanted to be his initiate. In his white leather fringe jacket and dark scarves, what was he? A kind of Eagle? A vision of turquoise ready to fly into the upper reaches of the spirit world. Do you bring word from my great eastern ancestors, Thundercloud?

I spent most of my time walking through the fields and the streets of the little town thinking that I was a kind of Hendrix, that I wanted to live my life like him, wear clothes like him, wear feathers and jewels like him, and, of course, play guitar like him —something that no one will ever do. In the darkness of my room I listened to the music move between the little GE turntable speakers. A small light from the back of the turntable gave off an eerie glow as if releasing a dark spirit that Hendrix would then enlighten. I felt a stab of sadness when on the TV screen David Brinkley said he'd died and there it was, not a photo, but a drawing of him, with the dates of birth and death written under it.

So, after only two years of knowing about him, his earthly body was no more. My music mates and I started playing his stuff on our guitars as much as we could. He was often in my thoughts. "Cry of Love" quickly came out. I have an image in my memory of the LP cover propped up against a wall, blending with the cheap panels of small town offices, which belonged to Jared Smallwood's father, turned into a rehearsal room. His physical death had left the teenage imagination untouched.

I imagined that I would move to New York and share an apartment with Hendrix and he'd show me all his licks and be like a big brother as we walked the streets in cool Indian Joe hats with feathers in them and met people like Mike Bloomfield and Steven Stills on Greenwich Village street corners, high fiving them and laughing and swapping stories about music, dope, women and the Universe.

So, somehow I knew he wasn't dead. Not really. There'd be no new recordings but he'd already said everything. Later, of course, record companies would release their backlogs and bootlegs that just went on and on for years as if Hendrix was an endless fountain on earth as well as heaven. Maybe he was.

Then, in an interview in this film I saw, one of the Isley brothers said, "Hey, maybe Jimi just went on into his alfa jerk, like when you first go off to sleep, and he musta just said to himself, 'Hey, I'm Jimi Hendrix. Maybe I'm so cool, maybe I could just die.' And he, like, just went on out." Then, in another scene, Little Richard, who seems more vulnerable in his flashing eyes, as if he were the High Priest standing beside Jimi in sacred space as the notes spill out in echoing reports down some Cascade Valley, said, "Everything I wanted to tell him before he died was good things. All good. You see Jimi was put back into the dipper and poured back over the Earth. "Second sight. The Dipper twice. Memory is genius. Remember twice as much. And bring news of Earth to the yet unpoured."

The once-poured ones who built the world didn't have second sight. Here facing the Great Plain at Europe's End, outliving Jimi by twenty-four years, I look out into turquoise twilights, out into winter's drear, to keep remembering, remembering for them, the ones who must destroy the old earth with their dark love. And Up From the Skies will begin the new one. "I wanna hear about the new Mother Earth. I wanna see and hear… everything."

Dear Samidha,

But the equation that measures so much of worldly life, becomes – in the end – master/slave. Someone is always taking or giving cues somehow. Master is lonely. Slave is empty. They go on dancing like a drunk with a hat rack. Suddenly the full force of life's tragedy hits you full force. Boom. Religion is a band-aid for the frightened. But band-aids can be attractive. Sex is a band-aid. And what is greater than sexual ecstasy with the woman you love? With a woman, you don't love for that matter? What can be more sexually pleasurable than a young woman's (or old one's for that matter) proffered ass swaying in the air, waiting to be fucked? Nothing.

Yet, I begin to see Mother Nature's brushstrokes as I advance more closely towards the canvas. She kept all her slight of hand tricks hidden from me when I was young —now she tips her hand. Winks. Ahhh, so THAT's how it's done!. She's just being merciful to an old man. To see through the Illusion is also to become less obsessed by it. Obsession is Illusion's slave. Illusion—when she diminishes—begins to reveal herself, her secrets. But then we cannot possess her and use our new Promethean knowledge because she is slowly vanishing! That is why an old man's final comprehension of woman's power is of no use to him. He must reconstruct her into that greatest illusion of all, the work of art, which is a kind of woman, but then you are back at the beginning. Which isn't the beginning. "In my beginning is my end", Doc said, quoting something. Such tautologies come from the limitations inherent in language—yet it's all we have!

We don't believe in unseen things anymore. I mean, I do, I guess—but it can be a curse or a blessing.

Tonight, was, I'm afraid, the final showdown with my girlfriend of three months. It just wasn't me, man. O lord please forgive my horniness. I avoided her text messages for only a week. This after telling her again and again that I could never fall in love with her and that sex was fine but that I could do it with her only in the context of friendship—or some line of crap like that. It seemed ok at the time. Shoulda known that shit never woiks.

Crip, my old roommate of fourteen years ago said months ago over a beer— and long before I met this girl—"It's nice to be wanted." A wiser and more empathetic statement I haven't heard since you said, "It's too bad women have to be people." It is indeed nice to be wanted. Especially after seven years of not being wanted, or yet being wanted by the wrong women and being too weak-willed not to take advantage of their wanting me, though I knew full well I couldn't fall in love with them, or "enter into a mature consenting, possibly live-in situation" with them.

Girls you asked me about: 1. Emese, the dark-eyed beauty. A bit of a phoney, though. Her wealthy Milanese boyfriend broke it off with her. Such a sweet loving woman. I love fat women! But something… phony? Just couldn't hang. Wish I could've. Then of course I tried desperately to get her back but she'd already found another dude.

2. Gudrun. Tall. But big. Not gawky tall. Very lovely face. Beautiful high cheekbones. Bit oriental. Like a Khirgiz princess! And plump. Much taller than Emese. Not the One. And I can tell she would never understand my relationship with my kids. If I had any sense I'd nix it tonight. But I probably won't have the courage. I knew she would feel hurt at some point. I simply said I need space-time. Physics type stuff. That shit. Within one week she starts texting me every day. I would write back lackluster replies. Just trying to be cheerful (whistling through the graveyard). Then, today I got a "Why don't men love me— Ionly give love—what is wrong with me? Why don't you love me?" text message. Hit me in the gut. Poor baby. So I said let's meet tonight if you want. She caught my phrasing and let me have it again: "If I WANT? And YOU?" She had me there. Checkmate.

Don't think ill of me, baby. I know it sounds sexist. But I TOLD her in the beginning that there would be no love! That I was a skirt chasing old man!!! We even laughed about it all the time. And you know how basically submissive I am. She's not very pretty. But such a good girl. Very good lover. If only I could give her what she wanted beyond all the sex. But I can't. Oh well. For one thing, getting in heavy with her would mean— like I said—that she would have to develop a relationship with my sons. I just don't see that. In the end, the boys take up so much of my feelings the person I share them with is gonna have to be inCREDIBLY special. And this chick ain't the one. Maybe there isn't anyone. Oh, hell, we'll probably screw tomorrow night and then when I walk to her office with her the next morning I'll kiss her at the door, walk home and then feel weird the rest of the day, feel like a liar and a coward. Oh, if only I didn't have to be a person. You can't be sexually satisfied or at peace with yourself unless you can love the other person. Anyway, I didn't respond to the "And you?"

You meet a woman that inhabits that border, below which you can't get turned on and above which she rarely wants anything to do with you. A handful of women I've known were above that border and I always kept a "gun" under my pillow, knowing my days might be numbered. Or they were slightly under it and I dreaded the day they would discover my lack of attraction for them—an amount of attraction just sufficient to get me aroused—but not really worked up, not worked up into a state of passionate LOVE.

The day of dread has come for me today with Gudrun. "But there's no laughs left coz we laughed them all." She was just on that border. As time slipped by she sank under it. Still, I hate to lose her completely. I enjoyed her company. "It's nice to be wanted." A man likes to accumulate not dismiss. But it's impossible. No woman will tolerate the presence of another woman—the One that I would surely have continued searching for. No man can give to more than one woman the attention that each of them demands. You'd be like the proverbial dude on Ed Sullivan, (much before your time, dear, I'll explain) running back and forth keeping a line of vaudevillian dinner plates spinning on poles, not letting them shatter all over the stage.

Well, baby, it's been over a month since I wrote the above crap. The holidays are gone but I still have my xmas tree up. It's always a bit hard for me to take it down. I have to be in the right mood. It was a good holiday. I got Ryly a new cell phone and a buncha little stuff here and there. I found a cool old Lakers b-ball with a cool silhouette pic of Shaq on it plus autograph etc. for Gordon. Plus alotta little gifts. They loved it. Helen and I gave each other ashes and switches, our usual gift to each other. Nothing weird happened. It was business as usual. Gigs were plentiful and predictable: people milling around big corporate parties not giving a shit about the music except as a background to their impossible to fulfill wealth and sex fantasies. We are the slaves. The "Committee" is the Master. Their god is in his heaven—all's right with the corporate world. No argument from me. Long as I get my check, I don't give a fuck if this place burns down! Nor do they give a fuck if I play another note. Free told me once, "Playing good on the geetar… not that important to the world."

I always think kids don't know stuff about life or people or sex or anything. But the other day Gordon noticed my new earring, I hadn't worn one in months after I'd lost my cool ruby stud one—at your place ?——but I had found this cool yin yang one at a shop the other day. As he examined my earlobe, he asked, "How come some people wear one in both ears?"

"Well," I said, "only rock stars and rappers wear earrings in both ears."

He kinda cocked his head authoritatively and bugged out his eyes comically, "And GAYS?" he said. I said, "Yeah. So?" Where do they pick this stuff up? at school, of course. It cracked me up. They both have very mature senses of humor. I was thinking soon Ryly will be the same age as me and Crip were when we first started to hang in a big way. Sixteen. How time…

Hi, again, after many many weeks. It's a cold, crisp February morning. Feels good. It was unseasonably warm a few days ago. It occurs to me, after just walking Gudrun, the Tender Amazon, to work, one must eventually love his lover—not just fuck her. Otherwise, it's too inhumane. The lover as plaything. Sure, it's fun but… We fucked all night and then, in the morning, I took pictures with her new cell phone camera of her sucking my cock and balls. She likes to see herself doing it. It's a laugh. But a look into the dark bottomless well of narcissism. "I see my melting face undulate upon the waters!" Look too long and one falls headlong with a vertiginous scream into the abyss. If one makes oneself into an object one is treated like one. Master/slave. S/M. It's all a laugh – someone sticking the wine bottle up her/his ass—a cock in her/his mouth, hands fastened behind her/him with a necktie. Blindfolded. Which is which? The dam of self indulgence bursting. Suddenly someone says, "How 'bout killing some Jews?" You see what I mean—i.e., where does it lead? Lust is insatiable. Until, finally, the body is thrown onto the dung heap. This is how it started, though, no? One step down the staircase. Suddenly the epiphany of Europe's horror. I hear the old dogs scratching behind the door.

How violent the World is (has become? always was?) For some reason, for me, the brutality is most embodied in modern automobile traffic. How ugly the trucks and roads and filthy salt-stained streets of the outskirts of Budapest! And the World! Here is man's selfish and fearful folly most clearly exposed… exposed in all its insanity. Most of my anxieties are rooted in my parenthood. Cars, all of modern life, seem so adverse to children. And now we're having a spate of car bombings. It's commonly said here that Hungarians love to exercise their power, of which History has so often deprived them, when they get behind the wheel. They're the most impatient drivers I've known. One guidebook I glanced at mentioned their obsessive desire to overtake. Of course driving feels more dangerous in the US now, too. God those huge SUVs! (Is that what they call'em?) I'd never seen anything quite like it, I'd been in Europe so long. Get hit by one of them and you'd be a distant memory very quickly. The supremacy of oil. It changed everything. It kills Palestinians.

Still, I'm having so much fun with the boys. They are so SWEEET!

Knocked out teeth and eye injuries worry me quite a bit as they go about their sports pursuits. I'll insist on them wearing mouth pieces—just like their hero, Lebron, —and Horace Grant/Jabbar style protective goggles. They really play rough here. And refs don't call fouls quite as cleanly. Their b-ball style is less elegant. The boys and I watched an intense, and very well-played I must say, sixteen and seventeen year old age group game the other day. The ref commendably called technicals on a hot-headed boy who started a fight. Came up fists flying after a dramatic scramble for a loose ball. He picked up another, he shudda been ejected for throwing the ball high into the air after being called for another foul. He was one of those scrappy players with a chip on their shoulder, full of intimidation, yet, not much good at putting the ball in the hole or even getting it to someone else who could. I told the boys that he was the epitome of what not to be on the court. They nodded in agreement. Then, of course, one has to agree with the guy who buys the cheeseburgers after the game (me) as a general (and I might add, pragmatic) rule of etiquette. As I say, the Hunkies like their b-ball rough.

The old barbarian cultures are less graceful (gracious) than the Greco-Roman, though their sensuality is purer. For Hunkies, food still seems a pragmatic thing. And it tastes good. But it shouldn't get too fancy, though it's fancier than the boiled meat and potatoes the Brits eat as a kind of penance! For the Italians, for example, food is not about nutrition, it's about art. Even a working-class Italian is a gourmet. They simply will not put anything into their mouths that isn't good. And non tourist Italian restaurants are about the same price as Reddy's poolroom in Edgeton. So, in this sense, their aesthetic is a form of decadence. But the Hungarians' growing decadence has been learned from the West (especially in the post communist era, which I witnessed almost from its inception) but still seems less pervasive. Even the Mafia, more Russian, Ukrainian and oriental in character, seems a bit more folksy here, less sinister. They say the Mafia in NYC is much more evil than its Sicilian progenitor. We forget that poorer cultures are more conservative. New ideas, whether libertine or not, often take root more slowly among the poor. They simply don't have time enough away from the drudgery of their work to adopt them.

West Europeans are probably suffering more from boredom. But the

Hungarians, in mad pursuit of Desire, are catching up. I should add that we are getting ready to see a Russia the world hasn't seen in awhile. More like the pre-WWI one.—Greco–Roman, renaissance humanism, the humanism of Erasmus and Shakespeare, which they themselves learned from the ancients, both Christian and pagan, doesn't exist the same way here. And that, my friend, is a most telling difference. It also doesn't exist, as we know it, in the middle East.

You'd find it interesting for your thesis I'm sure when I say that living here has made me see the character of the East more clearly, though Hungary's political leanings seem to still be toward the West, they differ deeply. One of the most telling ways is in the archaic sense of humor, though, when I tell them a standard American joke, they fall out with convulsive laughter. They like ours but I don't understand theirs. "The old rabbit shows the young one how to fuck; the young one watches the father, then, tries it himself. Afterwards, he says, 'I am sorry, father.'" That's it…. I don't get it, either.

Lydia said that Hungarians don't know how to have fun. Sometimes I climb up a hill a bit and look out. I can see the East quite well. When I see footage of Palestine, Lebanon, and Iraq, even, Kosovo, Serbia, etc, on TV, I recognize those streets, those buildings, those crummy looking apartment blocks, old Russian cars and dudes with high cheekbones and weird hats trying to sell you cheap stuff. You can get some great stuff that way! Then that's the sinister colonist in me, wanting me to say, glancing at the pretty gypsy girl, How much for the weemean, I vant to buy zee woman. (That's where you come in, boss! Ha ha!)

Now, the ordinary European girl might enjoy herself but not this girl in rags. No, she sees herself as an inviolable princess fit for a young Eastern prince, not a white scum bag like me. Yet, like you said, just to appease her dear poor father she loyally might well perform this, for her, disgusting, colonialistic act of prostitution. That's the great paradox of poverty. The colonialist himself, in reality, the real gypsy thief, always thinks the poor are promiscuous, immoral and less sophisticated. It's not true! But in time, after adopting his lifestyle, or being forced to, they will be.

Everything is cool, baby. Samuel Johnson said, "If a man talks of his misfortunes there is doubtless something in them that is not disagreeable to him; for where there is nothing but pure misery, there never is any recourse to the mention of it." Yet, I feel a sense of well-being only because of the children. Otherwise, it would be too claustrophobic. They connect me to the past. Where one's parents live, along with the memories of youth and friendship—that is the place that will always seem like home. Home is where someone loves you.

Hope you'll take my musings lightly. Still, I feel like I need to talk about real things, identify them. That keeps them from morphing into dark things. The only sin is NEGLECT. Otherwise, if there is a God, he wants us to be free. Yet, look at the vast prison the Earth can become… and one of our own making. I still gotta try and bust out.

Josh

Dear Carlo,

Man, been missing you madly lately… coz Euro rhythm sections are…. different.

I just brought home some succulent smoked bacon. Here you can get really great smoked spiced sausages and bacon, Kolozsvari style. "Kolosvar," pronounced: COL-osh, same sound as "cola," Var, but with the Hung. Long "a" which is the same sound Dracula makes. So, "Var" is pronounced like used to sayBela Lugosi used to say I "VANT" to drrrink your BLAHT! Kolozsvar is the Hungarian name for the now Romanian town of Cluj. "Var" means "Castle." Kolozsvar is in the (disputed and nostalgically romanticized by the Hungies) territory of Transylvania. They know they'll never get it back. Even though there's always a small right wing faction clamoring for its return.

They lost it in WWI at the treaty of Trianon, near Versailles. Romania supported the allies. Good Boys. Hungies bad boys slap slap. 2/3's of the Kingdom of Hungary was given to its neighbors! Bit harsh, but, gee, siding with the Nazis in WWII to get it back again? By the time they realized their political mistake, it was too late. Cudda happened to anyone —slaves to the decisions of their masters. Russians bombed the shit outta BP in '45 tryin to kill retreating Nazis. Anyone who loses something dear gets desperate. A national trauma they've never fully recovered from. They still use their own names for Romanian cities. Wouldn't it be weird if Kentuckians, defeated by Tennessee in a war, called Memphis, Yomama, or something like that, refusing to say Memphis, etc. You get the idea. Ah, Europe! So full of proud little silly nations. But it's slowly metamorphosing into one concept. Can the center hold?

But Kolozsvari bacon is kinda like what we call "country style" or, in other words, "better than anything else". Just made some pasta carbonara. Saute some onion and pepper (Hungarians call the whole vegetable "paprika," not just the sweet, or hot, red powder) and garlic—lots of it, like, four or five big cloves—then stir in a little tomato paste, simmer, fry the "bacon" cut up in smallish chunks, add to the mix along with some oregano, thyme, marjoram, a pinch of rosemary, a bay leaf. Simmer. Poor over a good linguine.

It's all waiting in the kitchen. But I'm putting off the feast in order to write. I feel good. I got gigs. Gigs in the cupboard. The band I'm in does "Shotgun, Sex Machine, Sexual Healing, Let's Get It On, Black Magic Woman, Oye Como Va, Tower of Power's, "Diggin on James Brown," alot of nifty kicks and such that reminds me of Sylves. God, I miss him so much sometimes, the humor, his hoped-for visit here that never came off). Pretty much my same philosophy of music... Pick Up the Pieces, Summer in the City, Al Jarreau's, Boogie Down... Soul Man, some blues. One band adds a horn section, another is just five-piece... or six or seven... piano, bass, drums, guitar, conga (I've gotten real addicted to that, gigs without conga seem empty somehow) sax, two trumpets and trombone. Sometimes I miss the cerebral stuff from Lacey's band, but nobody wants to hear that shit anymore. So, it's a question of survival.

Still think about Sylves a lot. He loved your playin' so much. Everything's gone, man. I'm clinging to these memories of sweet loving ladies as long as I can, to smooth the way to death. My life is going fast. Band is playing a lot. My throat is raw from screaming over the crowd (doctor doesn't like my x-ray).

Emese, the Romanian girl. Emese, I love Love. Maybe too much.

She's lying on the back seat, feet over the old Dacia's gear shift. The moon over a field of yellow grain, Venus rising. Finding that someone, like SHE once was. I keep searching. I tell her, "It's only memories I crave".

Why did Helen change, man? I guess I did, too. Somehow the space/time a couple creates a space of many years to have beautiful children just shrinks, shrinks away. Love happens when there's a space of time big enough for two lives to fit into—but only for a little while. Without space in two lives love can't exist! Emese has that same oriental yellowish skin that outside of the orient you only find possessed by Romanian and Hungarian girls. It's Persian? Turkish? Jewish? That very very black hair with subtly tinged saffron skin. The same huge brown eyes and dark circles.

Tales of sex and food, old friend. Forgive me. One of my favorite things to do sometimes is walk out thru the park behind my house and go to this little deli/grocery. In Budapest, there's all these little shops in every working class neighborhood where you get fresh pork chicken and beef, rarely fish. Magyars eat all kinds of river fish like carp (ponty) catfish (fogas) even trout (pistrang) but you have to go to select places to get it. Only certain bigger markets (Csarnok) carry fish and only out of the downtown area. Out in the malls can you get stuff like salmon (Lazac) or lobster or squid or red snapper, and that only very recently. (Probably fly it in from Croatia). I always go up and flirt with the sixty year old lady behind the counter who was obviously a babe in her day. Now she's fat and wrinkled with gorgeous, bright blue eyes. She always takes her glasses off when I make a comment about them so I can get the full effect. They are stunning. Ah, how many Hungarian men committed emotional hari kari over those baby blues! Mr. Deli Owner is conspicuously missing. Her son, thirty something is putzing about. Recognizes me as a regular, turns on a smile. "Ver r you frahm", mama asked when I first came in almost a year and a half ago. KenTUCky, I tell her. "Ahh, CANtooki. USA?" Yes. "Vould you like to fuck me? (Naw man, she didn't say that. She didn't and we didn't – but I would have).

It's obviously a Mama thing for me, a security thing. Big bosomy woman. Big protection against_____. "The embrace of poetry like the embrace of a naked body/ Protects while it lasts/ against all access by the misery of the world" - Andre Breton. So alls I gotta do now is get the earth mama and the slim Venus/ diana seductress in sync. Then all will be bliss (hell?).

On the other side of the shop they have a dazzling array of cold cuts and pickles. The shelves are full of packages of pasta (teszta) usually the Hungarian brands, not Italian—and bottles of brandies and liqueurs. You can sometimes get fresh bread at these places. So, I get three fresh thigh/ chicken leg pieces (they don't separate thigh from leg always. I mean, this shit was brought in and chopped up this morning. There's a bucket of chicken heads looking at me. (Where the hell'd yr body go, boys?) And something new: marbled turkey breast cold cuts. Turkey meat with streaks of paprika and fat? Walk back home, fire up the oven (only has one setting) put the chicken legs on top of this piece of a casserole dish I found somewhere (most of my kitchen furnishings were left by the departed Great Aunt of my land lady) throw in a coupla baked potatoes, whip up some frozen peas and voila! Supper. This is a pleasant change from cooking almost exclusively with a wok now. I was missing that slow southern roast style. What women can I lure in here with good food?

Sometimes I feel like I wasted my life. But sometimes it's hard to have enough faith in dreams and fate to really do something. I woke up this morning feelin wasted after the post gig celebrations and looked out my kitchen window at the two gold dust brown doves courting in the huge sycamore tree that stretches out across the pathetic little expanse of grass in front of my apartment building. I live sort of on the edge of downtown. Beyond me begin factories and access roads to highways and warehouses and shit. But if you walk the other way back towards town and the river there's this one parking lot behind a supermarket that reminds me of the one that ran from the back of the Presbyterian Church in Edgeton over behind Reddy's poolroom. When I was a teenager I remember walking through that parking lot thinking that it felt "urban" or somehow "outta the movies." The sun shone so yellow and bright. We played music in the church coffee house on Friday nights. Remember when that was, like, a big deal in Edgeton? A coffee house? Is that Christian? I remember dudes laughing in the kitchen, a light-skinned dude, blondish 'fro: "I never DID like white folks! I jes fucks they women!" You gotta love mankind.

The doves are circling each other around a branch. One seems to be sniffing the other's ass. They're sniffing each other's asses. The male hops up to a higher branch and spreads his wings above the female. She submits, hops up toward him. Then they fly away. Spring is coming. Then there's me trudging along the supermarket parking lot in the yellow light—only I'm in Hungary, not Edgeton.

Cheers,

Josh.

48

Hey Josh,

Thanks for forwarding. Good to hear all's well in Budapest. I'm staying with Aunt Pearl, who now lives in New Jersey, for a couple of months. Company I was working for folded so I'm chillin at her home for awhile after doing some gigs back in Medina. But sad news back here in the good 'ol USA: Carlo died this morning of a heart attack. Kinda weird. Very hot day. Played a gig in the park and then went home sayin he was really tired. I thought he was just sick of my guitar playing (ha ha, obviously we been missin' you!) He just died in his sleep. That's all I know now. Have no idea about your emails. Angelika has tried to get in touch with Sylves' ex-wife. I think she still has some contact with Carlo's wife. Hate to be the one to tell you.

Be strong,

Crip.

49

THE AMERICAN GUY BY JOSHUA CELESTE

To Mister Kovacs, Kreep,

Uzanet—Magyar Rendorseg (Hungarian National Police—massage for you IMPORTANT!)

19:55—(sender ou812)—Hello Kovacs mister! Please to office bring permission form from next of kin—and you are passport with foto for you. Mistur Celeste computer released immediately for yourself, for example.

Best … Lt. Nagy, Zsofia. Budapest Rendorseg. (sorry for my english).

271

50

THE AMERICAN GUY BY JOSHUA CELESTE

The night I met her was one of those balmy, late summer ones when the air feels like lotion on your skin and everything seems so mild and tranquil as if the City had become a garden after a gentle rain. Driving through Budapest's cafe district, I noticed all the girls in their summer dresses so I pulled my car over and parked on a little side alleyway, and started sauntering toward Andrassy St., hands in my pockets, carefully checking things out. Tanned legs, gorgeous hair, smiles, laughter, lips, tits bulging in cute blouses, asses swaying —guys and gals in their youth getting drunk, smoking dope in a circle over by the cafe's kitchen door. It felt like being in a kind of anxious heaven or mildly fatalistic hell since I would be too shy to dare talk to anyone. Everybody enjoying themselves in a context I only observed from the outside. Many were foreigners like me but they seemed to be blending in well. I suddenly wished one of my more extroverted buddies could be with me to somehow break the ice. I was at the breaking point.

She was turning the corner of Jokai and Andrassy. Right away—I don't know how—I thought to myself, I'm gonna make love to her, I bet. She was too tall for the kind of girl I usually hit on, and overweight, but not in an unbeautiful way. Her tallness (six feet?) helped her carry it well. She seemed big, but not fat. She wasn't pretty, but her face had some kind of enigmatic attraction. The cheekbones were high as an oriental girl's and her eyes were also rather elongated horizontally, squinty like a Chinese girl's, but then the corners of them turned upward slightly which just accentuated their bright intensity. Her tits seemed full enough, though not terribly sexy, and her ass was a little flat but not entirely shapeless. Not as shapeless and flat as mine I thought to myself. No, it was her full lips and her attractive streak-blond hair, her flashing, slightly arrogant and bored looking bright eyes… and her soft coffee skin tone. Cute, but not a knockout. And yet, still, she seemed homely—almost ugly with her weak chin and the gap between her teeth, almost—repulsive. I thought all this in a split second and at the same time stepped up a little hurriedly toward her. No one was closer than ten paces to us so I thought now's the time to say something without the embarrassment of being rejected in front of someone passing by.

It amazes me that I still have the guts to approach a girl on the street and say, "Excuse me, do you speak English?" after all the many rejections I've sustained living as a foreigner for so long, yet, I once again gave that workhorse line a shot. I immediately regretted it as she turned a surly expression my way and looked me up and down. She paused in her steps for a brief moment but then walked on saying nothing. I stayed behind her a few steps but then when I drew up beside her again waiting at the next block for the light to change, I couldn't resist trying to redeem myself.

"Sorry," I stammered in poor Hungarian, "I didn't mean to intrude. I have lived here for many years but still don't speak Hungarian very well, I only wanted to ask…"

"But you speak vell," she said. "Your pronunciation is good. Vhere do you come from"?

I started in on the condensed version of my life story as we walked slowly along, stealing glances at one another. I felt better that at least I hadn't given her the impression of a complete idiot. She listened.

"Sure we can't have one drink?" I asked, feeling more confidence. She didn't answer at first and I was preparing to give up and go my way but then as we passed a popular open air patio bar that had a rep for cheap live music. She said, in her thick, Hungarian accent, "Vee can go here if you vant."

What happens at that moment? Is it that some chasm opens and you're plummeting through the sky toward death but then you remember your wings, so small yet they still somehow keep you buoyed up? I see now, that I hadn't really looked at her. She had been only an impression, a Picasso-like swirl without shape. Slowly she came into being. I looked at her full on as we sipped Sangria at the bar. She wasn't pretty. Was it simply my horniness—I hadn't had sex with anyone for two years—that led me on?

We found a table and chatted. We both shared an interest in Hungarian folk music. I tried to impress her with some famous names I knew in that scene, people Crip had introduced me to years before and we had played some gigs with.

A few glasses of sangria later we went inside to hear the band. They were playing a sort of bad "world music" and wearing funny oriental hats—though they were local musicians, and much more "western" than their hats indicated on a badly lit stage. Still, there was plenty of conga drum coming through the bad speakers and the crowd noise. We watched. I stole furtive glances at her. I noticed her full kissable lips, round soft shoulders, coffee and cream skin tone, blond streaked hair, I knew something was happening. She's fine, I thought to myself. A fine, good girl. A horn squawked. A cymbal crashed. Someone was singing in Turkish in a flamenco-like style.

I asked her to dance and she accepted readily. After swaying to the music for a time I put my arms around her. After a few moments, I wrongly assumed she might let me kiss her. I tried ever so slightly to pull her closer toward me. But she resisted by pulling back very subtly. I felt embarrassed—then just as quickly it passed. No harm done I thought. She knows what I want. They always know. She must go, she said, as we stood in the courtyard again feeling the fresh lotion feeling of the late summer air. I was certain—certain I could maybe get a kiss— which I almost desperately wanted. I asked if I could walk her home. "No," she said, and she gently repelled, in that way girls have, my attempt to give her another kiss. So I turned away, holding the number she gave me like a little charm, glancing back once more at her tall figure disappearing into the shadows.

Not long after, we met again at the same place. She answered my text message I'd written in Hungarian asking her if we could meet again with a "very good!" in English. Funny how we tried clumsily to use each other's language. Later she would teach me many Hungarian words. I knew now that I had something. She was trying to show me that she wanted to learn a little English. But now I hesitated. A good person like her? You would simply make love to her on a whim? With no intention of being her companion? Such thoughts began to assail me. Like an addict I denied them. My perception of her changed. Or she was changing. Becoming something I could have. I began to think of her homeliness. Is this a woman I could fall in love with? The answer was no. Well, then you're a cad, I thought. Oh, why not just have fun? Let the chips fall. When I finally spotted her at a table near the bar, I could see one of her girlfriends she had confided in, looking me over. But then they both smiled and giggled and motioned for me to come over. Her friend excused herself. They both had such a sweet girlish air about them. Her friend was of a similar attractiveness, that Renoir-like softness, but less so.

She had to work in the morning, she said, walking away. Giggling, she winked her approval and gave a hand signal to her I didn't understand. I was in a kind of euphoria, intoxicated by perfume and the fact that after so long a woman might want me. I no longer noticed much around me. Suddenly I felt like a boy on the bank of the old fish pond on Water Maple Farm trying not to lose the little Breem fish on his hook, excited yet still steady, staring at the water. I stumbled with my Hungarian but it didn't bother her. She spoke slowly to me like I was a child. The orphan boy she'd come upon in the street.

We chatted and she smiled. I moved my face a little closer. Kiss? I kept trying to make inane conversation, still unaware that it was no longer necessary. After a few seconds, though, it became obvious. I tilted my face upwards towards her like a fish swimming up to the surface from deep water. We kissed in a slow gentle way. Her lips were so soft and tender it was like falling into a scattering of pillows in an opium den.

We decided to go out again onto the dance floor—only this time it was a band playing a kind of bad New Orleans style funk, the singer doing a badly Hungarian-accented version of Dr. John. "Voo do you laff"? he kept screaming in his fake gravelly voice." VOO DOO YOU LAFF!!!" Soon we were outside in the soft night air. We kept walking not knowing where I was going, feeling slightly nervous that I might lose my hold on her. We stopped at darkened doorways to kiss and I hugged her and pushed my hand against her breasts, pushing her a little roughly against the wall, running a hand along her thigh and squeezing her ass. She moaned gently like a train whistle far away on a windy night as she opened her mouth wide and I put my tongue as deep as I could down her throat, kissing her again and again.

Suddenly that wave of passion subsided a little and I came to my senses. "Do you want to come to my flat?" I asked. I felt a dionysian power over her now but her answer quickly snapped me out of it. "No, I must work in the morning, very early. I can't go with you tonight. I'm sorry". We then came upon a taxi stand and she opened the door quickly herself before I had a chance to do it for her. She smiled at me and blew a kiss and made a cute motion of her thumb against her ear and her little finger against her lips in an impression of a telephone, as if to say, We will speak soon.

Any uncertainties her sudden flight might have aroused were quickly put to rest when we met a few days later in front of the McDonald's at Moricz Zsigmond Square. She looked sweet in tight white jeans and a black fake designer t-shirt with some silly Italian words written on it in sparkly letters which I couldn't quite make out. Her lovely streaked-blond hair (how untouchable all the lovely Hungarian girls with their hair this way had seemed before!) fell across her forehead sexily.

It was a hot early September afternoon and little beads of sweat had begun to form very slightly on her upper lip. Her mouth hung open almost like she was panting gently, and her bright eyes had an almost scared expression in them, like a cornered little wild animal. Yet she was so tall in her heels. But the tight jeans couldn't quite disguise the fact that her thighs and her ass were unshapely. There was something round and strong and large and sweet in the roundness of her arms, the fatness of her weak chin, and the illusory way her large but unshapely breasts were pushed up by her bra so that her cleavage could show above her low-cut tasteless t-shirt.

I took all this voluptuous vision in as we walked along, glancing at her for a moment and seeing again the panting, submissive expression on her face that kept looking back at me. Slightly flustered I asked if she wanted to go to a cafe for a coffee (in this heat?) but as I turned to look at her full on she looked into my eyes and without saying anything shook her head, no, very slowly. "Do you want to just go back to my flat?" I asked, like a boy approaching someone who had been put under some hypnotic spell. "Yes," "Igen," she said in Hungarian. I led her along by the hand.

We started kissing in the elevator. Then I unlocked the door to my apartment and kept kissing her as I pushed her against the wall in the cramped hallway. Though it was a tiny apartment, I had pushed together the two single beds that my landlady's children had once slept in so that it gave the illusion, by covering the crack between them with white sheets, of a king size bed. The tight jeans, the t-shirt—suddenly it was all coming off and our fingers were full of buttons and zippers. She stood beside the bed in her sweet, lacy fake designer underwear and bra. I knelt in front of her, covering her thighs and knees and ankles with kisses. Her sagging shapeless thighs touched each other as she stood but I pushed them apart slightly and kissed the inside of them smelling faint traces of perfume, sweat and urine as I moved my mouth toward her pussy and the faint salt smell of the sea. She pulled me onto her as we fell back onto the bed but I wanted to savor her loveliness for a moment before getting up to get a condom from the bathroom shelf. She wrapped her legs around me and tilted her head back so that I could see and kiss and suck on her soft fragrant neck and blood-engorged jugular and I licked up further into her ear and temple. I rolled over and pulled her ass up to my face and began licking her pussy all over as she put my cock into her mouth. Then she did the sweetest thing which I will never forget and which no woman had ever done to me. As her vagina began glistening with my saliva and her flowing juices she turned around and leaning her face toward me, began licking and kissing those juices off my face like an affectionate cat or dog might lick the hand of its master.

Thinking back now I see it was just another expression of the kindness of her soul and her girlish modesty in regard to the smell of her own body, but at the time it occurred to me that she might be bisexual, so much did she seem to enjoy the taste of herself. Then she would kiss me with her tongue so that the juice might first go into her own mouth before sharing it with me. In the same way, I remember my wife, Helen, sometimes chewing food before putting it into the mouths of our children. Soon I could take it no longer and I put my cock into her pussy. I felt like a small ship out on a sea I could no longer see across as she rocked me and pushed against me with her round belly. She moaned like a wind in my ears and I remember chuckling to myself, as her moans became louder and louder, as to what my neighbors might think of all the noise we made. I felt as powerful as some sea god, though only moments before when I'd entered her we'd both let out a quiet moan of absolute surrender.

Yet when we finished and I gazed at her soft, satisfied eyes, what sad thoughts began to assail me. I wanted suddenly to be alone, so alone had I been for so many years, but I dared not show these feelings to her. Still, she sensed my withdrawal and she asked, timidly, if the sex was good. I kissed her and said, "Yes, it was very good." And it was. Still, I felt I needed to hide so much. Why, I don't know.

51

Like so many Hungarian girls, she still lived with her parents. But her apartment was separated from them in a kind of duplex. They lived downstairs while she had a few small rooms, a small living room with her few books, all in Hungarian, a kitchen with a little table, a hallway upstairs.

Gudrun called to say her folks were out of town. Gone on a brief holiday to Denmark. So Josh drove out of the city to see her. The suburb, called Saint's Wood, was a typically sad looking little enclave with row upon row of drab stucco one or two-story houses going along street after street. Old junky cars from the communist era were parked along the open ditches. Occasionally, one would see a new Western-style car, like an Audi or a Toyota or a Ford parked in a new cheaply constructed tin garage that barely covered the car.

Gudrun was waiting at the bus stop near her house waving to Josh so he could see her and pull over and she would get in and show him the rest of the way through the labyrinthine streets. As the headlights shown upon her, her face seemed stricken with the anxiety of someone falling in love. Josh felt almost sorry for her, but the neighborhood was so unfamiliar to him that he had to keep his mind on his driving and where he was going, even if he didn't have the slightest idea.

They talked awhile in her kitchen over a glass of wine. He rolled a joint which Gudrun giggled at and wouldn't try and then he took drags off of her cigarette though he'd given them up months before. The wine and tobacco and reefer tasted good. She made him a sandwich and he watched her hips move as she stood beside the sink. Josh came up behind her even while she held the knife she was using to cut slices of onion and sweet pepper. When she felt his hands sliding around her waist, she turned around to kiss him and throw her arms around him. She let the knife fall clattering against the dirty dishes into the sink.

Josh laughed and said, "I wasn't sure if maybe you wanted to kill me..." She giggled and opened her mouth wide for his kiss. She moved away toward the hallway and motioned to him with her index finger, wiggling it like a worm slowly undulating like a dancer toward her face, to come with her. He hesitated for a second and she stopped and looked at him quizzically like a bird. Then Gudrun cocked her head and tossed her forehead toward the bedroom like a girl tossing the bangs out of her eyes. He felt something give deep down somewhere in his chest, his heart, his gut, his knees. This time she was on top of him smothering him with her incredibly beautiful lips. He pushed his chest up so he could feel her breasts brush against it. Her pants came quickly off with one tug and he pulled the panty string aside and mounted her and rolled on top of her like the grassy hillsides of childhood memories but he could take it no longer and she pleaded with him. When he was inside her she began to cry out loudly like someone who was experiencing a great tragic event or as if she were a mother who had not seen a loved child in a long time and she cried and moaned rhythmically in gratitude for the reunification.

Once again after Josh lay still beside Gudrun, panting, he caught sight of her massive jowls and the rolls of fat of her thighs. There was something animal in her eyes that seemed to tell him that he couldn't talk to her about his feelings and suddenly he realized that indeed he wasn't fluent in her language at all, nor she in his. But he felt naked and alone very suddenly. He was cold. She embraced him and her warm skin felt good in the slight early autumn chill of the room. Autumn shadows played in the windows. She began to fondle his genitals, which made him giggle and push her hand away a little, because he was completely spent and knew he couldn't get a hard-on again for at least awhile so he said, sighing, It was so nice but I don't think I can do it again yet. But she laughed sympathetically and said, No, no, no— only we play a little. She kissed and licked his limp penis very softly and breathed softly against his thighs.

After a time they got up again and she fixed him another snack. Josh sat on her back stairs and had a cigarette. He was getting hooked again. He couldn't resist copying her smoking, she looked so sexy doing it. The September morning light had a gentle saffron melancholy way about it, as if, beautiful as it was, it contained the end of itself. Soon the fragrant smoke of morning fog disappears, people hurrying to work.

She would come in late she said. Her boss wouldn't mind. Her hours could be quite flexible. Yet there was much work to be done. But she could stay late. He was overwhelmed by the September light, by the memory of her love-making, the warm feeling in his genitals, the warm black tea in his belly. She asked him about his quietness, but he only shrugged. Why was something hurting him? Josh thought of his home far away. Nothing lasts, he thought, but I must love this moment, this yellow, honey, light even as it passes. Are you sure you're ok? Gudrun asks in Hungarian. "Yes," he says. "I'm ok."

Sometimes Josh suddenly awoke with some horrific vision still in his head like William Hurt in Body Heat. Only there was no husband to knock off. He lay there, looking up at the ceiling, arms folded, and remembered his college days. And the summer he and Lilian went to that party and finally he got up the courage to kiss her in his Mom's steel blue, Pontiac Catalina. That summer turned into lovemaking in the back seats of cars parked off country roads.

In autumn, it came time for her to go to school in New England. Josh went to the local small college in Edgeton but pined away for her, remembering summer. Another summer came and they started again, still in love even though she'd finished a whole year at Smith hundreds of miles away. It felt good to have her back. One day in the cool green of the shade of a grove of walnut trees he laid out a white sheet and there she was all creamy white and pale and naked. She was anxious about the possibility of someone seeing them, but somehow he put her mind at ease. A few moments later he looked up from their lovemaking and saw Ricky Boy and TLC watching him from behind the huge oak at the top of the hill. But he said nothing. He tried only to shoo them away with the expression of his eyes.

Again she went back to Smith. After another semester he couldn't take it anymore. They made love on her Christmas breaks back in Edgeton, but by early January she was gone back again. In February he decided to hitchhike to Amherst to see her. That was the snowstorm outside the I-80 truckstop in PA.

In Connecticut, a distraught guy (scarily drunk) in a little car picked him up. Soon the Story began. My wife, he sobbed, her and her boyfriend are tellin my kids that I'm dead! That I'm dead!

They stopped at a gas station and Josh let him put his head on his shoulder and cry while he muttered through the whole story—the love, the kids, the divorce. Finally, he fell asleep and Josh slipped away.

After a few more rides he finally made it to North Hampton. He found her dorm and knocked on the door they told him, curious girls walking around with towels around their heads and toothbrushes in their mouths. She was just waking up but he was so horny he pushed her back on the bed and started in on her right away. She made no attempt to resist him. "Josh, what are you doing?" They lay back. He lit a cigarette which she took a few drags from while he talked about the trip up. He thought she would be more interested.

Josh was too quiet around her friends. Other guys were more talkative and seemed to be tuned into her more. He found his mind wandering. Maybe they made lackluster love once more but then on the last day of his visit she wouldn't kiss him bye at the bus station. He knew something was up, but what? Something has ended, but he couldn't understand it. Weird bus ride to Cincy, thoughts of her as something gone. He hitched from there to Medina. Apartment felt empty. He was completely alone, he thought.

He visited Doc and his girlfriend just a neighborhood over. They had tea. Lilian is my girl, he thought, watching the rain from their porch, strumming his guitar. He refused to let go. He saw her Spring break but sensed now that he shouldn't even try for a kiss. He put their old love in a glass case and became its curator.

Josh couldn't get into Harvard, his SAT scores were just too low, but he must have just really wanted to be closer to her. Bertha, who was nearly eighty now, said she'd pay for him to go to BU. But he never enrolled. He just hung out in the clubs. That's where I met him. Playing Bluegrass music to himself to cure homesickness and hitching to Amherst every weekend to pray at the shrine of Lilian's dead love. He still thought it was alive. Poor dude. He vaguely remembered our bus rides to Medina, Aunt Pearl's apartment where Bertha used to bring them, and me hanging around his gigs. It was another lifetime ago. He thought about enrolling at Berklee. This was his chance to actually study music. I showed him the old Irish and Scottish songs I knew from my musicology courses. I played them scratchily on fiddle for him and the old Hungarian songs my grandmother sang. He loved it all. I got him some gigs in a few clubs doing his jazz and blues thing. He got pretty popular and I got good enough on bass to back him up a little. It was fun. We made enough cash to hang out and party and buy a bag of dope from time to time. I got food for him out of my dormitory cafeteria.

One night when Josh was visiting, some dudes came into my room kinda drunk. I sort of knew them but not that well. They knew Josh a little from hanging out but then maybe just to fuck with him they got talking about some girl at Smith that was, "really wild" and a friend of theirs had been with her a few times and said she was "really hot." What was her name? I asked as Josh sat nearby strumming his six-string. Lilian Carpentier, they said. I glanced at Josh. His face went someplace else. Maybe not a place but just somewhere. I didn't see him for a few weeks. Still, even though that cut must have hurt, he never went out with any local chicks, certainly not to deaden his pain. Summer came and school was over and we decided to do some gigs in Medina. Lilian was back in Medina at her parents' house. They were in California looking for a retirement home and he called her and she said come over I'm having a party. His heart jumped to think maybe he would get her back again but he didn't know how. Bring your guitar, she said. A few of us came, me, Harris, Free and Carlo. Josh was there, more than just a friend, but not her boyfriend anymore, that was sure to everyone. But Josh wasn't sure how to be and to her, he was like a sweet loyal dog that would stay beside you unless you whipped it and yelled Go away!

Her two friends from Amherst showed up. One dude was obviously her boyfriend. He didn't kiss her, like, a real wet one or anything in front of us but somehow you just knew it, I don't know how. What is it about that gut feeling? It's not always detailed Truth but it's the right Truth. Suddenly it became obvious: this was a shock treatment. As if she was saying: Now will you believe I have someone else? The party went on. I could see something strange in Josh's face. Me and Josh got back to the apartment we were sharing. I poured him a whiskey. I hadn't really realized that he'd been carrying a torch for her for so long. Tonight was the defeat. The surrender. There comes a time when all the illusions fall away and you're out in the open with no one.

I remember watching him pace up and down the sidewalk in front of our place. I practiced on his guitar. He never minded. He walked all the way down to just before the steps went down to the street and then kinda did this James Brown turn around pirouette and came back over and over. We sipped whiskey and talked. As the sun rose I finally talked him down out enough of his sorrow. He never saw her again.

52

Sex with Gudrun is amazing. When I'm fucking her doggie style, I like to hold both her feet in my hands and lift them up slightly so I can see that lovely ripple in her calf muscle. She's on all fours and I don't push her head down into the pillow yet. She's lifting her head up or turning around so I can kiss and lick her mouth and see her tongue darting into the corners of her mouth, her hands supporting her. Her tongue flicking and her ass wagging. I gather her beautiful streaked-blond hair into a handful of ponytail and pull her head back, exposing her peach-colored neck. She raises up off her hands a little, like a curious animal might start to stand on its hind legs, so I can better reach her neck, which I kiss, bite gently and lick. She throws her head down raising her ass as high as it will go screaming, "fack me! fack me! fack me!" in her cute Hungarian accent and her whole body shakes as she cums. She turns around to suck my cock but the stream of my cum hits her in the middle of her forehead and trickles down onto her lips which she starts licking gently. She clicks her tongue inside her mouth as if she were savoring some morsel of food.

After a moment, we tumble down into the covers giggling. Then I lay back in a kind of alfa state. I haven't felt this peace of mind for so long. She looks at me lovingly. But I told her I didn't love her. Her eyes shatter slightly when I say this, but quickly she sighs and laughs. O Joshie, she says, laughing. She seems unsexy now that I've had her so completely. Still, I feel almost some kind of pity.

They make love like this, a few times a week, Josh and Gudrun, for several months. He likes her but rarely calls. He'd gotten interested in a couple of other much hotter chicks. His heart leaps when the phone rings. "It's me," says, Gudrun. "I'm downstairs." He goes down to meet her. In the elevator, they kiss.

She comes in and immediately takes off her clothes and lays back on the bed.

She feels good under him, her legs swimming like a frog. He, like a frog crouched above her. Then he changes into a Rider, riding, riding the long way home, his head against the sweating horse's neck. But he's thinking of other women now. She straddles him and presses her soft hands into his chest. She suddenly looks at him, looks at him up and down quickly as if trying to take him in, hungrily, with one glance. She sighs and moans as she runs her eyes over his chest and belly and face. She's never had a boy with such a shapely body. Only the men at the factory where her father works, ones with beer bellies and foul breath. A desperate sigh of gratitude comes over her eyes and Josh feels in total control of her now. She cums in sweet staccato gasps and moans like someone crying.

Josh likes Gudrun but he remembers Lilian and Wanda… and then Helen. He'd rather not think of love, of Gudrun, like that. He doesn't see her for weeks. He laughs when she leaves a message on his phone, "I'm sick, baby. I have a fever! I'm staying in bed and having soup and thinking of you! Are you alright? I'm so hot for you baby. So hot under the sheets. I'm sweating. Fuck me BABY!" She feels like a little school girl she's so in love. She's a little afraid of him.

He doesn't call. One day she feels empty and sends him a message, "Joshika, you don't answer me. For two weeks now. It's too long time. Bye bye. I so feel empty. I try to give a little love… why doesn't the mans love me? Too long Joshika. Bye bye — U"

He feels a mild shock reading this. But then he thinks, it's better this way. Weeks pass. After all the serious years with Helen, he decided girls were now… sweet moments. Like the September light he remembered on Gudrun's staircase the next morning after they had made love all night. "A pretty girl is an oasis. The desert all around." He walked through the neighborhood, wistful. End of something.

He had already gotten what he wanted. Sex. It lessened the sting of losing Helen. He thought how coarse Gudrun had been, chiding him impatiently over his tendency to get winsome and depressive about his divorce, saying to him, "Joshika! You are warming up into big sadness again!" It seemed a bit insensitive.

The leaf strewn-streets were like old friends to Josh since he had been in his little bachelor apartment for a few years. He had money from his concerts with a little dance band that played nearly every weekend. He spent his mornings writing in his notebook, and writing songs and sending them to Harris in Nashville—but nothing ever came of it. He sometimes got work proofreading texts written in bad English.

The Sycamore tree outside his kitchen window took him back to Edgeton and the creek that flowed out from the spring behind his grandmother Bertha's house. The Rose of Sharon of Budapest summer streets also reminded him of her. So green in summer the sycamore was and then the leaves turned the color of sweet Tokaj wine, the same gold with tones of sunset green that bunches of ripe white grapes become. Then came the bitter copper of November and the gray ragged bareness of December. By March, as the green buds would poke out again, a few black leaves of late winter still clung. Months passed. All this he observed each year.

Josh sat in the Mona Lisa, his favorite cafe, and stared at his cappucino, bitter but cheap, and the Marlboro burning in the ashtray. Past the window walked the constant stream of Budapest, paying him no mind. He stared at the faces. Winter. Months earlier he had read Boswell's *Life of Johnson* and Sterne's *Tristram Shandy*. He didn't know why. He found them on Doc's shelf on a trip back to the States. The dry, stiff, sharp English reminded him of home. He read, imagining Johnson's voice sounding like Charles Laughton's as if listening to a very quiet, dull conversation taking place in another room. His eyes became tired and he rubbed them, staring out the window.

Weeks, months passed, looking out the plate glass window of the cafe, watching pretty office girls walk by, tough-looking businessmen with briefcases. Two months since he'd made love to her. The loneliness of realizing he couldn't find anyone else began to sink in. There had been that girl a few years before on the boulevard with astonishing red hair. Each time they met he'd been amazed by the exquisite beauty of her face. But often she stood him up. Still, he pursued her. Always next week, next week—they were to meet. And especially after Gudrun had sent her message of goodbye, in mild dejection, he pursued the redhead more diligently. But to no avail. He would have to settle for Gudrun. Just to feel her under him. He sat for many minutes looking at his phone. He looked far down the street towards the old Synagogue. Pidgeons flushed suddenly from its ramparts. He called her.

He hoped when he would first see her, he would see some kind of beauty he had missed before. He bounded down the apartment stairs and saw her waiting at the huge iron door. Her face was pretty, but there was something about it that hinted at some hidden ugliness, even decrepitude. He felt a twinge of disappointment. Still, she was sweet in her long black fake fur coat. Like a plump little lost black sheep. He gave her a small kiss in the elevator but decided it was enough for now. He wanted to savor her more.

Once inside his room, he realized how big and strong and tall she was. They sat talking at the kitchen table. Small talk. "Mindennak most jol van?" she asked.

"Is everything ok now?" She purred at him in Hungarian, touching his hand. He nodded yes, as they both giggled.

She smoked. He liked the way her upper lip curled as the smoke dribbled out. He could faintly see the childish gap in her front teeth. He stood up and walked toward her and she looked up at him shyly yet coyly as he sat down a-straddle her thighs and onto her enormous lap, kissing her long and full, letting his tongue finish off the last little taste of her lips. He gathered up in his hands a ponytail of hair from around her shoulders, and kissed her softly, like a deer nibbling grass, along the lightly pulsing vein of her neck, and where the downy hair curled in little swirls at the back of her head, as he bent it gently forward.

He fully possessed her again. He stood up and led her, just by her little finger, to the bed. Once they got their clothes off and were naked as saints, she got on her hands and knees and took him into her mouth. He bent down and kissed her and let some of his saliva dribble onto her lips. She sucked his cock. At one point, in the heat of the moment, he took it out of her mouth and slapped her rather hard across the face with his open palm. This increased her passion. She rocked back on her heels, hands on her thighs and her magnificent head tilted up, mouth open, and her tongue all the way out, in her gesture of total submission.

They met like this for several months, and the intensity of their love-making only increased. Gudrun grew very attached to him, but Josh purposely kept his own emotions in check.

Still, he chased the redhead. He wrote her a letter full of sex thinking it would interest her! She was elusive as ever. A few others. No dice. He groped the mother of one of his private English students one night in her car. She let him nuzzle her tits. But no kiss. Why do I have to wait? he asked himself. Still, he thought, I always have Gudrun.

He began to think it might be time to take her somewhere. A trip maybe. Still, he hesitated, almost embarrassed to be seen with her. But, alone with her in his flat, talking to her over glasses of red, almost black, dry wine around his kitchen table, he began to feel more at ease with her. He philosophized. Shared his thoughts with her about his family life in America, his love of poetry and art and music, his theories of culture, and the loneliness he often felt as a stranger in a strange land.

She sat and listened to this, smiling, not knowing what to say. He felt mildly disappointed by her silence, searching as he always was for some kind of deliverance. His knowledge intimidated her and she felt self-conscious; still, she liked him and found herself daydreaming about him at her desk at work, thinking how nice it would be to be married and have children. It made her sad to think that he cared nothing for such things.

"He talk only about Music, Art and Ideas!!" Gudrun said to her friends. "He say he don't believe in nations— not little one like Hungary; and that people are selfish and good people always crushed in the end, the weak always beaten by the strong."

Gudrun thought of ways she could bring Josh closer. He responds to my lovemaking, she thought, I must do it even more passionately. She remembered all the things her uncle had made her do so long ago. It made her shudder. Still, she thought, My Joshika is a man. This is what he wants.

But Josh kept his distance. Still pursued other women in secret. Once, while enjoying her company at the kitchen table, feeling he mustn't fall in love with her, he suggested they try something new. She was free, he told her, to see other men, of course, and would she like to screw one of his American friends? She stared at him for a moment, not fully understanding that now the stakes had been raised. Yet it confirmed some of her feelings about herself. She had liked it when, during their lovemaking, he called her "my little whore" and she felt herself opening so wide like a big bloom of rose. But to have it shoved in her face, she felt her temples tingling as if she wanted to cry. She didn't want to go back to that place he seemed to want to take her to—that dirty place of her Father's. It was okay in her fantasy with him but not in reality—not now. She laughed nervously at his question, not knowing what to think.

Josh felt embarrassed and wished he hadn't said it, but it was too late. She looked into his eyes. The eyes of a man, she thought. Why don't they love me?

Soon after this incident, Gudrun came to his door. Josh saw, for the first time it seemed, how beautiful she was. Her eyes were soft as a deer's and he kissed her cheek and giggled as he touched the lapel of her sexy new jacket she said she'd just bought for spring. They did their usual glass of wine but she seemed to only half-laugh at his jokes. She reached for his hand and seemed in a hurry to lead him to the bed. She quickly unzipped his fly and reached in to pull out his cock, which was just becoming hard, so his balls had not ascended much yet up into his scrotum. She did this at first while still kneeling in front of him, but then she pulled him onto his back and hovered over him, as he laid back placidly smiling at her.

After sucking the shaft for a few minutes, she then lifted it back and up, away from his scrotum, so she could more easily reach his balls with her lips, sucking and licking them. She listened to his soft little animal moans. She giggled to see him go into ecstasy. She became fascinated with how she could suck one of his balls downward away from the socket of his scrotum. She could actually make it descend—put her lips fully over it like it was a kind of lollipop—and then, with a hard kissing motion, suck it up into her mouth, just beyond where her lips met her teeth, and then release it with a rather loud popping sound. He smiled up at her as he lay on his back watching her. She would comically, almost mockingly, bug her eyes out and let her jaw drop, as she did this as if half imitating the fascination of a child. She giggled. Then, as she noticed one of his balls, of its own accord, would try to ascend up into the scrotum, as if running away and protecting itself from her searching lips, she let out a loud laugh of amusement.

He opened his eyes, as a sleeper who had been suddenly awakened would, and tried to figure for a moment what she was laughing at, but she just shook her head gently and smiled to assure him it was nothing important, at which point, being nearly hypnotized, he laid back and closed his eyes again. Still, she kept up, for a few more minutes, her little game of sucking one of his balls downward, releasing it with a pop, and then putting on a face of childish surprise and delight to watch it ascend again. She giggled more quietly, not wanting him to open his eyes and thus share in, what had become her little private game. Sometimes she even tried to take both balls into her mouth in the same way. This delighted her even more.

Finally, though, he sat up and started to mount her, but she pushed him back down as if to say, I'd rather do it this way. He was mildly disappointed because he wanted to be inside her, but just smiled and laid back down obediently. She stopped sucking and just masturbated him with her hand until he came on his belly. She turned away quickly to get a cigarette. The thought, She's changed, came to him in a flash of sudden insight but then it disappeared completely just as quickly. Usually, she kissed him. He noticed her laying turned away with her knees slightly drawn up. Now he jumped up quickly to get a towel to clean himself off.

The translation/editing project he'd gotten involved in grew more complicated and he wasn't able to meet her again for several days. Still, he thought of her often—and their last lovemaking. Could it be he was falling in love with her? Yet, he still never mentioned her to anyone, and, now, thinking of her as his secret companion, his secret possession, he simply waited, sometimes glancing at himself in the mirror—for her to call. But she didn't call. Not then.

He spent several days, so distracted had he become by their previous time together, pursuing the redhead, just for fun, now that Gudrun was "in the bag," so to say. But that was to no avail. He was called away for another week with his work.

He had gotten into the habit over the last several months of not calling her. She always called him. Tonight? she would always write in Hungarian in her text message. And once he had been so ambivalent about her! Had been, in fact, almost annoyed. Now it had been nearly two weeks! He felt the need to call.

There was no answer. He remembered her saying she was going through a big transition at her office—people being hired and fired—and would even have to attend an important conference in Vienna.

She answered with a dull, "Hello."

"Hi!" he gushed, really missing her. "How are you!?"

"Oh, hi Joshua," she said, in English, "I must to speek vish you. I very busy now I call five o'clock ok? You remember I say my boss not like I talk in office phone ok?"

"Sure, ok. Bye. Talk later." For a moment he listened to the pulsing beep of the phone. Then walked on.

He felt giddy. Her words had given him a stab of pleasure through his cock as it stirred in his pants. Surely they would meet tonight. It had been so much longer than usual between fucks. She seemed to grow larger in his mind, like big beautiful clouds, growing slightly sharper and turning steel blue. He used to lay on his back and watch them as a child flowing over the fields of Edgeton. Even the linden trees near his flat reminded him of her. The soft limbs of early May, the leaves like the skin of young frogs, the brightening light. The pungent smell of grass and mud, the sudden insect zipping past.

Josh kept walking, wondering how he could keep his mind occupied till five. I have a girlfriend and it's Spring. "It's Spring!" he called out to no one. Doc, his brother in the States, sent him a clip of e.e. cummings reading a poem about it. Maybe I'll call him tonight, he thought. He was in a silly, crazy mood. He just wanted to talk to someone. He talked softly to himself as he walked through the park, hands in his pockets.

He sat in the old furnished easy chair in his flat, the one with the sagging seat in front of the TV. He sat staring at his bookshelves, thinking suddenly how little they all meant to him now. He didn't want to read! Why should he continue to study such dead things?! Now. I want Now. Her. Now. Ten after five. Should I call? Then, the phone rang. He jumped up out of the chair.

"So, where have you been so long, sweetie? I was just thinking of you. Sorry I called you at work," he tried to say in Hungarian. "But I just suddenly got an urge to talk to you and… and… so, mi van veled, what's been happening with you? I'd almost think you had a new boyfriend or something!" He laughed as he said this.

"De van," she said, in Hungarian. "But I do."

His giddiness stopped suddenly with the knife thrust of her words. A pulse of sweat went suddenly from his gut to his fingertips. The tip of the blade seemed to start somewhere a few inches below his right rib cage and then slice quickly upward toward the middle of his chest. He sat back down and breathed out quickly as if he'd been holding his breath for some minutes without realizing it. She said nothing. "Hello?"

"Itt vagyok," she said. "I'm still here."

"Well," he said, into the receiver, remembering how he had told her that she was free to see other men, "This is good for you. I told you that once before…" his heart began beating very quickly. "Ok. Well. Yes. This is better for you. I am glad."

"Yes. Thank you. Maybe I call you, tomorrow, ok? I must go now."

"Ok. Bye."

Josh sat there for it seemed only a few minutes but then noticed the early spring sun setting. The air so soft like lotion turning cooler as it came in the open window. He got up and closed it.

He was like an actor still delivering his lines to an empty theatre as, later that evening, he wrote her a long text message telling her… now for the third time, that it was the best thing for her. After all, she was so much younger. She wrote back, the vibration of his phone startling him awake as he had finally dozed off in the chair, blanket over his knees, TV still on. "Don't be sad, little Joshika, you said you vere too old to have more children. And I vant children!"

He remembered their brief conversation months ago when she had said, "oh don't be sad Joshika, about your wife, your children, you should have big new family!" He remembered shaking his head and putting his finger to his lips. Shh. He had thought, don't speak. Only open your mouth for… and she submitted to everything. Wait! That's right! The guy at the door a few weeks ago.

"Who was that"? Josh had asked her.

"Oh, just a new guy at the office," she'd said. "He likes me."

"You like him back?" He looked pretty young.

"Ha ha …no"

But then she gave me no goodbye kiss! Josh thought. Because he was watching us! That's the guy! He's the one fucking her now!

But it wasn't that guy. It doesn't matter. Anyone would do in his fantasy-ridden mind. Her words were like a slow-acting poison. "De… van." She had spoken in Hungarian. "Ok, it's better for you," he said to himself.

He texted into the phone: "Good Luck! Have a great life, Gudrun! Yr young it's all ahead of u! Hope u have lots of kids! Call me smtm if u just want to talk, OK? C U smdy I hope!"

She never called. He was certain she would come back. One day, weeks later, talking to his ex-wife, Helen, about their kids' schedules for the coming week, he burst into tears. He told her about it all. Helen said poor little thing, and stroked his head. But why? he sobbed. SHE WAS SO SWEET! The poison had gone deep into him now. He was losing weight, chain-smoking, drinking. Still, he thought, She's coming back. I just know it.

After a few more weeks, Helen got concerned. "You need to get past this. Make her tell you if it's completely over."

"What's the best way to ask that in Hungarian?"

Helen told him, "You simply ask, 'Mindennak közünk végen?'"

He tried to call. No answer. (I am like the swallows. Endlessly careening against the air. No place to rest). He called from a payphone so she'd be more likely to answer since she wouldn't recognize his number. "Hello?" It had been weeks since he'd heard her speak. He felt the knife blade of her hello tracing the original wound, still fresh, but now lightly scabbed over. His heart started pounding. He imagined her sitting at her work desk.

He thought he heard laughter, briefly in the background when she'd said, "Oh, Hi Josh," but he couldn't be sure. "I only wanted to ask," he said, stuttering a little, "Mindennak közünk végen?"

Everywhere, Josh saw Gudrun's face. Every woman he passed in the street was her. He saw someone get into a parked car. Could it be her? Everywhere he heard laughter. But where? He felt somehow that she was watching him, watching him slowly disappear. Wherever he walked, he felt her eyes. He was afraid to leave his apartment. Soon she will come to have mercy on me, he said to himself. She taught him the word for screw, "Dugni." It was their private laugh word. Thinking it might touch her somehow, his sense of humor, he sent her a message in Hungarian, Akarom dugni veled. "I want to screw you."

That afternoon, after he spent the day holding onto his cell phone, she answered in her English, "We don't screw. I have a guy. Van a pasi."

Every spring dawn the pretty sun shone down on his bones and flesh, lying alone now in his bed. He wrote her long emails, detailing his theories as to why the relationship might have failed. Finally, he wrote, in his best Hungarian, "If you ever change your mind... please come back." She never wrote back.

One night Josh was walking past the huge old synagogue on Temple St. The streets were empty besides the cascading steel blades of the memorial sculpture. Something like the yellow light of the sun came down to him in a flash. A glint of slashing steel flashing and a loud popping sound. Something large and implacable struck his head. Pieces of things from everywhere began whirling about—the same place where so many innocent Jews had met their fate in WWII—the top of his head and his arms among them, the scalp stuck against a wall to the left of where he'd been walking. The lower part of his skull, just above the jaw, had a ball bearing about the size of a jawbreaker stuck into the side of it and lay on the pavement in a gathering pool of bright blood, the top part broken in two, a few feet away, one eyeball gone and something rolling away. Finally, after standing a few seconds... almost a minute? His legs collapsed on their own, but backwards, as if in a weird yoga position. They lay crumpled and twisted under the mass of his torso, about ten meters from his shattered skull and severed arms. Joshua Celeste was no more. Nothing left but fragments.

Josh sat on the steps of the great cathedral. He had wandered so long about the city that day—his legs were tired. He had the feeling of someone about to disappear. He wrote her a text message on his phone since he lacked the credit for an outright call—but he felt he had to tell her. "You big, big-hearted woman- I may have laughed at you. Maybe I mistreated you. I definitely neglected you. But – in the end—I loved you."

He stands in front of her, now, as she lays back on the bed, her legs opened wide, like one who stands at the junction of two rivers. One of her bare feet dangles in the air, slowly moving to a slow rhythm. Josh, on his hands and knees, reaches for it. He lets it move across his mouth, letting his tongue dart in and out between the toes, but his grip is made more difficult as the pretty barefoot jerks radically now because of the ever more forceful thrusts of the man standing beside him, inside her, at the apex of the junction. She pushes her foot against the crawling man's face, allowing him to kiss and lick it; but soon there is a rumbling in her womb, a grabbing, gushing sensation and she whimpers ever more loudly and smiles beatifically up at the standing man. The face at her foot now becomes a hindrance to her attention towards the standing man, and she gives the crouched man a swift kick as if to say, That's enough! And he topples backwards amid her laughter and ecstatic moans.

Josh awakes with a start. The body was that guys! The old friend of hers! What was his name? But the head (the standing man turns slowly. Josh can see his face clearly now. He's looking at him) The Head! He had a different head on him! It's that guy at the office! Faint sound of laughter. Wine. Dope. Sleep.

53

Hi Alisa!

I'm at work so just a short note. No, I didn't know anything about the American guy that was killed in the explosion. I hate reading about stuff like that. I'm sure it wasn't Joshua. He hardly ever leaves his flat! Big Baby! I'm sure he will try to call. Ha Ha! As always. I will ask him about it maybe—but then again, that will just egg him on. Robert says we can have a child in one year!!! Have fun in Rome…

Best,

Gudrun

SAMIDHA

I look like someone he used to know, he tells me. Oh, he lost somebody, that's for sure. He's got that little lost puppy look. How many times have I seen THAT one? Abdullah would kill me if he caught me giving my personal phone number to a John. Jaj, jaj! Such a pretty day. Buy fresh bread. Autumn leaves stick to the sidewalk. Like a little puzzle, little patterns I want to figure out. Autumn light. The light gets funny. Saffron yellow. Just because I have red hair (it's henna!) that's why he likes me, he says. I just changed it a week ago—it used to be blond, before that, brown. Why did I let him kiss me!!! There he is again. Sitting on the stone steps. Stone. Grey. Ok, you can come up. But not too long because he might come home. Old bread knife grey color. Old warped brown handle. I don't have much. A little butter, you want with it? I have a few pickles left. (That reminds me, I need to do the Cumin Chicken for the guy's next meeting. There's just something about him. Puppy. Lamb. Something. Kiss.

(unsent letter, found in computer)

Ah, Angelika—

Forgive my little tour of Old Hungary.

How odd life has become, still very engaging but odd. I suppose it's because it now seems unseen through the window of childhood and youth. That remains a prevalent feeling, a question often on my lips. Where the hell did youth go? I woke up this morning thinking of a girl I met in Venezuela when Carlo and I played there. I thought about it awhile and then realized that was 20 years ago!

Oh, I could go on but for many months now I've wanted to write to you about the boys. Helen and her mom, Madelene, and the boys moved from the spacious apartment that had been the backdrop for the biggest part of our relationship (all of our marriage), the house Helen had lived in from age eighteen on. As I say, they now live on the Buda side of the Danube, upriver (north) from me about a twenty-minute ride on the 18 Tram. The Castle sits high on its hill facing the river and behind the Castle at the foot of the Hill lies their apartment, overlooking a pretty, expansive park, five times the area of Water Maple Park!

Every morning, on their way to school, they walk up the winding street, and then a steep stone staircase, to the top of the Castle Hill. There are many staircases cut into the hill, but the one I'm thinking of that we usually take is actually covered, a bit like a covered bridge, with brick. The old granite steps have been worn smooth by hundreds of years of feet. It's rather steep so I'm pretty winded by the time we get to the top. As we come out at the top end of this, you might say, almost vertical tunnel, there is a lovely lane, a walking street, forbidden to cars, and covered with a soft line of Linden trees, with various little statues here and there commemorating brave soldiers, ancient mythologies and catastrophic events of the Magyar past.

We keep walking down a perpendicular cobble-stoned street (looking very classically European, like something you might imagine out of the paintings of Utrillo. I mean the urban density of it). We pass the Cafe Miró on the left, filled with tourists, not that great a place for the locals, though, just before reaching an expansive square where the magnificent St. Matthias (Matyás) Cathedral rises in front of us. My dexterity with the jargon of Architecture and Art History is scant, but I think it would be safe to call this a Gothic cathedral. It rises very sharply from a not so expansive dark stone foundation. The arches are very pointed. Most noteworthy, I had never seen anything like it before I came to Hungary, is the ornamentation of burgundy and yellow tiles on the roof. It sounds absurd but it almost reminds me of an American Indian ornamental necklace, as do many of the old Hungarian folk costumes. Yet the shininess of the porcelain tile "werk" puts one in mind of a Mittel Europe folktale. The image I always carry of two worlds separated by a dream of ocean.

It's usually not open this time of morning, though I've been in it several times; it's so ornate, the gobs of gold and wood filigree ornament look like candle wax drippings. I was told once that Russian and Nazi soldiers tommy-gunned each other right in the nave of the church, as they fought for possession of Castle Hill in WWII. Bloodied bodies lying about this way and that, the reality version of the war tv shows I watched as a kid. So, we go walking on past but then, right in front of us, is a statue of St Stephen I, not the Italian saint of the 4th cent, but the first king of Hungary (b.977, d.1038), on horseback wearing the Crown of Hungary, with a halo behind it, in reference to his canonization by the Roman Catholic Church in 1038. In his right hand, he holds the Cross of Lorraine symbolizing Hungary's conversion to Christianity.

This was the Stephen that brought Hungary out of the Dark Ages. The idea of the Hungarian nation was solidified under his reign. Hungary was a major power through the Middle Ages until, just after the death of good King Matyás, a struggle for power weakened the State, and most of Hungary was conquered by the Turkish Ottomans in the early 1500s. It remained under their control for nearly one hundred and fifty years. Hungary's relationship with Europe, due to its isolation from it, would be forever changed. Serbia remained under Turkish control almost another two hundred years longer and had been conquered one hundred and fifty years earlier in 1389 I think, well into what one might call the modern era. Parts of Serbia, Bosnia and Kosovo, remain significantly Muslim, an island of that past Ottoman era.

Various Serb movements have wanted to re-dominate both those regions since their defeat at the hands of the Turks in 1389. Shows how long proud Balkan (a Turkish word meaning "Mountain") nations can hold a grudge! Milosevic, in 1990, saw his chance, since such territorial ambitions had been muzzled by Tito in the commie era, to regain these sacred regions by military force. They would have succeeded had NATO not finally intervened against Milosevic's "police action" in Kosovo. Still, Serb forces killed (ethnically cleansed) here and in the earlier war with Bosnia, some 200,000 young Muslim men, women and children. Pretty gruesome. It's well documented, the mass executions, and mass graves later discovered are testimony. This was done in the 90s 200 miles away from where I now live!

As a nation—I exclude pacifistic, tolerant folk of the culture and there are many—the Serbs will never accept the loss of Kosovo, that poor, ethnically Albanian place that recently declared its independence. As I noted, these ethnic complexities, like their even older and more complex counterparts in Palestine, go back to the Middle Ages! Like the Palestinian Question, such ancient disputes resist a clear judgment of who's right and who's wrong. Such disputes lie dormant and then suddenly one side's sudden aggression sets off a war. I can sympathize with Serb frustrations and feelings of European betrayal yet the predominantly Muslim Kosovars were harassed violently by the Milosevic regime. It's hard to blame them for seeking geo-political release from that. Still, the ethnic Serbs who remain in Kosovo have had their country pulled out from under them, in much the same way as it was for the Palestinians. The region remains tense. And it's all under our noses. I walk past the old Serb neighborhood here on my way to teach a private English student every Friday morning over near the Synagogue.

Why are there so many ethnic Serbs living in Hungary? They fled, in a steady stream, since the Turkish wars with Serbia from 1389 till 1919 and the collapse of the Ottomans and the Hapsburgs after WWI. But I don't know for sure. Hey, I've been talking to some English-speaking Arab guys at the money exchange shop on Templom St. I told you about. I've even attended some of their meetings about the occupation of Palestine with my new friend Abdullah. But I'm not in sync with their hatred of Israel, and anyway, there's a girl there I like, ha ha! (I wish there were no nations, no religions, no political parties. Only people living as good, decent selves. Individuals going their own way-tending the children of the world. No "mankind," no "international community"—just men and women and their children—the fading sculpture of time).

So, let's continue our "historical walk" past the old sainted king, St Stephen, and let history make of him what it will. Corvinus, The Raven of Wisdom, freshly painted shiny black in a burst of BP urban renewal, sits high atop Mathias' Cathedral—looking down in amusement. As we turn left in front of the Fisherman's Bastion, a network of Gothic stone stairs and balconies and hallways looking out over the Danube toward the huge neo-gothic dome of the Parliament building that lies across the river on the Pest side, there's another grand staircase that looks like it might have been the setting for a coronation of some modern king like Franz Joseph, King of Hungary and Emperor of Austro-Hungary, from the time of the Dual monarchy, till its collapse in 1919.

For a moment, as Ryly and Gordon giggle over something the other said (which my bad old rocker hearing and bad Hungarian can't make out) dribble a basketball, or show me a secret spot where they and a friend had hid some old hubcaps they'd found beside the ancient remnant of the original castle wall. (It's amazing that we can walk so freely here, and that the old walls are completely free of vandal's graffiti). As I say, for a moment I feel like we're walking through history (as if we're like Woody Allen's Zelig in some black and white newsreel or photo from the Fin De Siecle); and I tell them so. They look around—only mildly curious—since I'm the one who, since I'm a grown-up, has a history; their own they barely know, yet. They wonder what history is.

We continue along a brick walkway—probably recently installed by some garden club of old descendants of nobles, though so much of that world was scattered to the four winds during the communist era; I have played shows in many of the old, noble mansions of Hungary (much like ones I once played in Water Maple County, like Waveland or Ward Hall). When I asked someone why there was so little furniture or paintings on the walls (they were nearly bare of any adornments), they replied: "Why, Joshua, the Russians looted them all after the War, all the silver, furnishings, everything!" and many of the old gentry changed their spots during the cold war, and some of their children have since re-changed them to fit the now 20-year old and first in Hungary's 1000-year-old history—capitalist democracy.

The walkway winds down the hill—remember, we walked up the hill behind the castle; now we walk down in front of it —and leads to the top of yet another staircase, that looks out in such a way that you are at the same level as the Parliament Dome, hundreds of meters away and across the river; yet you feel like you could almost reach out and touch it. I glance to my right and see where a small colony of street people, encamped at the foot of the castle wall, watching the caravanserai of Empires rise and fall, are hidden partially under the wide wooden staircase we now walk over, as we stand with Buda Castle at our backs and look out over the panorama of Pest: the neo-Gothic Dome of the parliament, it's old Churches, St. Stephen's Basilica, the old commerce buildings, some of which have now been converted into sumptuous hotels, theatres, restaurants plus an array of less attractive glass office buildings.

We say hello to an old man in rags —who looks as if, in his long filthy woolen coat and brimless cap, he might've stepped from the pages of Dostoyevsky. In fact he might be writing a novel. He often sits on the wrought iron bench, his every worldly possession no doubt packed into a few sturdy plastic bags around him, pouring over the besmudged and dog-eared pages of a notebook. I glance over his shoulder and see the myriad of runic, hieroglyphic letters he's entered there. God knows what message he's getting from somewhere or what he's trying to send out. Some days when we pass, he's sitting smoking his pipe, bemusedly observing the silly, ignorant metropolis that spreads out below him; some days he's not there.

But mostly I think of the light, the soft way it looks morning or evening, childlike itself as it creates the eternal moving picture of my children moving up and down a staircase of sky. I can't forget that first day of the new school year when I first walked them across the Castle hill, and suddenly the parliament

Dome appeared like a benevolent round-headed spirit across the river shrouded in morning mist; and the river, seen in brief flashes far below us, seemed itself like some gray blue snake of Myth. Yet the earthen bricks, solid under our feet, carry us one by one down to the narrow streets, and on down to Ryly and Gordon's school. Suddenly at street level, the Dome loses some of its mystique and I imagine dour politicians strutting its hallways tending to the quotidian duties of running a country. We walk up the short flight of schoolhouse steps. I turn an old brass handle and we walk inside. Not so long ago I knelt on one knee to kiss them goodbye, now they've grown so I need only lean my head down slightly. Goodbye, boys. Study hard, I say. I watch them climb the staircase that countless other children have climbed before them. They wave once more than disappear around the corner of the landing. I turn and walk back out into the Grown-Up world.

Yours ever,

Josh.

Dear Angelika,

I'm adding all this into the book. Hope you don't mind,

Krip

Hi Angelika—

Glad you liked it. Btw, he told me that he asked Wanda once if she minded all his flirting and she said, "Oh, no, a real man never stops trying!" I liked that 'real man.' I knew what she meant. I guess that's why I went ahead with it. I'm afraid I don't remember some of the things he said all the way, so I filled in things. I was in a trance almost the whole time. I still am. And we still have most of the records and poems, etc. Doc said he would have wanted it that way so I'm goin for it. Doc says I'm still looking for my 'voice.' And "Krip" was one agent's idea since it matches up with my last name, etc. I kinda like it. I guess… bit trendy maybe.

VEGE AZ ELSO RESZ.

PART
TWO

BY KRIP KOVACS

COMPILED FROM THE NOTEBOOKS OF
JOSHUA CELESTE, EDITED BY
KRIP KOVACS AND RYLY CELESTE.

INCLUDES THE LOST BALATON JOURNALS

1

I am Krip Kovacs. My friend, Joshua Celeste kept many journals. You could say I inherited them, along with all his files. As I have said before, for years I didn't know what I should do with them. But, now, I realize I must somehow tell his story, the story of a man. OK? It has been difficult at times to piece it all together. Sometimes I have made things up. Sometimes I have left things out—things I wasn't sure of or I was ashamed of. Still, my rule was this: write whatever the fuck I wanted to.

JOSH'S HOUSE IN BALATON

There was always a breeze. As he walked through the yard he thought of the huge lake so nearby. The main village lane, unpaved; the little stucco houses, some with their whitewash faded to a deerskin brown, side by side, with almost no front yards like you'd find in America, but only a thin shaded alley between them; the old man bicycling slowly toward the sorozo (beer bar) for a drink; the giggling barefoot gypsy girls walking to the grocery; the mother swallow darting under the eaves and into her nest of dried mud; the green vineyards on the hil—all this seems like a dream to him now. Years before I ever knew Joshua Celeste, "Uncle" ("bacsi" in Hungarian) Emil Schwartz, the writer, brought my mother and her sister, my Aunt Pearl, here in the summers of their childhood. Josh is driving, driving down the village lane in his old green Peugeot station wagon he bought in Budapest for 200 USD. The 2 child seats in the back are empty. He passes the sorozo (taproom), the protestant church, the catholic church, the little grocery. He reaches the hard road. The tall trees—they seem to tilt their uppermost branches over the road like a canopy. The tall lilies seem to lean their heads lovingly into the road as if strewing their seed before him, or waving farewell. A vast yellow field opens up before him, with neatly harvested squared hay bales in rows like a line of clouds. When he reaches the main road he is weeping. He can see how the valley curves up and he catches a glimpse of the huge lake nestled in the higher ground as if it sat in a bowl.

It was his crazy idea but she got into it. They would buy that place they saw in the real estate section—the old peasant house that looked like something out of Grimm's fairy tales, the place she insisted they buy. He loved her but he knew he was going to play around on her. The girls around the club scene were just too beautiful. Now he figured he would have a place to take his girls—to keep all that away from his new little family. And while his wife was staying at the country house he could pursue his little amours in Budapest. He hated himself for it but his willpower was too weak. Besides, he was dutiful enough. The boys were growing up. At bedtime, he read them Mother Goose and Edward Lear. He adored them. Just as he had adored their mother before something happened. Something changed. They stopped sleeping together. Still, when their arguing would subside, they would go through their apologies and hug each other tight in the twilit room, their sons napping, and realize how lucky they were and that everything would be alright.

2 THE NOTEBOOKS OF JOSHUA CELESTE

"We committed suicide in the US and were born again here."

JOSH

Wanda was my first death. It makes me shiver. Sickly, I think of who's making love to her now back in Medina ("I vander whuz kizzing her nooooowww", the old vaudeville number). I thought that from her first poison dart when she said, "Maybe I should get my own place." I thought she was just bustin' 'em on me but then one day I came home and she had split, like I said, with no explanation. Death. Long legs. For years after, I spun endless webs in my mind while drifting off to sleep. I bathed in the yellow light of memory. The light of growing up on Water Maple Farm. I had been instantly in love with her. I ran away into the electric maze of my mind.

3 JOSH IN BUDAPEST

After our little party, my tiny flat was trashed with the most luxurious scatterings of random things: the green tide-like shine of empty beer bottles, ashtrays, dope seeds, books, guitars, mandolins, cassettes, pillows, rugs, candles, incense burners—a brass lectern, books bound in Moroccan blue, blues records, huge gold crucifixes, a Kelmscott Chaucer, a Turkish Saracen, Vietnamese rice pots. Lydia was in my bed the next night. But then she was bound for Turkey the next day, dropping out of Budapest University. Before we made love, the thought of loving her had never entered my mind. But a few nights later, after she was supposed to be long gone, I began to crave her. Emese came to the club and so we went around from bar to bar. I didn't tell her that I was looking for Lydia in the old haunts. No dice.

Sydney was fucking her—I was sure. I'll bet her trip to Istanbul was a lie. She wanted Syd even though she said he was "just a friend". How many times have I heard that one? Axiom: it's much better to be lonely and horny than to get just a taste and then be denied. God, death is better than anguishing over a woman – isn't it? What did I want? To possess her even more than the night before? Axiom: The ones you want are the ones you can't trust. Even she had said casually, "Women can be so cruel." Was that her game? What should I write her? Dear Lydia, I am thinking of you often and wish you were still in Budapest, but … so it goes. I would love to talk to you right now. I feel like I just got to know you and then….

4 HELEN

A woman appears out of the drab winter dream of Budapest. She is the loveliest I've ever known: perhaps, the most dangerous. Who could know what she wants from me? She's just bored with the guy she's with. To her, I'm a "good-lookin' guy." Such a sweet Hungarian accent! Lovely trolley bus ride to Kossuth Square resting her head on my shoulder. Sometimes we kiss. I feel her sweet tongue. I feel in control more than I ever have before with a woman, yet it all seems headed for emotional chaos. Doc said if you want to find the truth look for the opposite of what you think is true. Chameleon truth pretends to be its opposite because anything else would reopen the wound. The REAL TRUTH would be too much. You'd bleed to death. The wound must close. It cannot stay open to the stinging world. The aged: first thing you see is the old scabbed over wounds, but still oozing pus. In an old coat near the dumpster. When we grow another skin can we still feel the way we once did when our skin was soft and smooth? Then the Equation would balance itself: we could love the thing we most want. Desire and fulfillment would come together. But what happens is just the opposite. The couple hates as much as loves. The infant reaches up to strangle the mother! The philanthropist plots the destruction of the world. The young girl seduces the cock that she will soon snap off with her teeth and engulf! Where do I get such bullshit thoughts?

5 Albert "DOC" CELESTE

Dear Krip,

Marriage is the end of Romance.

The cuckolding wife always kills her lover in the end—or she gets killed, or the cuck. The love act: for the man, the end; for the woman, the beginning. The male dies in his lover's arms. But through her he is reborn (reaches birth part of cycle).

The demon conforms to the contours of the addiction, efficient as a vine, entangling only what needs to be entangled. When you open your mouth for food it's the demon you feed.

Best,

Doc

JOSH IN BALATON

Time is running out. Must write it down. Peasant house in Balaton. Uncle Franz my next-door neighbor—his backyard full of geese and ducks and goats and mud, just like in everyone's yard up and down the street. No flies in his house unlike everyone else's. His wife fixed us coffee. We are new to the village. They are welcoming us. Speaking in quiet Hungarian only my wife can understand. No flies. His wife keeps 'em out, I guess. Our house was full of them the night we moved in. Bought flypaper the next day to no avail. Helen said the shop lady must have attached dead flies to the demonstrator strip hanging from the shop ceiling, ha ha. Went back to buy screens from her. Helen tacked them up. Less flies. Mosquitos. Maybe fifty bites from them in 3 days. You get used to it. Cool weather slows them down. Bagworms in the walnut tree out back. I picked them off with my fingers. Green goo between fingers.

DREAM

I am back in Kentucky with Berenice. We embrace slightly but feel guilty. A cloakroom? She kneels before me. Sudden shift to outdoors. Front door of my grandparents' guest house they called "the cabin". A woman is standing there vaguely looking like Helen, my wife, but it's someone else, I'm sure. Who? Dark reddish hair swept back. There's a vibe that she's a bitch. She's giving me shit about... what?... the way I live my life, my attitudes toward women. I take offense. Somehow I feel justified in lightly tapping her with a stick. Nixon appears! He seems strangely handsome. Young. Night falls. Front yard of cabin? A large rabbit prances by me. Curious, I follow. It becomes a wildcat. I feel a vague fear it will attack me. We grapple. I feel a sudden shock as if I'd been shot. The cat runs away. Still dreaming I remember my children sleeping upstairs. They, sleepy-eyed, curly-headed little boys come walking down. "Dad, a cat woke us up." A little kitten hops up the stairs.

JOSH PLAYING GIGS IN EUROPE

Train through S.W. Hungary at twilight, deer startled in the rushes. Sunset was beautiful along Lake Balaton. The conductor gave me some paper so I could write down some thoughts. I'd forgotten my notebook in Budapest! I needed more paper so I said, Meg? Meg? (More? More?) Which isn't correct. He didn't understand. Hungarian is tough to learn but I'm living here now so I should learn it. It's been so long since I learned anything. It makes me think back to when suddenly guitar opened up, started revealing itself to me when I sat in on some of Crip's classes at B.U. We jammed on Grateful Dead tunes, Paul Simon, James Taylor. I could strum chords. Then Bluegrass picking hit me. Doc Watson. Norman Blake. Tony Rice. Ricky Skaggs. My god, an endless fountain of notes. Clearwater banjo waterfall. Hills. River. Marshall's mountain stories. Then came jazz. Theory with Sylves. Same thing. Another big revelation. A new language. Like a rare humanist in Renaissance Italy knowing Greek. Clear water in a glass. Smoke. Rushing water saxophone screams. You can't hiiiide from Miles' muted trumpet. Child truth deep squeak. —But that's all been so long ago. Now it's me in a sleeping compartment on my way to a gig in Provence.

Train is neat. I can eat, practice, sleep—all in my little compartment. Night falls. I'm rocketing through Croatia in pitch black nearing Zagreb. A uniformed railway officer stands by the station, a whistle in her mouth holding a flag like the Statue of Liberty's torch. She lowers it quickly as we roar by. A train whistle screams. Strange to be in a country at war. To think it could all blow up in flames. A few miles away Bosnia is going up in flames. Good to know the U.N. boys, the ones I saw boarding at Keleti station in Budapest in their powder blue berets and all, are between me and the Serbs.

Strange how the mind leaps back in time to Medina, KY gig scene while on a train to Venice. I think of my old life in the States and I see a vision of Crazy Reddy standing in the hallway of his glorified strip joint, the Pickle Jar. Beer gut. Fat face. A little boy with gray hair. Boisterous, buoyant… but yet always seeming on the verge of some illness. Alcohol. "Turn that shit down!" he yells to the band. "Drank too much over the weekend. Never drunk in my own club, though". Later, upstairs, "I never turn down a chance to smoke some shit. My doctor said either quit drinking or my liver…." My liver continues to live. Finally me and Reddy had nothing to say to each other. He thought he could work me, power smooze my famous Mom, her illustrious family. Then the scandals. Reddy's picture pasted in the local news section as possible suspect in a drug case involving coke and other shit. Never did go to jail. But after the bust, he changed. His eyes collapsed back in his head or down his cheeks. Sad expression. Maybe he sang. Yeah, he sang to the cops I bet. Hard to live with himself.

I got to ride all alone in this compartment for so long. But what's this? Italian man with tipico long N. Italian face. Well, damn. His family, too. Cute teenage girl. She keeps staring at me. Afraid. I look so old now, I think. Forty. The wife is pretty, too, in a weird way. Black eyes, very blond, even for a Northern Italian. A sweet family. They all seem to cuddle as they pull out the couchettes. Girl's leg twisted innocently askew, a little virginal tuft of pubic hair is visible. A gentle kiss, embrace mama. She's so much darker. Like her father. Little red snappy dog she holds nervously between her fingers. Mama pat. Kiss. Daddy has a cold and turns toward the window. He's tired now but he's a nice guy at home. He works hard, tries to give them everything they want. The girl pushes her legs up like Jane Fonda in Life magazine. Did Kennedy try to fuck her? Bet he did. Maybe he fucked her. Back then the president could fuck anybody anytime. Nobody fucked with him. But they killed him. That's being fucked. Every so often his head exploding crosses my mind. Death so widely seen and so weird. To kill. To fuck. They say it's similar. A bullet like a cock. Fuck. Fuck. I don't know. I don't think so. Discredit Freud, thought all that shit up. Used laughing gas—or was that William James? Freud used coke. Freud sold coke. Mug shot in the papers. Freud. A Jew. Sold coke. Dead. Nobody killed him. He was old. Scared his patients. London. Who gets to be a genius? He was one. Midwife of an idea. Theory kills lots of birds with one stone. Kill. Stone. Bird. Fuck. Mama and daughter cuddle. Dad sleeps. She pulls her legs up. I can see the faint outline of her labia cupped tight in her panties. She doesn't know. Runs her finger across the elastic strap. It itches. Quick scratch with forefinger. Nice view now. Pubic hair black against dark cup of inner thigh like cloud shadow against the bowl of a valley. Turn my head. I think of Lydia. Legs spread wide. Train enters a long tunnel. Lights go off. Then on. Then off again. She finally gave in. Like a puppy growling with each push of her pink heels into the back of the soft round taught pillows of thigh. Finally came. Hair sweaty around her ear. Upper lip. Salt taste. Sigh. I want to roll over but she locks her legs. Calves into buttocks. Beautiful line down her calf where tibia meets, hangs, yet taught, lovely muscle. Dimpled. I'm getting old. Varicose vein. Wrinkled inner thigh. No exercise. Tv workout show. Steeetch that inner thigh! Burn some fat! But I like fat. Hands on heels. Push legs apart. Faint outline. Long legs. Big ass. Death.

6   KRIP KOVACS

On the train to Vienna, I can picture Josh thinking it all over. He had once realized that all those break-ups formed a pattern. The Equation: A relationship works because 2 (or more) people have created enough space between themselves for it to exist, to breathe. So for a relationship to exist there has to be enough space and time between two people. I fantasized about a girl once for a long time. Why didn't those fantasies ever come true? Because that girl was never going to give up enough space and time in her life to make it happen. Dig? Relationships with women end not because all women are the same – no, he was the same. It was him—not them. External events were absorbed by him and interpreted, in the same way, every time. If he could change, then his failures with women would change. He started thinking like this on the train.

But not only was it not the fault of Berenice or Wanda or anybody, it was just Life! What else could it be? He got up every morning and faced the music like everyone else. The music never sounds the same. But it was he that kept seeing it the same way, making the same mistakes. "Things fall apart." Again, he was back to the old brown copy of the "Collected Poems of W.B. Yeats" that Lilian had given him so long ago in high school. He remembered coming home in the evening from his day job with a road crew, driving up the fine crunch of the gravel driveway of Water Maple Farm, turn off the car and sit there in the shade of that old hollow Water Maple tree thinking of nothing in particular. He then went in the back door hearing that familiar "thwack" as it closed behind him. And there he sat and read Yeats, understanding little but still drawn to it. A line would stay in his mind. But it was the landscape of Ireland he imagined that attracted Josh. He could play "Michael Gorman's Reel" and "Farewell to Erin" on guitar from a record I gave him. The green fields of Kentucky he saw, he transposed to Yeats' Ireland. He remembered Lilian showing him "Ephemera." It was her way of telling him she'd be leaving. But he didn't want to believe it. Years after, when she'd been gone out of his life, he read it again and wept a little. Feelings stay where you left them. Then you come upon them one day, still in the same place. A woman has come and gone, he thought, but the poem remained. Like life. Life was life. The Gift. It was we who did all the crazy shit. Where did it go? A brief dust of snow and then the bright Kentucky sun turned it to clear water. I never meant anyone harm—not once, he said to himself in the train compartment, startling himself out of his daydream. Yet life comes crashing like a wave into the shore. It makes us do things because it's all we have. It makes us breathe. He fidgeted in his seat, arousing momentarily the Italian family from sleep. The train roared on through the night.

EQUATION

Graffiti on bathroom wall: "Whore: someone you fuck then go away from; wife: someone you don't fuck anymore but can't get away from." Yours ever, Doc.

7 DEATH OF MARSHALL CELESTE

When I entered the room my father was on a typical hospital bed/table, a white paper covering under him—the kind that seems like cloth, they make bibs out of, like the bib the dentist—or your mother—puts around you. The table was even like a horizontal dentist's chair, Naugahyde, black, flat but maybe curved slightly at the feet, resting on a porcelain white network of cabinets, drawers where the doctors and nurses probably kept supplies. Dad was old. 86. He'd had a gall bladder operation. Too old for that. He suffered a massive heart attack. He lay there now dead-still. I thought his cornfields, all the ears harvested, gray stalks, dry and broken as limbs before the gray- October clouds. But then some leftover electrical impulse from his ruined brained ran through him jerking up his feet or suddenly raising his head knocking open his lifeless eyes. He could always surprise you. They opened but the light had completely gone out of them. They were a dull gray as if covered with a thin glaucous film, no reflective light left of whatever had once animated them. The liquid brown expression they once projected was gone. Yet the tremors of electric life remained, making him jerk up out of his prone position, like a puppet on the end of a string.

"Can he hear us?" Angelica asked the nurse.

"We don't really know," she answered gruffly as if she'd been asked that question a thousand times by a thousand families standing around observing the expiring bodies of loved ones.

Every minute or so Dad's head would jerk up as if he was trying desperately to raise himself from the dead. The force of the jerk would push open his eyelids. It seemed as if he were looking at you but the eyes had no fatherly life in them— only the milky expression of a blind man. But he had seen things we never saw— the wind over the corn tassels. I remembered the groundhog in the high field he chose not to kill when I was just a boy riding with him through Water Maple Farm. He was a merciful man.

8 DOC

Agnes' father, the illustrious politician, Judge Daddy Demeter was famous for saying, "In all my travels, I've never met a Kentuckian who wasn't on his way home." But it wasn't like that for me. I couldn't wait to get away from it. All the shit about horses. Horse shit. Bank ads, team names—the constant image of the horse. And the self-righteous wholesomeness and inflated health-consciousness slathered in bible-thumping bullshit and all the bragging people did about how hard they worked and how the stupid lazy black people and spics were taking their hard-earned money and living on welfare, getting a bigger check for every new baby they produced, turning Medina, KY, a place where normally two-bit lawyers in pink button-downs and lime green pants and tasseled loafers ran around in BMWs into a slum that got bigger even as the wrecking ball got busier; and what was left of the antebellum mansions of the feudal times, they turned into overpriced apartments for rich college students who couldn't pass algebra or get into a Yankee school and when the developers ran out of money they left 100 ft cranes standing around in big holes in the ground. If you're willing to keep a tight watch on your social standing and pull the social ladder out from under your neighbor, work for the faux-aristocrats of the horse racing industry, drink their sugary over-priced whiskey, pay their outrageous rents and mortgages, then Medina, KY is the place for you. Marshall would've hated to hear me talk that way. But, still, I left the cold, effete, intellectual snobs at the University and headed home.

9 FLIGHT MORNING |JOSH

So strange walking through my new neighborhood the morning of the flight, so far now from Helen's neighborhood. I felt such a heightened sense of awareness. Could this be my last morning on earth? On my little 11th Kerulet (district) street? Suddenly the sunshine felt more beautiful than it ever had. Isn't the simplicity of walking down a street an amazing thing? I said to myself as I went to run a few last minute errands before the trip to the airport. Aren't the beautiful Hungarian women even more beautiful now? Why can't I be like this every day? The time-wasting bovine way I had spent so many of my days suddenly occurred to me and I recoiled in disgust. Now that I was faced with a long journey away from what I had grown so accustomed to, I suddenly felt sorry I was leaving. In a flash I saw the world I was fleeing as a paradise I'd never really noticed before. If only each moment I could feel this attachment, this miracle of the every day, I thought. But I knew it was impossible.

Trying to calm my distracted mind: organizing concerts, meetings, emails, phone calls. All things, faces, voices, songs, places, swimming crazily in my head. Only the sunshine in its profound beauty remains a constant. Otherwise, the world is full of desire, a Dante-like morass of pathetic imploring, my plea the loudest, most pathetic.

There's still so much to tell. A dream of ocean separates Europe and America. As you pass back and forth through that dream—you change.

Arrival "Home"

I just have to keep going. As soon as I entered the house, aside from a sense of great relief, to have finally arrived home, I felt a sudden pang of depression. Already, Mother was irked by the length of Krip's (my Hungarian friend's) upcoming visit. I had innocently tossed off the phrase "a few days" earlier to her on the phone when his visit would be more like a week or more. So right away I had failed in a woman's judgment. I had planned something—or not planned at all—inadequately. Once again the feeling of not being able to do something right in the eyes of a woman assailed me. The thought of how inflexible anyone, man or woman, could be occurred to me, and a wave of melancholy passed over me. But then, as I unpacked my suitcase and looked around, at home, at last, my depression lifted.

Coming back from Nashville

I felt the urge to write and consoled myself that my failure to conduct any substantial business in Nashville's music scene wasn't entirely my fault. I had set myself an impossible goal: to penetrate the inner sanctum of N-ville's songwriter's network and help Krip, my young musician friend who had helped me weather a storm or two in Europe, get his foot in the entertainment door—all in two days!

But seeing all the myriad songwriters scurrying around the Renaissance Hotel (a ludicrous name that had no point of reference that I could see—certainly neither desk clerks nor bellhops were attired in cinque centro garb) both endeared them to me and repulsed me at the same time. I sympathized with their delusion of "making it big" (even at my age I still held out for being "discovered", although I was beginning to have doubts as to for what) but the continuous drone of their twanging instruments, playing as a kind of backdrop to their narcissistic fantasies, began to grate on my nerves. I got bored out of my mind. Especially when I sensed that I didn't fit into their fantasies. Soon I began to hate them all.

Driving back to Medina I was struck full in the face with the reality (or dream) of where I was. The place I once called Home—could it ever be home again? So, now my alienation here equaled that of Budapest? So, where was Home? Nowhere and Everywhere. I thought of my childhood friend, Jared Smallwood. Once, I was following him down a deserted road near the airport. Suddenly he pulled over. We both got out of our cars for no reason. The wind was blowing and suddenly he yelled over the noise, in the fake Shakespearean actor voice he did so well, "Here we are! Nowhere!" Therefore, press on. After all, only 20 more years—if that—and then the gravedigger will "shovel me back into the human mind again".

Once, I felt some connection to the lush fields of the horse farms of Highway

69, Tranquility Pike, Moore's Mill and Old Capitol Road. Now it seemed far removed. The color of the asphalt, the look of the trees, the passing cars, the sky—all of it seemed strange and distant. Not to mention the sensation that my libertinism had no place here. This is a puritanically moral place; yet, under the surface lay chaos, murder and lust. A friend of the family's impending murder trial was in all the papers. His lover rejected him; he beat her; she called the cops, news of which got him fired from his job; out of revenge, he shot her five times. Only in such an atmosphere of repression—no matter the wealth of a man— could such a man be moved to carry out such a crime. Something is too ripe in this Eden – a place where social standing means everything and a fall from grace is irredeemable. Man is a born witch burner.

All those golden afternoons when I sat in the Mona Lisa drinking coffee and reading at the table beside the long picture window! It all seemed to start in January. That's the day I called Gundrun back. Before I called I sat and looked at my phone on the cafe table for a long, long time, cigarette burning in the ashtray.

10 MY JOURNAL

by Ryly Celeste, son of Joshua, friend of Krip Kovacs

An empty feeling after Krip's memorial and at the same time weary of my sorrow since his death only added a realism onto the artificial sorrows and melancholy I already allow myself to indulge in. So—he's gone- and I have reminisced with many of those who knew him. I think of Boswell's line, "Such was the life of Samuel Johnson (his "Life", my father read in the Mona Lisa bar over their cheap, bitter, but tasty cappuccinos). Such was the life of Krip Kovacs that I'm remembering now, just as he remembered my father, Joshua Celeste. The slide show of pics was especially touching. So many bands. And he started so young. And seeing myself as a child in some of them. I emailed a few to Angelica and Gordon. How we age! Such a handsome face when he was younger. Then the sagging older face. A beautiful life, I guess, even within its limits: growing up Jewish, sometimes in a Communist country, his withered leg. He took me in, in a way, after dad's death. Beautiful yet bleak, now, without him. He shied away from just hanging out. So many Budapests are like that—they just don't have time. Neither do I much anymore. No, Budapests are compelled to always look for an angle. But unlike many, Krip was always generous.

So now I go to meet Lydia, the "psychotic woman" Dad dated once. Geez, what will we talk about on the way to her home in Romania? I will try not to talk about my feelings, or my feelings about Death, now that Krip's death has made me sort of hyper-aware you might say of my own. Thoughts of mortality consume me! But I must constrain them in front of Lydia. She hasn't got a sympathetic bone in her body. Maybe it's for the best. I don't need sympathy. I need something, though. Love. An end to this gut-eating loneliness.

I follow in his footsteps. This is the rest of Krip's life of my father, put together from his journals, and which I have tried to complete as well as I could. Enjoy this life, as Krip said, of a man.

11 JOSHUA

Life after Helen. Yesterday the vast plains of East Hungary spread out before us as Lydia and I drove toward Romania. Even though we had had a pretty serious spat—she annoyed the hell out of me—after a month of not seeing her, she offered to drive me there so I could fulfill the Schengen Treaty Directive that says every foreigner must cross the border of a non-Schengen country (eg, Romania, Serbia, Croatia) every 3 months.

I had thought she was out of my life forever but here we were driving together down the pothole-riddled road, endless green fields of barley, corn and soybeans flowing out like a sea around us. She would touch my leg affectionately sometimes as she emphasized something in one of her stories, eg. Arany Janos, the great poet, was born in the sleepy village we had just passed or explained what something meant in Hungarian.

She seemed relaxed, not frenetic as she had seemed at Krip's party when we both got tipsy and then argued on the bus ride to my place. It all stemmed from my remark that I would probably just go right to sleep when we got back— implying that I was too tired to make love. I was. We had already screwed in the afternoon. I had wanted to make love really passionately one more time. But that's just it—she isn't that passionate. She's like a female version of slam bam thank you mam-type lover, women complain about, while I'm like the frustrated housewife begging for more foreplay. She likes it quick and in the missionary position only. I can't do it that way. Not until I've kissed and licked and caressed for at least a half-hour. But some little sexiness comes back from her—especially the spit curls around her neck when I lift, slightly, her neck-length hair and nuzzle it and give her little kisses. This for me is ecstasy. But she seemed uninterested in that, like a prostitute goading you to hurry up and finish. But today, driving, she's relaxed and as I said touching my leg from time to time as she talks. Occasionally, I've touched her hand if she's left it on my knee for a while and even brought it to my lips. Her skin is so soft and brown. Then I kiss her neck in the restaurant parking lot and goosebumps pop up along her arm. That's a good sign but stopping at a hotel or coming to my apartment is out of the question, she says. She must go home, she says to her children and her husband she no longer sleeps with. I'm not disappointed. A young man would have been. But I've learned to never question the actions of attractive women. It's foolish and futile. She had told me about this husband before and he was dimly sketched out in the background. I think she had lied once before saying she was divorced but she had forgotten she'd told me that. I used to tell people that, too, so I give her a break. Plus, she'd had some ten-year affair, off and on, with some guy in Dakar. Lydia—certainly not Ms. Reliable. Hungarians so rarely are. They don't feel that same compulsion to adhere to some basic rationality of relationships that western humanism—probably erroneously—implants in many of us. Perhaps they are more rational. Crip was the only one I knew who always did what he said he would do. Almost no one else.

12

I haven't written much about the trip back to Kentucky because I know I'm going to get emotional. I'm going to weep very hard and I don't want to. I've wept enough about my sad little life situation. I'm afraid of weeping. There's the summer humidity there. It hits you in the face as soon as you walk out of the airport. Then the ride down I-75, fast food the manicured perfection of the road. The shiny new SUVs. The border of the South and the Great Midwest. Then the drive down into Bluegrass Country. Mom at the porch. Hugs. Then a long sleep. I awoke early the next morning.

"How did you sleep?" Mom asked.

"Very well, of course," I said, glad to be back home.

When I was away I often pictured the little side yard on the northeast side of the house. The side with the screened-in porch off Judge Daddy's old room that faces the Milward's house next door. (The front door, which is rarely used, faces southwest. I walk through this yard every morning. I'm thrilled to be back in the lush vegetation of Water Maple Co. I notice every blade of dew-soaked grass, every bee, every butterfly, every bird that flits through the lilac bushes and Rose of Sharon, especially the bright blood red male cardinal. He never fails to get my attention no matter what I'm thinking as I pass by, no matter how big a hurry I might be in. (So many times I've tried—and failed—to get a good photo of him)! After raising the latch of the old chain–link fence, as I'm stepping over the calf-high brick wall, the old bricks slick with moss, I'm walking through the unclipped hair of Bluegrass yard that stretches out in front of the Milward's house. I pause at the smooth blacktop of Tranquility St. My gaze wanders out onto the long field that runs beside my mother's house. At this early hour, a bank of fog has nestled into the hollow of the field as it rises slightly toward the railroad track hidden by a border of trees. I've never seen it like that so close to town. When Mom and Dad were still together and we moved out to Water Maple I remember the fog out on the farm. Soon the sun will drive the humidity to a stifling level.

So, this was the first morning home. If only I could go back to that first morning—the others flew by so fast—and relive every morning. My mother worrying over every detail, beaming at my arrival, yet chafing at a new disruption of her daily routine.

That was many years ago. I always loved that part in the Wizard of Oz when the "wizard" is drifting away into the air. "Come back! Come back!" Dorothy screams. "I can't," he says, "I dunno how it works!" I can't get all my memories of those trips home to stay.

Back in Budapest

It was all so overwhelming like a jet plane in flight. 6 weeks! It passed so quickly yet it felt like a lifetime: the old tile-lined swimming pool with its mossy stone casing in decay. Looming above are the oaks, walnuts, pines and poplars, the magnolia and ginko, the rusted chain-link fence, the yard where I played touch football with Angelika and Doc and my little cousins when we were kids. The cabin behind the big house where we played, the paint now coming off the shutters and window sills, bird's nests in the gutters, stained walls and decayed shingles. Agnes, irritable over her heart medicine she says makes her heart pound too hard. A steady hysteria that never boils over. My shame at sniping at her. My anguish in the woods behind the house. An angel with a fiery sword stands at the gateway to the past. He won't let you back in. The place they call Fallen Springs, where I take the boys to play basketball, out the road by the factory where Berenice once worked, toward the sunset.

The Kentucky cardinal flits through the lilac

A sudden droplet of blood.

13

Gudrun and friend, Budapest apartment

When I heard the buzzer I went down the stairs to let them in just as I did in the old days when it was only sweet Gudrun alone. And there she was in the black fuzzy coat, which set off the gold in her streaked blond hair and brownish-gold skin, just as she was in the old days, looking up at me suddenly with her bright eyes but keeping them lowered very quickly, a gesture that gave her the air of a shy Mongolian princess, so much did her Hungarian and Slavic mix of blood suggest something oriental about her: a demur but coquettish almost wanton look.

He was handsomer than I had thought he'd be, which made my heart quiver and sink. He seemed slightly uncomfortable and stood a little aloof from her and didn't seem so protective as she'd said.

My kitchen was so small you could barely move without touching someone and Gudrun kept brushing against me on her way to the bathroom or wandering into the only other room which I used as a bedroom, living room, office, etc. She called to him to come look at all the books. "Yes", I said, please borrow anything you want. He passed on thumbing through any of them as he gazed along the many shelves, saying that he barely spoke English and was even less able to read it. She laughed at his modesty and laughed that masculine laugh of hers with a high-pitched tinge of Mongolian witch thrown in, at which point she hugged and kissed him in front of me. I watched them several seconds until she noticed and laughed her brothel laugh again.

"No-no, Joshika, don't look, you are bat boy, bat, bat boy!"

I chuckled and went back to my cooking. When I came back in to tell them the salad was ready, she had his pants down and was fellating him.

14

The Kentucky trip fades into dream. It's a dream that separates my two worlds: Budapest and Edgeton. The Ocean is the dream, a wide mist between two worlds. And if I should plummet into the Atlantic, I would only be falling further into the Dream. Like Alice tumbling down the rabbit hole, each world beginning at one orifice and ending at the other.

And the dream of Kentucky is the little walkway and stretch of grass that runs along the east side of Dennis and Timea's house (Agnes' brother and his wife). The little brick wall, only a foot high, made of the same ancient bricks I walked over as a child and the always perfect asphalt of the Milward's drive, emptying onto Tranquility St and Mom's front yard. Every day the sunlight is rich and yellow as safflower oil. In the early morning, I awoke and saw the fog again nestling into the field to the right of her house. Or I could walk on the sidewalk that splits Uncle Dennis' yard in two. Once, my departed grandparents Millicent and Judge Daddy lived here. Pines line the avenue. There was a tree with a small moat around it. We played in it often. What kind was it? A pin oak? On the other side a big burr oak whose abundance of acorns stifled the grass's growth. All over the yard, an assortment of hackberries, oaks, walnuts.

It occurs to me that I have two choices. Either come back to Edgeton and embrace that place with both arms or leave it behind forever. "The expatriate leaves everything behind". I can't go on living in Budapest with the Dream of Kentucky calling me back or being there and always knowing the Dream of Budapest awaits me.

The trip fades very slowly.

I remember running, running with my sons through DeGaulle Airport to catch the flight to Cincy. The strange feeling, after so long, of a big American car and a wide-open interstate highway 75 as Uncle Dennis drives us to Agnes' house.

15

I walked around the Cittadella in Budapest today, not knowing what to do with myself. Always hoping to meet some nice girl, a tourist, maybe, that I can show around the city, forgetting how old I am. Such city vistas! Budapest images jostle with Kentucky ones I've left behind. How can a man live in two worlds? Sometimes tears come when I think of home and my "dilemma". Agnes said, "I hope you solve your dilemma." But she didn't think I could.

Two worlds

With a Dream

Of Ocean between.

16

Tonight I went downtown to Gabor's house to buy a bag of dope. Self-medication. Such autumnal light along the 'Korut", the Boulevard, so early in September. The big yellow 4/6 tram makes big sweeps of the Boulevard. My mind is working very fast as I walk. I don't want to miss any beautiful girls (it occurs to me, a worthless girl-watcher, that there are so many, yet think of the ones one doesn't see) yet every face is a convoluted story—all of them forgotten a few minutes after they pass (Baudelaire's "The One that Passes" (sic?)—"and you knew"!) I remember the pretty blond middle-aged woman looking at the little child running back to its mother because she doesn't want to go back inside. The huge olive black iron door with the old latticed portal and the brass handle (the shape of a reclining girl's back as it curves to her hips) the gold of it blackened with the soot and street grime of a hundred years: and she looks down at the sweet little child and says: "Na! Mi van!" (Well, what's the matter!) And I stare at her handsome face for just a second too long and the man (35?) beside her (husband?) shoots me a quick look of anger with a trace of indignant shock. I rush past. Suddenly I come upon two butchers having a smoke in the shop doorway. It's 18.00. The day is winding down. A beautiful woman crosses the street. I cross, too, but I'm in front of her. I turn to look back but she's gone— into some store. I found a copy of A Moveable Feast in the bookshop with the pathetic little shelf of books in English. 3 bucks. I tried to read the first few pages by the light above my barstool at the Lanchid (Chain Bridge) Café, one of those ancient beer joints on the Buda side near the river. He putzes around Paris like me in Budapest. He's wistful as winter comes on and he thinks of his boyhood in Michigan. This is in a book. But me, I'm looking out the bar window as Fall is gaining significant ground on this summer of the long Kentucky dream. The sadness of the fading European light! What a beautiful thing is Death! I'm ol' "Hem" muttering to himself as I walk along beside the endless Danube. It gently starts to rain. And to think the girl he stared at in the bar must be long dead now—sunk into the forgotten decrepitude time sweeps away! All very dramatic. Later I will get into a warm bed with the book. It still has the original dust jacket—even if it's just a book club edition, it's beautiful. Suddenly, it's all I have. And the painting of the river on the cover is the only world I will know.

Life works out internally as well as externally. Externally it ends in death. Fine. No one knows for sure—like, if a girl colors her hair—if the internal life dies, too. But, still, I know something. The tragedy of the certainty of Death is eased by the joie de vivre of children. But something's under the flowing water. "The surface won't tell you/ what the deep water knows".

When Fate dealt a blow there wasn't a damned thing you could do about it. Still, reason intervenes and compels you to act, to correct the situation. Some don't have the tools to recover from Fate.

17 KRIP KOVACS, ED.

I went to see my Aunt Pearl Rabinowitz who used to read palms in her spare time when she wasn't sending poems and stories out to writing contests. She said girls came to get their fortunes told. "There were two I remember t that came in and wanted to know everything about Josh! Oh, I remember when he was just a little boy!" she said.

18 JOSH

Dear Josh,

It's like Crip is a schoolyard bully now. When he was a runt, he got knocked around by the big boys. Now that he's a man he wants to take it out on the girls. Not cool! Just a warning.

—Doc

19 JOSH

O those magical Budapest nights wandering near Moricz Zsigmond Circle with Crip! The magical 61 tram crawling down Villany Ut—that strange, lengthy stretch of Buda under the Citadella. And then the delicious, lonely walk down enchanting Karinthy Frigyes Rd. with all its strange shops and bars, nearly empty now on a Sunday night, except for students drinking beer and smoking in front of the grocery, too poor to drink the beer inside the bars.

How magical those nights long ago when I stood in Moricz Zsigmund Circle and waited for the 49 tram back in '89! An 89-er: someone who went to eastern Europe after the wall fell. How far away that time is now! What happened to that brown jacket I wore then that I bought in some used clothing store in America? It kept me warm as the October chill caught me by surprise. Etele Square was so far from downtown! How many hours I spent waiting for trams and buses in this strange, magical city so filled with women and pensive men with their collars turned toward the end of the year, turning cold! My ancient friendship with dear Crip. So many conversations with him about god knows what—usually just adding footnotes to how sadly delicious life is—how strange the passage of time!

The moon is out on this October midnight! Like the first night, I spent here in this lonely apartment. (How lonely all first nights are, like the lightning that flashed on the First Night of the New House on Water Maple Farm when Doc and I were children and slept in the same bed together). The same moon shone its milky white light down on my bed.

Always such a loyal friend! Diana, Athena and Great Mother Mary shine down your milky white light on my silly little life. Protect my sons!

Never let your judgment of a man exceed your compassion for him. For what good does it do to judge where there is no interest in caring?

20 "BULLET HOLES"

prelude to a play by Joshua Celeste (fragment)

Stage direction: A face on a blank stage speaks

Bullet holes. That was the first thing I remember. Blocks and blocks of sooty buildings, full of holes. Holes from machine-gun fire, from planes making strafing runs, but especially the holes made from the blasts of flak splashing against the sides of buildings. Russian planes flying in low—little resistance from ground arms—dropping their payloads on the lovely bridges of Budapest and the one Szechenyi spent his whole life dreaming of, before Kossuth drove him mad with politics and revolution. Planes swooping in. German troops running for shelter, torn apart by cascades of bullets into flesh, into the sides of buildings, bodies strewn in the streets, strewn among the aisles of Saint Matyas Church. Bridges fall in big chunks—they don't splinter like glass and mortar and flesh. So, you can put them back together again. All the king's horses. All the king's men. The riverfront of Budapest before me now. All the Stockholm-like calm and order of the facades, the Mondrian look of the checkerboard of windows and walls. Like a smile with a few teeth missing. The gray snaking curves of the Paris-like buildings, like the cupped parabolas of ruined Roman coliseums, a child's sandcastle partly washed away by the tide.

21 JOSH (NOTEBOOK AGAIN)

Lydia sits across from me in the touristy Magyar cellar restaurant flicking pages of her iPod with her index finger. At a nearby table the perky college girl, with her bald yet collegiate "date", kicks back a brandy and gives me a quick look. Now, as an old man I can tell, after so many years, when they "like" you, "find you attractive". So beautiful. And why would she look twice, I think, after catching a sidelong view of myself in the mirror, suddenly recognizing the bulbous head, the look of too much pink-faced sincerity? Even I know better than that. Some men will do, say anything to get laid. I'm beginning to be as big of a whore as any of my exes ever were. I drove them to whoredom by suddenly disappearing? Or they drove me. A restaurant is like a woman.

22

Gudrun always brings out the sharpest knife and flicks it at me vengefully. "De van", she says. She has a new boyfriend she wants me to know. It cuts. Yet somehow my thought of, "I was there before him" eases the sting. The way her lips part—her face relaxed for a moment in a half catatonic daydreamy dick trance right before she grabs it and starts sucking him. The show, the performance hurts and thrills perpetually. I am a privileged spectator.

23 BULLET HOLES: *A PLAY* (CONT.)

Stage direction: Warm black and white footage of the '45 bombings of Budapest segueing into '56 Revolution footage. The camera pans across blocks and blocks of urban rubble and the crumbling facades of buildings still riddled with bullet holes. These images are projected onto a screen at the back of the stage. After 10 minutes or so of these disturbing images, the footage switches to amateur-looking clips of a rock singer and a band. The music is of the singer/songwriter variety). Or then a face on a screen above a sleeping figure (as if the screen was the figure's dream) The figure wakens and sits on the edge of the bed, head in hand. A depressing room. Dark (winter?) morning. He then dresses and walks through the streets, sunny spring-like light. Now images of clean, new, reconstructed Budapest loom on the screen. As he walks, subway and tram images are projected onto the screen. He is on a trip somewhere through the city. Images of an airport. He is waiting for someone. People filing through an entryway. Suddenly he sees her. A medium-figured woman in her sixties with gray curly hair. She smiles. They embrace. And peck each other on the cheek.

Crip: The car is waiting over there. You can see they're rebuilding the old Communist-era airport. Everything is changing all the time. You feel like someone dancing at the center of a whirligig. Such sweeping changes. Everything was so different in the beginning of the collapse back in the '90s. You couldn't get western stuff hardly at all. Now it's all starting to flow in. But it was more fun before. We didn't care that we couldn't buy Crest toothpaste. Blenda-med, the commie brand, was fine! Now it's almost like back home. Let me take your bag. So amazing you're here.

Kiki: Well your letters were so sweet. And when you said you'd always wanted to get to know me better I just thought that was so nice to say and well (her face seems suddenly sad or distraught) I just wanted to come.

Crip: Really? You liked my emails?

Kiki: So fun to read. So fun listening to stories about Josh.

(They move out into heavy traffic. Crip lights a cigarette).

Crip: Mind if I smoke? (then, in a Steve Martin imitation) No, mind if I fart?

(They both laugh) Remember that old Steve Martin bit?

Kiki: Of course. How could I forget? (a few minutes pass in silence)

Crip: I always wanted to be funny like him. (He goes into another SM bit, then Robin Williams: "My penis on trial: 'Where were you on the night of April 13th?' 'I don't know your honor, first it was dark and then light and then dark and then…' " (they both laugh) But Jonathan Winters was my favorite.

Kiki: Oh, mine, too. (Krip tries to do a bit—faded laughter) So, tell me everything.

Crip: It's a long story I guess. Part of it was just Josh had this giant libido as big as his heart! (they laugh)

Kiki: I remember! (still laughing)

Crip: Then he met Helen and he told me he was just gonna focus everything on her she was so beautiful he was gonna play out all his fantasies on her. But then something happened after she had the kids. Things changed. He only knew how to play. Remember how silly he got? She lost all that playfulness. She got real serious all of a sudden.

Crip: Right. But something else. Some kind of fear, he said. And she got anxious about everything and very demanding. So many rules she made for him. He couldn't keep it all straight in his head. Remember how slow Josh was about catching onto stuff! He always said that he could play and sing and that was it! Sometimes people are good at one thing and terrible at everything else! She wanted him to study economics at night and computers and learn Hungarian. He flunked out of the night school, couldn't find a day gig. He told me one time he caught this look of disgust on her face towards him when she thought he wasn't looking. It got to him. They fell outta love. So they both started lookin around. He was just a gigolo (sings a few bars of that song). People gave him stuff, cash. He gave it all to his kids. What he tried to focus onto Helen suddenly went off in all directions. Gudrun, Lydia, you name it.

Kiki: I remember him as a little boy in Edgeton. A sweet little boy. But a naughty little boy.

Crip: I mean he always said, hey, the drive is there, you can't deny it. But she cut him off. She lost faith in him as a get-stuff-done guy. He was no good at that.

So, without her, he was just wandering around in a foreign country. Lost. Lost soul. He was just looking for love, like anybody. Anyway, they split up. It happens.

Kiki: Yeah, tell me about it. We're lost, too. A woman feels like she's gotta show a little backbone to keep a guy around. She's gotta house train him. I guess you can over-do it.

Crip: You can only control so much. A guys gotta have some freedom.

Kiki: Yeah, but how much? We try to keep you guys around with our bodies. What do we get for it? I loved Josh. I did. But he did it to himself.

Crip: But you can't be a control freak.

Kiki: But how can anyone be with anyone else? Some control. Some are controlled.

Crip: (sings)… "some want to be abused…" Remember that Eurhythmics thing? (laughter)

You know that was when music really started to go down. I mean boomer innocence started fading into decadence.

24 JOSH

Those late, winter nights when the moon rose over the thick clouds and lit them up from behind in dove's breast amber and rust and albino pink rose. Alone, this light greeted me so many times as I crawled under my blanket.

Leaving the children at their mother's: always the knot in the pit of the stomach, sting of salt in the eye corners. Ryly came rushing up to me as I started to close the door behind me. "Papa, I want to be a guitar player, a singer…. and a basketball player!" I try to teach Gordon the "little piggy" rhyme, but he seems to want to remember only the "roast beef" part. But I give him hints and he starts to remember the whole thing. Then he gets giggly and wants to lampoon it all: "This little piggy got blowed up!"

Another quiet Sunday evening. We did our usual movie at the Mamut Mall. The boys brought their new friend, Antal, along. He stayed over with us. Sweet kid. Just hitting the adolescent stage. Watching the way he acts seems good practice for when Ryly and Gordon soon get to the same stage.

It always feels strange walking through a downtown Budapest mall. It shouldn't, for all the years I've been here, but it does. Still an outsider… after all these years. (hums the Paul Simon tune). But is it me just seeing through the veneer of social intercourse after years of taking it for granted? (Krip practically yelling it at me, "There is no 'Joshua Celeste Story'! It's all in your head!") I start to see now how I assumed that other people knew better than me how to go about the day to day task of living; how I assumed they were right about most anything—and I was wrong. Suddenly that conviction is not so strong, especially now when I can so clearly see my fellow citizens' (and my own) transparent pursuit of self-interest. All's vanity. Like Jared Smallwood said of our first few years of high school, it seems like once again I'm "realizing shit out the ass!" I see Order's flimsy hold on society, the inability of anyone to communicate with anyone else, or be of any use to each other. I've become agoraphobic. I fear that I can't make a living. I'll wind up on the street.

The Big Bang Theory—could it have a counterpart in the human soul? Aren't we all just fragments somehow blown apart, coming together again, gravitating into globules endlessly circling each other in an endless void?

Doc said, "Men want to make love to as many women as possible—women want to make love to as few men as possible. Social construct?"

Marshall said, "When men join hands and sing, I am silent." Inwardly, I was always silent even if I was on stage singing my heart out, or trying to. Coming down from the stage, I always disliked having to greet people and chat with them, even accept their compliments, although I was often flattered. I also had to listen to their silly criticisms which so many audience members believe is their right to regale performers with. Some artists are cool-headed enough to benefit from it—I wasn't. It always offended me. I couldn't imagine doing such a thing to a colleague. But I never possessed a critical sense—except toward myself.

Another strange wave of melancholy comes over me again as the holiday season fades and everyone goes back to their old routines. Crip stopped by yesterday. It was balm for the soul. His youthfulness is so engaging. He makes me feel younger. We talked of this and that. Our big plan to "make it", make a trip to America, check out the scene and of course become rich and famous. His respect for me as a musician and the courteous attention he pays me as his older friend and quasi-mentor lifts my spirits and even assuages my loneliness being unable to connect with any good-looking Budapest chick brings. He gives me the feeling of at least being able to make some connection with Youth again!

My pursuit of musicianship, poetry, gentle women, a priestly detachment from things—all these things I thought could protect me from the "world". I wanted to meet gentle folk of my own ilk, people who shunned competition, but were, instead, caring, generous folk, accepting me and protecting me with their love. I found situations like this but they didn't last and the final dissolution brought on feelings of great separation and loss. The Equation: all relationships are negotiated. What do I get? What do you get? Until we finally divvy up the stuff. But wasn't I "just a gigolo"? The "kept man"—type relationship only lasts a few years at most. Some sort of independence must be asserted eventually. The man must bring home the bacon—right? Confidence is sexy they say.

Gordon whispered to me as we were going to bed: "I need to speak with you in the kitchen." So we went into the kitchen. "Sometimes", he said, "I have bad dreams."

"Aww, really?" I said, "What kind of bad dreams?"

"Where I lose you."

He meant, I realized later, getting lost at the Mall or the market. So sweet.

At first, I think I wanted to create, to compose a work, a work of art, maybe, that would include all the people I had loved in my life, family and friends. In this way, I must have reasoned, they would then all love me and be filled with gratitude that I had "gotten down" their lives on paper and so had given them a kind of immortality. Even loved ones who had passed on, I might have thought, would smile down on me from heaven, appreciative that on Earth voices still praised them.

But it was just another delusion. One forgets that the egos of one's fellows are plenty large enough to generate enough flattery and narcissism on their own. They certainly didn't need any help from me. Besides, it was my life, not theirs I was chronicling. The thrill of being an extra on another's "movie set" of life is a short-lived one. So, it is myself I want to preserve, while taking a few loved ones along for the ride to keep me company. To gather up all my memories and put them in a beautiful box or line them up one by one—in the same way, I once remembered all the women I'd ever made love to, daydreaming on a cloudy day looking out the window of the Mona Lisa Café. Is that it? To recreate myself, having grown bored with my present self, in memory? Or find something that was lost?

My failure in the music business. The reason becomes clear. When I was young I had no concept of entering into a competitive market. I never thought about trying to become the best. I started playing the guitar at 8. I barely remember a time when I didn't play it. It's been blood, breath—not something I competed about. My connection to Music was, to me, unassailable. I only wanted a "space" in which to pursue the art of music. It turned out that that was a taller order than I imagined. Many others had the same desire. "We can't all be great", I remember Crip telling me, once. I would have to fight for it.

Such a lift Sunday night having dinner with Lacy Corman and his band in Buda, a stop on their Euro tour. The band is all great young players, now. Yet, tonight, a few days later, I'm suffering from a backlash depression. The night of the show I was on a manic high, immersed in sentimental reminiscences, going back in my mind to what might have been, going back to that crucial moment on some such day long ago when I might have become something different than what I became.

At one moment during the show, whether he was playing something medium tempo, soft or introspective or forceful, letting his signature cascade of crystalline eighth notes spill and ring out into the room, I couldn't help stopping my eyes for a moment from darting around the room full of people, many grooving and dancing in the aisles, and staring at Lacy's spotlighted head and remembering all the years that I've known him, played with him, all the years I had occasion to simply recall my acquaintance with him, knowing he was the only musician I ever really knew personally who was possessed of true genius. A kinder and more magnanimous Lacy there never was more so.

Why did it make me feel good? Maybe it was because our reminiscences of a beloved time past gave that time a validity, my perception of which had begun to fade. I had given up those times for lost and yet here they were back again— the fond ones, the hurtful ones. But now I could barely feel the old wounds, so deeply had their poison seeped down, as Sylves said it would, into my "system," my memory, and which lay now in a dormant, inert state, a state of resignation. He had succeeded in his life, his profession—and I had failed. But tonight was no time for envy or a desperation to change the past and somehow right all the wrongs, the break-ups, the betrayals. People did what they had to do in the moment and they exulted or agonized over the consequences later. No, tonight I tried simply to enjoy this fortunate rare meeting of old friends, the moment of reunion with things past.

But, then, two days later, my manic joy subsided and a darker mood enveloped me. Suddenly, the full weight of my failure to make something effective out of my life pressed down on me. I want to do something significant… The endless solitude of my room wears on me. I think too much.

One must either play the game of life—play it warily and shrewdly—as Lacy did—or else withdraw and hope to make a living off of what the game players bestow. In an affluent society like America, the game players bestow a lot. In America, one can float through the deep waters of the wealthy and survive on their dross. Many Americans have too much and they're happy to get rid of it. They threw parties and had enough money to pay a band. A reticent man goes home, practices his instrument, reads great literature and then waits for the rich man's phone call requesting a band for his daughter's wedding.

25

Dear Josh,

People in your business, they don't like it if you just play the "loyal employee" all the time. On stage, they don't want you to be docile and just lay there. They want to fuck you in the ass and have you struggle a little while they do it. They want you to disagree with them, argue a little, and then…. they always win!

And Harmony in a relationship can be deceptive: when you think your mate is agreeing with you and "in synch" with all yr quirks, you come to find they were merely smiling and nodding their heads about insignificant things not really "at issue". When the real issues come up the discrepancies are much too large to avoid and the relationship quickly unravels. And then one sees painfully and clearly that one's mate has never made any real sacrifice for the sake of harmony but has only been pursuing their agenda all along. This is the case with most of us. There's a great difference between harmony and merely moving parallel with someone. For a time it's easy to mistake one for the other.

As ever,

Doc.

26 JOSH

Living in Hungary I've learned to live without so much! Yet, in the beginning, when I first noticed how impoverished my life had become I harbored the desire that I would be rewarded—here on earth— for the deprivation and loneliness. But now, after so many years in this drab urban wasteland, I see no reward is forthcoming. **THERE IS NO JOSHUA CELESTE STORY** with me as the hero/star and Fate on my side waiting to even up the karmic score. There is no god manipulating events. If there is a god surely he's more complicated than that! Yet, I can't let go. I can't let go of his hand. I can't help thinking I still might get lucky again.

My Way of Thinking About God: Childhood to Manhood

It follows me like the full moon out the car window,

its wan smile and yet on the verge of tears.

A flirtatious letter from Gudrun. But that will never come to anything. In fact, she's giving me the brush. She says she doesn't intend for me to be her lover again. (Karma from when I used to say, "I'll never love you!"). But she considered it. She's still smarting from the "dumping" Robert gave her. I think that's the source of her pain in her erotic letters to me. She talked about him all the time even when she asked me to meet her for a drink.

I'll always remember these lovely June evenings. The air so still. And I'm filled with the content feeling having gig money brings. Such longing for a woman—yet fear of falling for one and all the risk that brings. The random lay seems best. But so few and the loneliness between.

27 KRIP

Sometimes he just kept walking alone down the Big Boulevard (Nagy Korut) toward the Petofi Bridge. Head down, walking fast. Maybe it's Gudrun with her streaked blond hair darting down a side street toward Rossman's drugstore. But he walks up to some blond, back turned, fumbling with her apartment door keys and apologizes when he sees it's not her and he's startled her. What a gentlemen Josh was! I myself must admit to some feeling of pleasure when I see that moment of hesitation in their eyes when you've followed them to their flat door and looking nonchalant as you can, ask, "Is there a good place nearby to get a beer?" At least I can get my eyes full before they smile their Magyar Beauty smile, then look at you like the huncut you are and wave you away, annoyed, saying in clipped Magyar-accented syllables, "I cannot speak wif you now. Maybe there is someplace down zat strrreet derrr. "Care to join me?" "No, I cannot. I am meeting my boifren". That's your cue to get the fuck out.

And at this hour it's only Turkish kebab places that are open. He's walked so far from the expat party down at Lovolde Square he felt hungry. He got a veal kebab instead of his usual chicken one. It was delicious. Rice and salad of red cabbage, leaf lettuce, tomato and red onion marinade of oil and vinegar.

He thought of all the times they'd laughed in front of the Szirai, kebab cones in their hands, grease dripping from the tips onto the sidewalk that had itself become greasy with the grease of a thousand kebabs drop by drop twenty years since the Fall of Communism. Turks (Torok) coming into Budapest and opening shops. How many kebab shops in '56? Not too many. Now it's the best deal downtown. Cheap. Cheaper even than the Chinese places where we laughed and wondered about dog in the Szechuan pork. 2 pieces of Baklava tonight or should he be disciplined? Sugar made him sleepy and the hash-laced cigarettes made his heart race or gave him the feeling of a recurring panic, the "Claustrophobia of the Foreigner", which comes upon you when you look around the crowded street and realize there's no one who cares about you. He felt like calling Gudrun. He remembered her distant train whistle moans. Or even Lydia—her abuse and trembling clit above his face—just to talk to someone and know that everything was cool. But was everything cool? He'd see older men croak in the heat at bus stops. Someone threw the dead man's jacket over his face. Someone had called the ambulance. Buses came and went and still no one to claim the body. (Once, on Margit Island, one of those crazy motor carts ran over some old tourist guy. Killed him. His wife threw her jacket over him. The wind whipped up and started to blow the cover off but she rushed over to make sure it was anchored down, stricken look on her face).

Such thoughts came to him as he stumbled home. He wanted to go home— back to Kentucky—more than he'd felt in a long time. Agnes came to visit him in the early days, the days when the Fall of '89 was still in the air. In the yellow light of morning beside the Danube boat dock there she was waving at him. She had arranged for a boat ride to Szentendre and then a bus tour along Lake Balaton, long before he'd met Helen or bought the house in Balaton Kenese. He looked into the sunlight. There she was. His mother. Suddenly the savvy of her experienced traveler demeanor fell away from his eyes. She was simply his mother who had come across the world to see about her son and make sure he was alright. His heartfelt suddenly full and tears sprang to his eyes, but he was able to hide them as they embraced. Mama. So amazing to see you here. The light seemed to carry them away into the boat and lunch and the long day's journey until he kissed her goodbye at her Gellert Hotel room that night. Agnes always so indirect. She couldn't just come to Budapest, she must arrange a tour and stay at the finest hotel and be no trouble to anyone. A Grand Dame of the Old School. Senator Demeter's beautiful daughter. For a moment, Josh didn't want her embrace to end. But then the life around them came rushing in, the noise of the ship's engine and the traffic in the street. They were off to see his new world.

Now, here he was with her again—with Ryly and Gordon—in Edgeton at the old house where nothing had changed. Still his mom. But, still, the first split second of seeing her—the puffiness of her face, the slight rosy capillary damage around her cheeks and nose—he saw a first lightning bolt of mortality.

And so they had settled into Water Maple St. on that trip home in all its sunny glory. The mornings were foggy and cool. He walked past the oak tree in Judge

Daddy's front yard and looked out across the field beside Agnes' house at the tall pines and wild cherry trees vague in the fog. Agnes was forever talking about what she wanted to do with it—sell it or keep it, promise it to her children as inheritance or warn us that she would most likely need all the money from the sale of it to pay for her old age. Down Tranquility Pike Water Maple Farm was forever lost and Bertha and Marshall had been dead many years.

Those first few days back in Kentucky, Josh felt as if he'd been suddenly allowed back into Paradise, back through the flaming Gate, he felt so at home and protected, his family there and his two sons to lean on for energy all at the same time. Helen was like a shadow in the back of his mind, a voice, even, in a dark room that still called him back to Budapest, to Balaton, across the dream of ocean back to another world.

When he did return to Budapest he stood on October 23rd street, near the apartment he had taken. Now that he and Helen were separated, he felt that energy disappear and he was thrown back into the confused time before he'd left, a time he had been making sure all of the details of the trip had been properly dealt with. He had worried about the length of time ("It's not worth it unless you stay at least 6 weeks over there. Too far," his expat friends had told him) if the boys would be alright, if the plane would crash. And hadn't Mahamet, jr. and Abdullah, his currency exchange buddies, said that Budapest would soon be a terrorist target? Yet the war of words in the media between the Jewish intelligentsia and the rising right-wing was something he was glad to be getting away from. When Arafat came to speak, the right-wing, suddenly warm to non-Jewish foreigners, cheered. Such a strange, repetitive, amnesiac world. He remembered Aunt Pearl's words so many years ago," so much injustice in the world."

Now he remembered the manicured lawns of America, the air-conditioning everywhere, the clean streets, the perfect rows of shops and malls as if they'd grown there. Everything functioning perfectly in perfect America he glorified when he was away and that he'd only see for a few weeks. Only frightening if it should ever STOP functioning, some kind of anarchy break out. But Americans seem content to obey even rules that are rarely enforced. Europeans are amazed at the unity of the United States. "How does it all hold together?" they ask, puzzled. The pure joy of its functioning? The hatred of the government, the police, the army—and then the paradoxical veneration of them? The Civil War broke bones that healed back stronger perhaps? Once the crumbling edifice was shored up and unity restored, there was no bringing her down again? No, something is still festering.

The total aloneness of when he arrived back in BP hit hard. He should've just stayed in America a voice seemed to say inside. The idea of playing music in Budapest made him feel sick. Strange music in his hollow heart. Then he played a gig, went out with Lydia, talked to some buddies on the phone. The shame that he had left his home, his mother, faded. There is work to be done here, he thought, "My writing, my music". Then panic. "I'm of no real use anymore!" Helen took the boys to Balaton. "There's not one soul today in this city—this city that faces out toward Asia—who loves me!.... *Home is anywhere someone loves you.*

28 JOSH

I remember one morning in Kentucky, Ryly and Gordon were at the basketball camp sponsored by Medina Univ., so I took a walk into town. What a dream it is to be on Main St. Medina at 9:30 am. Shops just awakening. The yellow light of morning shining down on the American Town: corner of Short St. and Upper. All this given to me like a gift: The Joyland, the club I used to play so many years ago, Mistelbach Park, the classic American Main Street with its ugly parking structure and green glass bank buildings, the gift of downtown Medina handed to me.

I got hungry. I ended up eating a decent hot dog on Faulkner St. just past Main. After staring out the window for a while wondering if I was stupid/ horny enough to make conversation with the pretty secretary on her lunch break. I wasn't. I left and turned up Faulkner, turned left at Short and went towards Upper. I stood on the corner and looked at the city I had once lived in, worked in, loved in, hated in, despaired in. Some new fancy-looking restaurants: the Courthouse Café, a yuppie-looking fern bar sandwich place, Lawyers in ties, thousands working in new downtown offices. The old buildings of my childhood, some looked neglected, abandoned. I walked back to my car and drove to the old west end. Albertine's Deli was still there. There was the apartment Berenice and I shared back in '79. Did we eat much at Albertine's? I don't think so. We couldn't afford it. I got busted once for a joint. Taking a toke and looking in the mirror and seeing a police car. That was before Albertine's was even there. Crazy Reddy had a place there then!—that's right. Madame Fortuna's Home Cooking. Good bean soup and cornbread. That's where I went the morning they released me from jail. Some Deputy knew Judge Daddy and got me out. I remember that anxious morning I got out, pacing up and down in front of my apartment on Faulkner. A beautiful mansion, by the way, cut up into apartments. I wore my "Bob Dylan Live" double LP jean jacket around then. I would sit in Crazy Reddy's new place scheming big music biz coups with bandmates. But it had something to do with putting too much into a woman's love. Then when you got cut, you had no bandage big enough, no place to land when the trap door opened. No way to move your mind forward. Moments were measured in burning cigarettes. All you could think of was how to get her back, yet you knew deep down it was hopeless. Somewhere deep down maybe you didn't even want her anymore. That was what you couldn't face. And then some girl would come along and the cycle went on.

Why are you looking at me, Sylvester Moore, at the corner of Upper and Faulkner? A thin layer of white chalk covers your naked black body. We go up to your place for coffee. Your paintings hang on the walls. You hand me a new CD of your band. Still playing after all these years. John Hunt Morgan's statue is still beside the courthouse, "The Thunderbolt of the Confederacy". Some frat boys have painted his horse's balls dayglo blue. We talk over sandwiches and chips and cold, sweet iced mint tea. You're very excited to hear about my kids. You're shaking your head and wagging your finger. I look down to collect my thoughts. I look up and you're gone.

I keep walking. There's the corner of an infidelity to Berenice. Some girl in the Joyland Club parking lot. Black leather jacket and red lipstick. It was only a matter of time with me and Berenice anyway. I see Gudrun, Emese and Helen talking in the sandwich shop window. All of them have frizzed up their hair. What are y'all doin in Medina? I yell through the glass. They don't seem to hear even though they're looking right at me. I turn to look at a crow cawing over the courthouse. When I look back, they're gone.

I take the kids to Walmart. The sign on July 4th says "fireworks half price" but in fact, they jacked up the price TODAY and they were only going to be half price on the 5th! So I get kind of angry about it but then Ryly says, "No problem. Let's just buy more on the 5th!!!" Kids always see the glass half full – right?

29

The degree of the pain of losing Gudrun was surprising, but then the way it began to lessen once I got back to the States and then just disappeared altogether—that was even more so. It almost makes me think of the efficacy of prayer. So strange how, in Carlo's backyard in Cincinnati—we stopped in to see him on our way back to Edgeton—when the feelings of total emptiness beset me, I began looking up at the stars and bright Venus in the evenings and praying to Mother Mary. (And, later, at night in my bed in Edgeton I did the same, throwing in a few Pater Nostras as well). It must have calmed me deep down. Yet my cynical soul would never assent to the possibility of divine intervention—

especially in regard to silly love affairs. Yet I can never fully seem to disbelieve that someone is "out there". It's a feeling that seems to lie as a kind of protecting wall between day to day feeling and the "dark wood" of emptiness, mortal feelings, even insanity. Sometimes not being able to "have" her or to get her out of my mind drove me mad.

Ah, the last days of a visit home to Edgeton. Always a twinge of sadness. Just when you finally get the rhythm of the old home back—it's time to move on.

"Move on"—those were Carlo's words as I lamented the passing of my affair with Gudrun and asked him if I should try and win her back. At the time his words seemed harsh… but now I see that he was right. There's always that sense of panic and desperation at the end of a love affair. All the things one should have done but was too complacent to do are suddenly attempted all at once: compliments that were once withheld are blurted out, flowers are bought, all sorts of changes are promised and the desperate lover pleads, "I loved you then! I love you now! I never knew how much! But it's too late. One must "move on".

Summer smiles now like an indolent girl. Yet, a storm yesterday blew away the muggy, lusciousness and left the air cooler, almost chilly. I noticed leaves had already fallen from a small grove of beech trees.

Doc's books on the shelves in Agnes' house. How I will miss you! Poetry anthologies (Oscar Williams') Eliot's Complete Poems and Plays, The Collected Poems of W.B. Yeats, Rimbaud, Wordsworth, Whitman, Gibbon, Sartre… Bataille, novels, biographies, books of science and philosophy— all resting on that dark, rich paneled wall.

Now I'm remembering the first glimpse of the green, green meadows of Edgeton. As if the whole road from Medina to Edgeton was burned into my memory: my mother starting to look like her mother in her infirmity, "staying one stop past her destination", yet knowing that I, too, would want my children to deliver me from death. At sudden moments it becomes clear—and I understand the anger of those near death. I hope my sons are with me when I die. Yet I hate for them to see death. Doc and I, once, thirsty, searching for a coke machine in the hospital, broke our vigil over grandmother Bertha. When we returned she had rolled and lolled into a limp, round, vacant, wobbling corpse. Gone for eternity. The long struggle to live – ended. Agnes' father's house covered with photographs of his illustrious political career. If walls could talk. But they would tell the same story, from desire to death. Everyone in the photographs is dead now. I see the old man's ghost in every corridor. I want to speak to him. I look down to gather my thoughts, but when I look up—he's gone. The garden gone to weeds. No one can afford the gardener. Sitting around talking with Uncle

Dennis about the Palestinian question. I try to point out an injustice, but they see the Arabs as the perpetrators. It reminds me of the long talks with the Arab guys in Budapest in their "currency exchange" parlors. Budapest will have trouble someday they say. There is no compromise they say. A great battle brews—with rumblings even in this living room of middle America! But I am silent. Even my father evokes his sacrifices in WW2. I provoked him when I said, "My sons will not fight." He bared his jagged teeth and poked his finger in the air and suddenly he said I smelled too liberal! The seed of war grows within us all. Dr. Johnson said mutual cowardice was a natural deterrent. But the earth is covered now with machines men use to kill each other.

BACK IN BP

I feel little twinges. Again, I see Gudrun's face in everything. Water flowing under Elizabeth Bridge. Never ever returning. Still, something remains. But it's more than that. Every moment paints a thin layer over it. Like skin over a scar. Poison. Down. System.

Don't contact her until the season changes. When autumn comes we know who we really are. The earth, as a support, falls away.

I met her when I was vulnerable. I was so lonely coming back that year. I thought seriously that I might be losing my mind. The Arab guys near the Synagogue. They had no furniture to speak of in their "office" just a table and a few chairs maybe. But what I remember most was the guy chopping a salad on the table next to an adding machine. I mean, these guys beat the bank's exchange rate, or anybody else's in town, by 15-20 forints to the dollar. Amazing rate. They said to me: "Go out and tell yr American friends." Nice guys, but it always seemed like there was something fishy goin on. I never asked. Helen knew them from back in the commie days. It was easier for them to work the black market back then. The room smelled of chopped parsley and basil and mint. So, it was pure loneliness that let me start up with Gudrun even when I knew it was a crazy match. She sent me texts. "How you are beautiful Amerika boy?" And I wouldn't answer, partly because I didn't have enough minutes on my phone and partly because I thought, wrongly, that if I teased her a little she'd want me more. But it was that day in the Mona I finally called her again. That's what started it all. She called back. I felt like I had now stirred up a hornet's nest of old demons. I'm fond of the girl but is she "the One"? She needs a Man to answer Yes. One voice says, "Move on," another says, "Move on to what?" I pray to Mother Mary for clear-headed judgment.

Love is so sweet. That's why the risks are so high. The acrobat feels giddy with adrenalin. He knows that at any moment he can plummet to his death.

The lover entwines with the beloved. The beloved suddenly disappears. The raw flesh is exposed. The wind on the nakedness down to the quick, stings. Slowly the red, raw skin covers itself with new skin.

Autumn comes to S. Buda. Strange to think that Gudrun might come back. A sense of foreboding, yet one of possibility as well. It would be nice to have her companionship again. Like Crip said, "You're hurting because you miss her company." He said that his Uncle Schwartz used to say, "Vooman keep you varm in Vinter!" Winter's icumen in!

Wept this morning, remembering how old Agnes looked. Am I practicing for the inevitable orphan-hood that will come soon enough? I fear the shock of not having a mother. For so much of my life, I've been "someone's child". When that ends, what happens?

I went out to my car today and someone had stolen all four hubcaps.

30 XMAS MORNING 3 am

A child is born

What Beauty surrounds me. Surely she will grant me some companionship, allow me to possess HER just for a moment, to know that ecstasy again. To be lonely is blasphemous! To deny the splendor of each moment. The shatter lines in a slab of sidewalk, detritus gathered around a signpost, the indentation of the manhole cover, the coin copper name of the water company stamped upon it, all that I see in front of me, the urge to catalog it before death covers it in the great slab of the city's gravestone.

The old poem said "I am the master of my Fate" but it's not true. We are all bound together, one to another. And he who pinched the candle flames (in childish anger) one by one, he is master only of the dark, of emptiness, of disconnection—the Fate of his desire! Who dealt this hand? The Dealer swinging slowly to the ground in the hammock of his leaf, his answer is too much mingled with the voices of the dead. And yet the cupped hand under everything supports it all. The net under the acrobat—a network of interlocked fingers, fates, conversations, loves irrevocable decisions.

31

Dear Josh,

Loneliness and heartbreak make me fear death less. When I'm happy—fat and sassy—my anxieties about mortality seem to increase. This makes sense in terms of what I call psychic logic.

Pain and joy must, by psychic law, balance out, or cancel each other out. Just as the idea—the possibility—of death mars the complacent tranquility of the happy man, it brings the hope of joyous relief to the lonesome. Then, the weakness that allowed or ushered in loneliness metamorphoses into the strength that fearlessness of death can bring, just as the strength and health that led to joy and happiness becomes the weakness of the fear of its loss.

And at the very bottom, like a wild-eyed phosphorescent fish, lies the awful Self you don't want to face, knowing that now, at rock bottom, it's all you've got. The only net. The only place to land.

You found that you had left an awakened culture that was falling asleep and entered a sleeping culture that was beginning to awaken.

The lower you sink, the lower you will sink. (with yo' "brethren" standing by).

As ever,

Doc.

DOC (1999)

America is a lovely wife that everyone used to be in love with and wanted to serve and admire. But then she became too demanding, yet never proffering any reward or recompense for such loyalty. So, the love affair soured, turned bitter... then violent. The world will cast its lot with China. The world will turn against America, as it did Venice five hundred years ago. As the US weakens, her allies will fall away one by one. She will stand alone and the light of domination, her empire, will flicker and fade... and then go out. England will become a kind of brokering agent between the orient and North America.

DOC (APHORISMS)

Women never lose at the game of sex. They just stop playing.

Art is knowing there's someone else there. Art succeeds when the artist reveals himself as that Other.

32 JOSH'S DIARY 1967

Went to the movies with Kiki at Water Maple Theater. Her yellow shorts and little brown feet in sandals. Too shy darn it to do anything but touch her thigh. Then I went up to get popcorn. Her pouty lips. I kissed her and I was expecting a candy taste like in songs and she tasted like salt.

33

At the end of the jazz gig, audience gone. Footprints on the chord charts where they had fallen off the stand and onto the little stage floor. Doc says my lyrics should be gathered up and called, The Art of Losing.

34 KRIP

A girl I met at the Joyland, once: "You know, I've seen a lot of heavyweight cats duke it out on stage, but the opening act was this real mysterious cat. Like, he knows something you don't know kinda dude, and he proceeded to lay down some severely mellow shit for, like, a half-hour. This Bach-like chord changes type tunes that would build then flow back, weird gypsy jazz dissonances resolving into consonant, Prarie-like bluegrass orchestral rock panoramas and then you'd realize it was just piano, bass, drums and him. It totally blew my mind. The main event seemed like a real anti-climax for me after that. You should try playing with him". I gotta admit, sometimes I used to hate that.

For Josh, coming back to Medina was like the butterfly returning to the cocoon from which it flew. He said Medina looked like something dry and dead to him now. I dreamed, once, I saw him by Lake Balaton, dressed in priestly robes (of no known religion), everyone gathered to bid him farewell. He was going to ___(?).

35 JOSH

Gudrun is still on my mind. I think she's with a guy at the Arab exchange place. I used to disappear on her and not return her texts. I thought it would make her hungrier. Instead, she just got another dude! I thought I didn't give a shit. But I did! How could my own mind trick me like that? I spend too much time waiting for her call. Hope is the lover's opium. Months went by and I kind of got over her. Then she called: "Do you have a girlfriend"? she asked. "You haven't called me in ages". Equation: fear of loneliness makes us look for "insurance lovers." We met at the Mona. She looked even prettier than I remembered. Loneliness makes women beautiful. We had a nice chat. She let me fondle her a little—even while she giggled with friends on her cell phone. Then she would take it away from her ear a moment and shake her head and wag her index finger at me. On my knees, I kiss her feet in sandals but when I get up to her thighs the shaking and wagging begins again. She still has the guy she left me for—maybe it's him on the phone!—but she's losing interest in him. He's depressive. My experience: the quickest way to turn a woman off is to say you're depressed.

"In order to survive a woman's rejection, one must become an artist!"

—Doc

Saw an old street dude ("utcai bacsi") on my way home. I was walking from the Bertelen Lajos St. stop on the 18 tram, down Bercseny St. to my apartment off Baranyai St. He was asleep standing up, head pushed up to the wall, against the massive shining steel ribs of an enclosed exhaust fan blowing warm air from the back of a grocery.

36 DOC (APHORISMS)

"Men want sex without strings; women want sex with strings."

But is it true? About women, I mean. Isn't that belief prompted by the ingrained societal taboos? Without pressure from patriarchal society wouldn't they pursue meaningless quick fucks, too? Women are ceded the honorable morally responsible side of sex—but should they be? Do they really feel that way? Or is that they with their superior natural instinct already know the limitations of sex for its own sake and so adopt an attitude that goes beyond it? Is there a difference? There is no male or female principal of the Universe.

Men are collectors. Women are selectors. Men pursue. Women are objects of pursuit. All bullshit.

37

Balaton Journal May 9th. Hanging out with Dad's old band.

RYLY

After the gig, we looked out over the water into the darkness. No one spoke. Further up from the shore you could still hear people partying. I remembered that earlier that afternoon, as the sun had faded, I had seen a spectacular sea-scape, looking out to where a thin finger of land rises to a summit, not unlike Tihany, the hillside forming a kind of thin "C" shape; the other bank extending out into the water narrowing the passageway where the water flows through and outward as if it went on infinitely since, in that direction, it's impossible to see the other shore. One of the guys in the band had gotten word about Krip being back in the hospital. It dawned on me then that there was a chance that this time he would not pull through.

38 JOSH

Before singing in the Church the song the Bride requested, I had time to watch the wedding ceremony a few pews back from the alter. It struck me that it had been many years since I'd been in a church—though, in my mind, I am often in St.Jude's Church of Our Childhood. As I watched, it occurred to me that the tragedy and sorrow of Time—the sad fact that all living things must die—it's just too much for us. And so we make our suffering into a ritual. RELIGION IS RITUALIZED SUFFERING. That accounts for the somber way church ceremonies, even weddings and christenings, are held. The groom was very kind at the reception. He told me that my performance in the church was one of the greatest he'd ever heard. (He was a Beatles fan. He and the bride wanted "All You Need is Love" sung with the orchestra at the beginning and end).

Nice to think I gave someone something he'll always remember: a speck of immortality in a young couples' life together.

Gudrun has taken up a year of my life—half sex, half learning to live without her. Everything seems to balance in that way. Every moment of happiness we experienced had to be destroyed one by one in my memory until I felt ok again. I haven't gotten laid in a year. Even though that dark girl with the henna hair is nice I can't count taking refuge at "the Place" upstairs at the Arab dudes' exchange "office".

If yr lost you can't expect a woman to find you.

I wonder, always, about God. And lately, I've prayed to Mother Mary (the first time was in Carlo's back yard in Cincinnati on a Lacy Corman tour, when the pain of Gudrun's complete and surprising rejection of me was at its peak pain level). But do they exist? Is Jesus and his Mother, his Father and a Holy Spirit, are they looking out for me? I've been giving their teachings, as they've come down to me, an unorthodox interpretation, I guess. Yet the "menace" of life is palpable, the loneliness, the isolation, especially here in Hungary, so palpable it digs down deep into my gut, my genitals, my moods. I weep fairly regularly. I know I'll never be delivered from earthly pain. Sometimes it almost seems as if they're listening and making good things happen. I'm edified. But then it wears off. It seems to make more sense to hope for nothing, to believe in nothing. The world around me seems senseless, absurd again. I'm so cash poor, I'm paralyzed. Then, I take refuge in cheap used books in English if I can find them, music, my work. Doubt passes. But once again, nothing changes, nothing will be different. I'm waiting again for a woman's love that doesn't come, or else, no woman that I can love back. The beautiful women I chase don't respond to me, and the others, I feel guilty taking advantage of them just for sex. What nirvana is greater than sexual pleasure? It must be partly related to it—no? There is another life in which that drive is no longer there? One can't deny that it is there. Like Krip said, *"It's nice to be wanted."*

39 DREAM

Krip and I are sitting in a parked car in Edgeton. I begin one of my usual metaphysical discussions, telling him that in Budapest I'd often plug him into some of my images of my previous life in Edgeton. In other words, after having known him in BP, when I went back for visits in Edgeton, obviously I carried around thoughts in my head of my BP friends. For example, I might say, after some experience on a visit home, "Wait til so-and-so in BP hears about this!" In reality, I don't think I much experienced it that way. I tended to keep the BP and Edgeton lives quite separate, but this is what I was saying in the DREAM. I continued telling him this since I had often imagined him being in Edgeton with me (and he HAD spent a few years there growing up before moving up North). Again, in reality, I don't think I had much imagined this, although, yes, I had sometimes fantasized about BP friends coming to Edgeton en masse. As I say, since we are now in a car together (in the dream) and in the dream, I am speaking sincerely, I now tell him: "See? Now you are REALLY here. So, now, Krip, I see a very clear, strong connection between my imagination (you being in Edgeton) and the actual reality of you being here now. "Suddenly, (I'm saying in the dream—but I feel this way often, now, in reality) I see that reality and imagination partake very liberally of each other!" But this is also connected to my meditations on what it means that, for example, Bertha's house no longer exists, but in my imagination, I still see every floorboard, every stain on the wall, every table, chair, rug, piece of silverware, every wrinkled edge of linoleum, hear the refrigerator hum, etc.—yet the house has been absolutely RAZED, gone without a trace years ago! Which is the "greater" reality? The one when it existed physically or the one now still in my imagination, my mind? So, in the car, I was making this connection between the 2 situations: Bertha's house in my imagination and Krip's real "being" (as a noun?) in BP, carried by my imagination to Edgeton (in reality) and then "dreamed" in BP (as if real) as if being in a car in Edgeton! So many levels! Then, in my dream, after I've told him my little metaphysical flight of fancy, we are suddenly in a deserted street at night and Krip brandishes a set of "keys" that allows him to open manhole covers. He starts unlocking them. I also remember that sitting in the car he had on a white t-shirt, while now, as he's unlocking sewer caps, he's got on a black one. But then the dream thread is lost. I'm then walking alone and I see an obvious mugger approaching. I look around for an escape route and see another man approaching. I can't tell if he's friend or foe, in cahoots with the other mugger or coming towards me to my rescue. I see a crowd of pedestrians in the distance. I yell, "Hey Boys!" and it wakes me up.

I had felt a tremendous satisfaction in Krip's presence as if, finally, I had unlocked a metaphysical riddle. I felt at peace and unfearful of my own death. The mugger was perhaps a first taste of this newfound consciousness. "Are you really still afraid of anarchic reality, of random violence, of TERRORISM? Of Chaos? Now that you've found supreme order?" it seemed to ask me. I seemed to have understood that Reality was not so omnipotent. It's mixed up with the imagination. This comforted me. (Although, after all, Krip was merely unlocking sewers)! Yet the mugger had brought back an element of Chaos and the Irrational. But my metaphysical questioning had been the root of all that. Paradoxically, the mugger had in fact been Reality and the Rational posing as Chaos in an unreal dream attacking metaphysical knowledge (me in the dream). I felt a connection to Rational Reality for giving a sense of meaning to a Mystical Epiphany, which that same Rationality deemed worthless.

It occurred to me tonight, watching Krip's band at the Trafo in Budapest—people wanna have a good time. But they seem adrift, in a sea of what? "Forgotten teardrops" of course, but in their world, the world they must recreate from scratch every day. At least that's what the "foreigner" must do. He who is adrift is a foreigner, even in his own country.

There is a feeling in the air, a tension, a foreboding. The City can so quickly erupt into Chaos. It doesn't but the feeling is there—just under the surface. The siren wails, the anxious shopkeeper smokes in his doorway, the bar bouncer pokes an accusing finger into his money pouch, making change for a table of hoodlums on the terrace having a last round—the band sits among them telling stories of even stranger gigs.

Wisdom is by nature the absence of desire. Another little fish on the line lost? Womanlessness seeps back into my bones. Yet, I've become so used to it now!

Watching D-Day films on British cable tv. War heroes have such sad faces.

40

Now I live in this little apartment. I have a lot of time just to think. I lay on the bed and smoke and think a lot. Mostly about the past. Sometimes I try to think up ways to make money in the present—some scheme. I have to. Well, I don't have to. I cd die, just lay here until my energy ran out – like leaving a car running. Sometimes it seems like a good idea since nothing seems to come of anything. I mean, the schemes, my "projects" rarely work. But the thought that I cd feel myself dying—that's too scary. I wd like it better if it just ended quickly without my knowing anything. Just laying here letting life go out—that wdnt be easy. It wd take too long. You have too much time to think about it. It wd be like those crazy political extremists who go on hunger strikes. That always seemed childish to me – like a kid who threatens to hold his breath in front of his parents until they get scared of him being blue in the face and give in to his demands.

I don't like to go outside anymore. Sometimes I do just for a change. The light is very gray and weak. Even in summer.

Crip's got this lawyer girlfriend who gives me money sometimes. That's how I buy food. She wants me to go to a doctor to run some tests. She says something's wrong with me. Sometimes she wd rather just take me to the store and buy food, instead of giving me the cash. She wants me to have food. She's not sure what I use the money she gives me for. But I'm no druggie. I like to get stoned or drunk sometimes. That's about it. There's something about me tho I guess she likes. She's a nice woman. I think about what wd happen sometime if she stopped giving me money—the energy going out scenario comes to mind—but I doubt she'll stop anytime soon. I can keep things under wraps. I'm getting old. I used to never chase girls when I was young, or cheat on them, but now way past forty, I find it's the only thing I'm not too bad at. I found out that people are interested in 2 things: getting money and having sex. All the egoism in between can be boiled down to this; i.e. if a guy wants to tell his life story it's because he thinks by getting it out there in front of people, he might find someone who wants to hire him for something and he can get some money, probably to get sex (or "love") with. Or else just to keep a nice warm apartment so he can whack off when he wants and get rid of the whole mating urge- at least for an hour or so. As long as there's a furnace on, loneliness can be kept at bay. When it gets so cold the furnace breaks

down—then you got a problem. At least until spring—then everything returns.
Energy doesn't just go out. Energy starts coming back in. Then it might be nice
to take a stroll in the park. Even treat yourself to a 2 dollar Turkish sandwich. But
then you remember you shd eat the rest of the rice you cooked and save the cash
to put on the heating bill.

I can't let too much life energy go out. I have to think of the children.

41

I think of Gudrun's beautiful back. And when she reached her arms out across
the bed how the muscles around her shoulder blades rippled in gentle curves and
shadows, the shadows the deep muscular groove made down her spine funneling
to her ass. Watching the waves of her body as I pushed against her. Her breasts
gently swaying.

Sex is a drug. All that pushing and yearning that you open up in yr self just
goes down into yr nerves and the memory mechanisms in yr brain. Yr body keeps
thinking of how euphoric and perfect those moments of ecstasy are. It wants to
go back to that place. Then, one day an angel of the lord with a flaming sword
is standing at the gate barring your entry. Eve is gone somewhere. Maybe she'll
come back – but not for a long time. But you don't believe it. So, you go looking
for her. She has many disguises. Most of them you give to her yr self.

I used to be a good man. Perhaps I still am. But it's hard to tell because no
one asks me to be good for them anymore. When I was a child it seems I gave
people joy—but all that is gone now. I am far away from that place, the place
of songs. Here no one practices goodness. Every action must be calculated to
promote expediency and survival even. Behind every act of kindness, there is
an opportunity for personal gain. Now people are beginning to just take. They
sometimes now don't bother with the "give" and the "kindness" part. There is a
momentary joy in beating someone in a deal and knowing you've bought time to
survive. Time to keep your flat. Time to buy food in the grocery. But goodness
and generosity seem far away now, part of another life. The cashiers all try to
shortchange you. There's no recourse complaining to a manager, he's getting a
cut from the money they steal. He wants to leave the city and claim the Balaton
country house before his relatives try to sell it using a fake document from the
little village bank. His wife made a brilliant coup by getting the deed to the patch
of land next door to the farmhouse where the Gypsies had been squatting. They
had come to believe that it was theirs, then the wife finds out their deed was a
fake, drawn up by a shyster cousin who lived in another town. She coaxed the

bank to intervene and get possession. They did and then sold it to her at half the market value.

Nice going. The Gypsies were forced to leave their shack. The young daughter that used to walk through the square w such high breasts and long legs and strong feet, I used to hear her sobbing at night. Her father was crazy, a horse trainer with a black handlebar moustasche who wd drunkenly drive his team of horses through the village at breakneck speed. Somehow he managed to survive even though there were so many cars now—no one needed him anymore to break their horses. He started carting hay to the other farmers for their pigs. The mule-drawn wagon rattled slowly down the main dirt street. The girl's brother was retarded it seemed. One eye rolled in his head. The girl loved her father. He cared about nothing else but her.

Another gypsy woman next door used to curse at the wife whenever she saw her. The white men of the town said to ignore them. And so they did. Eventually, the cursing stopped. The land stayed empty. The pretty gypsy daughter walked by once and smiled. She was like the dark roses that bloomed by the side of the white-washed cottage.

42

Now, I am in the City again. Here in the little flat, I am losing weight. I may be sick somehow, I can't tell, just like the goodness or kindness. Nothing like that seems to matter as it once did. I am drinking ginseng tea constantly and smoking wild hemp Gudrun brings. I mix it w tobacco to take away the bitterness.

When Gudrun comes we sit and talk and I feel better. Her hips are so round I sometimes sit down on her lap and lay my head on her huge tits. Or we lay down and I massage her beautiful back muscles with oil. Then I lay my head on her huge ass and sleep. We wake up and make love. She smokes while I do cunnilingus on her. She squats down like an island woman. After a few days, she disappears. She doesn't answer her cell phone. Then, just when it seems I've overcome loneliness, she comes back. The cycle begins again.

One night she took me to the Turkish bath. She said it would give me energy.

43

I hate to leave my apartment. It means I'll probably buy something. Like food. If only we didn't need food or heat, things might be better. Are they bad? I'm not sure. They cd get worse. I used to do different things: play music, give English lessons. I worked at a vegetable stand. Crip used to come by and say hello. We don't talk about music anymore. The guy who owns it used to take a few English lessons from me. But he stopped. Not enough bread.

Bread. That's what no one seems to have. The streets seem a bit tense. If the currency drops pretty soon you won't be able to buy food with it anymore. And like Doc said, if you can't get food w money anymore then theyll be action in the street. People have always been grumpy here. Now they're getting downright mean. This place is like a second-rate summer camp that yr beginning to hate. You wanna go home but yr parents arent coming to pick you up—ever.

Crip's woman, I can't give away her name, is like a parent. She gives me money sometimes. She's very old. Except when she smiles she looks younger. She used to smile more it seems. I started giving her English lessons—then we started having sex. Notice I didn't say "fucking." Such a weird word now. Maybe I shd say it: fucking. I worried about it some. But she said her husband was cool. "He is a European man," she said. Which means I guess, he won't kick my ass. In the States, they kill ya. Like hangin a horse thief I guess. I always liked westerns. Esp John Wayne. Some painter told me the "light" in the old films is "warm yet spacious" giving the landscape that open feel. I guess they were all filmed in California or Nevada or someplace. I started checking out the light. And he was right. But now the cable co has axed TCM from my "package" so all I get now is CNN. Wars, terrorism, British announcers (tv journalists) and soccer highlights. People love to hear about how fucked up other people are. That way they don't feel so fucked up themselves—even tho they are. In fact, they're usually sloshed. Everybody in Europe is at least half sloshed all the time. It's a cool party sometimes, unless they're sick, comin off a drunk—which is often. Hence the meanness. Nothing got better while they were drunk. It all just stayed fucked up—to them—so they get mad about it—now that they're sober. I get mad sometimes. Sometimes I get drunk, too. I like the Other Drug better tho. But it doesn't cure that Lonesome Feeling. This helps—like I'm talking to someone— like Mother Mary. She's my best friend. She's different than the Woman. No money. But she looks out for me, it seems that way. I cd swear some things I ask her for—peace of mind, health to my family—they happen. I ask for Love alot. But that is trickier. Yr never sure if it's happening or not. Women come and go. Sex is great but Love... I don't know. It's more complicated. You think you give it. But then nothing happens. Maybe you don't give it right. Then you forget about it. The days go by. Then you feel that stinging feeling in yr eyes again. But then Mother Mary comes. But we don't have sex. The girls I have sex with – I try to see if there is any Mother Mary I can find. Usually, there isn't any. But I didn't give Mother Mary love either maybe. It's complicated.

44 LETTER TO ANGELIKA

You ever get the feeling the whole edifice is gettin ready to collapse? seems like many people trying to grab what they can get of what's left. And in the meantime, there's Hungary, where there's gonna be rioting like the Greeks soon enuff I bet. Is the jig up? It seems the system requires more cash input than it can get. So when it sputters and when there ain't no more cash OUTput... e' body's broke, things get unstable—people get aggressive and try to get back to that place they were before. But they can—there aint enuff cash—or jobs.

I don't wanna leave my kids or be separated from them by an entire continent. I live 20 mins away from them—yet I see them maybe twice a week at most—usually just for a few hours. Isn't that strange? Yet mainstream society is ok w it. Yet take a toke of pot and you're a menace to society—pay a fine, put yo' ass in jayail— you gwine tuh lose yr job, mother fucker, you ain't gettin no insoirance, boy. Yep. And so now if I move back to America—a place where I'm not an outsider—and voila! everything's ok again? Not likely. My children will be 3000 miles away.

Boy I cd tell you stories bout this Hungary place. Ain't no gettin ahead here. When I had kids I never thought fate wd deal me such a blow. But I see now: I wasn't master of my fate. I let other people determine alot for me. And then they forget you. You gotta be yr own man—chapter one that I didn't read right. I figured all I had to do was keep on strumming and SOMEbody wd rescue my ass—and now NOBODY wants to hear that shit. Not for money anyway. But the idea that I will have to be away from my kids—already I feel I was robbed somehow of the last 7 yrs w them. But I don't make enuff bread to support them anyway. So I shd consider myself LUCKY that I got jettisoned and Helen has the resources to keep food on their table! Right? Seeing them on Sundays and a Saturday afternoon now and again. They have been diminished I fear by my lack of influence. I can't be aggressive. I can't lead or tell people what to do. I can't insinuate or force myself into their lives. It's just not my nature it seems. And now they seem like they're drifting away from me and I can't do anything about it. My place is boring to them a little so I always gotta go over to Helen's and sit around like a fool. Crip comes by and the dog don't bark. Then maybe the kids and I go out somewhere. But I never have money for concerts or restaurants or almost anything for them. Still, they love me but... we just can't do real quality hangs it seems—real spontaneous quality hangs.

I hate even leaving my apt. now. There was a bomb scare in Helen's office. BP is so cold and strange. Lotsa foreigners agree. Crip's from here, but he says the same thing. My place is just too small for my sons to feel comfortable in when they come over. Maybe they feel a loyalty to their mom that makes them hesitate. That's fine. I want them to be close to her. A boy shd be w his mom. I just gotta talk to someone. That's why I'm paralyzed. Can't stand livin here. (Gotta call Lacey and see if he's got gigs. I don't even have his phone number anymore!) Can't stand the idea of leavin em. Hell, I never really got to be w them. Not like I wanted. Not like I always thought it wd be. I'm broker than I've ever been. I haven't worked significantly in 3 months. I've been scrounging and borrowing. Really have no idea how long I can keep this up. What a weird thing to happen. Have kids in a place you can't seem to make a living in. I've never made a decent living my whole life!!! Maybe I'm being dramatic. Or am I facing the truth finally!? Music is OVER man! Now what? 7/11 cashier? Ati the Grocer gave me a job working in his veggie stand. Cool. Aren't we 'sposed to like our lives? Not sure I can even do it. I don't have near the energy just to do whatever I feel like anymore. I gotta pace myself...

45 URBAN SPECTACLES OF BUDAPEST

I went to see a friend. He's a great sax player. But perhaps an even better photographer. He had been doing a photoshoot of one of the girls in the band I sometimes work with. We sat and talked in Hungarian. Mine is still poor but he's a good sport. Even tells me I speak well. But he's just being encouraging. He speaks hardly a word of English—doesn't seem especially keen to learn any from me. But he understands a little of what I say when I revert to English—which I do only because my brain gets tired trying to speak Hungarian. Like the Monty Python guy, "My brain hurts!"

I leave his place and get down to the street but the tram seems claustrophobic, the panic of the foreigner. The claustrophobia of loneliness. No one here knows me. A whole tram of people, not one knows I exist. Sometimes it's too much for me. It's spitting sleet and snow but it doesn't seem so cold. I decide to walk home. It's maybe an hour but worth it just to see the faces on the Great Boulevard. Soon I reach Blaha Luiza Square. (Louise Blaha was a great (light?) opera singer in the (20s?) It sits at the real heart of BP, a crossroads of the Great Boulevard and Rakoczi Road, a major downtown street. To get to the other side you can walk underground at a diagonal so you don't have to negotiate the maze of streets and crosswalks and car traffic above. But underground—it's a major subway stop—it's another world. I can't begin to describe the spectacle of it. A quick catalog perhaps of what immediately greets yr eyesight upon descending: Gypsy Prostitutes, and many other gypsies standing around not trying to sell women but just hanging out, talking, smoking. A cop is asking a prostitute for her "papers" and this is not even a red light district. It's the business center of Pest in broad daylight! The magazine shopkeepers making change w a snarl on their faces. A snack bar. Pretty office girls waiting to meet handsome office men. (Hungarian women are the most beautiful in Europe, except maybe for Serb women. Or Croatian. Or Moldavian. Or Armenian. It doesn't matter.) They stand looking at their watches in their winter clothes—smart long coats which they've had to put on again now that winter has suddenly returned. Hoods turned up like Tanya (was that the Julie Christie character in Dr. Zhivago?) uneasy in the subway filth, a filthy market beckons down a corridor, gypsy boys in rapper hoods, some evangelical Taiwanese shouting and singing songs thru a bad mic. Bums standing around with their hands out. And an old man with a guitar slung across his back. A gypsy man. The caseless guitar slightly wet from the wet snow. I follow him up the staircase and walk past. He's talking to himself. I've seen him in the metro many times, throw a coin into his case. He's counting on his fingers. Tabulating the day's take no doubt. He's not bad. Sings romantic songs. I mean, I've seen him before. Sometimes with a violinist. Surely he has a relative somewhere who takes care of him. He maybe lives w a daughter whose husband tolerates him. "But daaarling, Zoli brings in some money. He loves his music so…please, dear, let him stay." I press on through the throng. I stop at a used bookstore and buy a pretty nice book on Greek mythology and cultural history for 2 bucks. I started to buy a hardback King Lear for 3 but changed my mind. The chapter on Ovid in the 2 dollar one has aroused my interest too much. I probably won't read it. It will sit on the shelf near the window and when it's covered with a thin film of dust this Spring I'll pick it up and leaf thru it in the strong sunlight illuminating the dust flakes.

I met this girl in the Mona. Samidha.

46

What IS the story, man? It's spring. All I can think of is women everywhere. My heart has grown so full of lust I can hardly think straight. EVERYthing seems to revolve around finding the girl. Chat ups in the street only work sometimes. Like Gudrun. But she's so unreliable now. Why doesn't she just SAY, I have a new boyfriend, go away. What is she up to I wonder? I don't hear from her and then boom, we're at the Turkish bath together necking in the big pool outside. It's the inside of her thighs that look fat and some around the chin. For a brief moment she's unsexy but then as she's drying her hair with the hairdryer. She looks magnificently tall and blond with that ocean brown color underneath the blond streaks. She looks like Brigitte Bardo for chrissake! Then after a few hours swimming in the warmth nuzzling her huge breasts—she wants to go home. Not to my place. Had to wank alone when I got back to my crib. Why do I have to confess these privacies? (I told him he didn't have to… he continued…) I'm glad they're not easy. Not for me anyway. They're so elusive. Yet so full of love when they decide they want to be with you. So natural the way a woman's arms go around you. As if that was something nature had designed them to do. Embrace. Embrace Creation. Woman is holding all creation in her arms.

47

The waitress at the Mona Lisa looked so cute in her black sweater and black jeans. And black dyed hair. That wondrous just going over into fifty glow that women in their forties get. But they're always married it seems. The cute belly pooching out sexily implies gently the 2 children she has. She won't give me her number of course. And in this jeet (Hungarian hillbillie) bar, her hubby will probably kick my ass but it's worth it just to see how—now that she knows I dig her—how she teases me, goodnaturedly. I feel such a warm feeling that she deems me worthy of her little tease, which I can see is something she treasures a little. The little swing in her fanny as she walks away. But she smiles as I pay my bill and leave. Everyone wants love. She has enough. She seems prettier now that I know I can't have her. How boring her life must be—and unhealthy – in that smoky place. Standing all day. Waiting on all the old lechers like me. Right away I told her my life story w fake embellishments. Foreigner—divorced, 2 kids, too. She shrugged her shoulders as if to say, "Sorry. That's too bad." Was it in our minds together? the same lust? Maybe. Maybe not. She wd never give away a secret. A few good girls gave me a lot. And I was rich in love. But I squandered my fortune on windy things, daydreams, bewildered meditations. Lust. Why is it we men want pure lust just as we want pure maternity, pure virginity, pure prostitution.

Now I see I came here as a kind of colonialist! Ha ha! What cd I get out of this small European country? Fame? Sex? Wealth? Art? In what order? I got it all in little tiny unsatisfying droplets. Like Everyman. But I should talk about love, the Garden of which lust is but a key. Turn the latch. Yr in another world. Where many women become One. And Lust is the denial of Death, no?"

48

I'm a colonialist. This place would bring me everything I couldn't have in the

US, I thought. I needed to find people who were even more fucked than me. I can blend in here, I thought. "Everyone here is a failure," Doc told me, once. I seemed drawn to the country of the weak and when I found them weak and bitter and mistrustful. I exploited them as long as I could. I held out the possibility to them of "Success in America" as long as I could. Perhaps they never bought it. They played along until they realized I was a poser, charlatan, whatever. When I think of those photos I tried to sell! Going down to Croatia w my camera and getting the poor villagers to let me take their picture. Then I would use the computer to doctor up the prints by "antiquing" them, making them look vintage. Tried to sell them in all the tourist shops. Flopped. They're all sitting in a bundle underneath my desk. You'd think there'd be a market for all that kinda stuff the way Americans and western Europeans are always whining about nobody helps the poor. Well, here's pictures of them! You can start by buying the fucking picture—you wanna help so bad! The profits go to helping some poor village girl learn how to suck my cock! First step toward saving the fucking world. Suck my cock. Well, at least saving some prick from this gut-eating loneliness.

That's the big problem. Dealing with the ugliness of age. A whole city of wondrous women. Not ONE of them wants my cock! Yet so many good women crying out for love. In the end Woman's lonelier. How ludicrous Man's world must seem to her!

No, it's the past fifty ugliness—think of the bad breath, the dandruff, the hairs poking out of the ears!!—that's what isolates me. Makes me invisible. They laugh now. But you can't let it hurt your feelings. Bow your head and take it. Soon I began to like it. The way they got me to kiss their asses. I enjoyed being a cuckold most of all. That's the end fate of the failed Colonialist. He becomes the laughing stock of his former subjects. Once the freed servant finds his footing in the New Capitalism, he sees through the scams of his former Master. The Whore turns on the Pimp. But she who spends her whole life being pimped—becomes one herself in the end. And so they go on dancing around together like that—like a drunk w a hat rack.

Then I saw that the horrible Dance ends only with Death. Unless you can stop yrself from spinning before it. Then maybe you can live—really live. Death doesn't end the Dance—it just changes the tempo. But if you can spin away far enough—from where?—maybe you can Dance alone. And in yr loneliness, you must pray. Pray to Mother Mary in the morning of your loneliness. O Mary, our only help. Gather me in your milky white arms.

49

A human being is a seething cauldron of juices and acids and smells and gases and so many things inside that you can't perceive from a distance. Then sometimes by accident you get up close and smell the breath, the skin the hair. I smell that way too but you can't smell yourself. I don't know why but I think if I knew I would know many things I don't understand yet.

But a person is a petri dish of stuff—processes, piss, shit, cum. When people drive by on the street I think: There goes a stinky asshole. All those stinky assholes waiting in line for the light to change. The car that surrounds them drops away and there they are just an asshole with a body around it. A self in there somewhere talking to itself. Thinking, thinking, always thinking. Juices in the brain bubbling. Kennedy's brain got blown out into a car seat. They brought him into some room in a hospital w his brains all out everywhere. The doctors breathing, looking at him. A human being is a container filled with juice. Balls. Cock. A sour smell rising like piss from a toilet. The smell of pussy. The sea. Fish. The tangy burnt hair, oniony smell of underarms. A woman smiles. A little spittle in the corners of her mouth. A man. A man of middle age. The smell of aftershave. Yet the sharp smell of his sagging buttocks. The sharp spoiled smell of feet and toenails.

A sharp smell of anger. The smell of tears when someone is weeping.

A house of childhood. The smell of sunlight. The bright light brings the smell of old dog breath up from the carpet, the flesh color of face makeup. Dog breath and the tiredness of life seeping into my breath. The tired contents of my stomach, hamburger french fries coke. The delicious fried onions cleaning the filth from my blood, the sharp oniony smell of breath going stale and dull like fading flatulence in a smokey room.

I went to a zoo once. I loved looking at the monkeys. Not because I liked monkeys so much, but because there was a nice comfy bench right in front of this magnificent glassed-in cage. And I cd sit and look at the chimps as long as I wanted. I really just wanted to rest my legs. And having the chimps there to look at as I relaxed was not bad. One day this girl chimp and tired looking boy (old man?) chimp are circling around each other in the cage—or the girl chimp is— the male is looking tired. And heavy bored. He holds his hand over his forehead as chimps seem to do, almost like the way Jack Benny used to hold his hand under his chin, that nonchalant passive look that seems to say, "Well, what can you do?" They go on like this for a while. Then the female comes over and sticks her ass right up in the male's face. He does nothing. She walks away. Comes back in a minute or so and does the same thing. Sharp smell of chimp pussy. He does nothing. She walks away. Maybe they fuck each other later. I go home among the streets of sagging asses and swollen ankles and smells of human juices.

50

David is the sax player in the band. It's spring so I'm wandering around the 11th district not far from the Petofi Bridge. I knock on David's door. He lets me in and we have a smoke and I tell him made up stories about showbiz in America. It's not all made up but much of it is. I always sound like some second-rate lounge singer in a film about second-rate lounge singers. But David is only half listening. He's more concerned about survival. He wants to do a cruise ship gig but it seems weird to me, playing to weird drunks on a ship. Still, the money's not too bad.

The spring sun is shining everywhere. Lydia might stop in tomorrow so I keep thinking of that. She's six feet tall and a nervous big woman with a beautiful face. I stop at Fehervari St. and the tram suddenly comes roaring up and rings its child-like bell at an old man w a cane trying to cross the street. It surprises me, too. The green crossing man is not flashing at the crosswalk but still, you think the coast is clear—no cars—and then boom the Tram 18 is right on you. I step back to let it pass, cheating death again. I feel too high to walk around in the pre rush hour tumult. I take a side street but I linger around David's place thinking I might be having another asthma attack. But it goes away. I'm sober enough now to see the futility of life – the futility of fear of Death. We had watched some clips of Jackie Orsaszky the great funk musician and so he was my guardian angel. He's dead so I imagined him watching over me. And we had talked just before I got news he'd gone clear.

I'm too shy to make a pass at the millions of girls whirling by. I keep my eyes on the ground. They seem to want me to look at them but I'm too shell-shocked to return their gaze. This only infuriates them for a moment. It must be a fluke, they're thinking.

I think of Lydia again. I have someone now even though she's nuts. Let them come to me. I'm tired of their flippant rejections. Those little teen temptresses. You know the ones I mean. They hang out at the new party places, the ones that close a few weeks after they open, bumming drinks. And the goons at the door, I mean, it's a pickup joint for chrissakes! Looking at you contemptuously as if to say, Whadda YOU want in here? Huh? Some pussy? Is THAT what yr looking for? Well, kinda. So unfair they are. But I get the courage to face my drugged-out fears and walk on.

51

Attila is my new boss, the grocer at the corner a few blocks from my apartment. I stop in for another smoke. He gives me wine from Transylvania. Karoly, his buddy, brought it when he went home for a visit. It tastes like Tokai and champagne mixed together. It's homemade but not bad. A little sweet. A hint of greek retsina or Hungarian leanyka. Karoly has inherited a farm in Transylvania—2 acres. Not bad. Zsanette shows up. Her new set of teeth makes her look rather attractive. We go in the backroom and do shots of Vodka along with the wine. Attila comes in and plays with her ass a little. She slaps his hand. And he goes back out to tend to a customer. I play with her ass. She saches away and pours another vodka. For a minute I think she might blow me right here. But she and Karoly have this thing. Not sure what it is. She must go she says, I make you and Attila and Karoly a nice dinner. Attila calls you. Bye Bye. Attila has to close the shop to go and meet the black refugee girl from Angola he's got on the side… he's a colonialist, too, I guess, in his own country.

I don't know what I'm doing. I feel sick. I never see anyone. I don't want to, yet it's the old loneliness cycle again it seems. Go out and you see how frighteningly weird it all is, stay home and you get lonely, that stinging pre tear twitch in the corners of yr eyes.

52

Lydia bugged off. As we came home from this party I never shudda taken her to she got sore for some reason about me not paying enough attention to her. Kathy the willowy Canadian chick I had a crush on years ago kept talking to me—way more than just the oh how have you been type chat— and she got explaining things about her job, her childhood on Orchis Island, etc. I was lapping it up—careful not to be too obvious glancing down at her perfect breasts (just a masterful ornament, beneath the aqua halter top dress, decorating the rest of her.) I'm sure she caught me a few times. I think she cares nothing for me more than just the mildly curious fascination expats have here for each other.

But she's hanging over Lydia's seat at the bar too far so when Lydia comes back from the bathroom she can't sit down. I keep thinkin Kathy will wrap up the life story bit—tho I'm digging her and her voice immensely—and walk away so Lydia can sit down, but she just keeps on blabbing. Finally, she titters off somewhere. Lydia and I find a table. She says, Please concentrate on me—she means to say "pay attention to me" but her English is bad. It's all we can do to talk. And that's bad. Not because I wanna talk. SHE wants to talk. Blabbing in Hungarian—writing scripts, making films, blogging on talky political issues— this is her life. And she can't do it with me since I don't speak Hungarian well enough to really spar with her. She's bored. I can feel a big argument brewing. But it doesn't happen until we're almost to my flat and I say, I'll probably just go on to sleep. We'd already fucked that afternoon and I was gonna give myself the night off. Maybe pick things up in the morning—my favorite time to screw- esp if people on their way to work—those nosy people next door—can hear us. No, go.

"I will then be ALONE in yr flat!" she says.

  "What will I do?" "I don't know," I say, "read, maybe? Like you did while I was fixing supper this afternoon." Lydia's let herself get a little fat but she still looks pretty good. Not as good as when I met her a few years ago. She let me pursue her. Then I didn't hear from her for a while. Turns out she was kidnapped while doing a story on Dubai for some travel mag and some mafiosos beat her up and raped her. God. Why wd anyone wanna beat up and rape a woman? That's part of why I panic or have choking fits—there's something sinister about it all. But it happens. Sinister happens. Just like the Grand Convention of Death that's everywhere. But one night Lydia shows up at the gig. It's a smokey mafia-run joint called the Mona Lisa II, packed with handsome, horny young dudes and incredibly sexy women. I can't believe it's her. Hadn't seen her in 2 years. After the gig, when the last strains of Long Train Runnin were still hangin in the air and the dj guy had already started in on his schtick, it seemed almost a foregone conclusion that she was gonna come home with me. But as all reasonably good looking women must when out on the prowl, she had a girlfriend with her who was sweet but a bit plain. I'm sure lots of women put me in the same category, just under the libidinal borderline, the line under which almost all sexual attraction is impossible. And so it was we 3 are standing under the street lamp and it seems as if they're waiting for me to choose one of them. As if it won't be a problem either way. Choose Agota (her friend's name), Lydia seems to be thinking, And it's ok because, well, she's my friend and I'd like her to find a nice guy like you, or choose me and—as it turns out—I'll finally get laid after my boyfriend in Beirut dumped me. I went all the way there and DIDN'T get laid so—I'm due and it's ok go ahead. But I don't realize what she's thinking. I can't think of a line that will get her over to my place, esp since her girlfriend's there. Maybe they're a gay couple just coming 'round to say hello. I have no idea. (I don't know what I'm doing.) Just what Lydia will say 3 days from now after we've had our little fling and it was disastrous and then our little argument and: "Nem tudsz semmi" (You don't know NOTHIN). Somehow the way "tudsz" sounds coming out of her mouth sticks in my mind. It sounds deep and crass almost. Hungarian can get guttural and ugly sometimes. Usually, it has a kind of monotonous lilt that's quite pretty, like a girl you thought was ugly suddenly seeming beautiful—just for a moment, one lovely moment—then she goes back to being ugly. Like yr girlfriend! Weeks go by suddenly yr so horny she starts looking good, as yr going through the usual Sunday night fuck, yr thanking God you have someone. The next day you feel refreshed. Then comes that party where a few 20 something's show up and you see that yr girlfriend is zip, really— I mean, looks-wise. When standing beside those luscious babes you'll never have, she seems—ugly. But yr ugly, too. It's just not that apparent to you yet. But after so many years alone—I'm beginning to figure it out. Young girls remember their father's strong odors, his bad breath, his morning shit, his dandruff. You trigger all that and they flee but sometimes, and yr hoping soon, they become morbidly fascinated. Every girl wants to fuck her Dad once. No, it's just a Freudian tirade I've let myself indulge in.

Lydia's dad died when she was 4, she says, lying naked on my floor. Agota has just gone into the bathroom. They've spent the last hour juicing all over my face, facing each other astraddle me. Nice. I catch a glimpse of them making out as I look up between their breasts, squishing together like a bundle of balloons. I've already come and now I can't get it up even tho they want to be fucked. Something's wrong. I feel a tumor-like bulge in my abdomen. Jared Smallwood is dead I heard. Soon I will be. But suddenly I'm able to pull back Lydia's hair—she looks 16, suddenly, her wet spit curls clinging to her neck. I get instantly hard. But she only wants to do it missionary style. I try to change it up a bit. I like seeing that big fine womanly ass in the air. She doesn't. Doesn't want me to lick her pussy. What does she want? Agota has taken a cab home. Lydia and I sleep fitfully. Trying to avoid touching each other.

At dawn, I listen to her snore. Every struggling breath sounds like a rumble of thunder somewhere far away. Far away from this friendless place. No, I've simply lost my ability to find the people I once recognized as capable of loving me. I cdn't see it in Lydia but my horniness and loneliness overcame me so I made it up. I did a quick job of making her my "soulmate." But on the way home the center cdn't hold and things fell apart. It all started the afternoon before when she tried to play that shame routine about me not learning her language. After listening to that judgmental bullshit for a half an hour as she engaged a young Bulgarian boy in conversation at the bar, I decided to hit her with my "I don't give a fuck about yr language" spiel. Then we went home to fuck. I'm sure the Bulgar's shapely figure was running thru her mind. The bastard spoke fluent Hungarian. I managed to keep it hard but not that long, her tits suddenly seemed very wrinkled. And she didn't want me to suck them. Well, she did but then I pissed her off because I sucked too hard. I didn't bite, thank god, she might've killed me, didn't want me to fuck her doggie- style, didn't want me to do anything but give her a straight up fuck. So far so good. But I can't keep a hard-on. For some twisted reason I've got to see her ass up in the air—then my dick goes straight up, too. If she's flat on her back even with her sexy legs spread nothin happens. Only if she lets me lick and finger her for awhile then I'm ok. But she doesn't like that.

This goes on most of the day. But then at 2 am we're wandering the streets necking in little niches along the alleys. She turned on me. She let fly a barrage of insults directed toward my manhood, wagged her finger at my nonchalance toward her culture. (I put forth the proposition earlier in the day that her country's love of its "culture" was just another guise for its " nationalism" that infuriated her.) I didn't believe in Nations, I said. There shd be no countries no nations no ethnic identities no nothin. This infuriated her more. Finally, I handed her 10 bucks for cab fare and told her to stay at her friend's house. We walk into my flat and she angrily grabs her laptop and backpack and hisses at me as she opens the elevator door to leave" Why don't you find a young girl!!! Misterrrr Porrrrno website!!! She had rifled through my computer while I was taking a shower and found smut. Go figure. So long Lydia.

53

That's 2 things that arouse me in the presence of a woman I'm going to have sex with: lots of foreplay, esp around the vagina and the anus (I love to just put my head down there and explore those vast territories with my lips and tongue – like the girl chimp wanted her boy chimp friend to do) and she should be beautiful—looking. I respect beauty of the soul but it doesn't always give me an erection. I wish a woman's beautiful soul alone cd arouse me—but it doesn't—not always. And we're past any intellectual discussions now we're in bed, not a cafe. A beautiful soul, and attraction well North of the libidinal border I was just talking about, that's rare. Only Helen and Wanda had that power and Gudrun. The border got hazy w her. I'll amend these sophomoric fetishisms as it were and say, when I think of her, some women do have some elusive but substantial sensuality that is simply innate (Hey hey mama well the way you move) regardless of how well they conform to recognized notions of beauty. Gudrun was that way. Lydia wasn't. Some women haven't a clue about how to give themselves to someone. Instinctually, they don't even want to. She wasn't honest like the chimp. (She cdn't perform fellatio, kiss, allow me cunnilingus, hug, let me do her doggie style— nothin… for more than, say, ten seconds. She jumped around to different stuff like an episcopalian at high mass. And of course my hard-on wd fade with each new, ephemeral position. Finally, she let me finger her. Not that I ever reached the level of passion I did w Gudrun—tho, by conventional tastes, Lydia was much prettier. So, then, take heart— Beauty is in fact only skin deep. Or better, a woman can bring beauty to the surface of her body as long as it takes to really make love with someone. Though sometimes after lovemaking the illusion is more difficult to maintain. Like Kora, Demeter's daughter, Beauty must disappear beneath the skin, radiating almost imperceptibly from—where else is it coming from? The Soul. Lydia's Soul was like an embryo—so small and hidden it was. I never saw it. Gudrun's—simple as it was—was large and round—the sun … or the moon by turns.

Still, I'll miss her big round ass bouncing out of the bed suddenly, running off-post orgasm to the bathroom to take a piss. A plump woman, round, tall… big. And such an energy like hers I wish I had. But sometime I must speak about how typically tactless and inconsiderate she was—almost disconnected it seemed to any sense of proper manners I might have felt before when I lived in America. She was from a different world. She was Byzantine. I felt bewildered as the boy chimp with his mate—or I felt like I knew them better than her. My ignorance exposed something almost—sinister.

54

I don't know what I'm doing. A strong spring wind rattles my windows. In the storm last night, twigs branches and even whole trees were blown down into the pathetic little yard in front of my apartment complex. It's difficult to tear my self away from my computer—I keep reading my emails expecting them to say something different—to explain everything. But that doesn't happen. So I surf a few porno sites. How can so many women be prostituting themselves this way? Yet so many scenes remind me of those afternoons, those long evenings with Gudrun. I just want to relive them somehow. One minute she's dominating me, the next I'm humiliating her. First master, then slave. Always I imagine watching her w other men. Their cocks are much bigger than mine, of course. She reaches these imaginary ecstasies I could no longer bring her to. But then when I cum it all disappears. I'm glad to be at home alone.

I let my beard grow—only because I didn't wanna take a bath w the wind so hard outside and the super being too cheap to turn on the heat. Sitting around in a pullover and drinking tea is almost enough. I decide to take a long walk.

I walk up through the park walking fast so I can get the feeling of exercise. When I reach the square it seems full of pretty girls. One of them lets a bemused smile linger and I stare at her for a moment. The urge to follow her and make conversation comes over me—but somehow the feeling of futility is stronger and wins out. I walk on. Young girls probably like the scraggy beard. Their fathers, whom they hate, stay clean-shaven the way older women like them to be. Young girls chuckle as they pass, thinking how great it wd be to bring a guy like me home—to watch their father's reaction. For years they watched the old fifty-ish fart with his potbelly and eggy smelling flatulence, walking around in a towel, then she rubbed his chubby shoulders with linament, a loving pat on the head, running her fingers through his dandruff ridden hair, smelling his breath stinking of tobacco and onions. This is why she wants me, for a brief moment. But then she plays the whole scenario out in her mind in a split second and sees how trivial it all wd be. How to get rid of the poor man. Obviously, he wd turn into a complete dog in his devotion. And surely the lovemaking wd kill him. She's right, of course, on both counts. Death during sex, still, has its appeal. Sometimes with Gudrun my heart beat so fast after I came I wondered if it might just come apart at the seams. But it gradually calmed itself. Such a warm feeling in my tummy afterwards. Yet w/in a few minutes, I wd search for the soulmate she cd never be. Soon I felt cold and alone. She was like a little girl with no one to play with. She wd get bored and irritable. She seemed 14 one moment—33 the next. Her eyes were bright and sharp like a child's. Her plump body still exuded something girlish beneath the businesswoman demeanor. She always dressed like she was going to work. She left a pair of jeans in the flat. They fit me perfectly. I have them on now. I haven't talked to her in months. I started to call her but then I masturbated instead—and the urge passed. It will come back of course. But she'll never answer my calls. Maybe it's best. I don't know what I'm doing.

55

Who knows how long I've got? Walked up thru the park tonight—just to check the car. Since I have no legal residence I can't park in front of the apartment complex—only people w special stickers can do that—I gotta park about a ten-minute walk away. But that gives me time to walk up toward my old apartment of 20 yrs ago. I can tell when the emptiness sets in. I go wandering away from the city and toward the unknown neighborhoods in the south. I was here once before a few years back. But did I go past the old place? The Armenian girl, Paloma, then, the first few nights I spent here with Helen later in that winter of the same year. Paloma graduated and moved back to Yerevan. Then it all started. The whole situation.

The park is getting dark. A storm cloud rises up black behind me. I wonder if I can make it home before the downpour. The foliage is thick for Europe. The black blood stain of the mulberry, the thick heart shapes of Linden tree leaves hanging over the sidewalk, the plane tree's leaves as wide as hands already before June. The fecund pungent semen smell of the Ailanthus trees. The sidewalk begins to speckle with rain. 20 years I've lived here. It seems like yesterday. What have I accomplished? I'm still the same man but I feel decidedly more… tired. Yes. Where's that spring in the step of a thirty yr old? To myself I still look like that man. Long-hair, ponytail, cloth bag from Kolozsvár, jeans, white t-shirt. Suddenly I glimpse myself in a plate glass window in a row of shops my face, drawn, sagging. I try to start up a conversation w a cutee BBW walking by. She looks at me like I'm crazy. Am I? Crazy? Honey, I'm sorry, if you only knew. The pangs clench my gut for a split second. Is there something wrong with my pancreas maybe? My friend is gone. So long amigo. What happens now? I realize I'm headed toward the old apartment. I haven't really been at this very spot for almost 20 years. And yet I've come here so many times in my imagination, as I approach the wooden shuttered door on the garage and look thru the plate glass window up the staircase, the four flights I walked every day, thinking, I must stop smoking. Finally the hot summer came. I hung out w weird biker bands. Suddenly, I think of Wanda in her leather jacket. God, she was beautiful. Women always make the right decision—even if it seems wrong for awhile—or even if it's never right—they can transform it into the right decision. Just something they can do.

They've done a lot of new building but it can't eclipse my original memory of the place. The 7/11, the lunch stand, they're all gone now. Yet the street hasn't changed much, a new expansive bus stand, a disco. I gotta ask that girl walking by to have coffee with me. She's so cute in her white leotard and blue jean mini skirt. I ask her if she speaks English—she looks at me in disgust. Just like Gudrun did. Too bad. Eternity and I will never kiss her. No more kisses. Brown hair blowing in the wind—lead me to Death. The 18 Tram is coming over the hill. The rain starts pouring, pouring down.

56 KRIP

Let no man despair and have one melancholy thought in this, the glorious golden liquid light of late May! The new leaves of the plane tree proclaim it, waving their hands in ecstasy, Man will find his way to eternal holiness!!!

They took his children away! He lost his home and everything dear! Together we cursed the Muse and hardened our hearts to music. We wallowed in flesh and booze and smoke and years passed into oblivion!

Yet this holy morning, this First morning, survives. O Josh remember the holy morning, your Awakening, as you strode past Ol' Marcellus' mansion and the flowers drooped with blooms, the ash trees and tulip poplars!

Who knows how long *I've* got left? I'm the only one left to tell the tale. He's gone without a trace. Only these fragments are left. Yet he, just like I, was a man who only wanted peace and happiness, and that others should have peace and happiness. He wanted love and to give love to others. Ah, this is where chaos entered—melancholy and sorrow. Love! And Woman. Come near me now o beautiful pale goddess, master of Love and desire. Guide my hand as I write this. Guide my Steps in the world through its beauty, to which I am so blind and away from its endless desires, always unfulfilled, that I endlessly pursue. Today I will chant the Beauty of this new Day.

Come to me Woman! That I might know the truth of your earthly secrets— that I might know myself from your gift of your body to me! Let me not shun like the dead Puritans of old that great need within me, the renunciation of which led them to Death. In the holiness of our bed of flesh and Love may we honor these mornings of new yellow light and life—the great Jonquil Bloom of All Things— the gentle Jonquil perfume! – may it pervade every fiber of my Soul!!! O pale-eyed goddess Athena! O Mary! O lovely Spring Day! Guide my steps in Honor of my departed friend, let me cherish the words he left me. May I tell his stories, My story, may I tell the Truth as well as any dying man can tell it so that his children can honor his life, the life of a Man. Amen.

57 JOSH

Today was another empty day. Lydia stood me up. She's weird. And not a little dangerous. She's not malicious but in her need to survive she associates with questionable types. Across the border the situation is different than in the City, it's even worse. On the bottom lie the scroungers, the farmers, up a notch, the shop keepers, then the professionals, then the politicians, the gangsters, the bosses. There is no community. Only who can use who to what end? Money and sex and work and entertainment are undifferentiated. Real couples just trying to raise families are walking on rickety scaffolding. The corruption of the foundation has become too great. No one knows when it will collapse. And so their tensions run high. There's no supportive community for them to rest within. Extreme fatigue causes headaches and fever and mistrust. Everyone's alone with their desperation. But it's desperation under the guise of boredom or tv or porn or fashion or activism. The other day I saw on tv some chick being interviewed and at the bottom of the screen it said, so and so—musician, activist. I can see she wants to wake people up. That's ok. But does she remember what they were dreaming about? Only a few can remember their dreams. But worse, she thinks they don't see the horror around them – but they do! They just don't want to fight the horror illusionists—would you? But she will whip them into an army, her army, and they will go forth to face the horror illusionists. They will be slaughtered— but not her. She will write a song about it and live away from the war zone. The title will be sold on t-shirts. And then bootlegs of t-shirts.

The children are still sane because Nature and God protects them—but it might not be enough. Creativity is approaching midnight. There's nothing left to say that symbolizes or is an allegory for something else- so there is no Art— art now is just description. Description is needed just to record the beauty, but also some underlying sinister thing that is sensed but remains unseen. When the Pols and Gangsters and Artists and Cops finally meld – then the end is coming. Midnight is approaching. There was the fragmentation of faces. Nose where eye shd be. Moustache pasted on the forehead. Ass upside down. Face on ass. Head coming out of ass. Fish coming out of ass and mouth. Bubbles of gas with fishheaded men and women inside, puckering their lips, their pussies, their assholes. Breathing, sucking, then suddenly it all goes black

Now the sun's finally out. Impossible to resist trying to chat up the women in the street. The lovely woman this morning with the big derriere. I miraculously approached her with that silly I'm lost can you help me find the 33 bus schtick. I even bungled the whole line and er-ed and ah-ed for an eternity but then just blurted out, after of course asking her if she spoke English and then stupidly starting to speak Hungarian, "do you have a boyfriend?" "Uh, yeah," she said, and her eyes seemed to say, "So don't be gettin fresh." She fumbled with the keys to her apartment bldg door and went inside shutting the door behind her with a wan smile.

58 DOC

Dear Josh,

You see? A woman cannot be approached like that. It offends her because she thinks you take her for a whore. If she IS a whore, fine and dandy. I mean, people need money there now for their kids! And we respect her for that. But if not— well, then, it's no good. Even if she is a non-pro whore, she's not gonna go for that direct stuff. No, she's gonna wanna show you to one of her girlfriends, go to a party, a movie, THEN maybe she'll jump into bed or the back of a cab.

Cheers, Doc.

59 JOSH

Impossible—the girls in the street. Impossible with my stooped shoulders and limp, now, almost as bad as Crip's. Pain in my right side. Impossible. But still the sweet sunlight.

Look at the trees laden with fruit? Is it all for you? The cherries are ripe and sweet now. They sit out in boxes in front of the Mona like little wine-red nipples. No—so much beauty fallen ripened on the sidewalk—never touched. Left to rot. Time rots everything in the end. But the thought of Gudrun, of Lydia, of Emese—it keeps me going. Keeps me walking up Railroad Street toward the park. Even without a woman there's the solace of early summer. The liquid black shade I can almost taste. The cracked side walks, the pedestrians with their dogs approaching, the girl going to her lover or coming from there, pale voluptuous in her t-shirt, talking on a cell phone. Laughter. But then one reaches the main square. Teeming with lethal cars. Look round to your left as you step off the curb—one is rounding the curve there. Let's hope he sees you. Big Ass. Death.

Shadows of trees. I know no one here. Not really. Not well. But not just here but in the Universe—do I know anyone? The vast city to myself. Yet I have no one to see. 20 bucks is nothing in this town anymore. Used to be alot. I feel nauseous before I leave the apartment.

The apartment. That's a story in itself. My little kitchen. That's the best room. When Crip comes over we always sit in there. When Harriss came to visit from Edgeton. When Gudrun comes. How wonderful it was when the small talk ceased after about an hour or so then I would kiss her hand. Kiss up her arm. Lick her arm pit with its oniony smell. Nibble softly on her neck. Then lead her by the hand to the bed in the other room. O Gudrun. Please pick up the phone. Impossible. Doesn't matter.

The bedroom is filled with books and guitars. The sun comes only in the afternoon. Mosquitoes in the evening. So I have to keep the window closed. Otherwise, I wake up from an insect dream with bites all around my eyes. Salt. Sweat. I guess I'll never see her again. She came back once. Waiting. For what? The Equation. The Paradox. I can't unravel it. Her parents are demanding she marry somebody. Poor kid. I don't know what I'm doing. I was already married once. Twice. Three times.

But the kitchen is brighter. I put the veggies in the hot oil and stir them around. Some tomato sauce. Pasta or Rice. Doesn't matter. The ecstasy is the cigarette by the window where the late afternoon light pours in waiting for the veggies to cook. Waiting. Light on the fruit in the enamel bowl. Red blue green yellow. Hard tile surface of the cupboard's tabletop. With recessed circular finger grips to slide the yellow painted pressboard slats. All my landlady's stuff. Must've belonged to her dead aunt. Death. Waiting. Impossible. Big Ass. The cigarettes over and everything's ready. Pour the sauce and veggies over the rice. I watch the news. It's grim, of course. Poor Palestine. Poor Israel. Waiting. Impossible. Big Ass. People die. Everyone's desperate. Waiting for something to give. Finally, love comes— they say. Death. Big Ass.

The park benches are splintered and broken. Old men playing chess. I'm slightly high. Afternoon light is getting me that way, a dream, an aphrodisiac. That's why I spoke to the girl with the big ass. She looked like a combination of Gudrun and Lydia. You can spend hours licking flesh, pushing into it with your cock. But then the Other Person is there. She changes the position of her ass. She gets up to pee. She gets wet with an orgasm. Her breath is sweet and cigarett-y. The perfume on her neck is perfect somehow—always. The bathroom with its tub and the towels. What a vision of light and love she is there wet with bathwater.

60

Loneliness is relentless in the morning. But then the promise of the new sunny spring day slowly dissipates it. Still, yesterday the June weather turned sweltering and today was even hotter. I felt like I should venture out into the City but then this morning I got that tight feeling in the outside corners of my eyes, like I might cry. But I'm not sure why. Maybe it's because I saw my son yesterday over at his Mom's house. He's so innocent. And his faith in the world is so large—just like mine was. I can't bear to think of the sorrows he is yet to face. Yet there was a sweetness to it all wasn't there? My youthful energy and my love for my own body—it always carried me through. Somehow I had conceived of Helen long before I met her. In my ancient daydream of her she was also brunette, a little dark-complexioned. The way she seemed to know everything about me. The way she came into my life and fixed it up like she would the inside of an apartment. I knew somehow that someday I would meet a woman like that. It was as if she called to me from far away across the ocean "where the waters overflow:"

So often days are like a splashing flowing river full of light and understanding. But then one day something hurts you so badly that Time stops. Toxins build up. You can't move. Like in a dream when a killer or a rabid dog is coming toward you and you can't run—you want to but yr legs are paralyzed. The beginning of a cigarette gives you hope but by the end yr lost and wanna light another one just to kick start Time and get it going again. Yr thoughts dwindle down to the ember working its way down to the filter and the smoke drifting away into the room. Without it yr Nothing. Maybe you can get up and pace around the room clinching and unclinching yr hands but the Flow has stopped. Right before the cartoon character plummets he rests calmly in mid-air for a split second, resting on his elbow and the cupped hand under his cheek—then—whsssshhh—he disappears. That cartoon Air—that was the Future you once lounged in. Now it's gone. Ain't no. No Future. Unless you can put it back one piece at a time like I used to watch Agnes do with those jigsaw puzzles.

61

I just came back from America. If you could just connect the 2 worlds, the beginning and the end. But. Impossible. *The angel at the Gate barring my way with the Flaming Sword again.* Like the Budapest girls in the street. They want something but it's gotta be right. It's gotta be nice. Even when they let themselves go they come back to someplace nice. They can't play the whore for long. Men are different. They can keep going going down down up up until their wings melt. Ha Ha got that from that Greek story Doc told me. You know. Big ass. It's never enough. Possess! Possess! they seem to think. Clutching the woman's throat right before they cum. Twisting an arm round her back. Dominating. Searching for new Worlds of Ass. Not big enough. It turns into war. Searching for gold. Gold is sex solidified for a man, for the Colonialist. Girls wear it as a sexual monument. War is the last stop on the road to sexual frustration. No orgasm no matter how big can save you. So, Love the one you make love to. Or else it's the trenches for you mother fucker.

As I walk past the familiar cracks in the sidewalks, the pitiful sprouts of grass coming up thru the concrete, it hits me that Man has overlayed himself over the earth, covers it with something to protect his steps. He slowly forgets where he is. Earth is hidden by the pavement. Only little sprouts of grass in the cracks. Earth won't love him the way he wants. She gives to everyone, everything, not just him. It is. Only one thing, but he divides it into what's found there and what is a gift. "Lambkin was a mason good/ as ever built with Stone. He built Lord Weary's Castle/—But payment he got none." Woman he wants for his private earth. Round Belly. Big Ass.

So, that's the problem. Looking at the cracks, wondering how age made Agnes so bitter. I can't make my inner life match up with the world I see out there. The inner life is dangling looking for…?

62 KRIP

Now that his music student was out of town, he could spend Saturday morning wandering through sunny Budapest looking at all the lovely girls. He didn't have a care in the world that day. He knew it was some sort of gift. He tried to open himself to it. Was it ok or was it harmful somehow? What was he thinking? Will God bless me or punish me? But it doesn't matter, how can i know what's right?

And with that, he started murmuring to himself, "Guide my steps, Mother Mary, guide my steps."

How lovely Helen was! Her dark brown hair and her dark skin. Her dark brown eyes. She was an October when I met her. Something coming to full ripening perfection.

63

The staircase wound up and up forever it seemed. The wide floors of smooth marble worn smoother by a billion steps in a hundred years. The black iron banister ornamented in black flower shapes (fleurs de lis, I think) And then one came to an old wooden door that opened onto a ring balcony of different apartments facing inward into the courtyard as I said before. We walked into her parent's apartment, her father had been alive for one year since I'd known her. Now he was gone, cancer. Her mother, a serene woman who I rarely ever saw show any emotion at all—lived in the back rooms, which were filled with clothes on hangers and stacks of fashion magazine clippings and sketches of dress designs she used in her fashion design business. She was one of those typical fashion women, beautiful even at 65, a woman who had found exactly what she wanted to do with her life at a fairly young age, and so found other things in the world merely idle curiosities or things to pass the time with while she waited for the next fashion show or, her quiet obsession, a trip to Paris—a place that had an almost talismanic significance for her. Her youthful dream had been to become a Parisian designer. It never came true. But there was no trace of the bitterness of unrealized dreams in her. She had an earthiness to counteract all that. She loved to cook. And every Sunday found her in the kitchen hovering over a pot of meat soup or roast of pork, or cutting up chicken pieces and simmering the onions, and stirring the batter, which would become the homemade noodles (Gnocchi or, as the Hungarians call it, "galuska") for a succulent paprikas.

She was always in the background. Silently anchoring things. Helen, though, was always in front. It was Helen who ran the house. And it was a lovely house. A townhouse I guess you'd say. A penthouse – in that it had at least five rooms—a huge front living room, an office or study/library that Helen and I converted into our bedroom, another huge room adjacent to that where Monika slept and as I said stored all her clothes. Now, with much of her designing years behind her, her career had humbled itself a bit and she spent much of her time simply organizing fashion shows, which required storing and moving large quantities of clothing. She liked me. She was often catching me in a hallway holding, up a shirt or pair of pants up in front of me to check the fit and then giving it to me. She loved being around clothes. She handled dresses and shirts and jackets like she would a loved child.

Each room was entered through a great doorway, the paint on the doors having turned a bit yellow—but this only accentuated their beauty and austerity. One turned a substantial tarnished brass doorhandle to enter, though often all the doors were left open except of course Monika's back bedroom that was usually closed.

The room was, as the others for the most part were as well, graced with 2 huge elongated windows that nearly reached to the top of the 12-foot ceiling all the way down until about two feet before reaching the floor. They were formidable things that opened out like a door—not sliding up or down like the much smaller American windows did, and with the same substantial brass handles with which the doors did. A steel rod ran up and down the length of the window and when you turned the handle the tongue of the rod moved up into a slot at the top of the window casing fastening it shut. There were even 2 sets of these door-like windows overlaying each other! Both sets of doors were usually only shut in the winter. The strong winds of Budapest, strong as these windows were, still rattled them and whistled through their ancient cracks. The wind made a whirring sound that sounded like the unintelligible conversation of ghostly spirits long dead. The dog, Mina, would often cowl under the bed on windy nights like these. Opening the first inner window door gave you access to a broad window sill in front of the second window. If the second window remained closed, the sill provided a great place to put house plants or flowers on, since the window before them would be closed and would keep out at least some of the cold winter air or yet allow the plant to get plenty of light—even if it was the gray-blue European winter light. In summer the plants were taken out to the porch which faced out onto the courtyard. Usually, there were geraniums or tall irises. Different types of climbing iveys were allowed to climb across desks inside or even on the tops of tall bookcases the entire length of a room. A special long-necked watering can was then used to water them.

The entire front room wall, after one had passed through a small vestibule, where coats and hats hung from hooks and shelves and shoes were sprinkled about, was lined with bookshelves filled to overflowing—nearly all Hungarian writers and in Hungarian, except for a few English textbooks and novels Helen still had from her school days and whenever I stood in front of them and stared at all the books in a strange language I only partly understood in those days, I was still transported back in time to America, to Medina, and my old life there.

I sometimes found myself alone in their house—or else the children were asleep in the back rooms and I wandered around gazing at it all in that entranced way people have who are wandering around in museums. In fact it was a great fossil of the Hapsburg Empire long passed, just as its Communist era had also disappeared now, yet here it was, polished again and still shining in a New Day—a new day full of Brits and Frenchmen and Germans and Americans like me playing schoolboyishly in the old Ruins.

64

I'm in the Tilos Az A club ("This 'A' is Forbidden"). I catch a glimpse of that woman I always loved from afar. She was a blond sort of punker-looking girl back in the day—though continental punk always seemed something milder than the Brit version—typical euro teen: black leather jacket, maroon tight jeans, thin hips, peroxide hair.

Now she's a mom of a beautiful little son and a pretty older daughter. But is that her husband? Distinguished gray full head of hair, thick gray beard, perhaps the classic Magyar folk intellectual. She's middle-aged, but even lovelier now than in those lost days in the deep well of memory, the years just after the fall of the communist regime. Yep, even lovelier. Her low cut black top w/ a tasteful knit sweater of light green, lavender, black and olive colored stripes, the hair, still short, even buzzed over the ears, still blond-colored w the dark roots showing underneath, deep part along the side, but set high up on her scalp, like a windrow of new mown hay. And now some other members of the party start to come in, seating themselves around their table while the children go off to play at the nearby playground. A woman in a magenta long sleeve shirt—pretty but lacking my beloved's beauty in some intangible way. (What is it about the look of a woman you love immediately and yet the look of another, for some reason, has no arrows in it? What force, what event, even in childhood, gives the former her power?) Wait! Now I've caught sight of the gold band on my beloved's lovely white ring finger. If not the "Gray Eminence," well, somewhere in this city a husband thinks of her and she thinks of him. They will put their children to bed and then make love and hold each other through one of those vaguely menacing Budapest nights.

Luckily I've brought along E.H.'s "A Moveable Feast" to keep myself from staring at her. I knew it wd come in handy. I knew when I'd found it a few days before it had been placed there by Angels of Mercy—there in that little dusty bookshop on Kiraly Street full of dusty old Magyar books. "The English section?" I ask. I already knew where it was but I wanted to hear myself say something in Hungarian, like the way you might utter something in a dream just to know yr dreaming. The gray-haired proprietor points to the back wall. I pretend I'm just discovering the place he points to—perhaps he's pretending that I don't know either—there's a vague look of recognition in his eyes. I spoke to him just to break the spell of the relentless loneliness. The shop is a quiet chamber, like a chapel. The priest welcomes me in. Hemingway's book appears on the shelf. I remember Berenice trying to get me to read it years ago. But I never did. I feel good cause I just bought a new bag of pot from The Guy. So I make my way over to a friend's neighborhood on the Buda side. But he's not home so I wander up to the Cafe Lanchid (Chain Bridge) order a cheap Dreher, since I've only got enough bread for that and a pack of awful Pall Mall filters, and read the first few chapters. *Hemingway walks past in his brown suit from the 20's— contemplative, looking out past the 2 massive marble lions where the bridge begins.* The houses along Fö St. seem Parisian in the unseasonable September chill that makes you wanna zip up yr pullover. The cafe is full of men and girls with visions of men and girls making love in their heads in an alcohol dream. And cigarette smoke drifts through the old rich wooden rooms. And women laugh as they make love half drunk in my daydream. Summer's ending.

Weeks later and now the five o'clock sun starts to fade and the chill creeps up from the ground in the little cafe while I finish off Hem's bittersweet little book, making furtive glances at the woman I always loved but never spoke to back in those lost days. Her perfect head seems imprinted on an ancient coin, so sharp are the perfect lines. Suddenly, graybeard takes his leave—now's the chance to say something! But I'm too chicken and she's so engrossed in an animated conversation w her other friends: the lady in the purple top, a young boyish guy in glasses w brown curly hair and a scraggly young beard. Why do I do this to myself? I'm nothing to her!

But only her face can cure me from memories of Helen. She seems like Helen. The same kind of toughness, protectiveness. They would have to go through her to get to me. To destroy me. But it was mine not Helen's fault. She was a good girl with a beautiful face and her dreams of living with an artist like Josh weren't what she thought they were and then she wound up w me. Still, I take furtive glances at this woman I had secretly loved as she chatted with friends, sipped wine and then even tucked into what looked like a yummy caesar salad w grilled chicken pieces. I knew from the fullness of her now more matronly mother's body that she must have had, always, even when she had yrs ago affected a punker's thinness, a healthy appetite. You could tell it in the fullness of her calves and her feet, the wrinkled brown insteps of which were just visible in her low cut black ballerina-type shoes, as a glanced at them under the adjoining table. The "V" dip of her black t-shirt showed the fullness of her chest above her ample, motherly breasts. A gold pendant lay between them, like a golden bucket someone might lower slowly and carefully into a deep well.

Finally, they all leave together—the other girl, the 20-ish boy, and her. I saw the boy minutes later walking in the other direction and resisted the temptation to approach him and ask about her, who she was, her name. He wd've thought I was some nut, probably. Still, if I'd had one more glass of wine in me I might have done it. Walking home slightly dejected, at least the glass of Kék Frankos wine felt warm in my stomach. I thought of how nice it would be to lay my head on her chest and listen to her soft heartbeat. The story I heard was that her breasts had swelled with milk but then contracted again after an abortion, which left them drawn and wrinkled slightly and pulled down by the weight. In my imagination, I saw them as a great Roman ruin (even one that her Magyar ancestors might have once marveled at, before trying to destroy them!) gorgeous beyond words, brown as sand in sunlight and one wondered what they must have looked like when they were new and untouched. What might the fragments of roman walls we see today have looked like when they were first built?!

65

I went to Josh's old neighborhood today. He and Gudrun had lived in a "Domino house" one of the commie-era apt complexes. Concrete blocks starting up 8 stories or more like weeds popping thru sidewalk crevices. Endless graffiti everywhere. Anyway, hope Gudrun's happy now. She gave me some stuff that belonged to Josh, the old Audio Technica mic, we recorded alot of his stuff on that one. Some cables. She said she hadn't had the heart to go in the little music room at the old place but when she sold it, she had to. So I looked around. I thought about hitting on her, we had fucked once, during one of their many break-ups. She pretty much came onto me that time. I have no willpower when that happens. But right away I could tell she wasn't interested now. I hear her boyfriend is a pretty big dude. But I could also sense she wanted me to make a pass so she could reject me. She kept sticking her ass out whenever she bent over to pick up a box of Josh's old stuff. But as I looked around I could tell my tears were welling up and the corners of my eyes started stinging but I made it thru w/out crying, til I got outside, realizing I would never set foot in that place again probably ever—probably never see Gudrun again. I walked around the neighborhood. It was mid-October. The rain was still a little warm. Comfortable in my dark leather jacket and zip-up pullover. The leaves wet but still hanging on the limbs, the gold-orange deluge was yet to come in another week or two maybe, when the gold skins of leaves are sodden and spongy underfoot.

I looked at my reflection in the 47 tram car window as I sped away. October was in its full fading bloom. I remembered Josh's face—pale and sickly at the end—then the radiation would bring him back for months, even a few years, he would look normal. We grew apart. There was nothing to do with him. I couldn't get him any gigs. He was too sick to play. He spent time with the Arab guys and Samidha. I remembered the countless nights we had driven down the crumbling lanes and parking lots around this place. Where he had landed after Helen. I spoke out to him as I walked down the empty leaf-strewn lane. Are you there, man? I seemed to feel him come down to me, though I knew I was mostly faking it. He did feel closer. I felt that if I would meditate on it very diligently for awhile maybe he would appear to me. But I knew I would never try. Maybe I didn't want to know where he was. Or if he was nowhere. Both were too frightening for me, the mortal left behind. It seemed impossible to push either way. Then suddenly he seemed very very far away. That was what I feared, the eons it would take me to find him again. Yet Time is nothing. An illusion. And the pix of his son, the child Gudrun bore him, looked just like him. Far/ near. Maybe it had no longer mattered to him. After all, he was already dying! Maybe he just wanted to do something to make people see the insanity!

66 THE HOUSE IN BALATON

It was a beautiful place. You followed a long straight road from off the highway. He would remember the sun was always shining. They passed the endless string, one road deep, of quaint little sand-colored stucco houses. Some were old peasant houses whitewashed in smooth plaster putty. It was this kind of old house they had come to see—Helen had seen the ad in the Budapest paper. I drove them done from BP. They all got out of the car and looked around. A beautiful blond woman came out to greet them. Her husband, she said, had gotten a job working for the police in far away Budapest and so she had agreed to leave the place—her childhood home—to go and live in the city. It was very hard for her to leave, she said—and it crossed my mind as he looked at her that he could see the traces of long dried tears on her lovely face where she had often wept over the whole issue until she had finally resigned herself. Now she seemed cheerful in that fragile way people have who have made a great difficult decision that's now behind them. It wasn't a hard decision for her to decide on buying the place. In only an hour of looking around here and there and just taking in the whole beauty of the place, they were sold on it. She would telephone Josh later.

He had wanted to get away. To write. To write songs, to write about everything that had happened everything that made a man's life significant in some way. He wanted to be alone at first but eventually, he didn't mind, in fact, he almost welcomed it, when Helen became the ramrod of the whole "country house" project. After all she knew how to deal with all the Hungarian workmen, the carpenters, the painters, the plumbers. They would need a new heater in the house, not the tiny gas stove the previous tenants had used. And they would need to extend the gas line and hook it up. They couldn't use the bottled gas the poorer people in the village used—it seemed too dangerous, especially with the little boys, Ryly and Gordon, around. They would need to paint the place. Fix up the sagging porch. Put insulation in the floor. Take up the old rotted planks and put in new ones. (Josh had fought briefly for keeping the old ones, they were so beautiful but eventually caved in when Helen insisted they tear them out and the flooring man showed him how rotten the bottoms of the floorboards had become.) Still, it seemed a shame but there was no other choice.

But that was all a long time ago. You live long enough you see whole stories play themselves out. A whole era ends. You remember the beginning. "In my beginning is my end". Josh coming to Hungary, all the partying we did when he first got here. You shudda seen early nineties Budapest. We lived liked kings, eating in the finest restaurants, riding in taxis, playing in bars for peanuts but it was enough to survive. Aunt Pearl would send me 2 hundred bucks from Medina and I could get by on it for months! The Hungarians thought we were nuts. We got gigs abroad, Austria was full of rich music fans. Then I remember when he met Helen. Everything changed. It seemed like Josh had it made but somehow he was just withdrawing, disappearing. But I didn't know that then. We kept plodding along. He loved his sons so much he wept sometimes worrying about them. He missed the states. He needed his mom to help him understand fatherhood. Helen was a great mom, just not good at sharing her parenthood. She withdrew too. It went downhill as the boys grew up.

That's when Helen came onto me the first time. Josh had become so lethargic on gigs. Always so high. Forgetting lyrics. Saying smart-alecky things to the crowd. When they heckled him he would say, "We already got your money!" (we'd already gotten the door money) "So, FUCK YOU!!!" It got to be a mess. You never knew when he'd go off.

In Balaton Josh and I used to sit in the little green yard and I would strum and pick out country tunes and some jazz standards he'd learned from his mother Agnes and of course, Sylvester Moore. It gave him pleasure and took the edge off the grueling weekends playing in the Budapest Club scene.

Years later, in his tiny apartment in Budapest, Josh sickly and getting old, we remembered the Balaton sunshine.

Josh was great with his children. One day he found a few good-sized rocks and other things around the yard and laid them out in a diamond shape to use as bases for a little baseball field in the back yard. He'd found a Wiffle ball set with 2 gloves at the Siofok Tesco and so he taught the boys how to play baseball. Josh had said he only wished ol' Judge Becknall could see it, the old man loved the game. Both the boys had strong arms and good hitting eyes. Once Josh lobbed a pitch to little Gordon and the kid smacked it right back so hard it hit him square in the nuts and doubled him over in pain. The little boy had said, Papa, are you alright? And Josh, bent over looking down at his knees, threw up his glove hand and waved and called out, No problem son, just a minute, I'll be fine. And then let out a Josh-like Indian whoop, Whoooo-boy!

The other kids in the little village began to wonder what the two American kids were doing back there. One day Josh invited several of them in and showed them the fundamentals. The girls learned the quickest.

When it came time for Ryley's sixth b-day they decided to have a big game and invite all the kids in the village. It went ok until one of the girls kept swinging and missing. She just cdn't hit. She got frustrated and started saying that Josh was cheating. Even after he tried to show her how to choke up on the bat and to swing nice and straight and even and slow, still she got mad and stormed off. Many of the other children followed her. And so the game, and the whole day, kind of fizzled. As they were leaving, Josh decided to try and get them to come back so he yelled a heads up to the girl and tossed her a friendly well-intentioned lob. But it seems she hadn't heard his "heads up" so it wound up bonking her right on the head. That just further infuriated her. Josh stood dumbfounded by his bad luck, with his hand over his mouth like a child who'd just done something naughty. After that, he and the boys decided to keep the whole baseball scene inside their own gates. But whenever the girl or her parents passed by they ignored Krip's friendly "hello" and simply glared at him or looked straight ahead pretending not to hear him or even notice him at all. It was Josh's first experience with the implacable stubbornness of the Hungarian villager. When they had first moved into the now renovated little house, Josh's head was filled with community service ideas. He wanted to set up a studio and teach music, for free, set up a little stage and have a music festival. Teach them all about bluegrass music and jazz. But the baseball incident never really healed over. Though Helen and the boys were adored by the villagers—Helen, the country life bringing out her beauty to its fullest flower, was treated like a kind of queen. But they never could warm up to Josh much. Gradually, he began to withdraw with his guitar into the studio he'd fixed up in the storage room and in a strange reversal of intention—since he'd originally hoped the Balaton house would give him a meditative retrea—often jumped at the chance to get back to Budapest and plunge into the very nightlife he'd wanted to get away from.

67

It's so easy to think about it all now. Not sure how much time I got left. Doc said my liver is not in the best shape. My old friend Harris is coming to visit me for a while. He's retired and wants to see a little bit of Europe. So it's all a swirling miasma partly truth, partly fiction. It was as if I was a character in my own novel. First I'm this guy, then I'm that guy. I end up I'm everyone: well, the part that's in my head, anyway. I'm everyone but myself! God, the compassion I feel for my fellow creatures! But it's too late to do anything. There was nothing to be done. See, I had this world I made up in my head and it was all one thing. And I figured one day I would do something for everyone but everyone was just inside. I couldn't do anything for anyone outside. I just had to face myself and live. Let everyone on the outside take care of themselves, except for Ryly and Gordon, I mean, I wanted to provide for them when Josh was too sick—but I mean everyone else. I mean a man has to realize he ain't Jesus Christ for chrissake! That's what scares him. Not being Jesus. Then, what is he for Chrissake? That's what he don't get. It's not the loneliness and chasin women that scares him, it's the knowin that chasin women can't save him. I'm gonna have to drag my ass out there to the street, out to the market every day, and be just an old self among all the rest and try to come away with enough to get something to eat. I never said my will was strong! Especially with women!

68

I should go back to America and see Aunt Pearl. She's alone in Schwartz's old apartment, the one where she read little Josh's palm when Bertha would bring them there. She wd look quickly and say, Ah, it looks good. But I can't leave little Ryly and little Gordon now that Josh is gone. But she needs somebody to stay there with her—not just visit for a few weeks. The situation with Helen now seems tense. What does she want me to do? Leave? But where can I go? She says the boys are old enough now, they don't need me. But they love me. I know they do. Not as much as their Dad. And what can I do now in America? I don't know anyone there anymore, except Harriss, I guess.

But what a dark dreary place this can be. A gray stone sculpture from the street to the sky. None of childhood's friendly faces. So many are gone! Thank god Harriss is coming for a visit. I feel this isolation like I'm in this tiny room and it's shrinking. The morning light is so faint through the curtains. And outside, the poor, rummaging through herbie curbies, gray tattered clothes and matted hair.

The ancient Beggar's face! Rheumy eyes reflect a broken heart as he's shuffling along in that Charlie Chaplin shuffle. In the streets of an old black and white film, trucks go by carrying the City endlessly in endless flux, a banging sound as the tire hits a pothole, an old woman crosses the street, hurrying frail children by the hand. The train goes roaring by carrying glass and steel and plaster for a cheap apt. complex going up again and again somewhere but there's never enough places for everyone and finally, someone falls out of the nest and lands in the street in front of me and goes to pick through the trash and the man coming down the sidewalk has alot of things on his mind in a new black jacket and gray pants and he knows he must wrap up that deal today or it won't work out. Nothing is working out. Death. Big Ass. It's all coming together and then breaking apart like the tide going in and then rumbling out over the rocks somewhere far away. He'd kill me if he had to.

69

So when we split I realized I had built up this deluded world around me. Budapest was a true dream world in that few of the rules that applied to Edgeton applied here at all. One thing was American cash, it went forever in '91. As if money no longer mattered and it didn't. We rode around in taxis, went to the best restaurants. Just like we used to joke before that we were colonialists, masquerading as "artists." It was one big party, Americans, Brits, Germans, Austrians, French, Italians, Romanians, Slovaks and Serbs, w/Gypsy music in the background and bullet holes in all the buildings. They must've had a hell of a battle over this place. No wonder all the sexy girls (of all ages!) are not so easy. People are still shell-shocked here a little, just like my Aunt Pearl who grew up here during the war. All those gals must've heard all the horrible stories. There was an atmosphere of mistrust. The constant broken English. "I goat special permizson to go America vonce in 87! My son and I alveighs dream of to travel on zee root 66!" Everything here was broken, the phone system, the streets, the hearts, the buildings, it wasn't as easy to "get over" here as it looked. One day I woke up, foolin' around with my best friend's ex-wife, playing on the floor with his 2 kids and the party was over.

But I didn't know it yet. I was thinking all about Aunt Pearl back home and how proud she was, though a little skittish of me being in the Motherland, of me being able to go and visit her relatives and learn Hungarian (I was practically fluent now) even helping arrange another edition of old Schwartz' book of poems. It was all great fun. You could invent yourself into whatever you wanted to be. You wanna be a writer, a singer, a poet, a traveler, a newspaper reporter, a jazz musician, a photographer, fine. You can be any or all. Because you see there is no meaning here there is nothing at stake. One culture has just expired and the other one isn't in place yet. The money buys anything and nothing, food is just sitting around. There's plenty of potatoes. One morning I woke up and heard a guy chanting KROOOOOOOOMMMPPPLEEEEEEEE ("Krumpli"—that's the Hungarian for potatoes.) He was selling big bags of it around Kelenföld the neighborhood I was livin in for awhile, me and Josh sharing an apartment. Couldn't believe it, a guy actually hawking and barking his wares with only the power of his own throat out across the little narrow streets.

But that was a last cry, you never saw those guys anymore after 94 or so. Same with the Gypsy vendors in the underground. The women waving socks and sweet peppers and fake leather coats and Russian Marlboros and gloves and tomatoes and strawberries and water pipes and steak knives in yr face. (Tessék! Tessék! What wd you like? What the fuck do you like?) One of their tribe stationed like a sentinel at one of the entrances looking out for cops. But it was no use. The old little black market of Eastern Europe had to be shut down to make way for the BIG Eastern Europe black market that the government was busy assembling. I say good riddance anyway. All those poor gypsies waving that shit around. Desperate for a buck now that the actually quite efficient Communist welfare system was collapsing around them. Those that made it: congratulations. Did you make it to your cousin's in Toronto? Your Uncle Miklos from NY is coming back to start a drycleaning business in BP with all his own capital and you get one of the branches in Budaörs, good for you. As for the other members of yr family who didn't make it, Uncle Balint Bácsi got executed with a buncha counterfeiters (he didn't even KNOW them!) in Bucharest, I heard, and aunt Lilla died in a riot in Skopje. Too bad.

But if they had lived, if Democracy hadn't won, where would they be? Waving those socks in my face in the subway. Everything moves forward.

I didn't make it either. I didn't know I'd been dreaming it all. Josh said, I want you to have her now. Wow. I'd never had such a beautiful girl before. And she paid all the bills! Finally, I could rest that fucked up leg I'd been hobblin on. The place in Balaton. Unbelievable. And all my friends around, my Budapest music buddies, the folks at the embassy, Helen's family.

70 FROM "THE AMERICAN GUY"

by Doc Celeste

The yellow sunlight pours through the window into a small room with a stereo system, a desk with some papers on it, some poems crudely typed on an old typewriter, a guitar, an electric bass, a narrow, Shaker-style bed.

This is Josh's room. His "music room." He needs a room where he can close the door and be alone and work at his art, a room separated from Berenice's, his girlfriend of seven years. Berenice has redecorated the house Josh bought 3 years ago. She brought her paintings and sculptures to the house and put them on the walls. Josh didn't mind. He found them quite beautiful in fact. One painting was a huge swirl of yellow and orange and red that gave the impression of a naked woman curled up in a ball, her thighs tear-drop shaped, sweeping down from an s-shaped head like a Matisse cut out. Her sculptures were masks that had Aztec-like faces, frog-like eyes and small perfect o's for mouths.

Berenice was very beautiful, very cute and demur. Her hair was the color of the watery reddish goldfish in a bowl with sunlight streaming through it.

In the small room with closed doors, Josh practiced his guitar, read books and wrote songs and poems. He especially liked practicing Bach pieces and the melodies of Charlie Parker tunes. That was classical history. Then he would start listening to Jimi Hendrix and country players like Merle Travis and Doc Watson and try to copy their licks off records. He would sit for hours dropping the needle over and over at one spot, trying to copy all the notes just right, always thinking he must have missed something, humming melodies back to himself and sometimes feeling frustrated. At night he would take what he learned and try it out at the bars he would play with his band. His playing got stronger. He got a rep as a kind of local George Benson. He wondered if he would ever have the technique to be a great jass soloist or a classical concert performer. He doubted it. But night after night in the clubs he ground out his funky R&B bursts from his guitar. He had a small voice like Paul Simon but he still tried to imitate Stevie Wonder and Marvin Gaye and James Brown because that's what people in the clubs wanted. Nobody wanted that soft sensitive shit, he thought, not now, in the city, not the soft songs he sang for Agnes on the back porch when he was a boy. Like Carlo said, "We're playin for their crotches."

But the rhythm! That sacred rhythm that rock and roll and bluegrass had brought to him as a child gradually morphed into jazz, swing, bebop, Latin samba and flamenco. His guitar became a kind of receiver picking up sounds and images all around the world. In the little college town of Medina, he met drummers and dreamers, actors, dancers, African percussionists in the music dept. He came to realize, in the clarity and purity and wholesomeness of the life around him, that the religion of his youth, the religion Father Hozni had given him, the God his grandmothers, Bertha and Millicent had given him—was in no conflict with this sacred rhythm. The lilt of the Episcopal hymnal, the carols and chants, the lilt of Bach, was of the same substance as the piano of Chick Corea and the congas of Airto.

And so, he felt a kind of holy calling. That was the kind of musician he wanted to become. And so, the road began. He had come upon a sacred fountain. Yet now he must follow the river that sprang from it.

71

Dear Josh,

Wanda is afraid of intimacy. After a while she can't get turned on by a guy she lives with, has had sex with for a long time, had kids with, etc. It's just not in her nature. But she can still live with the guy under the same roof. They might never touch and she only speaks to him when she needs him to do something for her. Take care,   Doc

72 JOSH

I woke up this morning and as I laid there and stared out the window or up at the high 19th century Hapsburg ceiling I had this thought: psychological problems are ultimately spiritual problems. The idea of a holy spirit seemed clearer. We are part of it? Psyche problems are like insects: they're everywhere and in astonishing numbers. The mind is a seething hive. But the Spirit, which seems to be the part of us that, in the deep sorrow that surrounds me, partakes of what really is, soars like an eagle (St. John?) and yet is paradoxically the foundation under us. Is this the meaning, the manifestation, of the life of Christ? The mind is a house of Mirrors. The soul is a dark room blazing with light. But we can't get there yet, but it's where we're headed because that's where everything is coming from. Of course, it seems like bullshit. That's why we never feel right about anything because we don't feel right about that one thing. Every day we hide another piece of the puzzle (of ourselves?) and yet wonder why we can't solve it, knowing that when the pieces are all hidden and lost to our memory, it's finished—we've exiled ourselves.

73 WANDA

'Sup "Krip!" He could make 3 things: love to women, music on a geetar, and kids. But money—uh uh… never could make that.

74 JOSH

Then there were the records: the 45s of childhood, the LPs of young manhood. The little black 45 player was in my sister's room. When you stood facing the house on Edgeton Rd., in the center was a bright red door with a brass knocker. But this door was rarely used. We almost always used the door around the right side in the back. This door fascinated me. It was a "Dutch" door that could be unlatched and so it was divided into a top and bottom half. I suppose Marshall and Agnes wanted this kind of door so fresh air could come in in the stifling summers but the bottom could be kept closed to keep us kids from wandering out or animals from wandering in. But there was also an aluminum screen door in front of the Dutch one, a pane of glass slipped into it in winter. We were always playing with the latches on the Dutch door and so sometimes our parents simply kept it fastened in one piece. But my fascination with that, what you had to call a cheap aluminum "storm" door, had to do with the sound, the endless "thwack" over and over, day in and day out. In my reveries, tiptoeing through the light of memory, the toys on the floor, the faint sound of the television, the blue sky, wide out the back, over the rolling green hills, I listen to that sound. For a moment it swings silently and then if I make a little effort the sound comes back, faint but somehow clear. A creaking hinge, a child's musical voice, the skid of sneakers on the porch and then that thwack of the door. Walk in through the screen door of memory, through the back hall, through the kitchen and the rich walnut-paneled family room with its massive stone fireplace, down another small hallway, was Angelika's room. Though its window faced southwest and formed part of the front left wall of the house, it was flooded with noonday sun, a watery, light yellow, and then the rich hues of western sunset. It was here, because my sister inherited ownership of the little black 45 player, I remember listening to Skeeter Davis' "End of the World." A touching little melody. How did I listen to music as a child? The lyrics were so heartbreaking, but at 9 how was I to know that the words, in the coming days of puberty and kissing, telephones, passing notes in class, would be the landscape of my heart. There was another 45 called the little matador. A little boy fights "El Diablo" the bull. Mariachi trumpet flourishes. Does he kill the bull? I can't remember. Surely not. Marty Robbins' "Big Iron" ("21 would be the stranger with the big iron on his hip… big iron on his hiiiiip"). Jimmy Dean's "Big John." ("Well they never reopened that worthless pit, they just placed a marble stone in front of it. At the bottom of this mine lies a big, big, man, Big John"). There had to be a few Temptations records: "Ain't to Proud to Beg," "Beauty's Only Skin Deep." Johnny Otis'(?) "Boogaloo Down Broadway." Mary our babysitter would do the camel walk when she came in to see what I was doing. Her hand claps and finger pops locked me into the beat. The rhythm. Wanda's older sister, Yolanda, lived across the road. She was a little older and she taught me how to do the pony and the Shinga-ling. The rhythm was the energy that stayed with me when I started playing gigs. Sylves and Carlo always said, "If you can lay down the right groove, you can play anything over it."

75

These are the strangest days. I walked through the little hilly streets of the village near Lake Balaton this afternoon. My pain is immense. Then it subsides a little. I smoke. I walk. I try to appreciate the wonders of April: the frail cherry blossoms, the budding green linden trees. Balmy breeze. A storm is coming across the lake.

Dear Helen,

It was childish of me, coming to Budapest with Crip those many years ago. But then after so long playing in the cafes for tips and drinks, you came into my life, when I saw you working at Dragan's office. Remember our lovely building with the amazing Beardsley-like entryway! The spacious apartment the communist government had given your parents in the fifties. I guess I got too comfortable, eh? I did want to do things the way you wanted them done. I tried. I did. Now everything's all spoiled and ruined. How did I end up some sort of burdensome man? I feel like an unwanted guest now. The only guys that turn you on now are charismatic tough guys? You want energy you say? We can't recapture the old magic? Come back inside my arms someday. Please.

76

Strange dream I had the other night staying at Krip's in BP. I dreamed I was asleep and a door buzzer sounded somewhere outside Krip's bedroom. At first, I think, Someone's trying to get us to wake up and answer the door. Then I realize that someone's trying to rob us! Then I feel myself being wrapped in wires and sheets, like a spider wrapping its prey in spun webbing. Then I start up awake from the bed and look out on the sunny morning lawn, realizing it had all been a dream. There had been no buzzer, no burglars, only dawn in a different flat. Then I felt the strangest thing: I felt as if some winged creature—a kind of bird or bat or just a spirit?—had flown out of me, like some demon good or bad. Was

he one of the burglars? or someone trying to protect me from them? Or just a
visiting spirit? The buzzer sound had been so intense, but then when I looked
out on the little backyard filled with green grass and warm, yellow morning light,
everything vanished. I felt refreshed as if my soul had been returned or restored
somehow.

77 KRIP

So Josh and I are sitting in the Boston University dorm room jamming, listening
to my weird folkie record collection. I can still remember him sitting there on
the floor in a half-lotus so attentive while I tell him stories about my visits to the
Romanian/Hungarian border, staying with my dead mom's relatives (she died
at Buchenwald). Aunt Pearl is either back with our New Jersey relatives or still
staying at Uncle Schwartz's old place near Edgeton, KY. I don't remember totally,
but she arranged all these trips. This time I'm 15, starting to smoke a Hungarian
cigarette called Sopianiaes (aka "brown tigers") drinking Palinka, a homemade
brandy, and telling my relatives I can take care of myself. I'm wandering around
in the woods and this tank comes up! It's full of border police and they start
questioning me. They see my American passport. Take me down to the station
in Satu Mare. But I was too quick for them. My uncle told me to always carry
a pack of American cigarettes, a bottle of Jack Daniels and light bulbs. They
left me in the cell for more than an hour. When the guy came I gave him my
Marlboros and he let me out. They said I couldn't use the phone so a whipped
out the Jack Daniels and I called Pearl's sister, Eniko. Uncle Zoltan bacsi comes
up in the East German Trabant car and starts talking to them. Am I a spy? they
ask. Uncle Zoltan laughs and tells me to give them the light bulbs. Then one of
them asks me to give a message to his cousin in Queens. I say Sure thing and
they let us go. They were all ethnic Hungarians. But you gotta kind of keep quiet
about it. The Romanians don't like it. I got a huge hug from my grandmother
when we finally arrived at her doorstep. No more wandering around at the
border. This is the kind of stuff I told him in the B.U. dorm. See? Josh figured
that since he was a famous Senator's grandson and all that he would go to
Harvard. He thought that was part of the deal. People were supposed to help him
with that. But that didn't happen so he thought about enrolling at Berklee when
he heard I was at BU. It was the old "Boston fantasy." His grandma Bertha was
gonna pay for it. He wasn't an academic. I was studying ethnomusicology but he
dug that, too. He stayed in my dorm room sometimes. There was dope smoke
hanging in the air like clouds banked against a Smoky Mountain holler! Indian
cloth over the lamp. And Magyar music on the record player. Stuff I brought
back from visits: the band, Muzsikas, playing; the old fiddles, pipes, cimbalom,

humming of koboses. And with Josh's guitar playing it was like a land bridge between E. Europe and Appalachian Kentucky. (Schwartz must have had it all written down somewhere in Yiddish). Fiddle tunes spanning time and place. Someday I'll make a list of the ones we played. I taught Josh some fiddle. So, that explains how, when the years went by and I moved to BP, when Josh felt the sting of that woman thing, he called me. I said come on over to Budapest dumbass!

78 JOSH

DREAM

I'm suddenly in Edgeton in spring, balmy with redbuds heavy with bloom. I look out across the town. I feel really good. I am home. I go looking for Helen. She's in a room full of my relatives. Their eyes are on us as I try to be at her service, but something's disturbing. I'm laying down. Asleep? Helen cries softly. Yet the feeling of home prevails.

Maybe if I wrote some of this down. I wake with a strong feeling of emptiness. What happens is you get used to living with someone a certain way and you think of yourself a certain way. And then, boom, something changes. Somebody leaves you and everything you had created about your life just disappears and you are falling, falling. The structure, the guardrails are gone—nothing to hang onto. All the stuff you invented about yourself which you pretended everyone else knew about you, too—it all vanishes. Tears seem always about to come. I keep wondering if I did all that I could to save the marriage. Guilt over my mistakes plagues me. My loneliness seems almost as if I were dead. Depression is like a palpable weight on my shoulders. But then I realize how difficult she could be. Her annoying ways and her desire to control me. She hurt things, too. Maybe even more than me. Some of the things I did were prompted by her behavior. You tried to accommodate her, man, follow her rules. There was just no pleasing that woman. There was nothing you could have done to satisfy her. You don't realize, man, when they're done with you, you can hang around awhile—they don't care—but they are never going to change their mind. There's an air of contempt in anything you suggest. It's over. Amazing you stayed as long as you did. Then, when I think like this, I feel better. What is it with a man? He loses his angel and then runs after devils.

Things I still have, 2 kids, Crip's friendship, guitars and songs, wine, weed, cafes.

I'm still alive. But, god, the horror I feel when I think about my current situation, my perception of reality. Relationships let you pretend you're somebody else, somebody more successful, famous, loved by all. All the years that went by after I left Edgeton and the pain of losing Wanda and Kiki. I conquered it. And, now, it's back again. One is never immune to the pain of relationships. Whatever you invest—you can lose at any time. I have to keep pep talking myself. If only I could fuck someone—the lady at the fruit stand. Somebody to take away the pain of rejection and having to start again and wade through the loneliness. Remember the afternoon even a year before we broke up how in Spring 2000 when the veil of fantasy was lifted just like before when I saw the whole Wanda/Edgeton thing for what it was—and now, it was all back. Only now I'm in Budapest. So far away from childhood crutches. Crip says I don't have the "support group" here in BP like I had there. But the emptiness runs so deep this time. BP seems dry and dead now just like Medina did when Wanda and I split.

Helen was looking beyond me, to a life without love for me, a life free to live, a life where all the lost years of caring for children could be made up. Freedom. "I met a guy I went to college with years ago. We had fun reminiscing. He said Ryly was beautiful. We were out shopping. I gave him my phone number. I hope you don't mind". That was the beginning of the end. She had become someone else. First, the arguing; the sleeping separately. I think we had sex one more time. "For the Good Times." Why she allowed me that I can't imagine. It would happen out of nowhere. Perhaps she would meet with some guy, feel too guilty to go all the way and she'd come home not being able to take it anymore. Her icy ability to repress herself, her frigidity toward me would momentarily break down. Who could know what was going through her mind? Finally, she stopped letting me touch her. Many strange things were happening. She was gone a lot. Strange people on the phone asking for her. I started getting aroused by thinking of her with other men—then angry, then I would go numb. I was hanging by a thread. Just trying to survive emotionally. I was like a zombie waiting for the ax. But I began to want to sink, a paralyzed corpse of lost love. "Why are you doing this to me?" But neither of us could answer. Like good mules we bowed our heads and clomped, clippity clop, onward, dumb beasts bound for the inevitable.

79

Surreal walks along Lake Balaton. Still stinging from the Helen separation. Wondering what she might do in a divorce. Perhaps humans are just conduits of emotion, emotion contained in us but doesn't originate there. We are feeling intimations of what is, feelings which are just a fragment of the whole, just one consciousness of it. And the "Other" in a love affair is the unexpected bringer of joy, but also the inevitable bringer of pain and sorrow. Every moment enjoyed must be painfully let go of—one by one—if the great EQUATION of Life—the Balance, the leaving of no footprint—is to take place. Death removes everything. Yet a small life spark can always remain, just as life carries its own death within it. And Death brings Life.

Sometimes the pain and strangeness of where I live now, alone, is more than I can comprehend. I feel like I am at my limit of sadness, so intensely do I feel the absence of happiness and any meaning to my life. You can just hurt for a while. But how long? Harriss wrote a song for Lacy Corman ("But tell me when… and what do I do 'til then"). I'm lost. Hurt. Seeing my sons will be sporadic. I will no longer be under the same roof with them. They will now "visit" me. God, how she angers me with her strength! Her assured "this is the way it will be" attitude. How tedious it is being with her knowing how she really feels now. How strange a lover becomes when they no longer want you. Only someone's death can jolt the psyche to the same degree. Losing love is like death, but at least with death there is a kind of closure, a resolution and the platitudinous perspective of, "We all have to die."

She's relieved! She's free and in her home city! I'm free to do what? Lost. But it's the end of that world. Nothing left to chastise yourself for. She rejected your essence: mind, soul, body. There's nothing left there.

But deep down the Master wishes to become the Slave, the Controller, the Controlled. But then the slave conspires against the master and looks for slaves of her own to dominate. But those dominated she eventually collapses into and the cycle goes on infinitely—dancing like a drunk with a hat rack.

A trip to Balaton remains surreal. Seeing the places where we once loved. Ships pass by knowing nothing about me. But somehow in their slowness against the horizon, they hint at the long voyage ahead. At least I've exiled pain to the edges. It no longer wreaks havoc at the center of my mind. But then an unlooked-for glimpse across the vast future can startle me back to knowing my wounds are still raw. A line from a book: "My sorrow is so wide, I can't see across it."

Simple pleasures: aren't they the foundation of healing? But still one wonders what separates a man and a woman? The woman must think: "I can no longer give this man my body. I don't enjoy bestowing that gift upon him any longer". But she must give something. Perhaps, then, she immerses herself in her children's lives. But soon she must break free. But the man, the man like me, will wait, crouch in the thicket of unhappiness and an unhappy match, watch and wait, hoping her love will return. Sometimes, maybe, it does. Yet that moment of awful truth. I must leave this person—this person whose flesh clung to mine and whom I thought about, adored incessantly.

She rose up over the years as a great Image in the center of my heart, my life, all my impressions of the mad, mad world all around me. Now, I go to that place, the center of my heart, and the idol has darkened. It is twilight and the place seems empty and all that was alive and animated… has turned into something dry and dead. A feeling of hasty abandonment seems to pervade everything. I must leave this place. Yet, a few stray voices, lost souls, ask me, weakly, to stay, to come and lie down in ashes with them, die with them.

And yet, I'd been here before. I remember women: Wanda, Berenice. I remember how time seemed to stop. I played a gig at Crazy Reddy's with Hector, a Tuesday, Feb 14th. It was his gig. I wanted him to tell me to not give up, that love would come back. But he told me with some force in his voice to stop grieving over love. I wanted him to assent to my feelings, that a reconciliation was possible—but he wouldn't do it. I broke down and cried in front of him. He stayed silent.

But what is woman pain? I remember the end of the affair with Berenice. I was walking down Plato St. in Medina and I said to myself, like a good little philosophy major, Woman pain is that which occurs when a woman a man loves will not return that love. I was always too cowardly to break it off with a girl even if I knew things weren't right. Only once I remember breaking off a long-distance thing that had gone on too long—and it was easy because it was over the phone. Luckily I was too far away to do it in person—to deny someone the love they are desperate to get. There is a feeling of horrible power. I treated her badly. I took advantage of her sweetness to me. It was shameful. And so here I am, middle-aged sleeping on a friend's sofa in a little village near the immense Lake of the infinite, silent universe, using the Internet at Burger King to communicate with the outside world.

Feeling good tonight. The prospect of seeing the Slovenian chick on Saturday is making my blood flow again. "Please tell The Man I didn't kill anyone—just tryin to have me some fun". As Doc said, the drive is there. You can't just ignore it. It hurts to hear Helen say she's also ready to start having regular sex again. But I know how she feels.

Sense of time during pain seems distorted. I've been in Balaton for only a month but it seems much longer. Lenny Bruce: anger/ denial/ acceptance. I'm in a new era—moving toward the acceptance stage. Actually, it seems you experience them all at different times in a different order. It's not something linear I mean. It's fragmented.

Walks around Balaton. Still surreal. Hot summer. Hazy green faded parks. Rundown but pleasant and not too crowded away from Siofok. Empty side streets of the village in blazing sun. Learning the streets where the menacing dogs with heart-startling barks are. Sun-baked beer bar: 50ft Korso (pint) printed on an A-frame bill of fare on the hot sidewalk. Cheap, like a quarter.

So hot tonight in my flat I had to open the big door-hinge style window wide as it would go. Reading by the overhead light and tiny green gnats swarmed in. Unobtrusive but numerous. Nausea of "hive" perception.

Things you see at the beginning of a new experience, an experience still raw with some residual pain from the old life now dead, are not things that always remain a part of the developing daily routine. Going to a particular shop for cigarettes or finding a good cheap restaurant—these are things you lean on in the beginning for solace in hopes of regaining a foothold back into the world before the Shock. In your still vulnerable state, you cling to a friendly smile from a waitress, some kindly assistance from a gas station attendant, the touch of a pretty hairdresser at the barbershop. But then as time goes by you find that these first encounters fade to the margins of the newly developing routine of your new life. After a time you forget them as the strengthening impressions of routines take their place. But then out of the blue, you might come upon these first seminal impressions again, yet they seem somehow different: the restaurant is smaller than you remember, people in other places seem now less friendly than before. You'd been giving them the benefit of the doubt because you wanted to see them in a way you could take. Today they're busy with the hardships of life and you see it clearly. They don't notice you. You are no longer a new face to them. As if the first impressions you had were now less pure because of their contact with stronger routine impressions. How you "saw" things in the earlier beginning of your pain—all that has changed. You see differently now. And only on rare occasions are the original impressions, by a kind of squinting of the emotional eye, or a rare random re-alignment of scenes remembered, capable of being seen in their original light. There was a café in Budapest where Crip and I had an espresso or beer, once. I was on a visit there years before I decided to move. I still have strong impressions of the place, even a photograph, but I cannot for the life of me find that place now. Other early BP impressions I can relive—but not that one. (I think he might mean a place on Hollan Erno utca some 3 blocks from the Korut.—Krip)

My childhood street. Water Maple Ave. Time becomes less solid with an increased self-consciousness of it. Time. I'm in my mother's house in Edgeton. I'm on an airplane back to BP. Back in Balaton to my little room. But I'm not the same person. I was hiding out from Helen and the break-up. But now there's no reason to hide. What I should have faced, it doesn't matter. It's gone now and perhaps eternally unfaceable. I missed my chance. Still, I'm drawn to woman for solace. A new woman even if the bitter taste is still in my mouth. Sweet kisses to the metallic blood taste. The taste of failed Time. How lovely she was, bitter Time! Once, sweet as the yeast blown from the bakery. Breath of human time. How can she be gone? The wisp of brown hair. Darkened ivory sky. Dark brown moon. Skin like darkened poplar. No, only changed. Took on new form. The sky is whitening. Dark, blond, red, white, death. The old room that is my new home sends twinges of the past. How young we were in '89! What love we made in the bone-white buildings pockmarked with bullet holes left over from the wars. Love!

80

Josh didn't want to stop at the Peep Show but he needed a flesh fix. He had not had sex for a year and a half. He drove down to the gypsy neighborhood. He hesitated about stopping. He still had guitars in the trunk. There was little violent hand-gun crime here, rarely any shootings downtown. That was American stuff. Yet, if you were going to get pickpocketed or get your car ripped off, this would probably be the neighborhood it happened in.

Driving down Nagy Korut (the Grand Boulevard) at midnight on a Saturday night was like being underwater with little phosphorescent fish and eels swimming around the sides of the big current that swept along tides of metal boxes. Helen was gone for good. Or she wasn't. He no longer knew for sure. There she was in the same luxury apartment overlooking the Danube. But he couldn't fall back into the same old routine of hoping and waiting. Life continued with its implacable inertia unheedful of anyone's trifling personal problems. As far as that went he felt like someone standing around watching a robbery but too afraid to do anything about it.

Corner of Temple St. Right next door to a currency exchange shop. Peep Show. It sounded like something out of an old circus his Grandfather Dexter might have gone to, whistling and guzzling homemade whiskey. The big fire that Marshall had often talked about—the image of his father, age ten, standing barefoot in the snow, watching his house burn down, the fire almost looking like it was falling from the sky as the big sycamore caught fire. But that's what the Nagy Korut in BP was a freak show. Every café, in summer, was a little party, a conspiracy of gestures, of handsome waiters and tight-skirted waitresses, like sea froth, even in this land-locked city encircled by the River. After his gig, around midnight, the tide started to ebb. By one o'clock only the discos would still be thumping, as they would, along with a few nighthawks in small cafes where they dished out schnitzels and French fries, until dawn. Walking along toward the Peep Show he remembered the book Doc had given him, "Zorba said, 'What is a woman but a well. You bend down, you see your reflection, you drink and then you go away.'" He wondered if he shouldn't have gone away, too. Back to America. The Arab money changer guys on Temple St. had said as much. Why you not go back? they asked him. But he didn't go back. He stayed. "I ain't leavin' without my horse." A husband. A father. "Stay home with your wife and family." That old song was always a closing number at Crazy Reddy's, Sylves laughing and mugging like he was a Leadbelly character, buggin' out his eyes and pouting out his lips. "Stay home by the fireside bright!" He had tried. And failed. "Goodnight, Irene. Goodnight." Goodbye Helen.

Sylves had said to teenaged Josh hurting from Lilian: "Women can't save ya, boy!" Yet, when they gave their love, Josh couldn't help seeing them as the Great Deliverer. "I Fall in Love too Easily" he hummed as he walked along. But there would be no deliverance. Not now. No warm hand reaching into the infant's crib to ease the tears. Josh left everything in the States and came here to look me up. "Why did Wanda stop loving me?" he asked me, fresh off the plane from Medina, as we stumbled out of a Budapest beer hall. "Maybe she was looking for someone more stable," I said. "I mean, look at us, riding in a taxi through an esoteric European capital at dawn, half crocked, thousands of miles from Water Maple Farm!" He seemed hurt by that remark and I hugged him and said, "You know what I mean, man. It's all bullshit." And I remember how he smiled, that little boy look, yet the resignation of an old man as he bent down to put his arm around me and we tottered down Temple St. But Josh was stable. As if I could hear his great heart-thumping slowly. Slowing with a few more years from our boyhood. Who loved more? His women withdrew their love. But what happens to a woman? I wish I had known how to answer him.

81 JOSH

Samidha, the Indian girl. How beautiful she was. She remembered me. It seemed strange but then, what the hell.

When you come into the place, you go upstairs, go into a cubicle, put a coin into a slot. A light comes on and a beautiful girl starts to dance. It had to be her. The way Crip had described her. She hadn't aged very much. So then you say to her, "Can I have a private dance?" Then she leads you to a larger cubicle. There is a pane of glass that separates you from her, but there's maybe two feet or so open at the bottom so you can reach in and touch her, caress her. And if she likes you she can get closer to the opening and you can do almost anything. But you have to pay more. I was too afraid of getting something if I put even my condomed dick into her but she let me finger her, she especially liked me to pull her pussy lips gently and widely apart. Clit licking was ok but I kept safe and she liked it rubbed gently. No kissing on the lips, but licking and kissing everywhere else was ok. I loved licking her beautiful feet and up her legs to her smooth buttocks. My licking there, as it had on the bottoms of her feet, caused her to giggle. I was careful not to bang my head on the rather narrow glass opening. I told her a bit of my story. She was very kind. At the end she said, in the best English she could muster "I will give you VERY good blow job!" And so it was. The post-orgasm, circus streets seemed lonely as I wandered along. I turned back before getting to Temple St. (As she returned to her cubicle I had noticed a guy, didn't look Hungarian, watching us on a video screen—a kind of security camera I guess, just in case a guy tried to pull any funny shit on one of the girls).

82 MEMORIES OF ADRATO | PART ONE

by Krip Kovacs

Even the train cars seemed like something very old, at least they exuded a turn of the century feeling. The fittings were modern enough. Still, for someone who came from a country that no longer used trains much, it was like being in another time. Of course, Josh thought immediately of the War, all the people who must've sat in these same seats and all around was the Balkan countryside, the huge rock wall of the Alps in the distance, the smaller mountains in front of them, rolling green hills, forests and the sea never so faraway, one always sensing it somewhere. And as the train sped on through it all the great vista of the sea would open up as it does in Greece. Always the great overlooks onto the sea everywhere. He wondered where he was, like someone waking up from a dream. But to her, I suppose, looking back, it was only like being in another state, as if I was traveling in Arkansas or Tennessee. Hungary wasn't far. Of course, culturally it was different. The languages were worlds apart, though, living side by side for a thousand years, they had borrowed words from each other. Same word for dog, cat. Several other things I picked up rather quickly. But I would learn about things like that much later.

Adrato was a typical coastal town. It was like a miniature Venice in a way. The houses were all in the Venetian style—only the government buildings were built in the blustery baroque Hapsburg style—the Venetian stucco and wooden shutters above the narrow streets were, as we wended our way down to the center of town, replaced by thick columns and flowery convoluted ornaments on the cornices and architraves. You could feel the solidity of those squat granite buildings, as in Budapest, going on for block after block. But looking at the stucco and wooden shutters of the houses on the hill, with clotheslines braided endlessly through the alleys, it seemed as if the sea could wash it all away.

We glorify ourselves. In the past, the present and the future. We think the world before us is there for us, like a friendly stranger who would extend his hand in gratitude if only he knew who we were. And so you begin recounting your story, mostly to yourself, hoping the world is within earshot. And you see, if you bother to look, the remnants of other people's stories, every household, every building every street contains an epic struggle! You sense they are related to yours but you are caught up in your own too much to give them much thought. You take what you can use and then go on. You can use money, sex and Love. Your Desire for these things leads you on. Power is a kind of repository almost in which they reside. But it doesn't matter how to explain it. It's always changing before you can get a handle on it. And me, my glorified little subject, I'm changing, too. Slowly fading away and dying. At every stage, the Out There starts looking very different. Even the old way of me as the focal point seems to shift. The nurse will be here soon with the injection. That changes things. They disappear completely (and to think, in my fifties, I once complained about how the young people no longer responded to me!) But slowly the memory comes back And the enigmatic desire to say something. Anything. Even if you know it's only a fragment.

Falling in love with someone. That is the momentous event that propels everything else. Love points the way to money, sex, and the power they give you, the power even to love in return. A garden path of mellifluous roses, the thorns seeming less menacing, suddenly. Dragan had become so enraged with jealousy, I decided that Josh and Helen should leave town for a while until he calmed down. He told people repeatedly that he planned on having them both killed by his cronies in Ukraine and no one knew if he was serious or not. That eternal question mark that poses the unanswered question. (How many times years later I would thumb through my dogged-eared copy of Hamlet to consult the passage one more time. Somehow it always staved off the Inevitable!) Months earlier I had arranged for my old friend Goric to let Josh play guitar in his club for 300 Deutsche Marks a night. Not bad money. Josh would wear that black hat Emese had given him on our big trip to Italy years back that made him look a bit like an old blues dude and covered up his receding hairline at the same time.

One night, coming down from the stage on a break Josh saw her sitting by the tall handsome guy. She motioned him over. "This is my new friend, Ljubomir" she said, reaching up and putting a friendly arm around his neck. "He says he thinks Hungarian girls are really hot." His smile momentarily vanished into a sudden look of disbelief and fear. "Oh, really," Josh said. "Well, I agree." His smile returned when he saw Josh was to put up no obstacle to his flirtations with her. Not that he worried he couldn't waste him with one punch, (he was so big!)

he was probably just fearful of making a scene in front of the paying customers. The next day at his insistence they were to go looking for wild asparagus in the woods, something apparently young people did there in order to go hide and make out. He brought along his girlfriend. But quickly he and Helen disappeared down a worn pathway through the tall grass that led behind a hill. Josh knew she was having fun leading him on, yet it was also her way of insuring herself against any infidelity he might commit. She would then have a guy ready at hand. And she could test his jealous reaction. The other girl Josh hardly noticed. She spoke no English. Later, she was in tears—jealous of Ljubomir's obvious preference for Helen.

When they got back to the panzio they made love with very passionate kisses She was so beautiful it didn't take much time for him to get aroused. After, they could pet and talk. He said he didn't mind if she wanted Ljubomir. I think he might've even added that his feelings for her were beyond that sort of childish jealousy. This offended her. But eventually, after their quarreling subsided they laughed and she giggled telling him how funny Ljubo was, trying to kiss her. Then she said, "if I ever want someone else, you'll know it!"

The image that persists is this, her pure, white spotless tight jeans, the turquoise shirt with black flecks and the cute little loose-fitting black jacket she always wore. The mischievous child look in her eyes—her eyes that were browner than her light brown skin that made you think of October that would soon come and blot out the moist air of today's bright spring day. In October they would quarrel but today Ljubo drove them up the hill where they could look down on Adrato and see the orange mansard rooves like wreaths around the blue sea where a tiny ripple would belie a dolphin's splash and a tiny wave. Look north and the wall of the Alps stood, stoic and cloud -wreathed, snow-covered, grey and heavy, as if something terrible had happened far away, too far away to do anything about it. Look west and you could just make out the tiny buildings of Trieste. But there below them was the clear blue sea. He asked her to stop for a moment in the warm April sun which made everything, every fiber of green-yellow grass, every pebble on the road winding down to the little round piazza, every palm frond waving in the light salty breeze, stand out in sharp relief. The tanned skin of her forehead over the bridge of her Mediterranean nose had just begun to freckle very slightly and against the endless (ending on some Italian coast too far away to imagine) deep blue sea behind her face and fine strands of dark brown hair falling across her eyes, in memory now seem like an indecipherable landscape of some old story. She was holding the banister with both hands as she leaned her back against it. There was a playful look of childish anger in her eyes when she feigned a slight impatience with his constant photographing of her. She never liked being photographed but for him, she had decided to make an exception just for now. After he snapped it she turned quickly coming out of her pose and headed off down the little lane to the town. It seemed as if she walked over the orange rooves and he could watch her perfect backside sway girlishly, she was so happy with the Balkan freedom of the early nineties, as she walked. We had been '89-ers together. Now he had freed her from old communist Hungary and the world around them was their playground. And knowing he would soon be back in the panzio making love to her made him feel almost too giddy and weak, like a child consumed with laughter, to keep up with her as they made their way down.

PART TWO

Josh had been back in Budapest for some time. The bitterness of the divorce from Helen seemed to have faded. Josh was often alone now. It was the women of the city that had begun to fascinate him; he was, in fact, becoming obsessed with them. Many of Josh's musician friends had spoken of them. Hungarians were fond of saying "their women" were the most beautiful of Europe. But most other Europeans agreed as well. Now that the borders of East Europe were wide open, the coffee houses, the discos and nightclubs were filled with Spanish, American, Italian, Dutch, French and British young males looking for Magyar women. Josh was no longer really what you could call young but he didn't look it.

As it happened, Josh asked me to try and book him some gigs again. I thought again of the Club Losa near the Slovene border, near Adrato—Goric Goravics's place. Goric, they said, had sold the place years ago but that they would love for Joshua Celeste to play there again.

Josh wandered around the old Adriatic city. Goric' panzio was now a computer store. But the bar/restaurant, where he was still to play and had played so many years before, was still there and doing a brisk business, though the décor was now much more western and the posters lampooning the old communist regime were gone. As he wandered around toward the back alley and the kitchen door he noticed the stone stairway he and Helen had walked down. The dark blue of the sea, so far below, with the faint white traces of wave and dolphin splash, was still there against the white ring of new hotels that now ringed the beachfront. He felt the mild clench in his stomach and the slight sting in the corners of his eyes that so often in those long-ago days had signaled tears. But now he closed his eyes and smiled. Looking out toward the faint lights of Trieste, he sighed and started back toward his hotel. He thought of how ugly the communist-era hotels had been.

VILLAGE GIRL

The first time he saw her he knew they would make love. How he had known he was almost afraid to wonder. The stars align. You know it in one glance. There comes a point in the equation of attraction that a modestly pretty girl becomes, or lets herself become, eligible for pursuit. She crosses a threshold in her allure. She's not so untouchably beautiful that she becomes the quarry of only beautiful and/or extremely wealthy men, men that are near impossible for most more modest looking men to compete with, nor is she simply too plain looking to get worked up over. For Josh, lonely as he had become, recently divorced, at loose ends in Adrato, a less than warm-hearted city, she seemed, in children's story fashion, just right. Of a philosophical bent, Josh considered himself, an observant discoverer of hidden beauty. As he thought about her, and the sweet, fleeting kiss she would later give him, he began to wonder if his ability to recognize hidden beauty might be greater than most. "I've always thought I had a knack for finding pretty girls no one else thought were pretty," he said to himself. But then he thought, the skeptic rising up in him, everyman probably thinks of himself as a great discoverer, a voyager—Odysseus, in the end, though not always returning to find faithful Penelope. Every man imagines himself as a great lover, he thought.

She was a poor village girl. He noticed her as he was going out of the lobby of the hotel. A profusion of streaked blond hair flowing from her head tied up in the current reggae fashion. "vere are you vrahm?" she asked in a confident buoyant way. It seems so far away now to him: how they had drunk so much dark (almost black) red wine, how he had tried to kiss her outside the bar but she had turned her face away from him, how he then tried simply to talk with her and then, right before they reached the door of his hotel, she had flung her arms around him and kissed him passionately, then ran off saying, "I meet you tomorrow, ok?" He had then walked through the dark, narrow, deserted Adrato streets, feeling a sweet anxiety about the lovemaking that was to come, guilt and eagerness and joy and nausea, like a man not yet hungry enough begins to contemplate an imminent feast. He knew there would be no turning back, yet he knew, just as eminently, though she was a girl who would give herself to him, that he could never love her and be her constant companion. He knew that she would be merely an object ("victim" seemed to him too strong a word) of his predatory lust and that he would, soon after their lovemaking, abandon her. He knew, though he was too weak-willed to admit it to himself, that because Helen had left him, this was his revenge, not only against her but against all women that he felt somehow had mistreated him. I can remember Doc telling him, once: "It's a young girl's job, leave or get left!" Yet, he felt, though she was only 20 that she knew and accepted this as well, or would someday.

But who was she? Which old girlfriend? Lilian? Kiki LaSalle? Wanda? But it didn't matter—she was all of them. So, he was merely repeating something—some loose end in high school that had never gotten tied up. Some womanly deliverer that would only eventually lead him back to his self-hatred.

And yet, as she guided him down autumn-tinged back roads in his rented station wagon, and, when they had found a secluded place, and the white moon was rising over the cornfields, she stretched out her milk-white naked body over the back seat, with no words between them, she accepted everything.

So long ago it seems, he thought, now standing in front of the Mona Lisa in Budapest, post-gig, waiting for Gudrun who, though taller and older, looked very much like her.

To Helen

The white stone staircase

Above the Adriatic, vein blue

Did we somehow know then it would disappear?

April's Shakespearean sun awakened us

We hurried outside to the steps that would lead us

Down to the sea,

And Adrato,

A Venice in miniature.

On the landing above

The village floor of red-tiled rooves

Floating in air

You turned suddenly towards me

And I took your picture

In that light gauze shirt I liked

With dolphin flecks of aqua and turquoise.

83 THE COLOSSUS OF ADRATO

By Krip Kovacs

(The Budapest Week, April 1991)

If you walk out the back door of Dragan Jankovic's newly acquired panzio, you'll find a staircase on your left leading down to the sea, the Adriatic Sea, that unpredictable sea of the Renaissance imagination that was the inspiration for Shakespeare's The Tempest. One need only sail south to wash up shipwrecked on the Isle of Keriki (Corfu), but you won't find Prospero, Lawrence Durrell or Henry Miller either. What you will find are thousands of British tourists intent on putting as many miles on a motor scooter (dope heads on Mopeds is a popular song now) and kicking back as much Guinness stout as they can before getting back to work in Yorkshire.

Corfu, with the exception of the breath-taking views of Paleokastritsa, is a sham. But if hanging out in discos with Anglo Saxons listening to 80's hits mixtapes is your thing then you've reached nirvana (the place and the band— except Mr. Kobain, he dead).

The Greeks will have little to do with you, especially if you are not Orthodox, except maybe to smile and surreptitiously hocker in your Retsina, a popular wine here, part Olympian nectar, part Pine-sol (a popular US floor cleaner).

No, better to wash ashore to the north beyond the dagger-biting pirates of Dalmatia, beyond the Yugoslavian Civil War with its shaky truce, to the top of Istria, the crux of Europe—Adrato, Slovenia. Named by the Romans, the lost meaning of the name hints at the idea, as Dragan tells me, of a guiding fire on the shore, a lighthouse.

Dragan is a tall red-haired, handsome impresario who has returned to Ljubljana, the city of his college days, where he once was often seen, long-haired, strumming his guitar in local pubs and knocking back Lasko Pivos, the ubiquitous Slav beer, and chain-smoking Gaulois nonfilters. After all, Napoleon whipped the Austrians here. He has now turned his many talents to the tourist biz after spending years producing hit music in Budapest.

After Ljubljana and university, Dragan did a noble thing. He laid down his guitar, married a lovely Hungarian girl, and removed to her lovely coastal village of Adrato. They raised two lovely daughters in a lovely house over-looking the lovely blue Adriatic, which is wild and white-capped as a horse's eye in winter, calm as a sleeping kitten in summer.

As I walk down his back staircase I stop and look out on this sunny February morning, so portentous of spring, and over a Europe that has yet to be resolved. Looking North to the medieval, Venetian stones of the Church of St___, the snow-capped Austrian Alps rise in majestic steel blue. To the West, the curve at the top of Italy's boot, or bootstrap as some say, the faint cityscape of Trieste, and fainter still, across the vast water, I could swear I see a hazy, dream-like Venice/Mestre, only a one-hour hydrofoil ride from Adrato. This is the exact point where the Latin, Slavic and Germanic worlds meet.

Historically it has been a volatile mixture.

In Ljubljana I once asked an American-born Slovenian student what he thought of his parents' homeland: "The people here are a bit Alpine," he said. Fair enough. For sure, the famous Austrian stoicism, some would call it coldness, is tempered here by the warmer Slavic individuality, the Serb/Croatian variety of which has given rise to their current troubles. Indeed the Slavic temperament of the Karst mountains, a still somewhat unspoiled wilderness, is totally Karst!

Adrato is Italian but it would be an over-simplification to call it merely a small Venice, though you'll find the same catwalk alleyways and exquisite wooden doors and shutters on the stucco buildings washed in a watercolor of aqua, lavender, ochre and robin's egg blue. The difference for the tourist is simple. Think back on the plate of food that, in Venice, according to the menu, cost a 107, 965.52 Italian Lira, the bottle of wine that cost twice that, the whole scenario sending you running to the special tourist "Italian" dinner of Ragu sauce, limp side salad and a coke that still cost thirty bucks! Not to mention the piece of butter-splotched substance that resembled American Wonder bread.

At Dragan's new Club Adrato, which he opened not long after the fall of Yugoslavian Communism, is not only one of Europe's most exciting discos, but also host to some of Europe's most exciting jazz and blues acts, one of which is the currently performing Joshua Celeste Quartet (and with which I am proud to say I am the current bassist). You can get a pizza prosciutto or scampi risotto and so much more for a fraction of the Venetian prices. And then wash it all down with a Slavic "black" wine (reforska) or one even more indigenously Slovene, a tangy, rose-looking Svicek. Not only will this not cost a wheelbarrow of lira, nor will an angry Balkan spit in it, but perhaps Dragan will take you for a ride to a village near Celje in his newly restored 1967 Alfa Romeo "Guilica" (the only one on the Slovene coast!) to pick up a mere 50 liters of the said Svicek, five of which he will give you for free to enhance your view of the sea from the balcony of one of his lovely panzios.

Standing, now, at Dragan's back staircase leading down to the sea, I'm reminded of what one autograph-seeker from Split, Croatia ("the center of the world!") said to the musician, Joshua Celeste, backstage after his terrific concert: "The people here are still a bit sleepy with fear. They were beaten down in the Russian times. They don't understand your edge. They have no rhythm. They have only… Memories." Make new vibrant ones at Dragan's new Club Adrato!

LUKA, THE SERB SOLDIER'S STORY

(Friend of Dragan's)

"I was on patrol in an armored vehicle. We came upon 3 Croatian soldiers. They were trembling thinking we would execute them. But then one said, 'We know you. We watched you in our binoculars today eating lunch. We saw you but didn't kill you.' "What was I eating?" I asked. 'Pljeskavica' "OK," I said, "It's a deal. I won't kill you either. I let them go. There's a stone wall above the sea in Adrato. 500 years ago they threw prisoners off this wall. If you live you go free. If you die—you die. This was crazy shit they did 500 years ago."

84 JOSH

So strange walking through my neighborhood the morning of the flight. I felt such a heightened sensibility. Could this be my last morning on my little 11th district street? Suddenly the sunshine seemed more beautiful than it ever had. Isn't the simplicity of walking down the street an amazing thing? I asked myself as I went to run a few last-minute errands before calling the cab to the airport. Aren't the beautiful Hungarian women even more beautiful now? I thought, morbidly speculating it might be my last morning alive. Why can't I be like this every day? The time-wasting, bovine way I had spent so many of my days occurred to me and I recoiled in disgust.

Now that I was faced with a long journey away from what I had grown so accustomed to, I suddenly felt sorry I was leaving. In a flash I saw the world I was fleeing as a paradise I'd never really noticed before. If only, I thought, I could feel each moment this attachment, this miracle of the everyday! But I knew it was impossible.

85 KRIP

Trying to calm my distracted mind, organizing concerts, meetings, sending emails, phone calls. All things, faces, voices, songs, places, swimming crazily through my head.

Josh said once, "Only sunshine, in the end, in its profound beauty, remains a constant." Otherwise, the world is just full of Desire, a Dante-esque morass of pathetic imploring—my plea the loudest, most pathetic. I just have to keep going.

86 JOSH

As soon as I entered the house, aside from a sense of great relief, to have finally arrived home—or at least the home of my young manhood—I felt a pang of depression. Already Agnes was irked by the proposed length of my Hungarian friend, Krip's, upcoming visit from his Aunt's home in New Jersey. I had innocently tossed off the phrase, "a few days," weeks earlier to her on the phone, when his visit would be more like a week or more. (I hadn't, in my absence, realized how nervous mother had become about her heart condition).

So right away I had failed in the judgment of a woman. I had not planned things out adequately. Once again the feeling of never doing things right in the eyes of a woman besieged me. The thought of her inflexibility caused a wave of melancholy to pass over me. But soon, as I unpacked my suitcase and looked around, at home on Water Maple Ave., again at last, my depression lifted.

I was able to take a brief side trip to a music convention in Nashville where Harriss, my friend and former bandmate of years gone by, was working as a lawyer. Krip and I had set ourselves an impossible goal: to penetrate the inner sanctum of Nashville's songwriter network—all in 2 days!

Seeing all the myriad musicians, so many, scurrying around the Renaissance Hotel (a typically ludicrous name that had no point of reference that I could see, since neither desk clerks or bellhops were attired in any sort of Cinquecentro garb) both endeared me to them and repulsed me at the same time. I sympathized with their delusion of "making it big" but the continuous drone of their twanging instruments, playing as a kind of backdrop to their narcissistic fantasies, began, after a while, to grate on my nerves. I got bored out of my mind—especially when I sensed that I didn't fit into their fantasies as a fellow musician—and I began to hate them all. Even Krip and I were on the outs a bit after we began to sense the futility of our fantasy of breaking into the Nashville scene. But we got over it.

Driving back, in Jared Smallwood's truck, to Edgeton from Nashville, I was struck by the reality (or dream) of where I was. The place I called "home." Could it ever be "home" again? So, now my alienation here equaled that of Budapest? So, where was home? Nowhere and everywhere. Therefore, I press on. After all, only 20 more years or so—if that—and then the grave digger will shovel me "back into the human mind again."

Once I felt some connection with the lush fields of the horse farms of U.S. 60 and Pisgah Pike, Payne's Mill and Old Frankfort Road. Now, it seems far removed. The color of the asphalt, the look of the trees, the passing cars, the sky—all of it seemed strange and distant. Not to mention the sensation that my libertinism had no place here. This is a puritanically moral place. Yet, under the surface lies chaos, murder and lust. A friend of the family's impending murder trial was in all the papers. Provoked by his lover's rejection of him—he shot her five times. Only in an atmosphere of repression could such an affluent man be moved to carry out such a terrible crime. Something is too ripe in the rich yellow sunlight of the Eden of Water Maple County—the sunlight of the world! a place where social status means, as it means in the whole nation, everything. A fall from grace is irredeemable. Man is a murderous witch burner. I think of the gypsy riots years later on Temple St. in Budapest.

87

How can I encompass all my thoughts? Like the thousands of Jonquils that grew along the avenue to Bertha's house, I want to gather them into one handful that will unlock the secret of them all.

Here, now, on a trip "home" to Edgeton without my sons, without the fatherly/ motherly feelings that pervade, envelope me when they're with me day to day in Budapest, adult life seems cruel again as it did in '89 when I fled from the Past— from Kiki and Wanda and Berenice—with my heart like a tail between my legs.

But maybe it's just an illusion. The feeling that life is cruel could be just a result of lack of faith in God's love for us. With God, we needn't worry that destitution awaits us. He/She will provide. The American need for tangible proof arises again and again. We're forced to give it up and take what comes. We suspect our neighbor of plotting our demise. We shouldn't. He can't harm us, flung headlong as he is, along with us, into the unknown. I and my neighbor die and are shoveled back into the human mind again!

Does the very substance of Water Maple Avenue, Water Maple farm, Edgeton, KY seem thinner now? Was there a summer drought, now that I am here again with Krip, after so many years, that decimated the trees? Seems I remember a greater luxuriance, a deeper sunlight. I remember a trip back with Helen. Ryly was only 6 months old. I awoke in Mom's house at dawn on the sofa downstairs. The side yard was a vision of orange-brown leaf and blue dawn sky. Leaves burned orange by autumn death reaching down into me—an explosion of feeling. Fall Kentucky colors that Berenice said to me once that she could almost taste with her tongue.

88

My mind is racing toward death. The end of youth, of sexual attractiveness, has a way of narrowing the mind's once mellifluous thoughts. Solitude eclipses the once joyful hours of the daydreams of youth. Age doesn't bring wisdom, only the ability to "see through" the trivialities of young manhood. I can see why many of my old friends here back in Edgeton and Medina "just work" preferring not to think about things too much. Of course, age brings boredom, the feeling of having nothing to do beyond the necessities. No more passionate projects. Work becomes robotic and drug-like in middle age and beyond. One's job can become a refuge from another, freer, less routine, riskier world one cannot face. One can disappear from life's engaging events and still draw a paycheck.

In the end, I'm the loser, at least out in the "practical world" I am. Doc seems desperate, too, and mentally distracted. This is distressing because for so long I looked to him for guidance and stability. Still, he is a survivor. Am I?

89

I feel alone. Tuesday night's gig at Crazy Reddy's was flattering but the high of adulation doesn't last—especially when it doesn't translate into dollars. By the time Reddy got his cut and I paid off the sidemen—mostly new faces—there wasn't much left. In the end, even with Krip and Doc's maneuvering to make me look like a Euro star come back to his "roots", it was just another local gig for low bread. Some of my former colleagues—the number is shrinking—can survive on this. Once, I heard Agnes say to Sylves, "No memory of having starred atones for later disregard". She was always quoting some famous poem—got that from her mother Millicent.

90 KRIP

Only 2 things I screwed up on on the "Big Trip to Amerika!!!" 1) getting tired and frustrated with the Reddy gig, Doc (Mr. Big Email List) and I worked so hard on promoting it and then Reddy comes along and wants 20 percent of the door! which made me yell and scream in front of Josh. And 2) Screwing Wanda. She had that "fuck you" look in her eyes the "night after" when she came to the gig. I feel like I'm somehow diminished in Josh's eyes now that he's seen that side of me. I got sick of the whole N-ville smooze. But I knew he should talk to that big wig manager guy. I think it did him some good. He got some #'s to call. I wanted to help him like he's helped me. I got some money from Aunt Pearl. I knew the big wig manager guy had no interest in me, yet I balked at having to borrow Jared Smallwood's truck and driving 4 hours to N-ville. I was torn between wanting to help get him a good gig, constantly dealing with his mother's suspicions, since she doesn't much trust any show biz people, and feels like Josh is too old to do this anymore and just forgetting the whole thing!

The first morning in N-ville seemed strange. I headed downtown to the country music showcase thing. I parked my rented car at that crazy, hideously ugly Renaissance Hotel. It was early. Still, the ecstatic strangeness walking the early morning streets of N-ville. So, here was the town I had fantasized about for so many years!

91 JOSH

Finally, I got on the flight from BP to New York.

A San Francisco girl who had tried, and failed, to make a go of it as an opera singer in Romania was on her way back to California. During her years as a stand-in and singer of bit parts in Bucharest, she had managed to purchase a house. Now, she was trying to unload it.

I couldn't help glancing at her furtively from time to time, sitting next to me. She was a cute forty-something. She talked on and on, eventually falling asleep, a kind of self-hypnosis perhaps.

I had enjoyed listening to her describe her difficulties in Eastern Europe, they had of course reminded me of my own. At first, we love to hear shared experiences. Like me, she had thought of Eastern Europe as a new start, a place in which to become rich and famous in a round-about way. Like me, it seemed that she had committed suicide in the States and been reborn in another strange faraway place. But then that familiar wave of melancholy washed over me as I realized how well-trod my own life's road had been by so many others just like me. Here was another wanna-be, I thought, running home to save herself. But then we find that home has left us, Time stole it. Perhaps she was running back to commit suicide there as well. We always think that if we are deserving enough, if we have sacrificed something of ourselves, our pride, our life, others will take us in and say, There, there you poor creature, rest here awhile while I tell the world your tragic story and then we remake you into glorified genius god you always were. Something like that. Like Dorothy, we awaken in a new, strange place (before the massive renovations of the aughts, many streets of Budapest had been streets of Hapsburg yellow brick!) and we are exalted as strange avatars from a strange world, but then we find that, just like the exposed Wizard, when we try to ride the balloon back to our dreams, we don't know how it works either. The strangers we meet were, in fact, hoping we were their savior. And when the host and guest realize they have failed each other's expectations it sometimes happens that they turn on each other.

It always strikes me when I meet an attractive woman, and she was an artist as well, that perhaps I've met a possible partner, a lover, a soulmate. I start wondering if I should ask for numbers, email addresses and so on. But she slept a long time. As I glanced at her in the seat next to me I began to fantasize a life with her. I went through all the phases of a relationship. I thought of trying to accidentally awaken her and then declare my love! But my ears were stopped up as we started to land. I couldn't hear anything but the droning engine. I hesitated. I dozed off myself.

Suddenly we had landed at JFK. I went through customs first. She not far behind, I waited in the hall for her to catch up with me, pretending to fiddle with my baggage. I got a few stares from security people: What's he doing? Why doesn't he move on? These were the questions I imagined reading on their faces. Finally, she came up alongside me in the sea of passengers and yet I still couldn't muster the nerve to ask how I could contact her. Finally, as she was getting ahead of me I yelled out my website address saying, Get in touch if you want!

Ok, I'll remember that she said, and disappeared towards baggage claim. She never wrote. Another seedling sprout of man/woman relationship washed into oblivion.

Alone again walking through the dark JFK food court I caught up with the band: Carlo, Jared Smallwood on drums, Free playing rhythm guitar, all the old Edgeton bandmates Krip had assembled. They looked bleary-eyed and bored. The flight to N-ville had been delayed. It felt weird using American money after so many years. It felt weird to have traveled so far and then suddenly be in Tennessee and not Kentucky. That would come later. And then, driving up, there was Krip's smiling face. Someone to talk to! And so we got on the bus. Our "home" for the next 2 weeks. Like a flash, we are driving through the streets of Amerika! It was like every American city. How the same all cities are in Europe and America! In Europe, the monuments are raised to different events yet the Cathedral, the Parliament, the old city, the high rise apartments, in its way it's like the old downtowns of America, the strip mall, the KFC, the gas station. Like Doc said, All of Western Civilization is of a piece. I will never get to see the East, but somehow I bet deep down it's the same. All mankind suffers from the same malady. His speech, his shelters—everything attests to it.

AFTER NASHVILLE GIGS, EDGETON BAND
REUNITES TO ROCK LOCAL CROWD

(local paper headline)

Sadness at leaving home. So, there you have it. Heading back to Budapest and Europe.

92

My mother has always been a difficult woman. Or is it that all women are difficult for men to understand and one's mother provides the most complex puzzle of all? She came to visit me once in Budapest. Marshall had died several years before. The phone system in Hungary at that time was rather primitive. Many people didn't even have one. Every apartment door had a pencil tied to a string and a notepad to leave messages on. But she managed to call me from her hotel, wanting me to meet her at a tour bus stop beside the Danube. It felt strange seeing her there amidst the neo-baroque buildings of a strange city, in a bright yellow spring dress, waving frantically. She had already booked a bus tour to Balaton. Always so organized about things like that. At that time I knew so little about the Lake. I sat in the aisle seat half asleep while the guide told us the local history in English, German and French, so I couldn't see the things he was referring to out the window as well as Mom could. She poked me in the ribs at various intervals, Did you hear that? Did you see that? Beautiful. Such a beautiful place. I had no idea.

Is that why I felt drawn to Balaton years later? The memories of her yellow dress. The sadness a parent feels when your child leaves Home! A man leaves his mother but he never quite reconciles that loss. She either recedes into the past, a symbol of the warmth of childhood, or else, should she become more objectified, "just another person" who loves you and is loved as the body from which you sprang, she grows, layer after layer, into a vast complexity in your mind, is, in some ways, your mind. Seeing her yellow dress I suddenly feel an immense pity.

She seems too vulnerable, flying all this way to see me in this gray city—a city briefly clothed in spring, waiting for a long gray winter. Who was she, really? A man knows his father, that amiable guy who got lucky one night. As a man, you know him instantly once you outgrow the god-like esteem you once held him in. You either revere your parents like a saint reveres his god, or you become Prince Hamlet, always questioning, doubting and reverting to feelings of love that can never be revealed. Your life either grows like a pearl around that irritating wound or else like a cancer it spreads into the Self, slowly killing it by way of an over-abundance of reflection or the lack of it.

93

Back in BP I took my sons to Dilello's, the Italian place on Alkotas St. But to get there from their Mom's place near Ver Mezo park, we walked the side streets from Krisztina St. to Marvany. I'm so deaf now I could hardly hear their quick Hungarian patter between them, but then we joked around as much in English. Seeing the 86 bus reminded me of all those bus rides along the Danube to their elementary (altalanos) school so I could walk them home across the castle hill. Ryly seems a bit more pensive, self-reflective. Gordon isn't as separated from the world yet. The World, like a child, is innocent. A child, "in the world" and the world itself are almost the same thing—even all their unseen complexities. Like Doc said, Childhood reaches perfection and then it Fragments into adulthood. And an adult is simply a child expelled from the Garden.

The trip fades. Kentucky settles back into its photograph on the mantle, a scene under glass, floating in water with fake snow of memory settling down around it. Just as I fought back tears and depression as the days of my departure loomed, so do I, now that I've returned, feel as if I've made a grave error in returning, and I long to take again what now seems my long, futile journey across the sea, the sea of dreams, of wave ripples and Greenland's mountain canyons and the deep blue dolphin splashes that separate my mind, my two "homes."

94

A man who puts his whole life into being able to be with his sons treads a dangerous path. My sons' lives are their own now. Should the reasons to live my own life be dependent on theirs? For now, perhaps, but the hour of my separation from them looms large in my heart. During the tour, when I was at Agnes' house in Edgeton, I couldn't look at all the pictures she had of them on her bookshelves.

I missed them too much. Before waiting for Doc to take me to the Cincinnati airport I would think, What if I crash into the sea of dreams and never see them again? Always on these long journeys of mine, I think of Last Things. But yet it was the longing to see them again that kept me moving forward, through the "business" setbacks and the realization that I would come away with no real financially career-forwarding event or promise under my belt, only the sweet café concerts in the old bars of youth that were more like parties and reunions than real displays of serious music. Still, I felt the goddesses smiled on me and I tried to give them something special. I felt so sad I forgot to call Harriss and invite him to one of the after-gig parties. Seeing Wanda had knocked it out of my mind. I've always been too loony about women. Thinking of him made me realize that some friends—since I left home—have not fared as well as others. Yet Harriss seems happy, happier than other friends who are much better off financially. Several old friends, financially secure after working hard to pay off every kind of insurance you can imagine, exude such military gruffness and irritability that it's difficult to even be around them anymore. Hector comes to mind. Doc is tight-lipped and terse. The breezy comaraderie we shared as boys had disappeared. Alas, some are so focused on the present, their business at hand, our shared past has lost its significance for them or has been relegated to a few fondly, yet rarely, remembered high school jokes.

Maybe that's how it should be. Maybe it's all my egotism. I want them to still remember me, to bring me back to their "present" because I fear I have fallen downward like a leaf to just a memory and might drop another notch in their minds down to oblivion.

95

Dear Josh,

But they have wives—and, now, you don't. Wives change irrevocably the old Three Musketeers silliness and laughable sense of adventure among men. Married men look out upon their old comrades as if from behind glass. They become difficult to approach, un-spontaneous, arrogant. Marriage gives a great feeling of security but it can also stifle creativity. Perhaps I'm wrong but in your case, you seem to have written more in the last 7 years of "unmarriage" than you did in the opposite condition for 10. But IMO you never found the "right" woman. Helen let you be free—at first. The prison walls come down, the inmates inevitably rebel, etc.

Yours,

Doc.

96

Edgeton. Like a pleasant dream, it fades. The heavier air. Autumn wood smoke. Rotting leaves. Rain. Then that chilly bright sunny October day and a walk into town: the copy place to copy some charts for the gig, haircut (enjoyed flirting with the girl barber I had to talk into "just shaving it bald") Tilson's poolroom owned by Crazy Reddy now, I think, the colonial-style square with huge trucks moving through it though there's barely room for them. I've withdrawn. Something's not right. Now back in BP. No gigs. "Back in BP" the sound of the words chases away the Edgeton dream. Once BP was the dream and Edgeton was reality.

But every visit seemed rushed. I wanted to do so many things. You go on a long journey you want something to change. You want to bring back the prize. There just isn't enough TIME. Time. You become an editor. Like time is. You choose this or that engagement, searching for the ecstasy of friendship, sex or a job that pays! Anything that enhances life and makes it bearable. But often I simply slept. Couldn't keep but half my appointments. Crip seemed to give up on me. But I just couldn't go on. The pace was too much. The sun would go down and my energy followed suit. Even too tired to read my Faulkner novel I brought.

Remember the morning I left for Budapest? The September morning I mentioned before? I left my apartment and walked out into the sunny Indian Summer morning. The morning I didn't want to leave, to die to the place I was leaving. I didn't mean all the bad things I said about you, Place. Now I want to embrace you, go to my little room and see once more that same glorious September light pouring through the window of the morning I left, to pretend one of the beautiful Hungarian girls that fill the streets of Budapest was coming to visit me, to make love all day.

97 KRIP

Sitting here in my little room flipping through these notebooks that are really all I have left. I feel a twinge of guilt. I convinced Josh to come here—to be reborn with the rest of us 89ers in a new century! A new nation! A whole untapped ancient culture of gigs! I introduced him to Helen. Some good came out of that—no? You'd never understand dear reader. You would hold me accountable for a bit of typical male promiscuity. Go back to Puritan land. Thinking back to that "Big Amerikan Tour!" It's as if, as I sit here in the little room—I haven't seen anyone, haven't even been to the grocery, for weeks! I'd taken a long draught of America, the last guzzle of Kentucky bourbon, ice cubes lightly melted. The burn radiates from the guts. And spreads over time. And distance. One place mingles with the other. In the middle of the Atlantic Ocean, somewhere high above the dolphin splash, the one dream mingles with the other. America meets in confluence with the Europe I'd left behind—the Big Amerikan tour meets BP bar gigs, Berenice/ Wanda meets Helen/Gudrun. Slowly the waters of Balaton becoming a stronger current. Like the epiphany Josh told me he had once standing in front of the huge ING sign on October 23rd Street in Buda when he suddenly realized he was HERE self-imprisoned again by distance and there was no way back. No way past the flaming sword at the Garden Gate. That sudden feeling of irrevocable loss gaining power in your mind. Back here in BP, Edgeton dreams no longer nourish you. They die in the dry, ferrous air of Budapest.

   All very dramatic. But, now, no joke, the trip fades down to a little flicker of memory. The expansive, real feeling of it fragments into snapshots. I thumb through my camera, a push of the button brings each image, one by one like gravestones, substantial but weightless, without meaning, like an old grocery list you'd found in a book you'd used as a bookmark. You did go to the grocery that day. The date, some forgotten day of your life, is right on the slip of paper. What kind of day must it have been? Sunny. Autumn. Windy. The molding burnt cookie smell of leaves. Josh said that when he stayed at Agnes' after the "tour," every morning he would listen for the scooting sound the bottom of her bedroom door made when she came out in the morning in her bathrobe and slippers. A sound like someone clearing their throat as she hurried into the cold kitchen to light the stove. Another day closer to having to leave his "home" again. He laid in bed for hours, he said, staring at the ceiling, making up little prayers he hadn't thought of since he was a kid. Later, he would hear her calling him, "Woo-oo!" from downstairs. "There's a man from Nashville on the phone! Corman agencies? Says he needs to talk to you."

98 JOSH IN BP

   Fragile light peeping in the window. Alone. Far from home. The few people who know me in this foreign land see me as an outsider. They see only the shadow you cast from your former life—a life they never knew and see now only in the pale, bloodless disembodied thing they imagine that defines you.

99 NOTE FROM LYDIA

(Translated from Hungarian by Krip Kovacs)

If you must know why I traveled so much, I'll tell you. I love being fucked in the ass. Either by a dildo wielded (nice alliteration, that!) by a guy or chick or a cock, it doesn't matter just so it's cute and something going up my ass. But then on other days, it didn't interest me. I wanted to be fucked in the pussy by a real man. I want to sit on his face and wrap my legs around his cute, chiseled, dimpled chin and squeeze until I juice all over him.

Sometimes I went dancing. Sometimes I went off walking alone or stayed alone in the little room he let me have when he was gone, watching CNN (only the English language channel?) watching all the scenes of war just made me hornier. I wanted to balance all that militant imagery with sex! Sex! Don't kill, Fuck! That was my motto, like hippies used to say in America. Why do people kill anyway? Instead of doing more fucking. What are these chicks waiting for? So many guys with no one to fuck. It's sad. So, then, I guess they gotta kill something instead. So I've decided to promote World Peace with my pussy and my ass. PIECE OF ASS BE UNTO ALL MANKIND!"

I can see her walking through the gray streets. "Guess it doesn't work that way," she muttered to herself, loud enough that someone walking by heard it and turned, quizzical of whom might have said it. It was a man who paused for a moment and followed her toward the stoplight crossing. He stared at her body, her legs, her ass. She could feel his eye lingering on her, her tanned feet in sandals. She wanted to lift her t-shirt up slightly to expose her pantie waistband riding up out of her tight cutoff jeans. But she thought, better not encourage him. Annoyed, she walked across on a green light. A car suddenly whipping around the corner of the Korut and Baross St. screeched to a halt. The man who had stared at her was now stranded on the other side. She could hear him cursing through the traffic noise, "Whore!" She heard that distinctly. "He calls ME a whore," she thought to herself, "Somewhere he has a wife and kids and a mistress, maybe 2, and he calls ME the whore!

100 JOSH | DREAM

I'm walking down Plato Street in Medina. I step into a bar. The Tecumseh Grill? (Could that be a connection to Wanda's old workplace that was just across the street?) Suddenly I notice Krip but I realize I have to pee really bad, but instead of peeing in the bathroom I have to go outside and pee somewhere. But as I walk out Krip catches up with me. He seems worried that I tried to avoid him. No, I lie, I just really needed to pee. (The pee issue disappears). We walk together down Plato awhile (Could this be connected to where I always envisioned—and he described the street for me once, the place Krip told me his Uncle Schwartz had had a heart attack?) We are suddenly in a car driving through a lovely residential area, near Ashland, the old Marcellus estate but we must ascend a very steep incline. We stop but I worry the car might slip out of park and roll down the hill. Krip leaves. I then get lost in a maze of streets—like the Roma quarter in BP? A recurring dream I often have driving, driving, fear of never finding my way.

101

Day after Krip's Thanksgiving Party for all us expat orphans. I walked through the silent wee hours of early morning BP streets. My head was filled with vivid images of all the beautiful women at the party. I tried not to think about it. I walked through the beautiful empty canyons of worn-smooth, gray, soot-laced stone buildings, block after block down Kiraly St., passing an occasional cab, ignoring the cabbie beckoning me from inside, a student passing by, a street tough startled me as he stopped beside me—he only wanted a light—and then a pretty girl, nervous in the emptiness, trying to avoid eye contact, keeping her eyes on the sidewalk. The contrast of the Magyar beauty—her florid skin tone and astonishing hair and perfect clothes, walking among the somber buildings at such a late hour—a common site in Europe, but rarely seen in America, is a strong one. It takes hold of your attention. Like a rose blooming over a gray wasteland that nature has abandoned to stone and mechanical metal things. Yet, it is inappropriate to speak to them at this hour. Further down, on the boulevard (korut) the few prostitutes still out, in louder clothing, their toad-like pimp never far away in the shadows, are just as beautiful. But as Doc told me Dante said, the yearning for a woman's love becomes in time, the very soul's yearning.

It occurs to me that I've been living in tiny rooms, all full of books and guitars, for years now. Over 20, in fact. I think back to when I was around 10 years old when I decided to move into my 8 foot long closet. I can't forget its yellow sliding doors. They were forever coming off their rails, partly fastened by a magnet. I used my footlocker as a table, found a small chair and a lamp. Always a need to seclude myself. Bertha was like that. She spent so much time alone. Perhaps that's where I got it. Fate decreed it for her. Her husband died when she was thirty. Agnes spent the post-marriage part of her life alone, too. I set the lamp on the foot locker. I was setting up a miniature "study," a child's version of my parents' study. The lamp shining in the darkness, the way a light shone in the hermit's cottage, a beacon lighting the lonely traveler's way in the dark snowy woods. The time would come when I would brood in apartments and student ghettos in the same way. Years go by. I think of all those nights after concerts in Medina when I would stare at my reflection in my window in front of a small writing desk, (whatever happened to that desk?) out into the snowy night and I was safe and warm in my room—just like the warmth of the little closet room I made. Somehow, though, after setting all those things up in my closet I grew bored with my tiny retreat. My childhood room I shared with Doc suddenly became smaller. I didn't notice I'd grown. The chest of drawers beside the bed, a bed covered in one of Bertha's wine red crazy quilts, just to the right of the window that looked out toward the lake down the snowy hill, was room enough to hide my secret life: love letters from Lilian, ticket stubs, bumper stickers, diaries, even checkbooks. So I was a child and a man in the same place. 14 years. From 6 to 20 I lived here. The longest place I ever lived in one stretch. Of all my many places I layed my head down on a pillow, the Edgeton Rd house on the southwest side of Water Maple Farm was always the place I called home.

I keep coming back to that pretty September morning when, as I was getting ready to go to the airport and fly to America, I had such a vision of the beauty of ALL THINGS. I thought of how golden the sunlight was—like the first turning of the vineyard leaves in Balaton. The girls of Buda strode by among the shopkeepers hawking their wares, cars going by, the crisp autumn air.

And yet the intensity of that vision fades. And yet it persists in my mind, pressing its "Eternity" upon me. As if to say, there was One Yellow Morning and it never passes away. And so I carry that moment with me to the end—magical, sorrowfully beautiful in its passing, yet as if it had happened yesterday and not all those years ago, an event out of time.

102 KRIP | FRAGMENTS

Every morning the weak dawn light crept through the light green curtains beside his bed. His eyes would open and he would stare into the room and its fragile coming-to-life almost before his eyes. It seemed like only moments before he had put down his book, switched off the light and gone to bed. But as he searched for the clock face on the bookshelf he saw that it was 8 am. A full 10 hours he'd slept! It was time to face another day. But he closed his eyes, rolled over, snuggled into the covers and began a silent prayer: O Lord, have mercy on my soul, he said softly, And Mother Mary please come down and show me a sign. Guide my steps. Bring me someone to love.

His prayers amused him and he chuckled to himself. He added a few Our Fathers, the rhythm of which, for him, cushioned the blow of the coming day. He liked the part about forgive us our trespasses, as we forgive those who trespass against us. As he stared up at the ceiling he began to think. Always this last reverie before becoming fully awake: old friends in America, sad beautiful lost loves, and losing touch, men he'd loved who stood by him—would he stand by them?—and then how time had caused everything to fade. He would get on a plane and travel back to that world but so much had changed there. Many old friends had moved away. The ones left were glad to see him but there was less of the ecstatic joy of unlimited time to wander through cities and down country backroads, making up an autobiographical movie of each of themselves and playing it out.

103 DOC

"Change is the visual manifestation or objective reality of Finitude. We can see change. 'The leaves that are green, turn to brown'. But the infinite does not change. We cannot see the infinite. It is somehow hidden from us."

104 JOSH

Ah, the sheer joy of Christmas! The empty streets of Buda at 3:30 am Christmas Morning. Emptier than they have ever been! Krip's party. How many years? So many. How many are left? The huge snow and bitter cold. Suddenly it became warmer and rainy and foggy. A mist envelopes the whole city, a mist of oily poison gas falling like dew. Greasy on the windshield. My powers are diminishing? I'm afraid I'm actually becoming poor after years of playing at it. Now it's no game. Poverty seems very real. Yet, I am free to do what I want. Until the police come, of course. Yet there's something giddy about being poised to fly through the air on a trapeze—knowing there's no longer a net.

How fast Christmas passes! How fast everything passes! I thought of all the years I had waited for a Hungarian friend to come to my childhood home in Edgeton and share all those images of my past life with me. (Remember when Yolanda and Wanda came to play with me at the Edgeton Rd house? We taught little Wanda how to play monopoly?) Walking through your past life with a friend from your life NOW! What a fantasy come true! And yet, in the end, I only realized how empty and uninteresting my old life was to someone else. It was only my mother's house, her basement with a smattering of mementos in boxes wreathed in spider's web. Beautiful Water Maple Avenue. The true center of childhood. Nothing more than my memories, that endless parade of images, invisible to anyone else. And then, so suddenly, the visit had ended. I found myself in an uneventful Fall with the same money worries. And then so soon it was Christmas evening fading. I had thought, Now someone will understand my life and what it's been. But it's all going by so fast, doors closing, plates on tables gathered up and washed, tv shows murmuring in the background, clouds passing overhead, stars rising, falling. Your life is fragments no one else can fit together.

You don't believe childhood passes—but it does. In the same way, Mother Nature hides our own Death from us as craftily as a parent hiding Christmas gifts. But I knew it. I've always known it. But she sprinkled forgetfulness on my brow and only slowly did the solemn image form and I remembered.

And so I walked out into the European night—the moon's face hung so full of sorrow, and Orion hanging like the jangling light bulbs strung across a carnival ride with no one to meet, no one to speak to, only a beer and a shot, where lost souls sit beneath the benediction of a talk show, the inside jokes kept secret from us.

One wanders the empty street alone, undefined, left off the hook by star or moon. In the gas station, stalling for time, he examines things for cars: air freshers, oil, WD-forty; or Lays potato chips, a pack of condoms, a milky way, and spearmint gum.

The blood river flows by, the oldest color of blood, silver as moonlight, but he keeps to the street, mimic of moon and river, the young Diana abandoning her lamb lover, darting her deadly eyes your way, as if to say, "Enter my little finite paradise," or maybe, "My boyfriend is gonna kick your ass." But it sounds the same and so there's no way to know for sure which she wants. She forced down a jaeger and sent the crippled boy on his way. You, some second-rate Ionian, (Johnian, Ioanninan) watched it all. Where is it now? you say as you walk out into the empty street again, with its salt sheen, frozen (illegible) chalk. "Fuck 'em all!" someone cries (in Hungarian). She will not come to take you on your journey or await your return as she masturbates in the silvery tv light while her foot boy licks like a tame rabbit. Tomorrow night a new face. Or just now across the room, a couple making out. She heaps up her possessions, he examines them and tosses them aside. The competitive couple: whoever stays sexually attractive to the other, the longest—wins. And the other gets to be a martyr instead of villain.

105 KRIP

He could hear her having a petite orgasm in the next room. He was instantly hard the minute he realized what it was. Then, after he had masturbated, in the gloomy aftermath, he felt like he should leave. She didn't care. He could come and go (no pun) as he pleased. She liked that he shared the bills. If he moved out it meant his expenses would also increase and he'd have to pay more to keep his head above water and there would beless for her. He tried putting the pillow to his head, but still, he heard the faint thumping and moans off into the distance. He decided to get dressed and go out into the street. It was bitter cold and the wind was howling and blowing the snow around.

"Gudrun said, 'Musicians are the best lovers but they have no money and they never stay faithful.'"

106 JOSH

Wrote a letter to ___ (illegible). Waited on Gudrun. We didn't meet. Nem megyek, aszt mondta. My sinus headache dissipated. It had felt like my eyeballs were being pushed out of my skull. Then, I couldn't help seeing all my past failures lining up like the vid I saw of Ceucescu and his wife being executed in '89. Probably triggered by Gudrun standing me up. I have doubts about getting back together with her, but when it feels like she's leaving again I feel bad. Somebody yr not that turned on by anymore is better than no one, or is it? Maybe the thing is to just get stronger in your loneliness. Besides, the red-haired babe might be coming into the picture. Go out there and drum up some life, boy! Quit this wistful scribbling. So what if life doesn't respond like it used to. It used to give you freebies—now it don't. So, don't need freebies no more. I can pay my own way like the next guy. But what if I can't. Afraid to embark on another project. They never go anywhere! Dead in the water. Tired. Almost wanting Death sometimes. Then I think of my sons and I am afraid. What if something happened to Helen? Who could they turn to? No sleeping yet old boy! Go out there and show 'em!

And then my reveries. The pictures of the Great Past when Water Maple Street and Tranquility Pike were the scene of life's greatest moments. But when Judge Daddy ("It was only the biggest funeral in the fucking state" Jared Smallwood had yelled when he called me in Budapest) and Millicent died it seemed so unreal to me—I was so far away. Things changed after that. The Old Story ended.

107 DOC

Yes, of course, you are disappointed that there's no one to share the raising of your children with. It's a shock to see that no one else cares about your children that much. "Nobody knows but Jesus", eh? No one, no mortal man can share your joy or understand your sorrow. But there's a richer a pattern with you. Love soon becomes dependency. You make a foundation of the girl you love but you build no house upon it. Only a stone staircase leading up and down to nowhere.

Some people feel "put upon" by life, by their fate. They feel like life owes them a favor, while they themselves feel no indebtedness toward life, toward others. In my time in Hungary with you I felt as if people there felt put upon as a nation. Because they had been mistreated—and how they were mistreated! they needn't make a sacrifice to the rest of the world. On the contrary, they, the ones I chatted with at Krip's parties, seemed to feel that a sacrifice was owed to them. In richer, luckier nations there is sometimes a "desire to help." They want to share, out of guilt perhaps, their good fortune. The poor on the other hand want to make that good fortune their own. And if they could only achieve it, they reason, they would guard it jealously. Poverty doesn't ennoble so much as it creates small-mindedness. Read Shaw. About your woman problems: when one lover poisons another by neglect, the neglected lover, in anger, passes that poison onto another lover. We often imitate the lover who wronged us when we move on to another love. The survivor of abuse often imitates the abuser. I remember Gudrun. Exquisitely beautiful. That was the night she showed up at your gig in Balaton with that cute drunken brunette in tow. Andrea? Alice? It's the sudden pierce of the green-eyed goddess, the steady stare of grey-eyed Athena, the womanly patience of Penelope—all this in a brief glance, a heartbeat. You've always been a sucker for chicks like that. Remember this?

"So sweet, once,

The fruit now stuck in my throat"

108 JOSH

It's a bitter, wet cold in the streets. But the snow is lovely. It covers everything and rounds the sharp, metallic edges of the city. And then the temperature peeks over the freezing mark and it's gone. The sun turns it into gray droplets that well-up around the curbs. A mud/salt-encrusted bus splashes the mud/snow on an angry pedestrian.

Doc says we're alone. No woman can complete your life or steer you through it. The "couple" is a social construct, he says.

Now I live in this little apartment. I have a lot of time it seems just to think. I lay on the bed and smoke and think a lot. Mostly about the past. Sometimes I try to think up ways to make money in the present, some scheme. I have to. Well, I don't have to. I cd die. Just lay here until my energy ran out, like leaving a car running. Sometimes it seems like a good idea since nothing seems to come of anything. I mean, the schemes rarely work. But the thought that I cd feel myself dying, that's too scary. I wd like it better if it just ended quickly without my knowing anything. Just laying here letting life go out, that wdnt be easy. It wd take too long. You have too much time to think about it. It wd be like those crazy political extremists who go on hunger strikes. That always seemed childish to me, like a kid who threatens to hold his breath in front of his parents until they get scared of him being blue in the face and give into his demands.

I don't like to go outside anymore. The light is very gray and weak. Even in summer.

I met The Woman Who Gives Me Money. She thinks I am important. As an artist? She says, Yes. That's how I buy food. Sometimes she wd rather just take me to the store and buy food, instead of giving me the cash. She wants me to have food. She's not sure what I use the money she gives me for. There's something about me tho I guess she likes. She's a nice woman. I think about what wd happen sometime if she stopped giving me money, the "energy going out" scenario comes to mind but I doubt she'll stop anytime soon. I can keep things under wraps. The Woman Who Gives Me Money says she likes it that way. I'm getting old. I used to never chase girls when I was young, or cheat on them, but now way past forty I find it's the only thing I'm not too bad at. I found out that people are interested in 2 things: getting money and having sex. All the egoism in between can be boiled down to this, i.e. if a guy wants to tell his life story it's because he thinks by getting it out there in front of people, he might find that sex partner (and yes, love can develope from sex—I'm not heartless) or maybe find someone who wants to hire him for something and he can get some money, probably to get sex (or "love") with. Or else just to keep a nice warm apartment around him so he can whack off when he wants and get rid of the whole mating urge, at least for an hour or so. As long as there's a furnace on, loneliness can be kept at bay. When it gets so cold the furnace breaks down, then you got a problem. At least until spring, then everything returns. Energy doesn't just go out. Energy starts coming back in. Then it might be nice to take a stroll in the park. Even treat yourself to a 2 dollar Turkish sandwich. But then you remember you should eat the rest of the rice you cooked and save the cash to put on the heating bill.

I can't let too much life energy go out. I have to think of the children.

I think about the past a lot. I fantasize about it. Maybe I can explain why at some point. If I keep thinking maybe it will come to me. This morning I was remembering her beautiful back. And when she reached her arms out across the bed how the muscles around her shoulder blades rippled in gentle curves and shadows, how the shadows the deep muscular groove made down her spine funneled to her ass. Watching the waves of her body as I pushed against her. Her breasts gently swaying.

Sex is like a drug. All that pushing and yearning that you open up in yrself just goes down into yr nerves and the memory mechanisms in yr brain. Yr body keeps thinking of how euphoric and perfect those moments of ecstasy are. It wants to go back to that place. Then, one day an angel of the Lord is standing at the gate barring your entry. Eve is gone somewhere. Maybe she'll come back but not for a long time. But you don't believe it. So, you go looking for her. She has many disguises. Most of them you give to her yrself.

109

There's only one thing and one thing only, love. Walking down Temple St. my mind is full of images of the past. There's where Dragan smashed my guitar and pushed Helen over into a pile of trash. So long ago now. Suddenly the years come rushing in with a cold March wind. Memory tenacious as Winter yet silvered in the lack of sun, shadowy, sooty canyons of buildings and the boulevard at the end, seen far beyond as if through the wrong end of a telescope.

Nothing's changed. Except some of the buildings are re-painted. The palimpsest of memory still underneath. For so many years that loneliness of a man needing a woman. Once, there was the face of Helen always before me, leading me home, yet, still, the promise left unfulfilled. And as the days and the rain eat away this City of Time in the gray nothingness of Europe, there stands Love, all that's left. That which is eternally unpossessed. Always the figure of a woman leading, guiding my steps through the beatific streets, the granite heaven slowly decaying into night. The hoopla of Blaha Lujza Square opens to let the sunlight yellow tram snake it in two.

110 DOC

Hey Krip—Yes, God may be the Keeper of the Sacred but woman is the Keeper of the Sexual. Although Woman is vulnerable because of her current inferior physical strength, nevertheless she controls sex. She gives her consent and heaven opens. (Sex without her consent is not "real" sex, it's rape, or prostitution at best. Yet if Man were the Keeper of Sex he would inevitably defile it through his greed—no?

Faith is a manifestation of the Species' Memory of the End of Time. Faith and Poetry sensed (as in Dante's time and before) that the "things of this world would forever pass away" before Science proved it so. We, mankind, have always known intuitively that our planet and so we ourselves would eventually die. This is the Source of Tragedy and Science now concurs with this.

111 JOSH

I guess all I can do is record my wanderings through this city. Now I have no one to answer to. No one can shame me. So, I shamelessly go about doing whatever I want. I want a woman but what one woman could ever satisfy my all-consuming desire for flesh. I feel so much sympathy, sentiment, compassion for my fellow humans to be this lustful. Where does it come from? My desire to satisfy someone else's lust?

The idea that I can drive someone to ecstasy is what turns me on? The idea that my love-making is a gift to someone—is this what spurs me?

112 DOC

…Or these wild females that drive you to distraction—don't you just want to tame them like the guy who used to come out to the farm and "break" the horses? At first, you are like Yeats' Byzantine bird in the cage, someone's slave (*see Josh's poem*), your obedience affording some young girl a moment's pleasure. Then, you see that you were their beggar, and suddenly you are their master. You stare at every woman that passes by hoping for some signal of attention that never comes. Girls are capable of the intensity of male lust, yet they are more disciplined. Girls never lose control, ok, rarely. Girls never rape. They never allow their attraction to dominate them. Unless they fall in love. Then they are like a she-bear with her cubs. Woe to what comes between them. Nothing can stop her love. And nothing can make her love again a lover she has once spurned—unless she just wants to. Love is her domain she allows a man into. Sex is a way of securing that love once he becomes a citizen in her country of love. But like me, now, in your emails, you are sounding like a mathematician of sex as you walk the lonely streets, the foreigner——the colonialist, even!—trying to subjugate the local women with little success. You came to the Country of the Weak with your American dollars. You and Crip bought dinners, cab rides and prostitutes like the crazed ambassador of a banana republic or like that Russian ambassador driving around drunk with diplomatic immunity!

You've had to answer to no one but yourself. Now it's time for that answer.

113 JOSH ON WATER MAPLE FARM | KRIP

The boy walks across the meadow into a shady grove of trees. They form a ring around a hollowed-out place in the side of the hill, round as a womb. Round as a bird's nest. Small outcroppings of limestone rock shelve in layers among the rounded walls. A small still pond sits motionless below the hill—a few giant sycamores motionless in the mirror of its surface. At the top of the hill, just above the limestone, there stands the tree. It's not a very impressive tree. Of medium height it's perhaps a young wild cherry tree, or is it a hackberry? The bark and the leaves are too young to tell for sure. Marshall or Sylves would know. Bertha is probably in her house down the hill beyond the feed barn, sewing her quilts.

There is a thick vine wrapped around the young tree, wooden but snake-like, flexible, and little Josh pulls on it to test its strength. It seems strong enough to hold his weight. He starts to climb up, gripping it with the inside of his thighs. The vine sways slightly away from the tree even with his young, lightweight. Josh looks down at the ground some twenty feet below now and feels a giddiness in his stomach. The bark rubs against the inside of his thighs. He feels an ecstasy in his thigh muscles. To increase the intensity of it he can loosen and tighten his grip by turns. He looks out over the rolling hills of Water Maple Farm. Small tobacco plants with perfect leaves sit in rows, stalks of purple bluegrass wave in the breeze and cattle drink at the edge of the pond and sit in the cool shade flicking flies with their tails. He grips the vine harder, sees the finger-like tendrils of the end of the vines grip upon the tree. He knows he can't pull too hard or it might detach from the tree trunk. Easing down the vine to the ground he feels a wetness between his legs.

114 DOC

I feel like I must write to you about my feelings in regard to Josh's death. I remembered Lenny Bruce's thing where he said there were 4 stages of grief: shock, denial, anger and acceptance. I've felt them all simultaneously or separately in no particular order. You tell me the funeral will be in a week. I dread it. I don't want to think of how much I depended on Josh. I know only too well how a sudden feeling of irrevocable loss and despair can swoop down out of the afternoon sky without warning, bringing with it the certainty that no one can change the consequences his death will have on me and many others. And the sea of humanity I blend into on the street knows nothing about him. I look at people's eyes as they pass me by and think, Don't you realize he's dead? How can you just go on as if nothing happened? So. The silence is unbearable. To have lived to see the end of someone's life, a man I knew so well and truly loved, lived to see his end. Another person's death is like the end of a cosmos of knowing, only the stilled, memories remain like the remnants of a burned out house. The silence is unbearable. I can't look straight into it. I must avert my eyes. Just as no one can look at God, just as Dante couldn't look into Beatrice's eyes. And those souls who passed away from Earth are now part of that world that blinds earthly eyes. He made it to the other side. Toward the end, when they discovered the tumors and I came to be with him, he feared death. He felt ominous feelings he said walking down Temple St. for his doctor's appointments at the Szabolcs street hospital. You could feel the hatred from the shopkeepers. But soon he recovered his poise. He tried to keep friends and family around him, and music. I wonder how he survived. Did he weep for the life slipping away? Sometimes he got angry with me. I would live and he would die. But that passed. 'Not doing well,' he said over the phone. I started becoming fearful of talking to him. I thought I was annoying him with my own problems. But then he thanked me vigorously in that warm voice of his. Shamefully, as his condition improved, I began to forget him, so drunk and stoned out and absent-minded I became. I thought, He's got a few more years at least.

Then came a better death. Quick. If only I could have spoken to him one more time! No need to pick up the phone now. No one to talk to. So many inside jokes. No one will hear.

My prayer won't protect me from death. I hurt so many people and said bad things. Now he is gone. The wide Wheel's pattern we can't be sure of. And so, over and over I'm left to say, Mary, mother of the Word, the World, All Things I've seen and felt, guide my steps.

Best wishes,

Doc

DOC'S ADVICE TO JOSH'S SONS

"A woman, naked to the waist, once said to me, in between passionate kisses and while denying me access to her sublime lower regions, "I, being poor, have only one gift to give a man—my sex—so it is something I save for special occasions. I hardly know you. For a moment I was ready to give you not only my breasts, which you have rather skillfully, though a bit roughly, sucked, licked, and caressed, Sir; yet, now, when I think of the value I place upon my "prize," I think it prudent for the moment to refuse you."

This conversation comes back to me in my old age, one of the most enlightening of my life. More than any other it has given me insight into how women are different than men. And so, my "sons," may you consider that, yes, a woman has the same passionate drives as a man, yet "society" in its perpetually unfair way, prevails upon her to abhor promiscuity, for reasons men ignore, and at least maintain a chaste demeanor in front of the public. What she does in secret only God knows. Men are not let in on everything.

Know, my sons, that a woman's desires are equal to your own. But that doesn't mean she'll free of charge go tumbling into bed with you at the drop of a hat. Oh, no. The fear of being branded a whore, which might affect her possible long-term plan of settling down with a nice boy, is much too great—and the value she places upon her "prize" much too high. Someday women will not fear such societal pressures, rooted as they are in an inevitably dying religion's ideals of chastity, and the ills of thousands of years of male domination. No, someday women might rule the World again as they did in the mists of mythic Time. For the time being, though, respect their position. You just might win a prize. Yours as ever, Uncle Albert.

115 JOSH'S MOTHER

(Agnes Remembered)

The world seems the same everywhere at dawn. The same revving up of the traffic, either the big boulevards of Budapest with the small ant-like cars or the quiet idyllic morning streets of Edgeton startled by tank-like American cars and trucks suddenly hurling down them like a fat bumblebee whizzing by your ear in a field in bloom Josh remembers wandering through as a kid.

Everyone is inside themselves, whether in their warm bed or out on the street or in their car, waiting for death, the inevitable quick lunch, work, the afternoon, the tragedy of evening. The lunar sterility of the dead of night. And then that first eternal birdsong once again. Hopelessness drifts down like dust, covering everything except a tiny thumbprint. Josh's pen is like a flare.

Agnes is the most pitiable. But she doesn't ever see herself that way. Syles said, Some people hate life and they want you to hate it with them. Agnes smiles among the guests, but she's waiting for the inevitable moment when someone among her will test their wings and try to fly, at which point she will shoot them down with the arrows of her laughter, her mocking incredulity. She especially waits for the man, like her father, who will say he adores her, but who then ignores her and doesn't make good on his promise of eternal adoration. He's just a man, after, all, enslaved by his lusts, but she will take no pity on him, nor forgive him. There are other things, other desires, other women, perhaps. Let him go to them—their sparkling eyes and flushed cheeks. But leave her alone, she demands. Leave her alone in her mansion on Water Maple Street. The huge drafty rooms, the tiny fire in the fireplace, will dispel the awful memories of irresponsible men and their false promises.

Now she will reject all suitors, all love, even the love of her children, Doc, Josh, Angelica. It's not enough—this love—in the world. Even the love of the God she no longer believes in: the God of Fr Hozni, the little St.Jude chapel, fills her with hate. She wishes the dark disappointments of life upon her husband, her old lovers, her children until she knows that everyone has paid what she has paid in bitter tears and pain and dawn's tedious turmoil. She gets no satisfaction from this. She smiles wanly among her friends at the cocktail party. For now, she thinks, they have paid, though in their ineffective ways, paid for her presence here—her brief presence—until she can get back to 10 Water Maple Court and shut the door and be done with it all. Those same vodka-breathed discussions with middle-aged failures about the projects they plan to initiate, their dreams of wealth! The laughter and giggling stampedes of grandchildren, young mothers in summer, the lovely arms of young women holding the sweating glasses of cocktails, a frail gold chain around their slightly tanned, pink necks, the green southern evenings fading away in roseate sunsets out a kitchen window marked with swallows' flight or squirrels' leap into the tangle of trees, the female cardinal among the tiny forsythia blooms. On all this, she closes the door and sleeps a dreamless sleep.

116 JOSH

Sometimes as I rode along the Danube on Tram 18, the buildings looked like a jagged smile, in the jumble of spaces and facades. Smile, tooth, missing tooth—this was what the wars had done to the face of the riverfront. (I could see across to where Agnes had met me when she came to visit. Even now something cries out deep down: Time, don't take my mother away! She was wearing something yellow wasn't she—like the breasts of the meadowlarks in summer fields of Water Maple Farm). It seemed like death when I stared at the buildings and the gaps between them, knowing they were something distant and yet part of me. The City of My Sons—and yet Something Northern and Gothic. The great gaudy Gothic-ness of it all! I'd never seen a frozen river until I came here. Time stops. The foggy silver of air and breath turns to stone. The women here are too strong to need a man like me. I knew every day for the 20 years I lived here that someday I might return to my old life in Edgeton. Everything breaks up into fragments. Does that free us?

117 QUICK TRIP HOME

(American winter gigs)

Dear Mr. Celeste,

We can only pay a small concert fee and does not include hotel.

Best, Richard "Dick" Gozinia

Hector Sword Agencies.

It's snowing out Mom's upstairs bedroom. When I was young this was her bedroom. Now, unable to walk up the stairs, she sleeps downstairs in the old dining room, which Ricky Boy came and converted into a bedroom for her. I wake up looking out what was once her window. Through the snow swirling like mad, I can make out the intricate tangle of black tree limbs, like baroque cursive script, so dense it's unreadable. It seems like I will always come back to this room. Will my sons and their children think of me once sleeping here, staying with my mother during a snowstorm?

The snow covers all memory—good, bad—with a white watery ice that changes everything.

118 KRIP

Dear Doc,

Not sure how long I can hold out. After Josh, the interest in my gigs has dropped off. Helen and I seemed happy. It's too bad in a way that now we're on the rocks. After she broke up with Dragan again, I anticipated the time when sexual relations would be restored, haha. That time never came. It seems so long ago when she made that remark—what was it?—"You can't expect me to go running back into your arms". Other women on the road are the ones just under the threshold of attraction. It's The Equation !. Everyone wants a body to make love to that's usually just out of their reach. But the person we get is seldom "all we ever wanted." Helen was. Then she put herself off-limits. She won't even let me touch her now.

119 JOSH

Dream: Doc and I are in a car (he's driving) we're somewhere that feels like University Drive in Medina. We're near a tall set of buildings. They look a bit like the ones on Temple Street in Budapest. I suggest listening to Caywood Ledford announcing the Kentucky basketball game on the radio. But the reception is bad. Some great emotional pleasure seems to lurk in the background. We stop at an outdoor café. Jared and Carlo are taking a dish of ice cream and doing goofy things with it. I put my face in it, licking the melted ice cream and chocolate sauce, etc. lapping it up like a cat. Then I let huge gobs of it trickle out of my mouth, simulating severe drunken vomiting, (or am I swallowing semen?). Everyone laughs hysterically at my goofy mimicry, as I put the ice cream dish on my head. Then, I'm coming home from a tour. I walk through the first door of our apartment into the foyer. I can see Ryly and Gordon through the next glass-paneled door cheering my arrival. I seem to feel their same ecstasy over my return. I'm holding the packages of silly putty I promised them.

I woke up thinking that the apprehension of Truth that comes with age is only beneficial to the "inner life," not the external one. The wise man, the Master of the external world, the politician, the merchant, has only power—not Truth. The Poet, the holy man, has an internal knowledge of a spiritual truth. He has experienced internally a Revelation, a glimmer of Enlightenment, but has no Power to implement this knowledge in the external world, except perhaps to say a prayer, alone or among others, a communication and creation for its own sake.

DREAM

Helen crouches naked in the yard (Judge Daddy's house?) around some bushes. Suddenly, I know she's been unfaithful. Her lover approaches, a tall guy with an amputated leg. I'm sitting in a parked car with the door open and window down. It seems like summer. He hops toward the car with an air of cockiness, smiling. Helen is now Gudrun. He says something I don't remember—not malevolently. I feel somehow sarcastically contemptuous of him in a half-friendly way and ask him for a cigarette. He tries to give me a light but his face, like the wizard of Oz, turns into flame.

120 MARSHALL

After the whiskey still blew up I remember Bertha on the ground bleeding from where Dexter had hit her in the mouth. Money Joe and Cassandra from the Demeter's house in town were kneeling beside her as she comes to. Me and little Sylves at the time standing there. "Ish you awright, Miss Berfa? Ish you…" "Where's Dexter?" Bertha said, her blacked eye darting. "Uh, Miss Bertha", Cassandra then said, "I believe Mr. Dex has hit his head". Then I hear somebody shout, "Cotton, you get away from that whiskey, fo' I whip yo' fanny. Don't be callin' the law. These white motherfuckers ain't about nuthin'" And then, I heard,

"I likes my women, like that old geetar—big and fat!" Someone shouted, "Hey Joe why you wear old tri delta sweatshirt with 3 triangles on it?" He said, "That's how many people suck my dick! Shut up bitch!" Somebody said, "I been down so far, you know, when the Highway to Hell ends and then peters out into a kinda gravelly little road—I been down that, too!"

121

Hello Mr. Kovacs,

I commend your idea about writing a book about your friend. If you sincerely think it will assuage your recurrent feelings of guilt, then, yes, I think you should do it. I will be on holiday in Switzerland for the next two weeks. We will continue our sessions as usual after that. I will contact you on my return.

Best wishes,

Dr. Cross

122 JOSH

Balaton has never looked more beautiful to me. In the light of a May afternoon, clear, ceramic sky, she seemed so aqua and gently misted. We got lost on our way to Udine, not realizing the road to Redic ran to Kormend and the Austrian border in the opposite direction. We circled around lost between Sopron and Szombathely. But it was as beautiful as a Grecian vista of mountain and sea. The green somehow reminded me of Water Maple Farm even though it's such a different landscape. I daydreamed and gazed out over the water.

123 DOC

No one is irresistible. Allure is a thinly veiled desire for power. And one tends to want to make it absolute. One wants to become so attractive that one's partner or the attracted person becomes irrational, submissive and therefore able to be manipulated, corrupted, etc. One party maintains their rationality. Most rejections are not about looks but the result of a relationship being seen, by the dominant member, as impractical. An older man wants to be attractive, even irresistible to a young woman, but she might see a relationship with him as, not repulsive or un-erotic, but simply impractical and so to be avoided. But the rejected lover might feel that he is physically unattractive when it was merely a case of utility.

124 JOSH

Italian tour: There's no solitude quite as deep as a hotel room. This magnificent view from my room at the Lido Palace Hotel in Baveno! Yet when I wake I'm in a sweat thinking of my mortality. The phone rings and I hear Agnes and Angelica. Even as we laugh I think of the whole Celeste family story, the old farm, all of it gone. Ryly and Gordon left to carry the seed, English not even their native language. Time nurtures, then harvests. Everything swept away. Everything crowding in the dark. Embrace Death! Embrace Death! I keep saying to myself. Beneath the joy of their voices, beneath the beauty of the dark blue water of Lake Maggiore, lies such an aching nostalgia for what once was and the uncertainty of what will be! As if I wanted to somehow stop reality. It's enough! I've drifted too far from my home. I want to go back! Repair every failure. Put joy and peace of mind where all the pain and home's disintegration and rage and loss has been. But there's no going back. Like tears in the rain, it all fades into the Irrevocable. Where is love? Where is Youth?

Izola Bella notes:

Palace on island across from my hotel. "Christ and the Canaanite Woman by Annibale Caracci (1560-1609). Portrait of Charles Borromeo by Branchi. Borromeo family escaped the Plague. 2 statues of Venus by Pompeo Marchesi, 1789-1858. In the next room, Mussolini sat with the French at the table trying to work out a Compromise. (Does the tour guide seem to sympathize with Mussolini about the difficulty? She frowns at the Brit tourist who quips, "Guess we all know how that turned out")? The Conference at Stresa April, 1935. "The table cloth is damask, chairs covered with antique Genovese velvet. Napoleon rested here in 1797. Luca Giordano, court painter, 1632-1705). Hebe, Goddess of Youth by Gaetano Monti (18th century). Margherita Medici married Count Gilberto II Borremeo in 1529, sister of Pope Pius IV and Giangiacomodei Medici (a famous man–at- arms). The Unicorn was a symbol of the Borromeo family. Room of unicorn tapestries.

125 IDEA FOR A SCREENPLAY ENDING | KRIP

An aging expatriate man recalls events of his life while daydreaming and riding on the #2 Tram in Budapest. After a series of flashbacks, which include scenes of his childhood in America and also the childhood scenes of his future wife in Budapest, he recalls his loves, failures, his children growing up. At the last station the camera eye, which had floated over the city, focuses back in on the tram and we see that other passengers attending the old man, while others ignore him, who has fallen down. At the end, he lifts his fading eyes weakly into the eyes of a kind stranger, a young woman, who lifts his head slightly so he can speak. He smiles at her and whispers, "Beautiful, beautiful." The concerned passengers stay around the expiring body as unconcerned passengers de-board into the busy city streets. Tears appear in the young girl's eyes. The camera lifts over the city, a hive of activity. The now small cluster around the old man grows smaller and smaller as the camera lifts and floats away. Pigeons swoop past, we see the Danube and its bridges far below. THE END.

126

Dear Crip,

The thing you must know is that Helen got what she wanted, at which point she couldn't think of a good reason to keep him around. He became, like you, obsolete. You both became paralyzed in a dysfunctional mode, waiting for her love to return. You couldn't move forward until you could regain the secure ground of her returned love. That never happened. The years of stagnation and anticipation take their toll. As ever, Doc

127 JOSH

Nov. 24

Today was the first snow. I see now that one of the benefits (curses?) of writing lyrics is that it makes you see things around you more sharply, more truly (?) to make a better line. Editing, revising is simply seeing, seeing. The more you look at something, the more meaning it acquires. As if, in order to focus, and get to work, the Mind need only a smack upside the head. The mind sees into things the longer it stares. Illusion sloughs off and the thing comes forward. And then fatigue, illusion's ally, regains its lost ground and insight is covered over in scattered detail. Snow sprinkles down over everything. The snow melts as soon as it touches the black street. Buses, trams burst through its flurried curtain, ornamental trees cauliflowered with dust of snow. One snow-covered bough curves upward like an ancient mountain pass. Imagine the weary miniature caravan trudging up the limb toward the apartment window. Icicles on a drain pipe, a trick of the snow. The sun drips down, reflection in the wet cloth on the café table.

128 DOC

Extreme conditions, for example, the atmosphere of '89 in east Europe, create extreme liaisons. (His meeting Helen). Beauty and the times overrode his sense of propriety. It was a difficult match. But you must remember that they were carried along on a current of events stronger than they were. But Beauty came of it.

129 JOSH

The Ecstasies of Christmas!!!

Playing monopoly with Ryly and Gordon on the rug, just like Doc and I used to play, suddenly the Cardinal on the wall clock chirped like a real cardinal. Gordon said it's a "sampled" Cardinal chirp, Papa. Mama ordered it from Amazon. Ah, I remembered the cardinal that used to flit up and down Agnes' fence row. A vein of blood flowing through air. The forsythia around tthe house had been gold as saffron oil.

130 DOC

Your Hungarians are getting used to an "every man for himself" sort of atmosphere, now that the implacable authority of the Communist Regime is gone. That's why they couldn't work together. It explains why they are so critical of each other as well as foreigners. "Intractable" was the word Magris used. I even spoke with him about it at the conference. Once the harmonious union of mother and child is broken, the erotic becomes the only alternative for regaining this lost paradise. Yet it always equals something less than the original bliss of Mother/child. Sexual satisfaction, though intense and strong over a brief period, fades away more quickly than the bliss of infancy and early childhood. Hence the attraction of the Quest. Improvising jazz is sexual. The improviser plays over the body of the song. He intrudes upon its melody to enhance it. And, conversely, he can play a pre-configured "lick" or simply hold one note (riffin') and let the song play over him.

Crip,

Sorry to hear of your continued anxiety. I would just chalk it up. Don't go looking for loss. Just live and it will come to you. Actually, the fact that he doesn't exist makes God that much more fascinating. In some ways, I always thought you and Josh in Hungary were both a bit like Gulliver among the Lilliputians.

Finally, a woman clings to a young man, smothers him with passion, blushes in big red splotches, jumps on his genitals like they were the last bicycle out of hell and a young man thinks that he's the only one that she can feel that way about. But she could just as easily have jumped into bed with someone completely different. Such is the unpredictability of sexual love. Men can't see past the orgasm: women can. For men sex is the end of a relationship, at least that stage of it, for women, it's the beginning. [I heard him say that 100 times]. Men think short. Women think long.

If desire could be fulfilled in life, death would be impossible to accept. Successful people I have known, people who have had a great number of their desires fulfilled, were also people who, in the end, feared their death almost to the point of denial. The rest of us, when we feel our dreams and desires will never be fulfilled, resign ourselves to death, indeed, almost long for it.

You can still love, nostalgically, the person you thought your ex-lover was. But in time you see that she didn't exist. She was just an illusion you created. Perhaps she even played along with her perception of your fantasy of her. No need to dislike her. She was just being herself—a self you never really knew.

Music is like a woman you meet. The instrument: a lute, the strings, the kind of wood it's made of, the pearl inlay, these are her earrings, her lipstick, her rings on fingers and toes; the tone of the string when plucked, how long it rings in the air, the echo of the room: these are her lips, her hair, her eyes; the song plays, the chords move like medieval armies, a unicorn of ornament trills in an enclosure (the Unicorn tapestries in The Cloisters); the cardinal flits through the forsythia: these are her words, our conversation over coffee, life, work, love, the hidden mind now naked, slowly getting out of bed, picking up this and that, looking for breakfast.

As ever,

Doc

131 JOSH

Fun sometimes to get out of the center of Budapest. I had time to kill before the gig so I drove around the backstreets of Uj (new) Pest, a pretty little suburb. A place where many of the old buildings still stand, still in use, though not for the original reasons, alongside the newer ones, auto dealerships, fast food joints, etc., the western-style buildings that have sprung up everywhere since the Fall of Communism in, God, it seems like an eternity ago, 1989. Ujpest, like so many places outside Budapest, has the feel of a large Hungarian village, not a European capital. I decided to cruise around and look for a home cookin'-type place (Vendeglo, Gasthaus) where I could get a nice meal and read my book before having to get back to the gig.

I've always been fascinated by the ecstasies of Anonymity. Everything is new and unexplored but the newness carries with it a certain amount of fear. Is this a one-way street? one thinks, turning down a strange alleyway. But I'm already lost, pulled into an erotic fascination with a strange street. It's just too strong to resist. It will get me in trouble one day I'm sure.

Dodging the tail end of a Friday evening rush hour I finally found the perfect place, a Vendeglo with dark rich paneling and an old sign that had seen better days, neon flickering since the fifties no doubt but which had now ceased to glow and so just hung there. I could just make out the name in the dry, unlit tubing: "Kacsa (duck) Vendeglo. I walk in. A few beer heads are gathered around a back table. No food. Sign was just a relic. Only a beer joint (sorozo) now. A fragment of what it once was. Everything's changed. I travel on. Same fate. No food.

Then I saw it gleaming from across the backed-up traffic, Megyere Csarda. A real csarda. A Country Style inn. The kind of place Petofi or Liszt might have eaten in. I could already taste the simple gulyas I had decided to order for brevity's sake as I looked at my watch. The white-washed walls, the thatched roof, all there in splendid authenticity! I rubbed my hands with glee as I jumped from the car. I tried the door. Locked. The sign on the door with its awful finality, "Zarva!" Closed.

The world has changed, I thought as I pulled into a nearby McDonald's. Once there was less uniformity. Every place was different. Every movie house. Every store. Every person. The machine had won. John Henry dead. All over the world. I finished off a big mac.

Pigeons scatter before me. Cracks in the sidewalk remind me of the Atlas of Europe. A river flows 2 blocks from me toward unhappy children, Hungary, Romania, Bulgaria. All clasp hands. Between the sidewalk and the parking lot a trail has been worn by all the short-cut takers, a trail that reminds me of the cattle trails zigzagging through open farm fields I knew as a child. A different continent now, the same feet, riding on the fairy tale back of the stork over a dream of ocean. Cattle walking to lick the salt in the salt houses. When we used to herd the cattle to new pastures the salt house was hooked by a chain to a tractor and dragged on its sled-like runners to the new field.

After our lessons, Sylvester and I would get stoned and go to the art gallery in Medina where you can flip through this big catalog of modern paintings. Then if you like a print, Picasso, Klee, Gris, Feininger, Soutine, Matisse, Chagall, etc., they would order it and frame it for you. We would spend hours just flipping through thumbnail prints of every significant 20th-century painting ever painted. I could see where Sylves got his inspiration. But one day as we were walking in (and the manager rolled his eyes, knowing we never bought anything) Sylves suddenly said, "You know, it's funny to think how we will never be famous. We will never be perceived by the world as truly great. We can't all be great." I didn't believe it then, with so much life ahead of me.

In the tidal wave of European midnight, the roaring freight train takes everything away.

Each morning the affable sun puts everything back.

Life is a metaphor for something else. Death is what it is.

Love is all we have left of Paradise

A bridge between memory and earth

So strange how in the past I strutted around the neighborhood returning from a trip back to the States, glad to be back in my flat, to get some girl on the phone who would share my joy on yet another triumphal return from the invigorating environs of the Homeland.

But no girl answered this time. No expats in town to go get a beer with. I've been back a month and all I can think of is home. There are no more girls, no expats accompanying me on jaunts through their club district. Nothin. Nothin but me, here, in this one room in a foreign land.

MYSTERIOUS LADY

I must be what Hector said old carnies he worked with used to call a mark. They can see me coming a mile, or at least a kilometer away. You get lonesome here. You wanna get a coffee. I was reluctant to go back in. The last time I was in this place was 3 years ago. I never went back in after I had found one of those huge summer horseflies floating dead in my cauliflower soup. ("Hey Waiter! What's this fly doing in my soup?"). Funny. A real dead fly. Maybe the guy in the kitchen did it on purpose. Only a few days ago I realized that the cute girl at the cash register I had been flirting with was his wife. You know how guys are: life sucks, you gotta come in this awful place every morning and fix the soup, you're getting bored with the old lady, you're fantasizing about lotsa cute chicks coming around here and there, like the new busty one at the... Hey wait who's this pashi guy think he is talking to my… Then came the Fly. I had been so hungry. Now, I was queasy for 3 days. 3 years went by.

So many things happen in 3 years and yet not much. Nothing. It just seems like something's moving forward. Time is relative to how much of it we feel or experience. Without experience, Time doesn't exist. Does it exist outside human consciousness? I was reading this book about Sartre. Only humans have consciousness? If it ain't "in" human consciousness it can't exist—as consciousness. Of course, the earth exists even if we aren't conscious of it, but not like we see it. Only our consciousness is consciousness. Does that make sense? The World exists in one way and we in another. Me and Doc and Josh used to talk about this shit all the time. Maybe the whole thing doesn't even exist.

Such things ran through my mind as I ordered a coffee (skip the soup) in the Fly place 3 years later. And then, there she was. So beautiful. Dark coffee bean-colored radiance turning red, what's that dye they use? Dark buckeye brown to maple leaf red. Part Roma? but something else it seemed. But maybe I should have remembered my own axiom: beware of girls with glittery stuff on, bejeweled letters on a t-shirt, trim on blue jean seams, or sparkling cheap glass on a belt, etc. Is that a prejudiced remark? I mean, maybe these were the only jeans she could find cheap enough to buy? My gut was saying, Clear out, run the other way. But I didn't run. I stared as discreetly as I could at her smooth coffee cream-colored legs, letting my eyes slowly follow the shape of legs down to her adorable brown feet in fake jeweled sandals. But she seemed un-annoyed by my glances and as I chatted in America-accented Hungarian with the bartender. Three years had put totally new faces in the kitchen, the jealous fly-slippin' hubby long gone, she walked up beside me and, politely waiting for our inane conversation to end so that she could order another beer and shots of Jagermeister for herself and her friend (try the cauliflower soup?) (she was an old handsome woman in her mid-sixties—her mother?). She, after hearing my accent, asked me where I was from. So many young girls here find themselves fatherless in their mid-twenties. They are inclined or compelled as the case may be to form a bond of survival with their mothers. Their street smarts when pooled together in this way are formidable. But she seemed genuinely fond of her mother, who seemed to me to be coarser, more unrefined than the daughter. A thickness can come over a face as it ages, something bitter crusts over it.

"From America," I said. Her eyes brightened with surprise. She glanced at her mother seated at their table and turned back to me. "My English not good," she said. "Oh, no" I lied, not wanting to lose the seductive momentum of the conversation, "You speak well!" And so, as I joined them at their table, smiling at her smiling "mother," and pleased that I now had better access to a view of the perfect curve of the younger girl's neck, her dark round eyes, and little hints of perfume, I found myself yessing her each time she asked whether or not I could understand her English. I couldn't, of course, but I knew that if we switched to Hungarian I would lose my exoticism, so I tried like mad, filling in guesses and gaps with subtle hints in Hungarian, which I purposely spoke poorly so as not to arouse her suspicions of any fluency, and finally worked up the nerve to ask her if she had any plans for the evening.

"Yes, we are going…"

"Tancolni?" I asked, "To dance?"

"Yes! Yes!" she said excitedly, her beautiful dark eyes brightening, "You can understand my English words?"

"Yes!" I lied again.

"We will to go the dance club to…to…"

"Dance?"

"Yes. Dance. It is a charity dance."

"Can I come with you?" She hesitated and then suddenly understood my question. "Yes, come", she said. And so we all walked the short distance to the tram that would take us downtown. I tried not to stare at her legs too much, impossible as that was, as our train arched over the vast Petofi Bridge spanning the long mellifluous Danube.

We got off not far from the West End station and proceeded not to a dance hall but to a little café (kavezo) whose tables and chairs sat right beside the Grand Boulevard (Nagy Korut) the great ring road that forms a loose parabolic circle around downtown Budapest. It was a rather non-descript café and one that appeared to be temporarily slapped together like so many little businesses here that pop up then disappear after the tourist season has passed.

I began to meditate on how well Samidha (an Indian name?) filled out her skimpy black top and fashionably faded jeans. I fantasized about what she would be like in bed, how unimaginably soft her coffee-colored skin would be.

I bought them round after round, beginning to wonder if my money would hold out until we got to the Dance Hall. I was itching to get my hands around her. Surely then mother would be sent on her way, or even better, she would only be too delighted to stay with us and watch her daughter and I have a good time, delighted to watch her daughter arouse the amorous passions of an American man, a real native English speaking American man! The more the merrier!

The time wore on and I began to nod off from the heavy beers and liquors they kept ordering.

Samidha danced in warm red underwear that almost matched her heena-ed hair as an early autumn chill settled over the street. The wrinkled insteps of her feet curled like autumn leaves; her skin rippled like autumn wind. She raised her arms high to the failing light, a faint carbon stain in her underarms, shaking back her carbon hair and laughing.

I opened my eyes. The waiter glanced at me furtively. Everyone was gone. The place was completely empty. He walked briskly over with the bill. Dawn revealed the gentle swirling of leaves and filth. A rusty car bounded through an intersection on some hurried errand. I must find this woman.

I remember a few times when I would look at Helen and suddenly see not just my wife, a pretty girl, but her, a real person, not just an extension of my own perceptions. And there would follow this moment of revelation as if I was "seeing" her for the first time even though we'd been married for years. It was exhilarating. But, then, a sudden feeling of sadness would come over me. I'd never really known who she was.

[Here, a few pages are illegible—K]

UPDATE: There are no travel advisories for traveling in Eastern Europe at this time. Still, Anti-American feelings continue with some incidents reported over the last several months.

132 BALATON

One day, I had walked to the big embankment beside the Sio River, briefly catching a glimpse of a huge rabbit right before he ducked down behind the other side [cf. poem entitled "My Prayer"—K]. Coming back I was struck by the Eden-like contentment in the yard among my neighbors' chickens, the cat sleeping in the sun, drenched in the soft yellow light of early spring. Even the clink of my key in the outside gate seemed filled with Nirvanic purity. I tried to write it in a poem but it was un-writable. I couldn't make a point: I only cataloged what I saw, as I often did at that time. But, then, it seemed enough! Every object of nature seemed attuned to my thoughts. It felt like they knew! I thought by simply pointing the objects out someone, a reader, would instantly recognize the inherent drama in them. It's a common solipsism in bad poets. We tend not to know what the reader doesn't know or worse, what he already knows. We either explain too much or not enough.

At least in five years, I have moved beyond the grief. I don't write poems like that anymore. But I still walked out into the meadow, retracing my steps of five years before. I felt only slight tremors of the old pain. Helen still puttering around in the kitchen, only now with a new love by her side, one of her colleagues at the English school. But now I feel only a faint, almost sentimental jealousy. I had gotten over the loss of her love long even before they met. It was as if I almost pined for those painful days when I felt alive, not numb. Doc says one gets addicted to pain and becomes a chronic victim. It was a relief when she told me a year ago that she was in a new relationship. I had wondered for several years of our separation when I would have to face that inevitability and now here it was, much easier to handle than I had thought. Still, there had been some little twinges. Things irrevocable. Another deeper death of love.

But this morning I feel not a trace as he works on building, a small greenhouse behind the garage, and she prepares Easter lunch. The kids watch tv or play with the toys, especially the slimy stuff that sticks to walls when you throw it. I picked stuff like that up in Austria, coming home from a tour, where they have more American-style stuff. I continue down the same path of five years ago to a river five years older now as the backdrop to my old poem. But what is five years to a river? Still, the old brown, snaky god acknowledged me with a friendly glance. I looked around in vain for the old hare of my poem. Yet, something white in the distance caught my eye. I decided to get a closer look. It stood straight as an arrow, a marker beside the river, its whiteness in contrast to the still drab early spring landscape, shot through with a frost-bitten forsythia and pathetic trembling blooms of a lone pear tree. I crept closer. I made out the undulant, elegant S-shape of the body and the long beak pointing down toward the water, almost tucked into its breast. A blue heron. The Hungarians say "Golya" [cf. "O My Sister," one of Josh's poems—K]. I felt like I could get closer without it seeing me. I was fifty feet away. But suddenly, with no indication it had felt my presence, it spread its linen wings and flew away down river just out of sight around the bend. I felt sure I would see her again (it had to be female, the male usually has some black coloring) in the grove of trees I could just make out the tops of on the other side. As I bounded up the embankment, which must have been an old railroad bed, like the one Angelica and I played on as children, I flushed another one— the male? from the rushes along the bank. It flew in the same direction as the first one. I reached the top of the embankment and looked out over the adjacent field and down the meandering canyon the river cut through it all. Not a trace. I went no further. I didn't want to scare them. I turned back toward the house, retracing my old steps. Angelica and I, as children, had seen one day wandering the creek that runs through Water Maple.

Helen showed me more than anyone how children are delicate. I always thought of children as belonging to someone else, even if I found their company delightful. Now came the realization that ours were ours alone. My protectiveness of them created in me a sort of agoraphobia, instead of compelling me to go "out there" and set the world on fire. I tended the home fires. I became a "papucska," staying all day in my slippers and pajamas.

I had been at a continuous party since 1989. The Fall of the Hungarian Communist Regime had been like being given the keys to a beautiful decrepit old mansion and we—all of us expats and our Hungarian friends—wandered freely through its ruined rooms. Ten years later the party was ending. Life had caught up with us. Reality of western economics set in. I wandered the streets filled with only the unsustaining memories of the Fall and its giddy atmosphere when a beer was fifty cents and a month's rent was fifty bucks. All gone now as the Schengen Treaty kicked in. I went to a shrink, I felt so lost in the changes. But then something happened: I got used to being lonely. The poison that Sylves had told me about so long ago had like he said it would gone down into my system. I was numb to it. When the End came, surreal as it was in a foreign country, with only my kids connecting me to it now in any way, I realized that I had been carefully preparing for it. I stopped going to the shrink. She had barely understood my English, though, like many Hungarians at that time of integration into western ways, she feared repercussions among her superiors at the clinic if she admitted it. All Hungarians, with government social "nets", rapidly disappearing, feared for their jobs. (I was becoming a dinosaur on the music scene—the novelty of being American was wearing off on the public). I did all the talking. She nodded in agreement from time to time. And then I went back out on the strange streets that I had once felt at home in. Men began appearing in Helen's life. I even lost touch with Crip. And all that caused me to look for another shrink—the original one decided on recommending me to a male colleague, who, in keeping with the sweeping economic changes, charged a significantly higher fee. It was too much for me. I was on my own.

133 JOSH

It's five years later and I'm in the Mona Lisa bar scribbling this.

I stood in my little Budapest apartment kitchen mentally preparing my slightly agoraphobic mind for a walk in the 'hood and enjoying the play of new spring light on the bowl of fruits and vegetables sitting on the counter of the kitchen cupboard. First, there's the amazing purple of a red onion (lilla hagyma). It forms a teardrop droopiness that reminds me of genitals. With the yellow roundness of the perfectly spherical lemon next to it there's a sudden orchestral clash of color. (Is there anything more delicious than a few lemon drops over a slice of red onion? Add a pinch of Basil, some tomato, olive oil). I look back at the bowl again. The Zucchini curves away from the rim of the bowl, which is a hand-painted one from Transylvania (Erdely) of slightly yellowed ivory white with red and blue flowers and the bulbiness of one end gives it a dildo-like look along with its lizardy skin. (Crip told me about using one, once, as a sex toy with an American girl he met). But, no, slice it up and sautee it gently with some garlic and tomato. Pour it over pasta. Add grated cheese. Glass of red wine. The 4 plump tomatoes in the bowl complete the still life. I drop one on the floor and it rolls to the wall (their skin is the texture of red tile mixed with cloth, it's the new sun's effect: the same fruit seemed dry and dead in winter). But I ate it anyway.

Walking down a long lane in the park where I take the boys sometimes on weekends. It looks like a Seurat painting. The basketball goal has been tacked over the soccer one. I worry they will hit their head on it. Their one-on-ones get pretty intense. But years have gone by—no injuries. A father wants to protect his child from earthly pain! But it can't be done. (Marshall said he awoke in a cold sweat thinking of how the bluegrass thresher might have run over us, and the time I tried to pull myself up alongside him on the big Case tractor by grabbing the long-hand throttle! Almost sending the lurching tractor over me. There was another time I was thrown from my horse, spooked by a sudden calf running out of a thicket, and just nearly missed the wooden spike shooting up from an old tree stump). They must endure life's bumps and scrapes.

Sometimes I wonder how I will croak? Will it hurt? When Jared died of a heart attack did he feel anything? Or was it like a swift hammer blow? Carlo said he was probably dead before he hit the ground. Poor Carlo. A sudden flash of light coming down? All those Chinese zapped in an earthquake. Death's out there. Grim Puritan heritage makes it out like a stalker. It just happens? Like falling asleep. I was in Budapest but Agnes said Judge Daddy on his death bed started counting: One, Two, Three, Four! But then his old Virginia accent kicked in after Six—Seb'n!

But now it's Spring in Budapest! I shouldn't be writing this I should be out in the streets of the 7th district walking around hitting on the beautiful Magyar lanyok! I think of Baudelaire's poem where he passes the beautiful girl in the street and rhapsodizes about her. The one that ends, "And you knew!" That's why, karmically speaking, when I see an unattractive middle-aged woman in the street (rare in Budapest) I think: she's not going to get laid—but, oh, there's maybe a chubby, bald taxi driver or butcher somewhere out there in the city who loves her! Good! As it should be! But wouldn't she rather have a tumble in the hay with a slender, handsome 20 something? And she's not going to get that. So, why should I expect to get in the sack with the young hot female counterpart of my imagination? The Equation doesn't balance. Ah, women like her don't waste time: she knows a young swain wants nothing to do with her unless he's so drunk he can't tell the difference. She's resigned to not having him. So, why should I expect the girl coming toward me in the revealing tank top and cute shorts (her breasts are like ripe eggplants! One could spend hours just kissing her calves!)—to want anything to do with a middle-aged man like me? The young girl looks at me exactly like a young handsome man might look at the middle-aged woman. So, what did this ugly woman do, karmically, to be deprived of young cock she wants while I expect to be given—karmically, because of my past heartaches, or by decree of the gods of love—young pussy? In the eyes of the Universe, I and the ugly woman are equals. Therefore my expectations are self-delusions. But the refusal to give up, the addiction to hope that somehow women will love me, comes from memories of the isolated, infrequent amorous encounters of yore! Memory feeds me and I keep coming back like a stray dog. Big Ass. Death.

134 JOSH

I thought back to when Wanda and I split up. To see her on the street in the aftermath and know you couldn't go up to her and embrace her or even talk to her. I turned a corner in my car and suddenly saw her walking up Upper St. in Medina. I felt a lightning flash of pain in a kind of quick "S" shape from my chest down into my gut. Like a sword thrust and twist. Jared was with me and I remarked to him about it: "Oh, shit, there's Wanda." And he said something sympathetic. This was in his New Age period and he said, "Yeah, your Chakras are outta whack." But now, so many years later, I feel the same feeling thinking about Gudrun. An ache in the solar plexus that radiates up. I feel a constant nervousness and desire for a cigarette. Such a sweet girl she was! Even though there were moments when she seemed unattractive, dull. Just like when I first noticed Emese's ass was so huge when she bounded out of the bed to go to the bathroom. I wanted someone else. (Yet, now, too late, I think of how beautiful her eyes were.) I remember the same thing about Gudrun—the front of her thighs were fat and wrinkled. But the kindness of their souls radiated out from them. Gudrun's eyes were also beautiful. And her cheekbones were so exquisite like I said, she looked like a big Central Asian Princess! And she knew so many Hungie folksongs that she sang in her child's voice. Yet, aside from her street smarts, which were formidable, Hungie girls have to be tough as nails to survive, she lacked almost any interest at all in things of the mind. Completely un-intellectual. And she was never curious about my music; never asked me to play for her even though we talked about my gigs often. She seemed to have a weak capacity to understand such things. She came to one of my band gigs once and though she smiled at me on stage from a table near the corner window, she seemed not to understand what we were playing. But surely she did. It was merely the dance music of the day. Girls from the suburbs are less cosmopolitan than downtown girls.

Now I feel compelled to make a catalog of Gudrun memories. I see her standing at the sink getting a glass of water. Her heavy black furry winter coat as she stood at the doorway, looking again like a Russian girl from Kazakstan. Her girlish innocence in her black eyes so expectant of love. Standing, now at my sink washing my dirty dishes for me. (I did love you! Now, I admit it! I meant to tell you that I had changed my mind about not wanting a commitment! Will you come back? Ah, too late). Every memory must be brought out and killed one by one until the pain goes away. That's the only cure. I told her once that I could never fall in love with her. That must have hurt. More than I realized. It was just something I blurted out to toughen myself up and keep the upper "master's" hand in the relationship. Never show weakness, I thought. But now I am weak. Very weak. At least I tried to be honest. Honesty never assuages pain.

I'm looking at the clean sheets I put on the bed and spiffed up flat in expectation of her arrival that now will never happen. She never showed up. "De van." Or is it that I love her because now I know I can never have her. Big Ass. Death.

135 KRIP

Hungarians are in a difficult situation. For so long, ruled by foreigners they hated, they clung fiercely to their Hungarian-ness: their language, survival of their rich culture from the Dark Ages until WWII. But now that they are completely free politically (to express that Hungarian-ness without reprisal) it is that very Hungarian-ness they must now reinvent or even suppress in order to fit into the EU and new global re-alignments since 1989. But I've had it so much easier than them in this enchanted little country. I've perched above their culture (the culture of my mother, my father I never knew and who was rarely mentioned in our household, and Aunt Pearl and Schwartz) almost like a colonialist, while they, poor they, toiled in the depths of their nationhood, their history.

136 JOSH

Last gig on the Jazz from America Tour. The sudden illumination of a waxing moonlit sky in a strange town, Trnava, Slovakia. A "what am I doing here" moment. Walking the night streets feeling utterly alone (how far from Water Maple Farm I've come!) when the sky seems to rise in awful pain and joyousness of living; when woman can no longer be a deliverer when the heavens seem to come down near to your heart, your face, and yet say nothing. A truck roars past into the nothingness of the lamp-lit street. The stars! The moon says nothing. And the loneliness portends an even greater loneliness.

Concerts in Slovakia

Got to play with Lacy Corman again. He'd just returned from a tour with Jim Hall and Richie Beirach. But my "performance chops" are undeveloped. I just don't play many "concerts"— not enough to get good at it. My preparations are always a bit short-sighted because I'm of a "club" player mindset. "Café guitarist," one critic said. When I was practicing I kept resting on my laurels, practicing what I already knew and telling myself, It's enough; I'll knock 'em dead with this. But compared to Lacy it wasn't. It was weak. I practiced in fragments. I never composed a whole, flowing show. I never thought I'd be on the same bill with such a musical genius. But he was a gentleman. Reminded me of Crip with his jokes: "The Jew bends over and the Greek guy disappears"…. "How do you make a hormone"…3 musicians and drummer injured in car crash".

Yet, afterwards, I found myself on the tour bus staring out the window. Seeing the moon. Imagining it over Lake Balaton to the south and my sweet little family there's no time to visit. And yet her lunar love seems too severe. I wonder: is there nothing at which I can express myself with genius? Corman is not a wanna-be— he is.

As a teenager in Water Maple County, I would often end up at some party, say, out on some farm or on a venerable old Edgeton or Medina street, held in some crumbling antebellum mansion. The hosts were often "back-to-the-land" hippie types with a trust fund and plenty of pot and booze and wine, usually older than me and of a daydreamer bent more than they were practical or handy. Consequently, the old house, which had, once, perhaps 100 years before, gleaned from atop a bluegrass hill, had now fallen to ruin. The bohemian occupants may not have had the money, the know-how or inclination to fix anything. It was a brokedown palace as Sylves called them. The paint peeled and the ceiling leaked but a lazy country life went on with a kind of studied obliviousness. It wasn't unlike how I found Hungary in '89.

137 DEATH OF JOSHUA CELESTE | PART 1

by Krip Kovacs

He didn't feel much as he went down. Everything around him became One.

A woman, or a gentle Sylvester Moore-like voice over the ocean-like hiss of a cymbal coming from Temple Street. Driftin' on a sea of forgotten teardrops, on a lifeboat, sailing for… Yer loooove. Not up but out. He rose into All. The yellow light of Morning with Night at the Edge. The stage in his dream spread like clouds under the tour plane, prairies from the bus window as far as he could see in the Iowa-like universe of his memory. He could feel the star-spangled banner leap from his Strat fingers. My Old Kentucky Home. Rainy Day, Dream Away. He smiled at Jimi as he became him, their left hands twanging the highest lonesome blue note into the eternal pink dawn. Music trucked from his fender and struck onto the string in a rainbow of moist circular sound into the parabola of heaven. Even as he died to the light, he played the world.

And Josh passes into the world again but everything knows him already so he's a little higher. All he wanted, he received, until that, too, would be all over. Already he could hear the crowd cheering.

138 JOSH | BALATON JOURNAL

Back for a weekend. Indian summer is weakening. The nights have a chill damp feeling now and the fog hangs in the back fields, illuminated by the lone street lamp and the moonlight behind autumnal clouds. Farm life here harks back to an earlier time. Wonder what TLC and Ricky Boy would think of all this! Hay is ricked in the open. No one can afford to build a barn. I've never even seen one here. And the corn shocks my neighbor has propped up against his fruit trees are as charming as a Halloween decoration back home, only here it's for real. The stalks are grayish-yellow now. And the burgundy grays of November are starting to appear.

In our shabby little Balaton yard is Gordon's little plastic toy tractor. I think of Marshall baling hay on Water Maple Farm and Mama would say, Go take your father this pitcher of cold iced tea. And I would walk through the whirring insects in the red clover and hear the tractor noise, the hammering crash of the metal sides of the baler if it dipped into a small hollow place in the ground, perhaps an abandoned groundhog hole. The hay is swept into the machine by the metal arm of the baler and a golden bale comes out.

Had a weird dream which I've forgotten after the gig in Klagenfurt, though I sensed its power just below the threshold of consciousness. I notice Freud on the 50 schilling bill. (Ah, could you imagine William James on an American bill?) There is a sort of bored tolerance of sexual things in Europe. Austria is sophisticatedly jaded. Even the USA with all its seasoned consumeristic habits could never be so blasé. The surrounding countryside around Klagenfurt is simply gorgeous. (If only it wasn't in Austria! Krip often yelled). Such charming meadows and Old Empire villas and farmhouses wrought with exquisite stone masonry. The frost-tinged piney wooded mountains, the wide valleys. A baroque Appalachia. Yet everything here is so spiffy. The old pine floors in my pension in town were waxed and spotless—basketball gym spiff.

What a marvelous old dinosaur the train station dining room was. It was huge. I was due to catch my train to Vienna and I couldn't take it all in. It was so old, even the Austrians couldn't get those old granite floors to gloss up again. At breakfast, my waiter appeared from a time warp out of the post-war years. His slight build and bald though somehow handsome head and features were full of the futility of life. Witness having to serve this "foreign musician" he might have thought to himself. He thought I was gypsy I think. He seemed perturbed I had asked for potatoes with my ham and eggs. "French fries?" he asked. No, I said, just normal potatoes. "It's not normal to have potatoes for breakfast," he said dourly. I considered giving him a lecture about southern-style country breakfasts but then just smiled and passed on the fries. Why do I think dudes like him wanna hear about my past life? After nibbling on some tasty, though dry, Austrian rolls (those delicious braided ones) and sipping on some good strong black tea (rare on the coffee-drinking continent) he finally shuffled in with a beautiful plate of bright orange sunny side up fried eggs and garlic-smelling slices of glistening ham. When I saw the glorious, jiggling orange yokes I thought, Uh-oh, salmonella, but then just as quickly I thought, What the Hell and jabbed them with my fork and they squirted a yellow ooze over the plate. They were fantastic.

But what did these old dark pine paneled walls, high ceilings and smooth floors remind me of? Cigar smoke, beer served at 10 am (why not potatoes?) pork grease, flatulence, mop water? This was 1950 Medina with my father among tobacco warehouse men like John Buckley and Boots Rhodes in dusty three-piece pinstripe suits with pocket watches and a brown fedora, smoking pungent cigars among mahogany office desks and leather swivel chairs and old ledgers and papers with chicken scratch figures upon them. Everywhere, the smell of tobacco, wood, dust, wet mopped smooth stone floors, autumn light (tobacco-selling season) pouring through plate glass. The same here in this Austrian train station restaurant: tables of dark wood set with cloth napkins and old-style silverware. It was mostly empty.

139 BACK IN BP

Thoughts of joy and secrecy of 7 am subway ride. Strange faces. A distant culture and yet the same human longing and loneliness in each one.

I just wanted to write a letter to everyone I knew—all the time.

140 KRIP

Josh in the afternoon flipping pages of his datebook—all the names, dates, gigs, past gigs, then terra incognita, the endless white of un-booked future dates until you hit the cheap cardboard backing. The empty future. Blank. He thought of the white winter fields of Water Maple Farm, the herds of Herefords red as sunset against the snow, then the gray sky and the groves of trees where he wandered as a boy, penciled in thin pencil, the patches of plowed earth beneath, the rut and stitch of the tractor wheel in the nearly frozen mud, the white of the past, memories worn and rubbed in pencil. And the blank future. But he imagined into it. The endless bar gigs wreathed in smoke, the faces, red, pink, black talking, smiles of yellow teeth. Dark suits. Slick hair. Hoods wandering outside in the corner. Catching their eyes, even, on a solo. One hood elbowing the other saying, "Check it out, man, the guitar player sees us." Then turning away and only thinking to look again while he's at the bar on a break, talking to some kid.

"What kinda bass is that?"

"Oh, justa…"

"My brother's got a Yamaha."

"Good for him."

"Listen, turn your volume up halfway on your amp and your intensity and up to ten."

"Will do."

"You guys are pretty good."

"Thanks."

"No, I mean, no shit. You fuckers think I don't know what I'm talking about!?"

Everyone's a fucking critic. What the hell. There's no cover. Man's got a right to speak his mind. When you get up there and yer not a tv star, right away they think, "Struggler. On his way up? Or down. Cheap sound system. Bad lights. This ain't no Talking Heads concert. Clown." They're hoping you might croak or do something outrageously romantic or dangerous. "If I bled for all y'all all over the stage" 3 nights at Crazy Reddy's. Shd be interesting.

It felt strange when Helen changed and began to nag and demand. I tried to please her (God, she was the woman of my dreams!) but nothing worked. That's when I began sneaking out. I didn't wanna have an affair, just go to the wank tank and whack off and be done with it. Helen and I almost never had sex anymore. It didn't feel right. The skin of a woman that doesn't love you is cold. Her lips, cold. I thought, geez, with all these gorgeous chicks in the Budapest streets, maybe I oughta try and get some pussy. It's weird how much one thinks about pussy and how little you actually get. That goes for me, anyway. The biggest part of my lays were always "sympathy fucks." All those hours of walking, trying to disguise my limp, seeing if I could meet the love of my life just walking down the street toward me. Alcohol would give me the courage to drop a line at the stoplight street corner, or grocery or in a bar, etc. I often got withering stares in return.

But what if the submissive person mutinies? You take the abusive dominance of a woman for only so long and then you snap, you yell, you scream. But it's too late. The Jury of Dominance deliberates over the time you are kept in limbo wondering about your fate. You know the ax is gonna fall. But when?

The verdict finally comes in. Guilty. The sentence? Death.

141

Bertha made sassafras tea for the boys, Josh and Doc, lanky, teen-aged. The pure yellow light, light as locust honey, pervaded the yard and set the bees droning in the massive cups of the Rose of Sharon lining the fences now to the fields. She made toast in the oven, sprinkling cinnamon over it after slathering margarine on it. Bigelow's Constant Comment tea with orange peel and clove she also fixed for them. Or plain Lipton black tea, iced in summer, with sprigs of fresh mint. When he played in Brussels, once, Josh told me he haunted the Morrocan tea shops looking for Bertha's mint tea.

I heard some people in a café dogging down Josh's music. I didn't say anything. I realized that other people don't always love the people I loved. Have you ever overheard a cutting remark about a person you loved? Strange how the world can still crucify what you consider holy.

142 JOSH

Edgeton again. The Woman feels like I need to see my mom.

What a paradise here. So lush. The thick southern hardwood forest. Almost tropical. This is the garden spot. I see why Boone referred to the jungle-thick forest growth as "horrid." It still overwhelms in places, even though it's been "tamed." Think of the tangle of vines and the snakes he saw!

DOC

I have to disagree with my European friends who say that America is in decline. It's an easy judgment to make, obviously American hegemony will decline in Spenglerian fashion, but it's a premature one. To me, it just seems to be rising and getting stronger, perhaps not so much muscular as muscle-bound, but still robust, creative, energetic, fearless, morally engaged and decadent all at once. The country of Good. The country of Evil. America is full of wealth, poverty (of spirit as well) energy, depression, openness, congestion, greed, magnanimity, paranoia, generosity, gods, goddesses and devils of every kind. It's not the only place in the world, but what we call the world, its beauty, its horror, seems to focus here more than anywhere. The poverty of Africa and Asia is entrenched. Whereas in America poverty is active, restless, ready to transform or explode. People haven't lost hope though they often pursue empty dreams. The 3rd world by contrast contains little pursuit. It's an anemic form needing American consumers to reinvigorate it. Religion keeps it breathing but at the same time acts like a disease, a tumor, threatening to suffocate it. In America, the battle between the atheist and the evangelist is always at fever pitch. Yet, still America fears its freedom.

Dear Josh,

I realize that in Balaton you still feel moments of elation with her under the same roof again. She had said she hoped nothing was changed by the separation. And your childish, heart hoped you were still cared for. But it's all fake. It seems strange to me that you're still there in that house, in the same rooms you once paced in rhythmic despair. I know you've gotten over some of that. But don't you hear that lingering voice, "Get out! Go, man! Get away!" Do it for yourself!

Cheers,

Doc.

143 JOSH

Walking home alone on the Big Boulevard after a gig at the Mona Lisa.

There's a pretty entrance with marble figures… angels? on pedestals on either side of the doorway at Temple St., like the one at Semmelweis 13.

144

I remember lying naked with Berenice with an Atlas open on the bed dreaming about all the places we would go.

145 JOSH

Time makes a dream of everything.

146

I don't wanna let go of Sunday.

147 DOC

"Only before us does Death strike fear.

Behind us it is suddenly all beautiful and innocent,

A carnival mask in which, after midnight, you collect water

To drink or, if sweaty, to wash."

—*Magris at the conference in Budapest.*

148

Watching Gordon and Ryly sleep. Small boats gently swaying in Balaton Fured.

DREAM

I'm in one of those big communal houses like the ones I sometimes found myself in as a young man: different things going on in each room: sex, drugs, rock and roll. Some mulatto women, kinda like the ones I mildly flirt with on Temple

St, the money changers' place in Budapest, are trying to explain something to me but getting slightly frustrated. I'm on a second-story veranda—like me and Wanda's old Edgeton St. apartment in the old part of Medina? Some male figure, a kind of grim guru is present. A bird-like guy. He's not too confident in me in the dream. Questions my effectiveness, some vague objective I am unsure of. (The guy in the Turkish money change place that stared at me weirdly once?) But then at one point out on a beach, I hear him yelling, "Joshua! Joshua!" I look up in the sky and he is flying or more like standing over me as if ready to punch me in the face.

Another one of those nights of revelation walking around in downtown Budapest. The shadow of leaving for good casts itself wistfully, bittersweetly on all I see.

149

Ah, the squat stone buildings, block after block, some covered with soot, others freshly sand-blasted and painted in the spirit of progress, investment and EU accession, others fading into the gray of car exhaust. Tonight it's raining and cold after a hint of spring and sunny warmth only a few days ago. How dark, reptilic (I'm thinking of the oily slime on the streets) ominous yet joyfully dynamic this city is! "Up and Down the Big Korut" I should call my life. Ah, the long navy cashmere topcoats, the pudgy, round-faced working-class girl with a pensive expression, or wearing fake leather Chinese jacket, her glasses hiding in the glare her quick gray eyes, dishwater blond hair curling around a hairband. The sun doesn't shine enough around here. The young beauties gathered around the disco door, the yellow trams snaking through the square. Street people, criminals relaxing on the strip joint patio, short change artists. Foreigners blend into the nightlife.

Jazz is a beautiful woman I want to seduce, but she just won't give in to my advances. Sylves said, "It's a bottomless pit. Take it as far as you can or as far as Fate will allow you. You will meet others as you go down."

BALATON

It rained yesterday evening when we arrived. The next day was dark and cloudy but by the afternoon the sun began peeking out from breaks in the clouds and a pleasant breeze came in, as it does so often this near the lake. The boys and I tested out a new kite we bought in Siofok. We played board games and then kicked the soccer ball around a bit.

150 KRIP

During the war and the Russian occupation, in a psycho-emotional way, the whole country was damaged. The spirit of mistrust, anemia of friendship, general cynicism, despair of the positive, reliance on the negative, is palpable throughout the society. Suicide is common. Divorce is so uninteresting any relationship problem discussed hardly raised a ripple among my Hungarian friends. How much of the dark 20th century past did we bring on ourselves? Do they ask themselves that? Down Honved St., I always stop and look through the window at the old swastika-shaped tiles of what was once the Gestapo office—now converted into a law office. Old poet Schwartz said Hungary was like a pretty wing added onto the great Cathedral of Western Civilization which then Banu Khan, the Turks, the Austrians, the Nazis and the Russians blew up! It wasn't until the late 19th century that BP began to build itself up into the "Paris of the East". Blocks and blocks and blocks of robust granite trimmed in hardwood, eclectic Art Nouveau and Neo-Gothic/Baroque. The gorgeous gaudy imitation of an imitation, the Eiffel-built west train station, the Neo-Gothic dome of the parliament, the bridges over the Danube. "The great god-awful Gothic gaudiness of it all!" Josh used to say. But now all the buildings that survived allied bombs are fragmented, offices, apartments, museums, sex shops, Chinese buffets and Turkish sandwich joints, like huge sea shells beached in Time, giant dinosaur carcasses, all from a vanished era of the giants that once lived in them.

151 JOSH ON THE BUS

"The northwest corner of the old house used to get alot of shade in the early afternoon – as the sun made its way toward the pond below the house. That was where the field was – layin flat just above the south part of the pond where the water kinda pooled up—and it was fun to just pole fish there for brim sometimes and big globs of algae would stick to your hook. It was in that field I used to take a ball bat and pitch rocks to myself all day and knock em toward the house—but I was far enough back to where I never got too close to hittin any windows or anything like that. Mom wdnt've liked that too much. I was probably 10 or so. And I would announce an imaginary baseball game, 'Ok, folks, Gordy Coleman steps to the plate, the crowd is getting behind him, don't know if you can hear the cheers through yr radio but the hometown reds crowd here at Crosley wants a big hit—yep they sure do—as my old friend Judge Daddy Demeter down there in Edgeton, Kentucky used to say, 'He hit it a country mile!' I always love to hear the Judge's old stories so now Dalrymple, the catcher's, comin out to talk it over with Bunting—they don't wanna give Coleman anything to hit. Ok, heeeere's the pitch – swung on – and that is going back, back (shit getting close to Mom's bedroom window) that is outta here and the crowd is on their feet as Coleman rounds second and heads home for his... Time to try an ice-cold Burger Beer, this is Waite Hoyt and the Cincinnati Reds baseball Network.

"And so after a few hours I got a little tired of knockin rocks – and besides, they used to gouge big chunks of wood outta the bat and Doc wd get kinda pissed about that but, hell, you cdnt hit a baseball coz they went too far and then you'd have to go and fetch it which wd wear yr ass out after two or three hits – but down on the ground there was an endless supply of limestone rocks—some of them were too big of course, flat, Marshall used to pick me up and show me little shell marks in em, little perfect imprints of seashells, and he wd explain how the ocean used to be way over here and everything underwater and he even showed me sponges just like Bertha used to clean floors with only they were rock now of course, sittin on the ocean floor for a million years.

That day I guess I threw the bat back into the garage and started walking down the hill through the Apple orchard. And all the June apples were on the ground in the hot sun and big wasps and hornets and flies were crawling all over them sucking out the sweet juice. You had to be careful when you stomped on one and squshed it that some hornet didn't fly up and sting ya just like Doc told me he got stung real bad that time down at Aloyisius' house that time. One time I was climbing in the apple trees – they were so much fun to climb coz there were lots of sturdy low branches so it was easy to get a leg up and then it was great if the apples were ripe enough you cd just climb up and pick a few and suck on them—it felt great bein up there like a bird – sometimes even an ugly Starling or an angry Jay or a pretty cardinal would swoop in but soon as they saw you they wd fly away. And so many apple blooms and bees—o lord – they buzzed around everywhere but I wasn't scared but then one day a hornet 3 inches long landed right on my thigh just above the knee and started crawlin up my leg and I thought he gonna go up my pants and sting my balls—well, Marshall was down on the ground that day gettin his tools together for something and I started screamin, Daddy, it's a big bee, what do I do? Help me! Well, Marshall just smiled and climbed up on one the low limbs and he bunched up the pants leg of my shorts tight against my leg so the hornet cdnt go up my pants and then he just flicked it away with his finger and the hornet was gone. "See, no, reason to cry about stuff like that. Just use yr head a little bit—don't panic." Wow, I felt so happy after that. He saved my ass that's for sure.

So he was walking down the hill to the Springhouse which is where we pumped water up to our house—old Rue's old house. The spring came out of the hill and into a shady rounded little wooded place that was in the shape of a cup almost with a few limestone rock formations sticking out the way water rounds out a limestone place like that, sparrows and cardinals flitted in and out and the spring made a little creek which flowed on out to a watering trough and then on down to the pond. The field toward the pond was always flooded with deep yellow sunlight but as I said the wooded part was always shady though strong sunlight was able to get down into the shade, filter into it, and illuminate big broad leaves of burdock and elephant ear-looking plants and grasshoppers wd clutch onto the ironweed leaves, thistles bloomed with the same pungent purple blooms where bumblebees nestled deep inside. Occasionally an angus steer wandered shade -colored into the shade. The grasses—bluegrass and fescue sprouts and crab and grease grass and hog weed, stewed in the dew wet mud mushiness of it all, though where the sun struck it was dry. Angelica and I called this place "the marsh" coz we'd seen pictures of places like that further south and all the wild birds on tv shows. And—in winter—the marsh made a great 20 yard bobsled run (winter of 66 was a big one) And one day a heron had wandered up from the banks of the Kentucky River—and one of its fuzzy goslings—still tall and spindly—came toddling up the weed-bordered cow path one day. We thought it was a magical bird and we went to get mom, but when we came back it was gone. She shook her head thinking, What will these kids think up next? [cf. Poem, "O My Sister" Ed. Note].

But I saw Marshall with his wrenches workin in the Springhouse that day and I wanted to go and help him – sometimes he was mad and didn't want any company when he worked. I think he might've been putting in a water purifier maybe that day or just some random repairs—seems there was worms in the water coz of cow shit seepin into the spring. Maybe later Marshall put up a fence on the west side of the marsh so the steers cdnt wander in. He was twisting his monkey wrenches around and I was sitting on the cool limestone steps of the springhouse just chatting with him. He had his sleeves rolled up real high and you could see the white of his triceps just above the real dark tan of his lower arms. We were talking about god-knows-what. He seemed just a little grouchy coz of the work but nice enough. I'd learned how to kind of be easy around him when he was workin. And he got me to fetch him things like a washer or rubber ring out of the toolbox or an adjustable wrench. And then, BOOM! Water from a pipe burst out so sudden like it scared the hell outta me and I stood up real fast and saw the water hit Marshall real hard right in the Adam's apple and I took off up the steps, I don't know why I was so scared, maybe that the water was gonna get me somehow and I looked back and saw that spray hittin Marshall real hard in the throat and face and he just tried to put his hand over the busted place but water was gushing out too hard and fast so he just whooped like an old Indian brave and bent down to find a wrench. Finally, he shut it off. I stood at the top of the limestone steps and yelled, Dad? You ok? And he said, Yeah, godammit just wet as hell. Gope the house and get me a towel wud ye? So I ran up through the orchard not givin a damn about the wasps on the fallen apples, thinkin of that water just hittin my dad so hard in the face. But he's ok now I thought to myself so I jumped up in the air and clicked my heels in the sun out of the Orchard and brought a towel and a cold glass of iced tea Agnes had given me to give him. Water didn't mean to do it. It was stuck up in a pipe. Sun dries it. It flows. Dad's alive. Everything's ok. Still I got mad at myself for runnin. He laughed and said, Hey little helper, I'm ok! I guess he thought I was a 'fraidy cat."

152

Sitting here in this apartment staring at the walls I've reached a kind of perfection. Perhaps it's only me making a circle of thought by placing mirrors in front of each other. The corridor of reflections curves and I disappear around the corner and never come back.

Now, since the split with Helen, I see people differently. I remember the first revelation in adolescence that my father was after all just a man. He wasn't the God, I made him out to be as a kid. Not any more or less than anyone else, I mean. So, all my first perceptions of this place, this tiny, enchanted country, were illusory. I thought these good people would deliver me from my American sorrows! (I had wandered the streets: all my sad thoughts were of Wanda in Edgeton. I wandered the Wanda-tinged streets. And then when I kissed Emese that night beside the taxi stand in a drunken act of bravado and she kissed me back—Wanda seemed to suddenly disappear!). But now I see that I had invented a Budapest all my own to go with my personal quest to conquer the World. It was all just a personal mythology and they were extras in the movie of myself. Now they all seemed pathetic as myself, aging, mediocre, talentless, possessing no real genius. I've wasted some good years of my life here, I thought. I hid, like Jonah, from the eyes of the World, from God. What is Man but an ignoble, solipsistic loner! Why did I expect so much from myself, from "Woman", from powerful men?

Ah, the joyful, lonely nights in this 8th district, one-room flat! All the hours of contemplation! Surely beneficent meaning lies behind it all. But then it's so commonplace to hope for some deliverance, some revelation that would completely change you forever. Perhaps the beggars in the streets, rags around their feet, God has already revealed himself to them so why should they go through the motions we unenlightened must go through? Why, of course, they needn't wash or sleep under a roof! God has told them that just a few more days and they will enter Paradise! The sudden flash of light on the road to Damascus has made everything clear. You are changed forever and the past life means nothing. Yet, for the rest of us, there's only the daily grind.

I remember how, watching tv, smoking, the shiver of Death would come over me. For a moment I would panic, chastise myself for some excess, wondering how it might have infected me, destroying me slowly while I stared into the screen and its horrid imagery. Once an attack was so strong I called Helen so at least someone could hear my last words before I collapsed on the ground. Stranger in a strange land has his own special claustrophobia. Who but she or maybe Crip would have known what to do with my corpse?

There's something erotic in the Inappropriate. I keep chasing the wrong woman. She never responds to me but I don't give up. Like Wanda said, "A real man never stops trying."

The character in the Cormac McCarthy novel Doc gave me? The part where the young hero says, "I ain't leavin' without my horse". That's me. Still, hard to believe it's all gone. Where does love go? The corpse no longer animated with it. Soul leaving the body. Yes! Love must be shot down and dragged through the streets! Life feels more menacing. The wound of her love still weeping.

I remembered herding cattle with Marshall. "Oxen that rattle the yoke and chain or halt in the leafy shade. What is that you express in your eyes? It seems to me more than all the print I have read in my life."

153 KRIP

I remember Josh getting blown off the stage by Hector and his guitar at Crazy Reddy's. It was kind of a set-up. Hector had all these new-fangled effects. Sounded like a heavy metal record. People love power, to be over-powered. They wanna be fucked in the ass in a way by the sound, the spectacle. Then here came Josh with his beat-up Martin and just a little fender amp. Josh was a good rhythm player. That's how he got that road gig with Etta James and Lacy Corman— but drenched in dope.

154 JOSH | NOTEBOOK

Could it be that the girl you find after the gig is just a figment of your imagination anyway? A fragment of something that was once complete in itself? In the end, the mind is filled with images of the times we live in. The heart, the body filled with gestures of lust. But the soul—it hasn't changed. All the sexy garb attached to contemporary life, all its pagan-ness – it's all just ornament. The soul has not changed. Its loneliness never ends. Its wanderings never cease.

155 FROM THE MUSICAL LIFE OF JOSHUA CELESTE

by Krip Kovacs

The yellow light pours through the window into a small room with a small stereo system, a desk with some papers on it—some poems crudely typed, a guitar, an electric bass, a narrow, shaker-style bed.

This is Joshua Celeste's music room. He needs a room where he can close the door and be alone. Berenice, his girlfriend, has redecorated the house that Josh bought 3 years ago. She brought her painting and sculptures to the house and put them on the walls and set them up in corners. Josh didn't mind. He thought they were quite beautiful. One painting was a huge swirl of yellow, orange and red that gave the impression of a naked woman curled up in a ball, her thighs, tear-drop-shaped, sweeping down from an S-shaped head like a Matisse cut out. Her sculptures were masks that had Aztec faces and frog eyes and mouths shaped in Os. She was beautiful. Her hair was the color of the watery reddish gold of goldfish in a bowl with bright sunlight streaming through it. Josh practiced his guitar, read books and wrote songs. He liked Bach, Segovia and playing Charlie Parker solos. This was classical history. He would try to learn licks by Hendrix, Stevie Ray Vaughan, Merle Travis and Doc Watson off records. He would sit for hours, dropping the needle over and over at one spot on the vinyl grooves, trying to get all the notes right, feeling like something wasn't quite right, humming the melodies to himself and feeling frustrated. He took all this knowledge and tried it out in the bars he would play in at night with his band, which I played bass in after Carlo moved away to Philly. Sylves played drums. Josh became known as a kind of local George Benson, but mostly nobody much listened. He went on exploring "the bottomless pit" of jazz improvisation, but we had to mostly play pop/funk stuff people could dance to and so Josh ground out his funky R&B guitar bursts on covers of Stevie Wonder, Marvin Gaye and James Brown. Sylves said we were playing to their crotches, but it was still a Sacred Rhythm, he said, like those Indian sculptures he saw on jazz tours in Asia, and which he had learned from percussionists like Chana Pozo in New York. The bluegrass and rock and roll of Josh's childhood morphed into bebop and Brazilian Samba grooves and flamenco. His guitar became a satellite receiving and projecting images. In the little college town of Medina, he met actors, dancers, dreamers, African percussionists. He came to realize that the religion of his youth that Father Hozni had given him, the god of his grandmother, Millicent, was in no conflict with the Sacred Rhythm. The Episcopal hymnal, Bach—all was of the same cloth as Chick Corea, Keith Jarrett or a Weather Report tune. Airto, the Brazilian percussionist, performed in the Spotlight Jazz Series Sylves had helped to organize at Medina University. After the show, young Josh wandered through the park alone. He felt a presence in the Sycamore trees. He thought I must become this kind of musician. In his youth, he imagined he had found a sacred fountain. He drank from it. He followed the River that sprang from it.

156 JOSH

Sometimes the horror of my life here comes upon me with such force that I think that surely it happened to someone else. The earth seems a more fearful place. Sex and orgasm is a brief cure of the symptoms. Prayer is good as I drift off to sleep.

Cable tv. The misty sepia of Hollywood. Documentaries about the Golden Age, wealth of stars. Flip back to CNN. Explosions. Light of the World going dim. Flip to girls on catwalk. Chick looks like Wanda. There's always one biggie in yr life. Of equal status with the Mother. One woman stands at center stage—dressed in white. Helen stands a little apart, hovering slightly above in pastel space. Stop trying to figure out who she is in life, in a story. She fades in and out. They fade in and out together.

157 BALATON

Dear Josh—I found this the other day.

A lovely understandable spirit

Once entertained you.

It will come again.

Be still.

452

Be patient.

— Theodore Roethke

Love,

Mother

158 DOC

The sexual equation is often on my mind. I call it that for lack of a better word. Singleness= freedom. Marriage = prison. But they are interchangeable. Black is white/ white is black, is always axiomatic. In love opposites are important. What the lover says she wants is what she doesn't want. Eg., "He's only a friend" can mean, "I'm very attracted and may eventually let him have me." Flirtation means sexual intercourse is possible but not guaranteed. Never give all your heart. Never trust anyone completely. Just let things happen. When what happens is not what you wanted to happen then you are cast into the chaotic animal soup of Choice. The fool says a woman wants it as bad as you do! Yes, but not necessarily at the same time and not necessarily with you! The lover imagines the beloved is thinking of him—but she's not. Illusion rules in love. The girl that readily shares your bed is usually not the one you want. What you want is unattainable. Getting your wish immediately destroys the desire for what you wished for and the memory of why you wanted it. Desire is a woman. We are closest to god in harmonious relationships with women. If only there was one. This is the point at which god meets humanity. Isn't the body a temple? A godsend to man's emptiness. To condemn it is to invite suicide, defrock the soul, make it stand naked in the cold, shivering, dying without the mammalian warmth god created. The Passion itself is a kind of sexual love mis-told. A union of man and god producing the cunt-cleft world!

The body is the place from which evil can be expelled.

A man casts his line. The bait drops into the water. He can't see below the murky surface. Then the frightening moment—the fish bites!

159 JOSH

(brief visit to Edgeton)

Beauty of Water Maple Street and mother's house is indescribable and in fragmented, stolen moments I feel compelled to record my impressions. The almost tropical lushness of the black walnut leaves, nuts already coming out in June in a date-like hardness, wave outside the upper windows, a latticed canopy against the bright blue sunlight in the clear blue. Vast nostalgias. The decay of what was. The old life. Yet, the trees, the good old neighbor Uncle Dennis' ash tree, once used as a goalpost for childhood touch football battles, still standing, immovable in endless storms and deaths.

They are old now. All the ones who cared for us, watched over us in eternity of Sunday afternoon. We take their place in the middle age of parenthood. Other yards, other trees, their story mute, revealing only relentless Time. New blacktop on the river of street that runs through this jungle of hardwoods. The gleam of long cars in the circles of driveways, stained only by the splash of one bird dropping, white with a black cherry seed in the middle. The blood drop cardinal flitting through the darkening shrubs, the jay of sky fragment of the yellow morning, remembered now at sunset. All this—passing. My family—dying. The sunset is red-orange against the shadow of dark field.

The lost long-distance phone of old family wounds, scars of squabbles, a kitchen light, a silhouetted figure, pacing, opening fridge door, stopping, forgetting something, turning again. The boredom of Agnes and Dennis' second generation wealth, Marshall's farm in foreclosure, the hoarding of old stuff, stagnant accounts and furniture, fear of bad investment, grudges, defeats, and meaningless time-worn triumphs. The light flicked off. The memorized walk to bed, fingertips grazing the pitch-black wall.

160

Dear Josh,

Every man whose heart has been broken thinks he has attained some lasting wisdom about "Woman". But it's not true. There is no Woman. Only people. Every woman breaks a man's heart in a different way. And so the typical male, "take it from me" type advice that men like to banter around is essentially meaningless.

Cheers,

Doc.

161 JOSH

Back in BP. Edgeton is a passing dream. Almost hard to believe I was really there even though the impressions were strong. The end is near. I can feel it.

My young sons have so little connection to my old home, my parental attention to them seem to water down the strength of memory. Perhaps it has made me vulnerable to the intense urban immediacy of Budapest. I felt weak this morning. A wave of depression came over me when I awoke to face the day. My head was full of remembered images of the trip home. I had a good cry but afterward, I got out of the house and made a few calls and felt better. One mustn't succumb to the feeling that no one cares about you. It's not true. No one can carry another's burden but any decent man is aware of his own and so empathy is always arising. Loneliness is the anger of the man who has given up on believing that others also have feelings. Movement is, then, the only cure. Depression is stagnation and fear of movement. Doc says contemplation is not the absence, but the awareness of movement. To "stop" is to sink. A lover, seeing you sink, will not always help, but fearful, will abandon you or even help you drown. Emotional pain knows no age.

Interesting that Crip should figure in one of my dreams. But, after all, I'd often fantasized that he was fucking Helen so it figures that he would reside somewhere in my mind where the raw materials of pain and eroticism are. Maybe he never made love to her. Doesn't matter. Yet, remember the day I came upon him in the lobby of our apartment building by chance? (I had had to return to pick up something I'd forgotten?) He seemed flustered, found out. And the way he persisted, saying he had some tax business with her. "I need to go up, man" (to our apartment on the 13th floor). And then after our nervous chat, "Ok, man, I'm going up!" We said our goodbyes. I felt a twinge in my gut. But I walked away denying to myself I might have stumbled onto their rendezvous. But the greatest revelation is that even if you called him on it—there's not a damn thing you could do short of something crass. Who knows who she's had since the big split? Sad is the cuckold who runs around suspecting everyone. It's a bottomless pit. Remember the chimps at the zoo?

DREAM

Krip is standing above me as if on a staircase. (Probably at the Liszt Academy Concert Hall where he once arranged a jazz concert.) He's trying to persuade a woman, a vague feeling she might be pregnant (Why do men feel like kings when their women are pregnant?), to come to the concert. But then I am scaling a wall. Trying to ascend a ladder? He's talking to me from there? I'm possessed by the idea of getting my poems out of a thick folder and reading them aloud during the concert. But, then, like a klutz, I drop them onto the floor, but they bounce around like balls. I hastily try to pick them up, reassuring myself that they are all still intact, in order and still readable, yet feeling that he will not be interested in hearing them. Yet I have a feeling in the dream that they are better than his music. He thanks me for "helping" lure this woman to the concert. Scene shifts to me driving with Sylves. "I got no savings," I tell him. He seems sympathetic. I see Crip. Somehow he's playing electric guitar under a grove of Autumn trees. He turns in a way that makes me see how big his ass end has become. This must be related to when I got vaguely turned on that time Lydia jumped up from lovemaking to go to the bathroom and I noticed her huge ass. But did I subliminally wanna fuck Crip? Surely not. Freudian shit?

162 DOC

Dear Crip—Here's another letter from several years ago.

t"Helen and so many others I've met over the years, we worship different gods. Unlike her No-God, I can't shake the God of St. Jude of Our Childhood in Edgeton who praised life and promised that its inherent tragedy and suffering would end. I believed that he would be the good shepherd leading me to safety if I asked him. I said, "Guide my steps, Lord." And I have faith that he will. The pathway is of his making and why I must suffer as I walk along it, this remains a mystery. No-God World is a world of action. Reflection, it says, is silly unless it leads to more efficient action. Love, too, exists in this world, but it must always defer to action. In No-God World, love without action is a sterile thing that serves no purpose. It makes no one happy if they cannot act. A marriage between No-God World and God worlds is difficult. Mine failed."

The divorced man is like a lost sheep going from female to female, bleating, looking for his lost mother. He told me a guy came up to him at one of your famous ex-pat parties in BP: "And what do you do?" Josh was too embarrassed to say he was unemployed so he blurted out, "I run a sex training course for young girls!"

Josh was like a memento or some jewel someone sets apart on a separate shelf in some special place perhaps in a sacred vessel. Yours.....

163 JOSH

O moon, my love, you were always there in every late-night apartment window reverie, looking down with your pitying stare. Tonight you illuminate the white apron of winter clouds.

Went walking through the empty streets of Buda this morning—well, a few people shopping at the handful of open grocery stands. A few restaurants open.

Eker, the Turkish place was surprisingly closed, perhaps a Muslim holiday?

The yellow fallen linden leaves make heart-shaped mosaics on the sidewalks, stuck there like wet postage stamps. The colors are vibrant this year because the weather stayed fairly warm through October.

LOVER'S STILL LIFE *for Gudrun*

On the yellow table: 1) ashtray, one cigarette, crumbs of marijuana 2) a pair of earrings 3) half-drunk bottle of wine 4) condom wrapper, torn open, empty, 5) piece of honeyed walnut crumb from baklava slice.

164 KRIP

YOUNG WOMAN BLUES *for Joshua*

She said: "You can fall in love with the girl with the red dress on—I don't mind.

But I can love you better than her—better than anything you can find online.

The red dress girl went to a workout studio after work today

But I'm flippin' through a magazine in the back of a smoky café".

She walked out on the street, thinkin' 'bout me, tryin not to cry,

"I'm gonna go to the movies by myself—maybe find me another guy".

Then, she saw the leaves on the sycamore trees fallen to the ground.

She said, "I ain't no wife, but we got a life and my love is like rain fallin' down.

It falls upon the beggars, it falls upon the thieves,

It falls upon my own true love—but he won't give his love to me.

He always gives me money, his body I get for free

He puts his arms around me—but he won't give love to me.

My mama she loved me, my papa loved me too.

Hey ol'man why don't you love me when I give my love to you.

O I fell in love with an old man—20 years older than me.

I thought it would be fun to turn him on

Fill him full of jealousy.

165 THE END OF THE SONG

by Joshua Celeste (copyright Lacy Corman Enterprises, ASCAP)

Once, there were songs of love

That flowed from my guitar like wine

But in the summer breeze, suddenly I see

An October in your eyes.

O what a dream it was we'd never awaken from

We laughed, we played, never thinking of the day

The end of the song would come.

The end of the song and everyone's gone

The sound of laughter fades

We had our chance, we danced our dance

Our hour upon the stage.

One last glass we will fill

I'll look into your eyes and pretend

"There's still so much time—your love will still be mine

The song will never end

I write the final line

Kiss your lips of wine

The song will never end.

166

The city never sleeps. That's why it's insane.

167 DREAM

When he knew she was really gone he ran out the backdoor and started swimming toward the stars. He got halfway it seems when his arms gave out. She felt no closer. They seemed no further away. He drifted back on the river of heaven

A moon is over Hungary. For a moment its face is bright as night fish, then waves wash over it, turning gray. There are a million moons, he thinks to himself. A billion people trying to find each other.

Crip and I are standing in a Budapest square (Blaha?) there is a loose manuscript, large and unbound pages falling off a bit. There is a trial. A man is seated in a crowded room. An authority figure of some sort singles him out with a word. The man's face freezes in sheepish terror. He is then hoisted up on a sky lift which then becomes a gallows. A sad voice says, slowly, melancholic: "And if there is a blue sky beyond this one—he swings in it still." Final image of hanged man high above Crip's house: blue sky, yellow summer morning.

168 DOC

Dear Joshua—Lost love—it's the Mother you have lost. A remnant of Mother. It's the same as last night at a dinner party when I went out on the veranda and listened to that awful storm. The deep, deep rumble of thunder, deep into the furthest reaches of the sky, the sound of boulders crashing down mountainsides, I suddenly recognized them as a remnant of The Great Storm at the beginning of the universe.

169 BALATON

Go south on the M7 highway. After Szekesfehervar, the terrain changes. It begins to undulate a little more—not what you would think as you approach a lake region—and a more isolated type of village begins to emerge up the small slopes. The long stretches of Indiana-like plain with corn and sunflower fields are still there—but something barely perceptible changes. A lake effect.

At the party Samidha argued with some other Hungarians I'd never met about the difference between noodles (galuska) and dumpling (same Hung. word). Sometimes they are called Angyal Bogyoro (Angel's testicles). "I am the gardener who resists eating his best fruit", she laughed.

170 DOC

Dear Joshua—the artist has no function in the World outside his studio, except to allow his fellows a brief respite from their agony by taking delight in his creation. In the world of action, he's clumsy as Baudelaire's albatross. Instead, the artist must coax the world into his studio—like Sylve's painting in the tobacco barn on Water Maple—where, reluctantly, the world is transformed.

171 KRIP | THE EQUATION

(Tales from the Band Bus)

Cunt is the only cultural experience that seems to have any lasting value for me. How I hit upon this method of pullin birds I can't say. It was pure luck I guess—always a factor in these situations and one which alcohol can enhance, of course. Alcohol is a drug which allows you to walk into a room and in seconds be making out with someone's wife in the water closet!

I lived in Chausee D'ixelle upstairs above the movie theater called Le Cinema Lethe and so each night I could watch all the movies I wanted any time and as many times as I wanted. I started getting into the whole "story" thing that way. 'Blazing Saddles', 'She's Gotta Have It', the one I've forgotten the name of where Gena Rowlands plays an aging professor (it's patterned after "Wild Strawberries"), 'Blade Runner', etc.

But as I sat in the back of the little dark movie theater I realized that I had achieved by pure luck a rare vantage point. I would see the shadowy outline of a girl, alone. Right away you know she's single—right? I would hang out outside then ask her for a light (real original approach!). As I took the first drag I would ask something like, "Did you like the movie?" "Oh, yes." she would say, "I really loved it." Pretty soon I'm walking her home and we're discussing film and art and life and everything. I'm in her apartment. She asks if I want pancakes! While she's cooking I come up behind her and try to kiss her but she won't let me. Oh, no no no. But she's nice about it. After we have our little late night breakfast, she walks me down the hallway of her building and we say goodnight with a little peck on the cheek. Ok, ciao, ciao, she says. Everyone says "ciao" here. It's a good word.

The next day I find a little café across from her doorway and wait around. Here she comes home. As she's unlocking her door I come up and she laughs and gives me a hug and then a big kiss. The kiss of the summer. She makes pancakes and we make love for three days. Summer fades, the nights get chilly. I fall asleep one night with the covers off. She reaches out for me in the night. "O, ton cul est fois!"

I tell her I'm taking the train to Budapest for a few weeks—but I'll be back. She doesn't say anything, doesn't kiss me before she leaves for work. I walk up to Place du Petite Sable and have a coffee. Then I go waste time in Librarie de L'Imaginaire. When I come back there's a note on the door: I cannot for you wait in and you go in Europa far away and speak so with other girls. Adieu."

Josh opens his eyes and he is in one of those make-shift movie house/cafés in Budapest where they just set up a screen in an empty bombed-out lot, beside the bar. Kerts (gardens) the Hungarians call them. He's watching the Danube (Duna) flow by like a movie. It's like Josh is watching a movie of his past as if he was like me in the Cinema Lethe in Brussels. In his daydream, he looks down at the café floor, sticky with old soda pop spills and half-eaten candy bars and cigarette butts.

Medina Univ. Library. The yellow light pouring into the windows. Girls in shorts, no bras. It had been a long winter. He met Berenice through Hector and Free the guy who sounded like Jimi Hendrix. He liked her. He saw her talking to a dude in the library. When he walked by they laughed. "She must know I have this crush on her," he thought. "Must be a big joke for them. Well, fuck her, then. Guess that's a fantasy to forget about." To console himself he went up to his favorite spot, the 811 sections. Modern Poetry, which to him often seemed like indecipherable paintings on the cave wall of his solitude. Williams, Stevens, Pound, Eliot, Ginsberg, Kerouac, Roethke, Lowell, Corso. He remembered how Doc, back from boarding school in the east, had shown him stuff by Housman, Robinson, Frost, etc. He knew he should be working on something else for a class, analyzing pieces of music, but he couldn't resist the temptation, the quest to find out what all those obscure words meant. They must mean something. "This was I, a sparrow, I did my best. Farewell." Like photos penetrating his private pain.

He imagined Williams talking to him, patting him on the back. "Oh, yes, I know son. It's hard to get the 'news' from poems but men die every day for the lack of what is found there." The old Doctor got in his car and drove away.

Nodding off, studying, he suddenly opens his eyes and there she is standing before him with her cascading curls of auburn hair falling all around her shoulders in small waves like Lizzie Siddell in the pre-Raphaelite paintings she would later show him in books.

"Why didn't you stop and say hello when you walked by earlier?" "It seemed like you guys were talking about something important and I didn't want to interrupt." "Oh, that was just a friend in one of my classes. Actually, we had been talking about you just as you walked up. That's why I laughed. Suddenly you appear, like magic. If I looked funny it was because I was a little startled and embarrassed".

They talked. She gave him a ride in her green fiat. He remembered following her home from a bar, once. He'd lost her in traffic. Now here was that car again and he was riding in it. They talked in her parked car under the street light shade of a sycamore tree. He was too shy to make a move so she did. It was the first warm night of spring. She tasted sweet. She drove away. They met again the next night.

He stares down at the filthy cafe floor. He looks up at the movie screen in the adjoining room. Nola's doing the doggie with Mars. He sees a girl at the bar. Cute. A little fat. Big soft bosomy t- shirt. It's starting to rain outside. Excuse me, do you have a light? You like Spike Lee? of course you do, you are American. He's really funny. Did you know it was originally a student film? By the time they reach her house it's raining really hard. She makes popcorn(or was it pancakes). They make love.

"Bocsanat, Uram. Excuse me, sir," the Budapest barkeep says. "Zar ora van. Vee are closing now".

172 PULA, CROATIA

(Josh's journal)

From the bus, I see lovely old limestone buildings. Goats tied, grazing. Very Balkan. Suddenly, on higher ground a magnificent vista of the sea, peninsular thrust, then smaller islands in a fog-shrouded chain at twilight. The open sea seems to curve up toward the sky, the sunlight on its surface creating the effect of a golden road leading to the heavens. On every promitory, a stone church and capanile. The soil the color of chili powder or "Gulyas." Stone fences run everywhere helter-skelter. Old sheep pens. The stucco of the buildings in the villages is pure Venetian.

The sun came out as I walked toward the ancient ruins of the Arena and I noticed jonquils blooming in people's yards. I had driven by it in the cab coming from the train station on my way to the hotel and I was anxious to get a closer look. The old man at the ticket booth just waved me through. Nobody was there. The war had kept all the tourists away.

I stood mesmerized before it. There is a light, yet intoxicating feel to it even though it's made from massive limestones. When I stand before a ruin in Europe I always have an anxious feeling. As if the death preserved there could suddenly speak again. You think, they really did live here, just as I stand here now before this rock- hard testimony, seeing the pitiful little city around—celebrating its 3rd millennium, btw—going about its everyday life unaware of its own oblivion that surely as stone someday awaits it. And that awaits me.

I feel like I could cry like a child, man. For this is the childhood of Civilization I'm seeing. Look what's become of your dreams, your total mental energies, your life en total, you think, as you look into the empty spaces, the missing teeth in a mouth of stone, spaces in the remnant of wall curving into the shape of a bowl. I pity them as dead children, these people, so pitiless as they watched murder and violence for sport, such was their need, born before any Christ to pity them. But it is I myself I pity and mourn for. The incomprehensibility of all life. It was here, it thrived—it vanished.

Even now, little care is taken in this newly awakened once totalitarian country to preserve the monuments. They lay open, unattended and strewn with trash and defaced with spray paint. As I walked past the boarded-up archeological museum I saw an open gate leading into a little courtyard. I walked in and soon discovered I could continue unheeded past a dilapidated ticket booth and up the hill. I climbed half buried marble steps which jutted out, horizontally, like gravestones from newly green spring grass and jonquils and dandelions. I continued up until I came upon another site, a small ruined amphitheater of tiered, worn stones almost covered by the neglected shrubbery which was now an anarchy of thick brambles. I took a little dirt path but it lead into someone's backyard and the leer of the unknown tenant's pit bull turned me back. I soon found another footpath wide enough for a goat and continued up above the forgotten, half-buried fragment of amphitheater, brushing the overgrown bushes from my face. What I finally reached at the top seemed to be, judging from the kitschy looking cannons in front of it, an abandoned military museum, it reminded me a little of Ali Pasha's fortress in Ionanni, that appeared to date from the Hapsburg era. Someone had spray-painted a slogan over the crumbling doorway, "Give us bread—and Prosciutto." So I had the history of Istria all to myself with the exception of one green lizard who, darting in and out of crevices in the formidable cloud-colored limestone walls, guided me on.

173 KRIP

I looked down at the little stone marker Helen and the people in the Balaton village had put there. The tiny memorial, the gesture of people who hardly knew him. Did anyone? But what is a man's life? A brief light glowing in a fog, distant, barely discernable, at last flickering out. But darkness is still darkness. No darker than it was.

174 (ANGELIKA'S TEXT)

"Agnes used to rock little feverish Josh to sleep singing 'O Mary Don't You Weep Don't You Moan' to him."

175

Psalm 27, verse 14

176 JOSH | BALATON JOURNAL

What a wonderful pre-autumnal evening I passed just now. The quiet village spoke to me tonight in a way I don't remember it ever having done before. I knew everyone. I blessed everyone. The poor, the well-off. I listed them all and my family as I whispered my little prayer into the ever-faithful rose sunset of this evening mingled with the steel gray autumn-tinged cumulus clouds. Already the horse chesnut's leaves have begun to brown into the fading green. We've had chilly rains. The Danube is flooding to the North and West of us.

177 KRIP REVIEW

"Celeste's guitar moves through genres not from song to song but from bar to bar as if the whole of American pop music were boiling in the soup cauldron of his creative mind!" – Budapest Entertainment Guide.

178 MAY 1, 1962

(found in Josh guitar case)

Dear Sly,

I spoke with Marsh like I said. He's ok. Cried a bit. Then got angry. I was a little worried. He beat on the dashboard hard and yelled at one point. But then he calmed down and was sorry about it all. He's been so good to me. Really, I think he'll be ok. Still friends.

It's weird playing so close to home in Cincy. People I haven't seen since High School show up at the gig all the time. Not much has changed. Remember how Crazy Reddy used to say, "Let's talk money in the morning when I'm more coherent". He even came by and bought me a drink. He kicks back Tequilas with that same, "Hasta Lambago!" he used to say. He hit a little. Knew quickly it was hopeless. Come on. But the gig pays well. 150 a night. I feel sorry for the band guys. They're only gettin fifty. Miss you. Marvin Everett ('member him?) on drums. Good—but not you. Much love, Agnes.

179 JOSH

At dawn, a wan light comes through my bedroom window and I lay on my back staring at the ceiling. The lost, other world of past life comes to me, appears before me as if the light engulfing the shadow creeping across the room was a curtain being drawn slowly across a stage, each character motionless in some remembered pose.

Only a man who has left his past life utterly behind can see that same life as a complete whole. For hours, months, years, he can stare into his past, peeling layer after layer away until a certain truth appears, at least for himself, a truth almost too much to bear. He is Lazarus. He has seen the end of something—the end of it all. He becomes a Seer, seeing what others cannot. The End. The end of a time and so he knows that he alone can tell the story.

But perhaps the cowardice that made him lose that life in the first place, the fear of the rushing waters of life, that same cowardice now distorts that sight, that vision. He can only go on remembering, peeling away yet another layer but coming no closer, to what? A justification?

The Traveler is in truth a Searcher, searching for his lost childhood. The weekend traveler has only worked up enough courage for brief escapes but the true Traveler, the Explorer, is condemned to wander the world hoping (and pretending) that over the next hill or across the next river he will find consolation and the fulfillment of dreams that never came true.

He is condemned of course because what he seeks he will never find but he is also graced by the blissful inability to stop searching and is thus freed from the everyday constraints of other men, free to pursue his fantasies of heaven on earth which, if he is lucky should preoccupy him for the rest of his days. His passion for the New remains always unconsummated.

180 KRIP | INTERLUDE

I just turned 70. I've been trying to write this story for years now. I keep thinking I should write about me and not just try to remember stories Josh told me on the band bus. I can't remember them that well. I thought I could change a few names. But somehow it hasn't worked out. Make 3 people into 1, 1 into 3, make my own embellishments. But somehow it has to come out true because I really did live it.

I watch tv a lot and smoke dope and tobacco and drink coffee and tea and wine and brandy constantly. I live alone. Helen and I split up. It always surprises me how few phone calls I get now. But maybe it was always that way, I just never noticed because I was never alone as much as I am now. Sometimes it's fun. I can play guitar or write in my journal, but then the thin veneer of everything gets scratched and this scary feeling protrudes from all the illusions. I'll never be more than I am now playing creepy bars at 50 bucks (10,000 Hungarian forints) a night.

When the memories get too much for me I sometimes use Josh's old method of getting to sleep: I recite the Lord's Prayer laying there curled up under the quilt his grandmother Bertha made. I like the part where it says, "Forgive us our trespasses, as we forgive those who trespass against us." That seems fair. Just wipe the slate clean and start over again trespassing.

Seeing people with small children still gives me a twinge of sadness for the lost time when his kids were still small. How quickly the time flew, just like Aunt Pearl warned me it would! Sad the lost time Helen and I argued and mistrusted. But the boys grew! It's all for the best now.

FLIGHT

The good fathers have warm haggard faces with an ample gut, holding their kids like a big-breasted mom. Bad fathers are thinner, stay aloof, looking very stressed, sitting apart, reading a magazine. They metamorphose into each other as I drift off to sleep.

Awakened by take off, holding photos of the boys in my hand, how a crash or mid-air explosion would play out in an instant crosses my mind. Shock? Loud noise? Fire? Pain? Body parts strewn everywhere? I clear my head in resignation. Too late to turn back now, ha ha. Once we were air bourne the pilot said, "Anyone smoking will be asked to leave the plane."

181 JOSH | DREAM

I'm climbing a staircase alone. It's difficult but I get there. I have something with me—a guitar amp? I can't get down without abandoning all my stuff. Wanda appears. We're driving. She has smooth, sexy, light brown-skinned, brown- sugary legs. They're wrapped in cellophane. I am carefully unwrapping her. I wake up.

182

When I was young I anticipated ecstasies and revelations from traveling. Now it's just small joys, the mussels and squid pasta on our last night in Milan with Crip, Emese, and Igor the gourmet Russian/Italian translator/bluesman. Pizzoccheri di grano sarceno al forno. Just being in Piazza Duomo. Nothing else. No pretension. Aware of my genius self and my failed self. I love you both!

183

Leaving the disco, writing by the light of dawn.

How amazing the brown hands, the long soft fingers of the tall girl sitting on the tram at 5 am. She gets off with her boyfriend one stop before me. The lonely one still looking out the tram window. Let it go. It's no use chatting her up at this hour.

How amazing the homeless man, brown with smudge of endless streets, laying on the sidewalk (right in the middle of the square that in an hour will be filled with early morning Saturday shoppers and grumpy people headed for work! Is he dead? No, I saw his half-opened eye twinkle as the tram pulled out.

Dawn. Drunk. No girl. Yet, before, she letting me dance with her and run my hands up and down her arms, her ass, hug her and feel the soft cushion of her breasts, her perfume, enhanced by stale tobacco. How amazing her India linen skirt! Bobbing up and down like a belly dancer. I took a course in it, she said. Then, the faint light coming up in the open air. Two other guys wound up with her. But for one brief moment as my tram car pulled away, though I was resigned, dejected (yet joyful! to have touched her even once was heavenly!) we caught sight of each other and she smiled and waved! Eons hence some child will grow in her womb and be born in the sweet light of dawn!

Another Sunday morning. I wake up with my mind a-flutter with mostly elegiac thoughts. I suddenly burst into tears. Where are my children? We should all be living in a big villa in Croatia together! My shame at having not made more of my life. The prison of cafes where the sound of strings rings out and then dies. No financial foothold. Will everyone be alright without me? Does she know what children need? Of course she does. Ah, her again. How to get past old love? Hatred of her otherness that can't know me. My self-hatred. She made her decision. Let it go. There is no answer. "Everything put together/sooner or later falls apart". Ah, that Paul Simon line has been with me since high school: Berenice, Kiki, Lillith, Wanda... Helen. But it's true. Take care of yourself old boy. Nothing you could have done to change her mind. It goes back to the beginning, someone I probably would never have known, yet, the chance, the aberration or our meeting each other, it created a wondrous burst of LIFE!!! An explosion of possibility. Even if the flame dies back slowly... and even disappears.

184 BALATON JOURNAL

Agonies and Ecstasies of Balaton. The air has a hint of autumn. But it's only mid-August. This morning I awoke at dawn feeling awful. It seemed that the whole edifice of pain and failure and worry was going to come crashing down over me. The doc in BP has prescribed various pills. I wasted my life. Now it's over. It's not life but only survival from here on. I'm no one. My rumpled clothes lay across a chair. Helen and my sons sleep in the other room beyond the kitchen. Crip came by for a visit in the evening. I stand and stretch my arms. The sun pulls me upward. The village is quiet. The Sour Cherry tree's leaves turn red and gold at once. Sparrows swoop in to peck the last of the fruit in the treetops. Later, I walk down to the cornfield and feel of the ears. It seems to have peaked enough for us human folk to eat. It's still tender. Not as tender as the "Country

Gentleman" on Water Maple Farm but... But not ready. The village folk let it fill out much harder and tougher so to fatten up the pigs and goats and chickens. I marvel at the yard, the garden, the little paths, the road and the vineyard fields beyond.

I didn't see the big rabbit this year. Yesterday I saw the Golya (heron) of years past down where the Sio river curves. She suddenly springs again out of nowhere from the bank fifty paces ahead of me and settles in the top of an oak tree on the other side. Lake country. A small prairie. The corn husks are drying, buckskin and purple with strawberry streaks, the appaloosa splotches of Indian corn. The spirit of Marshall's old goddess moved at the edge of the field as the sunset. Pensive Kora making ready for the autumn descent into Hell. The beauty overwhelmed me for a moment and I felt a brief panic. Some pleasant thought came to me and I walked back to the thatched-roofed house.

Laying in bed at dawn I keep running over the events of my life. A sudden revelation: so that's what that meant, eh? That feeling of having figured something out, of having detected something deeper, sometimes ominous, some pattern of reality one had never come to grips with. This feeling descends on me. I need somebody. I can't take care of myself anymore. The hope of finding a woman buoys me up for a moment but then the wariness of falling in love snaps me out of it like a gunshot blast and I'm back to the beginning. What should I do with myself? Find a sugar mama, somebody out there freelancing like me. It's too hard. Working without a net, getting too old to do the double somersault. Yet in the face of it, a joyous resignation carries me forward. Someone loved me once. Many who loved me are far away.

185 DOC

Remembering when Josh and I pedaled our tricycles up past the big horse-chesnut tree beside Judge Daddy's big mansion, past the courthouse and the office that made him such a powerful man in Water Maple county and the parking lot of Chevys and Ford Fairlaines and falcons up to where the big green yard started and then the woods they called the Lost World. We were like little princes. Now I'm nobody.

186 KRIP

In those Budapest days, everybody read Pesti Est or Exit, the entertainment magazines. They advertised what was going on where. I'd get a copy and think what girl I could try to go to what event with. In the rare times, I got laid it was rarely with the one I really wanted. But I persisted. Always planning the perfect aphrodisiacal date. Every time I look at those magazines even now, in wracks at cafes and grocery stores, I sometimes get a hard-on.

The strange story of the 89-ers of Budapest. Almost too sad for me to remember now. Joshua Celeste, son of a farmer, thinking he could hit it big in Europe with his songs and his guitar. Just like Jimi in London! He was born and he "died" in Amerika! He was reborn in this reborn City! He flew toward the light of the Grand Tradition of European Art hoping to find the big bosomy embrace of the Music Mother. He found Life! The acrid, sweaty smell of Life he found in the endless cafes shrouded in nicotine and hash clouds and puke and shit and piss on the floor up to your ankles, crawling with roaches, the smoky wine breath of bathroom make-out sessions—such lovely girls, sweetly optimistic in a new society unknown for a thousand years of Magyar history! And love. He said, "My Grandmother, Millicent, used to say, 'When money troubles come in, love flies out the window.'" Waiting to get paid at the end of the gig, the pungent smell of money doled out to him, what Sylvester Moore called, "Doin' that Dance" in front of the club manager. Love cannot breathe there. The drunken walk home in the empty streets at dawn. He found jealousy and the bitter iron breath of those who felt they were owed by the wealthy West and never compensated. Did you rich Americans help us in '56? Why do you come here? they snarled, to fuck our women? amuse yourselves in our poverty? play among our Ruins!!!???

I've been here so long, the Americans have all left. The Magyar Amerophiles of '89, learning English, traveling abroad, have faded into invisible tech jobs, suburbs, bad marriages and bug houses. All the promises of '89 horribly exposed as bullshit, the fuel of capitalism, the fuel of Life! Which is all we ever had. Yet, I'm still here, the Straggler, The Rememberer, his friend, the guest who wouldn't leave. So many layers now since it came into my head to come here, since the late night phone call from broken-hearted Josh when I told him to come to me here and be reborn! I look for my dead Uncle Schwartz, but they keep killing him over and over. And so, too, Joshua dies many deaths. I wish I could go back to Amerika but it's too late. I lost the thread I spun from all I left behind. He said the only way to know life was to leave everything behind.

I awake from the music of my dream into the nightmare of disconnection. Amerika drifting away. I, the drowning man. The cafes are full of elektronik musick now. Nobody wants to hear Blues or Jazz. It's too Amerikan. It's a new World but there is no new Truth! I've seen both sides of the Equation, the Great Lie but now I cannot speak. Like a virus, one language creeps in and dulls the lucidity of the other. I go weeks without speaking to anyone. A little chat in

Hungarian with the vegetable stand owner, then, my room, bread with goose fat (zsiros kenyer) an onion, a clear brandy and sleep. I wake up in the gray light. This can't go on. My doctor said as much. And so I must get this all down before the light of the New World snuffs it out. I recite a few Psalms before I can face the day, the City, the metal surge that vomits itself over the bridge, over the Danube—even if it's bullshit, I need the rhythm.

187 DOC

Dear Crip, (I hope you don't mind if I spell it the old way, not your "show biz" way).

Being a foreigner can be an erotic thing. When I visit a foreign country I am, for example, much less ashamed of my womanizing because I hold little allegiance to the women of my host country. Much less than I would if I was a native. I can do what I want with them, exalt them or humiliate them without out serious moral recriminations. When a native jilts or is jilted his situation is more complicated due to the multiplicity of his societal connections—family and most especially, maternal ones. When you compromise a woman in the country of your birth you insult your own mother. Hence the hidden meaning perhaps of the term, Mother Country.

A Casanova or a Don Juan might say, A woman wants to submit. I don't know. What's more certain is that a woman requires something in return, some token of respect before dispensing any sexual favors. Without that she will surely snub you, often in a humorously flippant, friendly way, but sometimes very cruelly. Women are always on the defensive, old boy. They have to be what with awful men hitting on them constantly. The seducer should have thick skin but also know when to pitch the pistol and make a run for it. As ever, Doc.

188 LETTER FROM JOSH

I sometimes think of people I'd like to meet in the next life. Hendrix of course. But John and Paul. I felt like Paul. That innocence behind the observations of human nature in his songs—I wanted to somehow keep that intact. Penny Lane. Fool on the Hill. Obla Di. All the pageantry of life: the darker things too hidden and moving too fast to be dwelt upon too long. But they're there. Like a child might think of them. As a kid I remember the shock of seeing someone crippled or disfigured, particularly someone your own age. But I would avert my eyes and try to go somewhere else in my mind, so impossible was it to conceive of a world where this could happen. (Then you get used to it. But even if we joked I felt this chasm). Gentle, good Paul. Yet the feeling that it couldn't be helped, that he couldn't help you. Somehow this crept into the lyrics. He delighted you but couldn't take you into the inner sanctum of the meaning.

But I also felt like John. But years ago I was Paul and you were John. My feelings were more mainstream, my lyrics syrupier than yours. You were sharp, satirical, punful, clever—like Cole Porter. You even let some anger come out. I was still romantic. I regarded women as sacred, untouchable, abstract. Of course, I still do. We both do, eh? In your pain, you knew they were like us so all your songs put them on an equal footing. The girl and boy in your songs—I always imagined them as looking alike. Something androgynous. Erotic. I always looked for girlfriends like the ones in your songs. I guess I never really found one. Women found things in me I hadn't even understood in myself! And when they saw that I didn't recognize my own talent I think my lack of awareness turned them off. I was so out of it in those days. So daydreamy! But I was partly aware, like a child who hears his parents talking about him, but pretends not to hear so he can bask in their praise. They know he's listening.

But then, at the end of youth, you did a 180 and became Paul! And now I am John. The boho John, hippie John, the skeptical yet somehow spiritual John. You could handle the practical world, like Paul. I just never could feel part of all that. Even though I wanted to.

May is the loveliest time in Budapest. Tonight I strolled through the 7th district—the Jewish "kereulet." Where Helen and I first lived together. Such a lovely time. A kind of year-long honeymoon without going anywhere. It ended too soon. How lovely she was! And she loved me, then. Why does love fade? Is it the sudden awareness that one's destiny and the beloved's has become an obstacle to their mutual fulfillment? I'll always remember the corner of Dohany and Klauzal street sunlit in Spring. Bright, sweet May! I had only known her a few months. I strolled along, hands in my pockets.

The past is lost in useless memory. But it's all we have! There's Kadar, the lunch place, the Etkezde. What amazing meals we had there, me feasting on her eyes. And then the stroll back to the apartment to make love. Love. Where do you disappear to?

Yours,

Josh.

189 JOSH

(notebook)

The heatwave finally broke. The sky turned a more European gray and a cool breeze blew into Budapest after a night's rain.

The trip to Romania was great because I got to connect very solidly with Crip and Lydia something I'd wanted to re-establish for many years. Lydia is one of the liveliest women I've ever met. Few people have her buoyant outlook on the act of living one's life, though I can see in her eyes she's had her moments of despair and disappointment.

Crip remains one of the most generous people I've ever met. Whatever he was running from he seems to be running from it less now. I'd always hoped that he'd see me as a kind of refuge or oasis but I'm not sure he sees me that way. It's not surprising. I've needed him too much, depended on him too much. A squeaky wheel gets the grease but there's little faith in its turning. The needy inspire guilt more than hope. This trip remedied that perception slightly I hope. I made it clear to him in our conversation at the cafe in Cluj that I'd worked through most of my post-relationship problems. I think that won a little of his respect.

I recall that conversation now as the images of Cluj form a backdrop to memory. A canal ran beside our table some twenty feet below us. Looking past the bridge, over Crip's shoulder, the hot hazy center of the city bustled. Like the Milan tour the year before, the heat increased that suffocating feeling of urban brutality when there's no American-like airconditioning. Smoking became very unpleasant. There were times I felt, as I did in Milan, that I might have a dizzy spell. Something from the atmosphere around me begins to close in and I become too conscious of my breathing. Is it enough? I feel as if I could collapse and then drown. In the Milan heat I had thought to myself, "I could never live here!" The subways seemed like airless death traps. But then on my return in September, to hang out with Emese, it seemed mild and charming. When Ivan took me to an Italian "homecookin'" spot (he insisted we use the southern terminology!) I couldn't help wondering what it would be like to live there and I began to ask him about rent prices.

Cluj was of course much smaller than Milan, but I'm sure if I ever made an autumn visit I would feel the same way about the Transylvanian Capitol (Hungarian, Kolozsvar). I remember looking past Crip's shoulder, as we talked about the itinerary, and seeing how lurid the lovely, crumbling old facades seemed, the ominous new glass office building wedged into the middle of everything as the rush hour throng cars, office girls, tourists, gypsy wagoners, street beggars moved through the streets, a hot vision-warping shimmer rising from the asphalt. A world gone wrong perhaps, tempers simmering, but a present world, unrelenting.

Doc said that revolutions are the result of a terrible lack of communication. Trace back the mathematics of inadequacy and you will find the beginnings of hate. Recall some of the conversations with the currency exchange dudes in Temple street.

I accept that hurtful things happen. Yet, if I pick at the wound, I'm astonished at how they begin to bleed again. But they scab over quickly and I'm left with just a dull ache.

Oct 28. Just got home. Exhausted after gig. I sat at the kitchen table and thought suddenly of all the souls who waited to be born. Could the people of Bosch's time have conceived of a world war? Unborn souls waiting to die across the battlefields of Europe? The World-soul waiting as long ago as the middle ages for a great explosion. Suddenly past, present, future blend together. Time disappears and it all seems connected. I see how my era will be remembered: I disappear in the fire, the smoke and confusion.

My mind meanders like an old river. I got thinking of how Judge Daddy and Millicent used to sing the old spirituals. Judge Daddy was old and feeble when Mom got some folks from the choir of the black church down the road to come and sing to him, just doing a noble community service for the venerable Judge. 7 generations removed from the singing of their slave ancestors. Some of these folks were now well-off suburban types with nice cars, nice new 2 story brick homes in gated communities, jobs with computer companies or top blue-collar positions. You know what I'm saying. Things were changing, an era removed from the Judges. They finished a few more than competent numbers and the room was quiet for a moment. Agnes started to thank them but suddenly Judge Daddy tried weakly to stand up from his wheelchair. Agnes and Millicent rushed over to keep him from falling. He gripped the handles of his chair, gathered all the strength of 92 years and broke into the old hymn, "Steal Away." He bowed and lifted his head in a kind of "S" shape motion, trying to push out each note through the faint gurgle of his throat. When the last note had died away everyone—me, Mom, Millicent and the whole choir—stood stock still for several moments. What had we heard? Their grandparents would have remembered.

I drift back to Rylytown, the black town of Edgeton, Agnes bringing us home from school in the yellow afternoon light, passed the house Sylvester grew up in, the "broke down palace" they say once belonged to a rich white man who bought their whiskey, Shine and Money Joe sitting on the porch. Up and down, back and forth a thousand times on Edgeton Road. In fall I wore a sweater but by afternoon it was so hot and the air so filled with the smell of crisp dead leaves, the hulls of summer, the drone of lawnmowers and bees among the late flowers, you had to take it off and tie it around your waist. I left that green cardigan on the school bus once and Agnes scolded me. I never outgrew that forgetfulness. How I loved that place, playing in the yard, trying to kiss Wanda Washington. It's all before my eyes in this little room 10,000 miles away. Where are the years? I want to sift through them in a drawer, pausing to savor this or that picture.

190

Dear Josh,

But remember: there comes a time in a beautiful woman's life when she realizes men desire her, but her desire for them she can take or leave. She can control it. She's not addicted herself but constantly hit on by addicts. She's the dealer. She doesn't allow herself to get hooked. That's why, before she left, she said she couldn't believe she had this kind of power over someone. It is a drug. One you might need to get off of for a while.

As ever,

Doc

191 SYLVESTER MOORE

In his Studio

He stared into the center of the blue-black background, the smell of oil paint thick in the air. He dobbed on a smear of bright red in the shape of a mouth—singing? Yelling? Opening to give or deny, to praise or to ridicule. He stands pensive before the canvas. All the faces in the painting. Me in St. Jude Church in Edgeton. I look upward at Cotton in the sky, face in his hands, crying (?) His yellow hair and coffee skin, full lips, full nose, blondish brow, freckled forehead. Now he looks up at me. I hear him say something but I know not to look back. For chrissake don't look back at him! Don't make eye contact. Money Joe's face above Edgeton First Baptist Church, eyes gazing toward the alter. Sylves remembers a day, the rain pouring down the old house, the brokedown palace. He sees Money Joe at the kitchen table, the same face Sylves tries to put in the painting, staring ahead at nothing, and Sylves hears his own remembered voice saying, "And you never did give up the bread. Pops told you to give to my mama 2000 dollars a year, fucker! You was 'sposed to give to her!"

"Naw, naw," Joe said as he stared into nothing, "yo' daddy said DON'T give it all to her cause she don't know what to do with it! That's what he said, no shit!"

"Yes, shit. That's what I say! Don't know what to do with it? You know damn well she cudda fed little Cotton with it. And her workin at Irvine Air Shute AND takin' another job workin for Miss Millicent in the evenings, cookin', cleanin.' And you sittin there on your black ass every night gambling it all away at Crazy Reddy's, pimpin up in Medina. Shit is right. I'm glad the Demeters cut your ass off!"

"It raised yo' ass didn't it?" Money Joe said, raising his voice and coming up from his chair. "She never said she didn't like doin all them dudes!"

"Yeah, and you liked' at money. Why' ont chu money up on this right here! "Don't you come up outta that chair or I'll"... he stopped, dropped his head as he stood facing the old tired, rheumy-eyed man in the dirty white t-shirt, and ragged pants, the man of countless hours in tobacco fields, bluegrass fields of Water Maple county, hands swollen, fingernails chipped and yellow. "It's wonder you left enough undrunk up so I could fuckin' drink a fuckin' 2 cent milk at the goddamn school."

The old man sits back down and closes his eyes. "It's all bewshit. Why you give a damn about it now?"

Sylves stares at the canvas, the singing mouth now green, now orange. A tropical looking tree. Ailanthus swaying in the black background. White leaves bordered in purple. Kandinsky would dig this, he thinks to himself. If he'd grown up black in Edgeton. Then a green-yellow glow like a garden snake. Carlo playing bass, Crip talking to a babe at a cafe table, a hillbillie banjo player. TLC and Ricky boy in front of the barn door. Faces you see in church. The church floating high above Edgeton. Father Hozni flying like a flag, then a cloud, a streak of gray. The cassock and cotta mixed. Josh at the alter holding the wafer when he was an acolyte for Father Hozni. Christ knocking at the door. His burgundy robe against the blue stained glass. And years later the window with the angel, the flaming sword barring the Gates of Eden.

IN LOVING MEMORY OF JAMES "JUDGE DADDY" DEMETER
AND HIS LOVING WIFE, MILLICENT

Sylves is looking into a future he might never see. The yellow afternoon light pouring in through the window. He looks again into the center of the painting.

192 COTTON RETURNS

The tenant house was made of concrete block and sat beside the cornfield where Marshall had once said to Josh, making a sweeping gesture with his hand, "This is my god." Mud spatters had splashed up on the west side wall of the house because of the storms that had come in over Moore's Creek and up the valley toward Tranquility Pike. Sylves, wandering through the woods that day, had found a nice shady spot a hundred yards below the house and he set up his easel and paint set now that the sun had come out and made the droplets of rainwater sparkle on the tall weeds. Sylves eyed the western sky warily as it darkened with another thundershower not far off.

Looking out the window, TLC could see the fancy wine-colored Camaro pulling up to the house. He knew it was Cotton's car, the one they'd shot at one night when they reinitiated those after payday Friday night parties Marshall had put a stop to.

That was the time when Cotton had pulled up at the entrance to the long avenue of Water Maple Farm that wound down the hill over Moore's Creek and then up to the burned-out foundation of the old big house. Bertha now lived in the little house in the cup of a rounded hill where the spring flowed out and down the hill again where it fed into Moore's. You could park with a girl at the entrance, turning off the main road, and no one could see you for miles. You could pull off to the side of the farm road, take a blanket and lay down with her in the soft green grass, a grove of young locusts to hide you. If by chance you saw headlights coming up the hill, Ricky Boy maybe working late taking a truckload of sacks full of bluegrass seed to the warehouse in Cynthiana, you had plenty of time to back your car out and drive away. Josh hadn't been there that night—he had gotten his fill the night they scared Tim Boggle—but he heard later about what had happened. It had been one of those nights when TLC and the boys hid behind the big oaks and poplars and catalpas and waited for lovers to pull in and turn off their car lights. The trick was to give them enough time to get into it pretty heavy and then the boys, TLC and Ricky Boy, would come out yelling and firing off their pistols. "Oh, shit that's Cotton's car," someone said. "He must be home on leave. Hold fire boys!" But Cotton hadn't backed out and raced off when he'd heard the shots like most other frightened lovers caught in the act. The dark Camaro pulled slowly down the farm road everyone called "the avenue," beside the concrete houses where Ricky Boy and TLC lived. A beam from a flashlight had shone into the woods that night. The farmhands had hid behind the big tree trunks. They knew they'd pissed Cotton off in front of his woman. Finally, the car pulled away. Cotton yelled something out the window. Nobody could tell what he said.

And now, maybe a year later, here's that wine Camaro again. Only this time it's the bright yellow light of noon, neither Kiki nor Wanda are riding inside. It was Cotton alone. "Hey, you dim-witted white mother fucker, get your fat pink pimply ass out here. I got some whuppin to do!"

When Sylves heard this he turned to look up the hill toward the blockhouse, holding his paintbrush like a drum stick, "What in hell is that crazy black mother fucker doin' now?" he thought to himself.

Years ago Marshall had told Sylves, "They've never had runnin water inside. TLC and Ricky Boy—none of 'em. They just use the cistern in the side yard. Always have. They're different. I put faucets in there and they take 'em off and sell 'em. When it gets cold they get onrey 'bout goin to the outhouse to take a shit. They just shit in the corner somewhere and go right on. I told 'em to quit it but I can't do nothin' with them. I told them they oughta quit that shootin' and scarin' people. The cops were out here one night. Josh and them was just boys back then sleepin in the tree house. I told the boys no marijuana or I'd call the cops. Just kiddin' 'em, really. Well, Doc told me next morning they smoked one any way and soon as they got it lit here come sheriff Brown flyin down the avenue, siren goin', right passed the treehouse, headed up to the hard road ' cause he'd got a call somebody was shootin' up there! Boys thought the sheriff was comin' for them to bust 'em for pot! Hell, I just let TLC and them alone. I can't let them go. They wouldn't have no place to go! Try to take care of them as good as I can, you know that—don't I?"

"You hear me in there white boy?" Cotton yells, "I told you I was comin' back to kick yo' white ass. "

"You got a gun?"

"No, I ain't got no gun. I'm gonna whip you with my bare hands, boy!"

TLC came out in his dirty jeans and no shirt. His big, knotty hands grabbed the wire fence that bordered the yard from the road and he started to climb over. Faith came out and said something and grabbed TLC by the belt in his pants and said, "You ain't goin' over there and fight no black man. You hear me? We got enough to do right here with these kids. You can't act like that to me. You leave that sumbitch. I'm walkin to Marshall's and call the law right now." From his right side she saw the back hand coming but it was too late and she felt the dull ache and flash of light as she fell back. Her lip was bleeding as she started to cry. "Mama's all right," she said to the kids who had come out into the yard. "Y'all go down to Bertha's and fetch somebody up here right quick!"

"You go on and call the cops Miss Faith," Cotton yelled from the road, "By the time them lazy white fat motherfuckers turn off the goddam Kentucky ball game I'll have whipped an ass real good and gone on 'bout my business. Call' em right now. I don't give a fuck. I don't see Marshall's truck down there no way. He gone somewhere. No trees to hide behind now! He gonna get a whippin' from the biiig baaad black motherfucker!"

TLC climbed the rest of the way over the fence and when he turned around to face Cotton he saw the arm raised and the black jack way up in the air and sensed the flash of something soon to come down to him and the red, yellow light of the sun blinding him and Cotton's mouth open and the neck muscles tense. Sylves put the brush down and started to run up the hill. He saw something move in the trees

"Cotton." It was Marshall's voice. Sylves looked around and saw no one. "If you strike him with that thing it'll be the last thing you do on this earth."

"Marshall Celeste," Cotton says looking around for the voice. "I might have known you'd take my revenge away just like you took my daddy Joe's pride away. That's the way whitey does it, ain't it? Black man do all the work and don't even get half the bluegrass seed money or the tobaccah money or the whiskey money. Not a motherfucking thing. I oughta say Shoot my ass motherfucker, what do I need to live in this white shit world for anyway, but you're hillbillie ass would be just dumb enough to do it. Fuck you mother fucker!"

Cotton sees Sylves standing in the shadows. "And here come your other 'negro.' The artist 'negro.' The big black drummer. The negro who takes care of your horses so white mother fuckers can win money at the track where black people ain't allowed to go."

"Money Joe kept enough money to take care of your yella ass didn't he? When he didn't piss it away with them hoes up in Medina," Sylves yelled out. Marshall, stepping from the shade of the water maple, waved him back.

Cotton raised his hand again. He has TLC in a headlock and has gathered up his graying hair around his hand, pushing him down on his knees and pulling up the hair. Faith cried out from the porch. TLC put up his fists helplessly.

"I'm telling you Cotton I got a scope on this ground hog rifle and the x is right on your forehead. I watched you grow up, son. Money Joe was my friend. But I can't let you hit this man."

"Friend, shit. I don't want no white friendship. Neither did my Daddy. Y'all never did shit for his ass. We just fuck your bitches. That's all we want." Marshall continued to hold the rifle. Sylves turned his back to the fence.

He heard the black jack drop to the black top road. Cotton flipped a bird to everyone and yelled out "Fuck ALL y'all bitchezz!" got in the wine-colored Camaro and drove away. The bolt of lightning came out of the clouds and made a loud pop through the hackberries and water maples along the fence row. Sylves and Marshall both jumped and turned around as the thunder clapped and echoed down the hill toward the creek. "Fuckah nevah hurt me," TLC mumbled as he walked slowly to the house.

"It's awright, T," Marshall answered, "Go on back inside and see about Faith."

The rain came down very hard.

193 MARSHALL AND AGNES

She ran into him by accident at the car garage. She parked her green pontiac beside the Case tractor he'd driven into town. Tractor parts were laid out in pieces over the oily rags like body parts in an autopsy, Shine and Marshall bent over, holding the lantern to get a better look down into the skeletal insides, like a dinosaur being re-assembled bone by bone.

He seemed embarrassed to see her. He was grimy with dirt and grease and sweat and hay. But she enjoyed the earthy look of him, his waist slightly paunchy but his shoulders broad and his shirt clung with sweat to his belly. He said something like "Well, I didn't expect to see you here. I'd shake hands but they're so dang dirty". They smiled for a moment. Without taking his eyes off of her he turned his head slightly and said, "Shine, sir, wonder if you'd be so kind as to finish puttin' the grill back on that Case. I just might be able to finish that creek field by sundown. Or I may just go to the picture show, I don't know. Guess I'd better wash up a bit, though, if I do." He smiled at her, tipped his hat with a polite good-bye.

He courted her. She liked him. She liked the feel of his shoulders as he put his arm around her in the picture show. At her door they embraced. He always lifted her slightly off her feet. She let him kiss her. She loved his smell and the roughness of his neck when she put her cheek against it.

194 AGNES AND SYLVESTER

Her voice and his piano were the buzz of Edgeton High. In the yearbook the caption read, "We'll read about them someday!" Judge Daddy smiled during their duets, but he was humiliated when he thought of what his old colleagues at the courthouse might say. "But what goes on after the show, Judge?" He imagined the young lawyers snickering behind his back.

When the music ended in the parlor he would kiss his daughter. Sylvester, still seated thoughtfully at the piano, running through some chord changes in his mind, the judge would slap him on the back and say, "Son, we both know that's that ol' nigra music. You can citify it a little but it don't change much do it?" Sylvester would be startled by this. But regaining his composure, glancing at tight-lipped Agnes, he categorized it as a "You've never lived 'til you been a black man on Saturday night!" type remark.

"Can you play 'Steal Away', son?" the old Judge asked.

"Yessir, my mama sang that one."

"Oh, yes, I remember your Mama. All your people. Give Shine and Money Joe my best.

"Yessir, I will.

195

Dear Crip—In response to your discussion with Joshua about moments linked together. In an emotional crisis, time stops. Your usual perception of moment linked to moment stops, which is why you chain smoke. One contemplative cigarette leads to another and that restores a sense of well-being. Or, for instance, reefer gives you your reason to continue to the next moment. Filling the pipe is a ritual which takes up a certain amount of time, then, you smoke, then you're high and that in turn takes up a long series (a few hours) of moments and when you come down you simply load up the pipe and the process starts all over again. Other moments, even all the other things you do with your life are arranged around this ritual time. But something like a break-up or feeling sick—these can destroy the sequence of that cycle. You can no longer just float. You have to come down to an external reality that is more imposing. As ever, Doc

196 JOSH

When I was with Lilian, Crip and I went to live in NYC. His Aunt Pearl found us an apartment at West 158th St.near Broadway uptown. Marshall thought we were crazy renting a U-Haul (Bertha called it a U-Drive It!) with all our stuff and going up there, but we had to do it. She was enrolled at NYU for a summer course. I dropped off tapes at a few clubs. Never got any gigs. Lacy was no help. Besides, NYC jazz musicians kicked my ass. I did a few open mic singer/

songwriter things just for tips, Crip got a few bass gigs in party bands. So, we survived.

Lilian and I made love in the apartment. (Crip complained to me about it later). But then Lilian got distant. Then right before I had to go back to Edgeton for some gigs, she got downright weird. She would be weird on the phone when I called her from Edgeton. No more lovey-dovey stuff.

I knew so little about fucking then! Yet, it consumed me. I don't think she knew too much either. I got it in my head I just had to do it OUTSIDE! Like some sort of fertility ritual! We tried it back on the farm in Edgeton. She complained about the little bits of straw. And then she really got pissed when she saw Ricky Boy and TLC watching us from behind the big water maple tree up the hill from the garden.

When she spent a semester at Smith, I'd go down every morning to the mailboxes in the apartment lobby and look for a letter from her. But there never was one. Every morning for the whole year I lived there I kept hoping for a "I love you so"-type letter. Never came. And yet we never had that "Ok, it's over" talk. It just faded. White noise.... Shhhhhh. Mute.

And that's the way it was with the music biz. I kept waiting for a break, the call, the agent of your dreams—never happened. But like Doc described his reality as moment to moment, one step at a time, I was too scared to take a step in any direction. It was like when I used to sit beneath the shade of the big water maple back on the farm, my sneakers wet with the dew, Spanish needles clinging, burs on the canvas uppers, bees droning, rattle of the cattle gate and tractor throttle. The whole "out there" flowing in and out of me. I never knew when to move.

197 KIKI LA SALLE

(taken off my cassette player—Krip, ed.)

I tried to be a good girlfriend but it was just too much—especially when Josh went out on the road. I guess all those years of shaking my booty behind tinted glass 2-way mirrors at Reddy's got me all eternally hot and bothered.

Josh and Doc had me read all this Frenchy shit—Flaubert, Proust, Cocteau, Celine, who I actually liked, Kerouac and Henry Miller, etc. It was okay. They were trying to get me hot. It was honest. At least sometimes—as honest as a person can get, which is never totally honest. I've lived enough now to know that nobody knows. Even if they're as sweet as Josh was. But sometimes I would just get a bee up my butt and start cattin' for a fuck. I remember you coming to

Crazy Reddy's jerk-off palace, the wank tank. The reason I know is that there was this place in the corner of the mirror (another thing Reddy never fixed) where, if you looked just right you cd see the guy on the other side (or even a woman—yeah, there were some). Boom. I saw you.

198 JOSH

So then I thought, you're right! Sex is just another drug. When you get with a sympathetic partner, someone you "resonate" with, then the addiction becomes stronger. Lover=addict. You'll keep your hand on yr cell phone all night if you think yr gonna get a booty call. Sex energy is in a raw state. But sometimes it takes only a small event, a glance, a song, a drink—to get the process going. I can remember Doc saying once, "The digestive system starts at the tongue tip and goes all the way to the anus". That's kinda what I mean. The process. If both sides of the Equation are balanced. Flowing into one place. What ends in staggering orgasm might start at some mere suggestion. Like the spring that starts a river. The suggestion becomes more kinetic. Word becomes Flesh. It stands up. Then it can get purely aesthetic—struck by the sheer beauty of her body, the female form, celebration of male enjoyment of it. Once you feel that you can't completely possess this object of lust it becomes even lovelier. A beautiful poison floods your heart and goes down into your thighs. All encounters become this ONE encounter. Transcendent. Musical expressions. Jazz solos. My hour upon the stage. Born of the Whore. Lust. Then I reach up in the dark with her astride me panting and I see all their sweet faces, the creamy asses, the labia lips of flowers and I see a light (or ache?) on the ceiling. Like I could touch it. But I knew I had already touched it. Riding, riding. Waves over me. Something beyond the bodies! As if God said, Come! And I do! And come through the body to the real desire: a simple life, a breath. Empty your crotch ("Warm feeling in the tummy"—Berenice) and a spirit starts to fill the empty place, like grass licks the wound the plow makes. Weeds grow round the raw bulldozed earth.

Then, suddenly, boom—all gone. Poof! Withdrawal. Agonizing search for the new drug. Someday maybe yr cured. That wd be something different. But you'd have to be ready for it. The union no longer with Body but simply in the mind. A loneliness. Age? An emancipation?

199 KRIP

So, yeah, I thought, Good lord, I can't resist this shit: tall amazon chick, short, reddish, hair—like the one Josh got hung up on years later in BP. Was it dyed with blond streaks? I would just pop my cock out my zipper and let my swollen balls pouch out. She'd suck and then lift it up and take one ball at a time into her mouth, then try and wiggle both in. A bottomless pit. I lit a match once to see her doing it better and nearly caught her hair on fire! Everything about her I craved: the inside of her thigh, the pocket of her clit. Kissing up her arm, licking her neck. Jeans make that thhhwack! Sound as they slide off. Grab 'em just under the heel as they slip down off the round ass. Sucking as many toes as I can get in my mouth. All five! She giggles and says it tickles too much. The smoothness of her nail on my tongue.

But then one day I thought, What if I can't get past this and get to the next moment? In this ecstatic state, she controls each moment. You're like a dog with your tongue wagging, waiting for the treat. But then the Mistress disappears! Poof! Gone. "Make sure you've got something to look forward to," Doc always said. "The movie of YOU, the one you are still acting in (consciousness!), don't let it stop. Not before you, your mortal self does."

I thought of the voluptuous beds of America so absent in Eastern Europe. In Budapest always the cot like trundle bed. Laying there staring at the ceiling again, thinking of the house on Tranquility Street. Josh and I became roomies there— for a while.

"I didn't build a strong enough life," he told me, once, falling down the abyss of some lost interstate to nowhere on the band bus.

In those days girls would just show up at our place. There was no need to go out. We should've gone out. We got too nuts in there. Money Joe stayed over at one of our little parties, a little drunk. We got him high on reef, put acid in his rum and coke. He used to call himself James Brown, Jr. and spin around and dip like the real JB. Then he would come out of his spin, look a bit anxious and say, "Is that me or the record? Hey man! Shit be wrigglyin' on my arms man! Why you do this to me, Crip!" Finally, we talked him down. He called us all little Dick. "Hey Lil' Dick! Even if you HAD a dick, you wudn't have enough ass to sink it! You stringy-haired Jesus-lookin' Muhfucker! What you lookin' at?"

Then I looked over at Jared Smallwood and he had a plastic bag over his head, sucking it into his face and you could see the mold of his nose and eye sockets like they'd been popped out. Like a cyber-mannequin and making kazoo-like vibrations with his plastic covered mouth. Big Party.

200

He shouldn't have walked there. The old apartment. Just curiosity I guess. They'd been broken up for months. He crept up to the window. So strange. Just as he worried, or hoped, it might be! Berenice was a-straddle this guy. He looked much younger than her. The boy was on his back, arms extended out. Berenice was pushing herself up and down, her hands supporting herself on his broad, hairy chest. A faint layer of sweat covered her back, which he could see in the candlelight, and on her upper lip. He could faintly see them in the antique mirror slightly to the left of the cupboard. He reached down into his pants to masturbate as he watched. He could feel his heart pounding like a broken drum. They went on like that for some time. He had never seen her genitals from that angle, the way her pussy grasped the shaft of his cock like a mouth. The boy slid out from under her and pushed her head down. With her ass up he spread her out and entered her from behind, grabbing her curly hair and pulling her back while pushing her spine downward. He saw her eyes in the mirror. His own barely peaked over the sill. Did she squint in pain? Her eyes bulged out, then rolled back in white. She pursed her lips and moved her jaw up and down, breathing heavily. The boy first put his fist in her mouth and she licked his fingers and then he stretched her lips apart with both index fingers as if to simulate a smile. A car was coming. The light might expose him, he said, as he told me the story. He got on his knees in the hedgerow and knelt in the fragrant mulch and came in his hand.

Then I started gigging a lot. I had moved to New York so suddenly I got all these bass gigs with bad cover bands. I went with Josh on one Lacy Corman tour. That's the year he told me most of these stories. We'd drink. Get stoned. We could smoke reef in the back of the bus if we opened the back transom, like a polaroid pop up camera, accordion sides. Sometimes you could make out Orion through the crack). But I got fired before the tour ended. (Not as good as Carlo––I said that before). Then I didn't see Josh for a while. I heard he was not working that much anymore. The college party circuit we had both once depended on had dried up for jazz groups and had turned into a Neil Young kind of singer/songwriter thing. Every computer science major from Ohio to Tennessee seemed to have an alternative "grunge" band. Hence my split. And club owners realized these kids would play for even less money than we did!––free! Josh was cool, though. When he wasn't transcribing 'Trane solos or playing with Lacy Corman, he'd sit in with jam bands with guys half his age. Josh encouraged them, gave them guitar and jazz theory lessons for free, talked shop with them, etc. The girl singers in these bands (Wanda was in one of them) all worked day gigs waitressing in the Mad Farmer Café, a vegetarian place. That may be where Josh first saw her. All grown up. He would play there on off nights just for meals––stuff like tofu parmigiana, brown rice and brown bread, washed down with a pinot grigio or cabernet in winter, a hot cup of cinnamon coffee or a clove iced tea. Whoever reads this, get the broccoli crepes or the sour cream burrito and finish off with

485

Wanda's Italian Cream Cake. Wanda's mother grew up in Trieste, btw.

201

I imagine little Josh walking to the fence, looking out beyond Water Maple Farm to another man's land. "This is another man's farm. What does that mean? What is the land without fences? It belongs to no one." He thought of his father asleep in front of the TV—black and white scenes of a western going by. Cattleman vs. Sheepherders. He looked out at the dry tufts of ripe bluegrass stalks. They looked the same on both sides of the fence. Wild Cherry trees, Elms, Water Maples, Tulip Poplars, Kentucky Coffee Bean Trees, Sweet Gums, Hackberrys, Ashes.

202

Marshall in his office gazing at Dexter's old fiddle on the wall. Dexter played hoedowns, he remembered Money Joe's little mandolin, Shine dancing, little Sylves not more than 3 years old, dancing with him.

203

Aunt Pearl was disappointed when the rejection letters from Harvard and Yale came. But I did get accepted to BU. It was in Boston so I'd be near Harvard and not too far from her in NYC. In fact, at that time many Harvard philosophy profs had been lured into BU by the new BU president John Silber, who was something of a noted philosopher himself. Silber had a deformed arm. Taking a shit in the classroom building bathroom, once, I looked up and saw written on the stall door: "Silber swims in circles." I studied with Alastair McIntyre, Joseph Agassi and Erazim Kohak. I studied Jewish history with Nahum Glatzer and Gershom Sholem. It was pretty big time stuff. It had been Swartz's dream for me to go to an Ivy League school and so he had left Pearl enough money for that. BU was much cheaper so Pearl kept the rest in a savings account. It all seemed to work out because Josh would come up to visit Lilian at Smith. He called hitching from Medina to Boston his "long commute." He always liked telling the story of that one trip when he hitched through PA, getting caught in a snowstorm out on the highway and that guy who gave him shit for bumming a cig. Long-haired hippie Josh walking up to a stranger in the truck stop restaurant, "Scuse, sir. Do you have an extra cigarette?" "There's a whole machine full of them right there son," he sneered.

Shock of rejection. Visit to my dorm room. Some guys from down the hall dropped in. I didn't like them particularly, didn't hang out with them much, but the door was open. "Man", one of them said, "Crib, you wouldn't believe this Smith chick grad student we met at NYU the other night. Completely wild. Fucked us all.

"Oh, really? Who was she?"

"Some chick named Lilian Carpentier." Remember that one?

204

Sometimes your insides quake like the earth. Mountains slide into your heart. Love. Water Maple High. Spring day. Smell of sex. Stranger's breath. Legs splayed, lips grip shaft like a mouth. Making out at the bus stop. Images stick with you like honey and you get it on your fingers. Poison memories going down into your system. Big ass. Death. Shocks. Cattle prods TLC and Ricky Boy and the truckers used, herding cattle in the pens on the farm. She had tried to break it to him gently, "whole machine fulla dem right dere, buddy!" Farmboy Josh was young but still unaware of the urban world that had grown up around him and that he had felt compelled to plunge into. ("You can't play music to the cows." Sylves). The windows on the Greyhound icing up. He only had enough money to get to Cincinnati then he'd have to hitch. He thought of the pretty girl he'd talked to in the cincy bus station when he got there. Cute, short hair, dark Mediterranean eyes. He asked her where I-75 was. "Right over there," she'd said, smiling, pointing down the embankment. He had wanted to talk to her, to tell her how he'd lost Lilian and then she'd pity him and let him nestle his tired head into her arms and go to sleep, and when he awoke he would be home in his bed at Water Maple. (Years later, the old house was demolished but he could describe every room to me. Memory is greater than reality!). He woke up, turned to ask her the time but she was gone. When he finally got to Medina he was in a delicious trance of hunger and amazement. Joshua Celeste walking down North Street from I-75, passing Crazy Reddy's Fish Fry and Jazz Club. All the recovering junkie jazzers from Lexington played there. One day Reddy would let underage Josh come in and listen to Sylves' band over soda pop and a creole fish sandwich. If he'd only known, walking past it, that someday he himself would play there. Kiki La Salle would sing. She would say, "Let's get your mom to sing. That would be my dream!" Agnes had known Reddy in high school when they were both beboppers, so Reddy said, "Sure. Be great to hear her again."

They'd bring her up at Christmas parties to do "I'll be Home for Christmas" and some gorgeous ballads, the way she did them like nobody else. Sylves would play piano. But it was more of a free-blowin gig: Carlo would be talking about Bartok polyphony, Sylves would be trying out Cecil Taylor licks. I would come over, too, and sit in, even though I sucked on acoustic bass (was more comfortable on electric) but Sylves and Carlo had all this telepathy going on between them on stage all the time. They had decreed no electric bass on jazz gigs. Carlo only played electric on a country gig or a blues or rock type show when he knew the drummer would be playing too loud. On the jazz jam, they would often do Coltrane's "Moment's Notice". Josh wrote some lyrics and sang them for Agnes and everyone one night.

On these Sunday jams, we'd wear dark suits like the Marsalis brothers. We wanted to look like the folks coming out of the Soul Tabernacle Church, out of respect. Carlo would actually be coming from there, he was now the director of the church choir! He and Sylves would be the rhythm section. It was a black club. But no racial tension vibes. Maybe on a weekend night, but not on Sunday. On Saturday Shine said don't go up there, they kill yr ass. And some of Sylves' old high school girlfriends (they were in their sixties by now!) would make him sit with them on a break, look over at Agnes, and laugh and make over him.

"He shudda never come back from out there at Redd Fox's place. Ain't no good music places in Medina. Not any more. But we's glad to have him back even if he don't do nuthin' but foal mares and paint them crazy pictures! You see, Josh, we were the bebopper kids in high school: Monk, Bird, Diz, berets, sunglasses. People thought we was crrrazy! We listened all the time and we told Sylves, You can do it, man. Go out there and DO IT! And he sure do think the world of your family. You better get on back up there and play. Play Moment's Notice. That's a pretty one. Sylves likes all them kicks!"

After the gig, Sylves would treat him to a big plate of ribs with Reddy's special Doo Wop sauce.

And Josh would go to the tobacco stripping room and watch Sylves paint. "Sylves, how can anybody learn this music? It's too hard, man. I can't go up north and out play those Yankee cats."

"Then don't go."

"I thought you said, 'Don't play to the cows'?"

"You can play to them if you want. What do you want?"

205

So, Josh came to stay with me in Boston. We went walking in Cambridge one night and found a little jazz club called Uba's Too Strong Cafe. A band called Ghetto Mysticism was playing. We dug on the tenor player: an oriental-lookin brother with a button-down bebop cap and floor-length overcoat (place had no heat to speak of). Played a lot of soprano. It was like seeing 'Trane. Like, we could now put 'Trane in a body.

Josh said, "We went east. The sun rose later. The sound. The star. The stain. Never could shake it after I saw that dude play. That brother's shit got down in my soul."

That poison Sylves said goes down in yr system.

206 DOC

I have this thought a lot: the world is less responsive to me now. Or was the responsiveness I once felt—women nurturing my ego, colleagues making flattering comments—just a youthful illusion? The lifting of the veil of the spiritual beliefs engendered in me by Sundays at St. Jude of Our Childhood is now a source of feelings of loneliness. Josh feels the alienation of being a foreigner. Yet, it's that same alienation that strengthens one's feeling of independence. But is it, in the end, just another euphemism for loneliness? I always think of Williams' line: I was meant to be lonely—I am best so. I see clearly now such things prepared me for Now. Before, I was just a dilettante, an assimillado without knowledge of real life. Now, such lines flow through my veins. I hear them every day whispering in my ear, like pictures of my family. They sustain me like calls to a friend at 3 am.

Life is not a movie, directed by God and starring You. This is my great revelation of middle age. And one's concept of God—painful as it is to leave things behind—must adapt itself to these inner changes. Is there a moment when the child's God and the adult's God, the different conceptions, don't segue into each other and a chasm appears? A terrifying moment. Gazing into the bottomless pit. Is not this life's only real moment of Truth?

And God or no God, that perception of emptiness doesn't change. Are we different here on earth even if heaven's up there or not? Life is a waiting room. There's nothing more terrifying than this world. This is hell. The waiting. You can get out of it, of course. But wait patiently, or else run the risk of losing aeons of Karmic ground?

207 JOSH'S JOURNAL

This is the dead season. In the bleak mid-winter of Budapest now there is little separation of between night and day. A gray light covers all, day after day, until it finally submits to a pitch-black often bathed in fog with only the dim buildings and car lights visible. The street runs with a black liquid which freezes and remains black. A new snow is falling over it all. It's New Year's Eve. I don't have a gig. I look out into the corner of the building where the pigeons huddle to stay warm.

This is winter's vertigo. I need the lamplight as much in the day as I do at night. Night or day things look the same, the gray sun in morning, the pale street lamp at night. Day after day we move through the same light.

I never learned the ways of men, their stock markets, their politics, their world order, but I did, after so many loves, learn the ways of my own heart. And, so, I assume the hearts of everyone bare some similarity. So, I feel justified in thinking my feelings are universal.

I hung out with my high school friend, Crip, when he came back from Boston to Medina and enrolled at the University. I played gigs at the local cafes. We did what college buddies did: drank together, chased women together, although I was then going through a bit of an ascetic phase after Lilian and I broke up, which Crip snapped me out of. He rejuvenated my love of life. I even sat in on a few of his classes. Guy Davenport's literature course was one of my favorites. Crip taught me the joy of harmless cruelties toward other students. We loved blowing the cover off sauve bullshit artists as they attempted to put the make on an unsuspecting co-ed with pseudo-intellectual patter. We called it "cunt blocking" or "cb-in". Crip was quite good at stealing chicks away from guys. He had that rock star look of the day, curly hair, thin. We loved laughing at the world and exposing those we thought were imposters. But looking back I don't think we knew how to distinguish them. He would often turn serious and rail against his Jewishness and the way the Jews treated the Palestinians. We were only exposing things that needed no exposing. And our world was mostly contained within the campus.

208

A story of despair always seems to arouse more interest than one of hope. But I have sung so much Blues, told my sad story, wept more than my share of tears.

For now, let us change the tune to one of renewal, rebirth, if not hopeful at least truthful.

"We both committed suicide in the US. We were reborn in Budapest!"

He was right of course. How like a dream of rebirth my first days were there with the dry dust of my spiritual American death still clinging to my boots. I stared out our apartment window. I rode buses and trams rolling down a strange urban river of strange words hanging from buildings. People looked so different, a beautiful race of people with an oriental teddy bear cuteness about them, passing by, dressed in similar clothes, chattering a language of dream. Mist-shrouded bridges hanging fragilely over the gray waters, the jagged smile of the bomb-scarred waterfron—a mouth w missing teeth—the Hapsburg yellow of Castle Hill (and where Agnes' hotel was years later on a visit), the mustard and burgundy tiles of St. Matyas Cathedral spire, the looming strength of the dome of St Stephen's basilica seen through the slot of a narrow street looking down and across the Danube.

BALATON JOURNAL

I've been back from Budapest for one week.

Here, I reconnect with the insect past of my childhood. This morning, hoeing thistles, I heard the bees—their droning, a sudden whirring past my ear. I hadn't heard it in many years, only in a distant echo of memory and I remembered the fields of Water Maple Farm I wandered so long ago. And the hoe brought back the pungent odor of wounded weeds. As I write two huge flies buzz my head.

I wake up between 7 and 9 in the morning, sunlight streaming into my eastern window. Helen sleeps with the kids in the next room. It's not so bad sleeping alone. I can fart or wank at my leisure. But I miss the human touch. No woman has touched me for a long time.

My breakfast is a thick slice of buttered bread with cinnamon sugar or honey. I drink Lipton "yellow label" tea from a fruit jar. The boys are eating cereal a bit grumpy, they watch videos or cartoons. (Usually, kisses or hugs are not permitted until later in the day!) Gordon sometimes comes in and cuddles up in the cool morning. He seems to sense things people like and if he can he likes to try and provide it for them. He enjoys the feeling that he can make someone happy. He does. And he enjoys reciprocal attention. Ryly sees little gain from a mere regular hug, but he sometimes seems to surrender his independence a little and volunteers a hug on his own without any prompting from me. Perhaps he feels a twinge of loneliness himself. At any rate, it feels wonderful when he shows affection. He's not afraid of asking for affection, but it's rare that he seems to need it.

Lunch is borso leves (pea soup in a tomato stock) or paprikas csirke galuskaval (chicken stew with homemade noodles). Then the boys have a nap hopefully. They wake up grumpy, but then we shoot basketball or go for a nature walk, read, or play hide and seek. "Papa! Let's play hide and seeeek!" they yell with their sweet Hungarian accents. Gordon simply says, matter-of-factly, "I vant hide and seek." I close my eyes and count and hear them scurrying around for a hiding place. They hide in the clothes hamper or Helen's wardrobe. Suddenly you're aware of how small they still are.

It's supper time and the sun makes its way down toward the lake to the west of us. The sky pinkens then turns to fiery orange. My favorite thing is to grill chicken or pork (steak and hamburger don't exist) or wok something (chicken with carrots, peppers, onions, garlic in a tomato base) over noodles or rice. Helen makes one of her Magyar specialties I mentioned: a paprikas (lots of paprika powder), cabbage noodles (kapostas teszta) or meat soup (hus leves). All this costs but a few dollars. When I cook I love to sip a glass of wine. The dark, dark reds from Szeksard are my favorite but a few famous Magyar whites can also be good. Very good wines are also cheap. Wine and fresh bread every day I would miss that if I left here.

9:30 pm and the boys are wild. Getting them into bed consumes our last bit of energy. Helen has just bathed them. Sometimes there's time for a book in English. Mother Goose (Ryly calls it "Mother the Goose") has been a workhorse so far but sometimes there's "Green Eggs and Ham," "The Sleep Book" or Edward Lear's "Nonsense ABC." We fuzz out on some bad tv movie or variety show. Ryly is a tv nut and Gordon is learning from him.

"Kiss me goodnight," I ask. They hesitate because they know that now the light will go out and darkness means the day is really over but they acquiesce and already their eyes are heavy with sleep. I spread the mosquito net around the bed and go back to my room. (It also keeps the flies out. There aren't so many, now, yet even one can be awful annoying in the morning. Read. "American Tragedy" blew me away. Haven't felt up to another one since then. Strangely I found a copy of Auden's Complete Shorter Poems in a dusty corner of a Balaton bookstore. "Cheers, mate," it said in the flyleaf, "See you at the language school (Magyar bird magnet!) next summer!" pretty impenetrable stuff but it keeps me on my toes.

Where was it I was once loved by a woman? I must break out of my narcissism! I thought this today while watching the wind in the trees, "Will all my neurotic thoughts and silly memories just disappear? How I passed the eternal-seeming days, blend back into the black, forgotten, starless night?

209 JOSH AND BERENICE

The morning after Carlo's wake my memory wants to go back twenty years or longer when my beloved yellow spring light, sunlight the color of forsythia, shone over everything. And sparrows and starlings and the red cardinal flew in and out of the sprouting green bushes and a warm wind blew up into my shirt and my bicycle wheel splashed the puddles from the spring shower and so bright were the dandelions and violets, egg yolk and the royal violet of the veil when they veiled the alter and the gold cross with symbols of Christ's triumph over death. In a week they say He and His earth are reborn.

There was a group of us musicians. We played the college town bars. There is a perpetual youth that college townies can recapture every autumn with the return of thousands of students coming back to enroll. We played anything anyone would hire us to play. Anything that sounded good with a drummer, a bass player and a guitar I carried on my back as I bicycled through the eternal yellow light, the dandelions, the purple Christ-like violets of April, the white clover blooms spread out before me, the sun a gold cross veiled in purple—props for a Story all others descended from; the redbird in his black mask, a droplet of bright blood in the small green leaflets turning gold.

Her hair was yellow as golden thread. Tufts of it curled just above her pale shoulders. Eventually, we lay curled up with each other. The paleness and redness of her I breathed in patchouli and curry and sandalwood. In my passion, I almost fainted. My desire, desire for total possession, abated and love and devotion seeped in in the shadows. Love becomes a shadow and the sharp yellow light of the engulfing kiss, the dark pink tongues full of blood, feeling the softness of teeth, gently probing the throat and mouth, lips kissing and kissing, and brief sighs of breath, pink pomegranate nipples glisten with saliva, the whole pink-brown earth rises to meet the sun and the bronze moon rises and the swallow-winged sky, all of this brings love's afterglow. Finally, the traffic fades and the city lays its head in the crook of its arm.

The onion smell of supper simmers in the kitchen, the blue of the TV screen drones like bees. In the lamplight, the moth flits, the window goes dark and mirrors the ferns and the table set with silver. She leans to light a candle with one soft knee in a chair. She leans to kiss me. My bicycle leans against her bone-colored wall.

210 KRIP

The world seems to look at you differently when you get older even if you don't look at yourself that way. I can see I've aged but I don't feel very different. I only have a vague sense of having lost energy. That's all. I feel wisdom from having lived long enough to see recurring generational patterns. But Action can only benefit from the Wisdom of Experience after the fact. Therefore wisdom is useless in the world of action.

A man keeps constructing the same world, the one he was most loved in, over and over throughout his life. My life in Europe was a reconstruction of my life in America. "We committed suicide and were reincarnated here!" And vice versa. Everything I did was a version of what I had done. In both places, I started virtually from scratch. And yet think of the worlds before me that I sprang from!

Remember my silly notion of "the Equation?" the balance or duality or yen/ yang of things. Not opposites but dependencies. As a young man, I first broke it down into "looks/attraction," or "money/power" (and the resulting fame) but there is also self doubt/floating (Clyde in AMERICAN TRAGEDY) or narcissism/ martyrdom. The equation is based on what people will do given the situation they're in and their choices are few. Do/Should do. "All is number." But Father Hozni said sacrifice changes the whole system.

211

Little Marshall stood barefoot in the snow and watched his house burn down. Bertha, his mother, darted around from room to room but it was no use. She tried climbing in but flames shot up the ivy-covered walls where the old air conditioner unit sat in the window. She tried pushing it in but it was so hot from the flames inside the room she burned her hand. Finally, she backed away reached her apron up to her nose, coughed once and fell on her knees and wept. Marshall came closer to her but didn't touch her.

She sobbed and screamed, "If only that drunk sum bitch were here now!"

Together they watched their past drift away on plumes of smoke. Bertha suddenly looked down at Marshall's feet.

"Lorda mercy, child, you ain't got no shoes on!" Marshall watched the snowflakes disappear into the flames. She took off her sweater and put it on the ground for him to stand on.

"I think there's some old wool socks Dexter left in the tack room. I'll go look," Bertha said shivering and moving away up the hill to the barn.

"Thank you, mama," said the little boy. "O mama!" They felt so warm on his feet.

212 JOSH

The yellow light streams out onto the gray-white limestone gravel-paved lot in front of a workshop, with its metal, sloping roof painted dark pine green. The workshop is built of concrete block walls. You enter by a small pine door with a brass knob. Just to the left of the door is the large garage entrance, about 20 feet wide, with a sliding door lifted overhead on a greased track with one jerk of the arm. To the right, connected to the far concrete wall runs a large open-sided shed supported by 8 pine posts placed at intervals of about 12 feet. Each post marks off a ten-foot space. A basketball goal hangs over the next to last one. In these spaces 2 Farmall tractors are now parked, a New Holland hay baler sits 2 more spaces away. Marshall stands with a welders mask on, making some repairs. The apex of the angle of where the shed joins the concrete wall of the Shop faces almost directly into the western sun which has just begun its slow decline.

The back of the shed as you walk around behind it is almost even with the ground which rises steadily up as you walk. So, the roof on the back of the shed is very near the ground. All us kids, Doc and Angelika and I, could just take one step up and we'd be on the back roof, whereas the front drop off was some 15 feet. The same lower back roof faced a large open yard which was once part of the yard of the old house that burned. (There's a picture of it in famous photographer, J. Winston Coleman's book, Farm Houses of Water Maple County). Bertha raised a big garden here every year. I raised a garden for my 4-H project one year, but Bertha did most of the work. She liked to weed and hoe, she said. And she was always on the lookout for the ring she said she lost up by the big maple tree. What had been the foundation of the old house was now a big hole in the ground filled with weeds and brush. We were forbidden to play near it.

"Could be copperheads innair," Bertha would say. But Bertha's arthritis ("Artheritis") made her quit gardening and we used that backyard for a baseball field. Doc read a book about WW1, so, he took some whitewash from the shop and painted a cross on the concrete back wall and called it "Verdon Field". The wall made a fantastic backstop.

The field behind the shop sloped and rolled on and on westward down to what Marshall called the "dead cow gulley" where the carcasses of dead farm animals, unusable for meat, were dragged to by a chain behind a tractor. It was a real secluded place. It seems it was once a creek bed. But now it was dry. I went there to be alone and think.

The silence is broken by a distant drone of a tractor and fat pollen-soaked bees working holes in the shed posts. Marshall would squirt malathion into the holes and bees would fall out writhing on the ground. The baseball bat cracked with the sound of a baseball as me and Doc as Vada Pinson and Frank Robinson, 3 and 4 in the batting order just hit back to back home runs and lifted the Reds over the New York Yankees. "Swung on, deep to center field, back, back…

BALATON JOURNAL

The last night in Balaton for the summer. It was the best summer we'd ever spent here. The beach at Siofok is empty now. All the East German tourists have gone home. I wrote some long letters to Carlo and Crip, scratched the surface on a new recording project, took my jazz quartet to Slovenia. It was strange thinking of the times Helen and I had spent there in Adrato years before.

APRIL 21, 2000

Riding on a train out of Bratislava after the gig. Such misery in your thoughts about what lies ahead at home as you look at the pathetic garden plots under the vast open network of huge cylinders of oil and gas pipes winding through refuse and phone lines that resemble a giant's anarchic moonshine still!

Perhaps the illusion is thinking that if you let yourself go down a dark enough alley you'll find the light. But more darkness is all you find. Coming into the light is a sheer act of will, not an accident.

213

Josh pushed open the door of the Joyland bar in Medina with his free hand, puffing a little, while in his other hand, his stronger left one, he carried the old Skylark Gibson amp, the one Marshall'd bought for him so long ago at the Schwartz Pawn Shop for his thirteenth birthday. It still sounded good.

A couple of regulars at the bar, both lawyers it seemed from the way they dressed, made a move toward him as if to help, one of them eventually sitting back down and letting the other make the offer. Josh nodded his head in gratitude but motioned him away, stopping for a moment and setting down the amp against the door as a kind of doorstop.

"Thanks, man, but I'm just gonna set this here and go back and get some more stuff."

"Well, all right. Need some help with something else?"

"Naah," Josh said, I think I can handle it."

"Yeah, ok, me and my friend here are gonna hang around and listen for awhile if you don't mind."

"Don't mind a bit. Glad you're here."

"We hear you're the best geetar picker from here to Water Maple County!"

They both laughed and Josh looked up wondering why they thought it was that funny. Then he realized they were a bit drunk already, full of themselves, work done, big weekend.

"I did some work for your grandfather Judge Daddy once," the more talkative one said. "A lot of things going on now in Water Maple Co. Heard your Dad's place is going up for sale."

"I don't know a lot about it," Josh said. "I haven't been down there in a while." Foreclosure proceedings had begun on the farm. Josh didn't want to think about it. He figured every lawyer around was talking about it. The evening sun was going down. Downtown Medina nightlife was beginning to stir. Crazy Reddy drove by in his big Yellow Thunderbird and waved. He's out on the big town tonight, Josh thought. He brought in the rest of his equipment and grabbing the doorstop amp set it all down on the little barroom stage.

The vague light of beer promotion signs, passing headlights, street lamp light—all this reflected itself like broken glass on the little spills of beer that shone on the black and white tile floor. The leather of empty booths, smooth as polished stone invited escape into secrecy and conspiracy and the cover of night and idle conversation. The barback carried cases of beer up the stairs. A beautiful waitress in tight mini-skirt and low neck sweater, her hair dyed black, and her lips red as a fire hydrant, a vicious slash of rouge layed on, apparently, with a putty knife, looked at her black painted nails and shaking her tease-curled hair forward fingered the strands one by one looking for split ends, stopping to laugh with the bartender about something Josh couldn't hear and take a drag off her lip-stick stained cigarette.

In a moment's glance, Josh saw all this and then looked down at the pile of wires and sound-enhancing gadgets at his feet. This was the beginning of a digital age, which Josh could barely decipher, a new age of amazing machines that could manipulate sound and images, any kind of information, as a mathematician manipulated numbers. It was the Computer Age now and Josh wanted to stay current and marketable like any musician. Still, most of his stuff was ancient analog stuff he'd picked up here and there over the years, an old Peavey PA 400 powered mixer with some homemade speakers his Uncle Dennis had made for him. Along with the old Gibson amp was his Melody Maker guitar Marshall had also bought for him at Schwartz's. Marshall had always liked old Schwartz. Said he was a "smart trader."

All this Josh saw on the stage in disarray and breathed a sigh of weary resignation. Hope it works, he said to himself. He'd probably brought too much shit with him but he wanted to try out the new effects processor Tim Boggle let him borrow. It gave his guitar that watery sound he liked, that milky sound that reminded him of the first note of Hendrix's solo on "Hey Joe" that he'd heard his friend Free play note for note in Tim Boggle's basement all those years ago. He looked down at the intimidating wires. Why should I set all this up, he thought to himself. Still, something, a voice prodded him, "Get yo' sound, man," he seemed to hear Sylves' voice saying, "Get yo' sound." Miles' Tutu played in the background while the bartender grooved slightly, goofing with the waitress and drying some glasses. They don't give a shit what I play up here. Everybody knows that. It wouldn't matter if I played "Me and You and a Dog named Boo" by Lobo, as long as people kept drinking. I'm just a clown up here, an entertainer. He heard Marshall's voice, "Maybe playin' good on the gettar ain't all there is in this world." He took out a few chord charts he'd written out from his guitar case, charts he'd brought for me to use since I was subbing for Carlo that night, who was on tour with Lacey Corman. Jared Smallwood would be the drummer. He was Josh's childhood friend and only a part-time musician but the Joyland Club didn't pay well enough to get one of the really good cats from Medina University.

Josh looked at the battered chartbook. Charts fell out of the folder and sailed out over the stage like dove wings. He stooped to pick them up and saw how some were covered with footprints from all the shoes of all the many musicians who'd used these pages to steady the tightrope walk of a song, leaving them scattered like autumn leaves on the stage floor while they unplugged their instruments and packed up at the end of a gig. Nobody cares about your charts.

Once he'd gotten it all together, he plugged in to check out his sound. He fooled around with "Little Wing" and "Spain" and "Use Me" and even noodled a few jazz licks on "Darn That Dream," warming up and adjusting the controls. The guy at the bar turned around: "By God that IS the best pickin' between here and Water Maple County!" They laughed, coughing and slapping each other on the back. One gave Josh an exaggerated thumbs-up gesture.

"Thanks, man," Josh said and turned around to turn it all off. He went to take a piss but in the hall at the top of the stairs leading to a cellar storage room, the bar-back touched his shoulder. He wore a baseball cap and shades.

"Hey man," he said, I hear me some good black music uppair! Yo, I'm just startin' work here today. Them two asshole cut-ups ovair said you was playin' tonight. They ain't friends of yours is they?"

"No, they're just assholes."

The bar-back laughed loudly in two syllables, stressing the second one. "Ha HIGH!! Aw, man, that's cool coz I saw them bothering you and shit and I started to say something but…"

"Nah, they weren't bothering me." He was starting to look vaguely familiar to Josh when he turned and hollered at some men playing pool. "You all play pool kinda like I fuck—everything in but the balls!"

He turned back around to hold the door open for Josh. "Well, anyway, you good, man," he laughed, "too good for this honky place". Josh thanked him and headed across the parking lot to his car. Two hours till showtime, he thought to himself. Wonder what Berenice has got goin' for dinner? Then he realized who that dude was—Cotton.

214 JOSH

So how did I get to Budapest? It's a dull, small city, Midwestern US kind of airport. Not like the voluptuous train stations. You then take the airport shuttle (cheap) or taxi (cheap by US standards) or city bus (if yr a native, very cheap) through East Pest's very drab, run-down streets, reminiscent of the slums of Athens. But then the shell, the great spiral conch shell of 19th, early 20th century Europe begins to engulf you, Rodin-colored, squatty granite and stucco of Vienna and Paris. Cars. Cars. Buses. Trams. Ah, trams, yellow dream serpents. You approach the squat layered quarry of an east European city. The streets seem woven of sooty, dark melted wax that builds up at the bottom of a candle. Excretion of shellfish.

215 KRIP

Joshua Celeste? He was my friend. A strange cat. In a way, a strange case. But I wouldn't say "misfit." That's not the right word. He seemed to live completely for other people. Generosity and magnanimity were a natural to him as breathing, singing, playing guitar. Music was his inner life, deep, yet full of sun and shadow but outwardly he just wanted to offer it to someone.

216   JOSH | NOTEBOOK 13

Times are very bad. The dissonance of my marriage is deafening. My internal
dialogue seems like a screaming child. The dissonance of a bad marriage. I
remember how Helen once delivered me from the memory of old love. Now
the ground is moving again. She knows what she can or can't do for me, to ease
my suffering. The one she pursues doggedly, organizing her new life around my
absence, the other… well, it just doesn't exist for her.

217   DOC

But what makes the ground move under a man? Loneliness. And to know that a
woman's love is a fleeting moment of happiness. Another person can only give so
much and even that must be interpreted by an inner self.

We are alone. What is the response to this absolute loneliness? Religion?
Sex? Money? Fame? What a multitude uses this to distract itself from this one
inexorable fact! Anything anyone can say to ease this condition is just another
part of the distraction. Of course, it can produce earthly beauty, but, in the end,
only a beautiful distraction. Everyone's destiny is singular. To stand before God
(the Buddhist's void?) naked, without recourse to mortal earthly love, is this a
man's necessity?

218   KRIP | JOSH AND BERENICE

She was older than him. I'm not too sure by how much, but quite a bit. Now
that he had a job in Tim Boggle's music store Josh seemed even sexier to her. In
the evening she lit oil lamps and incense for him to play his guitar by. The soft
light spread out into the room while her friends from Medina U. and Josh's music
buddies and workmates at the music store would come over and watch Saturday
Night Live and listen and smoke and laugh and look at Berenice and Josh in their
new apartment in the lush woods of Sweet Gum Park. Josh played in the living
room and Hector flirted with Berenice in the kitchen while she fussed around the
stove with the coffee and the cookies and cakes.

Before Josh had finally left his little bookstore job and gotten a job at Tim's,
he'd had to ask Marshall for work around the farm and Marshall'd made him
chop burdock weed out of the fence rows—the same job he'd made Josh and Doc

do when they were boys. But after a while he let Josh drive the tractor out to the cornfields. (In those days Doc lived in Medina and worked on a master's at the University). The combine would blow the corn into the wagon and when it was full Ricky Boy would unhook it in the field. Josh would then come and hook it to the new Case Tractor and drive it to the barn where a machine would blow the silage into the silo. Josh would drive wagon loads back and forth all morning.

Marshall lost patience trying to explain things—the way you had to hook the wagon to the tractor which was then attached to an auger that forced the silage up into the silo.

Josh's mind wandered. This infuriated him. Marshall would bang on the tractor fender with a wrench to wake him up from his daydream and yell his instructions in the cool, cloudy October mornings, the bone dry husks of sycamore leaves breaking crisp under his boot, the feed conveyor roaring and rocking Josh to sleep, dangerously, in the tractor seat.

Ricky Boy's son, Kevin, ran around on the ground beside the silo shed doing all the work, shoveling fallen corn back into the wagon with a scoop shovel, making sure the auger didn't get clogged, etc. while Josh sat in the tractor seat falling asleep. He hadn't gotten home from the gig at Crazy Reddy's until nearly 2 am. Still, Kevin wanted Josh to be impressed with his work, his drive. But Josh was always so quiet. "Why was he so quiet?" Kevin thought. "I don't mind if he just sits there and don't do a lick of work. But I wish he'd look and see all of what I'm doin' and tell Marshall what a good worker I am." Marshall drove up. "Kevin, you are doin' everything just perfect. Y'all go on and feed cattle another hour. Bertha's got a big lunch down at the house for y'all. Ho! Josh! Wake up, boy, I wish Bertha'd fix a lunch for me like that. Whenever you come down and work she goes right to the grocery. I can't get her to even fix me a bowl of Campbell's soup seems like anymore. I'd pay somebody a hunnerd dollars right now for a bowl of soup. But today she's got fried chicken and green beans, baked apples, mashed taters, even sweet taters! And ice tea with big ol' sprigs of fresh mint in it. Doc's down there. Already ate. Won't eat anything but hamburgers from Burger Chef and drink pop and read funny books all day.

I remember those lunches, too. Aunt Pearl would let me work down there some summers. We would sit and eat a country lunch and the old window sill air conditioner rattling, smelling like the bottom of the pop cooler at Bessie Jane's grocery. That watery ginger smell. The same smell we'd sometimes smell in the bars we played. And after lunch Josh would be lazy with too much dinner. Marshall would say, "Don't eat no fresh onion at lunch. Make you sleepy out in the field. Marshall was too afraid to let Josh run the combine, especially after Ricky boy's cousin from east Kentucky came down to work one season and lost an arm. Marshall awoke in the night in a cold sweat thinking of how little Josh once grabbed the tractor throttle trying to pull himself up into Marshall's lap in the tractor seat, how he'd fallen off the Bluegrass stripper once. And that other time Josh's horse spooked when a calf darted from out of the brush and threw him out of the saddle and on the ground. He missed landing on a spike from a splintered tree stump by half a foot.

After lunch Marshall would say, "Well, let's see. Don't really be nothing to do out in the field now. Looks like a rain comin up. Ricky Boy can finish it out with Kevin later this afternoon. Josh, why don't you take the rest of the day off and drive Bertha up to the Medina Mall." All their lives Marshall had often thought, "Lord, my sons will never be farmers. Their soft voices and books and guitars. And Josh's beautiful hands!"

So, he had given them to Bertha. Agnes was often singing, working at her father's office.. Sylves played drums. And, so, they grew beside Bertha, on each side of her rocker, where she knitted her quilts out of snippets of her dead husband Dexter's ties.

The fat yellow and black bumblebees hammer the air and loll pollen-powdered in the cone of a Rose of Sharon bloom. Grasshoppers struggle to jump free of the road and the roaring combine swings wide and turns around. "I give you to my mother," Marshall would say to himself. "I can't teach you the ways of the farm. I can't remember how I learned. Shine and Money Joe showed me my father was too drunk but I don't remember their words. I learned by watching them. There were no words. Now they're gone."

And, so, those days ended. Home became the arms of girls in Medina.

219

Clipping from Down Beat Magazine, 1953. Quick hits.

Mr. Moore and Miss Demeter on tour with a USO Show which included stops in Belgium, Holland and France with an especially memorable performance of the band at the Palais Royale in Brussels.

220 1951

They lay in each other's arms for a long time. Sylves lit a cigarette and, gently stroking her hair, gazed down from the hotel room window at the traffic around the Place Du Grand Sablon. He felt better, now, about things. It seemed that now she really was his again and the jealousy he had felt over her "friendship," but was that all it was? the alarm, the adrenalin spurting into his confused mind again, her friendship with the trumpet player/orchestra director who sent her flowers, called her on the phone, bought her gifts—Sylves' jealousy in all this had finally dissipated. Still, the doubt lingered. Where had they gone after their "friendly" dinner the week before? She liked him, no doubt about it. His being twice her age didn't seem to matter to her, even though she reassured Sylves she'd never go for an old guy. And hadn't she just finished making passionate love to him, opening herself so completely to him, crying in ecstasy? "Let that Harry James-lookin' motherfucker do that," he thought, congratulating himself and watching the cute Belgian girl out on the square leaving the chocolate shop as he took another deep drag off his Lucky.

Agnes drew circles on his chest and kissed his nipples, sucking them lightly, turning them to little beads of sand. The lost bird in his thigh stirred and raised his head again. He could stand it no more and she raised her head to his lips kissing him deeply. She kissed in a line down his belly, pausing to lick into his navel before making her way slowly to his pubic hair she moistened with her tongue before taking him completely into her mouth. She swung her legs around so her buttocks swayed high and near his face. He licked her anus for a few minutes stuffing his fingers into her before pulling her into him like someone pulling a chair away from a table. Her soft flesh sent a fire through him and as he entered her she let out a sharp gasp like someone who had just nicked a finger chopping vegetables. Feeling him inside her she moved up and down in harmony with his rhythm until like someone who calms down gradually after a bout of hysterical laughter she let the waves of feeling and breath and cum subside in her and fell back onto him nestling her head into the crook of his arm, panting softly and finally going off to sleep.

By the time they got back to the States, he told me years later, she knew she was pregnant.

221 SYLVESTER MOORE IN HIS STUDIO 2

(the tobacco stripping room beside the barn on the hill)

Stand before the easel. Stare hard into the center of the blue-black background, the smell of oil paint thick in the air. Daub on a smear of bright red in the shape of a mouth...

Singing? Yelling? Opening to give or deny. To praise. To ridicule. Cotton's mouth, face raised up in his hands… crying? His yellow hair and coffee skin. The full lips. The flattened nose. Blondish brow. Freckled forehead. Money Joe and Shine in the background, a pew at St. Jude Church, eyes gazing at the altar. Remember the rain pouring down the old house, the old Broke Down Palace in Rylytown. I hear voices….

And me yellin at Joe, "You never did give mama the money Dexter Celeste said to give her!"

"No, he said keep it till I know she know what to do wif it! That's what he tol me no shit!"

"Yes shit. Shit. And her working up at Irvine Air Shute and takin' another job cookin', cleanin' for Miss Millicent in the evenings and you sittin' there drunk on yo' black ass every night gambling at Crazy Reddy's, bootleggin', pimpin' up in 'Dina. You owe me."

"It raised yo' ass didn't it!" Money Joe comin up from his chair.

"Don't you come up outta there or I'll…"

(Stop. Drop your hand. Don't hit that old man). "It's a-wonder you left enough undrunk for me to eat lunch at the High School." Always the same.

Look into the singing mouth now. Smell of paint. Green now brown-orange. Yellow light. A tropical tree. Ailanthus swaying in the black background. White leaves bordered in purple. Then, a green-yellow glow like a garden snake. Grand Place, Brussels hovering over St. Jude's, Edgeton. A trumpet. Everything floating above Edgeton. A cluster of faces. Josh and Wanda. A panorama of Budapest. St Stephen's Basilica. Father Hozni flying like a flag, a cloud, a streak of gray. His cassock and cotta mixed black and white. Bone. Josh at the altar holding a wafer. Christ knocking at the enormous doorway in a burgundy robe against the blue stained glass. Years later written under the west side stained glass window at St Jude's of Our childhood: In loving memory of Senator Xavier "Judge Daddy" Demeter and his loving wife Millicent.

Sylves sees all of this in the yellow light of afternoon pouring through the window. He looks into the center of the painting again. A European city. A man with honey brown skin.

222 SAMIDHA

I am from Goa, India. My mother died and my father remarried. His wife hated my brother and me so I decided to leave India and see Europe. I came to Budapest to study Gypsies who originate from India. I met an older woman there who took me in—like a mother to me. I would write a master's thesis on the connection between Hungarian gypsies and India. But after one year at Eotvos Lorinc Univ (ELTE) I ran out of money. It was no longer possible for me to return home. I met a Belgian man and he agreed to take me back to India where we were married in a traditional wedding which he paid for. We returned to Budapest where he had started a business selling Swedish saunas. We lived happily for a time but I later found out that he had another wife in Croatia.

I met Joshua at the place I worked on Temple St. near the Synagogue. He came in sometimes. Always very nice and a sweet and gentle lover. He said I looked like a beautiful gypsy girl. And so did the white girls there and so they treated me shittily. But Josh and I, we got to be friends. One day, a pretty autumn day, he asked if I would like to go to Lake Balaton with him and visit his country house. My ex-wife lives there with my two sons, he said, but it's all cool, as he put it. No hassle, he said. He picked me up in his red Zastava and we drove to Balaton. As he told me his story of his life in Hungary I began to sob in the car because of memories of my past. I was very wicked because when I had found out about my husband's other wife I waited until we were on a visit to Goa and I had him arrested under Indian law for adultery—I lied to the police that he raped me—and he was put in an Indian jail. After three months he wrote his parents in Vienna to tell them that he would kill himself if he was not released. At first, I did nothing. Finally, I gave in and he was released. I forgave him. We returned to Budapest once again and his sauna business was better than ever. Then I found out he still had his other wife! I came home one night to find that my awful husband had changed the locks on my apartment. He had already found a flat for me in the gypsy quarter behind Mester St. train station. I tried to have him arrested. I got Joshua to take me to the cop station where I filed a complaint against him. Again, I said that he raped me. Joshua waited while I wrote it out in pencil. Nothing was ever done about my case. But now that I lived in the gypsy quarter I made friends with a few girls who told me I could work at the Temple Street "place."

As I say Joshua and I went to Lake Balaton to his ex-wife's country house which she now owned as part of their divorce settlement. I played with his kids. And their dog. His dog loved to play in water and something made me giggle a lot: I would take a mouthful of water from the hose and spit it at the dog. He would jump up yelping for joy and take the water into his mouth. I wondered what his wife would think, spitting on her dog and making her kids laugh, but Joshua said only, Don't worry, she has her friends here also and I don't say anything to her about it so she will say nothing. I guess they had an open marriage. I remember the dark red wine we drank and the fiery rose bush. The gold moon rose behind the lilac bushes that run down to the gypsy neighbor's field where fish flop in the soap suds of the Sio River. A heron (Golya) flies before us as we walk along the river, sometimes alighting in the trees above the waves of rushes. On the way back to Budapest I sobbed again in his car and he seemed genuinely worried about me. I stayed with him for 3 days. One night we went to the Godor Club to hear jazz. It was good but the Americans are the best jazz players in my opinion, I told him. As we walked out of the club after the show a boy whistled because my dress was very short and tight. And Joshua laughed. He put me in a cab. Very gentleman. He said he would call me but never did. Years later I saw him again at the Temple St. market and we went to have a coffee at Mona Lisa. He said he didn't call because his son took his phone apart and the thin card got accidentally damaged ruining all his numbers. He sent me a note at the "place," "We will dance in a hash cloud/ In Goa and you and your Dusky sisters will dress me in the traditional robes And I will play nick nack paddy whack on my sarod!" He could be funny like that. When he began to hang around with the Arab guys at the money changers' place they would sing with him and he would play funny made-up country songs on his guitar with lyrics like, "We will fuck the camel under the tree/ in the UAE!" and we'd laugh and he would tell us all about Jimmie Rodgers and the guys would pronounce it "chimmy roshe." We also liked to hear him recite quatrains from The Rubaiyat. We loved him.

223 SYLVES | TLC STORY

It was a hot summer's evening. I was living in the old tobacco stripping room I fixed up. Made it into a studio. Had my drums in there, piano, canvases, everything. We didn't use it for the tobacco crop anymore no way. By that time your Daddy and me had set it up for stalls for the horses. That way I could do my thing, practice w headphones on, paint, read and watch mares all night, muck out the stalls—all that kind of shit. I had just got my phone line put in. They called from up in Edgeton at the little hospital. They said TLC had passed, pneumonia, could I go pick up Faith at the house? That was that old concrete block thing in back of the farm that stood up the hill from Moore's Creek up right beside the big cornfield and Tranquility Pike. You know that house. Not the one down the farm road from me, over the cattle gate but that other one. Your Daddy built that other one for Ricky Boy. It was way older, built of wood, had that shingle type siding, maroon, looked like dark brick but it was fake. Old screened-in porch was falling down. Thistle and burdock had growed up all around the front. You used to play up there and climb that vine that wrapped around an old Hackberry. Anyway, I said sure no problem. My heart was beating fast. Tears came up in my eyes real fast before I could think straight. All those years, man. That time

Cotton came out there and wanted to kill his ass. I drove through the farm in the old Mercedes your Daddy left me, passed the treehouse where you boys used to sleep out in summer, past Bertha's old house all in ruins now. One of the realtors said they saw a groundhog come out the downstairs room where Marshall used to have his office with that wall that had all those pictures of you all kids as you was growing up. Whatever happened to all them? I think Doc went down and got a lot of stuff out of there. They gonna tear it down I heard. It's for the best. It's falling down anyway. There's not one house left on that farm since I moved up to Medina. I used to love the shade of that big limestone wall behind Bertha's. The well from the side of the hill used to pour into a stone pool under her house and that as the best tasting water on a hot summer's day. On the inside wall, they kept an old copper dipper hanging. We'd dip it in there. You'd see a salamander or a crawfish every now and then crawling around there. Me and TLC would go down there after lunch at Bertha's. Then there was a pipe under that stone pool and the water ran out under the rock into a little creek before it went on down to Moore's Creek and you know that went on through Mr. Hired's farm and on down to the Kentucky River. And up to the Ohio, down the Mississippi into the sea. I was thinking like that, driving, looking at the pretty rolling fields of pink tobacco bloom over the broad green leaves with that big orange sun going down toward the river.

Faith didn't know he was dead yet. They didn't have no phone or anything. That's why they got hold of me and said can you go get her. Oh man, that was the saddest drive I ever made. Kids all piled in the back, all excited 'bout riding in Marshall's car that he never cudda got if he hadn't been Jody Lagrew's high school buddy down there at Lagrew Mercedes. Man up there trying to buy one asked Jody one time, said, is this thing rugged enough? and Jody said, Hell yeah it is, we got a guy down in Water Maple County that herds cattle in one! Shoots groundhogs out the window! Anyway, it felt weird driving a wife somewhere knowing her husband was dead but she not knowing it yet. I couldn't tell her. Didn't think it was my place. Didn't have the heart anyway.

And so when we got to the hospital and went up the hallway, here come the nurse out and Faith knew right away but she said, Aw naw is he gone is he gone? Kept saying that and the little girl started to cry. Other kids were looking scared. They went in the room. I stayed in the hall for a good while. Then the nurse come out and said they had made arrangements for Faith and them to stay the night there and they'd take them back to the farm the next day. The old mother come in about that time. Old bent-over man with her. I remember seeing them around Edgeton sometimes. Never knew they was his kin. Sad night. I went on back to the studio. Couldn't help thinking about death. It's like Time's a big scythe coming across a hayfield. Silver blade under the yellow hay under the blue-gray sky and the yellow light. Everybody got to go. Thought about Money Joe, Shine, Marshall, Bertha, Ricky Boy. Now TLC—all dead.

224 SAMIDHA'S TAPE

Mr. Kreep—When you hear this I will be many thousand miles away from Budapest and very far up and away in the mountains. And I will try to forget the terrible things and remember some small happy moments.

At that time he was very lonely I think. Like so many men who come to our place. At that time we also had a currency exchange office downstairs, the best exchange rate in Budapest! Joshua went there sometimes to change money he would get from Kentucky, the place he called his first home as you know. He still had various business affairs there, his children he said were in school there (or else in summer at his house at Lake Balaton), and so I mean he often had to change dollars into Hungarian Forints. And so he got to know the Arab guys there and he would joke around with them, they would cook big chicken Arab-style dinners and invite him. And they made the big Arab salads with fresh mint and cilantro and parsley that Homid would chop very fine with his knife and slice the tomatoes and tabouli style and with tomato and goat cheese. They would sit around on the floor and pass the dishes around and after dinner, me as well but not for free ha ha!—rice and chicken with cumin and parsley and the fresh Hungarian paprika and the sweet red powder and tea and simsimea the ones that look like shredded wheat covered in honey. Like the big chicken dinners Josh told me about on the farm of his American childhood! ha ha! It was there they would smoke and they would tell him the stories about the Israeli soldiers and what they had seen them do. Homid's young son was killed in one of the many bombings of Lebanon. So many things you American people never see because of Jews controlling your media. Sometimes I wanted to forget it all and tell them to try and forgive. It was life and how can they change the world which is so controlled by America? But then there would be a fresh bombing, some atrocity (I have footage that would be WikiLeaks like a children's show!) and I would think we must do something! And so Josh listened to them and he became more understanding. And then more militant. He was a gentleman but he could not say no. And so they convinced him I don't like they ask a man with family to do such things! Even if he was ill it is not right! But it is finished now. (long pause) But they assured him that no one would be near the Holocaust Monument on Temple St. at that hour.

It was a strange connection with the soldier Cotton. He said he knew Josh when they were young. He was a soldier stationed in Germany. He had volunteered for Iraq even though he was then a retired officer. He was then sent to Sarajevo as a peacekeeper in Serb civil war. He came to Budapest like many American soldiers for his, as they say, R&R. And so he came to our place. When he told me his story while we were talking in bed I said I know another man from your home he also comes here. His eyes became wide with surprise. It cannot be he said are you crazy he said and I said no and so—they met. Cotton had contacts with arms dealers so that is how the Arab guys got the explosives and the belts you can put around yourself, etc. Cotton and Joshua both came to the dinners and so the happy dinners became secret meetings and Cotton made a lot of money from the arms people he knew. And so he came to the place a lot, he had a nice car and money to travel he took me to Rome and Vienna and so we met and he gave me money that I sent home to Goa.

225

Department of Federal Prisons

Inmate Postal Services,

Box 812

New York, NY 10067

Hello Mr. Krip Kovacs—

Thank you for your letter. This is what I know, although my true origins are unknown. Cause you might have known the man known as my father, Money Joe Moore, and his brother Shine. Sylvester Moore, the musician, was kin to me in some way, but I never asked about it much 'cause that kinda shit don't mean much to me. Marshall Celeste and Money Joe and Shine worked the tobacco and bluegrass crops around Edgeton, KY. Joe used to say that onced they worked 85 days straight in bluegrass, sun up to sun down and they made 50,000 dollars that summer mostly on Water Maple Farm, which back then was some 2000 acres big I think. Well, they was making good money and they would get whiskey from where old Mr. Dexter Celeste onced had his moonshine still, the one that blowed up that time and ended up killin him but today I bleve they's a real whiskey distillery they built over top of it when the Celeste farm was sold. I know that 'cause Joe and Shine both helped pour the concrete. Well, all of em would come to the house on Saturday night after the work was done. I used to play in the fields with Doc and Joshua when they was little and when we gots a little older sometimes we'd have to ride the bluegrass strippers, stuffing the seed down in the sacks. When I got older, 'fore I went to the army, I'd help rick the big burlap sacks

of seed onto that big red International truck Marshall had and we'd ride up to
Cynthiana or Paris ky to the cleaning company where'd companys would come
and buy it. Bluegrass makes the prettiest green grass and when it grows out in the
field if you look at it right it has a purplish blue color. And when it gets ripe it's a
pretty gold color and when the stripper goes through and pulls off the seed head
and pushes the grass down a little bit it has the prettiest shiny color. Like I say on
Saturday night they'd come to our house in Rylytown which Joe got to calling
North Korea cause it looked like some villages he'd been to when he had to go
to the war over there. He got the purple heart and bronze star. I saw pictures of
him in his uniform my mother put by that piano Sylves used to come over and
play, but mostly I just remember Joe as an old fat fucker that drank. By the time I
went off to Nam he was always in Crazy Reddy's pool room drunk and bumming
nickels off white dudes in there. Crazy Reddy's was the onliest place a black man
could go into and shoot pool back then. Nobody caused no trouble.

Joe told me he remembered when Marshall'd bring Doc in there when he
was little and folks would bet on if little Doc could spell words right and shit
like that, showin him off for folks. Well, Joe got so sick drunk he couldn't get to
the toilet and he'd just let fly right there on the bench by the door. I remember
young brothers playing pool all a sudden look up and see Joe's face lookin funny
and then the smell and they would look disgusted and yell at Crazy Reddy, "Hey
Reddy! Better come get your boy! Man done shit on his self!" But like I say, years
before that they'd come to the house and carry on with my mother. They'd shoo
me outta there when they started drinking and there be a lot of carrying on
and the fan would be turning and so hot everybody'd be taking off their clothes
and I'd watch from the keyhole and Joe would get on her first and then Shine
and then Sylves and ol'Dexter, too. She'd get astride Shine while Dexter and
would take turns up on her back, riding her like a steer rides a punk steer in the
herd. And their skin shiny like bluegrass stalks in the light. I got to where I liked
Saturday nights the best! I don't look much like Dexter but I sho' got light skin!

My mama was a good hard workin lady and I made something of myself in the
Army and she was there for me even if she had to be a white dude-fucking hoe in
order to do it. But like I say they harvest fitty thousand dollars worth a seed one
year and that was damn good money back then and come time to settle up Joe
said, Marshall we come for our 25, 000 and Marshall said, Hold on, this my land,
I gotta pay taxes and fertilizer bills, I can give ya 10. And I still think about it, all
that work they done and I bet him getting pussy too and they was only gonna get
10,000!!!! Shiiiiit! Makes me mad still thinking 'bout it today. So, I guess I never
got over that shit and then I run into Joshua all them years later. I come back
from Nam and worked just awhile in Medina at this one fuckin place called the
Joyland Josh played at sometimes but I don't think he recognized me even though

I spoke with him. He probly 'membered me with curly blond hair but they shaved it bald in the army and I never did grow it back. But then I thought maybe he recognized me but just didn't give a fuck. And the Celeste's never did like me after that time I was gonna kill that hillbilly motherfucker who shot at me that time and Marshall pulled a gun on me. Fucker.

Well, I volunteered for a peace keeper job in Bosnia and I come one time into Budapest, the same town you said you was from and damned if later, after meeting this chick I'm gonna tell you about, I didn't see Joshua's picture in one of them damn nightlife magazines. Well, I hung around town as long as I could and later got myself transferred over there. I got in with them Arab dudes coz you could change money, dollars into Hungarian forints, at a good rate and they knew I had contacts inside the Army. They said they wanted to blow up a synagogue. I got them the explosives. And I got a fuck load of dough for it too—and rightly so. Well, I finally told Josh who I was and later met this Indian chick or gypsy or whatever the fuck she was. Turned out she already knew him! and all of us started getting together on Fridays after work I started working in their exchange shop on Temple St. after I got my discharge. Samidha and them would fix an A-rab style chicken dinner (reminded me of those big goddam dinners at Miss Millicent's when Money Joe and Shine had to put on them slave white coats and serve everybody!) but we would sit around on the floor on a big white sheet, eatin and then smoke a buncha hash and drink some Hungarian wine and a brandy they call palinka.

Well, pretty soon Samidha would do a dance and we would all be huggin and kissin on her and she would say what about Josh and they would laugh drunk and him all quiet and Samidha would tease him and say he had an ass like a girl and didn't we want to fuck it and the A-rab dudes would toss Hungarian money down on his ass while Samidha would hold it open for us. Made me think of when we was kids in Edgeton and they said don't open the cistern lid or the gas pipe and spit or throw things down into it, but we did anyway LOL! I would get up on that ass shiny and creamy as stripped bluegrass and man it felt good, like I was fuckin all that anger out from back in Edgeton when Marshall fucked over us. I'd get in Samidha's mouth and then his ass. Or she'd put that shiny steely dan up his ass while I put my balls over his eyes. She said my dick on his face look like a groucho mask! And this motherfucker was 50 some years old! but his ass still looked good. He didn't give a shit. He was sick or something. Said he just wanted to do something. Give back something. Yeah, he gave some "back" alright! Ha ha! Man, that was some good times. What the Hungarians and the A-rab dudes would call, "jo baszas." Good fuckin. Now I was getting back some fuckin' for all those years my mama got fucked and Money Joe and Shine got fucked! I said to myself, these motherfuckers owe me! And you know I think Josh thought he owed me, and the whole world! So, he gave up his booty! Ha ha! Hope this answers your questions. I did not get second degree murder. I'm in for conspiracy. You see, Josh volunteered even though maybe the A-rab dudes was gonna kill his ass anyway. You see, he knew they was right in a way. In the beginning I got to him with stories of some of the shit I saw when I was stationed in Palestine. But THEY was the ones that made him put on that belt of explosives to test the remote and the damn thing went off out in the street. See, I really think they was gonna shoot his ass ANYWAY no matter what he did and see, I think that Abdullah dude shot down on him from the upstairs window! So I guess he figured, might as well enjoy what ever they made him do. Dig? It was over for his sorry ass anyway! Mother fucker was gonna die had some kinda terminal shit. They said it might have been his sweat that made the wires fuck up and maybe he jerked something if he got shocked. I can't say no more cause my case is still pending.

—Cotton Moore

226   RYLY | DAD'S FUNERAL

A foreigner must look in amazement at the daily life of the host culture. I feel almost like a foreigner here now myself. But I grew up in the Lake Balaton region. Then as a teenager, I spent a lot of my time at "Uncle" Krip's house in New Jersey. I helped take care of his aunt, Pearl. But when you get back and start seeing the life of my childhood, every bus ride, trip on the metro, and, now, every pretty Hungarian girl's flirtatious look or sneer of disdain, the empty eyes of the street bum, every trip to the market, all these are like miniature epics in themselves whose full meanings are hidden. The Funeral is the most secret ceremony of all, a time when the Spring sun turns its blazing light inward and time, like the sudden slant of a galaxy, is visible as a veil- thin gauze that covers all things. I would never have known how to get there. Uncle Krip offered me a ride to the cemetery. Relieved of the daunting prospect of having to find it alone in the vast sprawling suburbs of Budapest. I'd only been back working my job he got me with the ex-pat English language paper, Budapest Week, for six months or so, I quickly took him up on it. I felt like I needed to revisit my roots a bit after "the accident" as everyone was calling it. I was finished with Medina Univ.

It was a beautiful spring morning. The plane tree outside Dad's old apartment (I guess I inherited), so barren of leaves through the long cold winter, was full now of sea-green leaves as big as the palm of your hand. The linden had already bloomed, covering everything with a thin layer of green dust. The white-winged crow, they don't have those in America, and the mourning dove and the sparrow flitted between their limbs, sometimes the dove flying right up to my window sill to coo and beg for the bread I had been putting out for her through the snowy months. The weather was so fine I became less concerned for them, surely they could find enough food on their own now, I thought. I ignored their prodding coos and soon they came less and less.

Krip arrived on time, rare for Hungarians, but, then, he was only half! and we drove across the Petofi Bridge to Barraros Square where he turned right and headed out toward the 10th District, to Pest Erzsebet and Ujkoztemető - the cemetery.

For years my father had carried his burden of cancer. For years the chemo-therapy had

prolonged his life. Every few years he went back to the hospital for treatment. But it never lasted. The cancer tenacious, bent on its own agenda it seemed always came back. I got used to the illness. It became such a part of him and of our relationship that I began not to question or even think of it. We never talked about it. But it was always there. A specter standing unnoticed in the shadows, waiting patiently. One treatment cured him for 2 years, another for 5, another for 3. Death was in no particular hurry it seemed. My father, though sickly, began to seem invincible to me. Death had come and gone. Too shy to claim him, but instead, conferring on him some kind of immortality.

But then it struck again. Quietly but decidedly. Drifting from his lymph to his lungs, filling them with water. After months of struggling to breathe, again the doctors were able to clear his lungs and his energy returned. He cannot die now, I thought. Death has tried and failed. Yet the pallor remained. The drawn skin. He fidgeted with his lip. Darted his eyes like a frightened animal. At 52, he suddenly looked eighty. I turned my head away from the photographs. At night I huddled in my blanket feeling a sense of invulnerability, reading my book, thinking of a thousand other things. What a wonder medical science is! I thought.

And it did give him a few extra years. Years of precious light, willowy yellow-gold light,

spreading its dust of light everywhere. Years of water. And the Moon. Of lovemaking with his lady friends. And thinking of nothing. Food. And work. Children on their way to school. A lovely traffic jam on the boulevard. A young secretary running to catch a tram. An Arab boy changing money. The stooped shopkeeper with a black moustache. The old woman at the market. The banker in black. Rain and clouds. And wind. Leaves. Blooms. A bottle cap. A twig. A dog turd. A used condom. And a million cigarette butts he'd long ago given up smoking all the detritus of Spring! The green grass combed by a quiet zephyr. A young girl's blond hair shining in the sun.

And then one day he opened his eyes walked down Temple St. past the synagogue and it was all gone forever. Fragments, Krip said. It doesn't matter now.

What throngs explode onto the streets of Pest every morning. Krip's old truck rumbled past the bright chaos of the Chinese market. I looked out the window at streets of endless shoppers and hawkers sifting through the sidewalk stalls looking for anything that would help them survive. Cheap clothes from India, hanging like washing from sidewalk racks. A lean-to spice shop. A thousand mobile phones stacked up on a table with a hundred cigarette cartons. Toys. Bags of fake leather. For a thousand years the multitudes buying cheap stuff from Asia from the Iasians, azsián, as they are known here.

As we got closer to the cemetery, Krip suddenly turned up onto a curb, making

himself a make-shift parking space up on the sidewalk as is often the custom here, and we walked the rest of the way, some 100 yards. But then it dawned on me, there is no cemetery! I looked around at the crowds filling the sidewalks, somber families walking slowly toward me down the small incline of a hill, dressed always in black or else black was the dominant color. Men on their lunch hours in dirty clothes, having already paid their respects to a loved one and now headed back to work. A girlfriend trying to give solace to a bereaved boyfriend by leaning on his arm, touching the tear on his cheek, letting the sun shine through her golden hair, a hint of sexiness in her black dress. I thought of the girl I left behind in Jersey.

No, there was no graveyard—only different stone, mourning rooms, 20 by 20 ft huts barely big enough to fit 50 or so people standing around the bier strewed with flowers, pictures, a stack of CD's, a guitar. There was Lydia. I sometimes wondered what had become of her. No one spoke. We all simply stood in silence thinking of him to ourselves—thinking of our own imminent death… most of all? But there is no understanding Death—his or mine. Silence. Then people began to file out.

Afterwards, I spoke with Lydia and shook her now thin, wrinkled hand. She looked stoic, perhaps the invincibility towards Death I'd ascribed to Dad was still living in her. I embraced her grown children. She gave me her card.

I stepped back out into the blazing spring light and chatted with a few old friends, Dad's bandmates. Beyond, there were the multitudes again walking up and down among the endless flower shops and stone cutter's yards. (Mourners can buy flowers on the way in and families barter with stonecutters on the way out. Always the living buying and selling here even in the temple of Death. But not for gravestones do they haggle. A crowded metropolis of some 3 million people hasn't room for that unless you are rich and can buy a grave in Wolf's Field. By the end, Dad was just a poor cafe musician. Krip kept apologizing. But I said it didn't matter to me. Mother sent a card she said to give to Krip. I would be going to the beautiful lake later to stay with her a few months. Agnes was many years dead and Judge Daddy's wealth long gone. A wall of smartly cut boxes, stacked like post office boxes, would be my father's final resting place.

Everywhere the Memories of the Dead! Outnumbering the living! Everywhere the weeping families! A Grand Convention of Death and Sorrow I had come upon the likes of which I'd never seen in America. No cars. The poor walking up from down the hill where they came by tram, the distant trams of the "projects," those crumbling high rise "domino" buildings that encircled the old city, whose numbers I'd never seen and seemed strange to me, having grown up in Mom's 1st Kerulet (district). The No.24. The No.8. The 13. The figures loomed out of the station like secret codes. Krip still called this his 'hood. I have dim memories of it. I remember jackhammers pounding, a lot of construction after '89 and the end of the communist era.

The Unexplainable, the Question, The Circus of the Unknown swirling about the crowd.

Krip had to get back to work so I offered to just walk alone to the metro. I told one last dirty joke Dad had loved—the one about the nun and the holy water. Krip always laughs as if he would keel over from laughter. His face gets red. And his eyes bug out. An amazing laugh. We embraced, shook hands and parted. I had rarely seen him in the last few months Dad's illness had come between us in an unintentional way. His health it seemed was the unseen bridge of our friendship. All the faces I saw, everyone had aged. A few middle-aged women, some weeping, comforted by Hungarian men in sunglasses.

A pall drifted through the sociability. A thousand years, twenty-five years, it hardly mattered. Time, the rumpled street sweeper pulled his creaking cart behind him, sweeping it all up - the dust, the sand, the litter, the clouds, the planets, the stars. When I left the place I saw the other multitude beyond the vast cemetery had taken no notice of me or of my Dad's death. They were innocent. Walking without Death in the sun. Not thinking of his Death, or mine, or theirs. Moving their pale spring arms. Sun glinting off legs. No one even seeing me. Death had thrown its protective cloak about me for the moment. Buses fill and then pull out in one burst of smoke. Quickly, another crowd gathers. Pensive mothers, their stricken faces softened by pale young skin, fathers and their eyes downcast, thinking out a plan for survival. Going up and down the hill, again and again to become ashes and then... the colorless gold of blazing spring sky.

227 KRIP | JOSH ON THE BUS

He remembers how in high school Doc fixed it so he got elected student council president. Doc had been the prez 2 years before him so he wanted to keep the legacy going. So, he rigged it. The day of the vote, with all the kids running around in the halls, he got Uncle Dennis down at the Edgeton Gazette to print out a bunch of handbills with Josh's picture on them saying, "Strong Joshua, Celestial as the sky! Vote Josh Celeste and keep our standards high!"

"Well, none of the other candidates had any handbills, so, when all the kids picked up all the strewn paper in the halls and lockers and saw my pic they pretty much figured they were supposed to vote for me. So, they did. I won by a landslide."

Kiki and Lilian and Jennifer Gardiner saw him in the hall the next day.

"Since when are you Mr. Politician, Josh Celeste?" Kiki shouted.

"Yeah, Mr. Music guy turns into teacher's pet?" said slender Jennifer.

"It was Doc's idea. I'm just playing along," I said.

"So, what are you gonna do for our school, Mr. Play-Along?" Lilian said.

"Doc's gonna help me deal with it."

"Doc?" said Kiki, "He's in college in Medina! What the hell's he gonna do?" I hope you got the trip to the regional finals all organized. You're supposed to help with the planning, you know."

"I just got word about that."

"No, you didn't you little fibber. I just made that up!" The other girls laughed.

"Come here and rub my shoulders!" Kiki teased, "those boys at Money Joe's are kinda rough on the dance floor!"

"Yeah, that light-skinned guy can dance his ass off!" Lilian giggled.

Josh scooted behind Kiki and massaged her shoulders, pushing aside her soft blond hair.

"Don't break my necklace, Mr. Prez. Mmmm, that's right. Oh, yeah, right there. Just a little harder."

"Hey, I want mine rubbed, too, hot stuff," said Lilian. She nudged Kiki aside. "Mmm, such warm, strong presidential hands."

"He gets that from playing guitar, girls. Trust me, I know. And other stuff!" They giggle.

"How 'bout a presidential foot rub," Jennifer said. "My feet are killing me after cheerleader practice!"

"Don't be taking those big ass smelly sneakers off in here girl!" Kiki yelled. "Oh, that feels so good," Lilian whispered.

The bell rang. Jennifer gives Josh a little pat on his butt as she grabs her books and hurries off, looking back and sticking out her tongue.

228 JOSH

When I feel wronged, a great anger wells up inside me. But just as quickly after a few hours of revenge plotting, I grow weary and just want to be left alone. When Marshall got angry with me unjustly, as soon as I saw a chance to get away from him I would walk down towards the pond below the house, where the higher field, the field where Marshall let me ride beside him on the tractor while he baled hay, slopes down toward Edgeton Rd. There was a pathway behind the pond that led to a grove of sinewy Ailanthus trees and a few young Walnuts, Kentucky Coffee bean, and Hackberry trees. I saw deer here a lot. It was secluded from passing cars and a little creeklet flowed near the grove, dividing it in two. I would walk there. Carp and catfish splashed in the pond and the creek widened the further around the sloping hill I walked. I came to a small fence which I climbed and realized I had crossed into Mr. Howard's property. His daughter, a pretty society lady Marshall flirted with and Agnes hated, lived nearby. She had lovely blond hair and blue eyes that shone brightly out of a ruddy tanned face. She was forty. I suppose I kept walking hoping she would find me and love me. Sometimes, riding with Marshall I saw her pass by on the little country road and I waved. Did she smile at me? I asked Marshall questions about her and he laughed. Everyone asks about a pretty woman.

When I realized I would never find her I would find a flat rock-face by the creek and lay down and look at the clouds passing, her hair and the blue sky, sunlight, her lips, the way her jeans looked, work shirt, gold chain. She opened the gate and we drove in. She leaned down to latch it. I could smell her fresh skin, some light airy perfume, or shampoo as she looked across the front seat at me while shaking Marshall's hand. (Did I ever speak with her? Did I dream it?)

It turned out that Marshall never raised her tobacco crop. Whenever he drove by her place after that he complained out loud that she never kept her fields mowed and the wind blew weed seeds over onto our place.

I kept walking. I poked a stick into a cluster of dead leaves damming the spring's flow into a lower channel. I squatted down to watch the water. I felt like God was somehow with me. But I didn't think about it much. I didn't pray. I looked. I listened. My head was yet to be filled with so much regret. Then, my wonder of the world was greater than my mistrust of it. I looked out onto the pond and years and years ahead. The killdeers called, the hawk swooped, the kingfisher dove. I walked back to the lights of "home". My father sat snoring in the cane rocker, his face propped against his big swollen farmer's hand, a cowboy movie droning in the background. Angelica played with dolls in her room. Doc read comic books in the twin bed on the left side of our room. Agnes was gone.

I must have dozed off. I awakened to the same old melancholy waiting for me. But I said nothing to anyone. Later, I pretended to be light-hearted. I thought how the pond, the killdeer, the hawk, the mouse, the kingfisher waited for my return.

229 RYLY

So many have gone! "Where are the years?" one of my father's lyrics goes. ("Ou sont les nieges d'un tant," Doc says). Whenever I walk past the Szabolcs St. hospital I think about him and the 89-ers, as he and Krip often called the many ex-pats in the Budapest of the late 20th century. He lay in his bed dying of cancer, (was it the poison air of Chernoble drifting west?) eulogizing in his quiet, weary way, America and a world so filled with injustice. In those days he was still hoping to do his "big tour" in Dubai where one of his Arab friends at the exchange office was from. Even one of his old friends from Krip's college years in Boston was from there and he wanted to ask his forgiveness. One night, he told me, they had played a phone prank on the boy in the dormitory. "When Mohammed picked up the phone we said, 'Come on down to the first floor. This is Delta Airlines. We'd like to give you a free plane ticket to anywhere in the world. We're waiting in the front lobby. Come and collect your prize!' Then we watched, giggling, from upstairs. He went to the desk. The student desk clerk shook his head, 'No, don't know anything about an airline.' But I got a call. 'Nope, no prize here, buddy. Somebody's pulling your leg, pal.'"

Dad had gotten too sick to get well. What happened next is not known. There was a lot of conspiratorial activity in those days. There was this atmosphere that the new administration gave off. Like the ship that attacked Tel Aviv. Mother said he was involved in something. She said she could sense it. He worked at the Arab

Grocery next to the exchange office. When Krip was still alive he said he hated going there, hated seeing Dad so old-looking and sick. He had stopped playing guitar long before, so, I guess this was the only way he could pay his bills. Mother sometimes gave him money. So did Krip. And the woman from India took care of him. I remember when they visited us at Mom's house in Balaton. He must have put on the belt of explosives inside the grocery, which means he had a key to the exchange office as well. There's nothing left of half the grocery but rubble. He was the only casualty.

But Temple St. wasn't my father's home. He lived in the 11th district near the Il Rege Café on Fehervari st. Almost everyday, as a much younger man, he rode the 86 bus down Budafoki st. toward the Gellert Hotel. I imagine him riding along the Danube toward Batthany Sq. where Gordon and I went to Kindergarten (before we moved to Lake Balaton). If he was early picking us up he had a smoke in the Izabella Café before walking up the alley and out to Batthany st. where he would turn left walk fifty meters to the school door, through the hallway and out to the playground where he would sit patiently watching us play football (soccer). He would talk to Tibor the janitor. Tibor spoke English well since he'd lived many years in South Africa. In the communist days, it was easier for Hungarians to immigrate there, not to the States.

"Oh, I don't know," I heard him say to Dad, once, "Now the big hobby for these kids in Johannesburg seems to be, look for tourists, fill 'em full of lead (he made his thumb and forefinger into a pistol) then pick their pockets".

"But I bet there's decent folks there, too, right?" Dad would say.

"Oh, sure, there's good and bad all over," said the old Hungarian.

230 LAST LETTER FROM KRIP

Dear Ryly,

Thanks for staying in touch... and for helping with the final editing. I haven't much time left. You can take it from here I think, right?

So, as you remembered, we got Josh to a final resting place. But as I walk through the old neighborhood, I can still see him standing outside the vegetable stand, leaning against some crates, smoking a Marlboro, wrecking what was left of that once gorgeous voice. And I also cdnt help noticing his hands a little blistered and gnarled by loading all those vegetable crates all day.

We never had that much left to say. I told him I was writing his life story, almost anyone else wudda said, Hey, when can I read it? but Josh just shrugged and smiled. He always asked about you kids and I told him Helen was fine and that you guys were coming up from Lake Balaton to stay with him for a few weeks. He wd silently slap me five as if to say, Awesome, man. His eyes lit up and he seemed suddenly 20 yrs younger. I never knew anyone who loved his kids so much. I never understood why he wanted to separate himself but I think I see now that he was afraid they wd become lone wolves like him. He must've thought that they wd be happier if they were raised by someone with a normal life. He saw me as a normal person now, now that I had the gig as editor of the magazine.

Everything seems so long ago. I lay in here in bed behind the curtains of my tiny apartment. I'm listening to the dull timpani thud of the morning traffic. Monday morning. A new day dawning. It's beautiful I guess in its way, the world outside. I feel so far away from it, yet it's there 12 floors down. What went wrong? I keep thinking. We cdve conquered the world, the band, the bus, all those gigs, all those promoter's wives!!! Forgive me, Josh! You hear, man? I tried, man! My mind and my dick—guess they ruined it. But I just don't know. Now I can't remember, man. It's the fucking pills! My fucking leg, man—it hurts! The world OWES ME, MAN! FOR HAVING TO WALK AROUND ON THIS SHIT!—Forgive me. This is all I can give in return.

Yrs. Krip

231 RYLY

Today the grey sky sank into my mood but I decided to run a few errands in the neighborhood and face the cold outside. The streets were chalked with salt and swept clean by the chill wind. I remembered summer. I almost started following a small line of people headed towards the 4 tram tracks and the gas station beyond where I cd re-credit my cell phone just to feel as if I was among people if only for a moment, even though it was the long way around but then the dark snowy path within the little wooded area beside the high-rise dormitory beckoned to me so I went that way instead. "I wandered into a dark wood"

When we visited Grandfather Marshall's farm, the snow-crusted field rose slightly as if you stood in a vast shallow bowl. The frozen corn stubble gripped the hard ground with its frozen root feet, like a cat tensing its claws. Between the dry dead corn rows lay tobacco stalks end to end to fertilize the ground.

Always the wood beyond.

In Budapest, beside his old apartment, the sparse little copse seemed like a place to hide—if only for a moment—a brief sanctuary from the traffic.

After my gas station errand to get a phone card I wandered on the little back street. The building, the block-long block of flats, was still soot grey from the communist time before western urban renewal money flooded in. Krip had said that back in those days the City did look more like a commune. Crowds, he remembered, used to move as one mass sometimes it seemed. Everyone with similar clothes, especially the odd central Asian style Russian hats, with the funny flaps. When Dad came here for his first gigs and first saw those hats Krip said he laughed and said they seemed like "grounds for institutionalization!"

Krip said he loved that one back street. So removed from the others. It was like traveling back in time. I implored it to envelope me in a blanket of memories and images. Why is it some streets, some places in the City, seem to know you and welcome you, to bring good luck—and other places give you a cold foreboding feeling?

The cold wind quietly drained me of my energy to fantasize, fantasize the history of all humankind as he had walked around looking for a home somewhere. And so I turned the corner and headed for the new shopping center. There's a delicious bread you can get there now—black bread with nuts in it, just like the kind at the old Joyland Restaurant in Medina where Dad used to play every Tuesday night.

The frozen fog descending on everything is like a forgotten dream image, making me forget man and all his endless anxieties and desires. Krip said the wind like a knife would cut him from his gut in an "S" shape through his chest. He cried out from inside sometimes: Lord, protect all the Children!

I walked on. A stooped-over old woman smiled as she passed. I smiled back.

I opened the box under Krip's bed. There they were, all in chronological order. I remembered the covers of some. I went down to the Danube and made a fire. It felt good in the chilly evening. One by one they went in and flamed up a little. Thin fragments of paper dancing in flame and up in air, like snowflakes falling the wrong way, and then drifting smoke.

232

Dad took us by the hand and we would walk up Castle Hill. Stopping along the way, Dad would read to us from a historical plaque tacked up on a wall somewhere or ask us about St. Stephen or King Matyas as we walked past statues and cathedrals. Just the way Krip said it in his book. Then we started down the other side of the hill, down the stone staircases, down, down to Vermezo Park.

After he would get us safely inside our apartment building I imagine him walking back to Krisztina Varos and catching the 18 tram to his place in the 11th district. I can see him getting off at Bereny Laszlo St. and walking the rest of the way past Karinthy Frigyes St. and the homeless people sleeping near the warm air of the exhaust fan at the back door of the grocery. But before all that I can imagine him looking out over the river to the Pest side and the waterfront buildings he said always reminded him of a beautiful woman, smiling, with a few gold teeth, shining out of the Gresham Hotel, the gold inlay in an ornate wreath around the upper façade. He saw his reflection in the tram window, the water front buildings floating behind his face. He saw the place beside the Danube where he told me once he'd first kissed Mom. He saw the boat dock where he had met Agnes on her first visit to Budapest so many years before. He saw her yellow dress in the yellow light of morning. She waved to him, then, and he ran to meet her and they embraced in the ocean dream that separated them. Seagulls called and took flight along the river. And the yellow light was like a bridge over the water.

POSTSCRIPT

KRIP: MESSAGE IN A BOTTLE

My last observations (found on Krip's desk - Ryly)

I walked my usual pattern tonight. I went up Hamzsa Bégi St and through
the park. The one that looks like a Seurat painting. It goes for so long in such a
straight line, I never saw a thoroughfare that stretched out like that. By the time
I reach Bartok Bela St I'm halfway 'cross the 11th District, and it occurs to me
that if I go left I wander into another world, I had bundled up and decided to
take a long walk. Now it's become a routine. To the left lies Etele (Attila) Square,
well, another five tram stops further, Bartok St. stretches out all the way from
Kelenfold, which has a kind of eastern Hungarian village feel to it, to down to the
Danube (Duna). That was the beginning of it all, those nostalgic walks through
my first neighborhood here. Before Josh, before Helen. All those cracked streets
sprouting weeds, it still looks unkempt, the part of Budapest urban renewal
forgot, at least for now. (But it's changing, there's a disco now where the bakery
used to be and a brand new bus station. I looked for my old haunt, a place that
wd now look like the vestibule of a toilet—the Inter Joy Cafe—but I think they'd
torn it down. I saw one girl, this was when Spring first hit, so tan in a white
sailor shirt and matching pants, a real bbw. So I followed her. I got alongside her
finally—was Josh still alive then? It was hot for April.

Excuse me do you speak English?

She fixed me with a withering stare but I was careful no one was around to
smirk. But I hadn't seen the pick up with some workmen in it. One of them
smirked. Or else he just looked. For all I know he might've meant nice try, I don't
know. He puffed his cigarette mindlessly – staring off into space. I wondered if

the Hungie guys talk to each other. I remember when I worked for the road crew in Edgeton. Nodding off in the shade. I remember the big black guy laying down crosswalk lines. Talkin to the old white dude who'd killed a man once who'd cuckolded him but was now out of prison—the old dude's voice in conversation vaguely in my ear as I nodded off in the front seat.

Naw, now you cant take a man's pussy

But it was her that did it, nah? — said the big black guy

Naw, now that's HIS pussy, ye see. Ain't nobody else's. Don't no matter she be throwin it on ya or not. It's hisn.

I'm walking at random now. Like a guy in that book who kept wandering around and finally the detective follows him and figures out that he's spelling words with the configurations of pathways through the streets he takes.

But I didn't go left. I went right. And after a few blocks or so I saw Gudrun talking to some woman. I figured she didn't want to see me so I went down a side street right before I got to her. Maybe she saw me. I decided to walk around the other block – but on the way, I suddenly felt like I wd pee in my pants so I walked back toward the park and found a secluded bush. Of course, as soon as I get my dick out and start pissing, here comes a cute blond, summer tan. At first she doesn't notice me, then she gives a start, look lady I ain't flashin you, I'm pissin ok? I look back over my shoulder, still pissin and notice that she realizes all this and has already forgotten me as she looks toward the trees—halfway plotting an escape just in case I really am a pervert—which I am actually but she doesnt know it. It feels kinda nice w my dick out as she walks by—I haven't had my dick out, even if it's by accident—in front of a girl that good lookin in years. Can it be that long? The time, I mean.

And so the fires of summer burn down. The cool fall nights dispel the haze. Once the air pulsated with thoughts of sex, the girls of the Blvd half-naked. Everything enclosed in the bright burning yellow room of an August day. Just a step from their passing smile to my bedroom fan—talk and wine coolers and cigarettes and kisses.

Suddenly it's all jackets and boots and wool skirts and thick stockings.

I keep thinking of the sea between me and Amerika. The sea that separates my 2 worlds. To pass over it is like passing through a dream – a dream time. As I fly through the mists above the Atlantic I'm transformed. So sweet was the July light of Edgeton. My Aunt and cousins and friends and old loves, old joys come back to me—old sorrows. How did it all pass away? All the info of the digital age, all the snares of its Net can't answer that for me, yet it's all I want to know.

I really don't give a fuck about Amazon.com. I wish all that computer shit wd all disappear! Where is Berenice, where is Wanda where is Kiki LaSalle where is Gudrun now I shudda said hello where is Lydia? Where is Helen? That's all I wanna know.

Time is absorbed into the sycamore leaves. In great cycles, the small sparrows return—and then disappear again. Now there is no cooing of doves at my window sill but they will return and the green that suddenly appeared over the park goes white just as suddenly, white with the black of the trunks of bare trees.

Everything is transformed. I'm not the person I was but, then, when I return, the person I was returns—dreaming of the person I became in the Edgeton summer. Where is Bill and Dave and Kenny and Joe? Where is Carlo and Harriss and Free and Sylvester? And now Josh. Yet, I'm too old for grief. Too old to play Faust. I'd rather play the devil. I know so much. And my reward is this relentless loneliness.

I wept this morning. Harder than usual. I'm not sure why it all just suddenly came out—unless it was that I saw Michael and his flaming sword standing unflinchingly at the Garden gate – barring my entry or reentry forever. I always picture the Garden of Eden as the backyard of the house on Water Maple St., right around where the blacktop ended and the addition hung over the driveway a bit and then the yard sloped down. This is where the guy in the Auster novel gets shot too. It's fascinating how different stories trigger the same childhood spot in our memory. I'm always there on a spring morning —the grass is still wet with the dew—always so thick in Edgeton but now I see the gate. Closed. Trespassers will be prosecuted. Adam is muscular, a young farmer and Eve is like a teacher I've forgotten or she has the brown hair of an old high school girlfriend. Michael's sword is always light silver like a cloud—I can't see the flame—and he himself is the same color. He has an archer's hat on? Probably images from some child's bible storybook. The last time tears overflowed was a few days after I got back from America. My America has become an emotion—a nostalgic longing. Because just like you never get over a woman until you find a new one—you never get over losing one home until you find another and then to lose the new home you've found and then be unable to get back to the one you had, that's the worst. But I got used to the loneliness and it goes away. Like guilt, it dissipates. Perhaps I'm meant to live in the Great Sea that separates all things. I am the King of the Kingdom of Separation. Yet, I'm free to visit either world for short periods of time like Kora from the Underground.

It becomes like a friend almost. So I guess I lied when I said it was relentless. I was meant to be lonely. I am best that way. I guess old people turn their loneliness into pets. But no one appears and takes it away, like it used to happen in American tv shows. It just dissipates over time. Some people go out alot – or outside themselves—and just find someone –or find some inner strength. I feel empty at night but then the well fills again as I sleep and I come back to his notebooks the next day with more thoughts. What I want is to go beyond all this repetition.

In Budapest The Woman used Josh but he said it felt good sometimes—to be useful. When I called she said, Yes, Josh told me about you. Now sometimes we go to the store and she gets me food—and that gets me thru another month. And there's always a language student or someplace to play guitar. Some people still remember Josh when I mention I used to play with him. I even use his old demos and say it's me. I saw street people picking trash at a dumpster once. I said That's me in 10 years. But the woman said, No, never. I won't allow it. but then one day I told her how little money I had and she said "I can't help you now." It felt suddenly like when Josh told me about Gudrun saying, De van (I have a new boyfriend) but then, later, The Woman sent me a text message, saying, You know I love you and will help you if I can." But she has to be careful of her husband finding out. She can't ask someone to find me a job, that brings the possibility of gossip among the other ladies of her circle at her law office—but it's ok to accompany her to the opera or a play—that's normal.

When I wake up I lie on my back thinking of Everything: folks in Amerika, faces, his kids—all the old scenes of life. The past is all we really have. But we shdnt keep looking back so much—like a miser counting and recounting his worthless money. The past is an abstraction too—it may have happened but it can never happen again. Yet because it's all we ever had we keep reliving it in our thoughts. The faraway past starts to infect the closer past. I looked at old photos last night. What do they mean now? It's only memories. His sons don't want to sit down and look at them, they become restless. I say ok go out into the Park, the green garden but come back in for supper. I put the photos away. One of Helen I keep in my mind, I start to burn it, then I put it away. I carry it everywhere I go. What is gone stays in the mind, indestructible till death. And then? I remember the inside of all the houses I lived in as a kid but now they're all torn down. Still every room intact in my mind. A place is razed, the memories all die with the rememberer? There's still a photo somewhere and so it goes on hanging by a tiny thread. But an imaginary thread stronger than a spider's.

Oh, I just like afternoon cafe conversations, nights in bars too but maybe it was all those yrs of playing at night and women seem so pretentious at night. I love to look at beeyootiful H women in the daytime, they look so vulnerable! (like the dead pope layin dere in aw dem robes in Derek and Clive) just kidding, I mean unpretentious and just going about their real life not acting a certain way to attract men. Women to me are such an aesthetic treasure (that's why I like to dress up like them!) I can't imagine that they are simply human like me. It just doesn't seem possible. I cd never quite submit to the conventional male wisdom "they're just like us but..." so I can see why there's all these traps and snares for me if you attempt to get too close. I think I've learned how to pet the tiger's head without getting bitten. (hmmm… pet the tiger's head… sounds a bit...) but maybe I'll settle down again one day with another (albeit older no doubt) beauty or two and as I get older I find myself praying to Mother Mary somewhere in the background— I'm like the peasant woman in the Flaubert story, " A Simple Heart", who adores the parrot in the cage— and then— I think the parrot dies (?) but eventually the parrot, still there on its pedestal, becomes God to her. Great story, you shd read it. So maybe I'm slowly turning all women into one vision, one entity, The Great Mother, the white goddess, Venus, Mary, Raquel Welch, Juliette Binoche, my next door neighbor… but as I was saying before I don't much like the frivolous courtship rituals people go through. I much prefer the "one look says it all" no need for her to put on the little black dress and fishnets (opaque whites are nice too) and bounce around "Catch me if you can ha ha!" After. We can do that after, break out the lingerie to renew that first moment of "Let's Get It On" the former, the flirty stuff, it's a dessert, the latter, the main course. But I'm not mooning about it. I have Mary (the virgin one? or...) watching over me. She's like my secretary. "Uh, Mister Lewis? Now, Mary, I told you, you cd call me Krippy pie" Uh, yes, Krippie dear, there's a Miss Anne Hathaway here to see you? Oh, yes, send her in right away...

I keep thinking about the girl next door. What is it about her? Is it the roundness of her face? The sturdy white muscles of her legs? I remember I used to think I would find a woman like that back in Edgeton. Somebody sweet—not wild like Kiki or Wanda—or too beautiful—like Helen. Even now whenever I write her name I feel that knife like Josh used to say, going in just under the ribs and then carving an "S" up toward the heart. But maybe it was just the drug of the PLACE, a place always there like home, like the Breast but not a giving out but a pulling in, an engulfing—that's what Doc said once, a covering over with earth and the ecstasy of thighs and ass muscles moving up like water thru a plant stem into your cock and then that hands free draining away of everything— everything that never worked out right or everything that made you ache and weep, all gone into her and all transformed in that cry of unity.

Josh used to tell me about when he was a boy he found the big thick vine wrapped around the tree—like a root that grew upward—somehow it was attached at the top somewhere—it seemed sturdy enough so he climbed it—it was the place near the tobacco barn—painted blood red—but down the hill toward a serene little cow pond—and the hill was hollowed out like someone had pushed a big round ball into it and then taken it out, leaving only the roundness—like the way a mama bird uses her breast to form the inside of her nest. —- he walked up to the tree and noticed the vine—it was one of those mornings—late mornings when he had simply started walking through the bright fields and the light was so yellow the world was a swirl of yellow green and blue and he wd always remember when he took a crayon once in Kindergarten and colored the blue eye of a duck with yellow crayon and it turned green. Not a soul around—just the distant drone of a passing car on Tranquility Pike. He stood there looking up into its branches—clouds like wisps of hair—and then started climbing. But after about halfway up he began to feel an ecstasy in his thighs up to his crotch—he had had an erection before—but this was different—it was deeper in the muscles of where the thighs met the crotch. Whenever he gripped the vine with his thighs the ecstasy would intensify and subside when he relaxed his grip. He did this over and over—always feeling the ecstasy pour out into his thighs and cock and balls—he'd hardly been aware of his balls before—- had his balls rubbed against the vine and given him a hard on? He cdnt remember exactly. He just knew it felt good. We laughed together on the band bus. " So, Krip, the first time I had sex— was with a tree!!

Another thing I've noticed about the digital age: now anyone is free to say — or post— THROUGH TEXT! — whatever they want— so we have all this great info but also, all these insane opinions. I'm interested now in only what rises to the status of literature and "MUSIC" all the rest is just people jivin on the internet. The audience is becoming one with the performer now, and the performance is horrible, their creations have little or no connection with the" ancient Wisdom" and are therefore stillborn. The jadedness of the audience has created a "Gladiator" situation in which they can't be satisfied until a human sacrifice is thrown to them. It cd get ugly. But I want to rise above that silly fray on the wings of poetry and music and literature. I didn't coz it, the impotent amnesia the World finds itself in, my principles went unheeded in the masses for the most part, the most important one being simply the old pre-raphaelite one of " the Work shd be WORTH doing" (i.e. a manufacturer shd not impose "WORTH" on something from the outside to satisfy his greed—-) so to be fair I shdnt suffer the consequences. But I probably will— still, I'll comment only thru the symbologies that were understood in a tradition from the Homeric Hymns to the Trouveres to Hendrix, so fuck it.

The 6 tram cuts right through the heart of the Pest side of Budapest. Such a fine Indian summer day. The women all have that faraway look in their eyes. The men all seem terse and uptight. They know the communication has broken down somewhere—still, they don't particularly care for me staring at their women. But mostly I'm invisible, too old. Youth got older but it got bigger too. And age sometimes gets squeezed out like the crush into the tram car—everyone breathing on each other, going home to supper—the rush hour fades. Back home Josh told me Marshall always said this was his favorite moment of the day. Rush hour relenting, the voluptuous secretary window shopping, suddenly started acting really friendly to me in the non-stop, readily gave me her phone number but then after waiting 3 days so as to not come on too strong, I text her. All day I've waited for her reply. It hasn't come. So the game begins? So China will be the master but they won't play the green game or they're gonna make up their own green game. Still, American showbiz will all get d-loaded into one file and then sent around so there's no help there. Budapest will become a whore playground for Chinese businessmen—don't stare at my girlfriend, like the old storekeepers back home with their merchandise, unless yr gonna buy somethin buddy dont read the magazines. But they'll bring over their own girls. Hungarian girls are beyond them. A new hotel on the big boulevard and all the pretty hostesses are Magyar girls from the countryside with long legs and streaked blond hair pulled back and the perky little purple Marriot uniform that says "Anita" just above the breast and the goon at the door. Fat Hungarian girls are the world's most beautiful creatures. But they just wanna get married and have children— the chinese finally gave up on all that. Colonialism is tough business—ask the Brits—they'll look down deep into their pint and tell you the whole story. The one we knew they were gonna tell but wished they wudn't—coz we knew it was the truth.—So now they're franchising all kinds of theme restaurants "fast food awks" little fermented birds the Eskimos dig out of the snowpack in spring. You pop off the brittle head and drink down the atrophied guts, a sign hangs out over the street a little bit "welcome to Gabor's 'Pop-an-Awk'" I peer into the empty room through plate glass, it's out of business, but already a new shop is going in, soft wear and coffee and DJ equipment. I cd swear the woman next to me in the packed tram is feeling me up. I just let her go on rubbing against me in the aisle – if I feel back she might get indignant—master /slave—there can be no other way. In the English bookshop one little row of paperbacks, lots of Maugham, plays, stories, Moon and Sixpence is not there anymore—maybe I bought it. It was great in the way it showed how little we really know other people – but he never looks inside with compassion—he's more at ease with ridicule and a moral lesson at the end that he's sure he knows. Fitzgerald is much better with half the oeuvre. But Maugham-wise old bird in his slim autobio—The Summing Up—what a life being a great playwright at the turn of the century. I know you got some pussy, mate. Well, tell us about it. But that's the difference, my colonialism is rotten with voyeurism, "I like to watch." Maugham and Hemingway wanted to be warm and they knew what love was, both needed mothers they cd love. In the end, they cdnt trust. Fitzgerald was more delicate. Miller knew how to take care of himself.

The afternoon sun on the bookshelf. All those days of reading while the world kept spinning and spinning out. I don't know what I'm doing. Perhaps the Chinese will be here soon. I leave the door ajar. Maybe they'll carry me out in the easy chair or will they dump me off the balcony like the Nazis did to the old guy in Polanski's "The Pianist"? Who knows? It's like watching a storm way off. And then the wind is upon you. Or suddenly the west is streaked in peach chalk streaks.

If I walk away from the River, go up to one of the big streets and turn right, just like the aging professor in the story I wrote—- I'm going away from western civ and heading toward something else—something that started in 1529 when the Turks took over this place. The Autumn sun is finally bright again—the factory gate and the parking lot beyond seems almost pretty—it shines down on working-class folks going by. I think Darwinian thoughts as I seem to see everyone in sudden epiphanies of what they are, like me, monkeys trying to survive, gathering food. The pretty plump girl w the Russian face, high cheekbones, seems waiting for someone. Such a pretty round face. All around the drab surroundings, volunteer grass growing in the cracks of the pavement—a strip of ornamental grass looking pathetic next to the busy street. The row of bushes full of weeds. That illuminates this vast anarchy. There's no order—look at the faces—the unwashed clothes, the unwashed anuses and pricks and pussys and balls and feet, and sour breath and flatulence lost in the sunny breeze.

I can't resist asking her, Do you speak English? She holds up her thumb and index finger to where they almost touch each other, indicating a small amount of something. I make like I'm a lost tourist. Once I get her in bed then I'll come clean with her. She's so plump and cute for a moment I think I'm actually getting somewhere but she indicates a guy approaching, her husband. He shoots me a dirty look so I tip my hat and walk on, half expecting him to yell, Hey! Come back here! To my back. He doesn't.

But let's look at this logically, why wd even a modest looking plump woman like that need my dick? She doesn't want sex, she wants security! Sex she can get if she's really that horny. Her sweet face—I bet when she gets scared or needs him to buy her something, THEN she starts with the strokes of her soft hands—how do women have such soft skin? and her cooing voice, and her legs opening. He hasn't got a chance. He's so stuck on her now – he can't stand it when other men are w/in 10 feet of her. But she's not lookin at the size of his dick you fool or the shape of his manly ass! she's lookin to see how rich he might be. But you'd never know, she only reveals what she wants you to see. She never gets caught being any way or lookin at any thing she doesn't want you to know about.

Her pussy and our mouths are wounds that just won't heal. The air, the sweet autumn air of dry leaves, just makes them more raw—sour breath, the salt smell of the sea the gulls on the Danube bring in, tipping their wings to the northwest winds. You can't possess anything. Getting laid is a process you have to commit to. It takes time, a thousand phone calls, an audition, a back rub, a kiss, no one knows.

I don't know what I'm doing. But each day is a gift. Life. And then the gift of death. The beggar approached me at the Mona Lisa. I had a copy of the selected cantos and the twilight of the idols in my pocket. I was in the mood for F.N.'s rant and knowing I wd get my fill w/in an hour or so I brought Ez along for a change of pace. I wonder if I will ever meet any of these people in the Mona Lisa of the Afterlife. But what cd they say? we'd probably want to talk about other things besides their books in that situation. Who knows? It doesn't matter but why did they write them? I bet it was just to be loved. I wanna be loved, too. But you cant carry around all the grief and lust along with the love, the love slips through yr fingers. The other stuff is like glue or the crusty skin I get now that I'm old.

So strange being in that club last night The Castrum Zapora—same place Josh and I used to play 15 years before. How is it 15 yrs suddenly feels like yesterday? It doesn't make sense the way time expands and contracts like that. All the BP gang was there. Except for Gudrun. I got a text from her that she was at a movie with her boyfriend and she's hurt her foot in a workout—wow those girls really do work out, eh—no wonder they look so good. 2 months ago we'd made out back behind her apartment and now she's dodgin me. Then I started dodging her. We go round like that, just like Josh said! dancing like a drunk with a hat rack. No problem, honey, if I had a nickel for every…. The dope and beer and wine starts to warm me. Everyone's from London – 'cept for a few American expats- Derek, Clive, Simon.

"Yeah, London's fulla tolerant people, mate. I grew up in London, mate, yeah—Too tolerant if y'ask me, I mean, no, I love London but, mate, if ya wanna see the real England, mate, you gotta go to Cornwall, you know down Devon way, mate. Oh, hey, mate, Roger fucking Waters, mate, is comin to fuckin Budapest, mate. Hey, like, I saw the fucking Pink Floyd show he did, with the fucking lights and all. It was fucking brilliant, mate but this time he's gonna do the Fucking WAW! The WAW MATE!"

So the beggar approached, I'm thinking, sitting alone—everyone bugged off to dance or go out to smoke a joint—thinking back to this afternoon sitting in the Mona Lisa reading FN—only I never really got started before he come up to me so I gave him forty forints, which isn't shit, only about 20 cents but it was all the change I had. The rest were like Hungarian 20's and shit but when I give him the

20 cents he just stands there, then pulls out a bag of socks wrapped in plastic and wants me to buy some. I shake my head no as if to say, I gave you 20 cents, be satisfied my dear beggar sir and go away. but he doesn't go away, he's like crazy glue crusting up on yr fingers—so I pretend to read—I almost half expect him to go, Oh, Nietzsche, he's so close to my shoulder. I wait a minute more. Then for some dumb reason I get up and say Will you get out of my fucking face you silly ass motherfucker I gave you 20 fuckin cents now get the fuck outta my fucking face besides yr not a proper beggar who shd know the Tradition—All beggars know that they shd accept what alms are proferred and smile and bug off—what kind of decent respectable beggary is this? or some such crap. Jesus I'm thinking as I walk down Baranyai Street, why do I do that? And I realized I shd have just calmly walked to the bar after asking my beggar friend what he might like, ordered him a drink, so I cudda busted one of the big bills in my pocket, and then given him some of the change. But no I had to get all colonial on him and cuss him. At least I did it in English so he didn't have the faintest idea what I was saying. But still, I had sinned against the gods of the Downtrodden. I had raised my voice to a beggar. He wasn't trying to annoy me w his bag of cheap socks, he was desperate, that's what he was. He was beside himself with the idea he cd maybe get 500 forints (2 bucks) from me. So I'm thinking this in the Castrum as the decrepit flower lady shuffles by our table. I buy some flowers from her and give her twice what she asks for them. O dear Lady, Mother of the Lamb of God born in a manger, forgive my sins. She nods her head in thanks. My friend has been eyeing the dark gypsy girl at the table across from us—she's beautiful in her black dress and black patterned stockings—the guy with her seems too young to be her pimp. Other friends pass by to speak with her. The guy gets up to go to the bar. My friend sees his chance and sits down beside her.

Today was autumn in earnest. The steady gray drizzle brought in a chill. The sunny days of the brief Indian Summer suddenly disappeared. But they might come back for one more curtain call—out on The Ed Sullivan Show-like stage. That same music they always played while a guy juggled or kept plates spinning on sticks (one of the plates as they were all spinning in a row wd eventually start to wobble and the distraught little juggler wd have to run over and give it a fresh spin) later one of those Broadway Danny Rose type conversations next day in the luncheonette—"Hey, what about Jerome on Sullivan last night?" "yeah, he only lost that one plate but he got it back on—standin there to the applause—wdnt Aldo have laughed if he cudda seen it—the old vaudeville gang—cue music: nyaaaahhh nyatta tatta tatta deee yata tata nyata – dah dah dah DA da DA!!!

Watched a young couple furtively on the tram—I figured I had punched my ticket, might as well sit back and watch the show but they didn't kiss much. And I wasn't in a horny voyeur mood anyway (reminded me of the old guy that watched me and Gudrun goin at it in the Turkish Bath that time—now I was him) The cold had come in and shriveled up my little cock and balls, anyway— still hard to get used to knowing that a young girl like that—giving her boyfriend a little tease, oblivious to anyone else around—that girl cares nothing for me. I even sometimes find myself envious of her—like, I wish some guy wd wanna fuck me and make over me like that, so young so strong but something always kicks in and trumps any bi thoughts. I don't think like that much now, a yr or so ago I used to think it might be nice—just to be with a young cute person, "ok, if I can't attract girls maybe some queer wd give me a try" but then all that dissipated. I just want a woman, maybe so bad I think I'd do anything for her, even sucka dood but she's not here so. Oh, I'll never know anyway. Men just don't turn me on like that—gotta be a chick—but that's impossible—and then, if The Woman finds out then maybe she stops givin me moola. Who knows? Men wd smell weird wudnt they?

Still, the loneliness, knowing yr body has been rejected by the universe, of people anyway. Just think, not ONE person on this earth, not even The Woman, wants to lick yr ass. So maybe if I lick an ass it's just coz I really want mine licked—it's really just selfishness—or ego—suck unto other as you wd have them suck unto you. I just want to be wanted by someone.

But why such obsessions? I'm too old now. Josh has been dead for years! I am a surrogate father now! Even tho when I said to Lydia that Ryly and Gordon were my best friends she said, I don't agree with parents being "friends" with their children. And I cd tell that all the Jewish psychology of the last 50 yrs had been lost on her. All the ideas about parents and children respecting each other's own worlds but maybe she's right, maybe I'm using them as a shield from the world— but is that wrong? but I shd be making a better living—giving them more money. I wanna make sure they know how wanted they are—and so I want them to want me. I see them only on weekends so I'm always being too melodramatic about it. You guys know I'll always be there for you, right? Yeah, "dad" we know.

I was sure that new chick at the grocery wanted to get it on. Then after phone number and touchy feely she pulled the I have a boyfriend routine. Weird. So now I get nervous talkin to her—my mind goes back to Doc tellin me about that time Kiki's boyfriend cold-cocked him. That musta hurt. So I just happen to walk by and there she is having a smoke in front of the store. That's when I make my move: Hey can we meet? And that's when she holds up her hand and shows me the ring. Oh boy. The conversation goes downhill. In fact this is her last night working at my local 7/11. Her guy is coming to pick her up at midnight, her last shift. I can call her "If you want" she says with a faint growl in her voice that seems to say, "If you don't mind the possibility of getting yr block knocked off."

So—so much for that. Cute eyes. Dark almost-black circles under them. Gypsy Jewish Mediterranean-something. Soulful. Too bad. But I don't wanna chase some dude's girlfriend. Maybe I will but later I noticed that sometimes you realize that yr so horny that girls not that good looking—like her, look really good to you. But then when at a party or in the grocery check-out line or a bar or someplace you see them standing next to an actual really hot chick—you realize they ain't so beautiful. It was just that, before, when they came onto you a bit, yr horniness built up an illusion of beauty and there was no hot chick around to compare them too. It's similar to when yr walking around thinking yr clothes and yr shoes, etc are pretty nice and then you go into a nice clothing store and start trying on a few things here and there— you look at yrself in the store dressing room mirror— looks pretty good. But then as they're bagging up yr purchases and you've put yr old clothes back on—you see how shabby they look to you now, even tho they had looked good enough to you before.

But I never looked that good in new clothes. And if you spill something on new clothes it always looks awful—whereas on old clothes it kind of blends in better. Ketchup stain, olive oil, wine, cum. I've been a little anxious over lack of gigs and I didn't wanna start whining about it. I'm mostly tryin to do this other writing piece I've been workin on. Music is so unfulfilling. I'm getting tired of the whole troubadour schtick, there's not enuff permanence of creation in it. I'm jonesin to actually create something lasting, not just another set for fifty bucks or a demo CD but I've been agonizing over it. Wonder if Im capable of doing it now that I know it won't be acknowledged in any monetary way. It's frightening a bit becoz not only can we see the live music scene dying as the machine asserts itself. ("Hey, I can play anything w this new program!" and maybe ALL art: actors and painters and musicians will be obsolete?) Seems under siege in that everyone, charlatan and adept, seems to be talking at once.

Civilization suddenly realized it had left half its children out in the cold and now, the children are outside the door with baseball bats, no time for fluffy stuff, no time for anything but throw them a cheeseburger and hope for the best unless the Chinese can mass produce it. We don't want it, there's no time for communication. People don't love anymore, they have relationships. Nietzsche said it was all a "Will To Power" and marshall McCluhan said the medium is the MASSAGE. That was the theory, now it's happening. You see, I told you I shd keep quiet for awhile. I'm getting apocalyptic again. Plus I'm finally starting to get comfortable with the idea of my own death, which is only 20 or less yrs away, not that long when I think that the last 7 and a half yrs of being split up w her seems almost like last week (not that it's been an all bad " last week" not at all, so that means I got a few more weeks like that to go and it ain't gonna be like when I was 17. Weird)

Metropoli are colder emotionally than small towns, the traffic, multitudes, pollution, very inhumane. Social networks for people my age and older are frail and Hungary has one of the highest divorce, suicide, and alcohol rates in the world. I can see why, they can't care about each other, they are too busy surviving… love, real gut-wrenching familial love… is instinctual maybe among families, esp gypsy families but affection takes leisure time. Hungary was like a prostitute in a cage for more than fifty yrs (of the 20th century and at various other earlier times as well) that was taken out and screwed occasionally for sport and then put back in the cage at the whim of various oppressors. Tartar, Turk, Austrian, Russian, American, a complete culture of emotional hazing. Hungarians are neurotically afraid of stuff. The 20th century was like electro-shock therapy for them. The history of the World has been a history of mistreating the poor. Now things are better but the psychological scar runs deep here and so I can only wonder at how deep the scars are in Africa and Asia, probably even deeper, all these people, these poor fucked up people were the objects of exploitation. But that was the only way Europe/Amerika cd pursue its Faustian dream! which it's still pursuing but now there's a buncha party crashers outside… did I already say that only half the people on the planet have ever made a phone call? So, hire them to make t-shirts!!! and pay em shit but it's still exhilarating to live here whoever ends up reading this: you shd come visit sometime, you know you have a standing invite of course, that goes w/out saying.

Suddenly I'm just dictating words from a static-filled radio broadcast I can barely hear. Every third word or so gets me wondering what the guy is saying. He's talking to a woman about the dampness of spring grass and how wet the air is and that leaves of grass glint purple in the new sun. She says that she should lay down and let the earth cover her with flowers— or did she say hours. And then the guy —I thought he was gone for a second — lost in static— but then he comes in again— and he says he had been weeping before but the woman said that it was ok. Then music played and they were gone.

HERE ENDS KRIP'S BOOK

I would like to thank the following people
who encouraged me on this undertaking,
and whose assistance and compassion greatly
facilitated its completion:

The Bluegrass Writer's Studio at Eastern Kentucky University

Attila Bordacs

Erin Chandler

Katherine Hilton

Celeste Lewis

and Dr. Jeffrey Lewis

www.ingramcontent.com/pod-product-compliance
Lightning Source LLC
Chambersburg PA
CBHW011112100726
47898CB00011B/3049